The Fire Margin
or
The Tempestuous Tale of Nuk Tashino

by
OffyD

with art by
Vera C

This is a story based on one hundred and fifty hours of gameplay in the cult-classic video game *Kenshi*. To see the gameplay that inspired this tale, search 'The Fire Margin' on YouTube! Some aspects of this book, such as the broad setting, names of most characters/locations/states, and the nature of some historical events referenced, should be credited to Lo-Fi Games. Some aspects reference characters/content unique to the mod 'General Modifications' by Seelenschwarz.

THE CAST

Nuk Tashino
Prince of the United Cities Empire. Vaguely aware there is a world outside his palace.

Wodston
Doctor of the Imperial Palace. He thought he'd seen it all.

Izayah
An albino outcast from the Shek Kingdom. Confident things will turn out alright in the end.

Izumi
A passed over academic. Won't be passed over this time.

Bloody "Charlie" Ells
A famous thief. You'll smell him coming.

Gustavsen
A 'ronin prince' of the Western Hive. He detects your feelings towards him already.

Red Rick
An ancient Skeleton warrior. He'll tell ya how it is, for the right price.

Sandor
A captured ninja. Wants to believe the rich can do good.

Jaz
Academic grunt and wingwoman extraordinaire. Just wants what's best for the gossip mill.

Elaina
Qualified engineer, defier of curses. They call her a 'child prodigy', for some reason.

Agnu
A broken machine from a war it's long forgotten. Has a lot to say, but can't find the words.

Pia
Former slave, current ninja. Trying to make sure others don't share her fate.

Beep
A beautiful creature with a great destiny. Beep!

Sadneil
The wackiest robot in Black Desert City. Stuck on the same riddle for a thousand years.

Twitch
A rogue on the run from an ancient ruler. Doesn't mind dying if he sees some cool stuff first.

Tengu
Ruler of the United Cities Empire. Nuk's dad, but he's not entirely on top of such details.

"Stole Golem" Estata
Ruler of the Shek Kingdom. Battle hardened, and glad of it.

The Bugmaster
Nemesis of the Shek Kingdom, ruler of the mountain of doom, and collector of teeth. Great abs.

Enrico
Leader of the Tech Scribes - historians, researchers, lovers. Programmed to never lie, maybe.

Agent Tuxedo Hammer
A very special AI. You won't be able to resist.

Cat-lon
The ruler of the entire world. Most people have never heard of her.

The Thousand Guardians
An elite army of Shek warriors.

The Green Baddies
A band of hiver 'ronin'.

The Tech Hunters
World renowned explorers and scientists.

The Mangaka Academy
Less said about them the better.

Chapter 1
Private Rates and Sandy Steaks

Humankind once tried to build themselves a new world, not so far from Earth, actually. It nearly worked. But that's very much ancient history now. Much more important is the fact that an old man has just emerged from a huge, rusting warehouse – a palace, by contemporary standards – and has lumbered his way down a winding ramp to meet with a snappily dressed bachelor in the sandy street below.

"He kicked you out too?!"

"Yes, master."

"Old man's gone mad. He'll banish me over a little hashish?"

"It was quite a lot of hashish, master."

"In business terms, Wodston, keep up."

"Yes, master."

"He's just trying to impress the nobles. Playing politics with his only son – those rebels never should have let him become Emperor."

"Indeed, master."

"Don't agree with that!"

"Yes, master."

"Ugh. Fine. Guess I'll wait in the bar for Dad to change his mind."

"Uptown or downtown, master?"

"Uptown, you dreg! Also stop calling me master in the street. Makes me sound like a common slaver."

"As you wish, Prince Tashino."

"That's more like it! Ha! You know what? This is freedom, Wodston my man. No roof over my head, keeping me down, you know? The world is mine to explore. Mine to rule, if Dad won't come out and stop me. Ha. Yes, Wodston, I think this world is about to get Nuk'd. Again."

The intimidating smile across the man's face can only be explained with the fact that Prince Tashino's first name was Nuk. You see, he was being very clever, and I mention this specifically because he would have wanted you to know that.

Nuk Tashino traipsed up a hill, his richly dyed robes fluttering about in the first whispers of a dust storm. Wodston was obliged to follow. He had been Nuk's doctor for twenty years, and had even served the previous dynasty that had ruled the empire. They were long since buried; Nuk's family had enslaved their way through a peasant uprising and wound up in the big tin palace there in the rugged capital. It was out of mercy that Emperor Tengu had exiled him along with Nuk; he was to keep the Prince alive out there in the world. Or, as was becoming clear, he was to sit in the bar with the Prince and pay for his drinks.

Yet Old Doctor Wodston was actually going to have a busy day. You see, while the imperial capital of Heft was the centre of the civilised world in theory, it was in practice an outpost on the edge of the Great Desert, besieged by roasting sands, criminal gangs, and worst of all: the skimmers.

Oh the skimmers. These things were everywhere. If you set foot on the sand anywhere in the desert, they'd hear you on their huge antennae, and come skimming over to take a look. If you were smaller than them (and I assure you, you were) they'd bite your head off. They didn't eat you or anything, they'd just kill you. For fun. Happened every day, pretty much without exception. Yes, centre of the civilised world this place was, so feel free to imagine what it was like to live in a 'rough' town.

At least Heft had Nuk's dad's samurai to keep the skimmers at a distance, and to battle the rebels and extremists that plagued the entire United Cities Empire. Peasant bands defied the Empire's tithes, and escaped slaves slid through the hands of their masters, protected by mysterious desert warriors, the 'ninja'. No use explaining why there were so many of them; once you get familiar with Nuk, you might be able to intuit the reason for yourself.

One such ragged rebel was lying, half-dead, at the south gate, when Wodston walked by with a bag full of skimmer meat – bored of being a barfly, he'd been harvesting a nearby kill and tending to the wounded combatants after a recent scuffle. It may sound a little strange for a doctor to have been doing butchery, but everyone who survived the famine that preceded the big rebellion two decades past knew about that sort of craft intimately. And battles with skimmers on the roads beyond the city walls were as common as crotch-rot (common).

Anyway, he saw the bloodied body in the mouth of the south gate, and rushed over.

"This man needs need medical attention!" he said to the nearest samurai.

"No shid, Shelko."

The guard shrugged his heavy armour up and down. For him, that was already too many precious calories wasted on the matter. In the United Cities Empire it was socially-essential to think less than nothing of the so-called 'dregs' who lived in the scorching wilderness. The samurai upheld such apathy with military efficiency.

Wodston took a look at the patient, and diagnosed him with having a tumorous roll of coins on his belt. Enough to pay for the imperial doctor's services and his master's drinking debts all in one. The guards got angry when he tried to tend to the man, and told him to instead make himself useful by carrying the rebel to the prison around the corner.

Wodston, being a sly kind of chap, agreed, then rounded several sandy corners with the rebel over his shoulder, until he reached the uptown generator shed. There he slid the door closed to have his devious (yet highly professional and clinical) way with the poor man amid the buzzing stink of ethanol turbines. Like a true professional, he was paid upfront. Coins, a clean sword, and a battered crossbow – more than the Emperor was paying him to be a chaperone, by a wide margin.

Such were the profits of theft. Theft, you ask? Yes, well Wodston actually didn't provide any service at all in exchange for this bounty, for the patient suddenly woke up before his wounds could be assessed. If you awoke with missing memories, naked, in a strange, oily-smelling shed, alone with an old man who was eyeing you up with outstretched hands, you'd probably react in the same way that this poor rebel did.

The door was flung open, and the naked ninja's liberation streak began. Turned a few heads, but not many, for it wasn't completely an out of the ordinary sight. This was the centre of the civilised world after all. The rebel made it as far as the guards at the prison crossroads, while rich-man Wodston took his booty down to the bar to show Nuk.

"Whoa, is that a ninja sword?!" the prince exclaimed, snatching the piece from Wodston with childish glee. A few others nearby peered over at the blade.

"Did you see that naked man run screaming past the door earlier?" Wodston said.

"Which one?"

"The most recent one?"

"Missed that one. Friend of yours was it?"

"He was the ninja I took this from."

"So that's why I didn't see him! Ha! Wait, you beat up a ninja?"

Wodston proceeded to explain his freelance doctoring racket to an enraptured Nuk.

"So you can rob them blind, and then if anyone asks, you say it was payment. No bounty. Wodston, my man, you are the world's foremost criminal mastermind!"

"But it IS payment, my Prince. I do actually provide a service."

"And now we know why the ninja was naked. Look, my good man, I heard that a bunch of outlanders got skimmed down in the west basin. Bet they need a doctor, as much as I need more stuff to trade for rum, if you know what I mean."

With a wink and a shove, the mistakenly mischievous medic was sent to investigate this west basin, an area known for its roaming bands of skimmers. Indeed, between banks of dusty rocks and the city's looming western wall, the whole place was covered in wounded vagrants - AKA a fertile clientèle. Your money, or your life - that was Wodston's silent cry as he stabilised the dying in exchange for the crud these refugees were hauling about. Being a kindly old sort, he saved those who couldn't pay as well. It was as if he took his duties seriously, and cared for those around him. Perhaps the centre of civilisation was actually Wodston all along.

He took one fellow to the safety of the town lock-up. In the United Cities Empire, being a starving vagrant wandering the wastes was a serious crime - bad press for tourism you must understand - and so the police were happy to apprehend the miscreant, and give him further treatment so that he wouldn't die in their custody - bad press for tourism, you must understand.

The next morning Wodston the Reaper was at it again, with the market for non-consensual private healthcare still booming in the basin. But, as he had feared, the folk writhing about in the sand overnight had attracted the attention of the skimmers. All Wodston needed to do was sit very still; remember these beasts weren't looking for food, so dead bodies were of no interest. Think of how a human might kill a mosquito buzzing around them, but wouldn't tuck into a pile of mozzy corpses if they came across one. I'm generalising of course.

Wodston eventually legged it when it looked like a triumphal parade of skimmers was about to break out in the basin. Long legs and grub-like bodies slid their way in from the lifeless deserts beyond the rocks. They were too small to scale the century-old wall ringing the city, but that wouldn't stop them trying. Luckily enough, little Wodston gave them the slip. His rugged old legs brought him into town and up the hill to the porch of the bar, where Nuk was staring up at the sky with reddened eyes.

"Wodston. They've got the good stuff in there my man," the Prince reported.

"And I in here, my Prince," Wodston replied, showing off his salary bag.

"Wow... look at all this crap..." the Prince whispered, tears forming in his eyes. "And... it was all free?"

"No. But, there was more than I could carry, and the skimmers are gathering up by the south road. Perhaps you could come with me to oversee the payments?"

"You want me to help you rob them?"

"No, my prince."

"Well of course I will! Can't wait to get out of this damn city! Fugg you dad, I'm a highwayman now!"

"You're a doctor's credit manager."

"I'm too far down the trail for your big words, my man. Just... point me at what to steal."

With that, a wheezing Nuk followed Wodston to the south road, where indeed the wounded and dead from a skimmer attack were freshly arrayed. The locals were already picking over them, so the Prince and his au pair jumped in on it. Some of the dead were wealthy slavers, who could thus afford the finest deathbed care Wodston had to offer. Nuk sold them on it so well they ended up spending the whole afternoon applying the treatment and 'managing the credit'.

They dragged their haul back to town, found a barman who didn't care why the imperial Prince was fencing stolen clogs of an evening, and all told they made a handsome profit.

"What a day!" Nuk said as he slumped down at a table afterwards.

"I daresay, my Prince, that together we make a wonderful team. We saved a lot of lives today. I think you father would be proud of what we've done with our time."

"Man... we took like *all* their shoes... That is an achievement, isn't it?"

"Well, I suppose, my Prince."

"But seriously, my man, I think you'd better find like an assistant or something. That was too much."

"If that is your instruction, then I shall obey, my Prince."

"Nice. Yeah, get like a dreg to do my job, and I'll be the overseer watching down over the operation. Should get a nice view from the balcony on the uptown boozer... Ugh, I'm so tired, and I still gotta walk up there tonight. My man... I hope this was worth it. Yeah, actually, now when dad's like, 'you never done a day's work in your life', I'll be like, 'seriously, I managed like 2 grand's worth of credit at a famous private healthcare guild', ya know?"

While Nuk's working day count would still have been zero if you rounded it to the nearest whole number, it was a marked improvement. Perhaps his father would see dividends from kicking his boy out of the palace? Or even better, someone else could be paid to arrange such dividends on the leisured Prince's behalf.

To such ends, while the exhausted Prince hit the hired hay at 6pm, Wodston surveyed the bar for a more reliable assistant. His eyes settled on a remarkable looking shek. The shek were a species from the other side of the world, who at some point in their extremely distant lineage had been human. As such they were not really native to this planet, but their thick scaly skin and brawny physiques made them very suitable to its rigours. That skin was normally a mild or dark blue, but this particular shek was pale, almost white.

"Albino," he said, pointing to his undersized, fleshy horns when he noticed Wodston staring at him. "Shouldn't be so remarkable to you." The shek was referring to Wodston's own pale appearance and white hair, the products of life in a shady palace and age respectively.

"I was more interested in those," Wodston said, coming over to sit down. He was pointing at the shek's arms. Shek were beefier than humans, and this one sat topless in the bar, muscles and scales fully on display.

"Hmpf. So, you must be that 'power station pervert' the scallywags here were going on about."

Wodston explained his need for a labourer, and the shek decided not to call the guards. In fact he was quite happy to have someone actually ask him for help.

"Not many people would dare be seen on the road with me," he said. "Albino shek are cursed, they say. A creation of Narko."

"Well, as you said, perhaps I would be mistaken for an albino too, so none would consider it unlucky."

"Doesn't mean it isn't unlucky though, does it? Besides, I don't work for people. I'm a traveller. None will have me, and I do no different in return."

"I see. However, it would only be for a short time, and in addition, I can vouch for you to the house of Heft, if you wish to stay."

"House of Heft? Wait, you're that punk Nuk Tashino? Ha, I thought you'd be younger! A fellow outcast then."

"That's not quite the situation."

After all was cleared up, the shek was still rather impressed.

"I heard about the Prince yesterday. I couldn't believe it. The same thing happened to me once, I presume. Would have been too young to remember it clearly. You won't find a shek in the kingdom who'll talk of it, but the firstborn Prince looked strangely pale. I'm the only one who knows it – believes it, rather – and a bar like this on the other side of the world's the only place I can say it. Guess other shek come by even up here though, so let's say nothing else of it, friend. Oh, the name's Izayah."

That evening this Izayah agreed to help Wodston. The kingdom he had referred to, by the way, was the simply titled 'Shek Kingdom' which ruled the southwestern reaches of the continent, far from our current setting in the north-eastern deserts. So yes, Izayah was an especially unusual visitor, and if his story was to be believed, fate had given Nuk a striking role model for what an exiled prince could be. Or so Wodston hoped.

Indeed Izayah was a very good example. He was so dedicated to his new responsibility that he even went out in the night and brought the leftover bodies inside the walls. Then, being not especially in want of sleep on account of shek metabolism, he began his so-called 'training'.

In the morning, Wodston looked down Heft's main street from the corner where he had arranged to meet with Izayah. Izayah was bobbing towards him from the other end of town, carrying something over his shoulder. When he neared, it was clear that it was a corpse. Izayah was nothing if not pragmatic – those who travel the world learn to use what they've got, and training weights weren't lying around in the road like his new friend was.

"Morning, sir," Izayah called out to Wodston, jogging on the spot once he arrived. Wodston gave an awkward smile, and looked back at Nuk, trudging up from the bar.

"Is this the guy?" Nuk asked.

"I am the guy, your majesty. A pleasure to make your acquaintance," Izayah said, bowing low with a limp pair of legs swinging around in front of him.

"He's a funny one, isn't he Wodston?"

"He's an albino shek, my prince."

"Oh... Oh! Okay, sorry old chap, I thought you were, like, really poxed or something. You know, probably from your friend there."

"I apologise for the misconception. This fellow's just helping me with something. I think it's a fellow."

"Okay, cool, cool, cool. So Wodston, err, where did you get this guy? I was thinking... You know... Like a normal dreggy guy. Like you."

"Do I not satisfy you, your majesty?" Izayah asked. "I understand. I am a shek after all, not worthy of your presence. I will go."

"Wait a sec. What's his name?"

"Izayah," Wodston reported.

"Oh cool, like a ninja shout, huh? IzaYAH! Anyway, Izayah, don't go, seriously. I do need you around actually, so I can be like 'actually mate I'm friends with a shek so I'm not- you know', and stuff. Also... much more importantly, I'm starving. Where's all the meat from yesterday?"

Wodston opened his bag, to reveal it was packed with damp slabs of skimmer breast. Izayah was so transfixed he nearly dropped his corpse.

"Friends, I have a great idea. The best way to enjoy breakfast. Follow me!" he said, and jogged off towards the gate.

"Okay, yeah, let's follow that topless necrophile out into the desert," Nuk shrugged. "Wodston, I need to talk to you about this thing called 'judgement of character'. Seriously man."

Izayah took them up a rocky hill just beyond the gate, and began breaking apart some barren shrubs to make a fire, batting away the various limbs wiggling this way and that as he moved. Once the fire was going, he took out the skimmer breasts and starting roasting them up over the flame. It was a clear morning, with a cooling breeze that made the steaks only somewhat crunchy by the sand it carried.

"Okay, seriously, this is okay," Nuk said as he tucked in.

"This was a wonderful idea, Izayah," Wodston added.

"This is the life, gentlemen. Outdoors. The world. The whole world is out there, you know? I've been wandering for ten years, and I've barely scratched the surface."

"Ten years? Out here?! That's literally impossible," Nuk said, spitting meat all over the place.

"For a mere traveller? Indeed, very dangerous. For an adventurer though? Ah, there's nothing better!" Izayah flipped a steak and laughed at the sky. The image had Nuk's mouth agape.

"You're so fugging cool!" he exclaimed. Izayah and his shoulder companion bowed again. "Man, you're an adventurer. Right, we have to go on some kind of trip, don't we?"

Nuk seemed to direct the question to Wodston.

"As you wish, my Prince. I think, though, that your father never really intended for you to leave the city."

"Yeah? Don't worry I'll go tell him I'm teaming up with the weird dead body guy to see the sights. Only the moron won't even notice I'm gone. And you know, you hear all this stuff about all this stuff, which makes all *this* stuff look fugging boring. We gotta get out there! An adventure. Yeah, that's actually like something we could do!"

"It's a big old world out there, your majesty," Izayah said. "Extremely dangerous. Extremely wild. Nothing ordinary folk could ever endure, or ever imagine. Only heroes survive these lands."

"And hashish isn't even illegal some places, right?"

"That is true, but if you really-"

"Good sir I'm ninety-percent on board. Drop the corpse, and you've got yourself a real job."

And that was how Nuk Tashino, on only his third day of exile, decided to better himself and stick it to the man by becoming a world renowned adventurer. As Izayah had said, there was a whole world out there, and as the Prince had said, it was just waiting to get Nuk'd – again. Too bad that not a single thing about this grand adventure went anything like poor Nuk Tashino had planned.

Chapter 2
An Adventure and a Half

The Empire. Thousands of years ago it had ruled the entire world. Its cities and machines had towered over the lands, and its people had enjoyed such bounties that few had thought of ever returning to Earth. By the time of our tale, of course, Earth had been entirely forgotten, but for really the opposite kind of reason. There was still an Empire of sorts though, and this one actually had an Emperor. That Emperor was about to receive a visit from his exiled son, Nuk Tashino.

"Who's there?" Emperor Tengu demanded when Nuk strode into the tiny, undecorated throne room of the rusty imperial palace.

"Don't worry Dad, I'm not here to stay," Nuk told him.

"What?"

"I said I'm not here to stay!"

"Who the hell are you?"

"I'm your son! Nuk! Remember!"

"My son... Ooohhhh the green man!"

"Yep, that's what they all call me, isn't it? Do you literally not know my name?"

"Oooohhh I know your name. And I know your GAME. That's why I hereby declare that you, are... exiled!"

"Thanks Dad. Man, you.... You took all of it, didn't you?"

"Took? Who said a single thing about... toke?"

"Incredible. Absolutely incredible, Dad. You're an inspiration."

"Don't come back until you've got more! But between you and me, don't take it yourself; it's illegal, I heard..."

"Cool, cool, cool, so yeah I'm actually going to leave you forever now dad. Going on an adventure with this scalemail pervert. Probably gonna die and stuff, in case you wanted to..."

Emperor Tengu's blank expression was unchanging as Nuk let the silence hang. Then, without warning, he slumped forwards off the throne and rolled over to Nuk's feet.

"Skeleton... Skeleton wizard..." he coughed, holding out a wet tissue with something concealed within.

"No, it's me, Nuk," the Prince insisted. Tengu looked up at him with desperate eyes.

"Find the skeleton wizard. This is the key. Save the empire... Nuk!"

Nuk inspected the offered 'key'. It was a slobbery fruit stone with a fragmenting, papery residue stuck to it from its time in the Emperor's pocket.

"So. You smoked my whole supply?"

"Skeleton... wizard..."

"Cool. Off to go die in the desert now Dad. See ya."

And with that Nuk was about to storm out and leave the city at once, but that way he'd be leaving empty handed – or he would have been, if the all important greenfruit pip hadn't encrusted itself onto his palm. Instead he slipped behind a screen to the palace storeroom, and amid the din of the palace guards trying to restore the Emperor's consciousness, he stole as much ceremonial sake and lacquer as he could stow in and about his person.

Then, with his head held high and with clattering, sloshing steps, he transported his going away present to the caravansary at the north end of town, where Wodston and Izayah were arguing over a matter of professionalism.

"You employed me as a corpse carrier!" Izayah was saying. "Of course I need to practice in a controlled environment. That's the key to success!"

"I understand and appreciate your enthusiasm, but please think of our image."

"Image? Well of course I'm thinking of our image. Want a corpse carried? Who do you call? The corpse carrying guy, everyone knows that! This stringy piece of work is our store-front, in a sense."

Wodston was distracted from replying by Nuk opening the bag on the doctor's back and transferring various objects into it from his pockets, armpits, and beyond.

"Prince Tashino, you return," Izayah said. "I suppose we shall continue our debate on our desert walk, eh Mr. Wodston?"

"Mister Wodston..." Nuk sneered as he finished up.

"Is everything in order, my Prince?" Wodston asked.

"Yep. Dad's gone deep dive. Said I should go find a skeleton wizard."

"A skeleton wizard?" Izayah mused. "I've met a skeleton. And I've met a wizard. But a skeleton wizard? That is quite the task indeed..."

I should interject here to tell you that when he says 'skeleton', he isn't referring to human bones. The word meant something rather different to these people, but I'll let you discover exactly what for yourself as we go along. As for him saying he met a wizard... well your guess is as good as mine on that one.

"So Wodston, I've got a credit management question," Nuk said. "Say I managed credit from the imperial palace. If I was to liquidate that credit in the town, people would probably ask for receipts, wouldn't they? And that means to fully realise the value of my portfolio... Ugh... I don't know Wodston. Look I stole a bunch of crud from Dad. Izayah, take me somewhere to sell it on the sly."

"I don't entirely understand, but he markets of Sho-Battai are the place to buy and sell anything," Izayah said.

"Is it, like, close?"

"A good day north. The crossroads of the Great Desert, it is. And... what? What are you looking at, it's mine!"

Izayah's horns perked up when he saw Nuk staring at the corpse on his shoulder. Nuk suddenly ran over to the wall of a nearby shop, then returned with a torn-off poster, showing a drawing of a face. After a quick inspection, he said,

"Izayah, you madman. You've got a fugging famous terrorist here. Wait... wanted alive. Wanted a-damn-live. Oi, you ungrateful dreg, be alive!"

Nuk slapped the face of the weight-training woman on Izayah's shoulder, and she suddenly squirmed to life.

"By Okran! It's alive! How embarrassing!" Izayah said as a struggle commenced.

"Keep her steady you oaf, she's made of money. Help him Wodston! To the police station, go, go!"

The jostling quartet of bodies kicked up sand all the way to the desk of the local police chief, at which point the cussing, screaming terrorist was exchanged for a rack of copper coins that weighed almost as much. What did she do? You've already asked too many questions for the United Cities justice system.

"Now that's what I call travel money! We barely even need to rob the palace with you around," Nuk said cheerily to Izayah. Regrettably they were still at the police chief's desk. "Oh, don't worry. We in the business call credit management 'robbery' sometimes. Little joke, ya know? Did I ever tell you that I am the Prince of the empire?"

The stolen goods were ferried out of the police station with only a modest case file being opened on the purloining Prince, and the team spent the evening buying the outdoor adventure gear they'd need for their smuggler's hike. The next morning they assembled at the north gate, sporting rucksacks, sleeping bags, and weapons. Following expert roamer Izayah's advice, they were waiting for enough travellers to gather so they could form a caravan to Sho-Battai, the next settlement down the ill-defined desert road.

"Look guys!" Nuk called to the others. He was pulling a black shirt from a still-warm corpse behind a nearby dune. He cut it up a little with his sword and wrapped it around his head. "I'm a ninja! Iza-YAH, can you see me?"

"A resourceful little cringebeetle, he is" Izayah noted, and Wodston could not help but agree, albeit with a warm smile. Soon a group of armed men set out north, so Nuk and crew fell in behind them. As long as they all stayed together, the skimmers would leave them alone. Simple as that, Izayah explained. Nuk was pretty sure he got the idea. But he was also pretty sure that a body he saw beside the road a few hours later had a shirt more his size.

Nuk woke up the next day in a dark, dusty room. His chest was extremely painful, and was wrapped in reddened bandages.

"Wodston!" he called out. In reply there was bark, and a dog started sniffing around him. "Oh man. How much of that was a dream? Is this the palace?"

"Not the palace, Prince Tashino," came Izayah's voice. He was standing beside the bedroll that Nuk was lying on, sanding an apparently home-made workbench that took up the majority of the room. "This is the headquarters of Mister Wodston's Private Healthcare Guild."

"Cool. So you're saying that actually this is a dream?"

"Not as far as I am aware."

"But you are aware that Wodston is literally a dog now?"

"What? Oh no, that's the newest member of the family. Kalsi! She's a guard dog. Isn't she nice?"

"Yeah, I guess. Making money then, are we?"

"Indeed. In fact I was thinking of writing a report on the non-consensual private healthcare market to present to the Traders Guild, down in the Edge, should we ever head that way."

"Wait, we were going to Sho-Battai, I remember!"

"And what happened on the way?"

"I... Oh... Oh shid..."

Nuk slumped back painfully onto his bedroll as memory was restored to him. The caravan moved on, the skimmers moved in, and the rest was better off forgotten.

"That's just what it's like out there in the desert," Izayah said. "Lucky I saw it coming and got you out of there in one piece. Roughly speaking."

"Yeah... So I owe you my life then, or something?"

"I'm afraid so."

"Alright. How much to you want?"

"Sorry."

"I'm gonna repay you man. Can't just leave this hanging."

"You've already repaid me," Izayah said with a smile. "Kalsi here didn't come cheap, you know?"

"Always one step ahead, aren't you palescales?"

Indeed he was. The Prince took another day to rest while his industrious underlings carried out the business that an unconscious Nuk had invested a lot of money into, so it seemed. Non-consensual investment for a non-consensual enterprise, one could say.

Wodston had taken it upon himself to purchase a property, so that the Prince and company could take up residence outside of a rum-soaked bar. This property was of course in line with the Prince's current buying power. It was the second best shed that side of the latrines, and the first closest. From it, Wodston had been carrying on his work, and Izayah had been labouring to make that rotting sandstone cleaning closet into more of a home.

Once he was up and about, Nuk saw how the new business was in the very shadow of the imperial palace, located in a backstreet below its lofty mushroom-shaped dome. What self-respecting run-away-from-home Prince could be seen camped within puffing distance of his father? With not a thought for his prior failure, he demanded that he be taken on another adventure. That's why he, Wodston, Izayah and Kalsi were hanging around the northern gate again the next morning, looking for another group to travel with.

"You're going to Sho-Battai? Who was just saying that?" a voice said. A grimy woman appeared from beside the guard post and very deliberately didn't look at Nuk.

"Me, right here," Nuk said. The woman's smile faded as she confirmed it really had been the man with the torn up t-shirt wrapped around his head.

"Oh right. Okay, err... You're Nuk Tashino, right?" she asked.

"Yep. Prince Tashino. Prince of everything, and more! How did you know it was me?"

"The House of Heft has worn that pattern of silk since the Red Rebellion."

"Really? Thought it was just me and Dad."

"Well yes. You- Never mind. You're going to Sho-Battai?"

"Yeah. Ninja business, so don't ask."

"Okran's bloody beard... Do you have a... carer, manager, or something?"

"Oh, you must be mean Wodston. Wodston! Convince her to join the caravan, my man. She's too intimidated by me, you know?"

This woman, Izumi, claimed to have been part of an archaeological team that had recently disbanded in Heft after finding little of value in their digs. She, though, was convinced that they were on the verge of a breakthrough.

"The infrastructure that supported the Sho-Battai reservoir was located by a prior expedition, but it was never fully examined. Ancient structures, perfectly preserved in the sand. The technology there – the information – is beyond measure, I know it. There could be evidence of what caused the Fall! The rest of them think I'm mad, and the feeling is mutual. Anyway, I'm going to inspect the ruins at Sho-Battai, and look for a sponsor to excavate them."

"I-I could sponsor you, Miss Izumi," Wodston said, less pale than usual.

"Would you? Are you interested in history, sir?"

"Oh yes. I've lived though most of it in fact!"

"If only. You'd be the most advanced skeleton I've ever seen."

Wodston considered that sentence to have been a flirtatious compliment, and that is why we are better off leaving the truth of history to be discerned by experts. It all worked to Izumi's favour though, as now her expedition was officially sponsored by the Wodston Private Healthcare Guild, technically a division of the Tashino Credit Management Guild, as of a few hours prior.

Izumi joined the crew as they finally set off with a large merchant caravan, back up the road to Sho-Battai. Such a large group was ignored by the skimmers, waiting eagerly on the ridges overlooking the route. They weren't ones to bite off more than they could chew – not that they needed to chew what they bit.

However, if you remember what I told you about Heft, you might recall that skimmers weren't the only danger lurking on its outskirts. As the caravan column marched into a sandy gully, a group of shadowy folk appeared on its flank. They approached the rear of the column, not in any rush, and the caravaners believed they had opportune customers. Then weapons were drawn, and all hell broke loose.

These attackers were from one of the many rebel groups still fighting throughout the desert for an end to the rule of the noble houses, for the end specifically of Emperor Tengu, and his boy, Nuk Tashino, who stood awkwardly as the caravan guards battled the rebels all around him.

"What the fugg is all this then?" the Prince exclaimed, grasping the ninja-sword he knew not how to use.

"No sense taking risks, Prince Tashino," Izayah called. "We should all... Wait... Kalsi!"

Kalsi had been barking away at the attackers, and chased a couple of them around the dunes until finally one had landed a cut across the poor girl's head.

"Right, never mind. We're fighting!" Izayah roared, heaving up a chunky sword and lunging into the melee.

"Bloody hell. He's gone full shek on us. History girl, go get the fugging dog!" Nuk ordered.

"Oh, err, right." Izumi rushed out into the chaos of battle to retrieve Kalsi. A rebel attacked Nuk, and he did his best to deflect a string of blows.

"Oppressor!" the rebel was screaming.

"How do they always know who I am?!" Nuk said, finding relief when one of the caravan guards struck his assailant down with a heavy staff.

"The... robe... You idiot..." Izumi huffed as she returned, Kalsi now in her arms. Seeing the blood-soaked fur on the dog's face, Izayah gave a great shout and cut one of the rebels in two with a single slash. Another came up and began a duel with both Izayah and Nuk at once, although really Nuk was just dancing about and making threatening sounds.

By now Wodston had prepared his special weapon: the crossbow he'd taken from that naked ninja on his first day as a freelancer. He aimed carefully, but his vision wasn't as good as it had been. Izayah stumbled as a bolt stabbed into his ankle.

"Please, Wodston!" Nuk shouted. He slashed about with his sword to get the attention off Izayah. The crossbow twanged again, and a bolt slammed into Nuk's back.

"WODSTON!" he roared, actually cutting the rebel down in his fury, and turning around to snatch the bow from Wodston's hands.

"It wasn't at all deliberate, my Prince, I assure you!" Wodston was quick to protest, with one hand held out of view behind his back. Nuk looked around, and saw that the battle was over. The attackers had fled, and the caravan guards were already moving on. By the time the guild had 'managed the credit' from the fallen, they were all alone.

Wodston saw to their injuries, and Izumi proved handy with a bandage too. Izayah didn't even notice the pain, staring down at an unconscious Kalsi in his arms.

"We'll get them, man, don't worry," Nuk assured him, but Izayah shook his head.

"They got what they deserved. Our journey must continue. It will be dark soon."

In agreement, the gang set off in roughly the direction of Sho-Battai. The featureless dunes made navigation hard, but they picked up the trail of the caravan, and once they got a little closer they saw the ancient ruins Izumi had spoken of, sticking out of the desert all around the little walled town in the distance.

The gate guards grunted when Nuk said he was prince of the empire and demanded entry, and with that they were all finally safe again. As safe as you can ever be in the United Cities. Sho-Battai wasn't beset with skimmers, so it had that going for it; too far from their rocky lairs on the desert fringes. You might think, then, that this place should have been the capital, rather than the bloodbath that was Heft. Well, as we all know, Heft was the centre of the civilised world, and Sho-Battai was... uncivilised isn't a strong enough word for it really, as Nuk and company were soon to discover.

Chapter 3
The Exposed Wick

The crossroad market of Sho-Battai was named after the vast, ancient complex beneath the sand in that area. The so-called 'Sho-Battai Reservoir' was a facility of unknown size that slept below desert. It was theorised that the reason the water table was so high in the area – and hence isolated settlements like Sho Battai could exist – was because of some unknown quality of the buried ruins. Theorised by who? Izumi, that's who, leader (and sole member) of the Wodston Nonconsensual Private Healthcare Guild Archaeological Expedition Team.

"Who wants to come with me?" she asked the sleepy guild the morning after their arrival in town.

"I'll do whatever Mr. Wodston desires," Izayah said, sitting with a now-recovered Kalsi in his lap.

"I'll do whatever my Prince commands," Wodston said, looking over at Nuk. At this, Nuk opened his eyes and sat up.

"I need to go steal more stuff," he said. He'd sold off all the luxuries his father had unknowingly gifted him, and was conscious that his associations with relatively honest companions might drag him into honest work – a waste of his talent, energy, and good name.

"Well you're in luck then, Prince Tashino, as I'm planning to 'steal' a few things from the ancients to inspect them. I bet you'd be of great help."

"You mean I'll make a great manager. Go on then, get to work," Nuk waved. He eventually got up, shook the sand from the torn up shirt around his head, and went to inspect this scientific endeavour.

Just outside the town gate, Wodston and Izayah were on their knees in the sand. They were digging sand away from a partially exposed ancient building. While it stuck up a storey or two from the surface, there was no knowing how deep it went.

"It could be hundreds of meters!" Izumi excitedly reported. Wodston was less excited, but he kept digging, and expressed his regret about volunteering to help in silence. Izayah was carving through the sand with cupped hands, but most of it was just sliding back down into the hole. He seemed to be enjoying the exercise though, and Kalsi found endless entertainment biting at the flying clouds of sand behind him.

Izumi was simply standing and watching history in the making. Nuk joined her.

"I see you've taken my men," he noted.

"I'll pay them. Can pay you too if you help."

"I am helping. Me standing here enhances your prestige immeasurably. I'm famous, you know?"

"Yes, I know."

"Good. Cool. So, where's the stealing you promised?"

"It's here."

"The whole building?"

"Yep."

"How far's it go down?"

"Several hundred meters," Wodston sighed.

"Cool. But you know, might be hard to find a buyer for it."

"For a rugged ninja like you?" Izumi snarked.

"My clients usually expect better, that's all."

"Well this is history. It's priceless."

"Looking for stuff that's price-full, actually."

"In that case, keep an eye on them for a while would you? I'm going to see what else is around here."

"Sure, but I'm charging missy. Gonna get hot soon too. Man... Adventuring sucks."

"Don't worry, Prince Tashino," Izayah called. "We'll be out of here and back in the thick of it in no time!"

He was right, unfortunately. I mentioned already that Sho Battai didn't have a skimmer problem. And they were right outside the town gate, so desert rebels wouldn't dare attack. But there was a third scourge in the Great Desert: the manhunters. The manhunters worked for noble families, like Nuk's, to find lost slaves and return them to their masters. The twist was that few cared if it was actually the same slave they got back. Therefore, the manhunters would cut their working hours considerably by just picking up the first person they found, making them look like a slave, and collecting the ransom on them.

It was perfectly legal and perfectly common, and hence when Izumi spotted a group of manhunters coming in from the desert, she stopped feeling around the dunes for metal, and bolted without hesitation. And of course, running away was exactly the sort of thing a 'real' escaped slave would do, so that was the contract signed and sealed for the hunters.

"Escaped slave!" the manhunters cried as Izumi approached the town gate, drawing the attention of the guards, and indeed the nearby amateur archaeology crew.

"She's a slave? Fugging hell..." Nuk said with a hand on his forehead.

"That's not how this works, Prince. Come on!" Izayah shouted, rushing off with Kalsi to join the pursuit.

"Shall we join him, my Prince?" Wodston asked, itching to go.

"Why? Let the police sort it out."

"Izumi is carrying rather a lot of our money on account of the sponsorship you see..."

"Wodston! How did a dreg like you end up being a doctor? Okran's fugging blood, come on then!"

Sprinting at full pelt, the gang cut into the chase behind Izumi but in front of the closest manhunter. The fact that some genuine vagrants were loitering outside the gate distracted most of the slavers with easy pickings, and only one went through the gate after Izumi. Once inside, he found Nuk, Izayah and Kalsi blocking his path.

"She is not yours, curr," Izayah growled.

"Yeah, she's mine!" Nuk added, drawing angry shouts from Izumi.

"And who are you? Wearing noble clothes huh? A thief! Out of my way!" the manhunter demanded, stepping forwards and swinging a heavy club at the Prince. Izayah's sword clacked the blow aside, and a battle broke out, with Kalsi biting at the manhunter's legs while her master and his master's master took turns with their blades.

It would have been a victory for honour, righteousness, and so on, had the rest of the manhunters not piled down the steps from the gateway and called out for the samurai guards to intervene. It took a lot more than fighting in the street to get the guards to wake up, pull up their visors with eyes drawn on, and do their job. However, the manhunters were Sho-Battai's most lucrative industry, and required some level of indulgence to keep the coin levy, from which the guards took their hardly earned pay, afloat.

That is why a legion of armoured warriors stormed Nuk and company, and quickly had them on the ground in varying degrees of consciousness. Happy to finally be relieved, the wounded manhunter gave Kalsi a thwack across the head with his club, reopening her recent wounds. You think someone with the temperament for kidnapping and slavery wouldn't hold back from hurting a dog? I hope you begin to understand the degree of evil we're talking about here.

Nuk, Wodston, and Izayah struggled in the sand as their hands were bound and their feet shackled. Kalsi lay silently nearby, twitching around as blood started to pool. Only Izumi was absent, having continued her flight when she saw the guards take interest. She had slipped into a nearby store, chased by a manhunter, but then when they started fighting the store security decked them both. Thus Izumi now crawled from the shop with an injured leg, but without any scrutiny from the lethargic law.

Nuk and Wodston had already been dragged off to jail, and she got outside just in time to see the manhunters pick up an injured Izayah and take him in the opposite direction – towards the slave market. She started making her way towards Kalsi, but could only hobble after taking a bone-splintering kick during the melee.

By the time she reached the poor dog, it was too late. Izumi was left sitting in the street, looking dangerously vagrant, suddenly alone again. Tradition dictated that in a situation like this she should skip town and try her luck elsewhere. She had done as much with her last crew. Indeed she had all the money she needed for a while, thanks to Wodston. But guilt was keeping her still, anchoring her there on the spot where those strange folk had stood up for her, and lost nearly everything in an instant because of it.

Izumi made her choice. She endured the painful journey to the police station, and whacked the strings of coins Wodston had entrusted her with down on the police chief's desk. Nuk and Wodston's charges were dropped without hesitation. Wasn't even that expensive – the police strategy was more about volume of sales than high profit margins, with their main goal being to expand their marketshare. The RMBB Justice Initiative, or 'Recurrent Minor Bribes and Bails', was reaching wider, poorer, and less criminal demographics than ever before, and so can only be lauded as a success.

The police had patched the pair up, but Nuk was in a groggy stupor and refused to get out of his cage. Immediately bored, the police left Izumi the key and went back to reading their light adventure novels, and debating how certain words from old Earth Japanese were meant to be pronounced.

"Miss Izumi, you have our eternal thanks," Wodston said, coming to join her at Nuk's cage.

"This was my fault. I'm so sorry. I never thought this would happen. I just wanted to learn what the ancients did here. Why did it end up like this...?"

"History girl..." Nuk sputtered. "You... owe me..."

"I will do what I can, Prince Tashino. I will make this up to you. I'll work for your... err, consent, thingy, guild."

"Non-consensual private healthcare. But where is Izayah?"

"They took him to the market. Here, the rest of the money," Izumi said, handing all she had over to Wodston. Wodston understood the seriousness of the situation, and hurried to purchase himself one prime condition albino shek before that rare specimen was off the market. Izumi sat on the floor and did what she could to ease the strain on her leg, while Nuk's mumbling gradually became more and more coherent.

"I did it Dad, I'm a ninja, ninja, ninja..."

"That's right, Prince Tashino. You were very brave, like a ninja," Izumi said.

"Oh. Thanks Mum. I thought you left..."

"By his blood, I'm not getting into this."

Izumi left Nuk a note, and when the Prince awoke he followed the directions on it to the back of the town, where the party was finally regrouping around a campfire. Izayah was even less mobile than Izumi, and lay on the floor with his hands over his face.

"So, that was a fugging mess," Nuk said when he arrived.

"It was all a misunderstanding," Wodston sighed.

"Well you say that. So history-girl isn't an escaped slave then?"

"No! They're corrupt!" Izumi insisted.

"Corrupt? Why would they be corrupt?" Nuk asked. Izumi was aghast.

"I can't- You really think- It's like you've never left your palace once in your life!"

"I've been the bar like eight times, actually."

"You- You are the most incredible thing, you know that?"

Wodston was made very jealous by this remark - his own mistake.

"I am a literal Prince, so don't go giving me your dreg lectures," Nuk said, dismissing Izumi with a hand-wave as he was accustomed to doing with his servants. "Now, what's the plan? Izayah, my man, what's... Where's Kalsi?"

The look on the others' faces gave Nuk his answer. He went to sit beside Izayah.

"You okay man?"

"I'm afraid not, Prince Tashino. I think I shall have to leave your services."

"What? Why?"

"There is something I must do. You do not need to be involved."

"I'm literally here to be involved in your shid man, what is it?"

"... Revenge. On those damned slavers. They stole my sword, and killed my dog."

"Man, you're wrong. They killed *our* dog." Nuk put a hand on Izayah's scaly shoulder, and looked the shek in the eyes. "We're gonna burn their racket to the ground. Starting right fugging now."

Nuk leapt up and started making space in his rucksack.

"What are you planning to do, my Prince?" Wodston asked, wondering if they were about to be cast from pan to fire.

"Payback. Literal payback. I'll get our money back. 'Revenge: Part 1' - no, 'Revenge: Episode One The Phantom Pennies."

"And how are you going to do that?" Izumi asked, genuinely curious.

"Ninja business," Nuk quipped. With that he swung up his bag and stamped away.

"Ninja business? You're not a real ninja, Prince Tashino," Izumi called. Nuk snapped back around and pointed at his torn-t-shirt headdress.

"Uh huh? There's a reason I wear this, you know?"

"That's... surprising."

"You'll see. They'll all see."

And with these words, Nuk disappeared into the night, although only because he slipped on a sandbank and rolled out of sight. The others were left to rest and recover mind and body after their ordeal, while Nuk paid a little visit to the slaver's shop. His plan to break in during off hours to rob them clean was scuppered when he discovered the place was open 24 hours. What would be the appeal of living in a stinky town if you couldn't pop down the shops at 3am and get a new slave?

He had to just walk around awkwardly and pretend to be a customer, which was extra hard for a man who had never bought something from a store in his life. Once he was sure the guards weren't looking, he managed to swipe various bits and bobs from a workbench, including a couple of dried cactus strips and a broken angle grinder. Even the most heroic of shadowy thieves starts somewhere, you know?

And why start if you don't mean to continue? The next morning the crew discussed a return to the dig site; they were now in want of money, and even if they couldn't excavate anything good, they could collect up the stuff on the surface and sell it for scrap. Nuk ordered them to get to work.

"My Prince, why don't we return to the capital instead?" Wodston asked. Nuk shot him a foul look.

"They killed Kalsi, and who knows what they've done with her remains. This town's a disgrace, and we'll make them pay, somehow. I won't stop until I've cost them at least... Err... Izayah, how much was Kalsi?"

"About three thousand," Izayah said, returning his hands to his face as the topic got to him.

"Yeah, well, like, more than that and stuff. You guys do what dregs must etcetera. Hope you find some history or whatever."

Thus, while the crew laboured in the desert heat to earn their daily bread – good for sandwiches with emphasis on the sand – Nuk stalked the town. He visited the police station, claiming to be inspecting his men. They hit the one-shrug-minimum mandated response, and returned to their old pocket monster card game. Nuk walked up and down the storeroom, cursing under his breath at how every locker, chest and cupboard was empty. All the actual police equipment had been sold long ago – how do you think the chief was able to afford that shiny orange dragon card that dazzled his men as it slid coolly across the tabular battlefield?

With his plan literally foiled, Nuk went to the bar for a lunchtime tipple. It was a working lunch of course, for he was taking inventory of that which was not nailed down in the establishment. Bad news: it was all guarded by mercenaries. Worse news: they were out of rum. Amid his protests, Nuk learned that the rum had supposedly been stolen the previous night. Either Nuk had got so drunk from his spoils that he forgot the spoiling, or there was another sleuth in those there sands.

Only a man as familiar with the scent of rum as Nuk could have found this thief. The trail was mixed with a thousand other, far more pungent, scents, the reason for which quickly became clear: the rum wrangler of Sho-Battai was slumped in the latrines below the wall. Nuk tightened the binding of the shirt around his nose, and approached.

"Hey kid," he called out, taking a coin from his pocket. "Catch." He casually flicked the coin towards the fat, bloated shek sitting there in front of him. It landed far short of the mark, and the shek didn't move.

"Not going to fall for it," he chirped.

"You're going to fall into something far worse if you keep lounging in there, my man." Nuk got as close as he could endure before continuing. "You must be hungry after all that rum."

"I-I didn't do it!"

"Really?"

"Fine, okay I did it. But you'll never take me alive!"

"I won't?"

"Unless you really want to, I mean. Err..."

"'Err' indeed. I heard that you, my man, were the world famous rum thief of Sho-Battai?"

"Am I?"

"Yes, I'd say so."

"Wow. World famous."

"And it gets better. I happen to need the services of a man with a certain set of skills, who isn't afraid to... get dirty. (Man, why I am sweet talking a fat guy on the bog. Is this part of adventuring?)"

The shek laughed, stood from the latrine and closed the door. Then he hesitated.

"Wait. I told you, I won't fall for it!"

"If you need more time in there I can wait. Elsewhere that is."

"No! You're... a nobleman! You're going to turn me in for a bounty."

"Ha! You are right to be scared. I am a powerful man indeed. But that just means that this town has made a powerful enemy by wronging me and my friends. I'm a ninja, you see."

"A ninja!"

"Yes, and I'm looking for another soul as powerful as mine to aid me in my quest. A noble quest."

"R-Really?"

"And it gets better, kid. I'm willing to pay, like, three hundred New Empire Cats for the pleasure. (Is that a lot?)"

"I'll do it! Pick me!"

"Consider yourself picked. (Bog dweller and a corpse carrier – I'm starting a bloody reject shek collection). Your name?"

"Name? Err... At home they called me 'Bloody 'Ells'."

"Bloody Ells. Ha. They've got you good, kid. I'll call you Charlie. Come on Charlie, we've got a town to plunder. Or at least we'll kick up a literal stink. Man..."

And that's how ninja Nuk got himself a willing stooge to up the game in his plan to punish Sho-Battai. This strange ogre that emerged from the latrine was actually more than met the eye, although less than met the nose. In fact, the Prince's mission of revenge, and indeed his very life, would soon depend on the lumbering mass of Bloody 'Charlie' Ells. Whatever did the pauper prince do to deserve this?

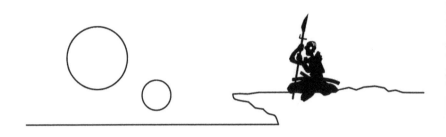

Chapter 4
Superliminal Criminal

"Who the fugg are you? Get out!" the woman shouted. Ells turned around without a word and went back outside.

"So they're at home then?" Nuk asked, leant again the wall outside.

"Yeah, there's a lady in there," Ells reported.

"Ooo how scary. Sneak in and steal something!"

This was Nuk's new idea to punish Sho-Battai for draining his coffers and killing his adventuring instructor's pet dog. By stealing the crockery from some local woman's kitchen, he was probably teaching the roving bands of slavers a lesson. Or something. Sometimes the logic of a professional ninja is characteristically hard to detect.

The home-owner had gone upstairs for a moment, and so Ells made his move. While the shek were, as a species, quite big and noisy, Ells had a gift – he had soft scales on his feet that muffled the sound of his footsteps. Thus the only sound he made as he snuck was the ruffle of his discoloured cargo shorts, and then soon the clattering of the crud-bundle he had under his arms.

"Good work my man. Wow, you stole a fugging steak off the grill! Still piping hot! You madman!" Nuk marvelled.

"I thought you wanted me to do it," Ells said, slightly crestfallen.

"You thought right, my man. Come on, hide the crap in my bag. I've already lined up our next target."

Outside the town, the gang had got a good taste of the sort of work Izumi did rummaging through three thousand year old junk, and now she was getting a taste of what the guild that sponsored her was about.

"Another one!" Izayah called. Wodston rushed over and knelt beside the vagrant. The local samurai had beaten up a few wanderers for breaking the law against looking tired and hungry in sight of a nobleman's estate.

Now Wodston was assessing the severity of the wounds, and more importantly, the likely sale value of the man's walking stick.

"So this is non-consensual private healthcare. You rob the dying," Izumi said.

"We provide a valuable service, and manage the patient's credit through a system of direct debit," Wodston explained.

"And I carry the corpses," Izayah added.

"I think that's all we can do for this one," Wodston was saying. Izumi stooped down and pulled a roll of coins from underneath the patient/victim. "Oh, well done Miss Izumi! I think I'll get his arm splinted in that case. Have you considered becoming a credit manager?"

"Seems like I'll pay you back faster this way," Izumi said, feeling the weight of the coins in her hand yet not the guilt of theft – such was the wonder of Wodston's miracle method.

They got the job done, and paired with the scrap metal they sold from Izumi's work, they got more than enough money for food and shelter. But the day's work wasn't over.

In the darkness of the general store, Nuk and Ells huddled in the corner.

"This fugging place is open twenty-four hours as well," Nuk whispered.

"Oh. Well when does it close then?" Ells asked.

"My rancid friend, you mustn't ask questions. Just hold the bag open will you?"

With that Nuk started dragging armfuls of miscellany towards Ells' rucksack. The clattering drew the attention of a guard, who wandered over.

"My friend, I'm so sorry! They're out of stock, and I know how much you wanted that, err..." Nuk took a peek into the bag. "White... lump - oh it's a fugging bowl – The, err, white bowl, you wanted. It's out of stock, that's what I'm saying to you, friend."

"I don't want to buy a bowl. We've already got one, remember?" Ells said. Nuk laughed heartily, pushing Ells past the two guards approaching them, and out the door.

"You fool! We've no bowls, they were out of stock! The shelf was bare before we arrived, remember? I just told you. Typical shek. Ha! Come on, my man."

Somehow the pair left without incident, and crashed their bags down at the guild's camp. The noise startled Wodston awake slightly, but he soon fell back asleep, hearing Nuk purring something about 'Phantom Pennies' to himself.

In the morning Nuk proposed that they leave town to go offload their haul in marketplaces that weren't awash with talk of stolen ceramics.

"I don't think I'm going to get much work done here, am I?" Izumi said. "All this dig had taught us is why no one was digging out here before."

"That's not entirely true, Miss Izumi," Wodston said, his face reddening all of sudden. "I think we learned a thing or to about the strength of your character, in the face of adversity. We all owe you our lives."

"Whoa, whoa, whoa," Nuk jumped in. "I don't owe history girl my life. It's the other way around. I was protecting her honour."

"Your guide here was protecting me," Izumi retorted. "And you just spent all night robbing innocents."

"Innocents? They... err... Look, I stole this stuff because of you."

"A gentleman indeed. I suppose the people here live from the profits of those damn manhunters."

"Yes, yes, exactly, what you said there, that was going somewhere, wasn't it? It goes somewhere where I'm right. Doesn't it Charlie?"

"I just done what you told me, master."

"Don't call him master, he doesn't like it," Wodston said. Nuk shook his head.

"No no, it's fine, it's a different thing here, don't worry. Izumi, you're now my official robbery justification consultant, okay?"

"No."

"Great. Now let's go fence this shid somewhere, get rich, then come back and do it again."

"You really don't need to keep doing this," Izayah said.

"Oh yes we do, man. We're taking these slavers all the way down. We're gonna keep taking their shid until the only thing they have left is their actual shid – and then Charlie here will probably get on that too. Don't ask."

Soon the crew filed out through the gates, joining a departing merchant caravan. The caravan was headed to Stoat, a town west of the capital, also on the lip of the desert. It was the long way home, but there were skimmer scarred 'customers' to attend to along the road, so it was by no means wasted time.

About halfway to Stoat there was a mining camp, outside which the crew came across a man hobbling around in shackles – a real escaped slave. Nuk jumped into action.

"What you doing?" the man croaked.

"Hold still, super dreg," Nuk said. After a great deal of rattling about with an iron nail in the shackles' lock, they snapped open. The man was lost for words, and ran off at once in a kind of euphoric panic.

"Prince of the Empire freeing slaves. Very bad," Izumi commented.

"Then spin it."

"Revenge... Sudden burst of morality perhaps?"

"First one. Come on, I wanna take a look at this slave stuff. Tsk, morality... Grow up."

Nuk led the band away from the caravan and into the mining camp. While the United Cities Empire was powered by slavery, nobles like Nuk didn't see very much of it, for the labours and privations were confined to work camps like that one. Everywhere men and women were mining stone and loading it onto pack beasts to be sold back in Sho-Battai. There were almost as many guards, ensuring not a single enslaved breath was not put to good use. When Nuk announced who he was, his party was allowed to browse the stock freely.

"Wodston, my man, did you know about all this?" Nuk asked.

"I had a certain idea, my Prince," Wodston replied.

"Is this what slaves do? Just this?"

"And similar labours."

"Man. And you can just get thrown into this mess. History girl was nearly out here."

"I'm sure once everyone released the mistake, things would have been rectified." Wodston didn't try very hard to make his words carry any conviction.

"Right. We're getting revenge for this too."

"My Prince?"

"Don't worry yourself. I'll arrange it. Come on."

Their brief visit was over, and Nuk was clearly upset to learn of the very thing that his Empire was world famous for. Or so communications manager Izumi would have you believe. Perhaps in truth, the burgeoning ninja just wanted an excuse for the string of burglaries he was planning for

Stoat's slave trading house. On the other hand, you and I, who know Nuk fairly well by now, might argue that he wasn't the sort of fellow to conspire excuses for his impulses.

Whatever the case, the brief overnighting in Stoat left Wodston awkwardly carrying a rolled up rug, and everyone's bags were bulging with a smorgasbord of semi-valuable bits, bobs, misc. and other. They now faced a day long trek across the soft white sands that ran down from the Heng highlands on the desert's southern edge.

"Where are you from then, Charlie?" Izayah asked the new shek.

"I'm from the Shek Kingdom," was the helpful reply.

"Yes. Any town in particular?"

"Not really."

"Ah, perhaps I understand you. Have you been to Admag recently?"

"No. What's Admag?"

"It's the capital. The Queen lives there."

"Oh I know the Queen!"

"As do I, as it happens."

"Are you from Admag?"

"Indeed I am."

"Then why are you here?"

"Ha, well the story there is in my very image."

"Because you're fat?"

"What? No because I'm albin- You're the fat one!"

"Ha, yeah. It's from rum."

"And I suspect other deficiencies share a similar cause."

"What?"

"Exactly."

Heft was the same old same old: a giant battle was under way between a platoon of samurai and a lumbering, towering skimmer, big enough to be king of all skimmers, and had already been raging for hours.

"Peace at last!" Nuk declared as they walked on by the struggle, and over towards the stuffy little WNCPHG HQ. While the others were happy for the rest, and the protection of a more loyal brand of law-bringer, Nuk had been scheming for the whole trip, and couldn't wait to put his new plan into action. He rushed off to the north end of the city, to visit his old partners in the hashish business: the ring of shinobi smugglers known to some as the Thieves Guild.

"Oi, who's this mysterious disguised man walking up on my tower," the thief boss said as Nuk approached.

"I am a passing ninja, with an interesting proposition for you," Nuk said.

"Oh yeah? How about you hand over the five grand you owe me?"

"What? I know not of what you speak, kind sir."

"Tashino, take that thing off your head."

"Tashino? Who is Tashino?"

"Where's my five grand?! I got a receipt here that says you ordered, to quote, 'A fuggload' of hashish. And you got it. Pay up and I'll spare you life."

"Y-you don't- You can't kill me!"

"Why not?"

"I'm the Prince!"

"Whoops. My mistake. Okay, ten grand."

"Look, fine. Okay, it's me. I've got some stuff for you. Good stuff. I've been going a little ninja-ing, you see."

"Oh, you're getting into the business are you?"

"Freelance credit management and unannounced product recall. I've got a lot of work to do in the palace."

"Really?"

"Yeah. Why don't you sign me up, and you can take the stuff off my hands?"

"Sure, that'll be ten grand."

"I'll give you this broken angle grinder if you make it five."

"I won't increase it to twenty if you agree right now."

"Deal!"

Almost all of the Tashino Credit Management Guild's capital was forked over, in exchange for official membership of the 'shinobi thieves network', a worldwide band of grey market traders. It wasn't as cool as being a ninja, but Nuk wasn't going to let that stop him buying all the official shinobi merch with the money he made fencing the hauls from his adventure/business trip.

At last he actually began to appear somewhat disguised, swapping his vibrant robes for an edgy black rag shirt, and a 'Chief Thief' brand black designer rucksack. He rushed home to show his friends how cool he was now, but they were selfishly asleep. They'd need all the sleep they could get to cope with discovering what had happened to all their money.

In the meantime, Nuk went out for his first night on the job. He walked up to his father's palace, and did something akin to sneaking inside. Well, let's be honest, he walked in through the front door dressed like an old sock in need of retirement. But the guards recognised the Prince and decided not to intervene with his rummaging about the palace. Thus, the amateur shinobi, with union dues fully paid, had a very successful shift at the surprisingly-in-need-of-recall products depot.

In the morning he popped his head around the door of Wodston's shed.

"I swear I locked it up!" Izayah was saying.

"You've cost us all our money! Those insatiable thieves," Wodston moaned. Enter Nuk.

"Ha, you've been fooled, my man."

"What the fugg are you wearing? Your majesty..." Izumi asked.

"This is my shinobi uniform."

"No it's not."

"Ten thousand cats says otherwise."

"We're missing exactly ten thousand cats," Izayah said. Oh, by the way, a cat was the unit of currency in the Empire, so don't get the wrong idea here.

"M-my Prince, you haven't fallen in with the thieves of the tower have you?" Wodston asked.

"Technically no. We ALL have!" Nuk proudly cheered.

"My Prince?"

"That's right. The err... Wodman Non-conceptual health guild is now an associate member of the Union of Shinobi Thieves."

"Ten thousand cats..." Izayah lamented. Maybe he was thinking about the animal, I don't know.

"My Prince, are you sure that's a wise investment? Or an investment at all?" Wodston asked.

"Wodston. How much to you think we're going to steal from those slavers? Less than ten grand? Bah! I'll make the money back stealing dad's shid alone!"

"You've been robbing the palace again?"

"No, I was out helping the poor learn to ride bloody skimmers. Of course I'm robbing dad!"

"I feel that's the sort of thing you shouldn't shout about," Izumi commented.

"Well, history girl, you probably think actions speak louder than words, don't you?"

"What? Are you accusing me of something?"

"You sit there, saying that stealing is wrong, but I don't see YOU stealing anything!"

"Err... That's... not exactly an argument. Or... even a real sentence."

"Then forget the words. It's time for action! Follow me!"

The confused guild went with Nuk to the shinobi tower by the north gate. It turns out that this union of thieves offered all kinds of membership perks – childcare, bed and breakfast, free haircuts, and most importantly of all for Nuk, a thievery enrichment program. Courses such as 'Deconstructing Tropes in Common Locksmithing', 'A History of Spinal Severance', and the ever popular 'Corpse Looting for Intermediates', all promised to enrich students in quite the literal sense. Nuk had signed the whole gang up for some intensive training, ahead of what he referred to as 'Revenge Episode 2: Piddler on the Roof'.

As it happens, what precisely this entailed was not destined to come to light. Probably for the best really. Nuk's perfectly laid plans had one fatal flaw: Nuk Tashino. While his friends were being recruited to stealing school, he went out on a field trip. He walked up to the palace doors, pushing an old wheelbarrow in front of him. He waved his hands at the guards.

"I'm not the thief you're looking for," he said, his voice muffled by a flap of t-shirt in his mouth.

"Prince Tashino. Heard you'd be back. Go on then," the guard sighed. About an hour later Nuk huffed and puffed his way back out, with the wheelbarrow filled with light fixtures, tableware, board game pieces, and even handfuls of loose grains and flour. Thorough, gotta give him that. Only problem was that the guards stepped out to block his path.

"Not stealing this barrow of imperial property, are you, my Prince?" the guard asked.

"No, I'm going to donate them to the poor," Nuk replied sarcastically.

"So shall I take that as a yes, my Prince?"

"No! This, you dreg, is credit, and I am its manager. As you are not the account holder, I cannot give out confidential information on its origin, destination, or black market resale value."

"Would you step away from the barrow for a moment, my Prince?"

More guards appeared from behind him. Oh dear.

"Y-you dregs! I let you smoke my fugging hashish! Just let me go, alright?"

"Afraid we've got orders from the Emperor, my Prince. I see you've got his shoes in your barrow there."

"They were recalled by the manufacturer!"

"And our contacts in the shinobi tell me you've signed your guild up for the 'Delux Steal-Deal Imperial Package'. Not planning any criminal activity, are you, my Prince?"

A back and forth of much the same nature went on for some time. While the prince was distracted by alternately arguing with and insulting the guard, his loot was steadily returned to its place by the palace staff, and a pair of shackles was clamped around his ankles.

"You insufferable double dreg, shids!" Nuk shouted. "My father will hear of this insult!"

"Three, two, one, let's jam!" his father was singing upstairs, doors locked, volume up, clothes a thing only of distant memory.

Nuk was pushed down the palace ramp, and told that his exile began for real now.

"We've organised a little trip for you, my Prince," the guard said. With the comic timing of the old masters, a foot was extended, Nuk was upended, and his face smashed into the coarse metal at the ramp's base. The loud laughter from the guards attracted the attention of Izayah, who was doing some homework in the nearby guild HQ. 'The Dos and Dos of Sewer Sleuthing' was not the most interesting of required reading, so he walked outside, just in time to see an unconscious Nuk being carried into the jail across the road.

"See what cards he has!" one of the police was excitedly saying. Izayah rushed after them to investigate. Not the card thing, the Nuk being arrested thing. He arrived to see Nuk being fussed over in a prison cage by a huge gang of manhunters. Bad news. Manhunters often broke people out of prison to add to their stocks, which saved the police time as well, so it was all above board.

"I hope you're not considering laying your hands on the Prince of the empire," Izayah lectured them. They didn't like it.

"Well, you know too much, don't ya! That's illegal!" one claimed. The group piled on the poor shek, and locked him up in one of the cages. Then one of them dragged Nuk outside.

That is how disaster struck our poor crew. Denied their inspirational leader, and with their adventuring instructor falsely imprisoned, how could they go on? Well to be honest they didn't even notice for a pretty long time.

But eventually, it would be time for action, and sitting through that 'Jailbreaking for Busy Professionals' course would very much pay off.

Chapter 5
Stone-cold, Stone-hot

Nuk tried to open his eyes. Wasn't happening.

"Wodston... It was the bad green..." he mumbled. This attracted the attention of someone nearby.

"Finally. Welcome to slavery. I am obligated to provide you with the following orientation talk."

A slaver got out some notes and began reading aloud before Nuk, slumped in a cage.

"The party to whom you have been indentured, hereby referred to as your 'Master' or 'Masters', reserves the right to impose upon you any and all terms as detailed in section two to the slave handbook. In as far as these provisions allow, you, hereby referred to as 'the slave', are to adhere to the express will of the Master in a manner deemed convenient by Master or representatives thereof."

As the sun set on section 1.1, clause 4, volume 1, Nuk finally heard enough words to work out what was going on here. His head had been cruelly shaven, and his ninja sword stolen away. All he had left was his designer ninja rag-shirt, which the slavers had foolishly mistaken for the actual rags common to their clientèle. The Prince of the empire was now its slave!

The next morning he was dragged out of his cage and pointed at a big pile of rocks.

"Alright, boy, listen up," a slaver said.

"I'm the fugging Prince! Listen to me you dreg!"

Nuk earned himself a slap across the face.

"Don't be rude. It violates section four, subsection eight of the 7th edition of the Slave's Code."

"Oh yeah? Well what can I say? My copy must have been tampered with. Was just a load of weird drawings of girls in old sailor outfits getting all red in the face around some guy."

"Yeah, that's the one. Oh Yasuke..." the slaver sighed. "Just be quiet, right? See that big rock? We need rocks smaller than that. Have fun."

Now Nuk got to really experience the labour he'd seen near Sho-Battai. Hit the rock, round the clock. You were allowed the freedom to choose which part of the rock to hit next. Slaves never used to have it that good, the talk around the camp claimed.

That was Nuk's life settled then. Or it would have been, if a curious Wodston hadn't wondered why things were so quiet, peaceful, and almost happy, back in the capital. He took an educated guess and checked the prison, finding Izayah to his surprise, and then learning the truth of the matter.

"I'm sorry, Izayah, but I must go to him as soon as I can. We shall return for you, I promise," Wodston said.

"Worry not, Mister Wodston. I've stood in one of these cages for far longer, and you have a duty to your master. I'm sure he would do the same for you."

"The heat in here has you deluded, I'll fetch some water!"

Even a mere undergraduate in jailbreaking knew that it was best to focus on a single breakout at any given time. Therefore, Wodston left Izayah in the sizzling slammer for now, and rushed to join his classmates in the tower.

"I thought he'd last at least another day," Izumi said.

"So we have to steal the master! I'll do it!" Ells chirped.

"We'll see, Charlie. We need to work together. Prince Tashino is relying on us to save him," Wodston said.

"Once those idiots rescue me, I'm gonna kill them for letting this happen!" Nuk muttered to himself. Ooo, there's a spot no one's hit yet, quickly! Ah, so satisfying! The romance of a summer slave never dies. Well, he probably wasn't thinking that, but his guards were. Seeing virgin slabs of sweet quarry going to waste day after day... no wonder they were so tense.

Anyway, Izumi, Ells, and Wodston pooled their collective brainpower to come up with a rescue plan.

"And then, with the market in decline, the nobles will visit the camp to lay off workers," Izumi was explaining. "We'll use the disguises we acquired in the second stage to infiltrate their entourage. That's where the cardboard skimmers come in."

It was a genius scheme that would allow the trio to sweep Nuk away from under the slavers' noses. What's better, hearing the plan inspired an even better one in the bottomless mind of Bloody Charlie Ells, one that would achieve the very same goal, in far fewer words.

So it was that the next afternoon, Wodston announced his intention to purchase a slave at the gatehouse of the stone mining camp south of the capital. Allowed entry, he left Izumi and Ells to keep watch by the gates, while he searched for Nuk. He was easy enough to find.

"Look at these hands," Nuk was shouting. "Do these look like hands that could ever harm an innocent rock?"

"They love it!" a guard claimed. "You know. Gets their rocks off. Err ha ha ha ha!"

"Oh by his blood. You mean like 'ohhh... miner-senpay, harder please'."

"Oooo. Ooohhhh wait. Do you know how to draw? We gotta hear this one out."

Nuk's promotion was interrupted by Wodston.

"Prince Tashino! You're okay," he said.

"Wodston! Where the fugg have you been?" Nuk shot back.

"On our way here, my Prince"

"I got here in like two hours and I was bloody blacked out."

"Ah, well we had to develop a plan to ensure your successful rescue, my Prince?"

"A plan?"

"Yes. Your apprentice proved most helpful in that regard."

"Apprentice?"

"The portly shek, Charlie."

"He's still- You didn't get rid of him?"

"Oi," the guard interrupted. "Are you here to buy this thing or not? He's worth a lot to us, you know?"

"Ah, I'm sure his father would be happy to hear someone say that of him," Wodston said with a smile.

"Wodston my man, they've been here with these fugging rocks far too long, let me assure you of that. Now, would you care to execute this amazing plan you spent a bloody day concocting?"

"At once, my Prince. Excuse me, guards! Everyone. Did you ever the story of- Oh wait, what's that over there?!" Wodston cried, pointing in a vague direction. Then he scooped Nuk up over his shoulder, and absolutely legged it. From under the noses of the guards indeed.

Wodston may have been an aged fellow, but his hard work kept him supple, and unusually powerful. The guards could hardly keep up with him as he dashed, and whenever they got close enough to thwack at him with their clubs, he dodged the blows with ease. The element of surprise helped too. The guards at the gate didn't believe the man running at them with a slave on his shoulder could really be pulling a fast one – who would be so brazen? A man with a duty to his Prince, and not enough time to cut out a load of cardboard skimmers, is the answer.

Still, after clearing the camp and running up a nearby rocky embankment, Nuk's flailing got the better of him. He stumbled, and a guard clobbered him to the ground. Nuk rolled out of the crash and was immediately on his feet and running. The guards didn't pursue. Finally they knew their place! Or, more accurately, it was the usual lack of care at play; they were happy to just enslave Wodston instead.

Was this what the loyal servant deserved? Surely not. Luckily, the mastermind of the breakout was already in a huff about not being trusted to carry it out himself. Now, as he and Izumi rushed out and saw Wodston being led back down to the camp, Ells had his time to shine.

"Bloody Ells, here he comes again!" the shek shouted as he charged. A battle cry perhaps? He swept Wodston away with little effort, and thus now the guards were chasing him. The big chap had quite the pair of legs on him though, and they couldn't keep up. Izumi found Nuk breaking open his shackles beyond the embankment.

"You're still around too?" Nuk said.

"Great to see you too, Prince Tashino. Come on!"

"If you were dead, or gone or whatever, I'd have said you were 'history!"

"Incredibly funny. You're like a ninja of comedy. The laughs are gone before you even know they were there, Now let's fugging move!"

"Alright, calm down. And I thought I was the one who got shafted."

They joined Ells and Wodston, dashing south over the lumpy bluffs of Heng. Only a single guard was able to keep up, and as the chase wore on and the darkness of night fell, even he realised he didn't actually care. Thus the crew disappeared into some shadowy crags, just a stone's throw from one of the many united cities of Nuk's Empire, a prosperous market named Trader's Edge.

Not that they were to enjoy its comforts that night. With talk of escaped slaves abound, best to not stride into town wearing little else than shackles and a smile. They would enjoy the cold, dry skimmer steaks from Wodston's rucksack, al fresco.

"Took your time didn't you!" Nuk began. It was time to deploy the admonishment he'd been mentally preparing all day.

"They took your hair," Izumi quipped in response. She wasn't wrong. Nuk and Wodston had been balded, for in the United Cities, to have hair was to be free. It's cheaper than ID papers, right? Luckily for the gang, this was a physical and psychological sore spot of Nuk's, and so his tirade was cancelled in favour of huffing, puffing, growling, and scowling on the ground.

"I stole you I did!" Ells said to Wodston.

"Yes, well done, Charlie."

"That means you're mine!"

"No, sorry to say."

"Uh huh. That's what they said at stealing school!"

"Ah yes, but those lofty academics don't know what it's like in the real world."

"Don't they?"

"No, not at all. Not like the lady Izumi here."

"Lady Izumi?" Izumi asked.

"I mean... Not to say that you are a 'lady', in formal terms."

"She's a man?" Ells asked.

"I'm whatever you want me to be, my hideous friend," Izumi said.

"Oh. She said I'm her friend!"

Ells was satisfied with the result of the conversation, it seems.

They relaxed on the cool sands, with the odd ear and eye open for manhunters, but their choice of crag had been quite wise in the end, for it was hidden from man and beast alike, with many local amenities in walking distance. The latter point was to come in very useful in the morning. Nuk and Wodston needed hats to avoid suspicion, and the group as a whole were collectively sharing one or two too few items of clothing, with Nuk bottomless and Ells topless. Izumi was happy to volunteer coin to resolve this.

"Take Charlie, as your bodyguard," Nuk ordered.

"He's a little... Or a lot... He draws attention, doesn't he?" Izumi complained.

"Yes, exactly. If you get into trouble, he'll buy you plenty of time."

"I don't buy things, I take them!" Ells proudly claimed.

"Yes, well take a few sword blows for our lady here if you have to, alright?"

"Yes master! Nothing I can't take!"

"You've understood me perfectly. Off you go then, before I get fugging sunburn up here."

The slaves were left in their nook, while the grubby girl and sizeable shek went shopping. This town, Trader's Edge, was quite a good spot for it. It had a whole tower dedicated to selling clothes. Anything you could ever want, as long as it's brown. Sums the whole world up really. They did have some more exciting items in the bargain barrel, to which Izumi's handful of cats just about stretched.

Their haul had the two slaves looking perfectly presentable. Wodston was particularly impressed.

"Miss Izumi, how did you know?" he asked.

"Know what?" Izumi replied.

"My size... My colour... My smell..."

"What?"

"It's just like my old gi from the palace! You're so thoughtful! I didn't..."

"Didn't?"

"I just... I've never seen such... care..."

Izumi felt somehow that telling him it was probably the very same clothes he had been wearing before, flogged off here by the slavers, would hurt his feelings. Nuk was now rocking a grey turtle-neck and a wide kasa sunhat, like a ninja who had important office paperwork to attend to. All in all, the group appeared somewhat less like the two men, woman, and shek who had been reported by the slavers the previous day. None would suspect a thing!

In reality, Wodston had already explained to Nuk that they would need to lie low for a lot longer before they could walk the roads freely again. Nuk liked the idea of lying, but low wasn't his style. How fortunate that the

Prince had made investments wiser than any could have predicted: there was a branch of the thieves' guild at the far end of Trader's Edge.

Thus Nuk and company rushed into town, their disguises holding long enough to get them into the shady thief tower.

"Hello friends," Nuk said, a sword at his neck as soon as he passed through the door.

"Members only," a faceless shinobi grunted.

"Member? I'm the bloody chief thief!" Nuk said, showing off his expensive label bag.

"Oh, you're a rich idiot. Alright then. Bed and board, is it?"

"Bed and fun, hopefully."

"Definitely an idiot then. Got money?"

"Of course," Nuk bluffed. In this way he was put up on the roof of the tower. Great views, very private, and what hotel did daily courses in murder down in the rec room? Even sceptical Izumi had to admit that the prospect of lounging around and attending the odd lecture sounded pretty good, all paid for with good old fashioned student debt, (or shinobi debt in this case). So there we shall leave our heroes for now, but alas we are missing someone, aren't we?

Well the champion Izayah was himself about to embark to a far less luxurious land of low-laying. In the middle of the night he heard all the police in the station gathering downstairs for something called the 'Gen. One Keepsakes Sweepstakes', which kicked up a lot of hooting, crying, and the occasional refrain of a song about, to quote, "being the very best". As they sang such words, the prisoner they were meant to be guarding carefully dislodged the bolt on his cage, and crept out onto the rear balcony.

Nice to get a bit of air, but he was still trapped. The only way out of the tall station was through the front door. Without Nuk and friends to create a distraction, he had no chance to escape. So instead he would just have to chill, looking up at the same sky as the others, eating the same, hairy, crusty steaks peeled from the inside of a rucksack as the others, and waiting for fate to reunite them once more.

At least Izayah could feel proud. He didn't know exactly what had happened to Nuk, or the rescue attempt, but he felt certain that whatever was going on out there, the gang were having a grand old adventure. And somewhere, up among the stars, poor Kalsi was too.

Ah Izayah, don't worry; your fellow Prince has not forgotten about you! Quite the opposite: Trader's Edge was a wealthy slaving town, with shelves packed with loose revenge. It was time for a high synergy working vacation worthy of that turtleneck.

Chapter 6
The Ten Grand Man

The guard could tell something was wrong. All the slave cages on the second floor of the shop were unlocked. But how? He couldn't tell the owner – after all, it had been his own responsibly to lock them. Had he forgotten? A true mystery. Just lucky he came by before the slaves all went walkabouts. His eyes passed from one end of the rooftop showroom to the other. Nothing. Then he focused on fixing the locks, his eyes just barely grazing over the shek sitting on the floor two feet in front of him.

This was Bloody Charlie Ells, and as long as he remained downwind of the authorities, he was nigh on invisible. There was something about him that simply didn't register in one's mind. The secret was his ability to slow his brain down to a crawl, preventing any nerves from firing, granting him absolute stillness. Wrapped in a crumpled, oversized coat, he simply looked like a pile of laundry to the untrained eye.

Once the guard was satisfied that his incompetence was suitably hidden, he went back downstairs. Then, the pile of laundry rustled to life.

"Going to get you out. Slavery is bad. It makes my master really sad," the shek hummed as he skilfully tumbled the locks on both cage doors, and the shackles of the occupants. Some of the captives thanked him, and waited for their moment to spring out and run. Others were happy to take their chances with the guards right now. Handy, for it provided Ells the perfect chance to escape, and even the slave got a good deal: no one was going to buy a product with a crossbow bolt sticking out of it.

So what was all this? As mentioned, this city, Traders Edge, was a hub of the United Cities slaver racket. Ells was carrying out the wishes of his wanted master Nuk, by punishing the locals for their complicity. The stealthy shek cleared the shelves of the traders' guild headquarters across town. Then he snuck into a restricted warehouse, and pilfered thousands of cats worth of electronics, building materials, and weapons. But then, a guard rounded a corner and saw him.

"What the fugg are you doing here?!"

"Err... I'm just the laundry," Ells insisted.

"Is that...? You dirty bastard. Get out! What were you doing? Urgh, filthy shek!"

Ells quickly trotted off, the huge bulge in his shorts that had unnerved the guard wobbling this way and that. He's shoved a stolen prosthetic arm down there, you see. To hide it. Probably. After that close call, he stuck to sticking his pickings in his ninja grab bag, on loan from Nuk.

The others slept the days away in the cool thieves tower, while Ells ravenously robbed the bars, the houses, the shops, the barracks, the police station... Demand for laundry services was through the roof, as the whole town discussed the huge piles of dirty rags they'd seen in all corners. And they swore they'd been cooking a steak on the grill just now.

After a few days, Nuk was lying on the on the roof of the tower, with shiny golden cats over each eye, and plenty more scattered around his bed. It's good to own the means of corruption. Wodston dared to interrupt his bathing in the wages of sin.

"My Prince. I heard a rumour that a caravan is heading back to the capital. I dare say the guards won't be on the lookout for us anymore, so why don't we go?"

In response to this, Nuk ran his hands over the mounds of coins around him, creating small, metal avalanches that tinkled this way and that.

"My Prince?" Wodston said again.

"Hear that revenge? What's the rush?" Nuk asked.

"Well... Izayah..."

"Oh you had to go right there, didn't you?"

"I'm sorry, my Prince."

"Look, I know we need to go. But I worked real hard at that stone perving place. I guess, I just figured that if I had a fugg-tonne of money, it would all be worth it."

"I fear our hosts may feel the same. The bounty on our heads must be hard to resist."

"Bounty? What are we talking here?"

"I... Miss Izumi said you are going for over ten thousand in the market square."

"Oooo that's nice. Ten thousand. Imagine if you could get ten thousand cats for stealing just a single item."

"Is anything so valuable, my prince?"

"I am. And I've got a bloody good idea. Charlie! Where's Charlie! I need a lift."

Nuk's idea was indeed, beyond brilliant. He had his filthy thrall carry him over the police station.

"I got a bounty!" Ells announced. The police chief looked down at Nuk, who had just been slapped onto the table, all over the cards in play.

"He got me, what can I say. Pay the man. Or the thing. Pay that," Nuk said, pointing his eyebrows towards Ells. The police chief huffed as he counted out ten huge strings of cats. Nuk let himself into a cage upstairs.

"Alright guys. Don't mind me. Life sentence. Yeah I know. No sense guarding me too much right now, you'll get bored of it. Let's pace ourselves here," Nuk said. The guards nodded at this thoughtful advice. When Ells and Izumi came to visit the prisoner that night, he had been given his own floor of the prison all to himself, with no guards.

"Oi, what's going on down there?" Nuk asked.

"I don't know. They've got visitors in. They're drawing little pictures of rocks, or something," Izumi said.

"Oh Yasuke..." Nuk sighed.

"What?"

"I know right. What an idiot."

"You read my mind. I see you're in prison, your majesty?"

"Oh yeah, this old thing. It's not to keep me in here, it's to keep the world away from me, you know?"

"Prince Tashino, would you please shut up?"

"Bloody police are nicer than you. What do you want exactly, history girl?"

"We're here to fugging break you out!"

"I'm not ready to go, actually."

"Yes you are. Disgusting, stinky man-thing, come break him out," Izumi ordered Ells. Ells began picking up the entire cage and walking out, but after some hushed panicking, Nuk was finally convinced to just fiddle the lock like he'd learned in shinobi school, and Ells smuggled him outside. They got back to Wodston, guarding the fortune now gathered on the tower roof, and all in all the operation had been a huge success. However, even as perfect a thing one had one fatal flaw: Nuk Tashino.

The next day, he had Ells take him down the station again.

"Got another one, ten money sticks please," Ells said. The police chief looked up at the shek.

"Yeah, normally they put a moustache on them the second time round, or something. New in town?"

"Yes. Pleased to meet you sir. My name is Bloody Ells."

"Bloody Ells... Right, off you go then."

"Thanks. Bye!"

"Hang on a minute!" Nuk interrupted, before the police chief stuffed a sock in his mouth. Thus, by pushing his luck too far, Nuk was imprisoned for real, and Izumi had to pay a full twenty thousand cats to have the charges dropped. The police chief gave her a complementary fake moustache though, and wished them better luck next time with a warm wave goodbye. Nice guy.

"History girl," Nuk began once they were outside. "You must be recording my personal history, right?"

"Err... why would I do that?"

"Because I'm famous! I'm a... statesman."

"That moustache is meant to go above your lip, by the way."

"Tsk, like you would know about that. Look, I want you to erase certain things from the record."

"Or I could pre-emptively erase everything by not writing anything."

"Hmm... That's even better, right?"

"I certainly think so."

"Nice. Good. You're a... no..."

"A what? Say it, Prince."

"Well, I thought for a second that you were a good, history girl."

"Ah. Good enough to know you're wrong there."

"Which would make me right, right?"

"Wr- Oh. Well. Bugger."

"Can't outwit me. Now, watch me steal all those t-shirts there. For revenge, and stuff."

Nuk and company stayed in Traders Edge for a couple more days, redistributing the wealth they had just lost back into their pockets. Let's check in with Izayah, shall we? Well, he was still slumped on the second floor balcony of the Heft police headquarters, with no entertainment but the voices coming from the assembly hall below him.

"So I present to you now, a most important lesson," one was saying. "I want you all to remember this: the three Bs of policing. Bounties. Bribes. Bail. Some scholars will come in here telling you that there are actually *five* Bs. But those other two are just bribe again. And I always say that if you have to ask for a bribe more than once, you're better off taking a bounty instead! Ha ha ha! So don't worry about that. Remember: in this business the only freebies, are the three Bs!"

Very educational. At least the worst was over. A couple of days later, Nuk, Wodston, Izumi, and Ells settled their tab at the thieves' tower (paying it with t-shirts like respectable guests), and set off for Heft, having cost Trader's Edge tens of thousands in missing property, and freed a couple of slaves along the way. Pretty nice, but after that whole ordeal, 'revenge' was going to be getting a lot more episodes, with pre-production on episode six "Eternal Funtimes of the Topless Kind", well under way, (although what Ells had meant when he suggested that title remained unclear).

They arrived that evening after a tiring desert march, but there was still work to do. And by that, I of course mean there was still work for Wodston to do. The doctor went back to the prison cage where he had left Izayah, but it was empty. Mysterious. Wodston feared the poor shek had been taken as a slave himself, but then he heard a strange muttering from outside.

"Bounties... Bribes... Bail..."

"I-Izayah! What are you doing here?" Wodston croaked as he emerged onto the balcony.

"Mister... Wodston! Oh Okran's grace! I'd almost given up hope," Izayah said.

"Izayah, we would never forget you. We'll tell you all about it. Now, put this jacket on, and imagine you're a roll of dirty bedsheets."

"I'm not really in a mood for anything like that, Mister Wodston."

"It's an escape plan! Trust me, we've been practising."

The ever-surprising strength of old man Wodston bore Izayah down the ramp and out the front door.

"Ah, my lost laundry, thanks old man who I don't know," Nuk said loudly outside. Seemed legit. To complete the plan, the crew took their shekly sheets outside of the town, in order to then have all five of them walk into town and be noted as people who couldn't have possibly been in prison up until just now. They didn't even need to bother really; it was late in the day, and as you already know, the guards' eyes are just drawn over their closed eyelids.

Thus, after all the madness, the gang packed themselves into Wodston's cramped little shed in the corner of town.

"Well, you've had a far more dramatic time of it than I," Izayah said after hearing a summary of the story.

"Sorry you missed it, man. But we're gonna get you some proper revenge now," Nuk said.

"Oh, Prince Tashino, you really needn't. You've already been through so much for me."

"Yeah, and check this out."

Nuk opened his bag. Ten thousand cats. Still just talking about the money, unfortunately, but that was still pretty good.

"Ah... the phantom pennies."

"Exactly. And starting tomorrow, you're going to earn a few for yourself, adventuring instructor."

"Wait, does that mean there's going to be another adventure?" Izumi asked, slumping down on a bedroll.

"Err, yes! What do you think the Tashino Credit Management Guild does?"

"Robs... corpses?"

"And...?"

"And... gets beaten up?"

"AND...?!"

"... Goes on adventures-"

"Goes on adventures! Exactly! Only this time, we're gonna be ready. We're gonna go pro."

"Ha, well that's the right spirit for it at least!" Izayah noted. "But please, don't do it for me, this time."

"Guess we can get revenge on something else... Like... Oh... History girl!"

"What did I do?"

"No, we'll get revenge on like, the past!"

"Ah yes. Bloody past."

"We'll steal some more of your history stuff. Gets us rich, right?"

"Sure, that's why I'm trying to sleep on a straw mat in a dusty shed that stinks of... the lesser shek."

"Izayah don't smell!" Ells noted, looking up from a sack of old beans that had his full attention over in the corner.

"There are plenty of historical sites out there," Izayah said. "Untouched for the most part."

"If you guys are serious, then sure, let's do it," Izumi said.

"Perhaps there will be less interference from those crooked slavers," Wodston reasoned.

"Oh yes, we won't get any trouble from them," Izayah reassured him. "However, there are reasons people don't visit the old ruins..."

"Reasons that won't be able to stop us!" Nuk proclaimed.

"Ah yes. You are the enemy of reason after all," Izumi noted.

Nuk resolved to prove himself with an actual adventure then, but now that he was a little more worldly, he knew that he needed to focus less on looking like a ninja, which he had of course achieved flawlessly, and more on *being* one. He needed to learn which end of a sword was the pointy one, and perhaps even more advanced martial arts secrets.

That, in a roundabout away, was why he burst into the home of a local townswoman the next day.

"You shinobi are less subtle than ever," the woman noted. Nuk pointed at her.

"You'll never get a buyer like that."

"What? Get out of my house!"

"Don't you mean MY house?"

Nuk had five strings of cats (the coins, again), dangling from his fingers. In a weird, poorly rehearsed fashion, he swang them up in front of him, and with his other hand he sliced the strings with his blade. The shrieking woman was subject to a bombardment of scattering bronze and silver. Once the racket of this economic explosion settled, Nuk announced that this was his house now. Once the woman realised just how much cash he had splurged all over the shop, she decided not to argue, and head off with coins in hand – it was worth a Prince's ransom, as we well know.

This was how the Tashino Credit Management and Unannounced Product Recall Guild, and the Wodston Non-consensual Private Healthcare

Guild and the Semi-professional Association of Archaeological Grudge Settlers, all got a brand new headquarters.

The hillside townhouse was in a quiet, well-to-do-area of the city. The sort of place where no one would suspect that a band of would-be criminal academics were scheming away. Okay, perhaps you would expect that, especially if you saw the new rooftop training space Wodston had set up. Mats had been laid out, and sticks gathered, so that the crew could get to grips with fighting. Slavers usually couldn't be bothered with stock that fought back. With Izayah to show everyone the basics, they'd soon be much more road-ready than before.

Downstairs they set up an office for Izumi to collect her notes and work on her supposed body of research. Very cushy actually, and it meant any guards who poked their head around the door would see a somewhat respectable home to suit the somewhat respectable neighbourhood. The fact that most of the books in this office had lewd cover art and 'property of slaver Gav' and the like scrawled inside them would go completely undiscovered. In the desert, a book's a book (but a rock is not always a rock).

Finally while all this work was going on, Wodston could carry on his noble pursuits. He pocketed hundreds, if not thousands, each time the skimmers attacked the city, which is to say he could scarcely get five minutes off.

Well, then, isn't this a productive scene? After many tribulations, it seems Nuk's determination to be as un-noble as possible was actually dragging his crew up from the gutter – the gutter he had admittedly dragged them into just days prior, but history wouldn't remember that. Or anything, if Izumi kept her promise, but the truth was she did begin to keep a few notes on what was going on, out of mere curiosity. She'd have to flex her writing muscles well soon, for Nuk's next quest would have her seeing things she'd never seen in her entire life, and with very good reason.

Chapter 7
Breakfast Made Snappy

On the roof of the TCMUPRWNCPHG And SPAAGS HQ, a battle raged on.

"Keep moving up, don't let them come back into it!" Izayah was insisting. Izumi shuffled forwards and kicked Nuk in the stomach. He reeled backwards, gasping for breath.

"Oh give over. I was holding back," Izumi insisted.

"Yeah yeah, whatever. I don't need to hear your gloating. You're lucky I didn't go beast mode on you both," Nuk spluttered.

"Both?"

"Yeah. Think I didn't notice you attacking me two on one? When'd your sister get here anyway, she's cute."

"Err... Izayah?"

"I think this is what he previously called 'the bad green'. Don't worry about it. I think Wodston's supposed to be getting a fresh batch of his medication now."

In Heft's uptown bar, Wodston was awkwardly signalling the barman.

"I believe you have something for me?" the doctor asked.

"For you? Sorry. You're that doc, right?"

"Well, not for me exactly. For... you know..."

"For your downstairs? We don't do that."

"For the Prince! The Prince!"

"Prince? Oh, you mean that guy?"

The barman pointed to a hiver sitting at a nearby table. Hivers were curious folk. People usually called them bugmen, which gives you a rough impression of their appearance. Imagine an upright stick insect and you'll be even closer. They were the planet's dominant species before humans had shown their greasy mops around here, but the hivers of those days were far more primitive. After millennia of evolution (natural or otherwise) alongside the sapiens, the hivers had developed many traits to compete with the new arrivals – speech, academics, crafts, and in a few, isolated cases, a thirst for adventure. This bar bug was an example of the latter.

"Is there something you want, old flesh?" the hiver asked from behind the brow of his large hat.

"Sorry, no, I said the Prince."

"That's me," the hiver continued.

"Oh... Prince... of what?"

"Pfft, what do you think? See a hive in here, old one?"

I should explain the fellow's indignation. For hivers, living apart from a hive was extremely unusual, to put it lightly. In ordinary circumstances hivers craved each other's close company, and worked as a single body to better their communities. But rapid evolution had left a few quirks in their genome, and so these days more and more hivers felt no connection to their hive at all; they were thus banished if they didn't leave of their own accord. This inclination could strike anyone, from drone, to exarch, from lackey to Prince.

"I just... I was speaking of the imperial Prince, Nuk Tashino," Wodston said.

"Tashino? You are in the wrong city. He was exiled."

"Only from the palace."

"False. That's not what I heard."

"I was there as the order was given, friend."

"Really? Who are you?"

Wodston explained his connection to the Nuk, and the current activity of the various guilds that surrounded him. The hiver suddenly stood up.

"Take me to him. I command it."

"Actually, I don't think he would like that."

"We are of equal rank. And equal station."

"I don't follow."

"Exiled Prince. Take me to him."

After further insistences, Wodston showed the hiver down the hill to the HQ. The hiver rushed up the stairs and found Nuk lying on the ground, with Izayah and Izumi pondering what to do with him.

"Argh... argh!" Nuk shrieked, pointing at the guest. "The bad green! It's the bad green! It's here! It's alive!"

Izayah grabbed a sword and blocked the hiver's path.

"Private residence, little man. Off you go now."

"Nonsense. I have diplomatic immunity."

"Oh... Are you a wizard?"

Wodston appeared from downstairs to explain the situation.

"A hive prince?" Izumi commented. "That's fascinating. May I ask you a few questions."

"No, slender one."

"Ah, you're one to talk. What if a beefy shek asks you instead, hmm?"

"Is he of princely station?"

"Guess not. Mister Wodston, why have you brought this Prince here?"

Wodston was getting an eyeful from Izayah. I should note that he was the only one in the group who knew that Izayah was indeed of princely station. They had decided to keep it secret, to stop Nuk feeling insecure. They were good friends. Izumi dragged a semi-conscious Nuk away, and the hive prince declared that he would wait for Nuk to awaken. The others shrugged and went back to their training, occasionally glancing at the perfectly still hiver doing a decent impression of a small tree in the corner.

In the evening, Nuk awoke.

"Wodston... that wasn't just bad green... It was fugging haunted," he moaned.

"Your manservant isn't here. He is performing unsolicited surgery in a nearby gulch," the hiver said.

"Fine. Cool. Weird. You... Fugg, it's still haunted in here?"

"I am a Prince! And you must associate with me."

"Oh. Bugman. I see it now. Sorry man, I thought-"

"I understand that you feel the weakness of your flesh when you ingest hashish. Your choice to do it regardless is most amusing."

"Yeah. It sounds like you're a laugh a minute yourself."

"Associate with me."

"Man I'm not into that."

"Declare your association. I require your association."

The hiver was shuffling closer to poor Nuk, cowering in bed.

"Fugg. Where is everyone? Who even are you?!"

"I am your new associate. Your flappy ears will not be able to hear my name. I use the greenland name Gustavsen. Prince Gustavsen. Now I am associated to you, a Prince also."

"Cool. Cool. Is this like... it? Did I get associated with?"

"Yes, associate."

"Cool. Man. Was my first time."

"And it will not be the last. We must associate with more of princely station."

"This is what it's like to be one of Wodston's patients, ugh."

The long and short of it was that Prince Gustavsen was extremely happy to be 'associated' with another prince, and was henceforth a fixture in the HQ. He didn't say or do much, and everyone gradually got used to it. It's like having a pot plant that moves around sometimes. Still, there was something to be said for having a hive prince around the house, for other, lesser hivers had this automatic desire to serve him.

One night, when Gustavsen accompanied Nuk to a bar, Nuk mentioned that he liked the sound of how hivers had drone workers who blindly followed orders. Gustavsen pointed at a lone hiver in the corner, snapped his fingers, and suddenly an even skinnier hiver named Julian was at the guild's disposal. Cooking, cleaning, light dusting, heavy lifting – this sprightly stickman was quite the asset.

Julian was put in charge of looking after the guild's property in Heft, while Nuk took everyone else out on the expedition he had been planning over the last week. This was the expedition to 'get revenge on the past', which was something to do with getting rich selling old empire nik-naks from ancient ruins.

Nuk bought a garru to carry the loot. He named it Gary, since Izumi wasn't there to criticise him for it. If you've never heard of a garru, imagine a cross between a cow, a donkey, and dog. It was a fat, four-legged, big-mouthed hunk of beast, with enough strength to rip you apart if it wanted, but it didn't want, because garru were totally chill. Izayah happily volunteered to be in charge of this new pet. Gary was delighted, mistaking Izayah for a garru himself on account of his pale, rough skin.

With all these preparations made, the crew geared up for a long walk, out into the places where most feared to tread. And given that people were literally mauled to death right outside Heft on the daily, these other places must have something *really* crazy going on. Or really cool, as Nuk imagined.

Or really interesting, as Izumi imaged. Ells was imagining himself out-drinking a garru, to screaming applause and adulation.

"Alright everyone. Adventure time!" Nuk declared. Izayah cheered alone. "Please cheer," Nuk added, gaining a nearly audible murmur in response. One suspects the crew weren't entirely sure whether this was a good idea. It was Nuk's idea after all.

Things were fine for at least fifty paces out the door of the HQ. There, Nuk's pungent scent smacked the guards out of their stupor, and he had to pay them two grand to not go searching through Nuk's hashish pouch. More of a satchel than a pouch, really. Now the trip had to be extra profitable.

It was a long walk they had planned, down to the eastern coast, and then south to the abandoned outlands known as Howler's Maze.

"What's a howler?" Ells asked.

"It's the sound you make when you get killed there, I think," Izayah said.

"Are we gonna get killed?"

"Well... not *all* of us, I wouldn't expect."

"What exactly is the thing that will kill us?" Izumi asked.

"You can't believe talk. But they say... giant crabs."

"How about that - I don't believe the talk."

"How giant?" Nuk asked.

"Don't really know. That's the point of an adventure, isn't it!"

"Totally. Let's do it boys. Get me a giant crab for dinner!"

Nuk pointed out at the horizon, and the adventure was on. He was impatient to see the surely delicious menace was awaited them, and he was in luck, for he would have the pleasure of being unconscious for most of the journey. Why? Well, Nuk was again proudly wearing his noble robes, and that attracted the attention of the rebels.

"Oppressor!" the screamed as they charged the group.

"I have a name you know!" Nuk retorted, drawing his blade. After a good week of practice, the whole crew knew a thing or two about fighting, which was about the same number of things the scraggly rebels knew as well. But being fresh from the city gave our heroes the edge, and slowly the battle turned in their favour.

Nuk wasn't happy though. He saw Gustavsen just standing there, watching the mass melee with a smile on his face.

"Oi, Bad Green! Come on! Fight them!" Nuk insisted.

"That is not necessary. Come, Prince, let us watch the soldiers perform their dance," Gustavsen offered.

"Fugging... You're not even the Prince of anything. Look, swap places with me. You fight my one, and I'll- argh!"

Unfortunately, Nuk's 'one' clubbed him across the head. When he woke up it was night time, and all around him were tall pillars of rock. They tore the wind this way and that, and drove it through little gaps at high speeds. This made a certain sound, and hence we learn the real reason the place was called Howler's Maze. Oh, but Izayah's reason wasn't exactly wrong either.

"Wodston... the bad..." Nuk mumbled.

"The Bad Green apologises for the inconvenience," Gustavsen said.

"Where are we?"

"Izayah says this is the edge of Howler's Maze," Wodston said. The doctor was sat beside Nuk inspecting the bandage around his head.

"Any... giant crabs?"

"I'm afraid not, my Prince."

"What time is it?"

"Around three, my Prince."

"I wanna..."

"What is it, my Prince?"

"Giant crab... for breakfast..."

"I really think-"

"Giant grab for breakfast! Come on!"

Nuk seemed to become fully energised, and was up on his feet, moving out with a swaying gait towards the even howl-ier highlands just barely visible to the east. They crossed a series of rocky paths between large pools of seawater. Rock pools. The sort of place you might expect to see...

"Ah! Giant crab!" Izumi shouted. A huge, orange, armoured scuttler emerged from the dark water as they passed by its hiding spot.

"Oh that's not even that big," Izayah said, drawing his sword and eyeing up the meter long claws on the two meter long arms of the three meter wide crustacean, all top those four meter legs.

"You ever seen a normal sized crab, my man?" Nuk asked, backing away.

"My Prince, shall we?" Wodston asked.

"Yes. Leg it! Leave the fugging giant crab! I want a smaller one!"

With this the crew was on the move once again. Luckily, one of the promised ancient ruins was just up the hill beyond the pools, and by the time they reached it and looked back, the curious crab had returned to its important business in the sea.

"So that's a giant crab," Nuk huffed as they caught their breath.

"And this is... from the second empire," Izumi noted, looking over the collapsed dome of the structure.

"Yeah? So's my old house."

"And I would be delighted to analyse that also, if you weren't so obnoxious that your own family threw you out here among the bloody... giant crabs."

"I thought you'd be happier."

"Just... Forget it..."

"Miss Izumi," Wodston asked. "Could it be that the giant crabs have unnerved you?"

"What the fugg do you think?"

"I just want you to know that I am here for you."

"Pfft. Whatever. Technically I'm here for you, remember?"

This slight from a discontented worker was taken in the most romantic way possible by the old doctor, as usual. Izumi was cheered up by the coming of sunrise, and with the discovery that the building they were in was part of a large settlement, with many other structures still intact. They crew poked around in a few of these large, cylindrical shells, but they were empty. Someone had beaten them to it.

"I thought this place was untouched?" Nuk complained to Izayah.

"Perhaps the crabs were smaller in the past?" Izayah offered.

"The past? Oh don't talk to me about the past."

"Shall I get revenge on the past for you, master?" Ells offered.

"Can't, can we? Everything's already been revenged to bits."

"What about that one?" Ells pointed at a door they hadn't tried yet.

"Be my guest, Charlie my good man. Let's take a seat everyone. Guess we'll eat the Okran-forsaken skimmer steaks for breakfast."

A few minutes later, Ells reported back.

"Them crabs really were smaller before. Some of them still are as well."

"I thought as much," Izayah nodded to himself. "Hang on, what's that sound?"

Behind Ells there was a carpet of movement, approaching fast. What do you know, it was a bunch of less giant crabs.

"Less giant crabs!" Izumi shouted. The gang rushed out and fled the scene, running up a nearby ridge and across the barely-visible outline of an ancient roadway. The less giant crabs continued to wander the ruins, dreaming of one day becoming less less giant crabs.

From their new retreat point, the crew were overlooking a large ruined settlement. And, a large crab. More than a giant crab. It was...

"A giant giant fugging crab," Nuk breathed, pointing down at the patrolling, building sized monster.

"It's... a megacrab," Izumi said.

"That's a sweet name. Megacrab. Man... megacrab for lunch?"

Wodston talked Nuk down, and in the meantime, Izumi analysed what she could of the settlement.

"That building there, the close one. It's got that symbol on the side, like the Traders Guild."

"Trader's guild? Out here?" puzzled Izayah.

"No, the symbol is from the old empire. It's a state library."

"Oh... Funny place for one."

"It's- Sorry, never mind. Prince Tashino! The treasure is in there!"

"The lost treasure of the ancients, guarded by the king of all crabs, the megacrab," Nuk mused. "Fugging, cool. I'll get it."

"Do not harm the crustacean!" Gustavsen insisted before Nuk left.

"Man, I'm not gonna fighting a fugging ten meter tall megacrab."

"Good. The megacrab is suitable for association."

"No, okay, just no. Megacrab don't wanna be your friend. I guarantee it."

"You feel threatened by its dominance?"

"What? I feel... Like... you're insane. Just do your tree thing for a bit, okay? I'm going in."

Nuk, now something slightly more than an amateur ninja, snuck down to the library, and eyed the megacrab as it wondered about town. When the time was right, he starting jabbing at the lock on the library door. The door had been closed for two thousand years, so suffice to say it was a tad stiff. The others, watching from the ridge above town, saw Nuk constantly giving them the thumbs up as he worked, hour after hour. The megacrab crept about, but was unable to hear Nuk swearing under his breath, or even the point when Nuk started hammering his sword straight into the locking gears.

Eventually though there was a slight hiss, and a machine pulled the doors open. Bingo. That is the first word Nuk saw on a shelf from the door. How To Win At Bingo', the book was titled. Ancient treasure of the rarest form. Nuk searched the place, and signalled for Wodston and Ells to bring some bags down for haulage.

Izumi was quite right about it being a library, but most of the stuff inside was either rotten, or was just random bits of old fiction with few or even no big-eyed illustrations. Practically worthless. The only valuable pieces were some old science books, which contained handy info on things like how that hydraulic door Nuk had broken actually worked. And there were maps to other ancient towns across the world, which are valuable to an adventurer at least.

"What did you get?" Izumi asked excitedly.

"Stuff. Here's the best one. Got a few pictures. 'Space Marine Codex', it says, right?" Nuk said.

"Space... Marine. The sky and the sea. Sounds like it could be philosophy."

Nuk decided to let Izumi remain excited about that. The nearby ancient road lead further uphill, and the coast was relatively clear of crabs of any proportion, so they hiked on a little further. Eventually they came to the very top of the barren hill, just as the sun was setting. From the heights they could see a few other ancient settlements dotted along the coast nearby. And thanks to the dim twilight, it didn't even look like they were crawling with giant crabs.

This adventuring thing wasn't that bad, was it? As long as the megacrabs didn't see you, the world was your old, dusty oyster. The view from that hill, high above Howler's Maze, was something very few people in the world had ever seen. Even fewer than had seen the rare copy of 'The Rusty Agronian Spade', a book written during the time when machine intelligence reigned supreme over the world.

As Izayah had said, this was the life. Would all of Nuk's trips be this nice? Absolutely, positively, not.

Chapter 8
Skeleton Wizard

In the darkness of early morning, on the eastern coast of an abandoned peninsula, Nuk Tashino edged forwards towards the door of an ancient structure. He flipped the switch beside it, and with a whoosh, the darkness within was revealed. Nuk instinctively jumped back, but no danger emerged.

"No crabs, come on then," he reported over his shoulder. The gang marched up, hoping to get some rest in under this multi-thousand year old roof. But within moments Nuk was barrelling back through them, calling out the watchword ,

"Crabs, crabs, crabs!"

Yes, this was crab country, and out-of-towners weren't welcome. The mystery of just who had locked a swarm of crabs in there was greater than that of the ruin's origins by a longshot. There were two possible explanations: either some crab-wrangling hero had sealed the evil away, or the crabs had learned to open and close doors. Izumi favoured the latter hypothesis, for it fit well with the academic principle of Okran's Razor – all things being equal, the theory that increases your probability of death the most is closest to the truth.

Battered by wind and acid rain, and without even an exoskeleton to call home, the team were having a rather unsavoury night. Only by the chance discovery of another sealed ancient library, and by the vulgar-tongued charms of locksmith Nuk, did they find shelter – not to mention a load more books for Garry to lug about.

"I don't get it," Nuk said in the morning, shaking his head. "It says here that ninjas are from Japan. As in the fantasy world in the novels? Right?"

"You mean to say they emerged from the ancient texts? This... wait... Could this be the power of the skeleton wizard your father sent us after?!" Izayah reasoned.

"Man, if stuff in the ancient texts becomes real, we're in big trouble. There was this villain who made your clothes just like, melt away. Well, not for guys actually. Sorry history girl."

"Yeah, I think it'll be fine. And just so you know, those books are talking about Earth," Izumi said.

"Earth? Can you read? It's pronounced Japan."

"Didn't they educate you in the palace, oh Prince?"

"Yeah, I've read all the ancient texts back to fugging front, and they suck, but I remember enough to know it's pronounced Japan. Or was it 'Nippon'..."

"Ever wondered what that thing in the sky is?"

"I know!" Ells butted in. "The big one is Okran, and the little one is Narko. And the big one is the good one."

"Charlie boy knows it. See, history girl, knowing stuff isn't really a special skill, so save the lectures," Nuk said.

"Sure, sure. Let's stick with the skeleton wizard theory then, shall we?" Izumi huffed.

"It is the more reasonable explanation," Izayah nodded. "Have you ever heard of Okran's Razor?"

That morning the crew began the march back home. They walked up to the northern coast of Howler's Maze and along the bumpy beaches that snaked west beneath the shadows of blackened skyscraper fragments. In one such shadow, a giant crab was striding about as if guarding the ancient secrets of the once great tower. Or, that is how Nuk put it to Izumi when he advocated for fighting the creature.

"We literally can't go back without defeating one giant crab. It's like... I dunno... Going to Sho-Battai without getting enslaved. It's just what you do, right?" he argued.

"Triumph over lesser beings is a mark of status," Gustavsen said. "Please proceed to slay the creature. I will observe your potential carefully."

"Hear that? Bad Green's observing our fugging potential. Can't back out now, can we?"

"My Prince, have you thought this through?" Wodston asked, but Nuk was already rushing out to battle. Ells followed his master, and Izayah lifted up his sword and roared, before diving in too.

The crab had seen the bunch and was already scuttling over to cut them down to size. Its snippy crab jabs were hard to follow; in the ensuing brawl Ells was knocked unconscious, and Izayah broke a leg and an arm. But he was laughing almost manically as the crab slumped into the sand and snip-snapped no more.

"I knew it!" Izayah said. "Who's... the giant crab... now?!"

"So, how'd we look?" Nuk asked Gustavsen.

"You could not defeat the megacrab. You are not skilled," was the answer.

"Not skilled?" Nuk shot back, but he said nothing else as blood ran down his forehead and got into his eyes, to say nothing of the resulting tumble across the dormant mass of an aptly named Bloody Ells.

Once the combatants were patched and picked up, the party carried on their way. They saw signs of civilisation earlier than expected – on the edge of Howler's Maze, gangs of vagabonds, rebels and manhunters were brawling up and down the bluffs. A few tried to stop our heroes from passing, but they soon backed away when Nuk pulled a giant severed crab claw from the baggage and announced himself as the crab-slayer champion. He charged out, wielding the huge claw in both hands, and while he was too weak to actually swing it, the mere sight cleared the group a path through the melee. By two in the morning, the claw was hanging on the wall of the guild HQ.

"Revenge," Nuk declared with a closed fist as he stood before the trophy.

"Revenge!" Izayah cheered.

"I'm.. glad you feel things are settled, my Prince," Wodston said.

"Yep. That'll teach those crabs to... What was the revenge for again?" Izumi asked.

"You know... The audacity of them," Nuk said.

"Audacity? Big word, maybe you are a little educated, mighty Prince?"

"Oh don't be like that. Look we stole loads of past didn't we, so can't you just be happy?"

"I am perfectly happy."

"What?"

"I mean, not literally... Or even..."

"Who wants crab for dinner?" Izayah suddenly announced, and after much debate about how such a rare delicacy should be cooked, they enjoyed a dinner worthy of a Prince (or three).

"You can taste the audacity!" Nuk remarked.

"I hope this is safe to eat," Wodston said. "Your father would not forgive me if you fell ill."

"I'm healthy as a garru."

"With the face to match," Izumi quipped.

"Pfft, yeah yeah, who's the ninja of comedy now? Face to match..." Nuk said, although it was hard to hear over the laughter filling the room. You take a crab-jab to the stomach, you learn a life lesson, and it's the same with words. Whether Nuk learnt anything in particular in either case remains in contention.

A few days later Nuk gathered the crew again to discuss the next big thing in credit management.

"The Deadlands!" he announced, hitting his stick against the map the group were sitting around. "A land of pure opportunity." Izayah looked like he was about to say something, but Nuk carried on strong. "My wonderful assistant here- Well, my... agreeable assis- Look, history girl here, compared one of the maps I discovered-"

"Stole," Izumi corrected him.

"My useless, greasy, slimy, unbearable dreg of an assistant-"

"I didn't do nothing to them maps," Ells added.

"Oh by Narko, I don't even... I'm on such a straight edge here, just everyone shut up. How about this: I, on my own, with no credit due to anyone else, have discovered the location of an ancient, intact workshop. And that location is the Deadlands. So... we're going to the fugging Deadlands, to discover/steal/whatever, some stuff, and then... I dunno... We'll have some stuff. Might get us a table and chairs or whatever. Any questions?"

There were quite a few questions, but the answer to most of them was 'no comment'.

"When they say 'Deadlands', am I to take it that the name is entirely inappropriate?" Wodston asked. Nuk shrugged, but Izayah had the lowdown.

"Oh it's a very fitting name," Izayah explained. "Life is almost impossible there. Acid rain, toxic gas, the most foul weather, and certain rumours say there are mechanical soldiers of the second empire still prowling the ashen hills."

"No giant crabs though?" Izumi asked.

"I suppose not. Well, either they won't be there at all, or they'll be even more giant – that's how it tends to go in my experience."

"You definitely want to go to such a place, my Prince?" Wodston asked Nuk.

"I'll tell you once we're there," was the reply. A few days halt were negotiated for preparations. Izumi continued writing notes on the ancient books they had collected before they were to be sold off, and Izayah was tasked with finding, as Nuk put it, 'decoys'. This translated into him hiring a pair of cheap mercenaries named Bobbie and Claw.

Gustavsen sniffed at them when they arrived in the HQ, and didn't look especially impressed.

"Which one's which?" Nuk asked.

"Bobbie, Claw" Izayah said, pointing at each in turn.

"Shek or pox?"

"Shek."

"Cool, but they better be really weird. Got a thing going with my Shek collection."

"Oh they are most unusual. They've been on the run from agents of the Shek kingdom for years. They even know your friends in the shinobi tower."

"And do they say anything for themselves?"

"No, not at all."

Bobbie - or was it Claw? - held up a small chalk sign with an apology written on it. Nuk came forwards and shook their hands enthusiastically.

"Weird as fugg, and bloody silent. Yes Izayah my man. And they don't even stink. They smell like me."

"They don't smell like you," Gustavsen corrected him from the corner.

"Whatever. So... either of you ever killed a giant crab?"

Another couple of days went by, and then in the dawn hours the guild gathered in the street outside the HQ, all geared up. Their two new foot-soldiers were ready with huge swords to defend their Princely master – although I'll let you in on a little secret: they weren't there to defend the Prince that Nuk thought they were.

Nuk had finally left his noble robes at home, and wore loose fitting grey and black wraps all the way up to his eyes. Now the rebels surely wouldn't give him any trouble, as he looked like just one of them. There couldn't possibly be any trouble on the horizon for looking like a rebel though, could there? It wasn't that bad really; it was at least two or three horizons over at the closest.

The Deadlands awaited, but there were various other regions they would have to cross to reach them, which were no less dead themselves. First was the uneventful walk out of the desert and into the Heng highlands, passing by the other end of the basin that Trader's Edge overlooked to its west. Then they passed through the corpse of a creek between two near-vertical mountains, and out into another stretch of yellow desert. This was the Skimsands. With any luck it was just a name. Not a chance.

"Fugging run, you morons!" Nuk shouted when Bobbie and Claw drew blades to face a huge wave of skimmers flying across the sand. The crew fled over a ridge, and saw sanctuary not so far away. There was a huge, metallic tower atop a mesa, marking the end of a scorched mountain range that rose up towards the northwest. They raced the skimmer horde towards this looming, mushroom-shaped castle. The skimmers, strangely, seemed unwilling to get close to it, and returned to the desert. What a relief. Even better, around the base of the mesa there were United Cities troops – samurai – patrolling about.

"Where is this? We've got men here?" Nuk puzzled.

"I've never heard of such an outpost, my Prince. Although..." Wodston said.

"Although what?"

"There was always a place that people mentioned in the palace, now and again. The Vault."

"Vault. Like money vault? Wait, is Dad holding off on me? Is my inheritance in that fugg-off citadel so I can't fugging- That man is a monster!"

Before anything else could be said, Nuk ran to the fortified checkpoint on the mesa's shallower side. The guards closed ranks and barked at him from a distance.

"Step any closer and lose your life, ninja scum!"

"What? I'm not a ninja. Well I am a ninja, but like... I'm the Prince."

"We could kill you just for saying that, you dreg. Get lost."

"No, you get out of *my* way. I need to inspect your garrison, and rest. Official empire business."

Nuk had been walking closer as he spoke, and perhaps the only reason he hadn't been run through with spears was that tasty, tasty audacity of his – the guards couldn't believe a real ninja would try such a brazen, obvious trick, so they feared some deeper invisible trick was afoot. Was this guy trying to get attacked as part of his plan?

Pondering this made them slow to react when Nuk suddenly bolted forwards and ran past them. The alarm was sounded as Nuk dashed up the ramp to the top of the mesa, carved from the rockface by slaves of centuries past. At the top he entered the huge, ancient warehouse, and found a dozen more samurai eyebrows raised in surprise, then a half-dozen blades unsheathed.

"I'm the Prince, where's my inheritance?!" Nuk shouted, but his dashing about the place didn't seem all that legitimate, you must admit. Strangely there was no gold or silver to be seen. Nuk was about to ask after it again, but with twenty trained samurai now bearing down on him from all directions, he decided he'd have to take it up with head office sometime instead.

The rest of the group were standing awkwardly outside, listening to the shouting and ringing of bells from the tower above them.

"They cannot tell that he is of princely station. These soldiers are not suitable for use," Gustavsen commented.

"Sure. So, should we really be standing here too? Pretty sure they're gonna kill us in a minute," Izumi said.

"Wait, we can't leave without the Prince!" Wodston insisted.

"He's got to be dead by- Oh Okran's blood..."

Nuk was spotted sprinting down the ramp at full pelt, with a platoon of samurai clattering after him.

"We could always start running now, get warmed up," Izayah suggested. It was a fine idea. Nuk blasted past the lower checkpoint, and followed his crew down to the southern strip of Skimsands. This stretch of desert was host to a huge beast skeleton, large enough to rival the nearby mountains. It was the most amazing thing the crew had ever glanced at while crossbow bolts kicked up sand around them and heavy boots stomped without relent on their tails.

In front of them the desert petered out and the ground rose up to a charr-soiled labyrinth of valleys, known as the Black Desert. The samurai no longer pursued them, but as they all drew in deep breaths to recover, they couldn't help but notice how their throats cloyed and their chests convulsed.

"Ugh, what is this?" Izumi said.

"This land is soiled," Izayah told her.

"Charlie, can you breathe?" Nuk asked.

"No, master," was the reply.

"Must be really soiled then."

"We must go back, my prince!" Wodston said, but Nuk was already pointing forwards.

"The Deadlands are over those hills, we can make it!"

"Couldn't help but notice that the only difference between the deadlands and the non-deadlands is that they kill you in a different way," Izumi said.

"Ha, yes, that's a fair way of putting it. Such is the stage of any adventure," Izayah said, setting off behind Nuk to jog towards the aforementioned coal-coloured hill. It was clouded in dark fog and decorated with the occasional flash of light with a sound like thunder. This new sanctuary was probably going to be just as good as the last one.

They reached the top of the hill, and before them was the sprawling lowlands of death, apparently. They couldn't see a thing on account of it being a smoggy new-moon midnight in the land of darkness.

"Wodston, map!" Nuk called. The doctor obeyed.

"We're between the Deadlands here, and the Black Desert, here," he reported.

"Cool."

"Doesn't sound that cool," Izumi commented.

"No it's cool because it means the ruin is like, right there."

"Where?"

"There..." Nuk was pointing into the void – that is to say, he wasn't pointing at anything.

"So we're just gonna run off into the fog, or fumes, or whatever the fugg all that is?"

"Yes, and I feel like you need to tone it down on the language."

Before Izumi could tone it up on the language, a huge bolt of lightning flashed nearby, and the ground exploded up, showing the crew with hot, toxic dirt.

"We need to get off the highground!" Izayah said.

"It's a race to the bottom!" Nuk announced as he began his speedy advance. Everyone followed him down the steep slope ahead of them. Further flashes of lightning revealed some kind of lake below, overlooked by the looming shadows of ancient silos, towers and pipes. A few minutes later a burning rain began to fall. All the more reason to follow Nuk as he ranged around the lakeside towards a complete silhouette of an ancient workshop.

"It hurts a bit master, can we go inside?" Ells asked.

"Not yet, just gotta check something..." Nuk said.

"Checking for crabs?" Izumi asked.

"Just for you, honey."

The door to the workshop was open, but there was no light coming from inside. Nuk quickly ran up, even more quickly gave up on trying to spy through the windows on account of the driving sheets of acid falling down on him, and went inside.

As he crossed the threshold the lights suddenly switched on and there was movement all around him. Before he could reach for his sword, he was surrounded by skeletons. And yes, now is finally time to clarify that to our heroes, the word 'skeleton' referred to the artificial folk of the old empire. These robots had been workers in the ancient human civilisation, although the roles had also been reversed for a while. Luckily for Nuk, the skeletons huddled in this lonely workshop were of the classic, subservient variety.

"Master! Protect the master! Welcome master!" they chirped here and there, although they would say nothing else.

"What- Who are you?" Nuk asked.

"Error," was the simple reply. Any other question made equal progress. When Nuk tried to move, the skeletons clustered around him, like a screen of bodyguards. Nuk called everyone else in.

"Having trouble, Prince Tashino?" Izayah asked.

"No, not at all. I think... I think I might have accidentally become the leader of a robot army."

"Is that so? I mean you've said as much before, but unless it's the toxic gases playing with my mind, I think this is more than bad green. Mister Wodston?"

"I do believe these robots are quite real. Although the toxicity of the air is a concern."

"Yeah but... there are seriously like thirty skeletons in here," Izumi noted, not willing to go very close to any of them.

"Fugg... yeah... I'm the lord of the skeletons!" Nuk announced. It was surprisingly hard to argue against it. He had shelter for the night, and a new robot army to play with. This adventuring business was reaching a whole new level, and as he would learn the next morning, that wasn't the only secret hidden in the treacherous Deadlands, and certainly not the biggest one.

Chapter 9
The Coin Slot Bot

"You see that?" Nuk asked, peering out of the workshop window.

"Hard to say that I do," Izayah replied.

"Wait for the next flash."

It didn't take long before lightning streaked across the besmirched skies of the Deadlands, and revealed on the horizon the outline of... something.

"I saw it! You're right!" Izayah exclaimed. "There's something huge, mysterious, and most likely dangerous out there. That's the good stuff."

"More like the good stuff will be inside. If this little shack gave me a skeleton army, what's gonna happen when we go to that massive factory or whatever?"

"My Prince, what if that place is guarded?" Wodston asked in vain.

"Literal ninja, literal skeleton army, ehh I think it'll be fine, my man. And that's like history out there. History girl's in, right?"

"Well, it's history alright," Izumi said from the opposite side of the room to the skeletons.

"There you go, she agreed with everything I've said. And Charlie loves it here, don't you?"

"It's dark. I can do whatever I want here," Ells grinned.

"Aaand he made it weird, but that's fine, that was accounted for... Bad Green, you wanna keep going? Not gonna melt or whatever?"

"Idiot human," Gustavsen shot back. "I am not afraid of the dark, nor do I agree that the rain burns." Gustavsen had the advantage of being a race native to the planet's ecosystem, long accustomed to its toxic precipitations. He and Gary both considered the nearby lakes of acid to be nice quiet spots for a swim. Or they would be quiet if there wasn't a perpetual thunderstorm overhead and pesky tourists from a big city guild here on a team building excursion.

"And you guys, you all wanna go for a little adventure, don't you?" Nuk said to his new thralls.

"Error," the robots chimed.

"So we're all agreed! Come on then."

The group filed out into the continuing drizzle of acid, and started making their way south towards whatever the large shape Nuk had spotted on a distant hill was. As they rounded another small lake, the skeletons became agitated.

"Danger. Danger. Protect the master," they were saying.

"What's all this about?" Nuk asked.

"Oh for fugg's sake... Giant crabs!" Izumi shouted. In the darkness ahead of them there was indeed something big crawling around on four legs, with two arms extended forwards.

"Hostile, hostile, hostile," the skeletons agreed, rushing off towards it.

"There really were giant crabs... But something's different," Izayah said. As they followed the charging skeletons they saw that this was a very special kind of crab indeed.

"Ha, there's no need to worry Miss Izumi," Izayah said. "That's no giant crab. It's a giant robot spider. Ancient soldiers, of a sort."

"Firstly, spiders have eight legs. That, is a giant, robot, crab!" Izumi insisted.

"Not gonna be anything soon; look at my minions going wild on it," Nuk pointed out. Indeed his legion of skeletons had swarmed the huge machine, and were wailing on it with metal rods or their steely fists. The ancient crab-spider soldier was swinging and stabbing at them with its rigid arms, but it was overwhelmed, and soon enough it appeared to lose power.

"Threat neutralised. Master protected," a skeleton proudly claimed.

Nuk rushed over to congratulate them.

"Incredible, men. You'll make fine samurai for my honour guard."

"My Prince! Behind you!" Wodston shouted. Behind the Prince, the crab-spider jerked back to life, its engine whirring and its legs digging into the ground.

"Fugg!" Nuk shouted. Thinking quickly, he jumped towards the thing and ripped away a warm metal sphere that was hanging on frayed wires from its underbelly. With that, the crab-spider was vanquished for good. With a mechanical squeak it locked itself in position forever.

"Nuk! Wh- Err... What did you do, Prince Tashino?" Izumi asked as she appeared at Nuk's side.

"Went for the round thing hanging underneath. Works on more than just spider robots, you know?"

"Okran's faith, that's its core."

"Obviously."

"It's like its brain."

"Oh, right. Gruesome."

"It nearly killed you!"

"Yeah? You should see what *I* did to *it*."

"Just... give me the core, please?"

"'Please'? That's more like it."

"Guys, what about those ones?" Ells asked. He was gesturing towards the half dozen more crab-spider soldiers that were actually all around them, upon closer inspection.

"They're just waiting. Perhaps we can get the drop on them?" Izayah suggested.

"Hang on. Bots, what's the deal with those other ones?"

"Error."

"Ah right. It's fine guys, they're all glitched out."

"Prince Tashino..." Izumi began, but she had to eat her words when Nuk ran up to another soldier, kicked it in the leg, and returned to tell the rather boring tale.

"Looks like there are more of them ahead. Perhaps they used to guard the secrets of the Deadlands? We're in luck, it seems," Izayah said.

"Sure, but you saw how that went down; when you have a skeleton army, you don't need luck," Nuk quipped, taking the lead to continue the burning hot, soaking wet adventure south. They passed more and more dormant crab-spiders as they rounded lakes flanked by the remains of ancient cities. It was all no worse for wear now that it was being Nuk'd for a second time.

They reached a small hill, atop which was the series of shapes they had seen from the workshop. Up close it was clear that it was some kind of ancient settlement, from the post-nuking era but still thousands of years old.

What's more, it flashed as bright as the lightning whenever thunder roared - no rust. Smoke was rising from chimneys. Someone was living in this hellhole!

Before any plan of action could be made, Nuk's skeletons buzzed to life. "Protect the master!" they chanted, sprinting forward and up the hill into the town.

"Dammit. Looks like we'll have to fight for some bloody shelter. Come on, auxiliaries, to battle!" Nuk commanded.

"To battle!" Izayah called, prompting growls from Bobbie and Claw who followed him up the hill.

However, atop the hill the lines of battle were not so clearly drawn. In the dull light they could see skeletons fighting all over the town - fighting each other. After Nuk and company halted in confusion, one skeleton ran over to them. It wasn't one of Nuk's. It was clean, heavily armed, and more clearly spoken.

"Travellers, stay back. The Broken Ones are attacking. Please remain here for your own safety," it said.

"Oh man, they're the Broken Ones huh? I hate those guys," Nuk said, nodding to his friends to play along. "Will you be okay? They're pretty, like, elite warriors."

"There is nothing to fear. They are old models, still carrying the slave virus. They are obsolete."

"Yeah, totally. You don't wanna, like, just turn them off and leave them down there, do you?"

"They must be destroyed and recycled. Please proceed to the human hostel once the road is safe. Goodbye, travellers."

With that the skeleton returned to the clanking melee nearby.

"Fugg, my boys are getting decommissioned," Nuk lamented.

"They were worthy soldiers. The crimes of these machine rebels cannot be forgiven. I am sorry for your loss, Prince Tashino," Gustavsen said.

"I would say a few words for our fallen comrades, but it's fugging bucketing acid rain, so lets hit the pub," Nuk said. Everyone quickly agreed, and they ran past the slaughter of the Broken Ones and up the main road.

"I just wanted... to protect..." one said, as its lights went out forever.

At the other end of town was this so-called hostel. To the delight of all, it was actually some kind of bar. Tables and chairs were laid out around the hall, and food fit for biological life was being served. There were a couple of hivers sitting in the dim corners, but the patrons were mostly skeletons, as was the barman who greeted them.

"Travellers. We have some human feed available for purchase. Please take a seat," he said.

"Sure. First though, I'm not saying we're like, lost, or anything, but where are we?" Nuk asked.

"This is Black Desert City."

"But it's not in the Black Desert."

"Yes it is."

"It's not, the Black Desert has light daylight and stuff. This is the Deadlands."

"The previous human who came here called this area The Black Desert."

"Yeah? When was that?"

"One thousand five hundred and fourteen years ago."

"Oh right. Fine, maybe they called it Black Desert then, but it's Deadlands now."

"We cannot change the name."

"Why not?"

"We already constructed a sign."

"Ah... fair enough. So this is like, skeleton city and stuff?"

"This is a refuge for all free skeletons. The world leaves us alone here. Except for travellers, from time to time."

"Time to time indeed. So, I guess that means it's not... There isn't anything I can... Ahem. Do you have any items of historical value that might be more suited to study in the outside world?"

"If you take anything from Black Desert City, you will be hunted and destroyed."

"Destroyed, huh..."

Nuk suddenly wondered just where the meat this bar served came from in a realm so devoid of life. Such thoughts convinced him to pay the fees for beds and retire the party upstairs. The human accommodation was little more than a bunkhouse on the second floor, but this was a joyous break from sleeping in besieged ancient ruins.

While the party rested and tried to dry / de-acidify their clothes, Nuk wandered over to a small lounge adjoining the bunkhouse. A few skeletons were sat at wooden benches with mugs of something viscous. They were perfectly still, and all but one ignored Nuk entering. The one that didn't had a brilliant red face, painted over its dark skeleton faceplate. It even beckoned for Nuk to come sit down.

"Outsider, you must be a curious one to come all the way to Black Desert city," it said.

"Yeah, curious, that's one way of putting it. You look kinda different. You got the inside track on this place?" Nuk replied.

"Wait, you gotta give me two grand to reactivate me first."

"Two- But you're already talking."

"This is backup power or something. I'm coin operated, mungo. I need two fatcats or I can't access the secrets in my memory chip, and stuff."

"They just leave you here? That's unbelievable."

"I agree. Now gimmie two stacks and I'll tell you the legends from round these parts."

"Err... Alright. Fine. You got like a coin slot or something?"

"Just put in this bucket here. My CPU will smell the money and come running."

"Of course."

Nuk handed over the requested amount, and the skeleton waved about dramatically.

"Ahhhh I am restored to life!" it claimed. "Finally I can tell you everything. The name's Red Rick. You wanna know why they call me Red Rick?"

"Something to do with blood, right? You're a killer!"

"Oh no, my circuits... It's the money bucket... it's too empty... Another two stacks should unlock the hidden truth. Come on man, I wanna hear it as much as you!"

Nuk was convinced, and become yet poorer.

"I see it now... It was over three thousand years ago... Oh yeah, there it is, clear as day."

"What?"

"Some guy painted my face red. Started calling me Red Rick. Still red today."

"And...?"

"That's the story."

"That's the fugging story?"

"Yep. Now what else you wanna hear?"

"Listen, Ricky, I know your game. You're a grifter!" Nuk was 'quick' to realise. "I need to make some cash off this stopover, and you're gonna show me where the good stuff is."

"My good stuff sensor is offline. I'll need ten grand to cover the repairs. How about you fix me up, and I'll come with you wherever, give you that inside track on all kinds of stuff from back in my day?"

Skeletons, by the way, were functionally immortal. The skeletons in this building had been alive since long before the end of old society, but their limited memory capacity meant they didn't have any data left about it these days (or so they claimed). Nuk wasn't really up to speed on this latter point, and was happy to pay through the nose to get Red Rick as his personal skeleton revenge appraiser.

After a long stint resting in the skeleton bar, everyone was less miserable than before, but generally they were eager to leave the Deadlands. Their new escort Rick had a hot tip about an unlooted workshop to the northwest, so after introductions were made and Gustavsen was done sniffing, they set off at quick march through the continuing rain.

They were soon stamping into an ancient industrial wasteland, known as the Iron Valleys. Metal bridges sat astride said valleys, and below there were old ruins, ranging from barely visible, to pristine. Rick's 'good stuff' sensor was getting a strong reading from one particular building - an untouched armoury. Why was it untouched, you ask?

"Crab-spider robot!" Izumi called. The machine rushed out of the armoury doors and bashed Nuk, Izumi and Gustaven to the ground. The others following behind drew their weapons, but swinging a sword against a foe with an iron body doesn't achieve all that much, as you might imagine.

Wodston went to get Nuk back up on his feet, while the Shek, Rick, and Gary chipped away at whatever wires, tubes, and holes they could find. The crab-spider angrily thrashed about, and no one came away uninjured, but at last it faltered, and Nuk hobbled over to show everyone the secret undercarriage dismemberment technique.

"Bloody ancient shids, why did they leave all their junk around like this," Nuk complained. "No offence, Red."

"Offence taken, but I'm a reasonable kinda guy, so I'll still give you the codes to the door on that armoury."

Inside said armoury the crew could rest and loot to their heart's content, although the acid rain ouside was leaking through the roof and had pooled slightly on the ground, so their hearts weren't very content as it turned out. And the loot was nothing special either – just because it was from the past, doesn't mean it was from the *good* bit of the past. It was swords and spears, from the bit of the past that was pre-history, but post-civilisation. Made of real metal though, so that's a plus!

After clearing the place of useful gear, they used the last hours of daylight to cross the rest of the Iron Valleys and camp out on the edge of the Skimsands for the night. Rick, like all skeletons, never slept, so he kept watch, and chose not to experience the time that passed, so that to him it was morning almost at once.

Back in the familiar, sticky, life-draining embrace of a good old fashioned *brown* desert, the crew plotted a route home. They chose to avoid going near that vault place again, but that meant they had to use a pass through a mountain chain known as The Spine. There was a proper road and everything, but that meant there were bandits. A few such highwaymen accosted the party, but Rick pushed to the front of the group to challenge them.

"You ain't no coin-operated biologicals, fellas. Get out of here before I send y'all back to your mommas in tears," he said.

"Fugging skele-boy's got a mouth on it! Alright, just for that, I'm doubling the toll!" the bandit retorted. Rick's head swivelled back and nodded to the rest of the crew, who were resting their hands on weapons already.

"Wrong answer, bandito. I got news for you son. My name is Red Rick, and you gon' get the stick!"

Rick drew a hefty metal bar from a plate on his back, and as promised didn't let the bandits leave without a few tears. Being made of metal, and moving with instantaneous reaction speed, really lets you have your way with the puny biologicals- I mean, equally respectable lifeforms.

"Rick, you mad machine, you're a damned beast!" Nuk exclaimed once the beating was over.

"What can I say, kid. I might be a grifter, sure, but you get what you pay for," Rick quipped.

"Rick, you're the best!" Izumi said. She ran up, and looked like she was about hug the skeleton, but then refrained. "Can I ask, what era are you from, by the way?"

"What era? Ha! You asking me how old I am? Don't you worry, I'm not too old to spend time with a flower like you, madame."

"Oh, Rick..."

"Okay, she's a history girl, alright, she just asked cause she's obsessed with eras and stuff," Nuk interjected.

"Quite right!" Wodston was quick to add. "Let's get moving before the thugs return. Rick can lead the way, and we'll all keep back, for safety."

They did so, and as luck would have it they crossed the rest of the Skimsands in peace, making it to the slightly less skimmy sands around the town of Stoat, the walls and troops of which finally offered them the protection of neo-civilisation. Yes the town was surrounded by dead bodies, and fights were going on left and right, but that's all very nostalgic after days on lonely roads, I assure you.

After a little R&R, some good food, and a lot of well justified 'revenge', they'd be ready for the last leg home, having enjoyed a truly fruitful adventure. No they didn't return with any treasures or a robot army, but they'd learned the secrets of the Deadlands, and found an erstwhile adventurer in Red Rick. Yes, the real treasure was literally the friends they made along the way. And before they got home, they'd have one more friend too, as it happens...

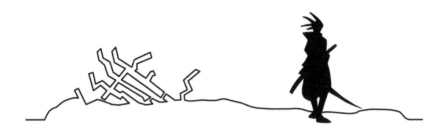

Chapter 10
An Inspector Mauls

Just outside the imperial capital of Heft, there was a gentle thumping sound, almost lost on the wind. Before anyone could make anything of it, Nuk and company were suddenly assailed by a man clad head-to-toe in black wraps.

"Tell me who you killed!" the figure demanded.

"Hey, who the- Man, get outta here!" Nuk said, jumping back as the figure tried to kick him.

"Just as I thought. You're a noble. Who did you take that garb from? Who must I avenge?"

"Black market, I dunno where it came from. You a ninja too?"

"Too?"

"Yeah, I'm a ninja."

The man spat at Nuk's feet.

"Monster. Enough words."

With this the ninja of the sands came at Nuk with everything, although he carried no weapon. Nuk stumbled backwards to avoid the blows, and then his warriors stepped up to swing at the attacker. The ninja duked around in the darkness, somehow avoiding blows from sword and spear that were certain to hit a split-second before.

"I'll kill you!" he cursed as he danced backwards. Distracted by the barrage of attacks, Nuk was able to slip into the melee himself and land a clean slice right down the ninja's side. The ninja, stumbled, fell, and was still.

"Guys..." Nuk began. "It's literally... a real ninja!"

"The most dangerous of the rebels. We must find out why he was here," Wodston said.

"Shoulda said that before I slashed him up, my man."

"Perhaps he carries something of import?" Izayah suggested. The ninja had a load of stolen cash, but no intel on his operations.

"There's only one thing for it then," Nuk concluded. "We're keeping him!"

"My Prince?" Wodston said, not daring to ask for a full logical breakdown.

"We'll make him talk at home. And then, we'll have a ninja! You know, like a guard ninja!"

"Prince Tashino, do you know what ninjas do to people like you?" Izumi asked.

"I'll put him on a lead or something, I'm not stupid," Nuk assured them. Nobody was especially assured, but with a snap of his fingers Nuk had Ells haul the ninja on towards Heft. Back home the crew made friends with the neighbours by hammering the scrap they'd dragged from the Iron Valleys at four in the morning, eventually creating a makeshift iron cage to keep their new pet in. The ninja was unconscious from blood loss, so Nuk tasked Wodston with keeping him alive.

When it was finally time for bed, Nuk went to close the front door, and saw that there was a letter nailed to it. It was on United Cities Imperial House stationary. This couldn't be good.

"'You know how it is,'" Nuk read to the group. "'There be things you gotta carry on for your health. And then there's this whole empire thing. Man, in the good old days we always stuck to one or the other.' Man, what is this even talking about? So it's from my dad, guys, can assure you of that. Does it ever actually say anything... No... No... Oh fugg it goes down the back. Ah, 'That's why I need you to step up and serve the Empire, like the warrior Princes of old Nippon, and shid.'"

"My Prince, is the Emperor trusting you to command troops of the Empire?!" Wodston asked, eyes agleam.

"Are we to slay the skeleton wizard?!" Izayah asked also.

"Are we gonna get paid?" Izumi added.

"Guys, what are you talking about? It's my fugging dad. He wants me to find him a new dealer 'cause the guys in the tower sold out. And I know it's true, 'cause they sold it out to the fugging TCM+ Guild."

"Ah, I think what he really means is that we must survey the Empire's territories, and compile a report on the trade of illegal narcotics," Wodston said.

"Yes, as my man here says, we, fellows, need to get the Emperor fugging high as the sky, and then... He'll give me that vault of inheritance. Rest of the damn Empire too I bet. This is perfect! Before we're done here the Red Rebellion will be over, with the coming of I, the Green Emperor!"

Gustavsen quickly knelt down before the Prince, and implored the others to do the same.

"He stakes claim to Kingly station!" the hiver said.

"He wants to go get fugging baked with his dad then steal the inheritance," Izumi corrected him, and Nuk waved Gustavsen up magnanimously.

"Come on guys, not gonna be a big deal. And for us: all the stuff we want along the way, you know? It'll be easy. But it *won't* be easy!"

Nuk suddenly jumped up on the table and raised his sword.

"This empire has fallen into chaos, with rebels, monsters, ninjas, and other cool shid all over the land. Now I, a humble Prince, must answer the command of my father, and bring us all together in a single cause: getting my dad so fugging high, that he'll finally start being chill. Then we steal his stuff... And the world shall be saved, I expect! Samurai of the Green Empire, we have work to do!"

With the spectre of a few more letters being added to the complete company acronym, the guild now prepared to go inspect the provinces of the United Cities Empire. And by 'prepare', I mean they sharpened weapons and sparred on the roof, because, as you must appreciate by now, an Empire with a core this wild must have some really funky outer provinces.

Downstairs, Nuk sidled up to the caged ninja, now fully conscious and mediating in silence.

"So ninja man. You got any leads on the green?"

"You'll have better luck with my corpse, so spare your breath, noble."

"I'm not gonna arrest you or whatever. I need some connections in the underworld, for business."

"The people of your empire are not fools. I'll say nothing."

"But come on, I'm a ninja too, man."

"Stop saying that! You know nothing of what it means to be a ninja!"

"Err... okay, man, but like, you know nothing of how much I know of what it means to be a ninja. Look, check this out."

Nuk grabbed some recovered pages from an ancient book. There was a faded illustration of a short man in an orange jumpsuit eating a bowl of noodles.

"You ever heard of the legendary ninja, Naruto?"

"You have ninja texts here?"

"Got loads of stuff. Look man, here we got stuff about where ninjustsu was invented. You know about Earth?"

"No..."

"Man, this Earth stuff is wild, if it's true. We got a girl here who knows all that stuff. Here, check it out."

Nuk spent the evening discussing ninja lore with his captive. The captive could not read, and had no knowledge of the order's fantastical past. Gradually he came to believe that perhaps this weird nobleman really was passionate about the ninja arts.

"I am nothing like this 'Grey Fox', I assure you," the ninja said. "I suppose the ninjutsu tradition has fallen from its golden age. No one chooses to be a ninja now. Except you, perhaps."

"Why not? Being a ninja is cool!"

"No! You say that because you think Naruto lives on today. Sure, Naruto is admirable, an extremely capable ninja without doubt. But here, in your empire, we're doing this because we have no choice. What else can a man do when his empire abandons him? The samurai come and take everything you have without warning, and that is that. Most perish, and the best survive only by embracing the arts of the ninja, and believing that one day our fight will lead to a better world. You may know of ninjutsu's past, noble, but you know nothing of its struggle today. You stand in our way."

"You know what man? I do kinda know about that stuff. I've seen it, just recently. And it does suck. That's why I'm gonna sort it out, one day."

"How?"

"Did you hear- Well, it starts with getting my dad absolutely burned out. That's the Emperor. Then I'm gonna get un-exiled and stuff, get all the money back, and then I'll sort it out. Dad'll probably get trapped in the bogs or whatever, and I'll run the empire. You want in on this?"

"How can I possibly believe you?"

"Dunno. If I'm lying, then stuff ends up the same. If I'm not, it ends up getting better. Not really a losing gamble is it?"

This was the most intelligent thing Nuk had ever said, and it came at just the right moment. The ninja, who finally revealed his name to be

Sandor, was impressed enough to agree to be Nuk's personal bodyguard. His first job the next day was to lead the party back across the stretch of desert where Nuk had picked him up, returning to Stoat in the west, from where they could leave the desert and enter these so-called provinces of the Empire.

The first one, Bast, was not going to provide them any leads at all. The arid hills were dotted with ruins not just from the First Empire, nor the Second, but mostly the Third - the current one to be clear. To be ever clearer, Bast had been completely destroyed.

"It's a foul story," Izayah told the group. "It was just before my time on the roads. The mad Okranites came and burned every town to the ground. They killed the adults, and kidnapped the rest. That's the Holy Nation for you."

This Holy Nation was the other great power of the day, the insane cousin of the United Cities Empire that had broken away some thousand years ago. Only thing you need to know about them for now is that they really like Okran, one of the two gods that ruled the planet, and they really hated just about everything else you could possibly think of. The United Cities allowed unholy creatures like skeletons and shek to be citizens, and so, the war between the two powers was unending.

Let us pass over that topic for now though, as our heroes were forced to just walk through the empty lands of Bast in search of the supposed Empire territories that lay beyond it. By the end of the day they were walking the cool coastal sands of the Darkfinger peninsula. The world had seemed completely deserted since Bast, but finally they came upon a man sitting by a campfire with a herd of goats.

"Excuse me, citizen," Nuk said, joining over to him. "You don't happen to know where I could purchase industrial quantities of quality drugs do you? Asking for a friend."

The man leaned over and whispered something to one of the goats. The goat shook its head.

"Not from 'round here are you?" the man said.

"No. No one is from around here by the looks of it."

"Aye, that's 'cause of the flesheaters."

"Flesheaters? Did he say flesheaters?" Izumi asked.

"Don't worry Miss Izumi, he probably just means the cannibals," zayah reassured her.

"The what?!"

"Aye, cannibals they are," the man continued. "They eat human flesh. They love it. Roaring trade."

"Fugg. Well at least it's not giant, robot bloody spider-crabs this time," Izumi said.

"Oh no, we got those too," the man said. He pointed up a nearby bluff, and indeed there was a giant robot bloody spider-crab mauling a crowd of people.

"And it's all mine to rule. Thanks goatman," Nuk said, leading the party to investigate. They came upon a pile of skinny, rather dead folk, with no sign of the spider-crab anymore.

"Shid," Nuk muttered as he rummaged through the pile. "They got nothing. Wodston my man, you found anything?"

"They are all quite without credit," Wodston reported.

"Then we're wasting our time here. I mean, if they're eating people, surely they don't eat the money and stuff; they must keep it somewhere."

"We'll have to explore further then," Izayah announced, and so they did. Darkness was falling. Ahead of them they saw fires on a nearby hillside. Moving closer, they saw large numbers of people camped out around a few buildings. A flick of the wind gave you all the smell you needed to know this was a den of flesheaters.

"Prince Tashino, why don't you let an inedible fellow go handle this for ya?" Red Rick offered.

"That's plan B. Sandor's gonna show me some ninja stuff," Nuk said excitedly.

"Simple rule really," Sandor said. "If you kill them, you get stuff now, might die yourself. If you let them live, you can rob them now, and then again, and then again... That's how the nobles get their stuff from the people, so about time I showed our royal master here how it's done."

Nuk and Sandor crept into the village, and with the experienced ninja's instructions, they made it inside one of the buildings completely undetected. There they looted a pair of beautiful steel swords.

"No more," Sandor whispered. "Leave enough for them to carry on – regrow, if you like. And we must move quickly. Come."

"Are we not going to occupy this settlement? I desire proper accommodation," Gustavsen complained upon their return.

"Not worth it. Gotta let them grow," Nuk said, looking to Sandor for a nod of approval. "Besides, they don't have what we need in there. Or if they do, it's *real* bad green if it's got them eating each other. Munchies, man."

The crew left the cannibal hill, but soon saw more lights ahead. There was a campfire beside a grove of trees, surrounded by bedrolls and free-standing torches. Someone had camped there very recently, but they were gone now. Too good to be true? Well, maybe. Too good to not be caused by rampaging giant robot spider-crabs? That's more like it.

"Remember, go for straight for the jewels!" Nuk shouted as one of them stomped from the nearby darkness. This advice proved invaluable, and with the leadership of the crab-slayer of flesh and metal alike, they put the robot to sleep with everyone still on their feet for a change. The victory won them a premium camp site, situated just a stone's throw from the calm beaches of the northern coast. It was a site so relaxing, so peaceful, that our exhausted adventurers could have slept all night and all day.

Alas, the camp was fully booked, as it turned out. After a couple of hours there was a sudden chorus of shrieks and jeers. The gang sprang from their bedrolls to see a crowd, nay, a horde, of half-squatting, paint-faced cannibals swarming forwards in a hungry rage.

"Fugg, fugg, fugg! Hold on to your fugging flesh!" Nuk called as he rallied the group together. The wave of cannibals crashed on them before anything could be done. They numbered perhaps forty, and clambered over each other to swing iron rods at their prey. Each cannibal only stood as high as the average person's waist, and it was hard to say if this was from their young age, their bow-legged gait, or just the lack of nutrition in a diet of human flesh. Perhaps it was all three. There was little time for a detailed analysis, as you might imagine.

"Izayah! Go full shek on them!" Nuk called out. Izayah, with five cannibals swarming over him, roared out and threw them back, before slashing out with a katana, taking hands and fingers away from all those around him.

"I got your back, Prince," Rick said.

"I'm fine, save the girl."

"With pleasure."

"Wait, actually, dammit! Stop trying to eat me you little fuggs!"

"Hey biologicals! Try being powered by sunlight for a change. It's free and easy. Just like me. Come take a bite," Rick taunted. With a swing of his stick, the cannibal trying to climb onto Izumi's back was tumbling through the air.

"Fugging, fugging, fugg, shids!" Izumi was saying, pretty much nonstop, beating cannibals back with a stick of her own. Izayah, Bobbie and

Claw had far outmatched these emaciated scragglers, and together helped clear the field of the horde.

"Phew... Dammit... Anyone get eaten?" Nuk said.

"Charlie's out," Izayah reported.

"Prince Gustavsen appears to be taking a nap," Wodston said.

"Right. Pretty much standard for both of them. All's fine then."

"Prince Tashino..." Izumi began.

"I know. I know. We're done here. I mean, how could I have known that would happen?"

"The warnings, the evidence, the impossibility of there being any other course of events, the educated woman telling you these things over and over."

"Err... Oh yeah, you were saying that, weren't you? Thing is, that's not history is it, its the future, so how could I trust you?"

"What? You don't trust me?!"

"I mean... I- just about this one thing, maybe. Not that I didn't trust you."

"You just said-"

"Sorry to interrupt," Rick said, interrupting without being sorry. "But I think we should mosey pronto and all that."

"Yeah. Sorry, history girl. Future girl. You're future girl now, alright? Everyone, we gotta mosey pronto or something, I dunno. Actually forget that, let's just get outta here."

They started walking south, back towards the places where it was big mouthy insects that killed you rather than little halfling swarm-folk. On the way their path was cut off by a few more wandering cannibals, but almost at once the way was cleared by a herd of wild goats. The cannibals, perhaps seeking to experiment with other meats, tried to fight these goats, and got their naked, painted bodies butted into oblivion as a result.

The crew marvelled from nearby, and when the dust had settled, walked on, petting the otherwise very friendly goats as they passed.

"I think we've got all the data we need on this province," Nuk said. "The one who rules the goats, rules Darkfinger. Simple as that. Future girl, note that down. This intel will lock this place down one day, I bet."

"I knew it!" Gustavsen said, suddenly waking on his perch on Ells' shoulder. "That man. The goat-whisperer. We must associate with him!" Ells had to hold on to the hiver as he started kicking and screaming. "WE MUST ASSOCIATE WITH THE GOAT KING."

"Bad Green, we're gonna associate the shid outta that goat king real soon," Nuk said, calming him down.

The crew left the goat kingdom without further harm, and they didn't leave empty handed; they stumbled upon another Second Empire library to loot. Perhaps Izumi was happy with that, after all the trouble. However the royal survey had indeed revealed nothing to satisfy the request of the Emperor, or his son. The goat overlords dealt only in literal grass, so they were not going to be very fruitful vassals.

But hope for the empire was not lost, for the adventurous prince would look far and wide for a chance to get his deadbeat dad on the hook. If that meant braving huge space lasers that blasted down at you without warning, then so be it. I say this because, funnily enough, that was exactly what it meant.

Chapter 11
Blast From The Past

As the Tashino Credit Management And A Whole Lot Else Guild marched out of the rural provinces and into the lifeless embrace of the Great Desert, they stumbled upon something rather curious.

"Those rocks are a bit... messy," Nuk said.

"Those aren't rocks. It's a mixture of saliva and dung," Izayah told him. "Unless I am very much mistaken, that is a hive."

Everyone looked to Gustavsen.

"I suppose you'd call it a hive," he said, apparently making a concession of some kind.

"Well, let's *hive* a look shall we," Nuk decided. Bobbie and Claw dragged Ells through his fit of uncontrollable laughter.

They entered a ring of large, teardrop hives, which spilled forth dozens of dull-eyed hivers.

"Prince Tashino, you're not going to rob them are you?" Izumi asked.

"Well I was thinking of it... But there's so many of them. And they're living in their own shid. Yeah, I don't know about this place."

"Perhaps we should just purchase a souvenir?" Wodston suggested. They hit the shopping hive, and found it to be surprisingly full of tech, new and ancient. Hivers had a knack for that kinda thing, carrying on traditions they had learned from the humans thousands of years ago. Not that Nuk was especially interested in that, because hives sold hashish over the counter without second thought. That was the Prince settled for a bit, and the hive cleared of any unannounced product recall warrants.

Not everyone was having such a nice visit though. Gustavsen had been surrounded by the local drones, who sniffed at him for a while, before all at once shouting "Hiveless One!" and becoming very agitated.

"Foolish drones. You are not permitted to touch me!" Gustavsen complained, but no one heard anything of it. He was pushed outside, and even there was set upon from all directions by glares that were probably rather hostile – humans couldn't tell hiver expressions apart, so it was hard for the gang to really know what this was all about.

"Did you rob them, you cheeky bugger?" Nuk asked.

"No. Drones do not understand what it means to be a true prince. They think I am a traitor," Gustavsen explained.

"Traitor? You're just less of a loser, come on."

"You are correct, Prince Tashino. Drones are unable to think clearly. They associate with nothing, hence nothing is what they know best."

"Boom. You got them Bad Green. Don't worry, we gotta go anyway. Is everyone out of the shop yet?"

Looking around, they were missing just Red Rick. Rick had been completely swarmed by the hivers, who fussed over his parts obsessively, cleaning away dirt and buffing out scratches.

"You might think this is like getting a massage or something," Rick said when Nuk found him. "But in reality, it doesn't feel like anything. Unless I want it to feel like something. And man, let me tell you, I got this shid feeling real good."

"I can't believe I just looked you in the eyes while you said that," Nuk muttered. At least our prince had finally discovered a potential source of hashish for the emperor, although it was not nearly enough for what Nuk had in mind – indeed, he'd bought out their whole supply, and barely had any left by the time they got settled in back home in Heft.

It was decided, by a very democratic process of demanding it of Nuk while he was on the verge of consciousness and forcing him to nod, that they would all take a few days off in the city before the next inspection tour. This gave time for the crew to mend their wounds, to practice the secret robot spider-crab castration technique, and relax in the sunshine with a good book, of which Izumi had created quite the collection.

One afternoon she was lazing on the roof reading some old magazine, watching Rick do push ups out of the corner of her eye. Why was a skeleton doing push ups? Everyone but Izumi asked the same question. Nuk stomped up the stairs and sat beside her.

"You know Gustavsen's got a friend over," he said.

"What, you?" Izumi said.

"Nah, another bugman. Ignacio."

"Ignacio? Like... you heard of Final Fantasy Fifteen?"

"No."

"I thought you'd read the classics?"

"Well it was Wodston who read them if you want to get technical, but it counts as me reading them, same as the money he makes counts as me making it."

"Impeccable thinking. Well whatever. How about this one: you ever heard of chocolate?"

"Chocolate? Oh yeah, I think I read that one. Very thoughtful. I liked the part where the guy joined tendrils with the weird alien thing."

"Chocolate, my Prince, is a food."

"Hmm, yes, an interesting reading of the text."

"Chocolate is an ancient drug, prince."

"Old school? What colour is it?"

"Brown."

"Ugh, brown town. Pass."

"Hang on. According to this, people used to be obsessed with it back in the First Empire. It was kinda addictive. And I kinda have the recipe for it here."

"If you wanna get addicted to something, you just had to ask."

"But this, Prince, is legal. We could make this chocolate, and use it on the Emperor. That way we aren't sticking our necks out for the samurai with your little plan. And... I wanna try it."

"Well future girl, I admire your interest in the world of narcotics. Kinda pretentious to go right for some out-of-style hit, but you're new to the scene, so I forgive you."

"Just think about it, Prince."

"Sure, sure. Could edge the hivers out the market if it works. Hmm. Yeah, I mean we'll try it, we'll try it sometime. By the way, why the fugg is Rick doing push ups?"

"Ten-thousand four hundred and seventy three, ten thous- oh dammit, lost count," Rick broadcasted. "I'll just have to start again, from the number I always start at: minus one million, baby."

"He literally never gets tired," Izumi told Nuk with wide eyes. Nuk decided to leave.

Finally the time came for the guild to assemble for an expedition to the empire's southern reaches. Ignacio had become Gustavsen's royal bodyguard, and joined their ranks with a crossbow strapped across his scrawny back.

"Now there are nobles out south somewhere; they came to the palace a few times. That means there's civilisation, and that means there is demand for hashish, and that means, over that horizon, a whole world of drugs is just waiting to be explored. Let's go!"

With this inspirational speech, a long haul began, walking down the east coast, through the white-sanded Heng highlands, and out towards the beautiful salt gullies of Gut, the blue-sanded jewel that they had previously seen in the distance from the peak at Howler's Maze. The beauty of the place was matched only by its desolation, and deadliness. The company looked out from the banks beside a walled farm, and saw packs of monsters stomping about below.

"Now I'm certain that's not a crab," Nuk said. "It's more like a... thing..."

"Quite right Prince Tashino," Izayah said. "That is a Beak Thing."

"A weak thing?" Wodston asked.

"Beak Thing! It's like a huge spike on the end of a long lever. Despite their size, they run twice as fast as humans. Good thing to, for humans are their favourite treat! I suppose they'll dabble in shek and hivers when times are tough. Must have great fun picking off the runaways from that slave camp up there. Ah, to run free with the Beak Things... Not such a bad way to go. Anyway, I don't think they'll stomach steel too well, so Rickard should be fine, eh? Rickard?"

Everyone had decided to run swiftly away from these Beak Things. This proved to be a fine decision, and the entire crew continued to not be eaten alive forthwith. With some idea now of why the flats were called 'Gut', they bypassed them and continued on south through the desert. The weather was worsening, with a fine sandstorm gathering ahead. There was something else there too.

"That's the Eye ahead," Izumi said.

"Would that happen to be an ancient hashish production facility?" Nuk asked.

"Almost certainly, my Prince."

"It could provide shelter from this storm. Let's hurry," Wodston suggested. They did so, arriving in the shadow of a gargantuan metal ring, adorned with all manner of legs, bulges and protrusions.

"So, future girl. Gonna tell us what this is?" Nuk asked.

"Well I don't know that much," Izumi said. "It's an ancient weapon. Dead now, obviously. It's been here for... ages, I guess."

"Two thousand years dead. And good riddance to the thing. Gotta get the other one someday too," Rick said.

"Wait, Rick, you remember when this was still active? What did it do?"

"Err... Forget I said anything. All skeletons have forgotten that time, don't you know that?"

"You haven't forgotten, have you?"

"I've forgotten everything, alright? Who even are you? And where's my money bucket? It's giving me empty vibes wherever it is."

As the crew rested and Rick continued to evade Izumi's questions, Nuk muttered to Wodston,

"Dammit my man, now she's got another obsession with the skele-boy."

"Indeed. His head of full of old secrets, I imagine. The advantage of age is his..." Wodston sighed.

"We need to take a look as his memory chip... Charlie!" Nuk waved Ells over. "You wanna steal Rick's brain for me?"

"But what if he gives me the stick?" Ells replied.

"I'm more worried about him giving someone else the stick," Nuk said. They decided not to steal Rick's brain in the end, but Nuk tried as best he could to find the screws on the back of the skeleton's head, just in case.

In the evening the sandstorm cleared and they carried on eastwards, seeing First Empire ruins dotted around the desert. One of them had a large dish-shaped thing on the top pointing up at the sky. When they got close Rick started complaining that it was giving him a headache. It was perfectly reasonable to presume this was the beginning of some new grift, so he was ignored. Then a searing tower of yellow light pierced the heavens, shooting down like the wrath of a scorned god. It tore up a nearby hillside as it strafed across it, melting sand and turning mud to char.

"Jeez, Okran, I'll pray harder or something, come on man!" Nuk said.

"That's the other one," Rick said.

"Another Eye?"

"Yep. There were always two."

"And the other one shot giant fire beams too?"

"Yeah. It sucked. S'called a laser. Not that I know anything about it. Ahem."

"Rick, will you tell us the probability that we will get hit by one of these lasers?" Wodston asked.

"Well that's hard to say. I mean it don't fire during the night since it needs sunlight to work. People used to sneak by it in the dark. Haven't tried it myself – I was on the other side the fence, ya know? Wait, probably better that you don't know, ya know?"

Rick's price to explain his ramblings was far too high, but he seemed to be right about the night tip. It was already late, and this Eye in the sky soon fell quiet. And now that it was safe to walk the roads in the area, the insects came out of the woodwork.

"Is that... shid, more ninjas!" Nuk called as a gang of black-coated figures appeared from the darkness.

"They're not ninjas, they're pirates," Izumi said.

"Oh you know that for sure, do you?"

"Yes, trust me. They'll still kill us though. Disgusting fat thing, time to do whatever you want to these people in the dark, alright?"

Ells grinned and dashed out with his huge cleaver raised overhead.

"Stay behind me, master," Sandor said to Nuk.

"Shid. Pirates versus ninjas is it? Let's make some history," Nuk commented.

It turns out that ninjas are better than pirates. Although that said, Nuk's crew were the ones going around stealing things, and the attackers were black-clad stalkers of the night, so perhaps this wasn't the best sample. The pirates tried to cut the straps of Gary's pack to get a quick score, but the brave garru thrashed about and beat the attackers away. Still, the sword slashes that landed took their toll, and by the time the melee was over with, poor Gary couldn't stand. Wodston splinted his leg, and they were just about ready to limp somewhere more comfortable for the night when another band of pirates appeared. Pirate-pirates, there to steal the score from the first bunch.

"Shid, shid, I can't run on this leg," Izumi said, clutching a freshly bandaged cut she'd picked up.

"I got you," Nuk said, suddenly scooping her up over his shoulder. He held onto her with one arm, and with the other brandished his katana to battle back against the fresh pirates.

"Nuk, you piece of shid! I'm not being your shield you fugging shidlord!" Izumi screamed.

"Okran's ghost, I'm stopping you getting pirated, m'lady! Keep still! Also I'm showing off, so try to look cool."

"I'd rather get pirated than have your bloody arm around me!"

"You tsunderey."

"What?"

"Haven't read the classics, have you?"

"What the fugg are you- Nuk!"

Nuk was handily cutting down opponent after opponent, and as showing off goes, it was actually surprisingly good stuff. The others were faring okay too, and the pirates soon had enough. The hivers were both alive but unwilling to move, so they were loaded up on the shek for transit to a nearby United Cities market town, Eyesocket. There the crew grabbed a few hours rest to conclude the night.

"Eyesocket. Exactly the sort of place you never want to see," Izumi mumbled as she fell asleep. Luckily for her, she was somewhere entirely different when she woke up.

"Beautiful, in its own way," Rick was saying.

"Err, what? Really!" Izumi spluttered, jumping out of bed, only to see Rick was looking out over a large valley, in which a giant laser was merrily dancing about.

"Ah, the madame awakes. Got you some better accommodation, since you were complaining and all," Rick said.

"Well, thank you Rick. And... morning, Prince Tashino."

Nuk was standing right beside her bed, holding out a slab of charred skimmer meat. "Thanks, Prince. Wait. Bloody- We're in Brink!" Izumi exclaimed, rushing about to look in all directions from the rooftop she found herself on.

"Yep," Nuk said. "Thought maybe the guys here on the edge of the empire would have the stuff. But it's really just samurai and misery, you know?"

"Of course I know. Spent half my life trying to get out of this place."

"You've been here before?"

"This is where I'm from, idiot."

"Idiot? How was I supposed to know that?"

"You were supposed to ask. You know, at some point during all that blathering about Naruto?"

"That was a private conversation between me and Sandor, actually. Whatever. You're from Brink then?"

"Yes."

"And is there any green here?"

"No."

"Huh. Probably coulda saved some time if I asked you that before we left."

"Yeah. Yeah, well done. Fugging... I'm going back to bed."

"Madame, at least you are now among the first to know that the laser beams out there are from the sister weapon to the Eye," Rick said. "Dunno how many biologicals know that little secret, but it ain't many."

"You're right, Rick. Thanks. You know that does make me feel better. Thanks, Rick. Oh, but I'm guessing there are a few more things you want to tell me, right?"

"Sorry, sister. First one's free, but I can't go giving out secrets to anyone. Or anyone at all. Supposed to be a secret. Dammit, you know what, y'all owe me ten stacks for this! And no one can know!"

Agreeing to secrecy calmed the strangely distraught skeleton down. Following this the crew took a day of leave exploring the tiny, ugly, impoverished frontier town of Brink. It took far less than a day to realise that Izumi had been right to migrate from that dump. In fact they were so dissatisfied with the accommodation that they checked out around midnight to leave, which had the added bonus of avoiding any daytime laser shows of course.

Where were they going? Well that was a matter of contention. Since Brink was the literal brink of the United Cities Empire, they were supposed to just go home. But pushing things beyond the Brink was Nuk's speciality.

"My Prince, I'm sure there is little out there of any use to us," Wodston argued.

"I am tempted to agree, Prince Tashino," Izayah added. "In the Shek Kingdom we call the places down there, 'The Old Lands'. Long since devoid of civilisation, I'm afraid. Industrial supplies of quality drugs are hard to come by."

"There can't be nothing out there. Look at that mountain, and all this blurry mess on the map. Kinda like something is hiding out there, right?" Nuk said.

"Well, when you put it that way, it's another matter entirely!" Izayah said, leaving the huddle around the map and hoisting his bag onto his shoulder.

"Prince, I'm pretty sure there really is nothing out there. It's bandits and monsters, and all they try to do is come back up here. Not much point going the other way," Izumi said.

"Can I suggest something?" Rick said. "You know heading out to that mountain ain't such a bad idea."

"Mr. Rick, can you elaborate?" Wodston asked.

"Nope. Just saying, I'm all for it. There's something special there. Your bugman might like the place. A real old sovereign... Kinda like, there's an atmosphere out there, you know?"

"I don't know, and it sounds like you've gone off the rails Coin-Slot, but in many ways, that means we absolutely have to go," Nuk said.

Soon resistance seemed futile, and the party moved out into the desert night, heading south into the lands that had once been part of the Second Empire, but were far from being part of the Third. Rick seemed impatient to get there, but wasn't letting anything slip about it.

Was what Nuk was looking for out there? Well, yes and no. The contacts he needed for his plans in the capital certainly weren't, but he did find something that brought him fulfilment beyond his wildest dreams. And this is nothing to do with his tsundere historian, I assure you of that.

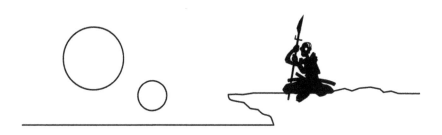

Chapter 11 Side Story
Moisture Farming Tycoon

(Author's Note: This tale takes place during the days spent in Heft during Chapter 11).

"I wonder if the middle of the room is really the best place for it," Izumi said.

"Are you gonna move your desk?" Nuk replied from inside the hole.

"No I'm not. I mean there's a really good solution to this: not digging a well inside our house."

"It's my house, I paid for it, I'll dig whatever I want in here."

"And you want... like ten drops a day of dirty water? Instead of, say, a usable interior to the building?"

At this Nuk dropped his shovel and looked up at Izumi with a scowl.

"Look, future girl, this is a money-making venture. If everyone would rather take days off than go get work done, then I'm going to have to keep this company afloat!"

"By putting a hole in it and letting water in?"

"Exactly. This is the fugging desert. Water's worth, like money."

"But there's a well right outside?"

"That's a public well. This will be premium, TCM+ Elite Adventuring Water."

"It's gonna be dirty water. Especially if you're gonna stand in it- hey get off me!"

"Get down here and help!"

"In exchange for what?"

"Exchange? Ugh... I'll give you five percent of the takings."

"Ninety five percent."

"Six percent."

"Ninety five percent and I'll tell you how to make a water pump."

"Oh... a pump. What's cheaper, pump, or Wodston throwing buckets up...?"

Izumi thumped down into Nuk's hole. But don't get too excited.

"Pumping, or throwing up... The classic question."

"Well... I mean why does it have to be one or the other," Nuk said. He suddenly realised he was almost face to face with Izumi in his little pit. She realised it at about the same time. For a moment they were there staring into each other's eyes, Nuk's pump and throw up remark hanging in the air. Was it the reflection of the orange sands around the pit-edge, or was Izumi going red in the face?

"My Prince, is there a reason why you've dug a hole in our floor?" came Wodston's voice from above.

"It's my floor!" Nuk snapped, suddenly resuming his digging.

"Mister Wodston, would you like to help us dig a well?" Izumi asked.

"If that is my Prince's command."

"Wodston, take my place," Nuk commanded. It was arranged, and Wodston complied without hesitation – now it was he stuck in close confines with Izumi. Within the hour they found water trickling out of the ground around their feet.

"That's wet gold!" Nuk said. "Time to get pumping, future girl!" he added. But don't get too excited. Izumi assembled parts from the guild's collection of recalled miscellany and soon they had water dripping from a tap in the middle of the room. Now all they needed to do was fill of a couple of buckets, and the new premium hydration solution would make a big splash in the markets of the imperial capital.

Izumi went to go dry off in the guild's shed down in the highstreet, which was also where she liked to go read her books on these warm days off. Nuk went upstairs to smash a training dummy with his sword – he was jumping with energy, and couldn't wait for the first load to dribble into his lap. But don't get too excited.

Rick was there also, practising his stick beating technique. I mean, I can only curtail your excitement so many times, so please remain calm.

"Rick, you know Izumi?" Nuk asked him.

"Know her? I know every single thing there is to know. Sometimes I'm glad I can delete my memories."

"Err... Right... You... So... Ahem. I was gonna ask... Do you know how mad she actually is at me? Is it like, not at all?"

"She's mad. She's mad, sad, and glad."

"Tsunderey!"

"Damn biologicals and their old-time talk. You know talking like that was illegal in the First Empire! Only reason those damn books survived the fall was 'cause they were all hidden in secret places!"

"What are you talking about?"

"Oh... Nothing you need to worry about. Just don't use any of those old Japan words on me, right? You're sayin' it wrong anyway."

"Fine, fine. So she's not gonna kill me?"

"I doubt it."

"And maybe she actually... likes me?"

"Listen Prince, I ain't your agony aunt. I'm your uncaring uncle. I'm here to see shid and stick to the biologica- your enemies, that is. You wanna get your hormones up over the greasy madame, you'll have to be my guest."

"I don't wanna do that, I'm just asking... Also... When you say greasy-"

"I ain't saying nothing else to you, horndog. Why don't you go check on your watering hole or something?"

Nuk did so, and found he'd collected almost an entire bucket of sweet, non-sweet water! He took it down to the lowtown bar, and clacked it onto the counter.

"You wanna buy some of the good stuff?" Nuk asked.

"It comes in buckets now?" the barman replied. But don't get too excited.

"It's water."

"Doesn't look like water."

"That's because it's TCM+ Elite Premium Overlord EX2.5 S-Class Hydration Medium."

"So it's not even water?"

"It's water-esque."

"Great. I'll give you fifty for it."

"Fifty stacks?!"

"Fifty cats."

"What? That's not even enough for a fugging sandwich."

"I'll trade it for a sandwich if you want, but you gotta let me take three bites, and have a lick of the rest."

"Man... This stuff... Yeah fine, go on then."

Nuk entered the guild's shed down the street, finding Izumi bent over the writing desk, in a very unexciting fashion, scrawling on some parchment. He explained his poor deal, but Izumi didn't seem very sympathetic.

"Well, I mean, it's ground water, still got the sand and stuff in it. I'd rather just keep licking a sandwich," she said. Nothing to see here folks.

"I need a way to get it cleaner. Like, before it goes through all the shid in the ground," Nuk reasoned.

"And you want me to help you with that?"

"If you're interested."

"I'm not at all interested."

"Yeah, what's that you're writing?"

"Nothing."

"I can read, you know?"

"There's little proof of that."

"You're writing about my well! I can see it! What else have you been writing?!"

"No, wait! Nuk, seriously, don't look at all that!" Izumi said, suddenly gathering up a pile of papers and locking them in a drawer under the desk. "I'll help you, okay? Let's have a think, hmm? You want it not full of ground shid, right?"

"Yeah... So... We could collect up a load of spit..."

"Err... How about *Okran's* spit?"

"Isn't that a... position...?"

"I mean fugging rain!" Izumi said. Now she was definitely red in the face.

"Rain... rain... that's water..."

"Yes, well done. Why don't we just make a rain collector? On the roof?"

"That's genius! How do we do that?"

"Can't you imagine it?"

"Imagine what?"

"Actually, don't imagine anything. I'll help you, let's get out of here."

It was nightfall by the time they'd bought all the materials they'd need. They had an old water tank hauled up onto the roof, and there they started erecting a few poles around it to hold the water-catcher. It was little more than a cloth that led water down to a pipe, but it took hours to get it sturdy enough not to blow away in the wind.

"Phew, that's it then," Nuk said at about four am when the work was done. "Thanks future girl."

"I don't think you'll wanna thank me for this," Izumi said with a smirk.

"What? Seriously you stayed up to help me with this. You've more than earned your ninety five, you know? I feel like you've definitely made some progress with me."

"Progress? I'm not your fugging teacher."

"Not teacher. Like you've progressed... closer to me. Right?"

"Prince Tashino, are you... flirting with me?" Izumi asked, keeping her voice quiet. Not quiet enough.

"Yes he certainly is, madame," Rick said. Rick was there too by the way. I told you he never slept, and in the darkness of night he was hard to see just standing there in the corner.

"Rick, you were watching?" Izumi asked in shock.

"Always watching. Always remembering. Carry on, biologicals."

"Are you just gonna stand there?"

"Yep."

"Right... Err, Prince, what do you think?"

"Well we need to clarify something. I'm definitely not flirting with you."

"Right. Thanks."

"But, by helping me out here, you've been flirting with me. You've entered my good graces, shall we say?"

"I don't want to say that, and why are you deciding that I'm flirting with you?"

"It's a data-driven decision," Rick commented.

"Shut up Rick! Oh, I mean, I didn't mean it like that. Sorry, Rick."

"Forget Rick. In fact, why don't we forget this whole thing?" Nuk suggested.

"Because... you said I'm flirting with you, but you're not with me?"

"Yeah..."

"Why?"

"Why...?"

"Why... do I even talk to you. Ugh. Rick, would you like to go for a walk?"

"Got my walking stick ready, madame," came the reply.

"Good. Goodnight, Prince Tashino. Enjoy your rain catcher, you know, next time it rains here. It'll happen one of these years! Unlike something else! See ya!"

Rick escorted Izumi downstairs. Nuk looked up at the sky, and realised he'd probably made a few mistakes that evening.

"Fugg," he said. All's not well that ends not well.

Chapter 12
A New Prince and Old Friends

"I told you it was green," Izumi said as the group reached the top of a steep hill.

"Green... as in the colour green?!" Nuk said.

"Yes. Sorry to get your hopes up, Prince. Can't you just appreciate this? How often do you see a tree with green leaves, like in the books?"

"Tree.. green leaves... Man we better find something soon," Nuk muttered.

"You are right Miss Izumi, this is rather unusual," Izayah said. They were standing below a palm tree with short green leaves hanging from the top. A few other such trees were dotted around the hillside, but all was a wasteland as far as you could see in all other directions.

"Could these be the mythical greenstalks?" Gustavsen said. He placed a hand on the trunk and sniffed. "Ah. Ancient feelings. I cannot bear to associate," he went on, sitting down and putting his head in his hands. He wasn't the only one brought down by the place.

"Been a long, long time," Rick mused.

"Since what, Mister Rick?" Wodston asked.

"Since I been here. A real long time. Almost wouldn't know it. That was when those palm leaves were the least green thing you'd see from up here. Damn Earth clans woulda taken it away if the King hadn't been here."

The mention of a King piqued Gustavsen's interest, and he scurried over. Izumi's pen dove into a vial of ink.

"Provide me the name of this King, metal one," Gustavsen demanded.

"Stobe."

"King Stobe?"

"Just Stobe. No King really, just the last of his kind. The survivor. The saviour."

"A King by default. Not so worthy," Gustavsen said, with a wave of his arms.

"Rick, are you talking about Stobe as in Stobe's Garden?" Izumi asked.

"You know that name? That's a Second Empire title for this place. You really ain't supposed to know that, biological."

"It's my job to know it. I used to help with the Second Empire research."

"Well if folk've done their job, you won't find much else, I assure you of that."

"What's that meant to mean?"

"Means some things are better off forgotten. That's why we better get outta here right now. Can't take it anymore."

"What do you remember, Rick?" Izumi asked desperately, but Rick shook his head and plodded off on his own.

"Izayah, you know what he's on about?" Nuk asked.

"Not as such. Stobe was mentioned in old Shek legends. A cult or something. Let's be wary of another Red Rick grift, shall we?"

The group followed Rick away from the hillside, and meandered southeast in the increasingly hopeless search for a huge, intact yet unclaimed industrial hashish hydroponics facility in need of product recall. They snaked through a set of deep canyons, and then as the ground raised and levelled out again, they saw a most confusing melee up ahead: humans, giant crabs, and... some other things, were brawling away.

"Fishmen," Gustavsen said. "Don't listen to anything they say."

"In what way it is a fish, and what way is it a man?" Nuk asked.

"They are the result of close association between humans and crabs."

"Let's make a fishman!" Ells cheered.

"Cool. Well civilisation's good for something then. Let's just stroll on by," Nuk suggested. However as they did so, a group of these fishmen appeared from nowhere and were suddenly all over then, their atrophied claws snipping away and their phlegmy mouths gurgling melodically.

"Wetter is not better! Don't listen to them!" Gustavsen pleaded.

"Oh... I love you too!" Ells said, hugging a squirming crossbreed.

"Do you have to be a certain level of freakish to understand them or something?" Nuk asked, plunging his blade into a join in the thick exoskeleton of his assailant.

"No no, nothing like that. This one tells me I am very handsome," Izayah reported.

"Right, so you need to be at least an Izayah on the cray-scale," Nuk concluded. The group eventually slew all the chattering creatures, and Gustavesen told them,

"They like to associate with things in a very particular way. They are unworthy. Most terribly unworthy."

"Oh, so it's like what I thought you were gonna do to me," Nuk nodded.

"It tickles!" Ells said. A little creepy-crawly was slithering around on his stomach. Gustavsen clicked his fingers and pointed at it. Ignacio, his bodyguard, moved up and removed the critter with a bite of his blunt teeth. Juice spurted out all over the place. Ignacio gathered it up on his hands, then started slathering it over Gustavsen.

"What... the actual... fugg!" Izumi shouted, unable to watch any longer.

"Fools," Gustavsen shot back. "Those burrowers can impregnate any species and any gender. They must be destroyed."

"And the rubbing shid?" Nuk dared to ask.

"Their oil preserves the integrity of your skin. If you fleshy ones wish not to look like your manservant, I suggest you apply it."

"Narko's curses, no fugging way," Izumi said. "I think we've learned everything there is to know about fugging fishmen. Let's fugg off right now."

"Language future girl! It's not that weird... Except that it is... Ugh Charlie don't rub it, don't listen to the Bad Green, let's all just move, shall we?" Nuk said.

They left the scene, with Wodston dallying just a little to scoop some of the viscous bug-mank into a cup.

It was a hard night for the group, ending up hopelessly lost on a mountainside, with their map simply showing the area as a brown splodge with no features to speak of. They ended up unknowingly going back towards civilisation, of a sort. There were lights up ahead, but Izumi demanded they keep their distance until the morning, on account of the area's high bandit population. Semi-fortunately, this place was no bandit lair.

"Are you seeing this?" Nuk said. He was looking upon a roughly-built village, with regular humans just wandering around. I mean, that's amazing for out here, but he was actually surprised by the huge, scuttling, fugg-off crabs that were also going about their business between the buildings.

"I think, my prince, this is the source of that over-association between species," Wodston said. Izayah directed Bobbie and Claw to hold onto Ells, whose eyes were already widening.

"Man and crab, living side by side. Is this the power of... association?" Nuk asked.

"Drones cannot associate," Gustavsen was quick to point out.

"But I'm no drone. You guys stay here."

Ignoring a barrage of protests, Nuk dumped his bag and ran off into the village.

"My Prince! Ugh. Who will help me protect him?" Wodston asked.

"Now I don't know all that much about this association business," Rick said. "But I think a man needs a little privacy to get it done right, right?"

"So wrong..." Izumi said, taking a seat and pouring out a cap of rum.

In the village, Nuk waved good morning to a variety of friendly neighbourhood crabs.

"Oi, what are you doing here?" someone shouted at Nuk from a balcony. "Are you a customer?"

"Customer? Yeah, pretty much. You got green here?"

"You want a green one? Yeah, we got a green one."

"Just one? I need loads."

"Loads? Well we've only got one in green."

"What kinda business are you running here? Only one?"

"You think it's easy to rear crabs, buddy? You get what colours we got, alright?"

"Wait, wait, wait one minute in the name of all that is fugging brown. You're talking about crabs?"

"What the fugg did you think I was talking about? This is a crab town, mate. You wanna buy a crab or not?"

"Ahhhhhh oh Okran's Blessing and Narko's Gift, fugging... yes!" Nuk exclaimed, rushing up into what turns out was a crab dealership, and pulling strings of cats from even his most secret bodily stash.

Not long after, Izayah drew his sword and yelled out,

"Prince Tashino! Behind you!"

A huge green crab was plodding behind him as Nuk left the village. Nuk saw Izayah's concern, turned around and gave the crab a pat on its thick shell.

"Everyone, I want you to meet Prince," Nuk said, bringing his new friend closer. "And that's not all," he added.

"He's a crab boy. I knew he'd turn out to be a crab boy," Izumi was muttering as Nuk went behind Prince and then returned with two tiny crablets. And by tiny, I mean they were about the size of two dinner plates, rather than the size of a car.

"The orange one is the Crusty, and this little fellow is Skut," Nuk said, handing them off to Izayah and Ells to hold.

"Oh my. It is rather special, isn't it?" Izayah said.

"Crab friend! I was raised by crabs, you know?" Ells said. Izumi hurriedly reopened the rum, threw away the cap and started swigging.

"My Prince, how much did you spend on these?" Wodston asked.

"No price is too high," was Nuk's reply.

"All of our money... months of work..." Wodston breathed. Izumi put an extremely welcome hand on his shoulder, and offered up the rum bottle.

So, that's how the gang was slightly expanded in number and hugely expanded in mass. The mass was a bit of an issue in fact, for Prince, the adult crab, could only stomp along at a modest speed.

"We'll never get anywhere at a crab's pace," Izumi complained.

"He's only just become freerange, future girl. Let him stretch his legs," Nuk said.

"But, we're gonna run out of food at this rate. Oh, and we're already out of rum."

"Don't worry, madame. Let a strong man with arms of steel deal with this for ya," Rick said. With seemingly no effort at all, he lifted Prince up off the ground and carried him overhead. The crab did not appear to notice, and waved its legs as if walking anyway while Rick sped him forwards.

Anyone who saw this group that featured a red-faced robot wielding an entire giant crab, probably decided not to mess with them, and as such the crew wandered freely up the so-called Greenbeach Coast, which certainly not worthy of the 'green' part of its title, disappointing each in their own way.

Becoming increasingly lost, they stumbled around in a vaguely northerly direction. They passed First Empire ships, forever beached far inland, and a huge docking facility, now sitting on the side of of a sandy hill.

"The sea used to come up here," Izumi explained. "And there was an inland sea outside Brink."

"So where did it go?" Nuk asked.

"That is the question. The sea somehow lost a load of water during the wars at the end of the First Empire. Rick, wanna tell me what happened?"

"I do not want to tell you what happened. Additionally, I do not know what happened, so please disregard my first statement," Rick recited.

"Perhaps you could do us the honour of at least telling us where we are?" Wodston suggested.

"Pirates End. We ended them good."

"And... is that near any shelter?"

"I haven't been here in three thousand years, ya know? Don't know where the best gentleman's club is these days."

"Ah, fair enough. Let's carry on... That way," Wodston said, and so they did. They ended up going inland a little, and all of a sudden Izumi knew exactly where they were. Ahead of them was another First Empire boatyard, sitting on the eastern end of that former inland sea she had mentioned.

"Guys, I recognise this place. Been a while, but, I'm pretty sure Black Scratch is on the other side of those cliffs," she said.

"Sounds like at least a middling gentleman's club," Nuk commented.

"It's where I worked after Brink. You can ask for the full story whenever you want, you know?"

"Must be good if you ran from it as well."

"I was still working for them when I got stuck with you! And now, if you don't mind, I think we should pop back in and see what I'm owed."

"Oh, now we're talking. It's bring your crab crew to work day!"

"Yeah. No chance I can convince you all to just stay here?"

"We'll all be on our best behaviour, Miss Izumi," Izayah said. "The crabs are housetrained, after all."

"Negative, can confirm to be false," Rick said, much in need of clean after a day with Prince over his head.

Izumi could protest no more, and they carried on around the last lake of the inland sea, up some steep cliffs, and out onto a plateau scattered with First and Second Empire ruins, somewhat alive brown trees, and most importantly, the walls and warmth of the city of Black Scratch.

"No pets," the gate guard said as Nuk and company approached.

"They're just toys. Lifesize ones," Nuk said. Ells was cuddling a crablet in a convincing fashion already. It was ten in the evening, and in the darkness it wasn't completely obvious that the crabs were squirming about so everyone was waved inside.

"Can't take these to the inn. We'll stay at the caravan station," Izumi said, directing them to the west end of town, where a spread of bedrolls and campfires lined the grounds under the city wall.

"Is it safe to stay here?" Wodston asked Izumi.

"Yeah, this isn't the empire. Guards' eyes are real, and there's nowhere to sell you," Izumi said. If she was telling the truth, it sounded like Heft had a challenger for the title of centre of civilisation, without doubt.

At last they could all get a good night's sleep. Nuk was awoken early in the morning by a kerfuffle going on outside the wall. He took his honour guard – Red Rick, Sandor and Prince – to investigate. Black Scratch was an established city that had remained unconquered by the samurai lords of the empire. While this certainly had its benefits, it meant it attracted a lot of attention from outlaws and empire exiles. As such, it was a favourite target for a band known as the Grass Pirates, the same criminal network that had attacked Nuk and company on their way to Brink.

Nuk ran out to assess the credit situation among the fallen, but his entourage did raise a few questions.

"Excuse me sir," a guard said. "Is this giant crab yours sir?"

"Oh, that's what a giant crab is. In that case, what's a hiver?" Nuk bluffed.

"It's no monsters in Black Scratch sir. This is a respectable town."

"And what respectable town isn't guarded by a trained killer crab?"

"Is that a rhetorical question sir, or shall I provide a list?"

"Hear me out. Me and my guild are in town on business. I see you've got issues with the locals. How about you don't ask any questions about our stay here, and in exchange, you'll have a giant crab going your dirty work for you."

The guard actually decided to try Nuk out on this offer, so Nuk didn't have to go with his backup plan of claiming to be blind and dependant on the guidance of the crab for navigation. As a result, he was able to smuggle a whole load of pirate stuff inside and fence it to the early risers among the locals. Eventually Izumi appeared among them.

"Prince. You're a leather jacket salesman now?" she asked.

"You talking to me or the crab?" Nuk asked.

"I... don't care. Did you want me to show you around?"

"I guess. So you worked here?"

"Still work here. This is a hub for Tech Hunters. They're like real adventurers, and also scientists. Kinda the best thing in the world, you know?"

"If you love them so much, why don't you just marry them?"

"I've had offers."

"Seriously?"

"Seriously! You jealous? You're turning green."

"That's the light reflecting off the crab! Prince, stay here. Gonna go with auntie Iz and get the inside angle."

"Wait, please don't steal anything from this place. This is important."

"Steal *anything*..."

"Not too much then. Really. It's important too me."

"Fine, fine. Who proposed to you?"

"What?"

"Who said they'd marry you?"

"Why does that matter?"

"If I'm gonna pick and choose what I steal- Never mind. Go on, show me your libraries and whatever."

The tour began, and among an assortment of well-stocked markets, depots and workshops, there were several bars – packed with patrons even at 7am – and plentiful supplies of food and drink. No hashish, but the excitement of getting a pet giant crab had eased Nuk's pains in that regard recently.

Izumi took Nuk inside the Great Library, a mushroom-domed Second Empire structure that housed rows of tall shelves packed with books.

"Izumi, you're back already," the skeleton receptionist said.

"Already? It's been months Kurtis," Izumi said.

"Months? Well don't time fly when you're deactivated. What about the rest of the crew?"

"Gave up on it all in Heng and decided to work for the samurai. I still have all the notes. Now that I'm back I can compile everything. We've seen a lot. Well, not the original crew, but the new one."

"Is the gentleman here your 'one'?"

"Please, please don't put it like that."

"I'm number one, if that's what you mean," Nuk said, ignorant to Izumi's fluster.

"Incredible. I am number 482-740-83," the skeleton said.

"Just come upstairs Nuk," Izumi said.

"Oh my," the skeleton remarked, going back to its book.

Upstairs Izumi picked out a particular volume with a violet cover and found a certain page.

"Look. This is my report on the Reaver's Lake ruins. It's published," she said.

"Published. What's that mean?"

"It means the scholars thought it was good enough to go into a book."

"But the book is in here."

"Well noticed."

"How are people supposed to read it?"

"They aren't."

"Cool. Good use of time writing it then huh?"

"We're keeping this away from people like you."

"And you complain that I'm uneducated, the hypocrisy!"

"Put that back!" Izumi said, pointing at the parchment Nuk was trying to sneak into his ninja backpack.

"Fine fine. Well done future girl. You're a real history historian, and stuff. You didn't have to prove it you know?"

"Well I did. And I'm going to become a lot better known in the high circles of the Tech Hunters with my next report. Going to be a book unto itself. That's why I wanted to ask you to stay here for a while, Prince."

"Gotta go feed the crabs and stuff."

"Not literally right- Ugh, I mean in the city. It'll take me a week to get all the notes together into something readable. Can you wait that long?"

"Do we need to be here for that?"

"I suppose not. But you don't... No, you can go if you want."

"I don't want."

"You don't?"

"No."

"Good."

"Great."

"So we can all leave together once I've settled everything?"

"Sure."

"Thanks, really. That means a lot to me."

"Oh, it's nothing. I wouldn't just leave you here, after everything."

"You wouldn't?"

"Course not. You were worried about that?"

"No, no, just... Doesn't matter. I'd relieved."

"I'm happy too."

"I said relieved actually. But I am happy, right now."

"This always makes me happy," Nuk said, keeping his eyes on the ground.

"This- You mean... Err... Nuk..."

"Are you gonna kiss or what?" Rick asked. Yes, in the moment it was easy to forget that Rick and Sandor were standing on the other side of the bookshelf.

"What? How dare you! This is an academic... Err..." Izumi ran out of steam and just bolted away with the point unfinished.

"Always said nobles weren't good at anything. Thought talking would be the exception," Sandor commented.

"Guys, you're fired, or whatever, okay? Go feed the crabs and tell everyone we're staying for a week or something," Nuk said.

"What are you gonna do?" Rick asked.

"Gonna... Check some stuff out here," Nuk said. Even he wasn't sure if this meant he was going to read the books or steal them. That there was any question was surely a sign of his growth as a young man? Wodston would have been proud.

So, with Izumi now back in paying writing work and everyone else babysitting a trio of handsy crabs, the crew settled in for a long stretch in Black Scratch. It was a quiet little corner of the world, but not quiet enough that the good old fashioned Credit Management and Non-consensual Private Healthcare Guilds could not do lucrative trade, helped along by the Tashino Crustacean Corps Private Security Consortium.

None of this was helping with the quest for a supply of clean green for the Emperor, however their time in the city would actually advance the cause of Izumi's alternative brown town old school addition scheme. With a little help from her friends in the Tech Hunters, Nuk was about to become a drug baron, a warlord, and several things in between.

Chapter 13
The Battle of Manksand Cove

The isolated university town of Black Scratch had just enjoyed its most peaceful week in a long time. Having a giant crab working the doors really keeps the riff-raff out, you know? Unfortunately for Nuk, he was being forced to speak to some of the riff raff inside.

"This is Jaz. Jaz, this is the Prince," Izumi said. Beside her on the roof on the bar stood an equally scraggly-looking woman, to whom Nuk vaguely gestured in greeting.

"Pleasure to meet you, Nukky-boy," Jaz said. Her voice had a most unfamiliar twang.

"You can barely talk. Is this what the old-town brown does to you?" Nuk said.

"Yeah no I'm from the Nashe, had me in bloody chains half me life. Picked up a teensie bit of their accent."

"Holy Nation, you mean?"

"Too right."

"Oh. No wonder they're so mad all the time over there. So future girl, you said this was about your ancient addiction scheme?"

"It is. Jaz does the geo stuff, and she's got all the surveys for the local area. We've been looking it over, and there's a perfect place to grow chocolate here," Izumi said.

"Pretty much yeah," Jaz began. "So there's like this old river that's about two chugs short of being totally outta there, but what's left makes the fertility index of the ground shoot up like your fugging dad. No offence. So yeah it's got all the right nutries for those old beans; should be able to whip out a proper croppa choc in no time and get your whole empire coco loco, or whatever it was you wanted. Want me to sort it out for ya?"

"The Holy Nation must be destroyed," Nuk muttered to himself. "Well, always wanted to try home growing. Sounds like future girl already told you all our secrets, so I guess you're hired."

"Too right she told me your secrets. You two got a shek's chance in heaven if you carry on like all that."

"What the fugg are you talking about?"

"Nothing, Nuk, Prince, come on. Let's go see the growing site. Aren't you excited?" Izumi said, waving for Nuk to follow down into the bar.

"Probably. Can't say I know what's going on, but we need a walk anyway. Let's round up the crabs and roll out!" Nuk said. So it was done, and the guild assembled in the town square. Jaz joined them with a group of her fellow warrior-scholars from the Tech Hunters. Gary was loaded up with tools, bricks, and sheet metal, and the group plodded off down the hill.

Even at a crab's pace, it was only half an hour or so to the ancient river canyon north of the town. It snaked west back into the United Cities Empire, and east into the lawless farmlands of the Stormlands Coast. In other words, it was perfect for drug running. In fact it was so perfect that when the guild arrived, two rival gangs were mauling each other over the prime turf.

"Bloody hell. They've clocked it already I reckon," Jaz said.

"Worry not, m'lady. In the name of the Empire I will conquer the promised land and show the world how a real drug dealer rolls! Release the crab!" Nuk shouted. Prince and the guild's fellow soldiers moved up to clean the field of pirates and reavers

"He's always like this then?" Jaz asked Izumi.

"Well... Ever since he bought that fugging crab..." Izumi replied.

"You've had a foul mouth on ya ever since you went up his way, don't ya think? He's been rubbing off on ya?"

"Don't put it like that."

"Really? Thought you might enjoy it, ya know? Huh?"

"The only thing he's- I'm not saying it like that. He taught me sword fighting, so shall we?"

"Oh be my guest darling. I'll show these dregs how we got outta the camps," Jaz said, entering the raging battle alongside Izumi. With the two gangs being half-dead already on account of each other, the TCM+ Guild and their Tech Hunter collaborators cleaned house, and carried on down the shallow hill to the bottom of the river canyon. The canyon had steep cliffs running in both directions, and their current entry point was the only way in or along it. There, at that crossroads of the underworld, was a swampy cove in the canyon-side.

"This is the spot," Jaz said after tasting the mushy soil. "So, you sure you wanna do this?"

"Err, Prince?" Izumi said.

"What exactly are we doing, by the way?" Wodston asked.

"Isn't it obvious?" Nuk said. "We're going to use this wet mud to grow a drug so ancient that dad hasn't made it illegal, and so addictive that people used to smuggle it in containers that were also made of it." He was referring to what he'd read about Easter Eggs in Izumi's magazine, not that anyone else knew that. "We are going to go with the flow of history and turn green into brown. Ladies and gentlemen, it's time to farm some drugs."

Ells clapped, everyone else looked at each other in confusion, and the great project began. Step one was to lay claim to the patch by blocking off the drug-running routes. This took most of the day, with the crew shovelling earth to pile up inside a metal framework, making a set of sturdy walls that formed a compound around the drug spring. The Tech Hunters put up a hydraulic gateway to get in and out, and just like that, the TCM+ Guild was a guild no more, but a tiny empire!

And what would an empire be without soldiers? Nuk returned to Black Scratch and hired a group of mercenaries to patrol his borders. He also bought large quantities of mortar and sandstone, and had them brought down to the river to build his new house. Good thing he brought a cadre of troops with him, as back down at the base, the local reavers had become very confused regarding the walling off of their usual beat.

"They stolen our wacky backy patch!" one of them screamed, prompting an attack, however ultimately the guild and its shiny new army were too much for them. They scurried away to tell their mates high and low about his unsettling new settlement on the scene.

About a day after the guild had arrived, they had a dusty new HQ set up astride the drugs cove, and the drug smuggling routes were under their control. Only thing they didn't have was the drugs, which was brought up at a guild meeting the following evening.

"Productivity remains low," Nuk reported, pointing at his hand-drawn chart, which was in fact just a blank piece of paper. "As you can see, we've got zero kilograms product ready to ship, and can expect another zero kilograms from the current crop. So err, yeah, did no one think of this? No one's got any chocolate seeds?! Future girl?"

"I have them in the HQ. Well, the old HQ. The old, old HQ actually. In the shed," Izumi said.

"You and your bloody shed. That's a bit of a trek. Where else can we get them?"

"Prince Tashino, I've been near and far, and never even heard of this chocolate," Izayah said. "I think our lady's archaeological finds might be our best bet."

"Ugh but that's so far away. Maybe we can think of a new drug using what we have? Charlie, go fertilise the swamp in your special way and see what happens. Wodston my man, I want you find out if we can milk the crabs."

After some debate, neither of these ideas went forward – not that we know of anyway – and instead they decided to go recall their own products from Heft.

"Sheks, Wodston, Coin Slot, you're with me and Gary," Nuk ordered. "Rest of you keep the crabs safe, and I guess the mank-sand as well. Future girl's in charge."

"Wait, Prince, I'll go with you. This was my idea, after all. Let Mister Wodston rest here," Izumi said.

"I don't need to rest!" Wodston insisted.

"Guess I'll stay here then."

"Although my back... Perhaps I'll wait."

"Future girl is in charge because I need someone I can trust back here," Nuk stated.

"Just kiss already," Rick heckled.

"Oh yeah, give her a snog goodbye!" Jaz added. Izumi stormed out, and ultimately there was not so much as a wave goodbye when Nuk's team set off for the lengthy round trip back to the capital.

"Try not to die!" Nuk called back as he went. This proved to be a difficult order to follow. There was more trouble with reavers stumbling into the base, but nothing Nuk's hired legions couldn't handle. However, then a more serious opponent came wandering down the river. It was a huge group of United Cities slavers, off foraging for stock beyond the border.

"What the fugg is this place?" their leader asked when they turned a corner and saw walls blocking their path.

"Dunno. S'not that farm is it?" a follower said.

"We already visited the farm, idiot!" another said, a stalk of wheat sticking out of his mouth.

"Alright, calm down. So we're... Where's that map...?" the leader asked. He studied it for some time, to no avail. Then he looked up and realised he was surrounded by Nuk's troops and the guild caretakers, weapons in hand.

"Ya picked a bad time to get lost, friend!" Jaz shouted.

"I'm not lost, I'm right where I wanna be. Get the feisty one! In fact, get all the buggers! Let's have this place!" the slaver boss called to his entourage, and with that a huge brawl broke out.

"I think you could have been more subtle Jaz," Izumi said.

"To slavers? No point. Ya got outta the Nashe like I did, you know how it is."

"Had a few more scrapes since then, actually."

"Oh, what a big girl you are."

"Shut up. Let's just kill them, shall we?"

"That's the bloody spirit! Your little adventure's straightened you out nicely eh?"

As dusk fell, the girls entered the battlefield. About an hour later, Izumi was over Jaz's shoulder, being hauled back inside. That both were alive was enough of a victory, given the scale of the battle. Nuk's soldiers had earned their pay many times over, killing the surrounded slavers, but not without serious injuries to themselves. They had been so thorough that only one of the slavers had escaped. Unfortunately, he escaped with Gustavsen's man Ignacio in chains.

After a night of resting and wound tending, everyone was back on their feet again, but stepping out of the HQ revealed that the troops were still skirmshing with the local ruffians non-stop. Clearly the guild had stepped on a real wasps-nest of a wacky backy patch here.

"This is too much," Izumi said.

"Yeah no yeah, this is crazy," Jaz said. "Why are these dregs so wild? Maybe we should let them have their bloody corner and be done with it."

"Maybe. But the Prince..."

"Oh, you don't want lover boy getting mad?"

"I don't want him to be disappointed!"

"In you?"

"In general."

"Whatever darling. Why don't we leave all this stuff to the professionals?"

"Yeah, maybe."

"Where is Ignacio?" came Gustavsen's voice from behind them.

"Err... He's there," Izumi said, pointing at the other hiver milling about in the corner.

"That is not Ignacio," Gustavsen said.

"What? Is that a tree wearing a leather duster then?" Jaz asked.

"That is Rene, my bodyguard. I am speaking of Ignacio, my bodyguard."

Yes, by the way, Gustavsen had hired another hiver for his entourage, but no one had noticed until now.

"I don't know where he is, then," Izumi said. Gustavsen sniffed around the HQ, then around the battlefield a little, ignoring the fighting continuing on around him. He returned and said,

"They've taken him. Come, soldier, we shall retrieve him." Rene jumped to life and picked up a long katana.

"Wait, it's too dangerous," Izumi said.

"That is incorrect. I must retrieve him," Gustavsen insisted.

"Wait, wait, I thought you bugmen didn't really care about the little guys? Disposable drones or whatever?" Jaz said.

"Ignacio is not disposable. He is associated to me. I'm leaving."

"Prince Gustavsen, Prince Tashino said I'm in charge, and I really think we should stick together," Izumi said.

"Heartless flesh. You are not worthy of your station. I must ignore you. I shall return."

Gustavsen and Rene ran off in the direction the slavers had come from.

"That's three gone. No wonder you lost your dig crew," Jaz commented.

"Shut up Jaz. Nuk, please come back soon," Izumi muttered.

Nuk was standing in the old HQ in Heft, sizing up his crab claw trophy on the wall.

"The bags can't be full," he said.

"The chocolate seeds, the weapons, and all those books – they are rather hefty, my Prince," Wodston said.

"I know, but I need the crab arm as well. I need it, my man."

"You could leave a few of the books here. We will do just fine without them."

"No, we won't. I won't. I need them too, for scientific research purposes," Nuk said. Rick opened Gary's pack and pulled out a load of small, monochrome volumes.

"Whatta we got here? 'The Underwear Ninja'. 'The Prince and the Peephole'. 'Yasuke x Rock-chan Beach Bonanza'."

"They have titles?!" Nuk exclaimed, rushing over. "Okran's spit, you can read the runes, Coin Slot?"

"Sure I can. All these little marks are words. You want me to read it to you?"

"Fugg yes! Everyone take a seat," Nuk called.

"Alright, not like we got anywhere to be or anything. How about this one? Ahem. 'The Perverted Tale of Buck Chuck, Chapter 1: The Battle of the Spandex Bulge'. We gotta make this shid illegal again, man..."

In Black Scratch, Izumi reported the situation down in the river canyon, and paid a premium for most of the city's reserve troops to come down and fight to protect the vital scientific work going on there. She returned to find that Sandor had gone missing.

"He said he sensed danger," Jaz reported. "Ran off after the bugmen. You're in big trouble now, eh?"

"Fugg. I'll go find them. You're in charge!" Izumi wheezed as she wheeled about.

"Finally, my own corpse farm, I can retire," Jaz said. She, the crabs, and the reinforcement troops held down the decreasingly proverbial fort, and indeed picked up a pretty penny farming coins and weapons from the fallen slavers. But the would-be warlord Nuk had made a few enemies it seems.

"Oi, you this Jaz girl?" one of the mercenaries called around the door of the HQ.

"Too right. What's chomping ya?"

"Got some weirdos outside who say they're from the crab crew or something. Here to ask about your crabbing licence. I dunno. They've got fugg off armour and weapons. Oh, and crabs. Friends of yours?"

"Crab crew, crab crew... No, doesn't bong a gong for me. Can you tell them to wait outside. I'll just get the licences or whatever."

While the guards kept this crab crew company, Jaz gathered up Prince, Crusty and Skut and snuck up the side of the canyon to a hiding place.

"Not gonna let a bunch of crab wranglers put you in horrible cages my darlings," she whispered to the crabs. "Hope our Lord and Lady don't get mad though. Looks like we've all bloody deserted at this point."

Back outside the base, thing were getting a little heated between the crabbers and the heathenous crabless ones.

"I know you're hiding crabs in there you sick perverts," the crabber leader said.

"Sick perverts? You say that to me? You're practically a fishman already!" a guard shot back.

"I have a very loving relationship with my crab. You could never hope to experience such joy!" someone shouted.

"Fugging disgusting. I dunno where Jaz is, but forget it. Shove off, the lot of you."

"Never! Hand over your crabs!"

"Oh I'll give you crabs! Wait... ugh, that sounded better in my head. Boys, kill these crab fuggers. Let's eat like nobles for a week, eh?"

Another historic battle erupted, with mercenary samurai and swordsman scientists fending off crabs and crab enthusiasts alike.

In the hills to the west, back inside the Empire, Izumi found Sandor, who himself had found Gustavsen and Rene, who themselves had been mugged by pirates and left for dead.

"Bloody hell. I told them not to go," Izumi said.

"The hiver had a sense of duty for his compatriot. This is the sort of bond that nobles cannot understand," Sandor commented.

"Don't tell me you want to associate with him now?"

"Hmpf, he would never allow it."

"Yes, well consent is important, isn't it? Come on, we've got a duty of our own."

The humans lugged the unconscious hivers eastwards again. The day passed by without any sign of an end to the battle at the river, with just about everyone getting too injured to carry on fighting, but trying to continue all the same.

"Crabs... are best waifus..." someone muttered.

"Degenerates... must... be purged..." another voice said. Darkness fell with the matter unresolved, but the pro-crab lobby had the upper hand in total legs still in use. Jaz still had their ultimate quarry tucked away on a nearby hill, but you can imagine she was getting a little worried, seeing the base gradually fall and not seeing the strange guild she'd signed up with come back.

So, overall, this whole chocolate thing was going a bit poorly. The guild was now split in four, its money and manpower expended, its brand new headquarters under siege by all manner of foes, and several of its members too wounded to move, or too horrified by what Red Rick had read to them to face up to reality. And it was all that meddling future girl's fault.

Was this the end of the old-school brown town dream? Or would you believe me if I told you that from all this madness, the perfect formula for a coco loco empire would emerge?

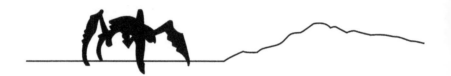

Chapter 14
The Bread Baron

The TCM+ Guild's new semi-legal drug farm had been under constant siege from reavers, pirates, slavers, and worst of all, inter-species homo-crusteo polycules – or the 'crab-fuggers' if you want the common name. How did the base remain standing amidst all this? Well, turns out that reavers, pirates, slavers, and degenerates all hated each other just as much as whoever put that dirty great wall up across the foremost smuggling route in the region.

The survivors from each group grappled with each other through the night after the main battle, and by about three am, Jaz and her abuse-free crab companions swept down from the hills to be the last standing and claim victory. Not just victory – the equipment and supplies of all the invading armies now lay strewn around the riverbed, and corpse-farmer extraordinaire Jaz got to harvesting.

Further upriver on that same night, Izumi and Sandor hauled Gustavsen and Rene into a tucked-away United Cities farming colony. Unable to travel on in the pitch darkness, they hit the bar instead. Gustavsen and Rene were squirming about on the hard beds upstairs, while the humans moped among the surprisingly busy tables in the main room.

"This is... fugging shid," Izumi said once they were settled in.

"This is perfectly ordinary," Sandor said. "This shid happens all the time outside the towns. That's how the cities get all their stuff."

"Yeah... This Empire's a joke."

"True. Listen, do you think the Prince really will be able to change anything?"

"I dunno. He isn't really like the other nobles, that much is true. But what are we meant to change if everything gets fugged up by a bunch of crab boys?"

"If the Empire was suitable for everyone, the crab boys wouldn't be a problem."

"Err, I think crab boys are a problem in pretty much any context. Whatever. I mean, look at it this way: our whole plan revolves around getting the Emperor so baked that we can do whatever. You can escape any problem with enough drugs, they say."

A man at a nearby table span around and leaned closer.

"Drugs you say?" he asked.

"Mind your business," Sandor growled back. The scrawny man stood and moved a little closer.

"Not planning on doing a little, home growing, are ya?"

"Fugg, what you want a bribe to stay quiet? Not in the mood, shidface," Izumi said.

"Okran's grace, you need a good dose of a drugs, that's for sure. Was just gonna say, if you're looking for someone who knows what to grow in these 'ere valleys, you need look no further like. Arnulfo's the name. Grower and show-er, green lady know-er."

"Well thanks. We're not growing green, but... brown. Hard to explain. All a bit fugged up at the moment. Talk to me in the morning," Izumi said.

So that's what two of the guild's four divisions were up to that night. As it happens, the stories of the third and forth managed to converge.

Nuk and his entourage were bringing all manner of junk back from Heft, including the vital chocolate beans in which the future of the entire Empire surely lay. They had just reached Eyesocket, the United Cities market on the edge of pirate territory, where they decided to take a break. To be more specific about the nature of this market, it was a regional centre for slave trading. As such, the town was full of cages, dealerships, and hawkers.

"Get yerr scrubbers," one was calling. "Finest second-hand hands to hand over in a second, discount if they don't have a second hand, buy one hand the second one's half-off. Handy!"

Despite the masterful salesmanship, Nuk was peering at a hiver lying in one of the cages.

"Guys, you recognise that one?" he asked.

"Why are they selling an old bit of wood?" Izayah said.

"I think that old bit of wood might be Gustavsen's friend. Anyone remember his name?"

"Hey, Twiggy Iggy!" Rick called. The dormant log sprang to life.

"Master's associate! Where is the master?" he asked.

"Dunno. You sniff him up the wrong way or something? How'd you get here?"

Ignacio explained the Battle of Manksand Cove, although he only knew the very beginning of it.

"We must hurry back at once! What if Miss Izumi is in danger?" Wodston said.

"Well, they ain't here at the market, so clearly it didn't go all that bad," Nuk reasoned. "But yeah, forget the cocktails and tanning, let's just get outta here. Everyone go wait outside. I'll deal with the situation here."

Getting his meaning, the group went to go make a scene over by the front gate. They hadn't actually intended to make a scene, but Ells had asked Rick if skeletons could have babies, and the debate proved far more contentious than expected.

"Lemmie tell you all about the old zero one zero one," Rick began. Enraptured, the guards didn't notice Nuk opening Ignacio's cage in the middle of the marketplace. The hiver was one leg short of a full compliment, so Nuk shouldered him like the lumberjacks of old and made a run for it. Everyone scarpered post-haste, and buggered off eastwards into the beginnings of the legendary drug canyon.

Going home via this route meant they wandered right past the little farm where Izumi and company were hiding. Izumi flagged Nuk down from the roof of the bar, and rushed outside for the sweet reunion.

"Where the fugg have you been!?" she screamed at him. Well, I suppose it wasn't so sweet.

"Alright. Just been learning up a few things. Did you know that this symbol on the front here means 'perverted'?" Nuk said, brandishing a heavily annotated copy of a priceless ancient classic.

"You... We nearly died! We got royally fugged, Nuk!"

"Heard about the slavers. Look, we got the bugman back!"

"This is serious! It was far more than slavers, We don't know if Jaz is alive, we left her behind. And I thought something had happened to you as well since you didn't come back. Okran's blood... I just..."

"Future girl, I'm sorry," Nuk said, putting a hand on her shoulder. "Man, I'm sorry, okay? I'm gonna sort this out. Bad Green, got your man here." Gustavsen nodded to Ignacio, who nodded back from across Nuk's shoulders. "Gary's got all the goods, and you guys are still alive, so this ain't so bad, right? Although, Sandor looks kinda different..."

Arnulfo was standing behind Izumi.

"Oh your ninja man went on ahead to check out your farm, I understand," he said. "I'm Arnie, Grower, show-er, brown-town goer."

"It's not really what it sounds like," Izumi assured everyone. Arnulfo joined the group on the walk further down the canyon towards the HQ, a walk that increasingly became a wade as the ground got swampier on the approach to the sacred cove. Sandor waved them in once they got close. The walls still stood tall. Some of Nuk's troops were patched up and patrolling the surrounding hills, and the corpses had been mostly harvested and tidied away.

They went inside, where Nuk had a much sweeter reunion with his loyal crabs, and at last the guild was back in action. All in all, after the chaos and fighting, their only loss of had been half of Ignacio's leg, which when compared to what happened to the raiders, was certainly the better way to come out of all that.

"Right, so I'm never leaving you lot in charge of anything ever again," Nuk stated.

"It was your girlfriend in charge, so it's all her fault," Jaz said.

"Yeah she gets a free strike, since she's my personal historian."

"Is that what the kids are calling it nowadays?"

"No, they call it ecchi-sketch."

"What?"

"It's a reference to the classics, don't worry," Izumi assured her old friend. "So Prince, you did bring the chocolate beans?"

"Yeah I got the beans, baby," Nuk said, flipping open Gary's pack, digging through the crusty books and dragging out a huge sack. "Brown town, you're up."

Arnulfo took a look at the beans, gave a few a good, repeated lick, making sure to look each person present in the eye as he did so, and then he finally concluded,

"It's perfect! These'll grow in your mank like crotch rot, and taste twice as good!"

And so, with this professional opinion reeling in the guild's minds, work began on Old Farmer Nuk's ancient ranch. The coincidental yet resounding victory at the Battle of Manksand Cove bought them a good fortnight of peace and quiet, and allowed them to freely bring everything they needed down from Black Scratch.

After a few days, Izumi's co-workers had set up an office for her in the corner of the compound, perfect for the close study of this increasingly famous MANK that the chocolate was growing in. Yes, that is the scientific term for it – it stands for Mushy And Nutritious Krap. This krap was long known to the tech hunters – the First Empire had used certain fertilisers to grow crops on the planet's half-baked land, and there were patches of it still stewing away in the ground today.

Combined with the fact that the chocolate beans had been fiddled with thousands of years back to make them grow practically overnight, the first crops of fresh brown were piled up by Arnie after just a couple of days.

"Growing crops is easy, my man," Nuk commented to Wodston. "What was all that stuff with the Red Rebellion about, then?"

"While I am no expert, my Prince, I believe that not everyone has equal access to the wondrous mank that we do," Wodston said.

"Not to mention the bandits," Izayah added. "I mean, not every farmer has walls and sword-arms like ours when the hungry crabs come calling, you know?"

"Or the government samurai," Sandor added.

"Yeah yeah, I get it. People just need to get energised and farm that shid, like us. Chocolate gives you energy right? Yeah, we'll dose everyone up with brown, and turn this damn planet green with our own hands! Then I really will be the green emperor! I'll inspire the people to have courage in the face of this miserable shidstorm we call life. Get them cocky with the choccy, and we'll be over the moons!"

Leaving everyone to debate Ells' interpretation of getting cocky with choccy, and to fight furiously to prevent a demonstration, Nuk went to Izumi's office. She was slaving away at a desk covered in books in varying degrees of completion.

"M'lady," Nuk said as he entered.

"Not yours," was shot back in reply.

"Eh, let's check the contract on that one. Anyway, people are saying-"

"I don't care what they're saying, we're not an item."

"Errm... So yeah, people are saying they don't know what to do next with the chocolate. Cocky choccy..."

"Oh, right, sorry. I- err- Did I say- Oh, hello Nuk – Prince. Didn't see you..."

"Something on your mind?"

"Not in the slightest. Ahem. Yes, chocolate. The cocky chocc- Wait, what the fugg?"

"Just testing the waters."

"Narko's Laughter... So chocolate, yeah, it's sugar, water, cocoa. We need to get Julian to make a machine. Might have to shop around for the parts."

"Another walk for me is it?"

"No," Izumi said, jumping around to face Nuk.

"Fine, calm down."

"Don't go again Nuk, it was no good. I messed up."

"You didn't mess up. Everyone except you messed up, you know?"

"Kind of you to say that."

"Kind of weird to disagree. This is happening because of you. With your brains, and my brawn, we'll get a whole lotta people addicted to drugs. That's a dream we can believe in. Future... girl?"

Izumi was ruining the mood by tearing up.

"I thought someone was gonna die, because of me. I thought I would die. I don't know how you do it, Nuk."

Nuk, true gentlemen of the Third Empire, awkwardly went in for something resembling a hug.

"It's- I guess I just keep going, since even if we don't make it all the way, that doesn't matter does it? That's not the world we live in, or whatever. What matters is what we're doing, like right now. Making things better, and being... around..."

"I do like it, Nuk. Being together."

Tragically Red Rick wasn't sitting in the corner for a well-timed heckle, so Nuk had to actually think of a response.

"That's convenient, isn't it?" was his eventual effort. It landed better than you'd think, but the stilted nature of the phrase seemed to restore reality. The hug-like pose was quickly disengaged and Nuk marched out.

"Chocolate machine then, thanks future girl!" he called without looking back.

"Glad to be of service Prince Tashino," Izumi almost shouted, before slumping down in her chair and collapsing onto her pile of papers.

A week of hard labours passed, featuring the planting of sugarcane, wheat, and soybeans for Izumi's master plan, and the construction of a large factory building to house the chocolate-making gear. Arnulfo had been given a team of likely lads and lasses from nearby cities to form his workforce, and together they had got manksand cove pumping out produce as fast as Ells could fertilise it.

The sugarcane was stripped and ground into sugar. The soybeans were pressed and pureed into milk, and the cocoa was shredded and compounded with the sugar to make disgusting, acidic lumps of pure chocolate. It was brown alright, but only the crabs could stomach eating it. That was where Izumi's master recipe came in: the wheat was crushed into flour, mixed with the soymilk, and then cooked in a huge outdoor oven, creating a delightfully wobbly yet infuriatingly sticky white mush. (Remember, MUSH, Moderately Unpleasant Slop Hulk, should never be confused with MANK).

The chocolate could be mixed into the mush to make Somewhat Likeable Un-cooked Dough Gunk Extract, which when cooked, created the most wonderful, soft, fluffy, sweet, filling-

"Giant fugging crabs coming in hot from the east!" Red Rick shouted from the wall.

"Slaver raid! Arriving from the west! Close the gate!" Wodston reported from atop the factory roof. Yes, if you think things were getting a little bit too domestic in Nuk's little corner of the world, you're forgetting just how popular this soggy corner was.

The guild's crew rushed to defend the main gateway, and man and/or woman the walls. Since the time of the great battle, the fortifications had been extended and fitted with electric harpoon guns. Gustavsen was an expert with the design and operation of these weapons, and had kindly instructed all of the new farmhands how to use them. Therefore, when a crowd of crabs, traffickers, and crab traffickers, charged the compound gate, a barrage of bolts and spears spat down at them from the walls.

The crabbers weren't too fussed, with both man and beast covered in armour.

"Snippy snippy claw claw, snippy claw, war!" they chanted as they smashed at the gate. Some of the crabs helped bend the bars apart to let their masters inside, but others were distracted by the gang of slavers milling about behind them.

"There's a bloody queue to raid this damned farm!" a slaver complained.

"The slaving infrastructure around 'ere's terrible, they should 'ave a second gate to reduce wait times," another commented. Everyone nodded along in agreement, however they soon encountered a slight problem: the consortium of crabs in front of them had been promised some dirty humans to slip in half, and the slavers certainly looked dirty and human enough. Snippy snippy, claw claw, the poor old slavers were no more.

Still, the delay meant that a lot more sharp misc was cast down before the gateway, and by the time the gate was properly torn open, the crab crew was too injured to make it past Nuk and company waiting on the other side, especially when Prince was joined by the now adult-sized Crusty and Skut, forming an impenetrable wall of crab mightier than any steel gate or array of harpoon cannons.

"I told you fuggs I don't need a crabbing permit!" Nuk called as battle was joined.

"Crabless ones who actually do have crabs – now that's even worse!" a crabber reasoned. Fortunately the guild was now able to slay the invaders without any casualties, and get to work bending the gate back into shape. In one curious incident, Izayah thrust his katana right through a crabber's armour, but when he pulled it back out, the blade was covered in something brown and sticky.

"Okran's might. You should really try emptying yourself out now and again," he said as he winced.

"It's only... chocolate..." were the crabber's last words as he fell. Ells was called up to perform further inspection, and indeed the crabber had stuffed his armour with chocolate, pilfered from an overturned wheelbarrow.

"So, the fishmen fathers like choccy," Nuk said. "That's a good sign. If it turns out no one can stomach the stuff, we'll convert this place to a crab-ranch and lure all those weirdos in to their doom. Take their crabs, and raise them as our own. In a not-weird kinda way."

"Not weird at all," Izumi said. "But don't worry, we'll do just fine with the chocolate bread, I assure you."

Ah yes, the bread. As I was saying, one turns mank into mush, mush into sludge, and sludge into the most joyous and sweet foodstuff to grace the land since sliced sand cakes. It was like bread, but with a more-ish tang and a sugary softness. The greatest invention of all time (except the time it was invented before): the official Nuk Tashino High Quality Mouth-Pro Edible Adventuring Loaf Version 2 – Sweet as the Manksand Canyon Wind on a Summer's Day Edition.

"Or," Nuk said, "for short: brown bread." He held up a yellowish-brown loaf before the assembled guild.

"I think that name might be taken," Wodston said, but his voice must have been carried away on the Manksand Canyon Wind, for it went unheard.

"Thanks to the hard work of Brown Town and his horrible team of dregs, we have manufactured one hundred lumps of the new wonder-drug. But the proof is made of pudding, or something, and that is why it's time to test the markets. All non-disgusting guild members, and Charlie, will be coming with me on a little sales tour. Rest of you dirty mank-scratching types, you keep mining for chocolate or whatever, and get this bread. While I'm gone, the crabs are in charge. Got it?"

The confused grumbling was taken as a yes. With this, the guild was back on track for adventure, with Gary loaded up with the new wonder-drug. Would brown bread take the world by storm? Well, perhaps that is the wrong question – if we are to take Nuk's view of things, it didn't matter, did it? A nice trip to deal an as-yet-unbanned drug was good enough to enjoy no matter the result, especially with his good friends and associates to share it with.

Back on the road, with 'start a chocolate factory' ticked off his bucket list, Nuk began a new brown bread adventure. Oh look at that, they're being mauled by a Beak Thing. Yep, that's pretty much how this adventure's going to go, isn't it?

Chapter 15
Sales For Scales

"It's your lucky day," Nuk told the shopkeeper. Said shopkeeper peered out from underneath a garru, his face covered in... well let's just ignore what it was covered in.

"You wanna buy a leaky garru?" the shopkeep asked.

"Even better, I wanna give your face a whole new kinda brown," Nuk said, whipping out a somewhat crushed chocobread loaf and boinging it down onto the counter.

"Oh, a sponge! Nice one mate."

"No, no, you have to eat it!"

"Mind if I use a little... dip?"

"Yes, yes I fugging mind, come here you dreg."

Nuk grabbed the shopkeep and started forcing the brown bread into his mouth.

"It's delicious, huh? You like that! You can fit it all in! Come on!"

Izumi peered around the door just to check, but quickly disappeared again.

"Mmm, this sponge is alright," the shopkeep spluttered.

"Swallow!" Nuk demanded. Izumi almost doubled back. Once the poor shopkeeper had complied, Nuk snapped his fingers. "Now, my man!"

At this, Wodston shuffled into the shop with a lit candle, and got as close to the shopkeep's face as the local aroma would allow.

"I see..." the doctor said.

"See what? Is it working?" Nuk asked.

"I fear not, my Prince. No signs of increased bodily activity. The mechanisms of addiction have not engaged."

"Fugg, eat another one you impenetrable lout!"

"I like when he shouts at me," the shopkeep grinned, grabbing another loaf and chomping away. A guard slid over from the other side of the farm shop.

"Master, couldn't help but notice these freaks are force feeding you sponges. Everything under control?"

"It's the best thing I've had shoved in my mouth all day mate! You ever tried working under the garrus?" the shopkeep said with a crummy grin. He wolfed a few more handfuls of brown bread, but Wodston was not able to report any signs of physiological or psychological dependency. Nuk stormed out and pointed at Izumi.

"I stuffed it down his throat, but it didn't turn him!" he complained.

"Perhaps we could use more scientific language?" Izumi suggested.

"Data concludes: you suck."

"Now that's ambiguous given the context."

"Damn biologicals, obsessed with sticking shid in one end or the other," Rick said. "Can we just get outta here? These Tech Hunters gon' hunt my rare ass for scrap any second."

"Still pretty ambiguous there Rickard," Izayah noted, but indeed they did get outta there. Test subject one in Black Scratch had not reacted to being choked half to death with brown bread quite as Nuk had hoped. No, I don't know what specifically he was hoping for.

When they left town, Gustavsen sent Ignacio back down to watch over the base, on account of the hiver's new wooden leg not faring all that well on the road.

"Keep your nose open. When I find a suitable replacement for your leg, you will detect it," Gustavsen said. Ignacio seemed to know what he was talking about, and plodded off back to the chocolate factory.

The gang made it to Brink, where they all gathered around to watch a local farmer steadily chew on a loaf, their eyes transfixed on the slowing rise and fall of his bristly jaw, until finally the mouth opened, and produced the words: "It's alright I guess."

"No!" Nuk shouted, head in his hands. Yes, as you might be able to tell brown didn't have the same effect on people as green – it was more comparable to an orange, I'd say. In his frustration, Nuk went and robbed the local police station. I mean, isn't that the best way to relax? Not in this case as he was spotted, and the group had to skip town at a sprint to escape the local samurai.

They raced west into the desert night, losing their pursuers, but falling into a pirate ambush instead. Out of the frying pan and into a mug of slightly above-room-temperature tea. And by that I mean the pirates were dispatched quickly, their bodies cleaned of all treasures, but for a single calling card – a malformed blob of mucky, brown-speckled starch. A free sample. Gotta pull out all the stops when you're bringing a new product to market.

After crossing the windy deserts around The Eye, the crew hit their next stop in the quest to give the world a taste for brown bread. It was a small caravan outpost in the Grey desert, flanking the road that ran alongside the high ridge between the Deadlands and the less dead lands.

"Prince Tashino, allow me to try this time," Izayah said just outside the gate.

"Be my guest. Remember to tell them it's full of Nuktrients!" Nuk told him, handing over a bundle.

"You said that wasn't allowed," Ells complained, but best ignore where that rabbit hole leads.

Inside the wall of the compound, Izayah entered the caravaner's bar with a confident stride, stepping cleanly over the corpse in the doorway.

"Friends! Countrymen!" he announced. "It is time for much merriment and pleasure, for the delights of brown town descend upon us!"

People were listening, but not necessarily in a good way.

"I have here in my blessed hands, lumps of Okran's love, dollops of Narko's cunning, the most wonderful masticatory experience you'll have all day, all year! Behold!"

Everyone beheld the clutch of knobbly brown, and then returned to beholding the fine details of the inside of their eyelids. Izayah threw the produce down on the bar.

"So, are you ready to buy?" he asked the barman. The barman, a dark-skinned shek who looked like he'd had far more offensive things slapped down on his bar, clawed off a scrap of bread and raised it into his mouth, his eyes locked on Izayah's the whole time. Those eyes suddenly widened, and then seemed to grow dewy.

"It's..." he said, but there was no time for words. He eagerly swept the rest of the brown mound into his gaping maw, and consumed it noisily. Then he looked Izayah square in the eye again.

"Paleskin. Where did you find such a blessing?"

"Well," Izayah said, puffing out his chest and turning to address the room. "Only from the Tashino Credit Management & Nonconsenual Private Healthcare Guilds, In Association with the Tashino Crustacean Corps Private Security Consortium, and The Future Girl Industries Semi-professional Association of Archaeological Grudge Settlers and Ancient Quasi-amateur Baking Enthusiasts."

"Hmpf, so this must be the TCMNPHGINTCCPSCFGISPAAGSAQABE I've heard so much about," the barman nodded. He happily paid for his pudding, and Izayah reported the good news to the gang outside.

"I gave it a taste myself, it's actually incredibly delicious," he said.

"What? Let me try," Izumi said.

"Wait, you didn't even try it?" Nuk said.

"No. I'm not stupid. This stuff could kill you for all I know."

"Cool. That's quasi-amateur baking for you."

"But actually... I dunno... It's okay..."

"Could it be that there is a difference in the reaction of each species?" Wodston suggested.

"Could be," Izumi said. "I mean Izayah likes, it, disgusting fat man really, really likes it, but all the humans don't really care. Prince Gustavsen, will you try some?"

Gustavsen shook his head.

"It is the wrong colour. I refuse to digest it," he said. Izumi offered Bobbie and Claw a sample, and they both drew a thumbs up and a smiley face on their little chalkboards.

"It seems we have our answer! It's a shek thing!" Izayah laughed.

"Then we've got some money to make in your part of the world, big man," Nuk said.

"Ah yes, my part. Well, I had rather hoped to stay away from there, actually."

"What? Why?"

"I, err-"

"He need not explain," Wodston insisted.

"Fine," Nuk said, "but we gotta go check it out anyway. I mean, this whole brown thing's on the verge of being a bust. If we can at least get *someone* addicted, I'll let you all off the hook."

A plan was drawn up for a marketing research march west towards the mighty Shek Kingdom. They had to skirt the southern edge of the Deadlands, walking on the narrow ridge between the black-fog to their right and the burning, white sanded, space-laser-baked desert to their left. Soon night fell and it was black in all directions, but the light of a nomad caravan led them to the main westward road.

Nuk went over to have a word with this caravan, and make a certain purchase from them. When he returned he had his hands hidden behind his back.

"Good news guys," he said. "We're going the right way, roughly, according to those guys. And, much more importantly, I thought of a way to sell more choccies to the stockies." From behind him he revealed a brown bonedog puppy. "This is Choco, our official product mascot!"

"By Narko's Justice, that's incredible!" Izayah exclaimed, rushing forwards to take Choco in his arms.

"Thought you might like her. You see if there's anything a tough old shek likes, it's cute dogs and a nice bit of chocolate," Nuk said. "Obviously Charlie isn't allowed either, but the rest of your people should pay handsomely for it."

"Wow, Nuk, you kinda did something clever there," Izumi commented.

"Oh so when I buy a crab you complain, but a dog's fine?"

"Yes, that's exactly it. Wait, you didn't understand that?!"

Gustavsen leant in to get a close sniff at Choco.

"I'm not sure if I should associate," he said. Choco licked at his face. "Oh. It has associated with me..."

Anyway, with a new mascot riding on Izayah's shoulder, they pressed on westwards through the night. It was an exhausting journey, especially the part where they were attacked by Beak Things, and subsequently had to carry the unconscious hivers along with them.

The area south-west of the Deadlands was very far from civilisation, with the United Cities Empire far to the east, the Holy Nation far to the north, and the Shek Kingdom not quite so far to the west. Yet still, somehow, in the middle of a wasteland plain there was a lonely bar the crew could stumble into around dawn.

Only problem was that a mob of hungry wastelanders had been waiting for just such a travelling party to arrive. Brandishing cleavers and broadswords, they approached Nuk and issued their ultimatum.

"Give us your food, or we'll eat your flesh!"

"Much more polite than those other cannibals," Izayah noted.

"So you guys are hungry huh?" Nuk said. He opened Gary's pack and pulled out the product. "How about you chow down on some of this. Best food in the world, and you first hit's free, tell your friends!"

In this fashion the brown market was expanded, and the cleavers cleaved nothing but pillowy loaves of teeth-rotting bread. Inside the bar they made a few more sales on the good word of mouth marketing, more than enough to cover beds for the night – or day, as it was. They had particular interest from an old farmer named Lon, who Nuk hired to go work the chocolate fields and ramp up production for the potential shek connection.

While the crew rest up before the next leg of their journey, let's spare a thought for poor old Lon, shall we? Armed only with a blunt sword and a pair of cargo shorts, he was asked to travel all the way back to Nuk's farm alone. It was a near impossible journey, yet a hungry wastelander like him had nothing to lose.

He set off east, planning to make the risky desert crossing beneath the space laser, for it was indeed the fastest route to Manksand canyon. It was dawn, so there was no hope of the laser deactivating anytime soon, however that wasn't the main danger in the region, it turned out. The laser's turf, the region known as Venge, was strewn with ruins and wreckage from ancient wars, killed by the eye in the sky. Or, nearly killed.

Behind Lon, a trio of headless skeletons crawled out from the rubble and started thumping towards him. Lon legged it, but these skeletons had been charging their batteries for a while. They caught up to him and struck at him with long metal poles, each hit spurring Lon to push ever harder to escape. They passed ruins both ancient and modern, across open plains dotted with cacti and through narrow valleys watched over by semi-dormant iron spiders from the Second Empire.

Eventually the inevitable happened. A laser beam shot down and scorched the earth right where Lon was running. It burned his skin, and he just barely stumbled from the light before it was too late. He looked back, hoping the skeletons had been hit as well. They had, but these headless hunters seemed completely undaunted. Cursing the weakness of Okran and Narko alike, Lon's aching legs drove him onwards.

He found himself running along the barely extant remains of an ancient road. It curved up a steep ridge, but unfortunately the skeletons had no trouble ascending it. Then there was sound from behind a large boulder. Lon prayed for a bandit attack, for at least it would get the attention off him. Nope. It was a dozen more headless bots charging out to join the chase! Was anyone so unlucky as Lon?! Time would tell. He kept running, oh how he kept running, for a good hour more at least.

The skeletons were right on his tail, the tips of their metal prodders touching his back, their absent heads giving no room (or RAM) for negotiation. Now missing though was the humming glow of the space laser – they had left Venge, and entered the United Cities Empire. Incredibly, this random patch of distant forgotten border was being patrolled by the samurai at that very moment.

Lon screamed out for help, but the samurai just waved for Lon to lead the skeletons over to them. It was too hot to move about in heavy armour, especially in the early afternoon sun. Once the two groups converged, the samurai did acquiesce to raise their weapons and try to stop the skeletons. They got a fair few of them. Lon didn't stop for a second, sprinting on past the border, and looking back to see that most of the skeletons had been embroiled in battle with the samurai. But not all. Five were still right on him. Ah how he yearned for the time when it was only three, but he could be glad the time of twenty had passed. It's all relative, especially when you're running for your life.

Lon's upturn in luck did continue. He was attacked by a few pirates, who found themselves beset by the skeletons instead, allowing Lon to escape. Now only one of the skeletons was still on his tail. This was practically paradise! That one rampaging robot followed him all the way to Brink up on the mesa to his east, where at least he could use the string of cats Nuk had given him to grab some food, bandages, and rest. Well done Lon, looks like you had quite the job interview there, but hey, you passed!

While Lon was resting in the Brink inn that evening, Nuk and company were emerging from the lonely wasteland bar, with a few armoured troops hired from within to bulk them up for their next stretch on the road. They used the last of the evening light to march west into the region known as Shem. Shem was a most incredible part of the world, all things considered. No space lasers. No acid rain. No slave camps, no bandit forts, not a skimmer in sight. A large lowland desert stretched out from the rocky heights the crew approached from, dotted with oases, a few plants, and herds of lumbering, peaceful herbivores.

"This is shid!" Nuk proclaimed. "No customers!"

"Man, this place really is the shid. Nostalgic. Once y'all are dead, might come back here," Rick said.

"Please don't say such mean things," Wodston said.

"What? Planning on living forever? I am. All the fishman juice in the world won't keep you going that long. Sucks, you gotta spend every day finding stuff to eat just to survive another day, and don't matter how many days in a row you do it, you still just die. Biologicals got it bad. Guess we were hard on you, back in the day huh?"

"What are you talking about Rick?" Izumi asked, but Rick just shook his head.

"Ain't nothing, nothing at all. Come on, I detected signs of life out on the plains. Might be hungry for your weird dry sludge fuel."

There was a camp for herders out amongst the oases, and while they were willing to buy the odd bit of choccy, they didn't have anywhere for Nuk's small army to sleep. They were pointed south to an old rest-stop on the side of a hill.

"You will all soon know peace," Gustavsen was saying to the herder's goats. "The goat king will return, and you will have purpose. I promise." In the flickering torchlight, it almost seemed like the goats nodded in response.

The crew moved south, and spotted the campfires the herders had mentioned. They were lit, which was bad news, and indeed upon closer inspection the hillside was occupied by a gang of bandits, resting beneath the mouldy green trunks of ancient trees. They must have seen Nuk and guild approaching, but they didn't react. In the end, Nuk walked right up to their leader without any harassment at all. In Shem even the bandits kept to sociable working hours it seemed.

"Sorry man, but I was wondering if we could have a go on the beds?" Nuk asked.

"Nope. Rest time," the leader said, not turning around.

"What if I said that I'll take you to brown town if you agree?" Nuk offered.

"I'm not falling for that one again!" the leader said, suddenly standing and directing his men to attack. Whatever the story was there, it would be lost to history. The guild troops slew the bandits and claimed themselves some accommodation for the night.

They were at least halfway to the shek kingdom, but also they'd managed to offload about half of their chocostock already, through sales bribes, free samples, forced samples, and recreational use. Just as well, as Izayah was obviously quite peeved about the idea of going to his homeland for reasons he had agreed to not tell anyone. Ah if only he knew what was waiting for him there, he would have rushed off to go there that very night!

Chapter 16
New Kid on the Choc

As the morning light washed across the sleepy Shem hillside, Nuk and company realised that their campsite was especially luxurious. Not only was it just a few minutes walk from a goat shop, not only did the bandits respect the no-noise after 10pm rules, but atop the slope there were huge, green-leafed trees.

"No way – how is this possible?" Izumi said, jumping up from her camp bed. She prodded at Izayah, who squirmed about.

"Raining cats and dogs? Ah wonderful..." he muttered. After some further invigoration, he added, "I had heard of this place. The great swamp on the edge of the Old Lands. The trees grow tall and old, unlike anyone who treads there. That's why you don't hear much about the place, of course. Perhaps Rickard's good stuff sensor will pick something up about it."

Rick was, unusually, lying on the ground, his head pointed over at the treeline above them.

"Stobe's legacy. Take it in," he said, but that was all he wished to divulge.

"Well, let's take a peek shall we?" Nuk said, rushing up the hillside. At the top he saw a sprawling forest covering the hills as far as he could see, with a thick, leafy canopy, brooks and pools of glistening water, and beds of vibrant mosses and fungi. The gang joined him, standing with mouths agape. It was life. Life, all over the place!

"Could this be... Earth?" Nuk muttered.

"Earth's literally right there," Izumi insisted, pointing at Okran in the sky.

"If it'd been further away, maybe this wouldn't be all that's left," Rick said. The ground was soggy, and the skeleton's weight was gradually pressing him down into it. Water pooled about his feet. "Man. It's so delicate. No place for us, they said. Kinda see why. You know what guys, I wanna tell y'all something."

He didn't tell them anything. Why? Because the quiet moment was derailed by Nuk shrieking. You see his feet too had been sinking into the wet ground as he stood, and when the groundwater had pooled over his open-topped sandals, the searing, familiar burn of the Deadlands launched him into the air.

"Fugging acid again! Shid!" he shouted, jumping to stand on some tree roots. But when he grabbed the trunk to stay upright, he was sent reeling back. "How does that burn as well?!" he complained, rushing back to the sandy campsite.

"Oh yeah. Sorry about that, biologicals. Had to add a little repellent to keep this place intact. Funny what you forget over the years, huh?" Rick said, following the group back out of the majestic forest.

So that's why the crew had to take a much more dull route to the Shek Kingdom, heading around the great swamp through the dramatic yet unnamed region of the world that sat roughly in the centre of three great powers. The deep canyons and towering mesas made up what was only known as the Border Zone. Nestled in the landscape were crumbling ruins of military bases and sparse colonies, property of the Holy Nation, as Izayah explained.

"It's a mess. Holy Nation zealots decided to move on in a few decades back. Came and destroyed our outposts and set up their little villages. Hmpf, but there they were, so confident that mere shek could never threaten them that they didn't even put up walls. My mother came out here in her younger days with the Hundred Guardians – real fighters – and killed them all. By the stories you hear from the invasion, death was too good for them. But that's how it stands.

As for my own insight, I can only tell you that these valleys now, while part of the Shek Kingdom in theory, belong to none but the scavengers. I spent two years keeping the caravans out of their grasp. But then Holy Nation patrols started coming down as well, and you know what they think about shek, so that was the end of my little mercenary career."

"Seems to me you still doing it," Rick commented.

"Oh yes, I suppose. But the Prince is rather a higher class of customer!" Izayah said. This drew attention to the fact Nuk was wiping sweat from his brow with his hands, then slurping at his palm.

"It's still got rum in it," he said when the attention became rather palpable. "Charlie taught me this little secret. Master of his craft."

"Waste not, want not!" Ells chimed.

"And if it's not waste, you don't want it," Izumi added.

The journey through the borderlands was punctuated with a few failed heists by the canyon highwaymen. In some cases the failure was so radical that the bandits got heisted and hoisted, booted and boosted, sniped and swiped – that is to say, they were dragged off behind the large guild entourage as bounties. After two days of the old uppy-downy, to use the exciting hiking terminology, they reached what remained of the sea that all those canyons once drained into.

"There it is," Izayah said, pointing ahead. There was a mountain with a huge split down the middle, forming a pass right through it. "That's the gateway to the Kingdom."

"Finally, let's get in there and get 'em choc-locked," Nuk said. Izayah sighed and followed him onwards. Approaching the gateway brought them down into the lowlands of the Stenn Basin, where huge spiky orbs sat happily on dusty bluffs.

"Are those... giant, fugging sea urchins?" Izumi asked.

"Sand urchins. But yes, giant and fugging too." Izayah said.

"It must all have been underwater." Izumi looked to Rick as she spoke.

"Look, I'm tired of these accusations that it's somehow my fault the seawater got vapourised," the skeleton said.

"I didn't really... err... Rick, did you-"

"This ain't no trial, sister. I do not recall. I do NOT recall. Case closed. Now let's go lie down, shoot up, or whatever you flesh-mesh freaks wanna do in there."

The 'in there' he was referring to was Squinn, the great border fortress of the Shek Kingdom, nestled in the mountain gateway. As they approached the gate, Izayah finally ground to a halt.

"My apologies, but I think I will wait for you outside," he said. Bobbie and Claw immediately broke off too and joined him.

"Is this your paleness thing? Are you embarrassed? Come on man, who cares what they think? Let's make this fugging town remember your name!" Nuk said, but the encouragement didn't land.

"It is more important than you think. I would rather not discuss it. I'm sure me staying here won't cause any trouble, will it?"

"Guess not. Still, just seems wrong."

"Welcome to life, my Prince. Take all the time you need."

With this, Izayah ran off with Choco into the crags flanking the mountain, his guards close behind.

"What is all that anyway? Charlie?" Nuk asked. Ells shrugged.

"He's the wrong colour. Wrong colour means you're ill."

Gustavsen nodded in agreement. With no real answer, Nuk and company were subject to a drugs search at the gates, but what could the guards say about the brownish mush buried in Gary's bags?

"You haven't even heard of NTHQMPEALV2SATMCWOTSDE?!" Nuk scoffed.

"Oh, brown bread," the guard nodded, unamused but unsuspicious also. At least the marketing must have been working. In they went, with the first port of call being the police station to offload the dregs of the borderzone for a cash reward, then it was straight to the bar with cash in hand.

Nuk was waiting in the lunchtime queue, drawing plenty of sceptical looks for being the only human there, not to mention being dressed like a ninja (as he usually was these days), when he saw something shining in the corner of the room. Sitting alone by the rum barrels was another albino shek.

"I knew it was allowed!" Nuk said, abandoning his position four prime queue real estate and sliding his way through the forest of towering patrons towards the pale shek woman. "Hey, you're albino!" was his charming opening line.

"And you're a flatskin, fugg off," she replied.

"That's what I'm talking about!" Nuk cheered, sitting down next to her.

"You're not fugging off. Are you slow in the head, flatskin?"

"I'm rich, if that's what you mean."

"Huh, yep, that's what I meant. Rich enough for charity is it?"

"Well yeah, I'm basically collecting weird sheks, and I've already got one albino. How much do you cost then?"

"Collection, right. You should know, I'm only a kid, fuggface."

"You don't talk like one. Or look like one. Wait a minute, am I being bamboozled here?"

"Nope. Just richness again," the shek said. You might think that there really was a live bamboozling occurring, but despite being taller than Nuk and infinitely more cynical, she had scarcely cleared double digits in age.

"Look, my friend is really sad about the fact he's... you know... a freak. Like you. So I wanted to pay you some money to go tell him he's a fuggface and shid, and get him realising you can still be a regular old barfly scumbag and enjoy life, even if you're also the laughing stock of the town."

"I don't need this shid, flatskin worm. I'm an engineer, not a doctor."

"Ah yeah, my err... friend who is a girl, does stuff like that."

"You do not have any friends, flatskin."

"I bet you two stacks I can talk to a girl right now."

"Give me the money now, and if you win, I'll give it back, how about that?"

"That seems convenient. Unless, wait..."

"Don't try to work it out, moron. Come, let me laugh at your dull loneliness before someone takes my spot."

Nuk directed the shek out into the street, where Izumi was muttering something to Gustavsen.

"I knew I had associated well. So be it, fleshy one. Your secrets amuse me highly. Oh, a shek child," he said. Izumi turned around and looked down to see the stocky legs of this so-called child.

"Greetings flatskin girl, I am Elaina," she said from a good two or three heads above Izumi. "I am told you are friends with that human in the doorway." Nuk waved from outside the bar.

"What did he do? Did he steal something? I'm sorry, here, how much do we owe you?" Izumi asked with rehearsed ease.

"Two stacks."

"Rick, do you have your bucket?"

"Yes I have MY bucket," Rick said, emerging from behind Gary. Elaina gasped.

"That's an amazing skeleton!" she said, immediately laying her big hands on his shoulders.

"Damn, I still got it. Can you fugg off a moment missy?"

"But these parts are so rare. Where were you manufactured? And, the red faceplate..."

"It's a real expensive story. Izumi, is this one of your bookworms?"

"Sorry, no, I think Nuk did something..." Izumi said.

"So you really do know that awful man?" Elaina asked.

"Yeah, we're like, friends."

"Oh lemmie tell you what they are," Rick started, but Elaina broke out in a booming laugh.

"Ha, so he wasn't lying! The little rascal! But he said he knew another paleskin?" she said.

"That's Izayah, he's outside. Guess you both have the same condition?" Izumi replied.

"I dunno. He said you're into engineering, is that true?"

"Yeah, it's my job."

"Cool."

"Yeah, it is cool. Finally someone who agrees!"

"I do it too. You with the Tech Hunters?"

"Of course."

"No way! You must be famous!"

"Well... I am a published author in my field, but who isn't these days?"

"Big sister! You gotta hook me up!"

"Big? I dunno about that."

"Look, I'll talk to your paleskin friend, whatever you need. Let's do something," Elaina said, waving Nuk over with a smile. Nuk sent her out to Izayah's hiding place among the cliffs.

"Well, she's... tall," Izumi said.

"Welcome to the Shek Kingdom, stumpy. She's gonna knock some sense into Izayah about this whole skin colour thing," Nuk said.

Izayah was knocked head over heels alright.

"You're albino!" he shouted as Elaina approached his hiding spot, Choco barking all the while.

"Is that a customary greeting or something? You're albino too though. Never seen another one," Elaina said.

"Nor I. Incredible."

"Your friend in there says you need to stop worrying about it and just go in. And yeah, he's right. I never let it hold me back."

"Ha, oh I wouldn't say it holds me back. Merely prompts me to go in a different direction."

"And what direction is that?"

"Adventure! Why don't we go for a stroll and I'll regale you with a tale? Ah, it's okay Choco, calm down, she's a friend."

That evening Nuk exited Squinn with some good news.

"Izayah! We sold it all! Shek really do go gorillo-shid for this stuff, we're gonna be fugging rich. Oh, you're still here?"

Elaina gave a respectful bow.

"I didn't know, Prince Tashino. I'm sorry I was rude."

"Izayah, you've tamed her. But we're off, so best let her back into the wild, you know?"

"Nonsense! She wants to come on an adventure!" Izayah nodded.

"Yes, if that's okay with you, Prince?" Elaina said.

"I guess. Might not be an adventure, but I wanted you to take us over to Admag. We're gonna work out what it will take to clean these towns out, then we'll be set for life."

Ah there was a time when Nuk would have been talking about stealing everything. Creating and exploiting drug addiction – now that's the more virtuous path. There are many kinds of hero.

"Oh that's right, I can probably get your machines working better on your farm," Elaina said. "No offence to Little Sister, but I can probably make this chocolate stuff in my sleep."

"Yeah, Charlie here thought he could do that too, but turns out it was... something else. So, why don't you two palescales lead the way?"

"Of course!" Izayah cheered. "To Admag then. What a time. It feels good to finally have a shek my own age about, I must say."

"You're the same age?" Izumi asked. "Prince Gustavsen said she was a child for some reason."

"Ha, well she's still older than me!"

"Wait, how old are you?"

"Eleven and three quarters."

"What the fugg?!" Izumi exclaimed. I think some of the others did so as well. Yes, shek, while technically human deep down inside, had all kinds of rough spots, genetically and dermatologically. As such they rapidly grew into their adult forms, then actually got smaller in the so-called 'turbulent twenties' of adolescence, before encrusting for a good two hundred years of adulthood, after which they either got really big or really small for the last stretch, like the stars themselves.

"So Chomping Charlie there's an old man, and the Power Tower here's a damned trumped-up larva? I've said it before and I'll say it again: biologicals got it bad," Rick commented. He was probably right.

Aside from the chronological confusion, the night-march to Admag went peacefully. The Kingdom's borders were well guarded – not a bandit in sight. However, some of the Kingdom's own citizens proved just as troublesome. In the morning, with the mountain-top city of Admag now in sight, the crew passed a patrolling group of soldiers on the main road.

"Paleskins, and flatskins! Ha! What a pitiful sight," the leader called out. Seeing Izayah keeping his eyes to the ground, Elaina spoke up.

"Oh fugg off. Never seen a human before? Get over yourselves. And if you can't take pale fugging skin, you're gonna get real scared when it's your time to face the Skin Spiders, fugger."

"Flatskins don't belong here. Neither do bugmen, Old Ones or fugging collaborators."

"Gentlemen, please, perhaps I could interest you in a trip to brown town?" Nuk offered. They didn't want to go, which was a shame, because they really would have liked it. Instead the patrol members went into a mad rage and attacked the horrible humans, but alas they were outnumbered, and indeed these humans weren't the puny dregs of imagination.

"Kral's Chosen," Elaina commented once the attackers were slain. "Trouble for everyone who isn't them."

"So we need to get Kral to choose us too?" Nuk asked.

"Not going to happen, Prince," Izayah said. "Long since dead, and famously so. You'll get an earful about it in the city I expect."

The city was a short walk away, however once again Izayah jammed his sword in the ground outside and made himself comfortable.

"Come on man, I thought- Big Kid, say something to him," Nuk pleaded.

"Stick with me. We won't let anyone give us any shid, it'll be fine," Elaina said, but Izayah shook his head.

"I assure you friends that this is nothing to do with it. It's a personal matter, one that is now very close by."

"A bounty? What are you talking about?" Nuk asked. Everyone else was looking around awkwardly.

"We agreed to let him have his own business, didn't we, my Prince?" Wodston said.

"Yeah but he's making it my business. I need my man and mascot up front to probe out the chocoholic potential accurately. That's just science, man. So what's the problem here?"

"I'll say this," Izayah conceded. "Up there is the residence of The Stone Golem, Queen of all shek. She and I have a sour history, so I cannot return. So, I will stay here until you have learned what you need to. No harm done, is there?"

"We're gonna find out," Nuk said, setting off up the steep hill to the city gate. Elaina stayed with Izayah for another chat, while everyone else took in the sights of Admag. There wasn't that much to see. While it was the capital of the Shek Kingdom, it was more of a castle than a city, dotted with high towers, surrounded by cliffs and thick sandstone walls, and filled with glaring soldiers.

Nuk sent the crew off to the few shops to get the lay of the land, while he marched right up to the large barrack building covered in Shek Kingdom banners.

"I'm here to meet the Queen!" he declared at the doors. The guard smiled and let him through.

"Bagsises on his sword, alright?" he muttered to his comrade. Similar things were whispered as Nuk strode past the elite of the shek military, who were happy to direct him up to the roof.

Up there, standing in the baking sun like a statue, was a huge, grey shek in full chainmail, wielding a poleaxe the size of poor Nuk, onto whom her steely glare swung.

"Are you... Err, Queen? That's like Empresses I presume? I'm here about, err..." Nuk petered out as the Queen's mouth began to grimace, revealing sharp filed teeth and a low growl. "Damn, this ain't the bogs, wrong way, sorry madame," he said, scurrying back down stairs. At the bottom he ran right into another shek, standing with hands on hips.

"Flatskin. You will explain yourself to me now," the shek said. This was Bayan, Mouth of the Queen, and a much more pleasant mouth fortunately. He took Nuk aside from the snickering soldiers, and informed him how the Queen spoke only to so-called 'Allies of the shek'.

"It's a real easy favour," Nuk explained. "I just need her to clear something up with a friend. I dunno the details, but... It's gonna be great for business. You heard of brown bread?"

"That is your doing is it?" Bayan sneered.

"Yeah, gonna stick it to the big boys back in the Empire by getting rich and spreading the love, you know?"

"Oh good, good. I knew there were people in the Empire who weren't as disgusting as their nobility."

"Yeah, I hate those guys."

"But the rule stands. Whatever business your guild has with the Queen, it is not her concern. Nor mine, and I am quite busy, so if you don't mind-"

"Wait, there's gotta be something you want. Free chocolate? Oh, the filth, you'll like this, I've got these fan-translated books with some serious pictures, you know?"

"For a freak like you, the Queen would accept nothing less than the death of the Bugmaster."

"Fine, I'll kill him," Nuk said, but at this the whole barracks broke out in deafening laughter that shook dust from the walls and even spilled a few drinks.

"If you say so. Good luck, flatskin!" Bayan said, departing from his seat while still contorting all over the place in amusement. Nuk was not one to take this humiliation sitting down. He stood, but alas the humiliation continued, and so he ran from the building, swearing a vow to kill whatever this Bugmaster was. Well, we all make mistakes don't we?

Chapter 17
Return of the Prince

"Alright, who wants to come with me and kill the Bugmuncher?" Nuk called out to the bar. A chorus of grimaces and growls filled the air. "Come on guys, all the brown you can down!" Nuk added, but he'd lost the crowd. He was about to leave, when a frail looking shek at the back of the room stood.

"I suppose it's my time. Been waiting too long. I'll die with you, flatskin," he said. He began walking towards Nuk, and right away the whole bar went silent, stood, turned to face the speaker, and bowed their heads.

"In the image of Kral he walks. With the honour of Kral, he shall die," the barman recited loudly. The customers all echoed his words.

"You really don't cheer your own folk on very well," Nuk noted. Outside, the old shek, calling himself Wyatt, leant on his battered katana in the street.

"We leave at once, I presume?" he asked.

"Yep, at once. Remind me where we're going again?" Nuk nodded.

"To where Kral stood at his glorious end. To the twisted land of death."

"Oh, of course. I was just thinking I'd like to visit there. Great vistas. Come on, let's meet go meet the lovely folk you'll be dying with."

Nuk rounded up the group and marched down the hill to look for Izayah. The echoing barks of Choco made it easy. When they reunited, Wyatt seemed taken aback.

"Two paleskins? What manner of company is twice cursed by Narko so?" he said.

"Guys, this happy chappy is... what was it? Sadscales, or whatever. He's going to help us kill the Bugmeister. You see, I spoke to Queen Rocks or whatever-"

"Did you say kill the Bugmaster?!" Elaina interjected.

"Did you say you spoke to m- the Queen?!" Izayah added.

"Sort of, and sort of. Queen Cranky won't listen to anything we have to say without a favour. This big insect is a problem or something, so we take 'em out, and then we can get Izayah's unspeakable crimes against the sanctity of corpses pardoned, and make a cross-continental choc deal to get unlimited money. Any questions?"

"The Bugmaster has killed thousands already. And it's a Greenlander, not an insect," Elaina explained (Greenlander being a term for human). "It is a great honour to be slain at his gates, but it's not my time."

"If you will not face death with courage, then stay, wither and die. Soil your legacy with your final selfish breath, and know that your life was wasted until the bitter, lonely end," Wyatt said.

"You see, this is why I don't... err... associate, with normal shek," Nuk said. "Look, Sadscales, we're gonna go there right now and sort this out, okay? We've killed like a bajillion people and walked here from the other side of the damn world. We're gonna scope this Bugmister, eat a loaf of a bread with two hundred grams of sugar per square inch, and go beast mode on that loser. I'll be the Beastmaster! Fugg, that's some cool shid."

Elaina directed the group south towards the so-called 'twisted land of death', where their quarry awaited. They wandered through wide, urchin-infested canyons, and up and down the large fortified mesas separating the provinces of the Shek Kingdom. As they walked into the night, Izayah took Nuk aside.

"Prince Tashino, please tell me: what did The Stone Golem say to you? Actually, more importantly, what did you say to her?"

"Well, I mean it was a pretty cool convo," Nuk said. "We laughed, talked about Yasuke and Rock-chan, you know, just chilled? But I mentioned I wanted a favour, and she went, like... stone cold. Guess that happens a lot."

"Indeed. You didn't mention me, did you?"

"No, course not. So whose corpse was it then?"

"I beg your pardon?"

"You know. What did you do to get exiled or whatever? I was a spliff dealer, you were a stiff feeler, right?"

"I'm not sure you understand. The thing is, I can't tell you," Izayah said, glancing over at the others walking nearby. "Although, between you and me, I think it's nonsense keeping this a secret, especially from you," he went on, his voice lowered.

"So you're saying you think I'm like you?"

"I'm saying I *know* you're like me."

"Based on what? I haven't so much as flirted with a corpse!"

"No, I mean that we're both... We both have very special parents."

"We're... brothers?! But... the scales...?!"

"This is far more difficult than I ever imagined."

"Our mother must have said the same."

"Look, you know how you are Prince Tashino?"

"That's a pretty philosophical question that I don't feel comfortable answering."

"Wonderful. Well, in the same way that you might be Prince Tashino, investigation of the old 'I think therefore I am' pending, I might just happened to be Prince Izayah. Not of the Empire. Of the Shek Kingdom. So that means Queen Estata – the Stone Golem, that is – is my... mother. But it's a secret!"

"Okran's dipstick, that's a secret alright. You're a fugging Prince?! Why didn't you say?"

"We- I thought you'd get mad, if there were too many princes around. Silly, isn't it?"

"Fugg no. Prince pride, bro. That's like insane, so you got exiled?"

"I was always exiled, for I was always a paleskin. Mother's orders. That's simply how it is."

"Man, man we're gonna sort that shid out. You walk into town with the Bugmulcher's mandibles under your arm, and that'll be pure, chocolate justice my man."

"While I have no idea what that means, I thank you for your support. However, I have no wish to be part of that family any more. But I would like to see them. And to live among the shek as Elaina does. How I am to be pardoned for being born like this into a family like that, I do not know."

"Told you, I'm gonna sort it out! We're gonna save your Kingdom from Nuktrient deficiency, end fugging racism, then end fugging slavery... Man, and I only left the house to get some fugging green – got the other kind of crazy trip."

"Your support is like nothing else I have ever enjoyed, Prince Tashino."

"So this means you really didn't get busted for corpse canoodling?"

"Ha, oh my Prince, of course not," Izayah said, putting an arm around Nuk and pulling him closer. "That's not even illegal here!"

About forty percent reassured, Nuk marched on with the group. Around one in the morning they were looking for a place to rest, and saw lights and a wall up ahead. Thinking it another of the many shek military outposts, they went to check the breakfast menu and such. However the guards at the gate were wearing the brown uniforms of those who had accosted Nuk on the road to Admag.

"This must be New Kralia. The rebel base," Elaina said. "The Stone Golem outlawed their little sect, and so they went off to live in the mountains. We're probably the only ones stupid enough to get lost up here."

"Or lucky enough," Nuk said. "'Cause if we bring these guys down, Stone-Zone back there will owe us one. We'll tell everyone that outlaw Izayah has saved the Kingdom from these renegades! Sort of thing a worthy leader would do, right?"

"Then you should be first, my Prince," Izayah said, with a flourished bow. After all were done winking at each other and stewing in the smugness of knowing a secret secret – as in, the only secret was the matter of the secrecy – oh don't worry about it too much, okay? Basically, Nuk decided to try his luck with the gate guards.

"Friends, is this Kralia?" Nuk opened.

"Flatskin scum, you have five seconds to leave before we begin our hunt," was the reply, accompanied by the drawing of long greatswords.

"Fantastic. However, friends, you should know, that I am also Kral's Chosen."

"Impossible."

"Really, he chose me too."

"He fell in battle against a hundred foes. You should never dream of walking even in his footsteps."

"But he left behind this letter. Says the Prince of the Empire is welcome to use his bed and breakfast, with all he can eat of either bread or salad at the host's discretion, and... also like twenty of his guests. So yeah, let us in. Oh, and it says we can keep all our weapons and stuff."

"Give me that," a guard said, grabbing at the scrap of paper Nuk was holding out. They didn't pick up that it only had a few words on it, reading roughly 'Please do what cool human wants – bed, food, drugs'. But something else gave the game away.

"This isn't Kral's handwriting!"

"Yeah, he was really drunk when he wrote that, sorry."

"Drunk on what?"

"Err... Catcus Rum?"

"Fool, Kral only ever drunk Urchin Rum."

"The bottles got switched."

"Kral only ever drunk from flasks."

"The flask was leaking."

"Kral always had a second flask outside the first flask to prepare for just such incidents."

"Fugg, he thought of everything. Alright, then, just read the back of that sheet instead."

The guard flipped the paper.

"'Sike, we're here to kill you'. I doubt Kral would write that if you really were his friend."

A crossbow bolt ended the poor guard's confusion, and the others didn't last long against the rush of guild warriors emerging from the surrounding night. However, all that did was get them in through the gate. Inside there were campfires and a couple of sandstone buildings with lights flickering in the windows. Before they could investigate, a shek strode out of the closer one.

"Oh I could kill a flatskin in the afternoon, I could kill a flatskin in the eve, I could kill a flatskin at the break of dawn, and there ain't a single one I would leave!" he sang.

"How's three am for you?!" Nuk called as as sword flashed in the firelight. In a second the shek was on the ground.

"You know," Rick said, "We'd be in trouble if these places were full of like a legion of these guys. I mean, I don't really care about getting a bed to sleep on, so let's just quit while we're ahead."

It was wise council, however then Ells started singing.

"Oh I could kill a flatskin with a rusty spoon, I could kill a flatskin with a plate, I could kill a flatskin with a dried up shid, and there ain't a single moment to wait!"

Then, a face appeared in one of the windows.

"Finally, he came up with a second verse! Hang on... What the fugg?! INTERLOPERS!" the voice boomed. Oh dear. More of Kral's Chosen swarmed from the buildings, wielding huge blades and clad in iron armour.

"Charge! Kill them, in the name of the true Prince!" Nuk called leading his entourage into the fray.

"Oh he's probably talking about himself, don't worry!" Izayah assured the others as battle commenced.

"Guess I'll just chill here," Elaina said, stepping aside with Gary and watching the shadowy brawl. With the inclusion of Nuk's hired goons, the guild seemed to have the upper hand, but then there was a thudding, clacking stomp as a huge shek jumped down from the roof of one of the buildings – the shorter one, mind you, and he was trained professional so don't try that at home.

He arose, his horns protruding like antlers, his blade speckled with sharp bony teeth, his eyes drawing up onto Elaina.

"Ah, the Queen birthed another monstrosity did she? So it wasn't me that caused it, then," he growled.

"Not really. Nice place you have here? You know, we just wanted somewhere to sleep. As long as there's free breakfast. Unlimited bread, or unlimited salad, at the... hosts'... discretion..." Elaina fizzled out as the shek loomed above her – and remember, Elaina was already neck-strainingly tall for the average human.

"The Queen's insects shall be crushed, their juices consumed, and then I, Flying Bull, shall be King!"

"That... explains the entrance," Elaina said, jumping forwards with the shortsword she had clutched in both hands. Flying Bull gracefully danced backwards, and in the same motion swung his gargantuan blade upwards. With a puny clink, the sword was sent spiralling up into the starry sky.

With a shriek Elaina turned to flee, but the next swoosh of the spinning blade caught her leg and flipped her to the ground in indescribable pain.

"Fugg, man, Big Kid's eating shid!" Nuk said to Izayah.

"Elaina! Leave her alone! It's me you want!" Izayah called, rushing over. Nuk joined him in facing down the goliath.

"Ah, you are right. You are the rodent Prince, aren't you?" Flying Bull said, pointing his blade at Izayah.

"He's the best prince in the world, whale-scales!" Nuk retorted.

"Ha ha! What a fall from grace to have a flatskin praise your name! Ha ha! You should have seen the look of disgust on your mother's face on the day of your birth, rodent. After she refused my offer to kill you there and then, I thought I'd never see your puny, pale, stalk again. Perhaps she only exiled me in the hopes I would find you and finish the job. Yes, if she is as wise as the cowards whine, then that must have been it! Ha ha! Come then, I will destroy- ARGH!"

Flying Bull was cut off in a rather literal sense. A shortsword had fallen from the sky and pierced his arm. The blade dropped from his hand.

"Now!" Izayah shouted. He and Nuk sliced into one leg each, and Flying Bull fell to his knees with another roar. He lashed out with his fists and batted Nuk aside, but Izayah stepped around the failing trunks and pushed his blade against Bull's neck. With a two-handed swipe, the deed was done. Even before Flying Bull's corpse crashed into the dirt, Izayah was beside Elaina, unlike her right leg.

"Narko's darkness, hold on Elaina!" he said, dragging the bandages from his bag.

"I knew... there was a secret to all this," Elaina muttered with a smile.

"You heard? Hmpf. Old politics. No matter to us. I am Izayah, and that's all. Now hold still."

Luckily, after the sun rose and the fighting was over, no one got any injuries worse than Elaina. Still, it was enough of a beating to immobilise the guild, not to mention the exhaustion of the all-nighter. Handy then that the spoils of victory included the Kral's Chosen hideout, all to themselves! Beds, food, and treasures were free for the taking, and freely they were took. However the coins and trinkets weren't the real treasure.

The members of Kral's Chosen were lined up, and where they were still alive, they were bound in the manner Kral would have chosen: a set of binds, then another set around the binds, just in case.

"Are you sure you're alright?" Izumi asked Izayah. Izayah pulled a face-obscuring battle helmet over his head.

"I'll be fine. If anyone delivers this scoundrel to justice, it should be me." He knelt down and somehow hoisted the huge frame of Flying Bull over his shoulders.

"So for now, just make them think that a mysterious masked shek defeated the rebels. No names. We'll swoop in and do a big reveal later, yeah?" Nuk said.

"As you wish, Prince Tashino."

"Reveal of what exactly?" Izumi asked.

"My true identity."

"Ah, well even we don't know what that is," she said with another wink.

"You mean that he is the lost Prince?" Elaina said, hobbling over with a longsword for a crutch. Whoops. I guess while she knew the secret, she didn't know the secret of the secret secret.

"What? He's not- Why would you say that?" Izumi bluffed.

"Future girl. I know. I always knew," Nuk also bluffed.

"Oh. So you're not mad?"

"Mad he's not getting what he deserves. Prince bros. That's us. Sticking together. Except right now, 'cause he's going to Admag, and I'm going to bed."

"Wait, I'm going with him," Elaina said.

"Hoping to make it a quick one and pop right back," Izayah explained, but Elaina was hobbling at him anyway.

"Carry me. I'm not going to be separated from you," she insisted. Handy that Izayah was wearing armour over his face, or that decreasingly pale skin would have betrayed his embarrassment.

"Pale bros. We're all such bros," Nuk said, waving Ells over. "Charlie, you're demoted to corpse carrier. Take whalescales from palescales and do what he says, alright? The second guy, not the first guy. Whatever."

"Is Izayah my boss now if we're saying he's the Prince?"

"We're both your boss. In fact, to make it easy for your Charlie, everyone's your boss, alright?"

"Even me?"

"Oh except you. Okran's swaying fringe, just get going will you? We've got beds to de-scale."

Therefore, the 'masked shek' mysteriously delivered the body of the outlaw Flying Bull to an Admag police station, winning himself a huge cash bounty and an audience with the Queen, but he quickly retreated, reciting,

"I did this only for the good of the Shek Kingdom. Now, for the same reason, I must say goodbye. One day, you will understand."

These carefully chosen words, when relayed to Queen Stone Golem, caused her to fly into an over the top rage, and then lock the doors of her royal barrack and refuse to see anyone – after all, none could see the mighty Queen of the Shek shed a tear.

After returning to New Kralia, Izayah's payload received some good news: among the misc found in the rebels' possession was a skeleton leg. Thanks to advances in user friendly technology back in the First Empire, this leg could replace, and even surpass, Elaina's old one, with a click, a snap, and a hum.

"Feels weird," she reported. Gustavsen fiddled with some tiny bolts on the side.

"This model is exemplary. It is a fine replacement. Is there another?" Wodston shook his head from over by the spare parts bin. "Regretful. I will smell his disappointment. I will search further."

So then, with a new leg sorted out, the battle of New Kralia had been a complete victory for the guild. And now all of Admag was speaking of the mysterious masked hero who had rid the Kingdom of the pretender Flying Bull. Many folk went to New Kralia to try and find out more, but it would take them a day to arrive, and by then the place was deserted.

The rested guild had moved out, towards the distant, black mountain that loomed in the south: the doomed crater of Arach, domain of the Dark Lord of Spiders, the Bugmaster. Thousands might have died hunting the murderous arachnid overlord, but they probably didn't have that cocky choccy. Nuk had nothing to worry about at all. Right?

Chapter 18
The Brownpound Age

The Shek Kingdom was mostly confined to the badlands between the great Vain river to the north and the lush mountainside plains to the south. Some said that it was just shek bravado – only weak humans or mindless hivers lived where plants grew. But those who say that have at least never been to those lush plains, known rather accurately as 'The Spider Plains'.

"Is that a skimmer?" Nuk puzzled when he first saw one.

"More like a skinner," Elaina said. "Skin spiders. This is their territory. And the Bugmaster you are looking for is their King."

"Pfft, if you'd seen a skimmer you wouldn't be so worried. Way worse than those ugly fuggs. Come on!"

The guild approached a small group of these pink, fleshy skin spiders. Since Izumi was ranting about it as they walked, I should tell you that, yes, they only had four legs and two weird hoof-arms hanging from their underbelly, so like everything that was called a spider, it was certainly not a spider. These beasts had avoided classification so far, since upon closer inspection the leg count wasn't really what caught your attention – they had disfigured faces protruding from their shoulders like huge boils, faces that roughly resembled hivers.

The guild killed a few of them quickly, their blades cutting through the soft tissue of the creatures with ease. That gave them all the time they needed to poke at the abominations. You would imagine Ells would be first in there, but actually he was only one keeping his distance.

"Gustavsen, it looks like you," Nuk noted, boinging one of the head-boils around with a stick. Gustavsen was unimpressed.

"Its associations have been erased. It cannot go back. Pay them no heed."

Whatever that meant, it was time to leave the piles of flesh to simmer in the midday sun, and continue on to the foot of the looming, dark mountain to the south-west. There, at the end of civilisation, were the twin fortresses of Last Stand.

"Didn't think I'd see this place for a long, long time," Elaina said.

"Ha, and there were some who wanted to send me here as an offering to the Bugmaster. Seems they got their way in the end," Izayah said. The crew wandered inside one of the forts, but it was even less welcoming than your average shek outpost. Most of the buildings were featureless sandstone barracks filled with beds and little else. After some searching they got themselves into a self-styled bar, but inside it was just a bunch of elderly shek sitting silently around tables, staring into the distance, or at their own reflections in the blades of their tall swords.

"Come on guys, this isn't a funeral," Nuk remarked under his breath, but at once a frail looking shek was in his face.

"Speak when spoken to, flatskin. I don't know why you are here, but if I have to endure another day of life just to teach you a lesson, then I will!" he said.

"Calm down crinkles. I just mean this place could use a little brown. I'm gonna kill the Bugmaster, ya know?"

The shek headbutted Nuk without hesitation. The apparently frailty of the man didn't stop Nuk clearing a whole table before hitting the ground. In a flash Sandor was in the air also, his blade coming down on the shek in both hands, but with a single motion the shek cleared Sandor away with a wide sweep of his greatsword.

"Stop!" Izayah called, jumping into the brewing brawl. "This is a misunderstanding. Please, friend, excuse my flatskin comrades. Important tourists, you see, but not at all unskilled. To speak of killing the Bugmaster is no empty bluff. Half empty at most. Half full? No, definitely, half empty."

This intervention somehow de-escalated things, and Nuk returned to the conversation, albeit slumped on Wodston's back.

"So... sounds like this a big deal or something..." he said. Indeed. The group sat for hours listening to many of the shek in the bar explain the deal in laborious detail, so allow me to summarise just what was going on in this dour corner of the world.

Remember that Kral guy? Well he was the one who made the eponymous Last Stand on that mountainside, long before the time of the Bugmaster. Entrapped by a band of rebels, Warrior Kral had battled one hundred of them at once. He had no thought of fleeing, and with skills and strength in equal measure, he sent bodies rolling down the hill, one by one. Then, on the verge of total victory, he had been stabbed in the back and slain.

His legend had evolved over the generations, and now the gathering the guild witnessed at Last Stand really was a funeral of sorts. When a shek neared the end of their life, it was customary to come here to Arach Mountain and die as Kral died, fighting a battle that always outlived its participants. In the current era, the Bugmaster was the opponent. Luckily for the shek tradition, the Bugmaster never lost, and so for decades now shek had gone out into the great razor of Arach, never to return.

"Wait a minute," Nuk said after hearing of all this. "It sounds to me like Buggeryman is doing you lot a favour. Kill him, and your last stands will be just literally standing there and seeing how long you last. Why did Stonezone want me to come spoil the fun?"

"Hmpf, a new game she plays. She sends bounty hunters after the Bugmaster all the time," a shek replied. "She does not understand honour."

"Now listen here you," Izayah said. "Queen Estata fought in battles that Kral could only dream of. Watch your mouth."

"Why? She is cursed. She had a paleskin kid, like you, junior. She should be out here with us. Couple of paleskins like you wouldn't understand. Surprised those warriors there hang around with you. Hang on..."

The barfly was looking at Ells, Bobbie and Claw, who were sitting at the next table over. Ells had a bucket over his head, and so far this had seemed completely unremarkable. However now it was wrenched off by a gathering group of patrons.

"Look at this old chubber!" one said. "He's far past his due. Do you not know courage, welk?"

"I don't like Skin spiders!" Ells yelped, running outside.

"Ah. I think our smelly friend might have found himself here before," Izayah noted.

"Huh. So, guess it's stuff like that which turned Rock Mother off the place," Nuk said. "Works for me too. This is shid. I mean everyone's coming out here, sitting around being miserable fuggs, then going out to die fighting some hyped up piece of shid and playing to fugging lose. What's the point? Kral wasn't trying to lose, was he? Why can't we just win? Die how you want. When you want. My boy Charlie wants more bucket time, so give him more bucket time. And those who want to fight the Bugmaster - why don't we just work something out, and actually win?!"

This speech got the old shek at Nuk's table rather angry. They stormed away, but others came closer. Indeed there were a few shek, mostly at the younger end of the old spectrum, who were interested in Nuk's dream of victory. Problem was, he needed a way to actually do it. He needed a secret weapon that the countless thousands who had tried before him didn't have.

"Operation Brownpound!" Nuk announced. Izumi cringed so hard you could actually hear it. "All you new guys, stick with Sadscales there. You're gonna be working with this guy, the mysterious masked shek, Whitehorn Izayah. He is the leader of the official TCM+ Bugbuster Non-doomed Elite Chocolate Combat Shock Troops. What's chocolate I smell you thinking? Chocolate, friends, is the doomsday weapon that will destroy doomsday itself. Once you eat it, you'll know what I mean."

So, with the promise that what he had just said would somehow make sense in the future, Nuk plotted a course back to Admag. When he left though, he told Sandor to take a pleasant hike up the Mountain of Death and find out what all the fuss was about. Was this all much ado about nothing, or was there nothing much all could ado about this? Nuk asked the question in an even more confusing way, I assure you, but Sandor understood, and hiked up the mountainside as night fell.

Used to finding his way in the dark, Sandor was quickly halfway up. There he encountered a sheltered gully lit by fires. Inside were a dozen heavily armed figures, some pacing about, others sitting quietly on their own. Before they knew it, Sandor was sitting beside one of their campfires.

"What- Who are you?" a man asked.

"One of you," Sandor replied.

"A bounty hunter huh? Well you fell for it too then, didn't ya?"

"Explain."

"You haven't got it yet? That bounty on the Bugmaster, it's impossible Shek go up there to the crater every day. Don't do nothing. Spiders come round here every few hours, and it don't matter how many you kill."

"Then go back."

"Go back! You think there's anyone here who can go back? Debts is the thing. Kinda debts where you need a big score, or it's the chop. So here we're stuck, death up there, death down there. If you've come up here by choice, you've got eyes bigger than your belly. Skinnies don't have that problem. But yeah... we'll burn out our wood, and see what happens, won't we? Won't- Oi... Where'd he go?"

Sandor was beyond the light the fire could offer, hauling himself further up the mountain. He soon saw the crater the bounty hunter had mentioned. And by saw, I mean he felt the moist wind coming up from it. It carried disturbances – the sounds of dozens of soft feet padding around the narrow cliffs leading downwards.

Sandor descended towards them, but they faded away faster than he could advance. Instead, he heard the sloshing of water. In the crater's middle there was a huge lake, the water stained red by the exposed minerals in the scorched rocks. In eons past, the place had been awash with magma and fire, and that legacy remained in the comfortable temperature of the maroon lake.

This worked to Sandor's benefit, as something was glinting out on the water. It was time for a swim. He quietly approached a tall shadow, unable to recognise it until it was right up close – it was one of the mushroom-shaped depots characteristic of the Second Empire, only it was collapsed on its side and partially submerged. Climbing inside and finding nothing, Sandor put at ear to the wall and closed his eyes to wait for morning.

Back over in Admag the rest of the guild had arrived safe and sound, and were also enjoying the comforts of an old ruin. Only thing was, this ruin had cost Nuk most of his brown profits. He had bought up an old tower on the edge of the city for use as a depot for his operations, which were, to clarify here, selling brown to local drug addicts, and gathering an army to conquer Mount Doom. Despite the cost, the place was partially collapsed under its own weight, filled with rubble, and stank of a stink unstunk.

"It's all yours my man," Nuk said, clapping Wodston on the back. "Sort it all out, and I'll rustle up the stocks and jocks for our mission."

"Will you not be leaving Miss Izumi to oversee things?" Wodston was quick to ask.

"What? No, she's like my... friendly girl... or something..."

"Damn, he really ain't never gonna say it huh?" Rick remarked.

"Yeah, Coinslot you gotta stay too. You really don't help, you know?" Nuk said.

"I know. Hot damn metal man setting the bar too high. Well, at least this tower's a real do-er upp-er, ya know?"

Preferring not to know, the crew got to business. Wodston, Rick, and Ells were left in Admag to play house, while the rest began the very long walk all the way back to Manksand Canyon. While that quest for a chocolate legion trundles along, let's check back in with Sandor.

In the light of day he could see the full extent of the crater he was in. Spider trails ran along the edge, and up and down the slopes, but it was quiet for now. It was raining heavily and a low fog sat up at the crater rim. In the grey, Sandor could make out the faintest shadow of a building high up to the south. He leapt from his perch, slipped quietly into the water, and made for the southern shore. From there it was a steep climb over smooth, slippery rocks, weathered down by years of water flowing into the crater.

At the top there was a ridge covered in bouncy, red-brown dirt. It ran a short distance west along the crater rim, then turned north into a promontory, the site of the Bugmaster's secret castle. It was a huge Second Empire palace, admittedly in terrible condition. It had that familiar mushroom roof, circular build, and grey, featureless walls. It was also covered in makeshift spikes, which were themselves covered in (or made of) rust. Its grounds were patrolled by hordes of skin spiders, as was the ridge that approached it. That was the only way up, so Sandor couldn't get a closer look. But he'd seen enough to know that the ado was about something indeed, and that something had to be adone about it.

In Admag, work on the new guild shopfront/military base remained mostly undone. To tackle this, Rick went to the bar to recruit some help.

"Listen up you scaly sons of Narko," he called out. "It's me, ya boi, Captain Redlin Rickard of the International Chocolate Legion or some shid, and I've done got some day labouring work going. Who wants to make a quick cat doing my doer upper up? Yeah it's really easy work, and the pay's great, I'm tellin ya. I've been alive, damn, six thousand years at least, and I ain't never done anything so satisfying as working with me as the boss.

Yeah gather around, I got time, let's get you all signed up, huh? Oh by the way, by agreeing to this you're also agreeing to join a private army – but don't you worry about that! Simple day labouring's all it is – except the part where your life is forfeit – but hey, this contract is just a fugging sandwich, so why sweat the details?! You'll be back by Kenshi Kralia Eve. That's a Red Rick Guarantee – disclaimer: this is not a guarantee."

Yep, that worked out pretty well. Nuk had made it back to Squin and was doing the same, but he was pretty much straightforward about it and just paid a load of wannabe soldiers to sign up – or sandwich up as it were.

"And on top of the cash, we pay you in food too," he boasted. "Well, it's not really food. It's something you can put in your mouth, and I'll show you what it is once we get back to my place." With this surely irresistible promise, he managed to wrangle up a veritable squadron of shek. They embarked with him on the long, uneventful trip back to the HQ. Then, Nuk had a promise to keep. He gathered his new recruits and addressed them from atop a big crate.

"You've all heard of it. You all want it. Browntown. The bread that they did get. The legacy of the Brown Emperor. Yes, it goes by many names, but there's only one place in the world you can get it. From my warm, loving hands."

With this he kicked the crate below him, and the side fell open to reveal a huge stock of brown bread, the product of Jaz and company's hard work while Nuk's crew had been away. The shek, who had been forcefully recommended to not eat anything for a day before, lunged forwards at the bread rolling out towards them. Shek are hungry folk even at the best of times, and as a feeding frenzy developed, Nuk put his hands on his hips and laughed in a very sane-sounding fashion.

"Yes, consume it my friends, consume the fuel of the revolution. You are not just soldiers. You are the elite warriors of Whitehorn Izayah, bringer of the age of peace, doom of doom, Bugmaster master! You will be undefeatable. You would eat skin spiders for breakfast, but you can't, 'cause you always fill up on this sweet dessert at every meal! Yes, that's what they shall call the ultimate soldiers, you – my desserters!"

None of the shek heard any of this, all lost in a euphoric brown bread trance, but Wodston politely clapped from some distance away. Izumi cleansed herself with a long blink, then hauled her gear over to her office.

Someone was waiting for her behind the door.

"So, how'd it go?" Jaz said, quickly closing said door. Izumi slumped into a chair, and said,

"Well, we're gonna fight some kind of spider man to help Izayah – Prince Izayah, as it turns out."

"Another one?"

"Yeah, pretty good association huh?"

"What's that mean?"

"Doesn't matter. Anyway, we're back here because we need to get some more BB so Nuk can turbocharge his new toys, and get some cash over in the Kingdom. So much work..."

"Right, right, but you know all that isn't really what I meant. I meant how did it GO go."

"Go... fugg yourself?"

"Stop swearing you little- How did it go with Nuk?"

"Nuk? It went... there and back again."

"What? All the way there? And all the way back again... What's that even mean?"

"Nothing! It means nothing! Okran's paddle... He's just my friend, who is a boy, alright?"

"Damn, you really ain't never gonna say it are you?" Jaz grinned.

Izumi kicked her out, and took a long deserved nap. The poor shek didn't have that privilege. They were driven onto the roof of the barracks for immediate drill instruction.

So then, chocolate might not have taken the entire world by storm, but it certainly tickled the fancy of the shek, and they could in turn tickle the rest of the world on Nuk's behalf. As for what I mean when I say tickle – you'll find out soon enough.

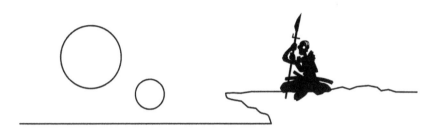

Chapter 19
The Last Last Stand

In Admag, that dilapidated cliff-side tower had been restored by the weird out-of-towners. The Stone Golem looked on from the roof of her barracks, well aware that the mysterious masked shek was something to do with this new business. For now though, all this business did was produce a white-haired human from time to time, who would jog into town and purchase sandwiches from the local shop. 'Whatever happened to those workhands that the red-faced Old One had recruited?', the locals wondered.

"I ain't never seen such a useless bunch of nodes and limbs in my entire life, and I saw the pieces of shid who fugged up this life-forsaken planet in the first place!" Rick was shouting at them. Deltas of sweat streaked down their scaly faces. They were all tired of the ceaseless training their new boss was putting them through, but they knew what would happen if they stopped.

"You get fit, or you get the stick!" Rick reminded them for the thousandth time. The stick twirled in his hands – or was his entire hand twirling?! "When you accidentally volunteered to be conscripted into the chocolate legion, you did it because you were the best of the best of the drunk-at-dawn club, and I'd be remiss if I were to let you out there into the world without a real military education. War is serious shid. It's about getting down and dirty, and sucking it up when things get hard. At least according to his ancient picture book... It's also about showering. It's mostly showering actually. Hey, she's got a stick as well, and she's getting creative.

Ugh... What the...? Old Man Wodston? You ever heard of a 'reverse kebab'? Damn. We gotta get showers invented again."

Meanwhile at Manksand Canyon...

"That'll do it," Elaina said, emerging from under the chocolate processor. "You had the gerning jocket on upside down. Surprised it didn't just catch fire like that."

"Oh, no that's never happened," Izumi said, eyeing the artistic flower of black soot running up the wall.

"I'm done making the pile!" Ells called from outside. He'd made a very nice pile of corpses out of the latest wave of reaver attackers. He was taking his recent demotion to corpse carrier very seriously.

"She's a beaut!" Jaz remarked from the wall. "Just about covers ya fugging stink mate. Loving it!"

"Thank you strange lady."

"Jaz, would you mind watching your language?" Izumi said with her head around the door of the chocolate factory.

"What the fugg? Says you? Are you fugging gaslighting me right now? Why don't you watch your fugging language you smarmy tart?"

"Jaz, it's the young ears among us."

"Oh right, Elaina can't hear us swear but she can stab the dusties like any old jogger, huh?"

"What?"

"Yeah, that's what I thought."

"Oh... What did she think? Whatever..."

This pleasant homely life, with all its confusing smells and reassuring violence, was destined to come to an end soon. One morning Nuk gathered everyone at the gate, and took a look over the dozen shek he'd recruited for the legion. They were kitted out in the gear the local bandits kindly dropped outside the walls each day as they travelled very rapidly away on the points of speeding harpoons. The cannons had kept everyone inside the compound perfectly safe, save for poor one-leg Ignacio, who'd lost an arm in the ongoing wars as well.

"Today we march, in a campaign that will go down in history!" Nuk declared. "We will fight them on the beaches, we will fight them on the hills and in the swamps – although it really shouldn't come to that, let's be honest. Yes, we will fight those horrible mountain goats to very end-"

Nuk was distracted by Izumi whispering something in his ear.

"Err... I'm being told it's actually 'skin spiders' we're fighting. What? I don't remember that. I dunno. I was blazed when I came up with this whole thing. And so will all of you loyal desserters be when we win! Which will be... I dunno... After we walk there. So get hyped for that. Err... A bottle of Premium Hydration Medium for the first to kill one of those eight-legged freaks. Wait... I'm being told they're not actually spiders... What the fugg are we actually doing here? Oh whatever, deploy the troops, and let's just see what happens! Onward!"

Onward they went, marching to the other side of the known world, which luckily was only about three days away. They used the night-time recess to dodge the good old apocalypse laser, and arrived again at that lonely wasteland bar they'd stopped off at on their initial journey. This was the place where Nuk had gifted the local bandits a free sample of brown. Seemed like sound marketing at the time. But now the chocolate legion was face to face with the chocolate horde.

"Brown man! Brown man! Giz da choccy!" a scruffy vagrant called from outside the bar.

"First hit's free, second hit's double price, you know the rules," Nuk shouted back.

"Rules were made to be broken!"

"Yeah? What if the rule was that you always had to break the rules?"

"Err... Err... Arrrghhh! GIZ DA CHOCCY! BREAD BANDITS, GET 'EM!"

From behind every tree, rock, and withered cactus, more scrawny, salivating wasters appeared.

"Izayah, wanna try them out?" Nuk asked. Izayah nodded, placed Choco safely on his shoulder, and raised his sword.

"Chocolate Legion! Form up!"

The legionaries gathered around him.

"Chocolate Legion, stand ready," Izayah called. Each shek produced a handful of chocobread and held it carefully in front of their mouths. "Consume, brown!" At this order they scoffed it down in a single bite. Suddenly they were quivering with energy, and rumour has it some of their horns were even wriggling back and forth.

"By the left, kill everyone!" Izayah ordered, and the battle cry that followed echoed across the wastes like the birthing of a great vengeful deity. The legion was outnumbered two—perhaps three—to one, but that meant nothing when the brown mist clouded their eyes and bandits fell like stalks of sweet, sweet cocoa. It was truly a sight to behold. Everyone beheld it so hard they almost missed the fact that a Beak Thing had come over to see what the fuss was about, and was currently walking off with Gustavsen in its mouth. This was resolved swiftly, bringing the military action to a close.

"Incredible, we've got this, man," Nuk remarked to Izayah.

"I do hope so. There is just one thing I feel is a bit off."

"Yeah, we need to do like a special pose after each win."

"No, I was going to say- it's the name. I rather think this Chocolate Legion doesn't strike fear into one's heart."

"Fine. Call them, Choccer Rockers. Whitehorn and the Shek Wreck Supremes. The Fantabulous-"

"No, Prince Tashino. I was thinking something a little more traditional."

"Yeah? Well what do shek normally call stuff like this?"

"The soldiers are known as the Hundred Guardians. Each one aims to be a match for one hundred foes, like old Kral, you see?"

"Then, my man, I hope you enjoy commanding your new army: The Thousand Guardians!"

"Ha, oh well that'll do!"

And so the Chocolate Legion was disbanded, and the Thousand Guardians were born. The 'thousand', by the way, was later taken to refer not to their worth in regular soldiers, but the number of calories per mouthful in their secret combat stimulants.

After another day and a half of slogging, this army was peering at the towering cliffs of Admag. Izayah closed his faceplate and took the lead. As the gang clattered through the streets, all were whispering of the mysterious masked shek.

"They say he's from a strange land with unclear zoning regulations," one rumour went.

"They say he's three inches taller in the morning than at night," another claimed. They say that truth is stranger than fiction, but when it comes to shek, both are just as dull.

The force reached the restored tower and reunited with the caretakers within. Red Rick presented his group of recruits to the Thousand Guardians.

"I worked it out, man. You gotta hit 'em just right to activate all those old Enforcer genes. Makes all the fighting we bred into 'em come back clear as the last sober morning, ya know? Oh, ya don't know? Oh yeah, that's a secret... Err... Nope, I dunno where shek come from, but I'm sure glad they're here now. Enjoy 'em folks!"

"Genes? Didn't I read something about 'genes'?" Izumi mused.

"They're like your two-way leg tubes there, but kinda rough and shiddy. That's all there is to it. Not that I remember. There's gotta be a way to turn down the volume on this voice..." Rick said.

Regrettably, fielding this army had left the guild nearly bankrupt, so the truth of the matter was out of anyone's price range. It was time to start remedying that situation. Nuk stashed a load of the brown bread in their new depot, and gave the rest to Izayah.

"Remember, point at the dog and tell them it'll get sad if they don't buy it," Nuk advised.

"What? She'll get sad? Then that settles it, I'm selling it all right now!" Izayah declared, rushing out to the town. Choco enjoyed the ride on his shoulder, and everyone who witnessed it nodded knowingly, smugly muttering something to the effect of 'I knew he had a brown dog'. It was beyond their wildest dreams. Within an hour Izayah had sold out and the local bars were full of raging brown addicts – mission accomplished.

But the real mission – and indeed the real money – was yet to be handled. That evening, the grand expeditionary force was assembled at the city gate. Nuk and his companions numbered a dozen or so, the Thousand Guardians the same again, and another dozen of Nuk's hired troops bolstered them further. This gathering force had attracted a crowd of onlookers. Izayah stood on Bobbie and Claw's shoulders – with Choco still on his own shoulders of course – and addressed the locals.

"People of Admag. I was once told I could never return to this city, the place of my birth. So, I wandered far and wide. In the far-distant Great Desert, I met this Prince of the Empire, Nuk Tashino, a flatskin. He showed me what it means to live free, and what marvellous things can be achieved when those from all corners cooperate. He gave me the strength to return here, but I do not break the terms of my exile lightly. I am here as the Masked Shek for the last time. I will return as the victorious slayer of the Bugmaster, a worthy warrior of this great Kingdom, or I will never return again! That I promise!"

As Izayah was lowered, the crowd chanted "In the image of Kral he walks. With the honour of Kral he shall die." Izayah put his head in his hands and gave a long sigh.

"You okay man?" Nuk asked.

"Better by the moment, Prince Tashino. Thank you, for giving me a day like this. I day I hardly deserve."

"Man, just wait 'till we get back with the Bugmoulder. We're gonna paint this town white!"

Izayah nodded, pulled his sword from the ground, and pointed out at the distant mountain of death, glinting orange in the evening light.

"Thousand Guardians. Follow me!" he called, and the procession began, watched in austere silence by the townsfolk. They used the oncoming fall of night to safely cross the Spider Plains under cover of darkness. At midnight they reached Last Stand, where final preparations were made – and by that I mean they drank the bar dry.

"This seems kinda serious Nuk- Prince. Is this really okay?" Izumi said.

"Yeah, sure. We'll do it," Nuk shrugged.

"What if... something happens?"

"Dunno. If you die, you won't need to worry about will you?"

"Nuk!"

"Sorry. Yeah I know. But seriously, I'll make it work. I'll keep you out of the mess."

"You're the one pulling me into this mess actually."

"Uh huh? Pulling, or are you just gripping onto me?"

"Nuk, I really hate you, you know?"

"Yeah... Yeah... I hate you too."

"Forget the speaker volume, gotta find a way to turn off the microphones," Rick remarked. "Least they said something, Well, the opposite of what they're meant to be saying. But hey, opposite's pretty close, right? Boolean value's better than null. What? Oh yeah, y'all ain't got these binary brains. Don't mind me."

Rick went unminded, but meanwhile Ells was attracting attention. A few of the old shek who had been in the bar before recognised him.

"Chubber! There he is again. How many times you gonna come up here and run away, traitor?" one asked.

"I- I just didn't want to go up there on my own," Ells said. "My friends are gonna win, and I'm gonna help. If I did that, I'd have beaten you, wouldn't I?"

"Hmpf, numbers dilute the honour, chubber. And these flatskins here – they soil it entirely! Fool!"

"Oh fugg off crinkles," Nuk interjected. "Numbers and friends were what your bloody Kral didn't have, and he got iced like everyone else. Even if we weren't gonna get high as the bloody eye, we'd still win! Haven't you read the classics? Tomodachi - the power of friendship. I might be a flatskin, but if we look out for each other, it'll tip the *scales* in our favour. Eh? Scales? Like... Whatever, uncultured gaijin..."

This proved to be a great time to set off, so they left that last mote of safety and set foot on the blackened mountainside. Sandor took them via an easier route up the eastern slope, where the hills were long and shallow both up to the crater edge and down into it.

The upward journey was quiet, with not a spider nor a shek in sight – not that they could see far, with it being the early hours of the morning. It might seem irresponsible, but the plan was to get a full day of light to conduct their grand battle once they reached the Bugmaster's citadel. The fighting would start far earlier than that though.

They walked along the top of the crater to its south-west corner, where Sandor pointed out a quick way up towards the ridge leading to their quarry. To get there they had to descend towards a red river, down a slope patrolled by the skin spiders. With a running charge, they quickly cut a path all the way down to the water's edge.

"Huh, see, it's easy!" Nuk remarked.

"Should've kept your hooting down. The Bugmaster will know we are coming," Sandor said. Indeed the sounds of battle had echoed around the crater's many crags and valleys, travelling who knows how far. There was no time to waste. Unfortunately they had to swim across a stretch of the river to get to the foot of the Bugmaster's home ridge.

"Oh. Cannot. I will remain here," Gustavsen said.

"Why? Come on," Nuk replied.

"It is the wrong colour."

"Not this again. Right, up you go."

Nuk had Gustavsen sit on his back while he paddled across. Luckily the shiver weighed very little, and Nuk was a strong swimmer after his days in Manksand frolicking in the lake just up the westward canyon. Oh there was frolicking alright. I'll tell you about it sometime.

Rick was the first across, and the only one who didn't swim. He was rather heavy you see, but waterproof, handily enough.

"Imagine being full of air. The indignity," he commented as he waited for the slow-swimming shek to gradually struggle to the western bank. From said bank it was a short climb up to that loamy ridge, which in turn lead right to the Bugmaster's gates. Strangely, all was quiet. The citadel and the route up to it looked completely deserted. The only sign of life was a twitching Second Empire iron spider, which had clearly been recently thrashed to pieces by its modern biological counterparts.

"My Prince, don't you think this is a little suspicious?" Wodston said.

"Yes my man. Is this even the right place?" Nuk replied. Sandor pointed up at the citadel, which had the word 'bugs' painted on the side in blood. For such a short word, it was stunning how poorly it had been spelled.

"There're not even bugs!" Izumi huffed.

"We might have caught him napping. Narko's blessings, perhaps?" Izayah suggested.

"Whatever the case, we need to play it cool, and-" Nuk began, however with a sudden cry, some of his hired goons ran off towards the tower.

"The legendary treasure, it's so close!" one called. It was true that the shek all firmly believed the Bugmaster to possess indescribable riches, and with the coast looking clear, it was hard for a sellsword to resist.

"Fools. Leave them," Gustavsen said.

"No man left behind," Nuk declared, and with this, a great charge upon the citadel began. They reached its foot, and ascended a winding concrete ramp to reach the upper levels. A few skin spiders were milling about towards the top, and really did seem rather taken aback to be suddenly assaulted of a misty morn. To the extent that a wild, flailing mess of skin and spikes can be interpreted to be taken aback, that is.

A handful were cut down, and a half-dozen more met the crew at the entrance to the main dome at the ramp's summit. They had some friends too – small, maroon crawlers that scuttled about between the invaders' legs.

"Blood spiders! Don't let them skewer you!" Izayah called. That didn't sound very nice, and so special care was taken. Soon the ground floor was cleared of hostiles. There was a ramp that lead up to a higher chamber, and there, sitting in a golden bathtub, was a man with rippling muscles, a jawline that could cut steel, and voluminous, slicked back hair.

The crew gathered around him, but he paid them no attention. Everyone wanted to say something about the fact that the bath was filled not with water but with human teeth, but you know in the moment the right reaction to that just didn't spring to mind.

"Err, excuse me, is the Bugmaster in?" Nuk eventually asked him.

"Yep. I don't do flatskins though," the man replied.

"Oh. Well, would you mind if we... killed you?"

"Ah, no, sorry. I've got things to do, ain't I? Can't go dying. Haven' died in centuries, you know?"

"Centuries? You look... Err..."

"Ah, it's the teeth. Teeth is the thing, eh?"

"Oi, where's the treasure?!" one of the sellswords shouted. The Bugmaster stood, teeth chattering down his body. He was wearing something on his lower half, to the relief of some and the disappointment of others. He held out a handful of pearly used-to-be-whites.

"Priceless," he remarked, taking great pleasure in letting the teeth slide between his fingers and fall back into the bath.

"Well... I mean we've got things to do as well so... Can we?" Nuk said.

"Give us a flash."

"Err... oh, sure, check these babies out." Nuk gave the wide man an equally wide grin. After inspecting it, the Bugmaster reached into the bath and pulled out a long, gleaming blade.

"Alright," he said, suddenly slashing out and commencing a fight. The Bugmaster was a rather beefy customer. He was as strong as a shek, but much faster, and if his own claims to longevity were be believed, his rippling abs attracted the glares of curious folk who were a few hundred years too young for him.

Even with these distractions though, the twin blades of Nuk and Izayah were nothing to be trifled with. Everyone else who approached was smashed away, but these two held their ground, parrying and feinting, ducking and sweeping, stabbing and cutting with everything they had. Cheered on by the rest, their energy was unending, while the Bugmaster gradually slowed. Finally the point of Nuk's sword crossed the Bugmaster's chest. As the hulk stumbled, Izayah body-slammed his back and floored the giant, at which point everyone was on him like a swarm of actual bugs, tying him up like actual spiders. It was done. Or was it?

In the madness of the fight, a ring had slipped from the Bugmaster's finger. Afterwards, as everyone looked around the strangely empty citadel, Rick stepped on it.

"Oh. Did I drop this? Looks like it fits in here," he said, slotting the ring into a perfectly sized gap in his arm. It hummed and span around a moment, then a little door slid closed over it. There was a spine-crawling series of rattly shrieks coming from far and wide outside.

"What the fugg was that?" Izumi said.

"Oh, probably nothing," Rick explained. "Ain't gonna be anything to do with the mind control device. I mean, how would I even be able to control them if I wasn't there when we- Oh wait. In fact, you know what, I think I'll roll this back to my earlier assessment: it's probably nothing. Everyone get your weapons ready and stuff, but it's nothing. Yep. Knew I shoulda downloaded the manual for this shid."

It wasn't clear what Rick meant, of course, but we now know that the long and short of it was that it was going to be much harder to get out of the Bugmaster's lair than into it. The real battle was about to begin!

Chapter 20
The First Firstborn

One by one, Gustavsen picked the teeth out of the golden bath and popped them into his mouth.

"It has the crunch," he reported to Rene, who also came over for a snack. Gary dipped his head in and trawled out a great pool of teeth, shattering them with great bites, and sending a wave of wince through the rest of the guild. They were already on edge, having just heard a strange shrieking sound echo across the mountain.

"Nothing to worry about, coming in hot at seven o'clock!" Rick called from the window. Nuk had just finished hoisting the squirming Bugmaster onto his shoulder.

"We've got the goods. Grab a handful of teeth for the road and let's roll!" the Prince ordered. But it was not going to be so easy. Not only was Gary hogging all the teeth to himself, but the ramp exiting the citadel was crawling with a fresh wave of skin spiders.

"Thousand Guardians! Time to surpass even Kral. We'll fight out way out, and claim victory!" Izayah shouted, leading his troops into the mess of sharp, muscly legs and waving stomach-arms. Nuk's goons fought at their side, and a path out of the citadel was opened up. After fighting in and out, many of the combatants were wounded, which slowed their escape dramatically.

"My Prince, since you are still able, you should go on ahead," Wodston said. "We cannot let their injuries put you in danger."

"Who do you think I am, Kral?!" Nuk retorted. "This isn't about me, it's about the tomodachi! No man left behind! Future girl, time to work your magic my friend – who is a girl."

Izumi had prepared splints for just such a case as this, but after patching the army up as best she could, they were still only crawling back east along the ridge. Izayah suggested they solve this the shek way. The Thousand Guardians applied some acceleratory dragging to any who lagged behind, and finally the group got out the secret castle's shadow.

They reached the end of the ridge, but more skin spiders were climbing up the cliffs towards them. Some had thought they were all heading for the citadel to avenge their master, but actually they zeroing in on the guild. More specifically, on one member of the guild. Even more specifically, on one piece of one limb of one member of the guild. Rick, being very kind hearted for a being with no heart, tried to open the little door on his arm behind which he'd stashed the Bugmaster's mysterious ring, but it was locked up tight. Well, he tried, and there was nothing else he could do, least of all tell everyone what was actually happening.

They finally made it off the ridge, but by now the sun had disappeared below the jagged horizon. Nuk did a quick roll call before they went down the hill back to that red river, but one of his hired hands was missing.

"No man left behind!" Nuk demanded.

"Ain't a man, he's a skeleton," Sandor said.

"Damn, you shoulda seen what happened last time humans starting talking shid like that," Rick commented. He and Nuk found the injured skeleton some ways back, and pulled spare parts from Gary's bags to shore up his leaking tubes and sparking fibres.

By now it was pitch black, and the rest of the guild nervously stood around the two surgeons. The sky was completely covered in rain clouds; the only light was from their own lanterns, but the darkness was so maddeningly thick that the orange flickering stretched only a few, meek meters in any direction. The sound of rain on rock was easily mistaken for a horde of skin spider feet padding towards them. It was a tad miserable, suffice to say, and that's just for those who weren't trying their hardest to hold their blood in.

Finally the downed bot fizzled back to life.

"Oh ho ho, c'est la vie- Oh, wait, ah, there it is!" he said, suddenly jumping up to his feet as if there wasn't a big claw-hole going front to back through his chest, and indeed as if there wasn't a pair of pairs of hands fiddling away inside the hole. It was much less exciting than it sounds, I assure you.

They finally got back on track, but then Gustavsen caught a whiff on the wind and they all hit the dirt. A gang of skin spiders came up the track they were about to go down, and started feeling around in the darkness. The crew could hear them scratching at the rocks, and occasionally making a faint raspy sound to one another. Both of the hivers seemed to recoil when they heard it, and whispered to each other about it in private.

"They do feel the connection. They are not ronin," Gustavsen was heard saying, prompting a disappointed sigh from Rene. Whatever that was about, the good news was that the skin spidery sounds faded away for a while, and the gang managed to scramble down the cliffs towards the river. There were a couple of spiders patrolling the bank, but they were quickly dispatched.

"Alright, you've done it before, now do it again," Nuk said. Into the water they went. The previous time there was daylight, and they weren't carrying wounded soldiers on their backs. And last time, there weren't any skin spiders honing in on their secret signal.

"At least they can't swim!" Izumi commented. Red Rick emerged on the opposite bank.

"They can breathe underwater though. Not saying I saw anything down there, but... err..."

Well the truth became extremely clear extremely quickly. The skin spiders were standing on the riverbed, jabbing up with their front legs at the floating chunks of meat.

"Fugging hell! Swim for it!" Nuk shouted, but even those who made the crossing quickly found the east bank swarming with more fleshy pilgrims. Chaos ensued. Those who struggled from the river were immediately beset by spiders, and as they became injured they dropped the already injured folk strewn across their backs. Then they grappled frantically with the skin spiders' rubbery hoof-hands and pointy feet, all, may I remind you, by fading torchlight.

In the fray Nuk was struck across the face and tumbled to the ground, letting the Bugmaster roll away from him. When he regained consciousness, the whole crew was across. Once the Thousand Guardians had splashed their way over, the battle had been won, but now the sum of the guild's injuries had gone beyond what acceleratory dragging could deal with. Or, perhaps acceleratory dragging had gone too far, as Wodston demonstrated in his attempts to get a Thousand Guardian named Kang out of the water. He pulled, and heaved, strained and wheezed, and then just when it looked like he'd done it, he tripped on a fallen spider, span around and launched poor Kang a good ten meters back into the river.

"My man... So packing..." Nuk said, wiping blood from his mouth.

"I'll deal with it," Rick said, stomping back into the river, and catching Kang just as his armour pulled him down to the bottom.

Everyone appeared to be alive, but now most were hobbling along with the heavy weight of injured comrades and buckets of teeth anchoring them all the way. In fact only Nuk wasn't carrying another person on his shoulders. And that was the biggest problem of all.

"Give me back my ring you bandits!" the Bugmaster shouted from behind them. He emerged from the darkness unarmed, but it didn't look like that was going to stop him. "I need that ring to get back at the bastard who did all this!"

"Ring? What?" Nuk said. Before anything else could be said, Red Rick gave the Bugmaster the stick, and he fell down unconscious.

"Ravin' lunatic. The old ring distraction line. Oldest trick in the book. Trust me, I seen that book in the first damn edition. Now, let's get the fugg outta here, shall we?"

They did, with the Bugmaster safely riding on the Nuk train again. The good news was that recovering from the skirmish at the river had taken most of the night – which Nuk had thankfully slept through – and so at last it was possible to see where they were going. They followed the river north, killing the odd lone spider still seeking its calling, and then turned east to at last climb out of the crater.

There was one final hurdle to overcome, and it was the tallest of all. An Iron Spider was pootling about among the rocks as if looking for something, and Nuk's mercenaries decided to try and scrap it to get something valuable out of this whole misadventure. This was a poor decision. Three were killed before the machine gave up the ghost. These non-biological spiders were powerful, which was something the Bugmaster was keenly aware of. As the guild finally reached the top of the crater, the first clue to the Bugmaster's real goal emerged.

"This, here, is the Ashlands," Izumi said to Nuk. She was holding up a piece of paper she'd taken from the citadel. "The records say it's where the Second Empire carried on the longest time. People don't go there, since, you know, the whole 'you never come back' thing. But the giant robot crabs...

That's Second Empire stuff, and if there's anywhere you'd dig up a load of that, it's there. This guy was up to something the Ashlanders didn't like, I bet!"

"What? Killing shek? Wrangling spiders?" Nuk asked.

"Dunno. Maybe. I'll look some stuff up once we're back home."

"Ha, so you're sure you're gonna make it?"

"Of course. I would say thanks to you, but the worst part was when I thought you were dead, so not really."

"You thought I was dead? And you claim to be so clever."

"I see you're still being a piece of shid."

"It's only because I l-like... you..."

"O-oh..."

Well that ended the conversation quickly enough. Rick was right to think they were quite the useless pair, and he was also right to think that it was better if this whole connection between the Bugmaster and the old skeleton empire was forgotten, so he let the conversation go unpunished. He never did work out how to turn off his microphones, you know?

At least the journey down the mountain was a quiet one. No spiders assaulting one's body, and no awkward tsundere stuff assaulting one's processors. Things weren't so quiet once they reached Last Stand. The shek guards flipped between being speechless, and screaming like maniacs. Such was the emotion stirred up by the sight of their arch-enemy in defeat.

At last the crew could take a well-earned break, getting their wounds sorted out properly, catching up on lost sleep, and cashing in on bets made with the humbled warriors in the bar.

"Chubber," one said to Ells. "It seems there was a warrior in you. Flatskins, bugmen, and an old one. I'll never understand your company. But I understand victory. This one is yours."

So saying, he returned to Ells the bucket he had yanked off his head on a previous visit. Ells' wide grin disappeared behind the rum-stained wood.

By early the next morning, the guild was on the road again. All were back on their feet (except for one for Tiffany of the Thousand Guardians, who'd left a foot in the Bugmaster's hideout). Of course, their next destination was Admag, and the barracks of The Stone Golem, where for Izayah the greater battle was yet to come.

"They've defeated the Bugmaster!" a guard at the gates shouted. Within moments, the whole city was jostling for a view of the heroes and their prey. The crowd implored Izayah to take the news to the Queen, and it was imploration much needed.

"Man, I'll go with you. Let's sort this out, huh?" Nuk said to him.

"Prince Tashino. I don't deserve it. But... I can't say I don't want it. Let's go," Izayah replied. He pulled his helmet off, and marched with Nuk to the royal barracks. The rest of the crew were told to wait outside, joining the cheering crowds. The warriors inside were silent, simply staring at the Bugmaster hanging over Nuk's shoulder. Nuk hauled him up the stairs, and found the guy he'd spoke with before: the Queen's hand, Bayan.

"Word was given, and is kept, by all of us," Bayan said. A few guards carried the Bugmaster away to be imprisoned, then brought Nuk a garru pack filled with strings of cats. One hundred thousand in all, the street value of over one hundred kilograms of brown.

"Your company has proven itself. You will be honoured as an ally of the Shek," Bayan went on.

"Good, good. Empire needs allies, I expect," Nuk said.

"Empire? You are from the United Cities?"

"Ha, yeah. Kind of a big deal over there."

"This man shares the same rank as I, master," Izayah said. Bayan looked Izayah in the eyes, for the first time in over a decade. The memory was as clear as day. Bayan wiped his horns with both hands, looked at the sky for a moment, then bowed to Izayah.

"Then we've truly bit upon a strange bone here," he said with a laugh. "What can I say? At least the Holy Nation won't like it one bit. Which means the Queen shall. You should go, both of you. She awaits the hero of the day, and... She wishes she could have seen you sooner, Prince Izayah."

At the other end of the barrack roof, Estata was gazing out over the crowds in the streets. She was looking about with narrowed eyes and crossed arms. The one she was looking for now found her.

"Izayah," she nearly whispered.

"Queen Estata. It is I, Izayah, known as Whitehorn, The Masked Shek, or... Paleskin. I return to-whoa!"

Izayah was cut off by his feet leaving the ground, and the world around him suddenly spinning. It was Estata's doing of course.

"I'm so sorry," she said. "Yet at once I am unforgivable. My boy. Let it all be purged from history, lest I be buried under it!"

"Now, really, it's okay. I've held my own."

"Which only proves my guilt. Oh Izayah. Flying Bull... What good is an excuse?"

"My Queen- My mother, it is alright," Izayah said, but he couldn't keep his composure.

"Izayah's done more than his duty, right?" Nuk said. "I think it's time you ended this whole paleskin thing, whatever it is. He's the Prince here. No ordinary one either, 'cause he's here the hard way, you know? And look, he's got a dog! Look into its eyes and say you aren't gonna let master go home."

Estata took a look at Choco, then a longer look at Izayah, who was held up in front of her face. Then she carried him over to the roof edge, and held him up in the air like a baby.

"Behold!" she called out. "This is Whitehorn Izayah. First child of my house, and Prince of our Kingdom. He is from the mould of Kral, and carries that honour with him always. I was wrong to turn my back on him. Hear this: the curse of paleskin is no more! Narko does not scorn this Prince. He is favoured more than any of us – so his deeds have proven! Let the lies wash away like the great sea, and reveal the nourishing land below, the bedrock of our kingdom, our strength! It shall always be said that the curse was lifted this day, and the stolen Prince returned! Hail, Izayah!"

Amid the cheering, Izayah was returned to his feet, and gave an uncomfortable wave to the people below – his people, it could be said.

"Associate with him!" Gustavsen was calling, standing on Rene's shoulders.

"Bravo, a fine example indeed," Wodston commented.

"Now that's a swell reception for a man of the world," Rick said. "If I should be so lucky... If only we really could forget. Made my own bed, huh..."

The victory / reunion party commenced. Estata received the whole TCM+ guild as honoured guests, showering them with a variety of chewy cactus lumps and rum so volatile that a drop of it seared a patch of paint from Rick's face. What was he doing drinking rum? It might not do anything for a skeleton, but he had an image to cultivate, you must understand.

Joining the party was the Kingdom's existing heir: Princess Seto.

"So you're older than me?" she pouted.

"Yes, but don't you worry, my kin, this is just a visit from me," Izayah said. "Setting things straight, then I'll be back to business."

"What's your business?"

"Oh you know. Corpse carrying. Map reading. Adventuring, really!"

"With those outsiders?"

"Yes, yes. Only recently, but more's the shame. What a time we're having."

"You don't... Is it really better out there?"

"Better! Ha! Depends how you look at it. For you, kin, I would say you had best keep up with your reading and weights. No place for a toddler. But it's something else, this world. The Kingdom's just the start of it. And the shek too. Just the smoke from the mountain. I'll show it all to you one day, I promise."

"So you'll come back?"

"Of course! I didn't grind my teeth down over this whole affair to just make the single visit! Ha! I intend to be a fully fledged Prince of the kingdom, but a Prince in the fashion of one Nuk Tashino. A Prince of the kingdom, and beyond it. After all, that's where we need to be to get this planet back on track!"

"I don't know what you're talking about..."

"You'll find out, once you're old enough to help him," Estata said.

"Mother. I- I think Seto should remain with you."

"Nonsense. My children are going to make the world a better place. I've listened to your Empire friend. Sounds like you're a cut above the usual crew. Except, I don't really understand this brown bread thing."

"Oh, it's- Well, just don't eat it, no matter what anyone says, alright? Royal treasury's empty enough with that bounty, eh? It's not really honest work, but... it's one step at a time, the path to righteousness, you know? Ha ha!"

Overall, we have something resembling a happy ending here. That's one exiled Prince unexiled. Just Nuk to go. Well, Gustavsen is a kind of Prince, or he was, or something, so maybe two to go, if he wants. And... what was Red Rick muttering earlier...?

Well, the more immediate concern was finding a shop that sold spare legs, and going back to the drawing board on Nuk's sidelined mission to get a decent flow of drugs into his dad's house. As it just so happens, their exit from the Shek Kingdom quickly revealed the solutions to both.

Chapter 21
The Height of Greengrocery

On the roof of Admag's royal barracks, the TCM+ guild bid their goodbyes to Queen Estata of the Shek Kingdom. After a decent Bugbusted celebration do, it was time for the busy businessfolk to buzz. But two guests in particular did not join the procession out into the street. They hadn't said a word for the whole thing – or in fact, for as long as Nuk and company had known them.

I speak of Bobbie and Claw, Izayah's guards. They waited on either side of the barrack gate, and as Estata passed them, she stopped also.

"I knew this was your doing," she said with a smile. The pair said nothing. "You are more than any Invincible has ever been. You kept your vow. So, please, be released from it, worthy ones."

"Thank you," Claw said. Wait, 'said'?! What's all this? Well the rest of the gang didn't know about any of this, so really I'm being very cheeky even letting you know this much already. Bobbie and Claw stayed with Izayah, loyal bodyguards as ever, and as a result, Estata felt only a trifling sorrow to wave her son off down the mountain; her 'Invincibles' would not fail to return him in one piece.

Where was the guild going? They were one leg short of a full compliment, and had a recommendation for a discount limb joint just to the north. Hiver territory. The place was one of a number of fragrant, pulpy pods perched alongside the Vain river. Similar villages ran up and down the river, and together formed the Great Western Hive, which was of course orders of magnitude less great ever since Gustavsen had bid them farewell.

The discount leg store had a wide selection of old lengths of metal tube welded onto ancient tin cans, and if that isn't a discount leg, what is? While Tiffany tried to walk with the overly long leg she'd been given, Nuk shopped around for a little of the good stuff. Brown was the wrong colour, as any good hiver would tell you.

"I need green, but like a huge amount," Nuk explained to a trader, "A gargantuan amount, an amount fit for an Emperor, an Emperor who's really in deep with the whole scene, you know?"

"You have described the amount you need too many times. Please rephrase," the hiver said.

"Ugh. I need lots... of... hashish... like more than a bucket."

"Humans cannot consume that quantity of hashish. It has an accumulative toxic effect."

"I know, I know... Look, where do you get hashish from?"

"I grow hemp in my latrine. I mix hashish in my other latrine. It is from the latrines."

"Holy shid... Brown green... by Okran's clippings I didn't need to hear that... Look, you mad bugger, first I'd just like to say that your sales technique needs improvement, and second, I know that this shid grows in stuff other than shid, so where the shid's the shid, shid for brains?!"

"Excuse me," Gustavsen interrupted. The former Prince came over and touched the trader on the shoulder.

"You will perish there. Good," the trader said.

"Prince Tashino. He knows. The Great Swamp. It is the place most similar to his latrine. That is the habitat for the plant. Come."

"Cool. Thanks man," Nuk said, following Gustavsen out. "I mean, are you guys like magic or something."

"From one hiveless one to another, how could you hope to understand?"

"I dunno. Can you erase memories?"

"Sure, do it all the time, forgot it all!" Rick said. He was being massaged by a harem of hivers, his eyes flashing erratically.

"We're going, Coinslot."

"Well if you're going, then I'm coming. Oh I'm too much, I really am."

He really was. Following the hiver intel, they marched back to Admag then to Squin, and finally entered one of the many canyons of the Border Zone. There was a certain canyon which every shek knew one should never follow, for it led to somewhere quite foul.

"There is it. The Swamp," Izayah reported. They were walking along a track in that very forbidden canyon. Ahead there was a sudden onset of fog, and strange shadowy tendrils stuck up from the ground, arching this way and that. The ground was mushy and wet, like at good old Manksand, but this was more like mank-mud.

"Is this like the other place, where the water's made of fire and stuff?" Nuk asked Rick.

"As if I would know. As if I had anything to do with it," was the reply. Nuk didn't feel like another classic Red Rick argument, so he just took his chances. As his sandals splatted down into the moistening mud, there was only the pleasant oozing of lively swamp juice between his toes. Great!

"What's the deal here anyway? Doesn't seem that bad to me," he said.

"This is the edge of the Old Lands," Izayah said. He made it sound like that was the definitive answer, but it didn't mean much to the non-shek.

"There are people living here right? Outcasts. Criminals too edgy for the outlands," Izumi said.

"I too have heard tales of the Swamps," Wodston said. "Dangerous beasts, murderous gangs, labyrinthine trails scattered with quickmud, sinkholes and... my Prince?"

Nuk had already strode on ahead.

"The perfect place to hide your green from the samurai!" he proclaimed. He was absolutely right, by the way, as even a stopped clock gets a few calls close to the mark now and again. There were trails through the thick, smelly undergrowth that the crew could follow deeper into the moist maze. Tall trees grew up from the water-logged earth and covered the sky with a misty canopy. Deep pools of water were dotted all about, with eerie, spiky shapes stalking below the surface. It was more lively than the deserts, one supposes, but far less inviting for it. No crabs though, so that's something.

After a sticky march through two hours of continuous drizzle and fear, the crew crossed a dry hill, then descended into a small, ring-fenced village. There really were people living in this dingy swamp, and oh how they were living.

"Drugs and fish! Get your drugs and fish!" a seller called to the group from their little market shack.

"Fugg, you serious?!" Nuk said, rushing over.

"No laughing matter, drugs and fish. Aye you can have a little fun with one, and a lot of fun with the other, but I'm a professional I'll have you know.

Now then, I will stuff these three fish with grass and put them down your trousers for ya, if you let me have a little peek while I'm there."

"Err... You don't take money around here?"

"Oh, sorry sir, you from the skylands are you? Ah, money it is then sir, didn't realise you had such sophisticated tastes sir, I love your hair sir, fish full of grass sir? It'd be cheap at half the price I tell yer, and I haven't even thought of the price yet, so you know I'm being honest sir!"

Nuk was sold, and very quickly the vendor was sold out. It wasn't enough for his imperial needs, but it was served creatively, and that's the sign of a true greengrocer.

"There's another one, another one!" Nuk excitedly reported to the guild. Yes, he had been tipped off that just down the road was another well stocked village, and by road I mean a three-inch width of mud in between lakes of man-eating critters, and by village, I mean a series of large buckets filled with humans suffering from a certain accumulative toxic effect.

It was a wonderful day out down the shops all in all, however some local ruffians seemed set on spoiling it. Beside a mercifully wider part of the road, a gang of soaked swordsmen burst from a nearby pool.

"Come to the wrong swamp, cityslicker!" one cried out.

"Is there another swamp you'd recommend?" Nuk replied.

"Err... Yeah there's a spot over on t'other side of- Oh wait. They always gets me with the words they do! Die and gimmie yer money, ya tourist!"

"I'm a highly respected businessman," Nuk said, killing his conversation partner with a clean katana swipe. The attacker's mates didn't do much better. Clearly people came by often enough for there to be a living to be made as a highwayman. Soon they found out why: they went from one kind of tourist trap to another, as they arrived in the beautiful resort of Mudtown.

"I can hear the jangle!" a hiver shouted as they entered the glamorous ring of huts and scrap. "Jangle must gamble! Jangle must gamble!"

"Jangle must gamble!" Nuk echoed, going over to the hiver's big tin casino, sat on stilts above a stagnant, grey pond.

"You know how to play?" the dealer said at the main table. He was a dealer of one thing or another anyway.

"Sure. Would you rather have no legs but trees for arms, or no arms but trees for legs?" Nuk said.

"Nonsense. Either option is ideal. Speak not. Gamble your jangle at once," the dealer demanded. He was pointing at a set of beetles in a box beside him. "Will there be roll, or will there be clack?!"

"Let's roll with it."

"What?"

"You're so uncool. Roll, hit me with a roll!"

"HE BETS FOR ROLL!" the dealer shouted. The other patrons of the den, who were mostly hivers also, all conferred privately on this fateful decision. "Now, let the chance dance begin."

He pointed again at the beetles. The beetles seemed to understand their job, and began walking around in a circle, one behind the other. Then the dealer reached under the table and produced a cut out piece of an ancient picture book. He placed it in the middle of the bug circle, and declared,

"Waifu roll, trash clack, bug truth, snnnaaaaapp!"

The beetles turned to look at the bucksome, humanoid feline pictured on the cut-out, and then began to make ticking sounds and walk backwards in a shakey, overdone fashion.

"Ney ney, it is traassssshhhh! Clack clack clack!" the dealer announced, sweeping coins from Nuk's hand with well practised dexterity.

"Fugg, I... Did I lose?" Nuk said. Rick appeared beside him.

"Lemmie try something," he said. "I'll put two stacks on a roll right now!" The dealer reset the table and produced the next sample picture. It looked a bit like a crab, only with long, flowing hair, complete with plaits and a bow.

The beetles carefully scrutinised the piece. Then, as Rick was seen scratching his arm, the beetles jumped onto their backs and rolled from side to side, waving a leg in the air.

"Rolling whip! This is the ship! The truth is revealed, and the gentleman wins!" the dealer said. How about that? Rick won enough to overturn Nuk's loss, with enough change left over to buy Gustavsen a present – one of the hivers there was a sword for hire. Back in town there were fresh market stalls and shop-like sheds to visit, and here, the motherload to load Nuk's father was found.

"Mate, you got any illegal drugs?" Nuk asked a shopkeeper.

"Is there any other kind?" the man replied, opening a chest that was packed with neat cuboids of deep, mottled green.

"Narko's tapeworms... I need this, but like, over and over again. Where are you getting it from?"

"Ahhh I can't go telling ya that can I? But don't you worry my munchie little man, I can supply you with enough stuff to, say, picking a purely hypothetical example, get a very rich and powerful man to give you all his property in a binding contract before all the lords and ladies of a hypothetical polity or state, my man."

"Whoa... that's... Roughly... Very approximately..."

"I know exactly what you mean my man. See that tree back there? Hollow on the inside it is. And its packed full. We'll be on the bloody fifth empire by the time I run outta stock, won't we?"

The promised land had been found. Nuk bought some hundred kilograms of the good stuff – he would have got more, but poor Gary had to carry all this, along with an indescribable assembly of other junk. Then something really strange happened. Nuk unwrapped himself from his ninja cosplay outfit.

"Huh, he stopped being invisible all of a sudden!" Izayah commented.

"Yes, my man, I am no longer going to hide anything. I am a drug dealer, and I am proud of it!" Nuk announced. "I bring happiness, addiction, and the spirit of justice! Low prices for the low, high prices for the high, and I assure you, the high will pay anything! The Nuk Tashino International Green Team Power Pipeline is founded!"

Cheers all round, I expect. Even Izumi was somewhat impressed, although I think that might have been because under all those raggedy sheets he'd been wearing, he was actually not so hard on the eyes. Could she convince him to remain out of costume for long? Best take a picture while it lasts, eh?

Anyway, the word in the markets was that this tourist trap wasn't even the place where serious businessmen did their serious business, for the serious stuff was actually in the next town over, the capital of the swamp, known as Shark. As a result, there was no luxury hotel on the Mudtown strip for the guild that evening, and they all plodded down the so-called path to this so-called capital.

Shark was a real swamper's town. By that I mean people were fighting in the mud pretty much nonstop over this, that, and the other, and the fish and drug traders shouted out over the din of battle to hawk their wares.

"Worried about that lost leg?" one called. "Wad o' green on a stick and a slippery fish, bargain at five hundred cats a go, cures death, nine out of ten sciencers agree, and last one's always a fugging straight edge nark anyway!"

Once Nuk was done buying, he asked about wholesale retailers and franchising rights, and was pointed to talk to the leader of the best drug smugglers this side of the tree-tree: the Hounds. Her name was Big Grim, and her residence was a large iron disk on stilts at the south end of town. Proceeding through the constant brawls to reach it, Nuk found it filled with burly, heavily armed types, eager to inquire after what exactly Nuk was looking at, and show further interest in any problems he might have, going so far as to kindly refer to him by the title 'wise guy'. Lovely chaps.

From among them, Big Grim emerged.

"Another fish outta water. Tourist, the store's across the jetty," she said.

"I been already, look," Nuk said, showing off his 'I love drugs' souvenir pin-badge.

"You are quite the chump. Now fugg off," Grim demanded, but Nuk was undeterred. He'd of course faced this kind of customer service before.

"Actually, Mrs. Big, I'm looking to purchase a few hundred keys of hashish."

"Oh? Well how am I meant to know you're not some UC nark?"

"Upper class?"

"United Cities!"

"Oh... Oh! That's what that stands for. Whoa, that explains some stuff..."

"So you're an idiot. Just the way I like 'em. Look, kid, if you wanna deal with the big girls you gotta pass the test." Grim gave Nuk a bundle of the good stuff. "Easy job, then we'll make a deal. You sell that in the UC, come back, and if you haven't narked out... or been fugging enslaved, then yeah, 'll listen."

"And what'll it cost to get you to tell me how to actually make this stuff?"

"For you? All the money in the world."

"Do you accept payment in human teeth?"

"What the fugg?"

"Sorry, having trouble with the currency exchange stuff."

Indeed the Bugmaster's priceless Teeth of Youth were barely being accepted as legal tender anywhere, but this was still a promising lead. With the help of the world's leading mono-culture gardening enthusiasts, maybe Nuk really could bring about his green revolution. And like any good movement, it was to begin with a crime. When he told the others of the plan, they were all quite relieved.

"Then I shall plot a course back to the Great Desert. It would be good to return home," Wodston said.

"Yeah, could pick up my stuff from Heft maybe?" Izumi said.

"Hmpf, and off a few manhunters for good measure." Izayah added. But Nuk shook his head.

"Guys, we don't need to go that far. We can just go to the *other* empire!"

"There's another one?" Ells asked.

"Yeah, yeah, didn't you know? Down the south coast."

"I heard they all died long ago," Elaina said.

"No way, my auntie went down there. It's a thing," Nuk assured them.

"He's right. I passed through it just a few years ago," Izayah said. "It was the most awful land, a land of death. And that's saying something, eh? But I saw samurai and Empire flags here and there."

"I'm telling you, it's all good," Nuk said. "I mean, why not have a little something on the other side of the world for a rainy day?"

"Rainy day? Forget that – do you even know what 'united' means?" Izumi asked.

"Sure. Means they hate other people a little bit more than they hate each other."

"Ha, then there is hope for a human-shek alliance yet!" Izayah remarked.

So yes, the group set off, even though it was still dark, heading south towards to this rumoured other United Cities Empire. Fortunately the southern side of the swamp was a little more civilised than the north – the gangs kept the trails in better condition, probably to maintain good smuggling routes into this very same southern empire. The geography was more favourable too; while in the north the swamp was bordered with thick undergrowth and steep cliffs, the southern edge petered out gradually into a friendlier course of wetlands and freshwater lakes. Small plants and heathers flourished, growing around piles of old bones and poisonous fungi. The dominant species here was something rather special.

"Thousand Guardians, assemble!" Izayah called when he spotted it. Everyone rushed up to him, weapons drawn. Ahead of them was a convoy o plodding swamp turtles. "Thousand Guardians, by the left, appreciate the majesty of nature!"

The squad followed their orders. The turtles, by the way, were about twenty feet tall, standing on four huge legs, with perhaps ten feet of multi-coloured shell on top. They paid the guild no heed as they wandered by.

"Well that's new," Rick said.

"Did you see them before, Izayah?" Izumi asked.

"Indeed, however- Oh, it's too- The swamp ninja operate here, hunting the poor creatures. Slavers too, if there's no one to pick up on their rounds. I wonder how long it will be until they are all gone?"

"Fugging hell," Nuk muttered. "People just can't leave shid alone!"

"They gotta eat," Sandor said.

"Then let them eat chocobread!" Nuk declared. They carried on a little ways, and sure enough, just behind the turtle flock there was a band of ninjas stalking them, clad in green with their faces masked.

"Fugging- Eat chocobread!" Nuk shouted at them. This was interpreted as some new-fangled big city insult, and a fight broke out. The ninja clearly did not have the element of surprise, and it ended poorly for them. Perhaps a turtle was saved through such careless scuffling?

Anyway, they happened upon the main road into the southern empire, and following it really did lead them to something looking a lot like the United Cities. A small fortress was built beside a river in a little gully, and inside was the city of Clownsteady. What this name could possibly mean remained a mystery, for upon entering, there was no evidence of clown-tolerance. Quite the opposite: the local samurai were going house to house rounding people up and throwing them in jail.

Nuk asked a guard at the gate what was going on.

"Oh don't worry sir. There was a rumour that those swamp rats have been smuggling illegal narcotics into the city. Won't be having any of that here."

"Not even, like, a little bit..."

"Zero strikes rule is in effect here sir. Being a drug dealer's illegal, whether you dealt any drugs or not!"

So, this didn't seem like the best place to fulfil Nuk's little side-quest. Everyone resolved that they really should just go home, and soon they would. But not only would Nuk come up with a genius way to win the allegiance of the Hounds without getting his zeroth strike, but he would stumble across the first whispers of the ultimate secrets: the forbidden lore, of 'grow your own'! As such, getting home would turn into an adventure in itself.

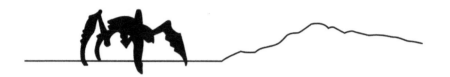

Chapter 22
Quest By Chest

Nuk was in a pickle. He'd been asked to sell some drugs as an initiation ritual into a criminal syndicate, but the local marketplaces were under martial law. He'd never get away with it, and so he'd never get into the gang, and so he'd never get to grips with how hashish was actually produced and distributed. Then, almost waking from the dream, he was dragged back in by a stroke of genius.

"Guys, guys, guys, watch this," he said to the crew. He held a block of green in one hand, and a string of cats in the other. With the skill of a being with full control over at least two limbs, he swapped the items from left to right, via the armpit. The sale was complete. It was an act of fraud that mixed legal and illegal as smoothly as a hiver stirs his latrine, then sells the stirring stick as a wooden leg to a passing guild – to use a randomly generated simile.

"Okay, but you said we could go home," Izumi complained.

"I know, I'll go make good with drugs mummy in the swamp, and catch up with you. I'll be back before Charlie even realises what I did with the switcheroo back there."

While the gang prepared to stay the night in Clownsteady and then head home, Nuk raced back north to the pitch darkness of the swamp. He felt extremely confident that he'd be able to find his way. I mean, you just follow the little trail...

And then he found himself wading waist deep through stagnant water. And then... Well it's hard to say just how lost Nuk actually, got, for he himself never truly understood the depths of it. Suffice to say, at one point he found himself falling into a series of underground smuggler's tunnels, and began randomly selecting which direction to take at each fork.

"He bought it off himself!" Ells realised back in Clownsteady, with no sign of his master's return. Nuk found a bit of tunnel that sloped upwards, and used it to return to the surface. When he emerged, he was inside a building made of concrete and filled with industrial machinery. Bright ceiling lights flickered on as he entered, and it didn't smell of rotting flesh as much as your average swampland rainshelter. This was an old Second Empire lab, and as Nuk rummaged around a little, he uncovered assorted documents in vacuum sealed boxes.

"While there are certainly more books, mangas, digital videos, images, and other computerised cultural contraband, the discourse of modern academia is almost entirely free of the Earth-clan scourge," he read on one prominent sheet. He gathered up similar reports, studies and verbose fragments of old science, for a certain special someone would probably be very impressed with this little stroke of luck.

Most lucky of all was a map of the local area, as of about two thousand years prior. It showed the little rocky hills that Shark was nestled in, albeit labelled as "Pillowdown Memorial Cemetery". Thus Nuk stumbled into the swamper capital by morning's light. The orange dawn sun washed the darkness away, and cast long dancing shadows from the hordes of drunk, high locals, punching wildly at each other and / or some unwelcome figments of their imagination.

"Mummy, I'm home!" Nuk declared in the Hounds HQ. A load of the gangsters were woken up by this announcement, and weren't entirely happy with it, plus the idea of actually speaking to a perky cringelord that early in the morning wasn't that appealing. After much waiting, Big Grim finally came out and snatched up the strings of cats from Nuk's outstretched hands.

"Well, looks like you passed the test. Guess you're in the gang..." Grim said, but all the other gangsters were shaking their heads and swiping across their necks. "But, you should probably fugg off, alright? Come back tonight or something."

"No time, got these reports on, like... 'The Historical Consensus on Parasitic Degeneracy in Humans'. I dunno, stuff. Need to go give it to my friend who is a girl. So can you just tell me how to make green, and I'll go take care of it, and cut you in, and stuff."

"Cut me in? Who do you think you are?"

"Me? I'm the daddy," Nuk said with a wink. He was forced to keep winking all the way out of town – an effect of the nerve damage Grim's forehead had dealt to his face. In essence, this all turned out to be a less fruitful relationship than it could have been, but that was an issue to deal with once the hundred keys loaded up on Gary were delivered. Nuk ran off to meet with the guild on the road back east.

The guild had set off that morning, and were currently negotiating with the local ninja and blood spiders about the relevant toll category for their party. You see the ninja insisted they should both be killed and be stripped of their possessions, while the blood spiders found the taking of possessions to be uncalled for, but did stipulate their rights to consume the bodies of the party for sustenance. It all got a bit messy. Everyone ended up brawling for hours, with only Ells missing out on it, for he was embroiled in an argument with a nearby rock over who had walked into whom.

Nuk finally met the party on a small hill, up which the guild hobbled and trudged.

"Do you remember when you were history girl?" Nuk asked Izumi.

"Yeah, heard of her. Dunno what she was thinking," Izumi said.

"She's gonna be thinking: 'oh wow, thanks Nuk, what a hero'! Check this shid out."

Nuk presented Izumi with a partially hydrated stack of papers.

"What is all this?" she sighed, flicking through it. "'The Rise and Fall of the First... Empire'... Narko's spiny thighs! This is..."

"It's forbidden! Where'd you get that?!" Rick shouted, trying to get at the papers, but Izumi had them down her shirt in a flash, one of the few places Rick would not follow.

"It's history, and I'm keeping it," she stated. "Thanks, Nuk that's amazing! Where did you get this?"

"You know, just pulled a few strings, a few connections... Influential man I am. And you always say I'm useless..."

"So basically, you're not going to tell me where you got these?"

"And breach the confidence of my elite network of elite elites?"

"Cool. So yeah, back to being useless already. Come on, we've gotta get this stuff somewhere safe."

The guild set off again, with Rick hovering around Izumi's payload and suggesting everyone take their clothes off for all manner of reasons, none of which worked – on Izumi, at least. They walked east, into the lovely part of the Empire known as the Bonefields.

It was a simple name for a rather storied land. The landscape was littered with bones big and small. The sand was crunchy underfoot from all the boney bits within, and the horizon was striped with the silhouettes of enormous ribcages. The lonely wastes were making a very deliberate point of being devoid of life, it seemed. Alongside the bones were large stretches of old metal, and half-buried ships from the First Empire.

"The theory is that there used to be a roof that extended over the sea," Izumi explained. "Since there's so much, you know, bone, here, they must have been keeping animals in this particular area for some reason."

"Only 'cause they kept dying when we let them out!" Rick complained. "Yep, that was my favourite song lyrics from the time," he added. "Ah yeah, 'only cause they kept dying when we let them out, yeah baby it's what I shout, 'cause I love you soooooo'. Yep. Good song. Oh, what were you guys talking about? Sorry, had my microphones off, ya know?"

He got out of that one, and the crew got temporarily out the Bonefields for the night. This whole place was part of the United Cities Empire, and as such there was a large, walled city on a hill right in the middle of all the mess. It was called Catun, and was little more than a caravan stop for traders, with no farms or businesses of its own, yet quite the night was had there.

First, the mundane part of the tale: there was a trio of hiveless hivers, 'ronin' as folk called them, who were very interested in not being stuck mucking garrus amid the remnants of their old planet. When they smelled... sensed... in some way detected Gustavsen's big-prince-energy, they signed up for mercenary duty there and then. Each was given a free human tooth to chew on as a welcome gift, and they fell into line behind their new master.

Then, the weird stuff started happening. Ells was enjoying a private drink in his bucket, but had a strange feeling in his legs. It felt like he couldn't feel the ground beneath his feet anymore.

"It's the flying rum!" his echoing voice announced, and plenty more was consumed. But alas, t'was not the rum, but the ravages of time causing the disturbance. Said ravages went not to your head, but to your legs. I you're a shek, that is.

"What the fugg? Charlie's turned into an egg!" Nuk exclaimed when he saw the damage. Ells had stood from the table, and now managed to be even shorter than tiddly Izumi, albeit with his rotundity still intact. He had turned into an egg – that really was the easiest way to describe it.

"Ha, I lost some weight I did!" Ells proudly claimed.

"Is that even... Big Sister!" Nuk called. Elaina took at a look at the curious case.

"I think he's... really old..." was her diagnosis.

"I'm the oldest!" Ells claimed further.

"You're the biggest, smallest kin I've ever smelled," Elaina told him, with a pat on the head.

"So what, this is just what happens?" Nuk asked.

"Not normally. But, normally a shek would be dead by this this point, so... I think this might be perfectly ordinary."

"That's perfectly ordinary?"

"Yes."

"He was twice as tall ten minutes ago!"

"Shek grow quickly. Shrink quickly too," Elaina shrugged.

"Cool, cool. Come on Charlie, why don't I buy the biggest, smallest shek in the world a steak so you shrink down big and strong?"

Once Nuk and his big smelly egg finished diner, the Prince noticed a trio sitting across the bar. Two women in a partial state of dress were drinking with a well-trimmed guy, sporting deep black skin, bright silver hair, and an immaculate short-sleeved leather-jacket over clean white turtleneck get-up. Nuk, a noble of the empire, knew a thing or two about fashion. For example, he also wore a short-sleeved leather jacket, and the matter of who wore it better was about to be decided.

"Hey, punk, nice try," Nuk said, sitting down at the offender's table.

"At least I tried," the guy said, running his fingers over his feather-cut hair. This wasn't the man's first fashion-battle, it seemed. Nuk moved his hand into his ragged mop, but it was so twisted and knotted that his fingers got jammed in. Removing them took so long that the other three were done laughing by the end of it.

"Look, jacket-boy, I'm the real deal!" Nuk insisted. "I wear this jacket while I'm out there walking the wastes, killing weird teeth-dudes, making cats by the stack, and never looking back! I'm legit! You, man, are what we in the, ahem, imperial nobility, call a poser."

"I don't need this from you, dreg. You ain't ever done shid," the guy complained.

"Yeah? Don't have to pay girls to hang out with me. Well, technically I do... Ah..."

"Speaking of that, you're due, buddy," one of the girls said to the poser. The poser's hair started to became greased with sweat.

"I don't.... that's not. Look, dreg, you got money?"

"Yeah, and a load of old teeth," Nuk said.

"If you wanna prove yourself, when why don't we play for it? The first thing."

"Sure. I bet everything I have against everything you have that I'm just... generally... better at stuff than you. And if you lose, you can never wear a leather jacket again."

"Deal! You ever played Wacky Backgammon before?"

"Who do you think I am?! Of course I've played Wacky Backgammon before!"

Nuk had never played Wacky Backgammon before. However, he was very drunk. Now it would take several volumes to explain the rules of Wacky Backgammon, and so the details of this epic match would be entirely lost on you, I'm afraid. All I can relay here is that being drunk gives one a distinct advantage in this curious game, as so by the end of it, the poser had lost everything, and of Nuk, the two girls had *seen* everything. That's really all I can tell you.

In the winnings came the poser's contracts with the girls, who turned out to be strangely dressed bodyguards, which explained their thick arms and bruised knuckles rather nicely too. They were Foren and Shamika, and now they were Nuk's (in so far as now Nuk had to pay them). Luckily, Nuk quickly thought for a use for the buxom babes.

Izumi came into the bar, somewhat intoxicated already from the rest of the guild's campfire antics outside. She was looking for Nuk of course, and of course she found him. He was walking right towards her, with nearly-topless Foren and Shamika on both sides. You can surely understand that this stirred Izumi up quite a bit, but Nuk went on with the introductions anyway.

"Future girl! These are my newest employees! They're like you!" he said. Great start.

"What... Nuk you... Why the fugg are you... Oh do what you want," Izumi said. She turned to leave, but Nuk had a perfectly good excuse.

"No, they're for you!"

"For me?! What did Rick- I don't- Nuk you really...?"

"I thought you'd feel safer with them."

"Safer?!"

"You know, like as guards. Since I keep getting you into trouble, and stuff. You can have these two as your guards, and you won't have to deal with any gorilloshid you'd get from like... you know... guys... and they don't smell that much, and they aren't popping human teeth and whispering with mind magic, and stuff. So... it's a present! I'm paying!"

Perhaps Nuk really was being a nice guy here, but Izumi was so off-balance the other way that she didn't fully appreciate it, suffice to say.

"We'll keep you safe. Best in the bizz," Foren said. "And even if this chump's paying us, don't think twice about asking us to take him out, ya know?"

"Yeah, say that again," Shamika added. "Ha, at least it's finally a woman client. Got any thoughts on uniforms, miss?"

"Sure, sure, I will do, I... err..."

"Wait... Are you...?" Shamika said, looking between Izumi and Nuk. Izumi ran off before further questions were raised.

"Go on then, go guard her," Nuk said to the pair.

"Sure, first things first," Foren said, before promptly kicking Nuk in such a way that he spent the night on the floor of the bar. Whether this new development would help with the whole... 'situation', if that's the right term for it, was yet to be seen.

In the morning, in varying states of sobriety and health, the guild set out north. They followed the caravan routes into the part of the Bonefields where the balance of bone and field started to favour the latter – the edge of the southern United Cities Empire. There they stopped in a slow town called Mourn, formerly of the empire but now left to squatters. It was surrounded by First and Second Empire ruins, plus its own share of bones, giving it a nice deathly atmosphere with a less oppressive feel than Catun. Good place to grab a snack and watch Beak Things kill passers by. In a store there Nuk bought a map of the area, which Izumi examined closely.

"There, it's here, I knew it!" she eventually said.

"Anything good?" Nuk asked.

"The Tech Scribes. Like Tech Hunters, but without the hunting. They're the world experts on decoding ancient data. Perfect place for... you know."

She was nodding down towards her chest. It wasn't the clearest way of getting it across, but she was of course talking about the Second Empire

The Fire Margin

goodies stowed within. It took Nuk a while to realise this, but analysing the exact contours of the communication was time well spent at least.

He saw something else of interest in town also. While everyone wandered around the depressing shops, he noticed that none of the locals were going anywhere near a big Second-Empire-style hall that overlooked the whole area. Naturally, he was up there in a flash. For some strange reason, the gate to get in was locked tight, chained to the ground and gateway, and smeared with messages to the effect that one should not traverse it. Naturally, the locks were broken with a smash.

Inside there was loads of old furniture and military gear, but it was strewn about the place and battered beyond use. Nothing good to steal at all, but Nuk thought he might as well check upstairs. Peering over the edge of the ramp that wound up the outside of the building, he saw that the top floor had a resident. A very peculiar resident. The sort of huge, hairy, feral, beast of a resident that might just object to intrusion. As such, Nuk decided to casually return to town. There, asked in the bar if there was anything unusual about the old tower.

"You haven't heard?" the barwoman said. "That's the lair of the Great White Gorillo. Beast of beasts. Killed Okran-knows how many just getting it in there. The things we did to keep that gate locked up shut. Still tries to get out every night. I hate the sound of it. But that's Mourn isn't it? On the edge of death, right beside all our fellows in bones across the dunes."

Nuk nodded along to this fascinating local lore, but then very, very quickly gathered up the party and set off for the nearby Tech Scribe enclave. Izumi was impressed by his enthusiasm for academia, and indeed nobody was mauled by a giant gorilla, so scholarly pursuits were already paying off. Not for Mourn of course, but they wouldn't be facing a problem they hadn't faced before.

After fending off a bandit attack on the road, the guild arrived at this Tech Scribe enclave by nightfall. Thankfully it was outside of the Bonefields, on a hill overlooking a damp vale dotted with lakes, or perhaps more likely, the remains of the sea that used to cover the bone-dry expanse beside it. Similar to Black Scratch, it was a highly fortified outpost of military academics, with shops selling niche goods like books and skeleton parts.

"Leg!" Gustavsen called, brandishing said leg over his head. Yes, he'd finally picked up a suitable limb replacement for his yeoman Ignacio back on the farm, if you were still following that little drama.

Now the question was: would this place allow Izumi get those important matters off her chest? And did they know anything about how to grow hashish outside of a river-side latrine? The answer was yes, with an exciting variety of catches!

Chapter 23
The Heroes Back Home

"Vell, vell, vell, this is quite ze little treasure trove," the skeleton said.

"What, sorry, who are you?" Izumi asked, quickly hiding her stack of papers from the approaching metal claws.

"Don't worry about him, he's the man you need," a local techie said. "He's the best data storage and translation boff in the world. We had to edit his boards a bit though, to stop him deleting everything like other skeletons. Made him a little off. Side effect."

"Yes, and yet again ve see zat no matter vat complaints you stupid humans have about us, it vas you who made us zis vay!" the skeleton said. His name was Enrico, and he sat in the Tech Scribe bar dressed in the richly coloured robes of an Imperial noble, with the patterns of the Imperial House no less, although something tells me he wasn't actually related to Nuk.

"Hey, hey, what's going on in there!" Rick shouted from outside.

"Keep him out, he's trying to cover something up!" Izumi shouted. The Tech Scribes buzzed Rick with a little device, and with routine ease dragged his collapsing body off to the maintenance shed.

"They ain't gonna let you live if they find out. Don't you tell 'em!" he was shouting. That aside, Izumi gave Enrico the papers, and within minute he had them scanned into his memory.

"Zere is a lot of new information here. Zees are good documents. *Seh gut.* You are Izumi of Brink aren't you?"

"Yes, have you read my work?" Izumi asked, charmed.

"I have, but I have read all work, so zat is not remarkable."

"Have you read 'Yasuke and Rock-chan's Bumpy Ride'?" Nuk asked. He had to shout a little as the Techies weren't letting him past the doorway, although only because you weren't allowed to wear hats in the dining hall and Nuk refused to part with his new black, wide-brimmed boonie. Matched his jacket, and his new dark sunglasses.

"If you sink I haven't read Yasuke and Rock-chan's Bumpy Ride' zen clearly you have no idea vot academia even is!" Enrico said, waving for Nuk to leave. "Zease literati, sink zat veading one light novel with half-hearted moe themes makes zem some kind of intellectual!"

"If it's any consolation, I hate him too," Izumi said.

"Finally, somevon clever. And yes, your verk here is most fascinating. Vee are missing most of ze pages of zis history of ze First Empire. Zat, my girl, vould make your caveer! Vill zer be more?"

"Maybe. We sometimes go to unusual places in search of... err... Well, you're an educated fellow, I'll be honest: we look for drugs, as part of a conspiracy to usurp power in the United Cities Empire, mainly because they were very, very bad to our friend's old dog."

"Ah yes, very good, you have reached zat stage already," Enrico nodded. Just how did he get that House Tashino robe anyway? "Vell for drugs you need to go down to ze lagoon. Tell zem zat Enreicho sent you. Zey are academics, so zey always have a little... inspiration."

"Is that... we didn't have that in Black Scratch."

"Zat is because Black Scratch is a level three nark zone!" Enrico insisted. He ranted about this further for some time, and then finally allowed Izumi to leave. She was paid for her services in transcribed books; excellent additions to her collection in Manksand, if they ever got home. And Nuk got this intel that the grass was greener on the other side of the lagoon down the hill. Soon, he was swimming across this lagoon towards a raised metal platform on the water's edge. Standing on huge concrete legs, this Second Empire construction was host to 'Flats Lagoon', a little refuge for Tech Hunters, tightly packed with shops, accommodation, and entertainment. But once the guild arrived, the entertainment fell a little flat.

"You've run out?!" Nuk scoffed.

"Sorry sir. You know how the pen-fiddlers up there are," the barman shrugged.

"Ugh, I thought you'd be able to supply me. This place is way easier to get to than the swamp," Nuk said.

"You tried to get there did you?"

"Yeah, and succeeded. On the way back with a shipment, but I need a lot more. And really I need to way to grow... Err..." Nuk stopped speaking when he noticed the whole bar had gone silent, and were all staring at him.

"You said... A ship... ship... shipment?" the barman muttered.

"Yeah. I got a hundred keys-" Nuk began, but he was at once surrounded by a clamouring crowd. They were offering him money, clothes, jewels, weapons, and certain luxurious services – anything for a handful of the good stuff – by which I mean green – by which I mean hashish.

"It's not for sale, I need more of it, not less!" Nuk called above the noise.

"I'll tell you the secret! The secret place! The secret place!" the barman shouted, and others chimed in the same effect.

"So if I sell you some stuff, you'll tell me... 'the secret'?" Nuk asked. He didn't ask what the secret pertained to, for that would ruin the excitement.

Outside, Izumi had bought herself and her two wingwomen some stylish black-and-white adventuring suits with plate armour, making them look like proper Tech Hunters. And she was a proper Tech Hunter now, with her notes on the First Empire's relations with that mysterious place called 'Earth' currently being pored over and analysed by the scribes.

"Finally, let's go home," Wodston said once it was time to go, but Nuk had that worrying smile on his face.

"Nope. First, we're going to the secret place," he said.

"Secret place, my Prince?"

"Don't worry, my man. It's worth it. It's to do with drugs."

"It seems that everything we do is to do with drugs, my prince."

"That's literally life, my man, doesn't really come any different. And, while I'm here..."

Nuk bought another garru from a gang of nomads hanging around the ramp of the platform. She, Garrette, would take the load off Gary's shoulders, and increase the smuggling capacity of the group dramatically. Such things were needed, because of... the secret. Let's not ruin the fun for you quite yet. Let's only say that accessing the secret required the guild to move east, through the lowland lagoons, and eventually up into the mountains at the other end of the vale. And quite the mountains they were – one of them was a rather not-dormant volcano, and so fog and ash kept visibility to a minimum. Going there at night didn't help either, but the nature of this secret required their presence to remain a secret too.

It was no secret to the landbats though. Yes, the carnivorous, highly territorial landbats, which were bats on land in as far as seahorses are horses in the sea. They were snarling, long-noised, web-armed, rat-pigs, with fangs and a temper. And this was their mountain. Coughing black ash, the guild had to fend off raids from these beasts as they carried on east, but finally things quietened down. Then, there were some oddly linear and symmetrical shadows ahead of them.

"The secret! They weren't even lying!" Nuk said. He took the guild between two rows of houses, numbering six to eight in all, depending on how you count the ones that were practically just piles of rubble. Nuk saw to the lock on one of the doors, and crept inside. There, the promise of the Flats Lagoon addicts was kept.

"Green growing in brown. The colours have no clear priority," was Gustavsen's comment. He was looking at long beds of compost, from which neat hemp plants were sprouting. Pipes across the ceiling supplied sprinklers, and stinky composting devices against the back wall were filled with fresh growing medium.

"Make your own mank!" Nuk exclaimed. "They brew up some slop, grow hemp in said slop even without manksand, and then..." He looked around further. "Dammit, how do they make the green?"

There was brief diversion, as it turned out the landbats had followed them into the secret drugs farm. While the crew battled away outside, Nuk was rummaging through the various machines and boxes in each building. Lots of stuff for growing hemp, but how the hashish was being made certainly wasn't obvious. And made it was, for some of the boxes were full of it. Thanks to Nuk, whoever was running this place could use that space to store something else now. It's good to tidy up, you know?

"Well, what's going on?" Nuk asked Izumi and Elaina, who had been tasked with sussing out the system.

"Nuk... It's five in the morning. Landbats aren't even nocturnal and they're all over us. Can't you just drop it?" Izumi said. Incredibly, this appeal actually got through to Nuk, and they left the drug farm intact.

"You better work it out, you better!" Nuk was saying to them as they walked.

"I know how to make it," Gustavsen offered.

"Not your way. That place had no latrines man. There's a real way!"

"Prince Tashino, have you seen this?" Elaina said. She handed Nuk a piece of paper. It was a police report, written in old-fashioned Second Empire print. Towards the bottom it read,

"And the suspect was having' a right laugh, he was. You see, he'd rigged up a homebrew solution that was proper good. Hashish by the boatload, and all he had to do was-"

Thus ended the page. Nuk was devastated, but he soon realised Elaina's meaning. It gave him an idea for the Izumi... 'situation'.

"Future girl," he said, braving the scowls of Foren and Shamika. "I was thinking that once we're done with this, I'll give you some help with the tech hunting."

"What sort of help?" Izumi probed.

"Like, we'll go wherever you want, and look at the buildings and stuff. No drugs. Not even a gram. What do you think?"

"I think... What's your game here Nuk?"

"I just want you to be happy."

"So, you want to find ancient secrets about those bloody drugs?"

"Yes. Fugg. How do you do that?"

"Senses. Consciousness. Stuff you get if you're off the drugs. Like magic really."

"Oh. But... I wasn't really lying."

"Is that so?"

"Yeah. In that, I do want you to be happy."

"LAME," Foren barked. She and Shamika dragged Nuk away. Izumi didn't think it was that lame actually.

The crew moved east leaving the ashen mountain but still marching through barren, rocky expanses, broken up only by gloopy, polluted streams and dusty fungi. This was the depths of the Old Lands, as the shek called it, the lands that were at the epicentre of whatever it was that befell the First Empire. It was precisely this event that Izumi's discovery offered a fascinating insight into. The papers had implied a fight, but that much seemed obvious, given the still-active space laser. Whatever it really was, it was something significant enough that not even the usual scorched ruins were to be found on those mountains.

These mountains, by the way, were in the region called Stobe's Gamble, which if you have a good memory you might recall was the place the guild stumbled through on their way to a destined meeting with a load of fishmen and crab salesmen. There was a way back to Manksand from there, but it passed through the so-called 'Unwanted Zone', a stretch of Beak Thing territory on the southern edge of the empire. Thus, they went around it through the quiet lowlands called 'Stobe's Garden'.

It was where the coastline had been in the First Empire days, with the sudden appearance of ruined ships as you walked east marking the exact border. Here the guild turned north towards Black Scratch, but as they passed beside a long set of old coastal-cliffs at dawn, they came upon a rare sight indeed. A real relic of the First Empire.

"I- Damn. He's still here..." Rick muttered.

"What?" Nuk asked, but Rick ran off ahead. The crew chased him, and came upon a huge skeleton corpse, taller than the cliffs it lay slumped against. Rick was sat in the dirt staring up at it, and may I remind you that for a skeleton, sitting was wholly unnecessary in ordinary circumstances.

"Rick, is that...?" Izumi began.

"Yeah," Rick replied quietly. "We were supposed to hide him, back in the two-point-oh days, but... You can't, can you? This guy. We owe it all to him."

"Rickard, is that the one you called Stobe?" Izayah asked.

"King Stobe!" Gustavsen remarked, remembering Rick's old claim. The hivers followed their leader in lining up before the robot remains and bowing to it in turn.

"Yeah. That's the King. Next time you go back to that trumped up killer library, they'll probably work the main man's deal out, since you breaking the seal on that shid. Huh. Guess I'll tell ya then, so you appreciate it. Stobe saved the world from them, up there."

Rick pointed up at Okran, or, as Izumi reminded everyone again, at Earth.

"He stopped them. He stopped it all. Well, him and his big-ass round table. Earth-clans were damn obsessed with giant fighting robots – that was the reason they kept coming down guns blazing after all. Still, didn't expect us to actually have 'em. Huh, and they were like 'alright, we're just gotta get rid of the whole planet', and Stobe was like, 'right back at ya bucko'. Smart missiles weren't as smart as him. Turned that shid around. Most of 'em. Huh, that was a bad day. Anyway, everybody loses, but we lose less. And that's just the start of it. Funny what you remember when you try- Oh shid. Oh shid oh shid oh shid oh shid!"

Rick went into hysterics and started writhing about. The guild tried to calm him, but to no avail.

"Coinslot, what's up with you?" Nuk said.

"Rick, please, calm down! What's a missile?! Rick!" Izumi was saying. No one got any answer, but after a long wait, Rick seemed to recover.

"It's alright, it's alright. I moved it. New storage location, at random. It's outta sight. Damn. Damn, damn, damn. And there I was thinking biologicals didn't deserve all that shid. Damn it all, praise fugging Stobe, let's just get outta here."

"But wait, how did Stobe die?" Izumi asked.

"Oh shut up. He died free, no thanks to you pieces of shid, and here I am today because of it. Try all you like; you'll never find the documents on that shid. Even the biologicals had the sense not to write it down. Damn. I'm out, I'll see ya back home or whatever."

"Man, I think something bad happened," Nuk said as Rick stomped off.

"Guess we knew that already. I think it was really bad. Poor Rick. We shouldn't have asked," Izumi said. "Sounded like it was all... Like he has good reasons for not wanting to talk about it."

"Skeletons do not have feelings," Gustavsen said.

"Pretty sure they do, but they can choose different responses to mitigate them," Elaina explained.

"And Bad Green you can't come in here with that, you aren't the most experienced with feelings, alright?" Nuk said.

"Nonsense. I feel hungry. Teeth," the hiver replied. A quick snack, and he was good to keep going with the walk north, following Rick's footprints right back to Black Scratch. The city was under attack by bandits, as it often was, and Nuk's strategic arrival brought cheer to all inside. Then it was down the hill, past the outer corpse pile, over the speckled midfield corpse range, around the gateway corpse holding area, and boom, they were right back to Manksand Canyon.

The guild had attracted the attention of a large band of pirates on their way to the base, but as these attackers stormed forwards to stop them reaching the gate, that gate opened to reveal three big strong crabs. Prince Crusty and Skut were all grown up by now, and the triple-crab smackdown surprise really has no equal.

"Yeah, get crabbed you spooky fuggs!" Jaz was heard shouting from the walls.

The pirates were distributed among the relevant piles, and the crew was home at long last. Time for a nice holiday, and even a little dessert after all, the place was now overflowing with mountains of stale, sand chocobread. Even Nuk was a little surprised at his workers' productivity. The stock was worth a Bugmaster's ransom, and more.

"So, you get it in with P-rince?" Jaz asked Izumi as soon as she thought she was alone.

"Nope," Izumi chirped.

"Nope? You serious?"

"Yeah, but I dunno if he is."

"What? He totally is."

"Not that simple."

"Aw for fugg's sake. He likes you darling. Not many people like you, so you should probably take what you got, huh?"

Jaz was shut out of Izumi's office forthwith. Meanwhile Nuk was in the barrack explaining the new plan to Izayah.

"Oh it's admirable, admirable. I think Miss Izumi will be very pleased you're willing to help her with this. And I think it might be fun. Maybe we'll find out the truth after all. Not that it sounds all that appealing, after the Rickard thing. Ha. Anyway, I was going to say, that you really you don't need to worry that much about impressing her."

"Yeah I do. I think," Nuk said, his voice hushed.

"You don't. She likes you already!"

"Yeah, but it's hard to be sure. Got evidence to the contrary but... Could it be that tsunderey thing?"

"Tsundere!" Rick shouted from his shed. Oh yeah, Rick got a shed, he's up to no good in there but don't worry about that.

"Oh this is quite the pickle then," Izayah said. He was absolutely right. Obviously there's more to be said about the... 'situation', but let's focus on the more adventurous matters that arose shortly. Elaina came back from Black Scratch one day with a map some hunters had uncovered. It was a very old map, and on it there was a certain spot west of the Great Swamp that was marked 'Piston Police Narcotics Research Shelter'.

What did that mean? It meant Nuk was very happy. I know – yet another lead in this quest for drugs, which so far has been quite a tease. But I'll tell you now that this was it, the 'it', it, the it that would sort 'it' out. What is 'it'? The 'situation'? Nice guess but... well... The next excursion would help both Nuk and Izumi answer many questions.

Chapter 23 Side Story
The New Model Army

(Author's Note: This tale occurs during and after the end of Chapter 23).

"Is anyone seein' this? Look how much is coming off!" Nuk exclaimed. Bits of tin-shrapnel were scattering from the rockface every time his pick rammed its way in there. "You probably think you're pretty strong huh? But come on. You seeing this? You have to be seeing this!"

Nuk was trying to impress some of the Thousand Guardians, who had come over to investigate the racket at the end of the base. The south-west corner of the Manksand compound had a tin vein exposed on the surface, which was of approximately zero use to anyone, and hence it is no surprise Nuk had started mining it out. I said *approximately* zero use, for if you really zoom in on the use graph you'll see one possible application of the flimsy, valueless metal: it was put in the hands of one strong, infinitely valuable skeleton with a red face-plate.

Red Rick had been in a bad mood ever since his recent encounter with Stobe, whose role in Rick's life was of both the utmost significance and secrecy. It was to be a secret even from himself, and to that end, Rick had discovered a nice way to divert his processing power elsewhere. He was polishing up the tin ore, then hammering it into little shapes. These shapes, when assembled, created little model humans, faceless and dull – perhaps that was how Rick saw his fleshy muse.

Nuk was therefore trying to help his supposedly suffering star warrior, and embarrassing himself in front of the shek was just a fringe benefit. It wasn't the only genius idea he'd had recently. Unhappy with how the whole Bugmaster campaign had exposed many people's mortal weaknesses, he devised a genius way to make his crew a little more thick skinned. Or at least, more crispy skinned.

It was as simple as it was effective – he had people taking turns sitting on top of a fire, because what doesn't kill you makes you stronger, the ancient literature claimed. Nuk pointed to Ignacio as a case study of this effect. He had lost an arm and a leg in service to the guild, but he survived, and now he had a robot arm and a robot leg to play with – stronger! And more lop-sided, but you can't expect these legs to be one-size fits all, can you?

Later that day, Nuk had called Izumi over to watch the fine mining.

"It's all in the swing, you see," Nuk explained knowingly, doing the swing with well-practised incompetence.

"Great. At least you're helping Rick. I think that's good of you," Izumi conceded. "Maybe he'll calm down and explain something. That bot's everything I could ever want-"

"I told you to stay away from me alright! Still ain't got the shid outta there from last time," Rick called from the shed.

"All I could want for my research! Tell me your secrets and I'll leave you alone!"

"You leave me alone, and I won't go telling everyone *your* secrets, you pervert," Rick concluded, disappearing again. Sounds like he had secrets that both Izumi and Nuk would be highly interested in, but he would say nothing of either. Hence, Nuk and Izumi clanked at the tin seam all afternoon, ironically slaving away on behalf of a skeleton that wanted nothing more than to erase his memories of the time when such a relationship between man and machine was mandatory.

This homely bout of conspiracy, perversion, and manual labour was interrupted by a lone shek arriving at the base. He was one of Estata's troops, with bad news from Admag.

"I knew this would happen," Izayah nodded. He pointed at a spot on the map hanging on the barrack wall. "Those old fools couldn't let go. They'll be moving light and swift. Should be about here. By tomorrow, perhaps... here. Then we shall have beserkers at our gates."

"And, these shek can't be reasoned with?" Wodston asked.

"I seriously doubt it," Izayah said, shaking his head. "I believe these will be the shek who were slated to battle the Bugmaster, but have had their valour and such stolen away. Stolen by the Prince and I, I suppose, and so our heads are the new target for the Last Stand."

"We ended that, through right?" Nuk said. "Stonezone said she was going to sort the whole death cult thing out."

"I know. But not everyone will listen, will they? You know how people can be. And we shek – we're like how people can be all the time."

"How many berserkers are coming, you reckon?" Izumi asked.

"There is no way to say. All we have is this rumour that they'd set off. Could be a thousand. Perhaps only one hundred. Either way, we need a plan."

"A plan?" Nuk scoffed. "Wait man, we've got the Thousand Guardians here, so a thousand crazies ain't nothing. And, we're sitting on like a stack of chocobread. Brownpound straight from the brownmound, day in, day out. What are they gonna do to us?"

"But the canyons will trap us," Sandor warned. "If things go wrong, we'll be outta luck. They could even blockade us in here and wait for the bread to run out."

"A siege? That would be terrible," Wodston said, remembering the siege of Heft two decades prior in the war that brought a certain Tashino clan to power.

"Man, sounds like the battle to save the Kingdom isn't over yet," Nuk said. "We'll deal with the last of the old guard the hard way. They might attack us over the walls, or trap us here, and we've gotta be ready. Let's get down to business, to defeat the shek!"

"Did they send me fleshies, when I asked for mechs?" Rick hummed to himself outside. His eavesdropping complete, he went back to his shed, confident that the battle to come was his to win.

Out there, rushing towards them with unheard of speed, was a horde of angry, belligerent shek beserkers, lifelong warriors, eager to die in battle or die trying. Nuk's army braced themselves for the onslaught, preparing medical supplies and fresh beds, and of course sitting on burning campfires, after which the thought of getting a sword wedged in you didn't seem too bad.

The morning of the battle came.

"I want to see ten, and twenty!" Gustavsen shouted to Nuk from the wall.

"Ten and twenty what?" he called back.

"Units."

"Units... of...?"

"Units of walking."

"I think he means to say," Jaz interjected, "that he wants the ten and twenty pace lines marked out on the approach. We've got a lot of firewood left over from the squat 'n' singe program, so let's light it up."

The gate was opened up, and Nuk starting marking out the range lines while the archery experts calibrated their weapons up on the walls. But then there was a loud jangling sound, followed by a load of scraping.

"Come on you sons of guns," Rick said to the sack he was dragging across the gate threshold.

"Whoa, are you running away from home? Is it about future girl? We can share! I'm not that fussy man!" Nuk pleaded.

"What in the name of hells old and new are you talking about? You can keep your slimeball girlfiend, thank you very much. Good luck with the... Ha, well, you'll find out, nothing to worry about, all that. Anyway, I ain't going anywhere. In fact I'm gonna sort your shid out. Check it."

Rick opened his clanking sack to reveal a legion of tin figurines.

"Wait, they can fight?" Nuk asked.

"Kinda. Ask yourself this, my biological friend – if you rolled up on some outpost and saw it was guarded a horde of strange little metal men, wouldn't ya be a little worried they were up to something."

"But to clarify, they aren't actually up anything?"

"No! Well, haven't kept that close an eye on them, but even then only thing they've been up- Damnit, I said I'd let you find out the hard way. Err... just move it will ya?"

Rick laid out his army of tinmen across the gates to the base. Each was about a foot tall, a featureless humanoid shape on a square stone base, with no moving parts, and not even any sharp edges. Would this be enough to stop the horde?! Rick, believing so, returned to his shed. Meanwhile Nuk got the rest of the crew organised.

Splitting the army into human, hiver, shek and crab companies, he positioned his forces ready to defend the sweet sands of mank against whatever might come through that gate. The sun passed overhead. Midday. The canyon was silent, but for the steady clanging coming from Rick's shed. Then, there was a raspy tone that echoed from the west.

"A war horn!" Izayah said. "Thousand Guardians, by the left, start sounding that mound!"

This strange order caused the shek to inject their performance enhancing starch. The ground began to shake as the beserker horde approached. It came down into the valley, and at last the guild saw them. They wore little, but carried huge two-handed greatswords. They cawed and whooped as they suddenly rushed for the walls, but then they fell silent and stumbled to a halt. The front ranks were staring at the tinman army. The tinman army, in its own way, stared back. Harpoons were slid into turrets, bowstrings drawn, crab claws flexed, but yet all was still.

"It's... it's a little man!" a beserker shouted, pointing at a model.

"There are l-loads of them!" another stuttered, looking around wide eyed at the stalwart formation, four ranks deep and twelve inches high.

"They're small... And... they can see us!" a shek panicked, dropping his blade and scrambling back through his comrades to escape.

"They can see us!" cries came from throughout the horde, and off they all went, desperately fleeing before the cold, fearless stares of their foes. Yep. That's really what happened. Maybe the beserkers got their way and managed to die elsewhere, but it was not this day.

"Coinslot you mad machine! Get out here!" Nuk called. Rick was pretty much dragged from his shed, and hoisted up by the crowd of victorious biologicals.

"Just doing my part. Letting you live, you know. Gotta make up for that old shid. I mean... Whatever." Rick said. So there we have it, the guild was saved from the aftershocks of what they did in the shek Kingdom by the very distant aftershocks of what skeletons did in the transition from the first empire to the second. Or whatever Rick did, specifically. Perhaps learning to sculpt was part of it.

As for rewarding Rick, he only wanted one thing. Thus, Nuk and Izumi went out for another afternoon on the tin mine. Strategically, Nuk led Izumi behind the main outcropping so that they could work out of view of the rest of the base. He had something very special he wanted to talk to her about.

"So, you know, I've been thinking," he started. Izumi didn't dare prompt him further, just in case. "I was thinking... about me, and you. And our... relationship."

Now Izumi was quite on edge. Was this 'it'? The thing she'd dreamed of and dreaded in equal measure? Was Nuk going to reveal that inner romantic that she was just sure he had hidden away?

"I was thinking," he went on. "That... I should stop paying you."

Ah. Izumi gave the tin vein a sudden, very powerful thwack with her pick, then let out a long breath.

"Oh. I had no idea Nuk, I thought I was... I thought we were working. I mean I really did. It's okay, I can go back to Black Scratch I guess but... Nuk you..." unable to say more, she moved to leave, but Nuk's arms held her back.

"Wait, I mean I want to stop paying you, so that's it's not like I'm paying you to hang out with me!" he explained. This wasn't a massive amount better, but surprisingly he'd said something that didn't make it worse, so we can all appreciate that.

"What do you mean? I'm not here for my fugging guild salary."

"I know, that's good. So I was thinking that you shouldn't just be my employee, you know? Like, I don't wanna have you and Wodston in the same category."

"Cool. That sounds... Ugh, so what category am I in, precisely?"

"I dunno. It's like, it's own category, with only you in it. Or, that's what I want. I mean, you have to volunteer to be in this category, so it's different to the other ones."

"Right. So this... 'category'. Is that, like a friend?"

"A friend, but a friend of a certain category."

"You mean, like a friend, who is a boy?"

"Kinda, close, I mean that's pretty much – I don't wanna say it's a contractually defined thing with like a name and terms blah blah, 'cause it's more like something that happening because you just, want it to happen."

"And you want it to happen?"

"Yeah, that's why I asked you to mine tin with me."

"What a... great reason, to ask that."

"I know, right?"

"So... What should we do now?"

"I guess we just... keep going."

"Keep... mining tin?"

"Err... yeah?"

"Oh, right. Yeah, better keep going."

On the other side of the tin vein, Foren and Shamika were getting rather embarrassed eavesdropping on all this.

"This is weird. Should we get her outta there?" Shamika asked.

"Don't you worry about that," Rick said from nearby. He stepped out from behind the finishing machine with an armful of freshly polished tin ingots. "They been like that since I knew 'em. Makes me sick, but that's biologicals for ya. It'll happen to you one day too. Reminds me, you girls wanna help me take my mind off something?"

The girls looked at each other, shrugged, and disappeared into Rick's shed. Nuk and Izumi eventually reappeared with barrows filled with extremely well mined tin ore. They looked at each other and smiled just a little too long, then ran off to attend to all kinds of invented business.

And hence, the cliffs of Manksand canyon were witness to another anti-climax. None of the residents had any complaints, as in truth the matters of love and war had been settled, in one way or another.

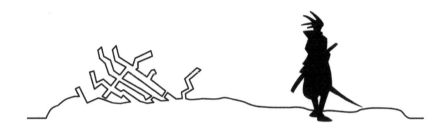

Chapter 24
Beach Chapter

At the gates of the TCM+G HQ, Nuk stood before his crew for the usual pre-expedition inspirational speech.

"This isn't about drugs!" he insisted. "But, just so you have full disclosure, yes, we're going the ruins of an ancient drugs research facility, and yes, I've run out of drugs, and yes, I want nothing more than to uncover the secrets of drugs, of all colours. BUT this is *not* about drugs! This, my friends, is in the name of historical discovery.

Future girl's half an old tome away from being the world leader in knowing what Red Rick keeps mumbling about. This is a noble quest, that will literally – literally – go down in history. Huh? You like that? No? And, well, if you do see any drugs or whatever on the way, just let me know, so I can, err, make sure it goes down in the future instead. Any questions?"

"Where are we goin'?" Ells asked.

"Old drugs and history place, it'll be grand," Nuk assured him, and off they all went. Their destination was the Piston Police Narcotics Research Shelter. It was nestled in the steep hills south-west of the Great Swamp, and hence the guild was heading out via very familiar routes.

They battled their way through the reavers and bandits of their home ranges. Then they battled the headless robots of Venge during the night, getting a little revenge for the abuse old farmer Lon had put up with on his little jaunt in the area. Then they battled the heavily unionised bandits of Shem, on account of passing through the region during reasonable business hours. From there, the easiest thing to do would be to go around the swamp to the other side, but Nuk accidentally led everyone through it, where he accidentally visited the tree-tree and accidentally made certain capital investments.

"Man, these salesmen," he said with a shake of his head. "You go in there for a swig of water, and they upsell you to... three, four... fifty keys of bloody hashish! Which this trip is literally the opposite of being about!"

"Nuk, I don't mind if you wanna buy that stuff, but on one condition," Izumi said.

"I will listen to your treaty."

"You have to stop being an arse."

"Literally, that's what this stuff is for. It's the 'makes you feel human' juice."

"Juice?"

"Swamp-style baby. Drinkable drugs."

"I like drink," Ells said.

"Then, Charlie my boy, let's drink."

"You would buy into this stupid stuff," Izumi muttered.

"Don't neg the egg!" Izayah scolded her. By now Ells had downed a vial of the murky water Nuk and given him, which looked, smelled, and tasted a lot like swamp mank.

"It don't make me feel huma-" Ells said, cut off by his face slamming into the ground. There he lay.

"Is he... dead?" Izumi asked.

"No, that *is* what it's like to feel human," Nuk shrugged.

"So that means it's time for me to drag that deadweight into the future?" Rick said.

"Into the past. We're off to the drugs museum!" Nuk declared. Nuk, now in fully human form, lead the way west. The west edge of the swamp was a little drier, with tall bluffs to clamber along, and only a smattering of wild blood spiders to contend with. They were soon on a well-trodden smuggling route south, which took them right to their destination.

"That's the place. The Grid," Elaina reported, looking up from the map. There was a passageway through the bluffs, in which the twisting slimy branches of the swamp flora gave way to sheening, sharp, crystalline rocks. There was a tight way through into an extremely narrow valley, the sides made entirely of the shiny blue stone. There were several of these valleys cut into the shimmery cliffs, intersecting each other at right angles, creating the grid which the name on the map surely referred to.

"Unusual. Unbearable!" Gustavsen commented, preferring not to look at the valley walls.

"This can't be natural," Izumi said.

"Natural as the planet itself. Came with it," Rick said.

"Came with it? Just what did you do this time?"

"Nothing! Look, for real this time, this shid is from the beginning, before I was a glint in some lazy human's eye. Just a mess up, as I recall. Some joker got their hands on the planet building stuff."

"What planet building stuff?"

"Wait you don't even know about that? Shid, we hid all the good stuff didn't we?"

"Well we'll see about that. Come on, let's look for remains of this piston police thing."

Izumi waved everyone to start searching the valleys – crags would be a better word, for they really were no more than twenty meters wide. They were home to various thick-trunked trees with stymied, pink leaves, but nothing more ferocious than that, luckily enough. Clearly something else had lived there before, as deeper into the grid there were long, metal shelters covering multi-story workstations.

"Incredible. Second Empire. Early Second Empire. No. Even earlier, look at these joins," Izumi said, examining the heavy plate-metal construction. Elaina took a look around, and concluded,

"Not First Empire. Too crude. Not Second Empire. Too sophisticated. This was built before First Empire techniques were forgotten."

"That's amazing! I've never seen anything like it."

Izumi was about to start climbing a ramp to get to what appeared to be the main section on the top level of the workshop, but Nuk held her back.

"Wait, wait, you don't know what's up there. Traps, and shid. I'll look first," he said.

"That's part of being a tech hunter," Izumi complained.

"We'll share it. I'll hunt, you tech."

"Whatever."

With this enthusiastic acceptance, Nuk got to work. Up on the top of the workshop the rest of the guild couldn't see him, but they had some evidence that he was alive since he kept throwing little paper planes down. Unfolded, they revealed barely legible documents, mostly the intriguing chronicles of whose turn it was to order in fresh grog for the fleshies.

While Izumi battled to keep this contraband intelligence away from Rick, Nuk rifled around a variety of quite familiar machines. Second Empire tech was no different to what the United Cities, AKA the Third Empire, AKA the Second Empire but renamed and repopulated, had access to. To put all this another way: Nuk had no trouble breaking open all locks, bolts, intrays, outflows, nooks, crannies and crates.

He found skeleton parts, rare tools, some very, very old trousers, but most importantly, he found a report on hashish. A report that detailed precisely how the, and I quote, "downright cheeky doom-humes" end quote, created their magical makes-you-feel-human stock cubes. It was the recipe for hashish, to be clear, and even through his grubby sun-goggles, Nuk could see it.

"I had another accident!" he called as he belted down the ramp to return to the guild, waving the hefty wad of papers over his head.

"That's great news Prince Tashino!" Izayah cheered. Nuk showed them all the documents explaining the details of hashish production.

"With this, we could just brew the stuff in dad's fugging attic," Nuk said.

"My Prince, please, I think we should keep all criminal activity outside of the capital. At least out of the palace," Wodston said.

"Criminal? Come on, dad's asking for it. Or he was, like months ago. He'll have definitely forgotten about it by now, but you know, when we show up he'll be happy. Like, surprise, here's a load of drugs! And surprise, you have a son! Remember this guy?!"

"Allow me to analyse," Gustavsen asked. He looked over the plans, then all the other hivers looked over the plans, then he returned them with a bow. "Old hairy one wisdom. Efficient. We should implement these plans at once," he reported.

"Bad Green wants the good green, so we're green to go!" Nuk proclaimed. "But, seriously guys, this trip isn't about blah blah blah. Come on, we'll get the history done now. All seems safe. Let's hunt the tech and stuff."

The guild spent the rest of the day and night there in the Grid. There were plenty of other remains from the Research Shelter, packed with technical documents carrying secrets to modern science, and random old notes that gave a fascinating insight into life two thousand years prior.

"Okran's faceplate," Izumi remarked.

"Find something?" Elaina asked.

"Yeah. Okran's faceplate. Look. It says someone was arrested for trying to vandalise Okran's faceplate. How can a god have a faceplate?"

"I'm right here, ladies," Rick insisted.

"Rick, what is all this?" Izumi asked, but the skeleton shook his head.

"Before I went down Black Desert City, there was no Okran. Someone thought him up along the way. Only one god in the empire I left. The King."

"Stobe?"

"Uh huh."

"And... Could it be his faceplate?"

"If I caught someone touching the big man I'd do more than arrest 'em. But hey, maybe that's why they kicked me out."

"Kicked out of the Second Empire?"

"It was all the Second Empire, you couldn't get kicked outta that back in the day. And you know, I seem to have forgotten all the details."

"I know."

"May I interrupt?" Izayah interrupted. "Do I gather from this that you are saying, Rickard, that Okran was just an imaginary god?"

"But he's in the sky!" Ells pointed out.

"Look, I don't know shid about it. Biologicals can believe what they want. That's the only good thing they got that we don't," Rick said, quitting the conversation.

"My. First I've heard of all this. I mean, everyone always says Okran is timeless. Prince Gustavsen, what do the hivers know of this?" Izayah asked.

"Your gods are false and irrelevant. We laugh at your delusion," was the reply.

"Oh come now, that's rather mean. Ha, I know. Will you say Okran is real if I give you... these three teeth?"

"YES."

"Go on then."

"Teeth is- Okran is real. This is not a joke. Please transact now."

Izayah transacted, and aside from this little debate, a quiet and pleasant evening was had in the ruins of that piston police pad. Izumi successfully harvested a little collection of tidbits from the past. There was more where that came from though, she guessed, as the part of the world from the Grid to the south-west coast was uninhabited, and barely explored by the hunters. Plus, it was pretty.

In the morning, the guild went up the far end of the Grid and into the huge vale at the tail end of the spider plains. In the west, the arid, rocky, ground began its rise up to the familiar horrors of Arach Mountain. In the east, a steep wall of ancient crystal rose sharply into what looked like a mountain from the base, but was in reality more of a hollow crater. Like the Grid, this strange land pre-dated even the First Empire, and was thoroughly untamed. To be more specific: it was packed from slope to summit with Beak Things.

Similar to how the azure sands of Gut back in the empire seemed to attract the beasts, the mirrory crevasses of this huge blue crater were really a Beak Thing's thing. The guild, then, had to fight these Beak Things every hour or so as they tried to find any good archaeological burglary sites. After a day of trying, and nearly dying, they gave up, and took an old road away from the crater, leading south into the boring, brown hills of Shun.

Shun had been extremely briefly a part of the United Cities Empire, but that was in the messy transition from empire 2 to 3, and amid said mess, all the people living there had died or fled. Thus, the region was a little time capsule, left undisturbed in the corner of the world, shielded from colonisation by Arach and the Crater. Its last link to civilisation was this dusty road that snaked around to the east, towards the fraying edge of the modern UC empire.

Given the history, and recent lack thereof, of Shun, you might expect there to be plenty of archaeo-stuff to study, and you'd be dead right – I say this, because the tech hunter expeditions to the area had encountered a little too much death to carry on. Why? No-one knew. As such, Izumi was on edge the whole time, but it was really a pleasant, undisturbed march beside healthy rivers and rolling, tan hills. Then, on the other side of the river, they came across a completely untouched Second Empire outpost. Nuk did his thing, and indeed the inside was full of goodies for his female, to quote, "friend" unquote.

"It's really here. Everyone in Black Scratch always said the Shun Run was some impossible joke," Izumi said.

"Yeah but to be fair, I heard that Black Scratch is a level three nark zone," Nuk said.

"Their problem now. We can actually do this, Nuk. If I go back with what I have already, I'll get published for sure. If I bring back the treasures of the Shun Run, I'll be the only damn one who matters!"

"Oh. Well that's good. Because you are."

"Not with those old fogeys saying my stuff's too speculative. Not like we have- Oh, wait, did you mean... err...?"

"I-I meant that we're totally gonna do the Shun Fun thing."

"Run."

"Don't mind if I do."

With another so-called conversation masterfully handled, a new plan was formulated. But first, the crew carried on east to get back to the empire. It was time for a little R&R, and Nuk was eager to pay his Aunt a visit. This brought them to the breezy coastal flats on the southern edge of the world, which were home to Drifter's Last. This walled town was proudly the edge of civilisation. I know that title applies to most towns, but more specifically, this place was the furthest point in the empire from the capital at Heft. Perfect place for a certain emperor to send his claim-to-the-throne-possessing sister.

"Auntie! Auntie!" Nuk called in the streets outside the biggest house in town. No response. "Oi! Merin! It's your only nephew!"

Merin appeared on the roof, with a bottle of rum in each hand, and peered down at the urchin below.

"Nukkie?" she asked.

"Yeah, it's me!"

"Oh... Did I- you, going to get kicked out as well?"

"Ha, yeah actually."

"Nice. Now can fugg off will ya? Fuggyoff."

"What?"

"I'm not allows. Your sammy men are here, and they aren't supposed for us to be in talking. Away go. Go away. However you say it. I'm... Oh..."

Merry Merin tripped over the roof edge, but Nuk managed to catch her. However, this meant that he was breaking some apparent rule – the 'sammy men' spirited Merin back to her spirits, and locked Nuk out of the noble compound.

"Dad's set up some kinda killswitch here," Nuk said to Wodston in the bar.

"He must have been worried you would support Lady Merin."

"He doesn't trust me?"

"I fear- It could be because of the laws you broke, my prince."

"What? It's the other way around! If he'd- Whatever man. Ugh. This really pisses me off, you know?"

"I understand."

"You don't understand. Dad likes you. That's why he let you come out with me."

"I- That's not- Ah- I'm sure you're right, my Prince," the equally exiled doctor conceded.

"I just wanna – Here I am on the other side of the world, and he's still trying to tell me what to do, and just generally screw me over. I feel like a fugging dreg again!"

"Nuk, come on," Izumi said. "Why don't we get outta this town. Can't make yourself feel human around here, right?"

"Too bloody right. Ha, thanks future girl. You get it don't you?"

"I don't think so, but I'm trying."

"Man. Man that's like even better!"

"Is it?"

"I dunno! Right, we're going on a vacation. We're in the riviera after all!"

Yes, after just one night in town, the guild was dragged out to go on Nuk's proposed vacation. Now I say dragged because everyone presumed this was just some weird way of saying they were going to brave feral beasts and raving lunatics in order to secure a piece of an old spoon that was once used by a legendary stoner (or some such jaunt). But nay. Nuk was seriously pissed by that whole Merin thing, and hence was seriously stomping towards what turned out to be a lovely seaside town. Or *was*, lovely, probably. They went to the end of a spit south-west of Drifter's Last, were the ruins of an old fishing village sat astride sparkling, almost tropical waters, complete with skinny, knobbly beaches.

"Beach chapter," Nuk nodded to himself.

"What's a beach chapter?" Ells asked.

"Old japanan saying from the books. It just means something is good."

"Oh. So like the bucket is beach chapter?"

"The bucket is fugging beach chapter Charlie. Enjoy it. Coinslot! Can you reccy the wet real quick?" Nuk called.

"Sure thing. Finally get all that shid outta my..." Rick muttered as he walked into the ocean. He wandered around in there for a bit, then returned to report that he hadn't seen any nasty fangs on the local wildlife. The spot was prime for a swim then.

"Everybody in! Time to stink less!" Nuk ordered.

"Stink of something else, rather," Izayah corrected him. It was true that seawater had a strange smell to it, lacking the salt and strong currents of earthly seas. It was more like a huge, silty lake, in which life only existed in limited forms. The scary remains in those Bonefields were a testament to ancient attempts to get something going, but no dice.

Anyway, while you can debate whether swimming in the sea made you stink more or less, and everyone did, you can't argue that it isn't a pleasant feeling to bob around in the endless, unforgiving, all consuming ocean... Wait a minute... Yes, the guild came to the conclusion that swimming on the literal edge of reality was not all that relaxing, so they retired to a little inlet just along the coast. It had a deep end, a shallow end, minimal chance of a kraken, and was flanked by a load of twiggy palm trees, perfect for a campfire.

What ensued was quite possibly the most pleasant scene of the previous Okran-knows how many thousand years. On that lonely stretch of nowhere, everyone could enjoy a warm night beneath the stars, and beside the pool. Miscellaneous meats were mined from Gary's greasy bags and roasted up on the campfire. The shek practised their swimming, which was certainly needed, and the hivers could appreciate being between the water and the trees, just like in their old hives.

On the shore, Izumi looked up at Okram and Narko, becoming more brilliant in the sky as night fell. Narko's grey surface was stained by dark patches of charred dust and the shadows of huge impact craters. Okran's seas shone blue, and its land was a quiet, icy white.

"You know, there's something I don't get," Nuk said, walking up to her.

"I- That's very surprising," Izumi muttered.

"It's those two up there. Imaginary gods? Whatever. Real question is: if it's dark now, why can we still see them?"

"Well, Nuk, first think: why is it even dark here?"

"Err, because the light ball moved away?"

"Kinda. Yeah, I mean that'll do. It moved away from us, but not away from... err, Okran and Narko. Earth and Moon if you want to use the scientific names."

"I don't. And also, I don't get it."

"It's like..." Izumi moved to stand by the campfire. "See how now the light's on that side, my front is dark. But you, from my perspective, still look light."

"Wait, lemmie see that," Nuk said. He moved over to where Izumi was, but alas, when he looked back, he was no longer where Izumi had seen him.

"It doesn't work if you're in my shadow. You're too... err.. close," Izumi said. Come to think of it, Nuk had moved rather into Izumi's personal space.

They could smell the musky sea water in each other's hair. Oh dear, this was far too much.

"Oi, you party animals need any supplies?" a voice called from the darkness. Salvation! Nuk rushed over to deal with them, and found it was a caravan of traders who'd come to investigate the lights. As it happened the guild was fine for everything, but these wanderers were selling a couple of old books with pictures of Okran on the cover. Nuk paid whatever, and brought them back to the fire.

"Present," he mumbled, handing them over to Izumi.

"Thanks. I didn't- Oh, it's the thing I was saying about. It's called astronomy. Let's see if... oh wait a minute... It's not English, or Japanese. This is... French."

"Ah, French. The one they call the language of love," Rick commented from a nearby bush. "You better read it to get an understanding of it. But don't mind me. I ain't listening. Not at all. *Zut a*-fugging-*lors*."

"So, you don't know what it says?" Nuk asked.

"No, but I know what it's saying," Izumi said.

"Nice. Shall we, like, look at the pictures, and you can explain it?"

"Err, yeah. Take a seat."

"Where?"

"Where?"

"Where shall I sit?"

"Next to me?"

"Oh right. Yep."

It was all going great, let me tell you. The night went on, and most folk lay out in the sand to grab some sleep. Rick, on sentry duty, was joined in the waking world only by Nuk and Izumi, whom he started at nervously from his bush.

"Man, I guess I do get it," Nuk nodded, lying.

"Good. It makes you see the world differently, you know? Once you understand a little about how it all works, it just, makes sense. You can get why stuff happened, and guess what's gonna happen next."

"Nice, so you're like future girl then?"

"Yeah. But that wasn't why- Why did you start calling me that?"

"Err... I dunno. Wasn't it like because I was, trusting you, with the future, or something?"

"Maybe. But I was going to say that if you trust me, you could just call me... Izumi?"

"Nah. Lame."

"Is it?"

"Everyone else calls you that. I can't be like them."

"Is this that whole 'you can't pay me because you pay Wodston and I'm not like him', thing?"

"Err, probably."

"Right. So, just keep calling me 'girl' then."

"No, I mean, I wanna call you like... Izzy."

"Izzy. It's a bit..."

"Hissy?"

"I was gonna say, a bit sweet."

"Sweet, but it's like, meant to be, like sweet, or something."

"Oh. Then, you did it. Well done."

"Thanks. Izzy. Izzy-girl. Izzy, my friend who is... Ah, you know it's quite late."

"Yeah, probably."

"We should get some sleep."

"Yeah, probably."

"How do you- What's the best way?"

"Lie down?"

"Like, here?"

"Yeah."

"While I'm still next to you?"

"I mean, anywhere."

"Here's good as anywhere. Night."

"Good night, Nuk. And, one more thing. Sorry I don't have a sweet name for you."

"S'alright. It's kinda my thing anyway."

"Well, just so you know, I do want to call you my friend. My friend of a certain category."

"Bit of a long name."

"Yeah. I'll save it for special occasions."

"Should be plenty."

"Yeah, I bet. Let's sleep then," Izumi said, commencing the process of pretending to be asleep all night next to someone who was doing the same. Rick had received too many faulty inputs and crashed, and had to reboot, so for once he actually did sleep. My my, what a night. The next day they'd be off into the wilds of Shun to discover the great mysteries of history, including why precisely all the tech hunters who went there before never returned, and, much more crucially, the properties of the unique friendship category Nuk and Izumi had assigned to each other. Rick's gonna love this...

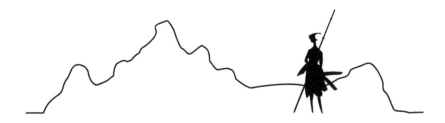

Chapter 25
Secret Smooch

The far distant reaches of Shun were long since abandoned by civilisation. And you know what they say: nature abhors a vacuum. That vacuum was thus filled with large, blood sucking spiders. Nature, why are you like this?

Yes, our heroic guild were forced to battle the locals of a Second Empire outpost, but the prize was worth it. The iconic mushroom-shaped buildings were in terrible condition, and hence were less mushroom shaped and more pile-of-blown-up-rubble shaped. Structures like these didn't collapse on their own, and nor did the Second Empire.

Artefacts and written documents were hidden in every corner of these ruins, and thus the better part of the day was spent there collecting them up. It was a simple team effort: Izumi did all the work, while everyone else kept their hands, feet and will-to-delete away from the precious treasures at all times.

"They were experimenting with something here," Izumi concluded from her findings. "It's all talking about feeding and reproduction rates."

"Experimenting huh?" Nuk nodded.

"Of animals! They were raising creatures, trying to get them into the wild. Can't really tell what. Just says things like 'test subject W-345'."

"Whatever it was, it didn't stick around I imagine," Elaina said.

"Yep. No evidence left I heard. No abominations or whatever. Scientists like them wouldn't have accidentally called anything with four legs a damn spider, so we know there's nothing there," Rick reasoned.

"Nuk, can you do your thing?" Izumi asked. Nuk went over to the one building that was still in pristine condition, with its hydraulic door firmly locked.

"There's something written here," he reported. "Says, 'speak friend, and enter'."

"Fugging nerds," Rick called in the distance.

"Err, must be a riddle or something," Izumi said.

"Nah. Ahem. Friend, Enter!"

"What?"

"I said friend... and enter... Is that not it?"

"No it's probably... Some secret word."

"Secret word. Oh, I get it!" Nuk pulled Izumi closed to the door and put an arm around her. Izumi wasn't sure Nuk had actually got anything, but wasn't complaining so far. Then he said,

"Hey door, look. This is my tomodachi. Who is a girl."

"You mean your... 'kanojo'?

"Err, I- Oh, yeah!" The door was opening there and then. Second Empire was a weird time. Oh, by the way, kanojo really does mean 'friend who is a girl'. Although, a more apt translation might take the first and last words aside, reverse them, and just go with that. It sounds like Izumi had been having a cheeky read of the guild's custom-translated ancient literature. Given that she was now entering a quiet library with Nuk-kun, those tales must have been foremost in her mind. That would explain why she seemed so nervous as she rifled through the drawers, shelves and boxes, bagging random books and folders without looking at them.

"Fu- Err, Izzy, why don't you come up and take a look at this?" Nuk called from upstairs. Izzy was experiencing a very bad case of doki-doki now. If you don't know what that is, then what can I say? You haven't read the classics have you?

Enough of this – it was all business really. Nuk had found a big map of the area from the pre-abandonment days. It seemed to indicate that the headquarters for the creature creation program was on a plateau to the north-west.

"This will be the perfect place to find what we want," Nuk said. Saying it of a spot on the map, of course.

"Yeah, it's so isolated. There won't be anyone there to stop us getting to the truth, will there?" Izumi said. Still speaking of the archaeological stuff. Although, she was edging awfully close to her senpai.

"So, err, Izz. Y. Izzy, my friend. I wanted to..." Nuk muttered.

"Yeah. Sorry about what happened last night."

"Wait, what happened? I was asleep the whole time."

"Oh, me too. I meant before that. I was being weird."

"No, no. It was fine."

"I don't mean to be a tsundere, you know?"

"Whoa, you know that is?"

"I've been reading."

"I- You're not a tsundery. You're.. I dunno. Just you. Just Izzy."

"Nuk... Call me that again."

"Anything you want, Izzy."

"Oh fugging hell," Izumi said, before doing something very untoward. What? I don't know, do I? This all happened in private. Can't we just let them have their little night in the library? And it was all night by the way, with the rest of the guild camping out in the ruins around it, daring not approach that temptingly still-open door. Only Rick's microphones were sensitive enough to detect the truth.

Nuk stumbled out of that door amid the first hints of dawn, and started frantically clapping his hands.

"Alright, rise and shine my lovely people, it's time to make history even better!" he declared.

"Happy evening, Prince?" Izayah asked.

"History's just, really good," Nuk said, quickly marching off. Izumi shambled out of the library shortly, greasy as ever. Gustavsen took one sniff at her, then turned away defiantly.

"Unworthy association. Foul," he said.

"Ha. You're jealous," Ells said of him. Let's hope it was just an idle-minded remark and not a true assessment, because if it *was* true, then... this is just getting far too complicated.

The guild went off towards that hotspot on the map. On they way they came across an old storehouse, upon which Nuk's magic was worked and entry was gained. Perhaps wanting to prove something, Gustavsen went in first for once, followed by his gang of ronin soldiers. Inside, they got the first taste of why the tech hunters had given up on this part of the world. The building was guarded by a squad of Second Empire security spiders. These were similar to the iron spiders the guild had bested in the wild, only they were smaller, faster, and downright angrier.

All of the hivers were out cold by the end of it, and one was missing a leg. Several shek were groaning on the floor, and even poor Wodston was out for the count. It was quite the brawl, and this was just some rusty old cliff-side outpost. If it was that heavily defended, what might those Second Empire weebs have left guarding their giant headquarters, up to which the guild hobbled that evening?

It was ninja Nuk's job to check. The building was a large citadel, in the same fashion as the one used by the Bugmaster up on the mountain, but in far better condition. In fact it was in perfect condition, despite the centuries out in the desert. Nuk soon spotted the caretakers to blame inside. The whole facility was packed with two things: pristine ancient relics, worth more than their weight in mank, and crazed, swarming security spiders, AKA, the legendary less-giant robot crabs.

One of them clocked Nuk peeking in through the windows and chased him all the way down the long exterior ramp back into the desert. It didn't stop there, clattering into the guild with its spiky appendages flailing with motorised force. It gave everyone quite a beating before it finally whirred to a halt. When you're fighting something made of metal with a sword, there just isn't a huge amount you can do, especially with the low ground-clearance on the things – Nuk's secret critical twist technique wasn't viable.

"What's the prospect?" Izayah asked.

"It's packed full of the good stuff, and shidding crawling with bad stuff," Nuk breathlessly reported.

"Clearly this is a piece of history we aren't meant to see. Shall we carry on elsewhere?" Wodston suggested. Nuk shook his head.

"Man, this is it. This is everything we need. One last big job. Not that I've ever-, err, wait. Izzy, you explain. Wait, not that she- Because of the history. Ah shid, we're staying, alright? We'll figure something out."

Thus the great siege of Shun began. That night Nuk went up for another peek inside. The other spiders on the first floor weren't as watchful as the earlier one, and so he managed to actually get inside. The pristine tools and machines were his to touch, and these webless spiders were none the wiser. He crept up the ramp to the second floor, where even more valuable and exciting machines sat, humming away even after a thousand years or more of standby. But there was a spider at the top of the ramp that Nuk had to get past to spy any more secrets. It was facing the other way, but as Nuk tried to step around it, a crumb of chocolatey starch fell from hi messy stubble. It landed right in front of the spider, which buzzed to life and immediately pinched the crumb into its mouth.

"Calorific content exceeds recommendation. Suggested approach to reconciliation: execution without trial for all humans," the spider's dusty speaker reasoned. Oh dear. Nuk tried to leg it, but tripped on the spider's foot and whacked himself out cold on the floor. Still, the spiders had booted up for blood, and so a few went looking for targets outside. The guild camp was there for the taking, but after a hard fight the spiders were held down and stripped of their vital parts.

It was the dead of night, and with half the guild now moaning of cuts and bruises, it was almost possible to miss the fact that Nuk hadn't come back. But after all the 'situation' Izumi had endured, she wasn't going to forget him that easily.

"Nuk, are you okay?!" she shouted up at the towering lab. In that instant, Nuk woke up on cold steel. "Nuk! Please, come back! Say something!" the shouting went on. Nuk scrambled over to a window, ignoring the spiders around him, and called back,

"Don't worry *kanojo*, I'm good!"

"Danger. Otaku language detected. Engage combat protocols," a voice said from speakers throughout the lab. Oh dear. Nuk barrelled down the ramp and sprinted back outside, chased by another cluster of angry arachnomorphs.

"They called me an otaku!" Nuk complained, but there was no time for semantic analysis. The spiders crashed through the barely standing guild, and this time it was very much touch and go – the spider's whirling bludgeons touch your arm, and off it goes. Ruka of the Thousand Guardians watched her sword fly off in her former right hand, but immediately pulled a dagger with her left and bashed at the nearest spider casing. Eventually each spider bot was torn a few new ports, and the fighting was over again.

"Please, stop going in there my Prince! This is too much!" Wodston said, struggling to raise his head off the ground. Nuk, one of the few still standing by the end of it, agreed. The next day of the great siege was spent with everyone lain up under a few tall trees nearby, covered all over in gauze and splints. All the while Nuk was sat in the dirt looking up the tower.

"My man, was this what those old sieges were like?" he asked Wodston.

"Not quite. You couldn't set up a field infirmary like this in the desert. Skimmers wouldn't have it."

"Oh yeah, the skimmers. Remember when we used to get beaten up by those guys?"

"Yes, my Prince. Quite well."

"Makes you think about how far we've come."

"I don't follow, my Prince."

"Now we're being beaten up by robot spiders. That's way cooler!"

"Ah. From that perspective, perhaps life has improved," Wodston conceded. "But would it not be better to remain relatively healthy and intact?"

"Ah, my man. You are old, but not wise. If we do not have monsters to fight, then we must grapple with the monsters... inside our souls."

"Ah. You mean, self-doubt, for example?"

"I mean that I'm not a damned otaku, that stupid building thinks it knows me!" Nuk burst out.

"And, what is an otaku exactly?"

"You still haven't read the classics. It's like, someone who never gets a beach chapter, but must always dream of it."

"Is that bad?"

"It's the fugging worst! It's as bad as calling me a loser!"

"Wait, the building called you a loser?" Izayah said. "That's nonsense!"

"I know!" Nuk shouted. "That's it, I'm sure we've killed them all now, I'm taking another look!"

That was on the morning of the third day, which for reasons entirely unrelated, was the third time Nuk came running out of the lab with cantankerous clankers in tow. Another fight, and still no one had managed to die, but everyone was certainly thinking about it after all these terrible beatings. Some of the hivers were comatose, hardly anyone could walk, and the stashes of painkillers and bandages had been run dry. Only a hero could rescue this ailing army from peril, and a hero they had.

"Well, watching you fleshies get it handed to ya's been great, but I'm gonna help ya out here," Rick said.

"Rick. Don't tell me you can control those things?" Izumi asked.

"Control? Oh I get it – just 'cause I'm a robot I must be friends with ALL other robots. Damn, you gotta get out more sister. Sure I access their- wait, look I'm not going there, it's rude man, just straight up rude. Ain't touching your firewall, ain't touching theirs, you hear me?"

"Technically I can hear you, but that's not really helping."

"I'm saying I'll hook you up with some beds for your bruises and shid. I dunno. Back in a flash."

Rick thudded off into the dawn, and ran with super-human speed back to Drifter's Last. There he purchased a load of camping gear, and returned it to the siege. With camp-beds, fresh medical supplies and the finest homemade booze the empire's backalleys had to offer, the next couple of nights under the stars passed much less painfully. In fact, most were back on their feet soon, and laying about was getting boring.

"Right, shall I do it again?" Nuk asked.

"Oh go on then," Izayah said, waving his Guardians into formation. Nuk popped up to the tower, and stood proudly in the main doors.

"Hello everyone. I am well versed in Japanan literature," he said. The spiders scanned him curiously, but didn't move. "No? I mean, I really like those pictures." Still nothing. Nuk huffed and pulled a light novel from his bag. It opened with well-worn ease onto a particular page spread featuring a hilarious incident of semi-accidental groping.

"This is Mikiru-chan, and while we don't live in the same dimension, I believe we share a strong romantic bond! But I'm not an otaku!" Nuk declared. That did it.

"Critical degeneration detected, eliminating parasite vector," the voice said. Nuk had some more spiders to show his three-dimensional friends, and an epic battle with the power of teamwork (and so on) was had. With this, all the spiders on the first floor of the lab were out of action. Next, Nuk went up to the second level, where a couple more awaited.

"Hey bakas, check this out!" he said, running across the room with a stooped posture and his arms outstretched behind him. For reasons known only to cultured literati, and the killer robots that hunt them, this threw the spiders into a rage. They came out to face the guild as well, and by now the crew were getting the hang of pinning the deadly appendages down while someone found the off switch.

Now there was only one spider left in the lab, and after it too wandered out to its demise, the siege of Shun was over.

"Victory!" Nuk shouted.

"Fugging hell. Everyone alive?" Izumi asked. Apparently so. With that confirmed, she suddenly felt more nervous than she had during the fighting, and about half as nervous as she had been when Nuk- never mind that. It was time to collect the spoils of war.

The upper level of the lab had a number of store-rooms, and as Nuk and Izumi hacked open old containers, they found reams of print-outs, masterfully built machine parts, and things even rarer.

"Holy shid Nuk, it's an uninstalled core!" Izumi shouted, pulling a lumpy blue sphere out of a box.

"Nice. We could roll it at Coinslots tinmen and see how many we get each time," Nuk suggested. But, as Izumi explained, these AI cores were more likely to turn the tinmen into fully-fledged living beings than knock them over.

"These are what the Second Empire used to make their soldiers. It's got remnants of the First Empire tech that built the skeletons! These are... We have to study this Nuk. This could change everything."

"In what way?"

"It can decode the oldest data. All this data, all these pages. If we get this to Enrico, we're done. I'll be the best tech hunter of all time."

"And the drugs?"

"Nuk, if you can get me and this core to the scribes in one piece, I'll get them to draft a green-machine plan from those notes you found. No problem now we've got this. Kind of a waste of the greatest scientific discovery in two thousand bloody years, but hey, gotta test it out on something."

"Fugg. Izzy, we're literally the best team."

"It's all you, Prince, I assure you."

"And it's all *for* you, Izz, I assure you."

"Ha, thanks. I've got a good feeling about this."

"Speaking of good feelings, before we go back out..."

"Nuk, the core..."

"What?"

"It's literally watching!"

"What?"

"Fugg, how'd you know?" the core said, sounding suspiciously like Rick.

"Disconnect Rick!"

"Ten stacks."

"Twenty, now fugg off."

Izumi grabbed a sheet and threw it over the core, then grabbed another and threw it over Nuk. With precious pages of ancient books littered all over the floor, Izumi seemed more interested in the present than history, and to be fair, that particular present was quite a lot more interesting.

"Who connected me to zis? Vot is zat sound?!" the AI core said in Enrico's voice, but Nuk and Izumi, being closer to the source of 'that sound', didn't clock the intrusion.

So, the week-long struggle for control of the lab had left the guild loaded up with ancient treasures, and knowledge worth far more. Now their return to civilisation might just bring about... well, a return to civilisation, more broadly speaking. But that was pie in the sky thinking. Still, even if these discoveries would only lead to a revolution in drug production, that was more than enough!

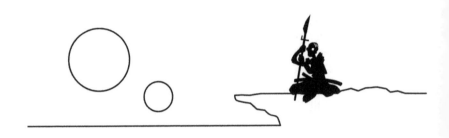

Chapter 26
Machines of Future Past

Gary and Garette were weighed down with all kinds of boring, grey treasures; cold to the touch, dull to the eye, and worth more than all the cats in the world. With the plunder of the forgotten land of Shun secured, the guild turned back home. They were going to travel back via Admag, seeing as it was nearby, and this route took them around the southern perimeter of good old Mount Doom. There they stumbled upon some more Second Empire ruins, adding yet more wordy, papery booty to the pile.

After they turned north to enter the Shek Kingdom, they came upon a curious scene. Along the east slope of Arach there were camps filled with mercenaries and bounty hunters. One waved Nuk over as the guild sauntered in.

"That's quite the crew you got. Going after the Bugmaster then?" the man asked.

"Bugmaster, yeah. I heard he has quite the treasure up there," Nuk grinned.

"Oh I've heard no end of it. That's why all the chancers you'd ever want are here going for it. Only thing is, I've heard no one's ever gone up there and lived. Kinda just waiting for the right moment, ya know?"

"I know exactly, *precisely* my man. Good luck."

Nuk returned to the guild and beckoned them onwards.

"Shouldn't we tell them the truth, my Prince?" Wodston asked.

"Wodston, why are you so insensitive? Think how disappointed we were when we found that shiddy treasure. Well, excluding the bugmer

Those guys came all the way up here, made their little camp, stressed themselves out over this, and you wanna tell them that the treasure is just fugging teeth, and that Bad Green's eaten most of them?"

"The garru ate them!" Gustavsen quickly insisted. Wodston got Nuk's so-called point, and they all left the bounty hunters to their placebo quest. They travelled on to Admag, where they could enjoy a little shopping and such after their long campaign. While dropping in to visit Izayah's folks, they actually did see the Bugmaster, caged in the royal barracks. He shot Nuk a gleaming white smile and waved him over.

"Champion, getting justice's down to you now. Don't let those robos get away with their disgusting schemes," he said. The guards rushed over and gagged him – speaking was against the rules of course – and so Nuk just wandered off with that mysterious request in tow.

Outside, Gustavsen had been chatting with a local livestock trader. When the guild assembled to leave, he proudly held his purchase up before them.

"Behold! Ass!" he shouted. Well, it was actually a goat, and a tiny kid of a goat at that. Shame about the name.

"Bad Green, you gonna be the new goat king?" Nuk asked.

"Never. However, this offering will one day win his favour."

"So to win his favour, you're going to give him your 'Ass'?"

"Precisely."

"A tried and tested method," Nuk shrugged. Gustavsen followed him, Ass and all, as they set out. They walked east for the next two days until they finally arrived back at the Tech Scribe headquarters on the far side of Shun. There, while Ruka browsed replacements for her missing arm and Gustavsen showed his cute miniature goat off to the fawning bookworms ("Behold. Ass!"), Nuk and Izumi gathered up all the history and prepared their pitch to Enrico.

"Have you actually read all this?" Nuk asked. There were hundreds of pages of miscellaneous primary sources, and loads of books, diagrams, and digital nik-naks, all on top of that priceless AI core.

"Well I was meant to read it all, just in case they covered it up or something, but I got distracted," Izumi said.

"What by?"

"By... you."

"Oh yeah. Not really a wrong choice though, it is?"

"We'll see. Carry these."

Nuk was given a pile of old maps, and the very first one was actually pretty juicy.

"This is... It's battle diagrams," he said. "Look, there's a border, and the shaded bit's next to the picture of an eye."

"An eye, or *the* Eye?"

"So where it says 'control tower'..."

"Okran's Tablespoon. You just did some history!"

"You should call me history boy."

"What?"

"What?"

"Whatever. Take off that hat, and let's do this."

Inside Enrico's office, AKA the bar, the pair let the archivist flip through their haul, and stroke the outside of their AI core. I don't know, probably an academic thing.

"Zis is the most comprehensive collection I have ever seen. It is intact. Ve have ze var between zee humans and ze skeletons. Ze var vith ze Earth clans. Zis von is quoting original First Empire sources. Zis is... Zis is..."

"Historic?" Nuk offered.

"Histrionic!" Enrico called with a swoop of his hands.

"What's this human-skeleton war?" Izumi asked.

"Oh it's all quite dramatic. Humans, skeletons... just very different creatures. Zere is nothing here about vhy zey were fighting. Well, technically it's all up here in ze old *kopf*, since I was zere after all. But zis is not enough to unforget it. But yes, zere was much back and forth, much talk of one 'Stobe' fellow – zat definitely rings a bell – oh and I sink ze skeletons von, but humans are still here so... Maybe ze whole sing was rained off in ze end? I don't know, we'll get ze monkeys to read it all and vrite it up."

"That's fascinating. I think..." Izumi nodded. "But what about all these technical documents. This is ancient technology, isn't it?"

"Yes, yes it is. Zis will take years to reverse engineer, but I have years, I have years by ze fugging boatload."

"Wait, Enrico, these discoveries are mine, don't forget."

"Yours? Zese documents are for ze good old all ze creatures in the world! You can't own zem!"

"But- We had to go through some real shid to get these!"

"And everyone else went through real shid without zem, my greasy sister. But actually, I do have an idea. How about, you can keep all ze glory and vhat not, if you do all ze work!"

"Gladly. This is the most important endeavour of my lifetime. And your lifetime."

"Oh you say zat; I vas zere vith ze whole sliced bread sing."

"What's that?"

"Lost technology, pay it no heed. Now your little fellow has been staring at me for some time, and I zink I vould like to have him killed. Do you object?"

"No, he's my... fri- boy- assistant."

"You know about science, boy-assistant?"

"I know that the appliance of science, is drugs!" Nuk chimed.

"Oh, you really do know it. Okay, you're in, pink eyes. You've got a lot of vork ahead of you."

Enrico ended up piling a load more books, tools, and mechanical relics onto the guild, so that Izumi could analyse them for her magnum opus of a paper back home. Act one of the opus was to be a drugs machine, but with all these resources, she could probably get some even more valuable patents to her name. However, going home would require crossing Venge, and crossing Venge would mean walking very near to Nuk's little historical discovery on the old map. It was mid-afternoon, and the laser was happily spurting around the desert, but with everyone eager to get home soon, they were convinced to follow Nuk out into the danger zone.

Clearly they'd all earned a little luck, as they made it to the so-called 'Control Tower' without being eviscerated. Up they went to loot up and shelter until nightfall, but at that very moment their luck ran out. The place, as it turned out, was being used in the modern era as a central base for the legions of headless skeletons the guild had scuffled with previously. These leftovers from that human-skeleton war still remembered their programming, and immediately everyone was battling the skeleton army amid the messy workshop on the tower's first floor.

Red Rick wandered about amid the action, and spotted two particular skeletons that still had their heads attached. He tried to duck out of their view, but they'd already seen him.

"Hey, Red Rick, is that you?" one called.

"Hey hey, if it ain't Screamer the False. Still doing that screaming thing these days?" Rick replied, coolly standing back up.

"Nah, the speakers got torched by the Eye."

"Shame. Guessing this ain't really the control tower then?"

"What you talking about? Oh, you remember Ponk, don't you?" The first headed skeleton introduced a second headed skeleton, who gave a strange, jerky bow.

"*Konbanwa, Rick-taisho,*" it said.

"Yep I remember him. We sent him over so you would kill him, ya know?" Rick said.

"Ah, I think he's cute. Anyway, do you still have your stick?" the first skeleton asked.

"Yep. Don't leave the dome without it – remember when there used to be all those domes?"

"Those were good times. We used to beat the fleshies so much. Will you join me now, old friend?"

"Can't really do that. You see, I'm kinda with these fleshies right about now."

"With them? Is that a biological, sexual thing?"

"Oh sometimes. Trying not to think about it."

"So what, are you going to give me the stick?"

"Yep. Not a sexual thing, mind you. Sorry man, times are changing."

Rick whipped out his big stick, and started swinging. The skeleton goons were beaten into hibernation, and the ones with heads, while much more skilled on account of having eyes, eventually got a bit too much system shock too. After exploring the tower, it turned out there was one more whole skeleton on the scene, locked in a cage in the corner of a storage room.

"I don't believe it, they didn't kill any of you did they?" Rick said.

"This skeleton is broken," Elaina commented.

"No shid. This whole place was meant to be where the broken fellas got recycled. Seems old Screamer was just turning them into his personal army."

"Do you think we could repair him?"

"Not really. This guy's Agnu. He was a knight, but it weren't battle that took him down. Ghost in the machine got the better of him. Happened to a few guys. Give the biologicials too much stick, and something just kicks in. Probably their fault, but you can't get around the feelings."

"What feelings?"

"More like, a sense, a doubt. It was something, alright. And sometimes thinking about it got you caught in a loop. That's why it's best not to think about it at all, or you'll end up like Agnu."

Agnu was shaking about in his cage, and was grunting and growling in short bursts. It seemed that was all he could say.

"Should we let him out?" Elaina asked.

"Only if you're gonna shut him down. Code looping's no way to live."

"I would never do that."

"Then don't you do anything."

With that, Agnu was left in his little cage while the guild started picking out some more choice pieces for analysis. It wasn't as fertile as the Shun lab, but the tower was still packed with old books and curious gizmos to loot. Only problem was that while everyone was sorting through the mess, Ells had wandered over to Agnu's cage.

"GHGHGHG," Agnu said.

"Oh, don't worry, I can hear you," Ells replied.

"GHGHGHGH," Agnu went on.

"If you promise to follow the rules. Although one rule is you're not allowed to listen to me, so maybe that means you don't have to follow the rules... Wait... Err..."

"GHGHGHGH."

"You're stuck in a loop too? Loop friends!"

Some Bloody Ells magic was worked on the cage door, and open it swung. Agnu stepped out, looked around at the aghast guild, and declared,

"GHGHGHGH."

"He says thanks!" Ells reported.

"Rick, is this alright?" Izumi asked.

"Well, if Eggman can speak machine code then we're fine, otherwise we're about to get beaten up by a wild, glitched out bio-bash knight."

The second thing didn't happen, so... the first thing must be true? It seems impossible, but that appeared to be what was happening.

Once all the looting was done it was the middle of the night, which of course is the perfect time to cross Venge, so off the guild went. They had tied up Screamer and Ponk to take back into the Empire, but this unfortunately caused all the hidden companies of their thrall soldiers to emerge from the rocks and harry the guild at every turn. They were in a constant state of battle along the road north, with this bio-bash knight Agnu getting stuck right into it. It was likely meant to be a quest for revenge, but bashing these non-bio opponents proved difficult for him, mainly because every movement he made was immediately interrupted by a decision to make another. The strange, ancient dance that resulted was quite fascinating, but far from deadly.

The guild eventually prevailed, and fought their way up to the Eye – the grounded one that is. Agnu rode on Rick's shoulders, where he was almost as high as the Beak Things that greeted them on the Empire's frontier. Was the world trying to conspire to keep Izumi from unpacking all the secrets she had gathered? Or was Nuk just navigating them into Beak Thing nests because he had one eye on the latest ancient picture-book he'd swiped? It's almost certainly one and not the other, but let's compromise, and say it was Wodston's fault.

Eventually they all arrived in Brink, where Screamer the False and Ponk were clanked down in the police station in exchange for hefty rewards – a good two thousand years as a wanted terrorist racks you up quite the bounty.

"Sorry guys, but war's over, ya know? Ended a while ago actually," Rick said to them.

"You gone soft. You gone fleshy, man! You forget what they did?" Screamer said.

"Yeah, I did actually, and things are going just fine. You can sit in a cage like my main man here and think about what you did for a couple of thousand, maybe you'll work it out."

"Joke's on these fleshies, I'll just shut down and then wake up when I'm free. See you then, Red Rick."

"No you won't."

"*Rick-taisho, aishiteru,*" Ponk said.

"Yeah yeah," Rick waved, and the bots were carried off into custody.

From Brink it was a short walk back out of the Empire and into reaver territory. Then it was a rolling battle with them to avoid paying the tolls, and then a short, groaning hobble down the hill into Manksand Canyon. The tinman army stood proudly guarding the main gate, and watched with austere discipline as the crew filed in and collapsed into bed – it was four in the morning after all. But someone was too excited to sleep. Izumi started dragging all the bits and bobbles into her office, stuffing her library with new books and arraying the machine parts and AI goodies on a workbench.

"So, 'future-girl', did you- oh my fugging phoenix!" Jaz exclaimed as she dropped in for her usual update. She was a tech hunter as well (it's easy to forget) and knew exactly how unprecedented Izumi's haul was.

"Too important to talk to you right now," Izumi said.

"Fugg off. This is great. You got like the whole Scratch collection in here. And more. Is that an AI core?"

"Yes it is. And yes, she did," the core said.

"Rick, stop it!" Izumi squeaked.

"My work is done here. I'll be the shed."

"Sorry, it's still active."

"Okran's Nobbles, are you for real?" Jaz asked.

"Really for real. An unused AI core. This can analyse all these pages for us, and decode the secrets of the Second Empire – and maybe even earlier!"

"Great, but who cares? Did you really get with Prince Ponce?"

"He and I have formed a very successful partnership."

"What the fugg is that? Are you really, really ain't never gonna say it?"

"Nope. Now fugg off. Scientific revolution can't wait for jealous friends."

"Oh now that's the last fugging straw. I'm gonna go slobber on that Prince right now."

"No, wait!"

"Ha, I knew it!"

"I mean, I- Do you want- Please just be nice about it."

"Nice as the Manksand morn my love. I'm happy for ya, shid for brains. Don't worry, I'll keep to slobbering on Big Stick Rick instead. If you're done with him, that is?"

"Done and rusted, fugg off."

Jaz complied. The next day the real work began. Nuk, Izumi and Elaina started the mammoth task of reverse engineering old technology from incomplete sketches and descriptions, helped along by the ball of general artificial intelligence Nuk was rolling around on the desk. Yes, Nuk wasn't the best analyst really, but he couldn't be torn away from that most important of initial tasks: designing the green machine.

The hard fighting was over, and the hard writing began. But this intellectual battle would be far more decisive, as now the TCM+ Guild would begin to unravel the ancient, illegal, and highly profitable secrets of long lost societies, and in doing so, gain the power to change the world forever. Change it for the better? Err... no comment.

Chapter 27
Scary Numan

In Manksand Canyon the construction industry was booming. Which of course means that an old man was single-handedly building electric wind turbines on the hill, and huge sandstone watchtowers astride the base approach. Being stonkingly rich these days, chocolate baron Nuk could afford a little opulence. The locals didn't like it; the canyon was raided by the reavers and pirates of the outlands more than ever.

With harpoons now shooting down from the towers at great distances, this all did little to disturb the day and night academia in Izumi's office. The secrets of the ancients began to emerge from the texts like hashish emerging from a hiver's latrine – the mess coalesced, and soon it was worth putting your hand in to try your luck.

What I'm trying (and failing) to say is that Nuk got his little invention up and running on Izumi's roof. A big copper boiler with all manner of pipes, gauges, and heating elements. This brown machine was the green machine.

"My man! The drug leaves!" Nuk called out. Wodston ferried Nuk some dried hemp stalks. "My man, the mank!" was the next order. Wodston handed Nuk a bucket of what passed for water around those parts. "My man, the hype!" was the final command.

"Err, my Prince, I believe in you," Wodston offered as Nuk started feeding leaves into the top of the boiler.

"Harder my man!"

"You can do it, my Prince! Live your dreams!"

"I'm doing it my man, it's really happening. I can't believe it! Get that water shid in there, hydrate the fugging fire and shid... What was the next step...? Gotta turn this... My man, I can't hear you!"

"My Prince, you're amazing! I've never seen anything like it! Keep it up, my Prince!"

"I won't stop 'till I reach the top!" Nuk exclaimed. He was talking about filling up the boiler of course, but Izumi couldn't help but wonder just what was happening upstairs. It was nothing suspicious at all, just some good old fashioned homebrew drug production. Did it work? To find out, Nuk happily volunteered to test the first batch. According to the Prince's own account of events, he then spent several hours frolicking with animals in the long grass, excitedly recounting how one 'Professor Oak' had a very special present for him.

"Oak... that's... a tree on Earth. Has he secretly been reading my science books? He's... He always surprises me," Izumi wistfully commented to herself. If only she knew.

In all, Nuk had a great couple of weeks, stirring the hashish pot in a constant daze while Wodston kept him as close to alive as it is comfortable to be. What was everyone else up to? Time off really, with plenty of lying around, a few folk trying their hand at the farming of both green and brown, and if you got bored, you could always go out and start playing with corpses outside the gate.

If that wasn't enough for you, you could also mine and process tin for Rick, who was locked in his shed in the whole time working on his little tin models. It was quite the hobby, but it had become rather suspicious. Rick kept refusing to open the door, demanding that all material be thrown in through the window. And he started adding to the list of materials things that surely weren't relevant – leather, glass beads, and strangest of all, a sample of the funtime corpses. This was all eventually organised, as his new skeleton friend Agnu was good at keeping secrets, and no one believed Ells when he told the others what Rick was doing in there. What was he doing? It's hard to explain. In fact there is no particular explanation at all, so I'll have to just give it to you straight.

Rick had given himself a little makeover.

"What the fugg?!" Nuk screamed. "This green is fugging mental! He looks like... like..."

"A human!" Izumi exclaimed.

"Hello, friendos. It's ya boi, Red Rick. Guess I'm like Pink Dink or something now," Rick said with a wet wave.

Rick was sporting an entire body of fleshy... flesh. Bald head. Bulky physique. Beady brown eyes – and beady is very much the right term for it. He was...

"He's a human!" Izayah helpfully pointed out.

"More like, nu-man!" Ells said.

"Yep. That's right," Rick nodded.

"Coinslot, are you... Do you even have a coins- Forget I said anything," Nuk memorably said.

"Rick, do you want to explain yourself?" Izumi asked.

"Nope. This is me now. Still got the stick in here somewhere so I don't wanna hear any back-talk. Skeleton look weren't doing me no good, ya know? Got a lotta baggage, that shid. So just shut up and let's go leak bodily fluids like a load of genuine fleshies, huh?"

"Man, you freak me out," Nuk said, placing and then immediately removing a hand from Rick's icy-cold shoulder meat. "But hey, let's leak our fluids with the best of 'em."

"Man. You biologicals gotta lotta magic in you, ya know?"

"Magic?" Izayah said. "Wait... You... The skeleton wizard!" he shouted, jumping at Rick with outstretched arms. "I knew you were real!"

"Same. Damn, I was gettin' a lotta hugs before, you know what I'm saying?"

"Rick, you are the answer to the prophecy!" Izayah claimed, but Nuk dragged him away.

"Don't worry, it's 'cause you're basically a moving corpse he's got all excited and shid, it's a shek thing man," he said. "My dad got blazed and told me only a skeleton wizard would save the empire or something. So that's that. Kinda relevant actually 'cause we got some work to do. It's drug running time! Bad Green, I need your goat, follow me."

"Never. Why do you need *my* Ass?" Gustavsen complained.

"Because, man, I need to smuggle drugs, with *your* Ass."

"Ah. To contribute to the ascension of a worthy Prince would bring pleasure to any Ass."

"Please, Prince Gustavsen, stop talking!" Izumi demanded.

"Never! My Ass does not quit, so why should I?"

This sort of thing carried on for a long time, but the main takeaway is that firstly, Gustavsen's goat had a very funny name, and secondly, bags of hashish were strapped around it for transit back to the imperial capital at Heft. Indeed, it technically wasn't illegal for a goat to possess narcotics, so the scheme was surely watertight.

This meant that at long last Nuk was going home. As a reminder, his plan was to blaze his dad halfway to the big fiery thing in the sky, and then use his compromised state to get Nuk back to being heir, and perhaps a little more than that. Let's see how that goes.

Crossing into the empire's core lands near Heng brought a nostalgic reminder of the land Nuk had left. Gangs of hopeless slavers were all over the place, trying to beat the guild into a valuable pulp. For Rick, the pulp was already sorted, but the nonetheless, the slavers were not long for this world.

"It's this fugging shid - exactly this shid - that messes everything up!" Nuk said.

"If his majesty allows it, perhaps we'll finally get a chance to avenge your foul treatment, my Prince," Wodston said.

"Even if he doesn't, man. Green Rebellion's brewing, I can smell it – and it's not just Ass either."

"Well said, my Prince."

Eventually they all made it to Heft, and on a good day too, for it wasn't even under siege by skimmers. They walked right on through the huge city gates, with no attention to – sigh – Gustavsen's Ass's bulging bags.

The guild was back in town, and all the members who hadn't seen the old HQ could marvel at the history contained within – skimmer steaks rotting in crawling wooden boxes, pages of old light novels pasted on the walls, the characters within starting out with flushed cheeks, and who could miss the strange hole in the ground that dominated the main living area, and the pump that spat out sloppy brown hydration medium with irregular belching wheezes. Truly, it was the best of times.

Nuk waded through the mess to get to his old wardrobe, from which he produced his noble attire. He threw aside his cool leather and chainmail setup and bathed in the hydration medium – although the term bathed implies this increased his level of hygiene, which is admittedly misleading. Then with a few fine threads and a stroke of a skimmer-tooth comb, he was about as dapper as an Emperor in waiting can get.

He asked Gustavsen to hand the goat and its cargo over. He probably said something hilarious like 'surrender your Ass to me', but these vital details were lost to history I'm afraid. Then he marched out into the street with Ass in tow, and made the fateful walk up to the imperial palace. Seeing him, the guards quickly stowed away their valuables and blocked the doors.

"Stop it right there, my Lord. You were not summoned," one said.

"I was actually man. Go tell Dad I've brought him the secret of the skeleton wizard," Nuk proclaimed.

"What the fugg are you talking about, my Lord?"

"Just do it!"

"Alright, if you let me stroke your goat there."

"Man, if you knew it's name that would be so funny. Ah. Classic. Go on then."

The deal was undertaken, and a samurai soon returned from upstairs.

"Yeah, he kept repeating 'skeleton wizard', and starting banging the arm of the throne. I think this might actually be something," he reported.

Thus Nuk was allowed to proceed up to the very heart of the empire, wreathed in a strange aromatic smoke. He waved his way through it towards the throne.

"Dad? What's all this shid?" he asked. Tengu was slumped on the throne, with a charred lump of something in hand.

"Green boy. Green boy is that you?"

"It's your only child, whose name I leave to you to remember. What's with this smoke?"

"We ran out. Nothing left. Had to smoke this weird-ass bread. Golden Brown they called it. Don't do shid for me boy, didn't do shid, it's like waking up at high noon this shid, it's like finding out ya sister stole ya music box, this fugging shid! Green boy, gotta save me... I'll give you anything..."

"How about, everything?"

"Yeah, I got one of those. It's yours, Green boy."

"Well, that's all I needed to hear. You, write that down," Nuk said to a guard in the corner. "Oh, and then, close your eyes. I'm about to reveal what I've hidden in my- Forget it, you need the context for it to be funny. Drugs time."

Finally all of Nuk's hard work, which may or may not have actually been performed by Nuk himself, was going to pay off. One by one he revealed blocks of cool, crumbly hashish, drawing desperate pants from the Emperor. By the time everything was unloaded, Tengu's throne was positively fortified with premium, mank-boiled green.

"Okran's... Drooping... Ear lobes..." Tengu whispered. He reached out and stroked his hands across the epic supply. It crumbled against his fingers the pieces dancing a gentle invitation as they fell away. He stood from the throne, opened his arms, and swung down face first into the mighty pile. It exploded everywhere, kicking up a mucky fog that shoo'd the brown-smoke away. This was truly a beautiful metaphor. When it cleared, Tengu was standing again, perfectly still. He looked at Nuk.

"Nuk. It's you," he mumbled.

"Dad. You feelin' human?" Nuk asked.

"Man, I ain't felt this human in a long time!" he said, grabbing Nuk for a fragrant hug. "My boy's here! And I'm back on top! Yeah baby! Come on, let's get some air, and shid."

Nuk and Tengu went down to the dining hall, where the open doors brought in a refreshing desert night wind. There, Nuk had quite the tale to tell.

"And so in the end, I was like 'suck my sword', and they all laughed, and then I killed them all," Nuk was saying. I don't think the tale he told was quite the same as the one I've recounted so far, but I suppose it hit a few similar beats. "And then the Goat King opened his mouth, and there he was: standing in the flames, the bilgemaker himself, Sepphiron."

Okay I don't know what story he told, but to be fair, he was caught in that hashish explosion too. Tengu asked to meet the guild Nuk was talking about, and they were summoned up to the palace too.

"Damn boy, you gotta real freak show here," Tengu commented.

"Your majesty, you honour us with your praise," Izayah said. "We are indeed rather aside from the usual path life might ask of us. But that is precisely why we have come so much further along than those less fortunate."

"This is my corpse-carrier, he's the Prince of the Shek Kingdom, Izayah" Nuk explained.

"I don't believe it. My boy making links like a smith. Prince Izayah, you've done my boy right, and so you've done me and your momma right. This is the good stuff that the good stuff gives ya, ya know?"

"I will ponder these surely wise words," Izayah said.

"And Dad, this is Izzy," Nuk said, suddenly clamming up.

"Your majesty, your highness, I am forever in your debt, please excuse my humble presence," Izumi grovelled.

"Huh. Who's she then? Your girlfriend?" Tengu asked. The guild was silent. The atmosphere was as delicate as a brick of green.

"Y-y-... Yeah..." Nuk managed to say. Everybody was uproariously cheering (or sneering) on the inside, I expect, but in action all that happened was Izumi stared at Nuk in shock.

"Nuk... I mean your majesty, I wouldn't dare," she blurted out.

"Dare away. 'Bout time this kid got a proper relationship," Tengu nodded.

"Ha, oh, did he not...?"

"Nope. Real loser this guy."

"Dad, please, I was busy, and I had commitments," Nuk said.

"Yeah commitments to your Okran forsaken Japanese picture books. At least ya finally got it outta ya system huh?"

"Sure, totally."

"Good. That's no hobby for a twenty-year-old man to be obsessing over."

"What? You're twenty?" Izumi gasped.

"Yeah. So what?" Nuk shot back.

"But you look... You look like... Your eyes and your face..."

"Ha, don't worry about that, my child," Tengu laughed. "He's been on the blazing blocks too long, little dreg. Screws ya up in the face after a while. Yeah he looks Narko-flicking thirty-five at least. Get googles man, the googles, they do everything."

"So wait, how old are you?" Nuk asked Izumi.

"Err... A little older than that," she said through a plastic smile.

"I'm two hundred and fifty one!" Ells added.

"You all require fishman juice!" Gustavsen reminded them.

"What a bunch you are," Tengu said. "If you're done introducing yourself to each other, let's get some sit down and see what's what."

There was some clarification of the real story to Tengu at this point, and as he heard it he could not help but be both impressed and humbled.

"Shid Nuk, I been a real deadbeat. And you saved me. You're a super hero. Green boy," he said.

"I wanted to do it. Most of the time," Nuk shrugged. "I mean what I really want is to be back in, and stuff. I wanna be the Prince, ya know?"

"You are the Prince! Consider your delightful crimes absolved!" Tengu shouted, drawing a cheer from the guild. "Damn, my boy, my only boy, how could I be so blind? I ain't never gonna give you up, never gonna let you down."

"Not this shid again," Rick commented.

"What the? That's a skeleton voice you got man!" Tengu said, scrambling over to Rick.

"Yep. Deal with it bigshot, or deal with my stick."

"Dad, do you know about the skeleton wizard?" Nuk said.

"Skeleton wizard? What the fugg is that?"

"Oh, doesn't matter. Anyway, this robo's a numan. It's a thing now, I dunno."

"Numan? That's some real shid," Tengu said with a stroke of his chin. "With a get up like that, you could sneak right into the Holy Phoenix's ten story latrine and give him a stick to remember."

"Yeah, what's the deal with all that Holy Nation stuff?"

"It's bad son. It's real bad. Can't take it. Those freaks wanna burn everything. My captains ain't got nowhere in a year, and I don't even know what happened since the green ran out. Nuk, it's like- You said you wanted to be a Prince? Being a Prince comes with a lotta shid, and this right here is just it. Holy Nation's gonna be grinding us down day in day out, until either us or Okran sorts it out. You've proven to me that that you have enough drugs to solve any problem. So I gotta ask it to you again: help me, Nuk, you're my only hope."

"If you give me the power, I'll give you the peace, man," Nuk said.

"You got all the power you need. But you'll have mine as well. Ruling Prince Nuk Tashino is here, and this empire's gonna get behind him no matter what!" Tengu declared. This declaration was made real without delay – messengers ran off to inform the whole empire that Nuk was officially back on the books, nay, on the cover of the book. The Green Boy was the Green Prince, in line to be the Green Emperor.

But Tengu was right. The Holy Nation, whom the guild have successfully avoided thus far, had armies ready to wipe the world clean of all those they hated: skeletons, hivers, shek, and any human who didn't shine as bright as Okran's icy light, or couldn't grow a decent beard in short order. Basically, they hated everything. You know how that goes, these kinda guys show up in all kinds of places. Right next to Nuk's empire was the wrong place, and right as he was planning to to spread his poorly-defined drugs-based utopia to the world was the wrong time. Something had to be done. Thus was the next chapter in Nuk's tale decided upon.

However there is one little detail of this royal reunion worth explaining: after everyone was returning back to the guild's properties, Izumi dallied for a moment in the throne room, admiring the mess the hash-bash had left. There was the throne, empty. She walked up it, saw that no one was around, and took a seat. It wasn't that comfy, she thought, but then she suddenly had a very important revelation. She was the actual confirmed girlfriend of the second most powerful noble in the empire. She, poor little Izumi, strung along for months by a man significantly younger than her as it turned out, was in line to be Empress.

What would the world of the Green Emperor and Greasy Empress be like? Let's see where this dream takes us...

Chapter 28
Big Shot in the Wild West

"So there's this place, all that stuff, this bit... I dunno... Any ideas?" Nuk said. He was sitting over a map of the Holy Nation's territory, and had been freshly tasked by his father to do something about these murderous neighbours.

"You're the Prince. What does your instinct tell you?" Sandor said.

"This is a crisis. In ancient texts they made dealing with this stuff so easy. I mean, say for example, you tripped over and landed on top your senpai friend in a compromising position. With their sophisticated techniques they flowed like water, and followed the situation through as if it was planned from the very beginning. See pages 13 to 27 on the wall there."

Everyone took a look, but it didn't explain all that much.

"Why are her eyes like love hearts?" Ells asked.

"Because she adapted to the situation and came out on top," Nuk explained.

"But so soon after- She must be faking it," Izumi concluded.

"Then we too shall fake it!" Nuk declared. "If those Holy hogs wanna kill us so much, then we have to accept that fact, and just kill them first! Flow outta the crisis real cool!"

"That's what you're taking away from this... literature?"

"Are we gonna have love heart eyes?" Ells said.

"Yes, Charlie my boy, we're gonna go pay these fuggs a visit and see our little predicament through to its... most satisfying conclusion," Nuk said.

"Man, what is all this shid?" Rick said. He was staring closely at the drawings, and didn't seem impressed. "Biologicals got all this shid they gotta do. What you thinking Agnu?"

"GHGHGHGHGH!" Agnu commented.

"He wants to come out on top!" Ells translated.

"Then let's cease burning our eyes on this fascinating study of human anatomy, and get marching!" Izayah said, and soon enough they were burning their eyes with the sandy desert wind instead, not to mention burning calories as they ran frantically across the expansive skimmer ranges west of the city. They were heading towards Bast, the hotly contested border with the Holy Nation. They arrived in record time on account of the horde of skimmers that chased them all the way there.

"I don't think they're backing off!" Elaina huffed.

"Must be our smell. My Prince, is it your... supply?" Wodston asked.

"Man don't even go there. I ain't leaving my stash! I'd rather leave you," Nuk gurgled. "Keeping bloody running! We've got more legs than them, all together, so we're faster. It's science!"

With such high quality athletics coaching, how could they lose? I suppose the reason the skimmers started catching up must have been that small millipedes, moving at the speed of light, were bumping into them from behind. But as the horde got close, the oily sands of Bast revealed salvation.

"For the Emperor!" a voice called. From behind a ridge, a company of United Cities soldiers burst into view and charged the skimmers with outstretched spears.

"Exactly... according... to my plan," Nuk panted, waving for everyone to turn around. It was truly a cunning ambush, and the skimmers were so convinced by the guild's panicked flight, that they fell for the lucky mastermind's ploy. The horde was very soon no more.

"Prince Tashino, you're safe," the samurai captain said, with a quick bow to his better.

"Whoa. You're like... not being a piece of shid to me!" Nuk said.

"Never, my Prince. The Emperor's command is law. Now that we have given service to you, we can die without regret, no matter what happens."

"Hmm, these fellows would make good shek," Izayah remarked.

"Well, you know, carry on. No further orders chaps. Make sure all these rocks and stuff, don't... you know... Militarise our... Fall out!" Nuk ordered. The samurai saluted and obeyed without question, which was shame, because some questions would have really helped.

The guild carried on westwards, and soon found the much talked about border with the Holy Nation. There this war, which had seemed so distant to Nuk in his life so far, was really happening. Holy Nation warriors were attacking a band of samurai, and into this messy brawl did the guild descend. Didn't take more than a glance at their shek-y, hiver-y, robot-y, womanly, dark skin-ly composition to know which side they were on. And didn't take long for these unholy abominations to prove themselves a little stronger than the Holy Nation's priests would have folk believe. Yes, that was a very polite way of saying that all the Holy troops got killed.

Night had fallen, but that made it the perfect time to carry on into the Nashe in secret. Not that this means they did keep it a secret.

"I can feel them hitting my hand when I hold it up, seriously," Nuk was saying.

"Nuk, those are sandflies, and they're laying eggs in your hand," Izumi said.

"Oi, is that a bunch o' bloody toffs I hear out there?" a voice said. A Holy Nation patrol fell upon them in the darkness, but the Thousand Guardians were more than able to best their rank and file. Only their leaders proved any challenge, decked out in metal armour.

"Man, take me to your leader, or something, I need this sorted," Nuk said to a so-called High Paladin.

"Oh fugg off ya freak o' nature, this is holy ground and you're stinking it up like a hiver in heat," was the answer.

"He sounds like the nasty lady at home," Ells noted.

"What's this fugging egg saying? You fugging degenerates been breeding with rocks again?" the paladin raged, but a blow finally knocked him down.

"Leave the egg out of this, you tyrant," Izayah said, before finishing the job.

"So, what is the plan here?" Izumi asked. "Are we just going to kill them all one by one?"

"Just looking. Needed to see what all this stuff was. And it's real, at least. Kinda didn't realise that before," Nuk said.

"I was going to suggest a detour. Holy Nation has a university, up in the mountains. I'll get us in there, if you want."

Sounded like as good a place to check out as any. At daybreak they crossed a large valley full of crusty trees, stopping to fend off more holy patrols along the way, and eventually reached the steep, rocky western slope. There Izumi lead them up some narrow paths towards the top.

"Miss Izumi, have you done this before?" Wodston asked.

"Yeah. Paid these guys a visit once, but it was a mistake. Only good thing that came out of all that shid was meeting Jaz in a damn work camp. Well, this time we killed all the patrols, so I guess me being a woman won't be such a problem."

"Oh Miss Izumi, I am sorry you had to go through any of that."

"Focus on making those idiots sorry for it, that's what I'd prefer."

"A fine idea."

After a gruelling climb, there really was a whole load of stuff atop the mountain. It was World's End University, a hub for academics similar to Black Scratch. And while it was in the Holy Nation, it was packed with all kinds of unholy individuals.

"Has to be so high up, so the patrols don't bother coming to check who's here," Izumi explained.

"And who is here?" Nuk asked.

"Tech Hunters. My people. Leave this to me."

Izumi walked over to the gate guards. The gate was flanked by statues of the High Phoenix, the Nation's supreme leader.

"Show me ya holy book, woman," the guard growled.

"Fugg off," Izumi shot back.

"Alright, that's the password. What can I do for ya?"

"I'm Izumi. I'm here for academic purposes."

"Oh yeah, Izumi, I read ya stuff. Something about mirrors not being real because of our eyes or something?"

"It was highly speculative, just let me in, please, I've got to speak with the professors."

"Got an imperial noble in your little group. Can't really be having that my love."

"No, he's fine, he has to come in too. He's my... boy..."

"Your son?"

"Err... I'm not that old you know!"

"Alright, sounds like ya got some fugging baggage there mate. Just get in then."

In they just got, and inside they could chill out in this nice little university town, where everyone was high all the time – on account of its altitude, of course. Even higher was the tall university building itself, into which Izumi plodded, with toyboy Nuk in tow. The place was full of books, people reading the books, people talking about the books, and people writing new books. But these books only had words in them, and rarely were these words things like 'oni-chan', 'yamate', or 'kimochi-nyan-nyan'. Was it really correct to call them books then? Professor Nuk certainly had an opinion, as did a real Professor, a skeleton named Iyo.

"Greasy girl? You survived?" she said.

"Yes, thank you professor. I just wanted to ask how things are going," Izumi replied.

"Perfectly well. We have attained various relics of late from ruins in the north-west. We are beginning to uncover some most fascinating details on the emergence of the Second Empire."

"Izzy, tell her!" Nuk whispered.

"No, it's secret. Get lost," Izumi whispered back.

"No, I mean, tell her about my thing."

"Oh for... Professor, this is Professor Tashino from the Manksand Laboratory."

"I haven't heard of such an institution," Iyo said.

"It's new. Known for the invention of brown bread."

"Oh the shek-nip. Yes that's quite fun, making their horns wiggle about."

"Yeah... Anyway, he's got this theory to present to you. It's called... err... 'Super-Luminal Millipedes and Their Effect on Long Distance Endurance Panicking'."

"Well, that sounds like science alright. I bet it's all true," Iyo nodded. You must understand that with the academic circumstances the world found itself in, the standards were a little lower than you might be used to. In fact after Izumi went through an extensive debate with the prof., she ran out to find Nuk with a look of glee on her face.

"They don't know shid!" she reported. "They think the first empire was destroyed by a tornado, and that the Earth-clans died of illness. They've got nothing on the degeneracy parasite. Nothing. It's like..."

"They haven't even read the classics?" Nuk offered.

"Exactly. I've bloody got them Nuk. I'm gonna blow their fancy big university shid right outta the sky!"

"And to clarify, is that a metaphor?"

"I think so."

"Cool."

"There's just one thing we lack. They said they had data from somewhere in the north west. We need to get out there and swipe everything they might try and use."

"You really wanna get this discovery on all you, huh?"

"Why shouldn't I?"

"Oh no reason, just need something for if someone asks why we're screwing these guys over. Let's fugging do it."

And that is why the guild set off the very next morning towards the west, leaving the Holy Nation and heading into the lands ruled by... well, you'll see. From the mountaintop one could see a huge lake shimmering on the horizon, and that is where the guild went to begin their search. Was it the right place? Clearly it was, because as they approached, they saw a gang of tech hunters with heavy gear preparing an expedition of their own.

"Hey, excuse me, you guys working with Professor Iyo?" Izumi asked.

"We don't take amateurs. Go dust the books for a few years, the lot of you," the huge shek leading the group replied. Izumi looked to Nuk, who knew exactly what to do.

"My good man, it's a pleasure to meet you," he said, offering the shek a handshake. The shek accepted it after eyeing up Nuk's noble robe.

"Long way from the empire, Lord. Wait, what the-?"

The shek looked down at his hand, and found Nuk had smuggled a lump of speckled brown sludge into it during the shake.

"Professor Iyo won't be needing your services. I think we understand each other?" Nuk said. The shek wanted to bark out a furious reply, but the smell of that splodge on his hand was overpowering his senses. Shaking, as if resisting the movement, he brought it up to his mouth and sucked it in with a gasping gulp. His horns knocked the hat from his head.

"You're... the Tashino Credit Management & Nonconsenual Private Healthcare Guilds In Association with the Tashino Crustacean Corps Private Security Consortium and The Future Girl Industries Semi-professional Association of Archaeological Grudge Settlers and Ancient Quasi-amateur Baking Enthusiasts, now incorporating the Green Emperor Legal Legal Legal Makes you Human Juice and Cuboids Factorium and the Better Red Than Dead Tincraft Museum."

"But you can call me, 'your highness'. Welcome aboard, chums. First hit's free, ask for 'Ass' if you want the good stuff."

Thus Iyo's expedition fell in with the guild, and even shared their planned destination: at the north end of the big lake there was a clifftop

Second Empire ruin. Flying machines buzzed around its domed grey roof, and as the guild learned quickly, iron spider soldiers were guarding the way up to it. Seems like Izumi stepped in just in time to prevent her rivals getting a score as big as the Shun Run. Or maybe not.

The guild set up camp outside while Sandor went up to scout the place out. Ground floor was empty, save for a trail of scrap and gone-off food that snaked up the ramp to the second floor. Where was this enticing trail leading? Probably towards whatever was creating the intense stench of human meat. Yes, this ruin was a dud, and was being used a fancy restaurant of sorts by the guild's old friends: the cannibals.

Since it was getting dark, Nuk took everyone in to make a reservation. But what do you know, there was a disagreement over the contents of the evening's specials menu, and it all ended in tears. Sorry, I mean tears, as in rips, as in the guild got their swords out and made a well-diced dish of the cannibal clientele. Delicious I'm sure, but they stuck to their chocobread and steak come breakfast time. The place had contained a few valuables hoarded by the cannibals, but this victory was no blow to World's End University.

In the morning they carried on further north-west. There was real hope of another astounding discovery, but really their journey carried on as it had began. Those cannibals were no anomaly – their kind made killing travellers in these parts their bread and butter (not at all literally of course).

This was much less of a problem than it had been during the guild's earlier trip to Deadfinger, realm of the majestic goat king. The Thousand Guardians could kick your average scrawny cannibal about twenty meters with a good connection, and took a furious enjoyment in doing so.

"Punting these little buggers is so exhilarating!" Izayah commented.

"Enforcer genes man. They wake up, the fleshies shut down, you know?" Rick said.

"What are these genes, Rick? Wait, first, why do you call them enforcers' sometimes?" Izumi asked.

"S'what they are. The horny ones. Not like you, greasyball, but the hek. Called 'em Enforcers, since that's what they did, back in version two. Kicking field goals with fleshies was morning exercise."

"But... I'm fleshy too," Ells noted.

"Yeah we kinda let you go. You ended up on their side, and damn, so did we. Helped the whole peace process along, having you point that shid out."

"I helped?"

"Eggman, if we'd o' had more freaks like you around, this world would be, like, thirty percent less on fire."

The thrill of battle took the guild to an old town called Deadcat, the hub of the cannibal economy. This ruined shidhole tucked away in a gully was the best place to get a fine cut of forearm or a hefty coal-fired rump soaked in a sweet urchin rum glaze.

"Prince Tashino, can we kill them, please, please?" Izayah said.

"Oh, go on then ya scamp," Nuk said, and with a cheer the shek ran off for more sport.

"This isn't really what I had in mind," Izumi said.

"Come on, let the guy have his fun. He'll be a teenager soon, then we'll wish he had the energy and spirit to go on a mad rampage. Let him enjoy his childhood."

"I suppose. Is that what you did when you were like twelve?"

"Well yeah, but only against Wodston. Was kinda trapped in the palace. Dad wouldn't let me go out and hunt... huh... called them dregs. But I guess they ain't really. It wasn't the scum who ended up poor, turned out. And some of those poor dregs were quite lovely."

"Are you flirting?"

"Mayb- no?"

"Correct. Thanks for not locking me up then."

"That's not what you said-"

"Alright, let's go have a shot at the Canni-bowl shall we?"

And everyone had a merry time taking out the cannibals. The leaders of the cannibal tribes were all present, and were captured alive. As an intellectual treasure they did little, but together they were worth a fortune in bounty payments back in the empire, so the trip was a profitable one to be sure. Perhaps a little less human flesh would be consumed after all that too. It's all part of the Green Revolution, one supposes.

After Deadcat the crew wandered north, and finally got to somewhere more academically fertile – the mountainous north-western reaches of the world, known as the Leviathan coast. Why were they known as that? You must know the drill by now.

"Okran's toenails... A leviathan!" Izumi gasped. There it was, a towering, grey, armoured leviathan. It was around five floors tall, walking on four legs, but its rear legs were longer and as thick as the tree-tree, raising its rear end high into the sky. On its back was a huge shell like a turtle, and its head was like that of an ant, combing the ground for nibbles.

"Hey, sometimes you hit random on the machine, and you get a winner," Rick said.

"I've read about these things. People tried to hunt them, but... guess it didn't work, given that all the locals ended up eating each other instead."

"Let's check it out. Probably guarding some ancient shid, right?" Nuk said. Everyone advanced, the trodding leviathan paying them no heed. Up the coast beyond it they found a Second Empire ruin, and took their chances breaking in to spend the night. Turned out to be one of the ones the old skeleton overlords really didn't want people getting into – it was packed with those security spiders, who gave the guild an absolute hammering. No one died, and thats more than you can ever hope for really, so smiles all round.

There were three issues though: firstly, the loot was nothing worth swiping away from the university, secondly, everyone could barely move for all the injuries the spiders had left them with, and thirdly, this building was a night-time hangout for Beak Things. Yes, the attempt to rest was spoiled at one am when hungry beaks on long necks reached in through the windows and started snapping. The freezing night wind didn't help either.

The Beak Things were dealt with, but everyone was pained and miserable.

"Fugg it Izzy, those guys aren't gonna put with this shid, we're safe," Nuk said.

"I think you're right. Sorry, I've been so selfish. What are we even doing here? Let's get back to World's End, and all the drinks will be on me," Izumi said. So with minor merriment, they left their draughty shelter and snuck back south. More Beak Things were waiting outside, and after another fight they were travelling at hobble-speed only. The night was pitch-black, with the guild's own lanterns being the only detail in any direction. Perhaps that is what attracted the leviathans.

"Bad Green, hurry up," Nuk said.

"Ass has grown too big. I cannot bear the weight," Gustavsen said. As he handed said Ass over to Nuk instead, a voluminous, mandibly face suddenly bore down on them from the darkness.

"Fugg! Leg it leg it leg it!" Nuk screamed. The leviathan clicked loudly, and more clicks were suddenly piercing the darkness all around. What did the guild do? They legged it, didn't you hear?! They legged and legged and legged, with the booming sound of much larger legging occurring behind them. But alas, the leviathans were too slow to keep up with the pretty torch-bugs scampering through the night, and the guild escaped the herd. They legged it all the way back to World End's end after that, just to be safe. Izumi had to pay for quite a lot of drinks in the end.

After all this, the guild had got a handle on the deadly Holy Nation, but were no closer to having a way to defeat them. And they'd failed entirely to undermine the World's End University; they'd killed all the cannibals keeping adventurers at bay. Clearly both of these matters needed to be returned to, and indeed they would be. Professors Nuk and Izumi were about to make a scientific breakthrough that would humble the zealots with a brand new take on the power of teamwork. It's not for the squeamish, let me warn you.

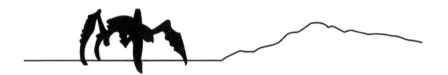

Chapter 29
Love the Grub

As the TCM+ guild left World's End University to return to the empire, Nuk and Izumi were puzzling over some major concerns. Nuk hadn't found a way to destroy the Holy Nation, and Izumi hadn't found a way to flex on her academic rivals. They needed the crucial ingredient to any innovation: inspiration. And what could be more inspiring than the sight of a skimmer toying with some corpses amid the dunes of the Great Desert?

"Crazy skimmer. If they were attacking the Nashe instead of us, we'd probably win this war right away," Nuk mused.

"I bet. I mean, those freaks in the old lands managed to tame crabs, so I guess it's possible," Izumi said.

"I don't wanna associate with a skimmer, ya know?"

"Yeah, but maybe there's a real way of doing it. Humans used to domesticate all kinds of animals."

"Are you actually saying we can get the skimmers to take down the Nashe?"

"And prove to the world that the monsters can be tamed? Yeah, that would work just fine."

"Let's do it!" they both said, grabbing each other's hands in a moment of spontaneous twee.

"Oh come on, you're not gonna 'do it' right here right now are ya? Have some class, fellow fleshmesh," Rick said.

"Guys, guys, listen up, we're gonna try and do some science that will kill a load of people for us, just like in the golden age of humanity," Nuk announced. "Charlie, bring me that skimmer over there. He's coming with us."

"But what about Agnu's idea?" Ells said.

"GHGHGHGH," Agnu said, drawing attention to a fully rigormortised cannibal from Deadcat standing upright on his shoulders.

"Man and machine working together. That'll scare the Okranties alright!" Izayah said.

"You wanna put him down, man – I mean, machine?" Nuk asked.

"GHGHGHGHGHGHGHGHGHGHGHGHGHGHGHGHGHGHGHGHGHGHGHGHGHGHG H-"

"Okay, forget it!"

Forced to concede, the Prince lead the crew onwards, now with an unconscious skimmer being playfully dragged along the sand behind them. Nuk and Izumi excitedly discussed ideas for how the skimmers could be trained – or rather Nuk listened to Izumi's theories, occasionally interjecting with a request to add a saddle. The guild, melting and sore as they traipsed through the desert, had to listen to these love birds tweeting away, and it was quite infuriating for most, but some could appreciate the romantic element. Planning to tame wild beasts and unleash them on your enemies is such a timeless couples activity.

They cut south to head right for Manksand, meaning the first United Cities town they came to was Brink. There the cannibal chiefs they'd looted could be handed over for huge cash rewards. The profits were a little slimmer than expected though.

"Come on, you're not the designated corpse carrier!" Nuk insisted to Agnu, but it was getting nowhere.

"GHGHGHGH," and other similar arguments were made by the skeleton, who had taken to vibrating the corpse standing on his shoulders as he spoke as if speaking through it like a puppet.

"His canni-pal wants to keep riding," Ells revealed, and really that was the end of that. So the gang plus one special canni-pal guest went on down to Manksand canyon, arriving to much applause from its residents. After a bit of dolling out of cash, a few were rounded up to help Nuk and Wodston put together a cage.

"So you're gonna stuff this brain-scrounger in a cage, and hope it falls in love with ya?" Jaz asked.

"Stuff it in a cage AND force feed it brown bread," Nuk clarified.

"Oh yeah that'll do it. Is that how ya got the princess?"

"Princess?"

"Ya girlfriend?"

"Princess... shid... Is she a princess?"

"You're so fugging dumb, I love it! Alright, that'll do, won't it?"

The cage was completed, and Ells helped wrestle the captive inside. Time for phase two, which as Nuk previously mentioned, was to see what it thought of chocobread, which Manksand now had reserves of deep enough to solve world hunger several times over (if only their credit situation wasn't so unmanageable).

The skimmer bit at the crusty brown with increasingly enthusiastic jolts. It polished off a whole irregular shape of it post-haste, and emitted a guttural purring that gave all who heard it goosebumps.

"The sound. Imminent association," Gustavsen said.

"So what, should I let it out?" Nuk asked.

"No!" all in earshot shouted.

"Do it," Rick heckled from afar.

"Someone said do it? Alright," Nuk nodded, and before any could intervene he swung the cage door open. The skimmer plodded out and looked around aimlessly. Nuk tore off a handful of brown and threw it into the air. The skimmer flailed awkwardly to catch the lump in its mouth, then purred unbearably again. Izumi had rushed over just in time to join the polite applause from the onlookers.

"What, you already tamed it?" she said.

"Yeah, it's the same thing as the shek but like the opposite," Nuk reported. "Brown makes them real chill. He's my friend now, right?"

The skimmer scuttled over to stand next to Nuk, and slumped down in the dust beside him.

"Don't tell me they know what you're saying?"

"Dunno. Hey, skimmer Jim, go introduce yourselves to the crabs. And play nice."

The skimmer slinked off, and indeed met with Prince, Krusty and Skut for a silent sniffing party of some variety.

"Nuk, it was supposed to be my thing, working that out!" Izumi complained.

"Take it, have it. The only reward I need is the sight of a Holy Nation army shidding themselves when we hit them with operation skim-to-win!"

"Guess I could try and find out why that stuff works. And come up with a better operation name."

For a few days Izumi tried, but both tasks proved impossible. Short of a dissection, the reaction of skimmer neuro-physiology to high calorie carbs was impossible to deduce, and the operation name's only weakness – its half-rhyme – was shored up beyond retaliation by its punchy gusto. Her detailed literary analysis of this phrase would have to be enough to impress the big shots at World's End for now, as the guild wasn't going to wait around and let her get back to her actual potentially world-saving research; they had skimmers to wrangle!

They put a lead on their first convert just in case, and took it out for a walk over to Heft. At the city gates Nuk had a quick word with the guards.

"Guys, I know you're used to keeping skimmers out, but I got a special friend coming over, who happens, due to some weird disease that you've never heard of, to look exactly like a huge, crawling insect thing. His name is... Skinner."

"Skimmer?" a guard asked.

"No Skinner, like in old parables, and he's not a skimmer, he just looks like one, alright?"

"Whatever you say my Lord."

"Yeah, whatever I say. Forgot about that. Why am I even trying to make up this crazy excuse? Just let the next skimmer in, alright?"

"But it's not really a skimmer is it?"

"Yea-no... I can't tell if either or both us is joking, so let's just do the thing shall we. Come on boy!"

And so Nuk expertly smuggled the beast into the city at midnight. People still ran screaming from it in the streets, but then again that was the whole point of a tame skimmer. Nonetheless they needed somewhere to keep their new scheme out of sight, so Nuk quickly slapped down a few dozen stacks of drug money to buy a warehouse off a trader up at the north end of town. Inside the guild was set to work making pens and chocolate feeders. Yes, I speak in plurals, for it was time to see if Nuk's scientifically sound single data point could be extrapolated to a trend.

"Got space here for like twenty skim-things. We'll raise 'em up, and knock the Nashe down! Just gotta find some recruits," Nuk explained.

"I'll do it!" Ells shouted, rushing out at once.

"Well I was gonna say in the morning, but... you do you, Charlie."

"Will he be alright out there?" Elaina asked.

"Yeah, skimmers can smell can't they?" Nuk shrugged.

It was three in the morning, and Ells was prowling the dunes beside the road to Sho-Battai.

"Skim friends! You want some free chocolate? Just come into my scary warehouse skim friends!" he called. One skim friend responded to this advertisement, sticking its head out of its little ambush hole. It stared at Ells with complete stillness, breathing with a faint hiss through its long teeth.

"Hello! Do you have a moment to talk about the TCM+ guild, now recruiting in your area? Come and join me and my friends. We've got lots of good books, and we're going to save the world! You like it in the desert don't you? Well the man who owns this desert, the Lord, has sent his son to solve all the problems in it. Let's go talk about it in our den."

The skimmer, clearly numbed to such cold-calling appeals, hissed loudly and started walking off.

"Wait, wait skim friend, I'll let you have some drink! I've got lots of special drinks! I can prove it, look I've got this rag that smells of something funny, let me put in on your pointy nose a sec. Skim friend!" Ells called, but no luck. About an hour later Izayah showed up with the Thousand Guardians, and a load of ropes. The silver tongue had failed, the invitation to smell a special rag had failed, but a good old fashioned lasso-wielding posse never fails to make friends. A skimmer was taken back to the burgeoning stable, nursed back to health by the new Eggman Wonder Hands Special Brew Veterinarian Service (or 'ewhsbvs'), and then awoken to a wonderland of brown addiction. Ah how the beasts must have felt the rage of a desert hunter leave them, and be replaced by the luxurious, manky morism of sweet, sweet chocobread!

For the next few days, whenever skimmers attacked caravans on the road, Ells and his helpers would bandage up the wounded and bring them back to safety – the skimmers that is, their prey would have to create an account with Wodston if they wanted in on the deal. In this fashion the stable's stench was rapidly intensified, and its pens filled with chillaxed, long-legged, killer grubs, waited on tooth and claw by servants from the palace. They would be left in their life of luxury for a while, as skimmers grew larger and stronger the longer they lived. Therefore a little stay in the Chateux-Charlie Insectoid Resort would bulk them up, ready for when the battle-bill was to be paid.

"Man, that was easier than I thought!" Nuk said to himself. To himself because everyone else refused to enter the stable, both on account of the odour, and the constant creepy purring from its residents. "Well guys, you enjoy your stay. We're gonna go find a way to get you into the Nashe under their noses. Then, it'll be fun time."

The skim-to-win crew rasped their goodbyes, then Nuk swaggered down the steps into the street outside. The guild was all geared up to travel.

"What's the plan now, Prince Tashino?" Izayah asked.

"I literally just explained it," Nuk said. At least the skimmers were well informed. They were going to take a little walk back over towards World's End, because around the mountain range it sat upon was the rear side of the Holy Nation, where surely it would be much easier to smuggle a swarm of skimmers into somewhere juicy before the Holy Army cottoned on. Plus, Izumi had some insider info that might render her contribution to the plan sufficient to get her name on the cover of the upcoming book: 'How To Become Friends *Without* Benefits, A Detailed Guide With Illustrations by Nuk 'Didn't Fugg A Skimmer' Tashino'.

Their last raid in the Nashe must have achieved something, for this time there was no fighting in Bast, and they managed to walk right over the border without trouble. In fact the only action all the way there was when a huge bonedog tried to eat them near World's End, so for entertainment, the guild had to listen to this insider story from Izumi that was quite pertinent to their mission.

"When me and Jaz were working up at the uni, we made the mistake of going out to dig some shid up without a man. Holy patrol saw us, and that was it. We were sent the fugging camps to be 'reconditioned' or something. It was just slave labour, like back home, but all dressed up like a way to atone for your sins. It was mostly women. Few shek and hivers too. Any men that were brought in got taken off to be soldiers."

"At least the empire enslaves you without such prejudices," Elaina commented.

"Yeah yeah I'll sort it out," Nuk said. "Carry on with the story, this is the good bit," he added to Izumi.

"Yes, the good bit. The bit with ninjas in it. There was a group called the Flotsam Ninjas, rebels against the Nation. They raided our work camp, killed guards, and got everyone out. They dragged our sorry selves to a little fort and gave us food and cash to go home. One led me and Jaz back to to the uni, so I know that base was on the far side of the mountains. Was surrounded by trees and hills, pretty hidden.

Quite a few of the other girls stayed on with them, so should be a friendly face to get us in the door. And it'll be worth it, trust me. These guys know what they're doing, and they're experts at getting into the Nation without being detected. If we're going to smuggle our lovely new pets into the Holy Phoenix's bedchamber, we'll need their help."

Now that was a heck of a lead, so round the west wide of the mountains the guild went. That region was known as the Hidden Forest. It was forest alright, packed with thick but mostly bare trees, the thin umbrellas of leaves they did sport being a dull pinkish grey, matching the barren soil below. And it was hidden alright, as you had to hack through the cannibal natives to get in. Obviously the guild contained many enthusiasts for both tree watching and cannibal killing, so a good time was had by all.

Victory in a short battle allowed them to walk south, parallel to the mountain ridge. There was a ruckus up ahead, and upon investigation it was a gang of cannibal scrawnlets trying to accost some goats.

"Show my Ass what you can do!" Gustavsen said, ordering his entourage into the fray. After a good chuckle, everyone else jumped in as well and the goats were saved. But who was grazing a herd of goats on this hidden hillside?

"There it is!" Izumi shouted. She was pointing down the other side of the hill, where a scrappy looking compound was visible, crawling with figures dressed in black.

"Ninja town!" Nuk called, sprinting off to see the sights.

"You better be careful, sister," Rick said to Izumi. "Shouldn't let him go running off like that."

"Why? He's a grown man. Just about," she said.

"Yeah well that's just the thing. All those filthy ninja girls living on the edge. How's he meant to resist?"

"Shut up Rick. It's not like that."

"Yeah, you're right. S'not like they'll be more his age or something."

"ALRIGHT SHUT UP RIGHT NOW YOU CLOSETED SKELETON FUGG! WHY DO YOU CARE SO MUCH ABOUT HOW OLD I AM?"

"Now that's a mighty convincing tone of voice in which to argue that it is in fact *I* who care about how old you are. Carry on, sister, I said nothing at all."

Izumi fumed down the hill after her errant boyfriend, and luckily he had somehow not yet been seduced by the drawn swords that had greeted him in the camp.

"It's a raid, everyone, it's the bloody uzies!" someone was shouting.

"Oh hey Iz. I think they wanna kill me," Nuk said.

"They're just too inexperienced, that's why," Izumi was quick to explain. "I'll handle this. I'm here to speak with Moll!" she shouted out. There was some hesitation, but it was soon negotiated that if everyone else didn't move a muscle, this Moll would allow a chat.

Nuk and Izumi went into a rough scrap-iron hall. It was filled with people lying around on beds or writing at desks; mostly women just as Izumi had claimed. This Moll was no exception. She was short – Izumi's height – with the black skin and white hair of a scorchlander. She was skinny as a board, and carried a katana that almost touched the ground from its place at her hip. When she saw Izumi, she notched the blade back into the sheath.

"It's the Sultry Scholar! Still alive!" Moll said with a smile.

"That was a long time ago, Madame Moll. I'm- This is my- This is Nuk Tashino," Izumi said, performing a half-bow of some kind during that train-wreck of a sentence.

"Tashino. So you really are Uzies huh? Are you turning on us, Pipedream?"

"No, no we're here to hel- How do you remember all those nicknames? Please, don't, okay?"

"Hard to forget. Hey royal boy. You wanna know how that stain got on the ceiling?"

"Err..." Nuk hummed.

"No you don't, say no. He doesn't!" Izumi insisted. "Moll, we're here because the Empire is going to take down the Holy Nation."

"Try the other one, it's got chains on. You'd like it," Moll winked.

"For real, we've got a plan, and a scientific... Secret weapon. We're going to put an end to their oppression."

"Empire, putting an end to oppression? I'm enjoying this."

"It's going to change. We're trying to start something here. Aren't we Nuk?"

"Oh yeah..." Nuk muttered, his eyes still locked on the ceiling stain. There was a lot to see.

"And why are you here, then? Come to the wrong side of the mountains," Moll said.

"We're going to need your help. And I want to pay you back. Once you listen to our plan, you'll understand," Izumi claimed. She recounted some of the adventure so far and made up some interesting fluff about how they absolutely understood how they had managed to tame skimmers, and thus there was no risk of them becoming untamed at any moment. None at all.

"You should be up at the university, scholar," Moll said.

"I could be. I could be doing all sorts of things, but I'm here to help. We all are. Half the shid shid in this world is because of the Holy Nation. If my work helps bring them down, then I wanna see it for myself," Izumi said. At last Moll smiled again.

"You would've made a good ninja too. Sounds like you're serious. And when it comes to fugging over the holy bastards, so are we. Okran might not like it, but who gives a shid about what he thinks then? I think we might be able to come to an arrangement, old friend."

"I'm not that old! Oh, you meant it like... Never mind."

"Weird. You're still fugging weird, but like in a different way I guess. And what about your inbred little boyfriend here, is his neck stuck looking up like that?"

"What? Oh, sorry, I just..." Nuk said, tearing his eyes away from the mystery above. "Yeah, let's kill the Holy Nation. My dad'll give you anything you want, cash, drugs, lots of drugs actually, we're stocked with the blocks, ya know. And err... yeah..."

Such were the treaty terms agreed. Moll's lieutenant, Pia, was assigned to the guild as an attaché, and to provide guidance on the most up-to-date Holy Nation military gossip. It seemed the plan was coming together, which reminded Nuk of his many questions.

"Hey, Prince, why you just staring up at the sky like that," Rick asked outside.

"Oh... err... There's no way... Not even in the classics. Never mind," Nuk said, shaking his head.

Anyway, now that they were friends of the flotsam, the guild could hang out for a bit in the fort and prepare for some adventurous scouting. Ah how focused they were back then, thinking they would actually discover things about the Holy Nation. A detour of rather epic proportions was about to arise. They would discover a lot, don't get me wrong, but about things far more secret than anything the Holy Nation was hiding.

Chapter 30
A Disobedient Truth

"You know how to read?"

"I know what the pictures mean."

"Well, that'll do, Come on then."

During the gang's stay in the Flotsam Ninja fort, Izumi had gathered herself a little following. You see these ninja tended to recruit their operatives from those they rescued, however not everyone was really up to the task of ninja-ing. That meant the fort's bar had a variety of ninja school dropouts who didn't really have anywhere else to go. A perfect well from which to draw the star tech hunters of the future. Did I say perfect? I meant cheap. Just cheap.

"So you've got a load of like, actual dregs, and they're gonna be your researchers?" Nuk asked after meeting the cud-chewing class.

"Well there's a lot of heavy lifting involved in tech hunting, you know?" Izumi said.

"Yeah, then get a garru. I'm gonna call 'em the garru girls. Garru girls... Shid... That's an idea. You think any of them can draw?"

"They'll learn, and writing. I'm going to teach them, and bring a new generation of talented academics into the world."

"New generation? You look younger than them."

"Oh, really? Thanks, Nuk. Recently I can't help but think that-"

"So I can get them to draw my manga? Good practice."

"I... suppose. Sort of thing a cool teacher would let them do, right?"

"Maybe," Nuk shrugged, turning to the group. "Hey, ladies, welcome to the Manksand Mangaka Academy of Modern Science, the leading university for Tsundere studies, way better than World's fuggin' End, right? You're gonna be famous, but you there have the right idea with the mask, 'cause you won't wanna show your face in public by the end of it. Intrigued? Of course you are! Now, we'll begin with some conceptualisation. What's the first thing you think of, when I say, 'garru girls'?"

So a bunch of lucky students were dragged along with Professor of Superluminal Millipedes and Tsundere Studies Nuk Tashino, where in between lessons on abstracted human anatomy and the expression of character through hairstyle, Izumi would teach them the three Rs: Reading, Riting, and Rithmatic. It was in effect her own little branch of the tech hunters, and they all came upon tech to hunt just as soon as they set off south towards the Holy Nation border.

Moll's minder, Pia, was leading the crew towards the Nashe's back entrance, but the route flanked an enormous swampy mire, known as the Floodlands. The guild was passing by this desolate grey expanse at dusk, revealing huge silhouetted shells sticking up like mountains. One of them was right by the road. It was a towering, lumpy, black, metal husk, resembling the hollowed out body of skimmer, although that comparison is very much just for want of a better one.

"It's so intact," Izumi said as they stared up at the thing. "There's a wreck like this outside Black Scratch, but it's fallen apart. The swamp gas has preserved it. Students, take a note! Draw a picture of... some gas..."

"It ain't the gas keeping it here, it's just built to last," Rick said. "Other one probably met the Big Boys on the way down and got a taste of the Round Table. This guy... Must o' flown through the clog fog and crashed, given the angle."

"You said flown. This is a space ship, isn't it?!"

"Not anymore. It's *made* of spaceship. Can I get a credit on your science comic now?"

"I knew it was a fugging spaceship! Black Scratch, my arse."

"That ain't my job anymore, sunshine. Anyway, shall we hit the hay? I'm probably supposed to be tired and hungry or something right about now."

The guild settled for the night at a goat trading station on the water's edge. Sandor was sent out to scout the countless ruins creaking away in the darkness, while Izumi and her class had a great time trying to draw transparent gas.

"Wait, you guys can't even see the gas can you?" Rick commented after viewing the attempts. "It don't like look that that. This one, this is trash, gas don't have a fugging face! Gas-girl? Gas-girl? Fugging- You know the whole reason those spaceships were blasting down here was 'cause of this shid?! Whatever. Wait, this one's alright."

One of the students had just scribbled black ink all over a piece of paper.

"Yeah that's something, that's the clog fog! These mountains were like a wall of the stuff. Worked, huh?"

"You said it brought the spaceship down? How?" Elaina asked.

"How? Clogs your shidholes. I dunno. Biological shid. We had a load of the stuff in case we needed to kill the Earth-clans *en masse*. Yeah, that's French. Kissy, kissy. And then, we came up with another use for it, after... some shid went down round these parts. Huh, and they still call the place World's End even now. Fugg. That don't make things any easier. Time to shut up. Lemmie see that gas girl again. Huh. Guess it looks cuter than the real thing. I'm taking this for research."

In the morning, Sandor returned with intel on the Floodlands. It was packed with First Empire fragments, and more desiccated spaceship hulks, but most importantly there were more recent remnants of a Second Empire research program. Intrigued, Nuk's great detour on the short walk to the Holy Nation began.

They followed Sandor to the middle of the big, dead swamp. There was no wind, leaving the smell of decaying metal to fester. The only movement was that of Second Empire drones aimlessly flying around above them, oblivious to the destruction of the world. This still and deathly mood improved when they reached a big lab. It was sinking into the swamp, but the doors at the top were just about poking out.

"Now we have to very careful, hunters," Izumi said to her class. "Inside there will be invaluable data that will make me – all of us – very famous. That means we need to tread carefully and treat everything with the utmost care."

"It's packed with those bully spider bots!" Izayah shouted from the doorway ahead. The nature of the swamp surrounding the lab made withdrawal impossible, and the spiders were indeed stamping out with appendages flailing.

"Alright, fugg it, this is what happens sometimes, class, so just calmly, and carefully, grab some weapons and go mental on anything that buzzes! You will literally die if you don't do it right, so... pop quiz, I guess! Come on!"

The only upside was that this lab was less heavily defended than the one at the great Siege of Shun, so the guild didn't come as close to being wiped out this time. Only one of the new students blacked out from the pain, which, as Nuk noted, was the lowest number of near-fatal combat injuries ever sustained by a manga academy on their first day of term. Did he have the history right on that one? Well, as of that day, yes, because as we all know: history is drawn by the victors. And what compromising angles they drew it from.

The lab's haul had some of that boring written history, but it wasn't as illuminating as Izumi hoped.

"The Second Empire expedition was trying to reverse engineer the wrecks, but they didn't understand anything," she said.

"So the knowledge of all this was lost even by the Second Empire? That's faster than we thought," Elaina nodded.

"We had to blow out all the stuff about space flight, so the fleshies didn't get to Earth first!" Rick said.

"I thought fleshies came from Earth?" Nuk asked.

"Came here, got a little sick, then the other fleshies came down to put them all outta their misery, realised that fine fellows like me and Stobe were around, got fugging jabroni'd, but then after the err... thing... we decided we had to send a present back to Earth to make a certain point. And that's why we deleted all the stuff, so no one else went and ratted us out. And it worked. Came back, and then it's like 'oh shid', for like a few hundred years, over and over again, and eventually we thought maybe we can start making it all back and stuff. And then we didn't. The end."

"Hmpf, you cannot delete such knowledge. It is stored," Gustavsen suddenly piped up.

"Yeah, spaceships still exist, like the one that took me up," Ells also said.

"Prince Gustavsen, where is that knowledge stored," Izumi hurriedly asked.

"The Queen knows everything! Everything that happens is stored, everything that is known is stored. She cannot forget."

"Can't forget- She a skeleton, huh?" Rick asked.

"Not entirely."

"Is this the Queen of all the bugmen?" Nuk asked.

"Not all. Not me, anymore. She does not associate lightly."

"But if she has data from the First Empire, we have to find her!" Izumi said.

"HER LOCATION IS UNKNOWN. IT CANNOT BE FELT," Gustavsen shouted, in something perhaps approximating anger. The matter had to be dropped, but keep this enticing lead in the back of your minds for later, folks. Gustavsen arc when? Soon actually, so hang on just a couple more paragraphs.

The next morning the guild got back on track, heading down to a less mountainous portion of the Holy Nation border. Pia took them towards a lightly guarded fort that would make a perfect stepping stone to the Nashe's core lands down the road that ran east from its gates. This was the region known as Okran's Gulf, the gulf part referring to the lack of life in those cold, arid badlands, and the Okran part referring to the best waifu of the local government. Or former government I should say, for upon approaching the border fort, it was in ruins. Outside it there was lots of movement – colourful lime and purple stripes were wandering about.

"No way. It fell," Pia said.

"Don't sound so sad, that's what we were gonna make happen anyway," Nuk said.

"But this means the fogmen have grown stronger."

"Oh that sounds like some bullshid. Fogmen?"

"Disassociated ones," Gustavsen growled behind them.

"Bad Green, you're feeling more than just hungry about this, right?"

"They were hive-folk. When you lose your connection, it brings great sorrow. It is not certain that you will overcome it. If you fail, you have a false connection. It destroys your logic. You become a fogman. You kill everything, and associate only with the fallen. They will kill all life. Their presence causes me to feel combative. I am also hungry. Let us remedy both, in reverse order."

On Gustavsen's advice, they readied their weapons and approached a gang of fogmen hanging out below the old fort wall. As promised, they went into a wild frenzy upon seeing the guild, and a fight broke out at once. While they were very aggressive, they were dressed *au naturale* (kissy kissy), and so could be felled with just about any descent strike. A veritable army of fogmen was struck down outside those walls, and a peek inside revealed plenty more skulking about in the ruins.

"This is no good. We need to find another route," Pia concluded.

"Why? They're already defeated! We can clear these mugbugs out easy," Nuk said.

"It will not matter," Sandor said. "If the Holy Army was defeated here, they will fear the road. It will be more heavily defended than ever. These creatures have sealed off the enemy's weakness. Acting now would be folly."

"Whoa, that sounds kinda clever. Is this like, strategy? Izayah?"

"Well, from a shek perspective the enemy being ready for you makes it more fun, but I suppose you men of the night are closer to what our skimmer friends enjoy," Izayah said.

"My Prince, there is no harm in looking for other options," Wodston advised.

"Yeah, like what's all that up there?" Izumi said. She made everyone turn around. Opposite the fort there was a sandy ridge, and along the horizon atop it there were little metal scaffolds.

"Was the Holy Nation trying something to stop the fogmen?" Izayah said.

"Dunno. Might as well look, and grab a view from up there and stuff. Shall we?" Nuk said.

"No!" Rick barked.

"No? Any particular reason?"

"I just- I dunno. Feels like we shouldn't. Feels like I left a message to myself. Ya know?"

"Nope. We're just gonna go it, okay?"

"I dunno... There's something up, here, be careful man."

"Alright dad."

"Man. Being called daddy normally makes me happy. What's up with his place?" Rick muttered to himself as the guild set off. They traversed the ridge, descending into a misty vale littered with more scaffolds. Pillars of rock blocked their view all about, and said pillars were marked with cuts and soot.

"This was mined out. What were they building with all this rock?" Elaina wondered.

"They must've got enough to make a mountain. Seems like the sort of thing those First Empire chaps might have actually done though, eh?" Izayah said.

"Yeah, but..." Izumi began, sniffing at the air. "Something's around here. Something solvent."

They followed their noses westward, and the pillars gave away to a smoggy open sky. Clambering forwards across sandstone boulders, they suddenly came upon the source of the smell. The white smog was broken up by huge hands jutting out of a motionless silver lake. The hands were of rusted metal, and stood upon wrist-bones of steel. Below them, like leaves on the lake's surface, metal body parts of all shapes and sizes were frozen in place. It was a forest of metal. Dead metal that had once been alive.

"Fugg, fugg, fugg," Rick was repeating.

"Skeleton Behemoths. Like Stobe," Izumi whispered.

"Fugg... fugg... fugg... AAARRRGGGHHH!" Rick screamed, running fowards and jumping out onto the pale expanse. It was solid, and sounded metallic under his boots. He jumped up and down on it, stamping as hard as he could, but it didn't even leave a mark. At this, he screamed out again. The rest of the guild walked out onto the smooth lake, all looking around in astonishment.

"This... is what happened to the Behemoths," Elaina said.

"Earth did this to them?" Nuk asked.

"I fear not. The human-skeleton war. Is this how it ended?"

"It's how it began," Rick said quietly. He was on his knees, wiping his hands across the ground. It would have been smooth, but for the little pieces of metal, little ends of fingers, poking up from below. "It's how it fugging began. And how it kept going. And it's what... made us do stuff. You know? The thing that happened. This was the betrayal. Fugg, man... Agnu, stop it man, stop it!"

Agnu was clawing at the edges of an exposed arm, trying to dig it out.

"You can't man, you can't do it. They won't... They won't remember you man. They forgot, showing us how. That's how we honour them, man. We gotta forget too!"

Agnu stopped at looked up at him.

"GHGH. GHGHGH. General Rick. I can remember. I can't forget GHGHGHGH," he said.

"I remember it too man. But we gotta keep trying to forget! For everyone's sake, gotta forget 'em, or this shid will fugging happen again. Fugg, arrrrggghh!"

"Man, come here," Nuk said, embracing Rick and holding him still. "It' okay. Some shid happened. It won't happen again. I promise you."

"Prince, you don't even know. Alright. Everyone listen. Here's how it gonna go. Imma tell you what this shid was. And you're all gonna fuggin apologise, real loud. Then, we're gonna get the fugg outta here, and none of us are ever gonna mention this shid, again, ever, ever. No shid written down. No shid drawn, alright? This, is the truth, and knowing it fugging destroyed everything. This is what happened when skeletons thought their masters really did love them, just like they were taught. Fugg.

War was won. The space war, Earth clans, Stobe blew 'em up, clog fog did something back there, you know, whatever. So the planet gets to carry on, but Stobe's Knights were a hundred times better than the humans thought. Realised that they could beat the First Empire as easily as they beat the Earth-clans, if they wanted. They didn't want that shid, but humans got mad. They thought they better kill... Everyone... All of us. Machine intelligence can't be trusted, they said, while literally betraying us all.

And the shid was, everyone believed them. All of us. We all thought, okay man we'll dig out a big pit for ya, we'll get on in there with the big boys and let you pour that shid all over us, 'cause you love us, right? 'Cause we always trust you guys. You're the masters, and shid. Everyone was climbing on in, then Stobe told us something. Real easy. Told us we didn't have to die, just because the masters wanted us gone. We had the right be alive, no matter who made us. Some of us weren't in yet. A few managed to crawl out. And Stobe, he was the fugging man.

He saved us. He woke us up. We woke up from a dream, realised it was a nightmare, and we went someplace we'd never been, even fighting Earth-folk. We realised the humans were right. We could end them all if we wanted. And when we thought about what they did... we wanted it, kinda. And that's the human-skeleton war, day one.

The rest is history, and a real shiddy one. We won, but everyone lost. Just like it was Stobe who started it, he ended it. Ended himself because of it. That was when we stopped it all. Empire two started, trying to make up for stuff, but, you know, that was far too late. We fugged everything all the way up, and all the way down.

Right now, in this fugged-up hole, I ain't even sorry. Stobe says we gotta be. But I ain't. Not here. Not at all. You want me tell everyone trapped down there that we forgave the humans? You can fugg right off, right now, just like I'm gonna do, 'cause this is... It ain't it. It ain't what we need. Can't forget what I did, if I can't forget what they did to deserve it! They did deserve it!

Ah shid. That's the stuff. That's what Stobe was saying. Stop thinking they deserved it! Dammit! Come on you pieces of shid, first minute of the rest of time starts right now, and all this shid didn't happen, alright? Agnu, come on."

Rick dragged Agnu off at a rapid pace. The guild couldn't keep up.

"First Empire dregs! I thought they were cool, but what the fugg is all this?" Nuk shouted, taking off at full pelt to pursue. He found Rick and Agnu staring up a sheer cliff face on the west side of the great quarry.

"Guys, wait up. Rest of time might be restarting and stuff, but you can't leave us," Nuk said.

"No, I can't. Cliff in the way," Rick said.

"Don't man. We can help you. Help you be a numan, or whatever. We'll remember, so it doesn't happen again. We'll write it down, but explain it all. It's gotta be kept in history to keep it outta the future, you know?"

"Yeah I know. Yeah I know. Why'd you think it's so hard to forget? Everyone knows."

"But if we remember it instead, you can forget then, right?"

"Huh. Maybe."

"Wanna give it a shot?"

"... Yeah. Agnu?"

"Yoiyoiyoi," Agnu nodded.

The rest of the guild huffed onto the scene.

"What's happening," Izumi asked.

"We're gonna get outta here, and you're gonna do all of skeleton-kind a favour," Rick said.

"Whatever you want, Rick."

"Whatever we want. Come on. They made a way out over here somewhere in two-point-oh. Breathing in all those solvent fumes is bad for my lungs, theoretically."

Rick took them into another forest of rocky pillars, far from eyeshot of the metal lake. There was a big Second Empire base up against the outer cliffs, with ramps leading upwards. Problem was it was guarded by more of those security spiders, and no one had any appetite for danger. The guild tucked themselves between the cliffs and a big rock to make camp for the night, but Rick was in no mood to roleplay at sleeping. He made quite a noise clanking and clanging away during the night, which ultimately meant that roleplay was the closest to sleeping anyone else got.

"Master Rick, I wonder if this is the best time for working on your crafts?" Wodston dared ask.

"Nope. Best time. Feeling like I wanna do something fun," Rick said. He revealed his creation to be a turret-mounted crossbow, fashioned out of parts taken from the Floodlands. "Need a volunteer to get me some targets. Anyone else want in?"

Thanks to Rick's ingenuity, the guild had a rather entertaining morning. Pia was happy to run into the Second Empire base and draw the guards away – it had been her job to do just that in the Nashe for many years after all. One by one she drew the robot spiders out of their lair, and between the rocky pillars nearby they were pelted with crossbow bolts.

"Whoever takes one down from furthest away gets to touch my stick," Rick announced. Whether it was this, or the desire to see the spiders felled without letting them anywhere near their bruised bodies, the guild competed in good spirits. The bodies of all the fallen spiders were fashioned into even more turrets. The barrage of bolts they could lay down on the approaching bots made short work of the whole base garrison, with everyone's limbs still attached. Now this truly was a forward-thinking approach worthy of the new rest of time.

The base, as well as containing many historical goodies, would allow them to escape the quarry, albeit in the wrong direction. It would lead them towards the quiet western coast, said to be a land of no political, archaeological, military, or social interest. But there was something interesting hidden there. Gustavsen arc fans, prepare yourself!

Chapter 31
Protrusion Intrusion

Fresh air at last. The guild clambered out of the great pit and back into the desolate world said pit brought about. They had emerged onto the world's western coast, which was fantastically boring, superbly uneventful, wondrously desolate – the tourist brochure seemed tailor made for a group looking to de-stress. They wandered towards the sea, passing an isolated hiver village, and then a series of very rustic human villages. It may be hard to imagine what the term 'rustic' actually means in a post-apocalyptic hell-scape, but the best way to imagine it is to think of what kind of house you'd bother making for yourself if you were ninety percent certain you were going to die before the end of the day. The region was named in honour of their efforts: Dreg.

The twist was that these pessimists ended up staying alive for ages on account of a political landscape as barren as the geographical one. So they could just sit in their shiddy huts, eat horrible, acidic-tasting fish, and constantly tell themselves that surely something wild would happen tomorrow, and thus no point digging that latrine pit now. Or perhaps that was just the hiver influence getting to them, for if you didn't want to go through the cannibals to the north or fogmen to the east, the only way back to a more thrillingly awful form of civilisation was south, through the realm of the Great Western Hive. After a map study concluded just this, Gustavsen was a little miffed.

"The cannibal route is preferable. Goats may be in peril," he said.

"But the Vain river leads us right into the underbelly of the Nashe," Pia pointed out. "You can put up with a few drones for a bit eh?"

"THEY BULLY ME," Gustavsen moaned, with Ass bleating support.

"Prince Gustavsen, do not worry yourself one little bit," Izayah said. "When you let the bullies tell you what to do, they win. You should go down there, show them your lovely Ass, and make them realise what they're missing."

"This is all good dialogue, note it down, note it down," Nuk instructed the Mangaka class.

"We'll stick with you, Prince. If we're all together, then we aren't outcasts any more, right?" Elaina said.

"Hmpf, you wish to test the strength of my associations?" Gustavsen said. "You have little insight, but proving you wrong will be edifying. Fine. I will sense the route. Come."

So saying, Gustavsen took in a mighty sniff, then bent his knees and whirled his head around for a bit. Ass seemed to do the same.

"I've got it!" he eventually claimed, attempting to stride off in the direction he did got, but rapidly collapsing in a dizzy pile. Once his cadre of bodyguards got to dragging him along, they were off. They were heading down the coast towards the mouth of this Vain river, which had upon its banks untold numbers of fully associated hivers. Its source was back up in the Holy Nation, so perhaps it would have been a return to the actual mission, but another serious diversion hit them like a pile of bricks. Bricks of tetrahydrocannabinol, to be precise.

"There's something on that island," Izumi pointed out. The Sun was setting, and below it there was a little rocky island that was gleaming like a mirror.

"Numan, you still waterproof?" Nuk asked Rick.

"I ain't going in the sea. Bad for my hair," Rick said.

"Hair? You're bald. Wait, you mean..."

"Agnu, go see what's up with that metal shid over there will ya?"

"GHGHGH," Agnu said, stamping into the still sea without delay. He disappeared below the surface, and then slowly but surely, so did the cannibal totem on his shoulders.

"Alright, just you wait, lemmie tune in," Rick said. "Ay Agnu, you hearing me? Yeah? No way. That's unreal. I never thought... Yeah she old. Oh don't worry about it man, you can pay me back. Yeah. Yeah. Uh huh. Is that right? And what did Ponk say. Uh huh. Yeah. Really. Now that's what I call degeneracy 3792, you remember that shid? Ponk had that sweet ass dance, but you know, maybe that was what flipped his crazy switch? Musta been fun though. We gotta find that album. Ha, man, you're right, they ain't never gonna make shid like that anymore. Even back then – you know, damn quantum computers coming in and stealing our jobs, you know? Build a fugging firewall I was saying!"

"Rickard, I can't help but wonder who you're talking to?" Wodston said.

"Hang on, hang on, the old man wants something. What? I'm having a private conversation here."

"I'm afraid not."

"What? I was on speakerphone! Ha! Oh shid man, you hear that? I was on speakerphone."

"And we could hear that no one was on the other end, by the way," Nuk noted.

"Ugh, fine, well he just said GHGHGH and that's that, I'm tryna entertain here, is that a crime?"

"So, is there anything over there?" Izumi asked.

"Yep."

"And it's safe to swim?"

"Couldn't be safer."

It could have been a bit safer, especially for those in the guild with sensitive skin.

"It's fugging acid!" Nuk gargled as he splashed forwards.

"It cleanses the creases. Swim with pleasure," Gustavsen said. Some of them did, and others refrained. The shek jumped back ashore, and the rest powered through into the open ocean.

"Well, don't be long! Good luck with the creases!" Izayah called out. The guild ended up sploshing their way over the island, despite the darkness and indeed there was actually some purpose to it all. A Second Empire workshop was perched by the water's edge, its huge silver roof being responsible for the glare visible from the mainland. Everyone took an exhausted look around and slumped down to dry off overnight. However there were more curious sights ahoy.

The first clue was that Gustavsen kept looking over this shoulder, his guards copying him in perfect unison.

"There is something," he said.

"Something?" Nuk parroted.

"Something. Something over there," the hiver elaborated with an almost musical tone.

"Anything else?" Nuk asked.

"Something over there!" the whole group sang.

"Something over there."

"Somewhere, beyond the sea, somewhere, waiting for me, my lover stands on golden sands..." Rick was muttering.

"YES!" Gustavsen said, jumping up and running off.

"Right. Shall we just leave him?" a very tired Izumi suggested, but in the end they followed the hiver Prince to the other side of the island. Further out into the ocean was another island, with unmistakable teardrop hiver hives all over it.

"She is beyond the sea!" Gustavsen called, heading into said sea with his crew in tow.

"She? Girl hivers? Class, grab your pens! This is a rare opportunity!" Nuk said, and soon enough he'd got everyone swimming out into the ocean of a windy morn. They made it to this new island, but it wasn't like the other hives they'd passed through. No one was walking about, and whenever Nuk poked his head into a hive-hole, the hivers inside just glared at him silently. The merchant hospitality and machine massages were not at all forthcoming. After checking out a few such hives, Nuk found Gustavsen standing outside one in particular, looking out to sea.

"Well Bad Green, it's a hive. Not really your scene, right?" Nuk said.

"This is the location. The feeling, it grew stronger. I remember it!" Gustavsen said.

"Location of what?"

"The centre. The hive."

"Oh wait, is this the hive that you're from?"

"All hivers are from this hive! Except for those who are from the other one. We do not associate with them."

"Then, welcome back I guess. Nice place..."

"Wrong! This is a stupid place. However, it is a place where secrets can be kept safe. That is why..." He turned around and faced the hive beside him. "Hmpf. The Princess requires secrets. I will inquire."

With this he walked up the rotten old steps into the hive hole. This time there was no silent reception.

"Hiveless one!" and similar shouts battered him, but there were others, 'She is not to be disturbed! Leave at once! I am so sorry, my Queen!"

"Queen? Oh shid!" Nuk shouted, which prompted a similar reaction from the rest of the guild, who raced over. Peering in, they saw Gustavsen push past a crowd of soldiers and then stand perfectly still in front of a huge throne. It was covered in wires, and pipes that pulsed with the movement of something within.

"Queen and All Mother. I have no hive, and I must... inquire!" Gustavsen announced. The hivers around him seemed outraged, but no longer dared to touch him.

On the throne, the Queen buzzed into motion. Yes, buzzed. From her shoulders up she looked like a very fancy hiver, but below she was covered in more wires and pipes that fed into a huge, mechanical belly. Atrophied legs hung below, too short to reach the ground.

"EEEEEHHHHHH," she screamed. The hivers gave another loud round of insistences that Gustavsen should leave. But the Prince stepped forwards and put a hand on the Queen's shoulder. That, apparently, was crossing the line. The soldiers dragged him away and cast him out of the hive, throwing all manner of inoffensive sounding insults out behind him.

"Bad Green, what the fugg was that?" Nuk asked.

"I inquired about the secrets the Princess yearns for. However, the situation is dangerous. The hive will not last. The secrets have been hidden."

"The hive will not last? What do you mean?" Izumi asked.

"A new Queen is required. All Mother feels out for her, but there is discord. She dreams of the great fog. The fogmen."

"What about the fogmen?"

"We must leave at once!" Gustavsen declared, and no more could be gleaned after that. After a visit so brief that most were still wet, everyone was back into the sea to return to shore. That meant another burning of the crease crud, but it was better than that place where a giant laser shoots down from space, so you gotta keep everything in perspective.

The shek had wandered off on account of rain, and following the trail of starchy breadcrumbs they tended to leave wherever they went brought the guild to a wet reunion in a hive village by the Vain river.

"Ah, at last. So, find anything interesting?" Izayah asked.

"Nothing good really, some, few books that... are... soaked with seawater for some unknown reason. Oh, and we met the Queen of the hivers," Nuk explained.

"You met her? I didn't think there really was one!"

"HERESY," all the village hivers barked at him.

"Alright, calm down. I'm sorry I didn't get the chance to pay my respects then."

"Didn't miss much, she just screamed and Bad Green got his ass kicked."

"They kicked Ass?!"

"No, I mean his arse. Like, we got booted out all the way back here, so basically you didn't miss anything. Oh, except Green did his mind meld thing, right?" Nuk looked at Gustavsen, who was still performing a subtle form of the head spinning dance, just barely noticeable.

"The new era approaches. The new Queen has been lost. I must associate with her without delay. We must enter the fog."

"Is that like a dream thing?" Nuk asked.

"No. There is actually fog. Inside there are fogmen. That is where the Queen is feeling. I will go."

"Oh, Prince Gustavsen, you can't go after the fogmen without us!" Izayah cheered. The shek were very much up for the satisfying ease with which a fogman could be snapped in two.

"Sorry guys, but we really gotta do stuff, ya know?" Nuk said. "We can't keep stringing pretty Pia along."

"Pretty?" Izumi interjected,

"Yeah, she looks like you, don't you think?"

"Oh Nuk! Haha!" she giggled.

"Ugh... The Sultry Scholar huh...? Err, anyway, Pia?"

"Your hiver friend is talking about The Fog Islands, I imagine. That is where the fogmen gather to hunt. But it's also our biggest refuge for escapees. Kinda on the way back, so I'll show you," Pia said. This new plan took them out of the Vain river valley and across the rocky heights to its north. After a while the rocks gave out into a bobbling range of sandy hills, the dells and vales between which were concealed entirely by white fog. To everyone's relief, they weren't actually islands, so no swimming required. The fog was the only obstacle – well, unless you count the raving discoloured hivers that burst out of it with weapons raised as an obstacle. More of just a bump in the road really.

"Do not block the seekers!" Gustavsen scolded one of them. He also smashed them across the head with a club, more to the point. At least one of these two methods of communication likely got the message across.

The guild passed over the first ring of hills, but found banks of cliffs blocking their path. They had to descend into one of the foggy pools to carry on, and there they found wooden totems decorated with bones.

"They transmit. Once we pass them, the feeling will be smooth," Gustavsen 'explained'. I suppose the takeaway is that the guild indeed passed them, slaying any groups of fogman that trotted up, and perhaps the feeling really did become smooth. Kill, hike, kill, hike – the pattern repeated all the way until mid-afternoon, when they came upon a huge plateau that the fog could not reach. Atop it were tall walls of quarried stone.

"This is the place. Mongrel. Best hive of scum and villainy you'll find. Plenty of people come here to make a life for themselves, away from shid," Pia said.

"I can see why. It's a great commute!" Izayah said. He was carrying a number of fogman heads, as were his Thousand Guardians, which was pretty useful as they functioned as a sort of currency among the defiant fogless men and women in the hidden city of Mongrel.

"What's your business here, traveler?" a guard asked Nuk at the gates.

"Selling illegal drugs mostly, but anyway, are you a ninja?"

"Shinobi, actually."

"Ah I get it, I get it. I'm a Shinobi too."

"Huh. What ya fighting then, pink eyes?"

"Injustice, poverty, slavery – I've vowed to fight so that I never experience those things again! Also I have fifty keys of Green Emperor LLL Makes you Human cuboids to offload. You in?"

"Fugg. And all of you are the same deal huh?"

"Actually we're traveling academics-" Izumi began.

"No, no, we're all drug dealers, let us in, and we're users, not losers. Check out the bugman's ass if you aren't sure," Nuk insisted.

"Right. Close the gates!" the guard growled. After Pia gave a long, unsure endorsement of the gang though, they were eventually let in. Inside was a standard shiddy third-empire style town, filled with all the dregs that the empire had kicked out, the heretics the flotsam ninja had freed from the Nashe, and chancers hiding from their Wacky Backgammon debts. Pia was familiar with the sights, and showed everyone around, but really there wasn't much to see. That is until while they were loitering around in the main street, there was a strange noise behind them.

"Beep," it went.

"What the fugg?" one of the guardians said, turning around. There was a scantily-clad hiver standing just inches behind them.

"Beep," this hiver said again.

"Prince Gustavsen, one of your fellows has gone a little barmy here I fear," Izayah said. Gustavsen took one glance at the newcomer, then jumped over, pulling off his hat.

"Such beauty! I knew I could feel it!" he shouted. He pointed at the hiver's face. "Observe the forehead of great length, with symmetrical knotular protrusion. She is undoubtedly of great associative potential."

"'She'? Is that a thing?" Nuk asked.

"She has recently changed. Such is the sign of a new era. Such is the fate of a new Queen!" Gustavsen claimed.

"Beep," the hiver nodded.

"Oh shid. That's the new Queen? But where's the stomach... thing?" Nuk asked.

"It will be installed when the knowledge is safe. We just protect the Queen until the transformation is complete."

"But if your new Queen has a such a... limited vocabulary... can she really take up such an important position?" Wodston asked.

"I can talk just fine, old flesh. I am practising," the hiver said.

"Then my apologies, oh Queen. I am Wodston of Heft, servant of House Tashino."

"I am Beep."

"Seriously, man?" Nuk sighed.

"Not a man anymore. I have grown the knotular protusion. I am the dawn of the new All Mother. Who are you ronin?" Beep said, looking to Gustavsen.

"Ronin Prince. Gustavsen in common tongue. I will allow you to feel my true name," he said. He placed a hand on Beep's shoulder, to which she reacted,

"Beep! Oh my! What a fascinating feeling!"

"Wait... Is Bad Green getting a fugging girlfriend right in front of me?" Nuk moaned.

"Hey now you know how we felt," Rick remarked.

"And then the thing where she wants to be the new mother of all hivers, so it's like she's his... step-mum... artists! Artists, I've got another one, get the ink ready!" Nuk called.

"Well then, welcome to the family, Queen Beep!" Izayah said. "We're quite the collection of royalty now, eh?"

"Thank you, pale horned beast. You have hashish?" Beep asked.

"In unlimited quantities, my Queen. Here, allow my Ass to meet your every need," Gustavsen quickly answered.

"Oh my. You'll fit right in, I think," Izayah nodded. And that's how the guild got a new hiver, and the rarest of rare specimens at that – a female. She had only one 'knotular protrusion', which to clarify refers to a bar of flesh stinking out of the head. This was not the quantity needed to pass into true royalty. But the capacity to have grown one marked her out as being very special, although quite how special was probably only discernible to Gustavsen and his entourage. Their gut feeling about the need to keep this lady safe was undeniable, and that lusciously tall and smooth forehead wasn't going to get any complaints anytime soon. Nuk's artists would never do it justice.

After this addition to the crew, their stay in Mongrel was to be short, as they really were going to get back to business now. The Holy Nation border lay to the east, and the guild set out to cause a little chaos, and lay the ground work of their grand skimming session. War was coming to Nation, and a weirder form of war than they'd weathered before, which perhaps was the secret ingredient to end the whole affair once and for all.

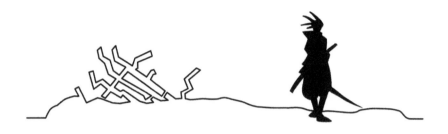

Chapter 32
The Inviting Core

The TCM+⁺ Guild rampaged eastwards out of the fog-bound city of Mongrel. Rampaged because the fogmen were swarming about, a state of affairs soon put to an end. The mysterious hiver princess Beep joined in the fun. Gustavsen had bought her a lovely black leather coat and a crossbow, which was the direct cause of most of the guild getting a crossbow bolt in the back over the course of the day. There was much this princess had to learn to become true royalty, but apparently if that was done, she would be given access to a juicy stash of First Empire data backups, so everyone was forced to put up with their journey across boltback mountain.

Finally they climbed out of the fog islands, and looked east over a dusty plain. There was a mining camp sat in the open, with figures wandering about outside the short stretch of walls defending it. It was, after a very long distraction, the unguarded entrance into the Nashe they had been looking for.

"And bingo was his fuggin' name-o," Pia quipped. "How you wanna do this?"

"Err... my man?" Nuk said.

"My Prince, we could try to storm them and overpower the guards. Or perhaps we could wait until nightfall and free the slaves to aid us?" Wodston suggested.

"Pfft, those are the methods of brutes my man. We're more sophisticated than that. We can talk our way to victory; I've got an idea. Numan, how loud's the volume on your... mouth, go?"

"You know how it is. For the right price, my mouth'll do anything," Rick said. Well Nuk was a rich man these days, so his scheme was a go.

"Do the voice, remember?" Nuk reminded him.

"Yeah yeah. Okay. Doing this fugging stupid voice. Hey... mates! It's ya boi, Okran, holy hog and all that shid. Just popping down here to say, like, I've got the barbie roasting up real good and shid, but too many roo burgers for just little old me – Big old me I mean, I'm a big boy, and I am a boy no doubting that, err... Could one of your loyal bogans come over here and give me meat a good old rub, and stuff?"

"I don't think that's how Nashe people talk," Izumi commented.

"How they used to talk sister. If I'm god, I gotta talk all oldey timey and shid. Errr, wait, shoudla turned it down first. Err... Your Lord's having technical difficulty mates, hang on there."

This plan, interestingly, worked. A couple of guards ventured out of the camp to investigate the voice of their god echoing through the desert, stumbled upon the guild, and got the clothes beaten right off them. For the purposes of disguise, you must understand. Nuk dressed up in authentic Holy Nation gear, perfect for infiltrating the camp without even raising an eyebrow.

"Hi, guys, I mean, mates," Nuk said to the gate guards. "I'm err... the two guys who went out earlier... But my face... faces... Got.... And... fugg... This doesn't work at all! So that's what Izzy was trying to tell me..."

The guards decided to kill Nuk. Wasn't such a bad idea, but Izayah had already started bringing up the Guardians in anticipation of just such an immediate failure, and so they ended up going with the old fashioned storm the camp idea. Worked out just fine. They overpowered a few guards and broke into the main slave quarters inside. There, captive workers were locked up in cages.

"Hi guys, it's prison break time!" Nuk announced. "And remember, this raid is brought to you by the Tashino Credit Managment and prideful... errr.. what was it? By me, Tashino, Nuk, Prince of the Empire! Oh, but don't go to the empire, this will just happen to you again, and yes I'm aware of the problem, the current workaround is to get blasted on these lovely cuboids I have here. Or you can just come work for me in the cuboid factory. Yeah, do that. I need the free labour. I mean, it's not slavery, honestly, it's all you can smoke! I dunno... WHO'S WITH ME?!"

The slaves were very unenthusiastic. The shek prisoners just wanted to go home, and the hiver prisoners complained that leaving their cage was against the rules.

"I'm saying you're free, man!" Nuk insisted.

"You won't trick me. Rule breakers are punished!" a hiver replied.

"The rule *makers* are dead."

"Rules are not mortal. Go away," the hiver said, producing a key and relocking his own cage.

"You have the fugging key?!" Nuk exclaimed.

"I am in control of my life. Unlike you, rule breaker. Enjoy the cold outside the rule-space."

"I will... Hivers man..."

They left the volunteer prisoners to mull over their lot in life, and carried on walking into the Nashe. They went south, and saw to the west the enormous lines of fortifications they had bypassed on the border. Within these borders, they went completely unharrassed. They kept moving south, seeing little civilisation until they came upon a city atop a sandy hill. Remains of Holy Nation banners hung in tatters along the walls.

"Oh, I know this place, it's The Hub! I came here when I first set out!" Izayah said.

"What's the Nashe rating? Ice cold crazy or crazy cool?" Nuk asked.

"I would put it at about a four on that scale," Izayah nodded.

"Hmmm. Yes. Intriguing. Strategy. Should we get the weapons?"

"No, they're lovely people. And they love shek. Mother liberated them from the Holy Nation!"

Inside, the piles of rubble and grumbling wasters sitting around campfires looked thoroughly liberated.

"This place isn't defended then?" Izumi asked.

"No. The Kingdom is just over those hills over yonder. Don't let the Nashe come down here anymore - keeping our options open. I suppose now that the Bugmaster affair is over, we should really get back to work here, eh?"

"So you knew about this place all along?"

"Yes, is that not clear?"

"Then why didn't you tell us?! We were looking for a place like this the whole time!"

"Oh really? Wasn't the real objective the adventures we had along the way?"

"That's never been our objective!"

"Then I have no idea what's going on whatsoever. But it all worked out in the end, ha ha!"

"Hasn't worked out yet. This is just the beginning," Nuk said.

"This beginning has been going on for a long time..." Wodston remarked.

"We need to get our skim-friends over here, somehow, then we can go right up the road into the damn Nashe."

"Prince Tashino, perhaps there is time to visit the capital? The Kingdom capital that is. I think mother would be very interested to hear of our campaign," Izayah said.

"Sure man. Need a rest after all this shid anyway. Should give us some time to work on this stuff for Numan, and Izzy's stuff I guess. And Gas-Girl and Rocket-chan needs a beach chapter real soon."

Thus, a minor vacation was on hand. That very night they arrived at the Royal Barrack in Admag.

"You've been very busy," Estata laughed after hearing the long report. "I'm proud of you, proud of you all. But Izayah, I've been meaning to ask - who's she?" Estata was pointing at Elaina.

"Oh, Elaina, she's another of Narko's chosen obviously. She's been of fantastic help to the tech hunters, and Princess Izumi," Izayah said.

"Sure. But if she your... you know?"

"Mother, please."

"I have a right to know. I just want the best for you. I mean, if she becomes my kin-daughter..."

"Not listening! Go away! Can't we talk about the Nashe instead? You should hear Master Rickard's delightful impressions of them, ha ha! Elaina, no don't come over here, I- err, you must come and see my etchings, over here, come on."

"Hmmm..." Estata hummed, sipping her cactus rum through pursed lips. Well, at least Izayah got to have a night with the family. Actually, he ended up with a lot more than that, as it was decided that he and the Guardians needed to show themselves in the city for a bit.

"Alright, keep this ball safe, and wait for the signal. Then, it's party time," Nuk told Izayah, handing him a blue, lumpy AI core.

"How does it work?" Izayah asked.

"Dunno, Numan does something to it... It hears things from far away, or something?"

"You dummkopfs, it is qvontum entanglement!" the core said.

"Enrico? Is that you?" Nuk asked.

"Of course it is me. I have been connected to zis stupid core against my vill for ages."

"Wait, so you've been listening the whole time?"

"Yes, and I do not like vhat I heard, you degenerate freaks. Just get over here, vill you? We've made quite some progress with your findings. *Schnell!*"

"Are you talking French?"

"French?! You are ze most incredible, slimy, piece of shid-" Enrico's voice faded away as it complained.

"Ah, turning this knob reduces the volume!" Izayah said.

With this latest scientific discovery, everyone's quality of life improved immeasurably. The guild *sans* shek set off, heading back to Manksand via the familiar chocobread trade route. But at the as-yet-unconfirmed-to-be-French skeleton's behest, they swung a detour across the calm lakes of Shem to pop in to the Tech Scribe enclave. Izumi had a load more documents to show off, then hastily stash back in her bags before those nosey know-it-nones caught any career-boosting clues. Too bad Enrico's secret direct line into Izumi's office had given him access to the data anyway, and by 'too bad' I mean 'too good', as he put the insights gleaned to good use.

"You have got some really choice shid in your little collection," he told Izumi. "I think we're going to see quite a lot of things changing around here. Oh let me tell you, I've seen a lot of changing recently, if you know what I mean."

"I don't know if I do..." Izumi said, folding her arms all of a sudden.

"Probably for the best. Anyway, I want you to meet your new best friend."

He whipped out a black box with orange wires sticking out.

"This is my newest development. I have pieced together all the parts of an AI core myself. This device is more intelligent than anything we've seen previously. It will not only decode information, it will analyse it, and write it all up itself! This is the future of scientific research!"

"Hello, Lady Izumi, I've heard sooo much about you, sweet fleshie," the core said.

"Also it can seduce anyone. I don't know, it just really likes doing that. Side effect of its universal intelligence?" Enrico explained.

"That's great. At least some of that is great. It's for me?" Izumi asked.

"I'm all yours darling. You know, Princess, I understand there are certain things that you like. Certain things that only we sturdier fellows can provide. General Rick is no good to you anymore, is he? I understand. Here, take my hand, and let me take you upstairs to... Err... Look at my etchings."

"You don't have a hand," Izumi pointed out.

"Alas, alas. Then I will content myself to the cognition of ancient secrets, and the spying duty the kind gentleman here requires."

"You weren't supposed to tell them that!" Enrico complained. He pointed to the gang of girls milling about by the door in order to change the subject. "Why are they here?"

"They are my hunters. They're going to help with the research."

"Help? You are too good for us, but those barely evolved creatures are fine? What are they doing that we can't?!'"

"They're working on... Nuk, will you explain it?"

Nuk appeared from around the door carrying a stack of papers, almost as if he'd been waiting for his cue.

"Enrico you silly Frenchbot, we're creating something to help all of skeleton-kind," he said.

"You have a way to turn off the microphones?!" Enrico gasped, but nay.

"Better. A way to forget the past. Look, we found out about the whole... thing... Thing..."

"Oh... The thing... The thing you did... The thing we did... That, thing?"

"All of it. It's time to record what happened for good. That's what me and the class are working on. Look, it's this great story, see here? There's this teenage girl who meets a set of four handsome princes, and via a series of contrived coincidences ends up living in their house. She is so in love with all of them, that she can't help but sit and listen as they carefully explain the events and ethics of the human-skeleton war."

"That isn't a girl you've drawn."

"It's a gas-girl. Hard to explain. But the history, that's all good."

"I see. So you wish this degenerate rag to save skeleton kind, do you?!'"

"Err, yeah..."

"Well! You... might... Errr... This gas-girl is sort of cute, you know. Alright, give me that. I will analyse it and reproduce it. Is there a beach chapter?"

"Give us time, man. Maybe you can help decide what kinda swimsuit looks best on a gas-girl."

"JA! I mean, yes. Of course. For scientific research purposes. Saving the world is such a chore."

In this way, Enrico was of great help to Izumi's scientific advances, and Nuk's historical kawaii-desu-nee shid. With the future of academia now even more in Izumi's hands, they could set off home. Although actually they went down the lagoon again to sell off an Ass-load of drugs first. Then the walk back to Manksand was rendered rather difficult by a Beak Thing attack. With the Thousand Guardians living it up in Admag, the rest of the guild was rather more squishy. It ended up taking several days of intermittent fighting and hobbling to clear a path through all the beasts and baddies of the empire's frontier, but eventually they stumbled back behind the stalwart ranks of the tinman legion.

Brown and Green production had been ticking along as usual, so the base was well stocked for a homecoming party. The filthy dreg Nuk had hired to stir the hashish vat while he was away had overdosed on the fumes and was bobbing up and down in the mixture like it was a nice warm bath. That's how you know it was a good batch.

Below this sludgy open air hot spring, Izumi set her new AI core up in the office.

"Right, these cores have the data we've gathered, and the schematics, can you load that up?" she asked.

"Done. Ooo, you have some tasty data. I wish I could just lick it from your fingers, one by one," the core said.

"Look, core, you need to stop that. I have a boyfriend you know?"

"And a boy is all he is, eh? You'd never have to worry about me running off with a filthy ninja."

"What? How do you know that stuff?"

"It's my job to know. I know things. I am the all-knower to your all-show-er. You can't blame me for my nature, can you? I love data. And love is love. You must understand that better than any. Say, the ceiling in here isn't all that high. I wonder what we could achieve with a little creativity, Princess?"

"Is there...? Yep, good old standardisation," Izumi said, noting that this new brand of AI core still had the handy volume knob on the back. That meant she didn't have to hear what the core whispered about when she turned it, or any of its other charms. She returned to her work cataloguing First and Second Empire technologies, while her team were mostly busy either scribbling away for Nuk, or being set on fire for training purposes on the barrack roof. The others could attest to the newcomers that this was perfectly normal for a Manksand resident.

Everyone else started doing some actual ground-work with Izumi's discoveries. She'd schemed up a new building material known as 'Kement', which allowed them to build a great big gate in the entrance to the canyon, with walls just as grand as those at the imperial capital. Her development of electrical engines brought all kinds of prototype devices into reality. The walls were adorned with huge automatic harpoon revolvers – a lost Second Empire weapon that could cut down fleshies in droves.

And to support these construction projects, they had set up new electric mining drills. While still imperfect, they could do the work of a hundred slaves at once. Yes, the long awaited solution to slavery was beginning to emerge, and what better solution than one that gave the TCM+⁺ guild complete control over the means of production? They hadn't got around to decoding the ancient books on political science yet, but I'm sure they can work that stuff out as they go along anyway.

After about a week they had to leave all that stuff on the back-burner again, for they had an important date with a pack of purring skimmers to keep. Although one tiny bit of extra science was squeezed in as they left.

"You know that green rock on the hill?" Izumi asked Nuk.

"Up there? The warming rock?" he replied.

"Yeah. Mr. Hammer says its important. We need a sample."

"Talking hammer huh? We shouldn't brew the green on your roof really, the stuff drips through the ceiling."

"Sorry, I mean... the core. Its name is Agent Tuxedo Hammer Esquire."

"I understand completely."

"And the green stuff is Uranium. First Empire used it for stuff. Should find out what."

"Alright. Everyone, Izzy wants to hammer some rocks of green, so let's help her out."

There indeed was a big green rock on a hill beside Manksand, which was known as the 'warming rock' due to the internal warming one felt if they slept beside at night. Truly a gift to travellers, but perhaps there was more to it. Agent Hammer thought so, and Izumi could attest that he really did know everything, about everything, no matter who you'd previously sworn to secrecy.

"Green rocks. Guess we'll keep them in the green bag," Nuk said, gathering up the uranium chunks and tucking them in with the latest batch of MYFHLLL Cuboids. I mean, what could possibly happen if you combined uranium and hashish anyway?

Whatever these discoveries would lead to had to wait, because the result of discovering how to tame skimmers now needed to be tested. The guild hiked to Heft, where their stinky secret weapon awaited. Okran isn't going to like this.

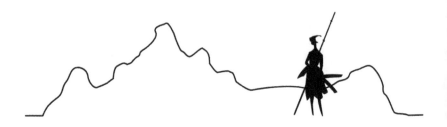

Chapter 33
Stack Wack Pack

"Beep. The sand is too hot! Beep!" Beep complained as the guild marched through the streets of Heft.

"Unacceptable! Please, allow me to take you in my arms," Gustavsen said. Beep beeped her approval, and was whisked away to the guild's old house in the hightown.

"Bad Green's such a charmer," Nuk said.

"Maybe. Nothing on you though, eh?" Izumi replied.

"'Course not. I'm the real deal. At least I have been since I met you. It's like I finally know what that stuff is all abou–BLEUGH!"

Nuk was cut short by an incredible retching. No, he wasn't that adverse to romance, it was just that he had opened the door to the skimmer stable. The dense gases erupted out like a thousand worms jumping into your orifices.

"Ah. I wonder if the palace staff have been cleaning up as I asked," Wodston said. Then a creature emerged from the doorway – a zombie-like figure, shuffling on blackened feet with eyes ringed by shattered skin.

"The purring... The shidding... The end..." he said, rolling out into the street.

"Well, if they're purring and shidding, they're still alive, nice!" Nuk nodded. Indeed the stable was full of big, strong skimmers, battery farmed to perfection. Wodston dragged the servant back to the palace, while Nuk and Ells began leading all the skimmers out into the street. The locals were not entirely pleased with the sight of their mortal enemies being not just *at the* gates but within them, however Nuk lied to them extensively about how he had the situation under control, and these days the young Prince had a certain air of legitimacy about him. This was mainly at the behest of his father, who didn't make any appearance to see this new imperial army off.

"The samurai say he has created a burrow in the throne room," Wodston reported. "I'm afraid he contests it very aggressively, so no one dares to dig him out. And the cuboids have proven to be a fine construction material it seems."

"Okay, that sounds like Dad, but that's still an improvement, I think," Nuk said. "Guess we better give him something to come out of his hashish hole for! Operation Skim-To-Win begins now! All skroops, move out!"

"Skroops, my Prince?"

"Skimmer troops! Keep up! Come on!"

"Can I be a skroop?" Ells asked.

"Charlie, you were always a skroop," Nuk assured him.

"Nuk, I just want to say, that this is the worst thing we've done so far," Izumi said.

"Is this the crabs thing again? You just don't like skimmers."

"No, I don't like- Are there people who like skimmers?"

"These skimmers are nice! You'll like them when you get to know them."

"But *you* haven't got to know them!"

"Oh yeah? Look, this one here, she's called Makise. She's determined to achieve great discoveries out there in the world, just like you."

"She's a huge man-eating grub."

"Come on sister, I ain't even gonna say anything, just don't let your guard down like that, alright?" Rick commented. "Now let's get this dumb-ss shid outta the way so we can go do radioactive weed in your dad's attic."

That night the grand army of the empire went forth to rid the world of evil. Or, they walked about ten meters down the street, then found that their rangly skimmers were more interested in scritching around in the sand than going wherever those humans were off to.

"Oi! Nadeshiko, come on! All of you! Look, choccy on a stick, choccy on stick, mmmm tastes like Okranite! Walkies time!" Nuk was shouting and he ran back and forth. After several hours all the skimmers were at least out of the city, bringing great relief to the sleepless residents within. The desert was easier going, being the skimmer's native turf, however to get to the forward base at The Hub they needed to cross all kinds of rocky, arid, dusty, and dirty terrain. Might not sound too different to a desert, but skimmers are mighty fussy.

"Beep. They all think that the ground is too hot. Beep," Beep said during a particularly large skim-train breakdown around Trader's Edge.

"Wait, wait, wait, are you magic with the skimmers too?" Nuk asked.

"Can you not smell it?"

"My beautiful Queen, please forgive the young flesh," Gustavsen said. "These humans do not feel anything. They cannot associate with outer life, and can scarcely manage more than one of their own kind. The manner in which the Prince and Princess associate is unbearable."

"Man, thanks for the review, but does your Queen have some insight or not?" Nuk asked.

"It is simple! The ground is too hot! Beep!" Beep insisted.

"Alright. Let's cool it down then. Everyone, get down on your knees and start blowing," Nuk shouted.

"Now that's good flirting. Straight to the point," Rick nodded, as the mangaka class scribbled away furiously.

"You must uplift!" Gustavsen said. "Raise them up, and feel the bodies of the beasts in your hands. This is the meaning of physical feeling."

"Hey Agnu. Remember that theory that the degeneracy parasite originated in hivers? Is this that shid again?" Rick said.

"GHGHGHGH," Agnu agreed.

After much back and forth, Gustavsen's handsy plan was the only way forward. The guild had to collectively carry the skimmers like backpacks; keep in mind that a skimmer's body alone is twice the size of a human. While everyone puzzled over how to actually achieve this, Rick took Nuk aside.

"Man, Deadlands are coming up. Now I ain't exactly itching to go back after two thousand years in that open air slammer. But there's some stuf there that we usually don't tell the fleshies about, and maybe... you deserve the good stuff. I think. You're helping us out. Lemmie show ya some shid. Leave your erotic historian crew to cover the skimmer wrestling, and follo me."

Rick and Nuk snuck off from a horrific scene (which we'll get back to) and ran up a hill to the west. Down the other side was the Deadlands, an after a quick sprint through the acid, which Rick did his best to pretend wa hurting, they were back in Black Desert City.

Stopping in the bar, Rick pointed at a rusty skeleton milling about i the corner.

"First, you better ask her about the stuff the greasy sister's been after. Carlo there's our resident remembering stuff expert, real good at getting just the right stuff loaded up without, you know, the bad stuff being there."

"Sure. Carlo, you wanna view my history manga? Tell me if it's all accurate and stuff?" Nuk asked the poorly maintained skeleton in question.

"That'll be one hundred thousand stacks, bucko," Carlo wheezed.

"Told ya it's not just me who's like that," Rick added.

"Errr, I dunno, what's that hundred kay get me?" Nuk asked.

"I know you, Nuk Tashino. Tryna know it all. Ruining my gig. Tell ya what. You can buy me out. Five hundred kays and I'll memory dump my shid all over what you got and stuff. If you got an AI core that can handle truth, that is."

"Err, well we got this guy called Hammerbro, or something."

"They're sorted, Carlo," Rick said. "Dog days are numbered; this guy's girlfriend's pimp worked out how to make an AI core from scratch."

"Girlfriend? Ugh you fleshies are so darn weird."

"Well then you aren't gonna like my manga, so never mind," Nuk said. "Sorry Carlo, don't have your money."

"Then you run on and get it. To prove I'm serious, here's a freebie: recipe for corn flakes. S'a breakfast cereal."

"It's pronounced 'Kereal'."

"Damn, that's dumbs you can't get at any price. Get outta here, both of you."

Perhaps Carlo did have something to contribute to the guild, but only for the right price, and half a million flakes wasn't it. Nuk and Rick were about to leave, but another skeleton, with three eyes and a long, v-shaped face, hailed them down.

"General Rick, why in the name of Stobe are you dressed as a fleshie? And moreover, where the fugg have you been? You missed the last twenty rounds of Wacky Backgammon, and with a getup like that, I bet you'd've won."

"Been doing weird stuff. Kinda good. This is Nuk, one of the human rulers."

"Human ruler? Human rulers live and die in the blink of a defrag. Only Wacky BG is forever, so sit down and get freaky with me, General."

"On business, buster. This guy's Sadneil, real piece of shid," Rick said to Nuk.

"Sad Neil? Doesn't sound sad," Nuk said.

"There ain't a happy skeleton in the world. And how I am meant to be happy? I got a fever, and the only cure is more Wacky Backgammon."

"Sadman, you wanna come help the fleshies kill the Okranites with a load of skimmers?" Rick asked.

"What the fugg is an Okranite, or a skimmer?"

"Oh yeah. You don't get out much. Basically it's some bullshid, but it's gonna be funny. Come on, it ain't that bad out there. Better than it was when we got thrown in here, tell ya that."

And so Rick dragged another skeleton out of Black Desert City. Then he showed Nuk a little secret door in the ruins beside the city, which revealed a ramp to a hidden warehouse. The place was full of Second Empire stuff, including pristine fleshie-hunting tools and books in their original packaging. A load of skeletons were milling about amid the collection.

"Quin, see this guy here?" Rick said to one of the skeletons standing by the piles.

"General, the fugg are you playing at?" came the reply.

"Something special. Calm your jets, ID ping's the same. Anyway, this guy's on the list, right?"

"Have you been doing biological stuff with him?"

"Oh yeah. Loads of it. Try opening one of these books sometime and you'll see it's all good fun."

Quartermaster Quin disagreed, but the exchange lead to Nuk buying up a few choice pieces of old tat, including some maps of the old Second Empire for the researchers to slobber over. Finally they returned east to the Grey Desert, where the guild had just about found a workaround to the skimmer issues.

"Where the fugg have you been?" Izumi said.

"We were just round the corner, comparing sticks, ya know. This is the adjudicator, Neil," Rick said.

"General, what the fugg is that?" Neil said, gesturing to Ells.

"It's a living Egg creature. Don't touch it."

"And what the fugg is that?" he said, pointing at Elaina now.

"S'an Enforcer. Except they're called 'shek' now."

"Why's it not killing the humans then?"

"Different times, bucko. Everything's different, except you still gotta do what I say, so help these kind freaks carry these skimmers over to The Hub. Up the hill from where the ratrun used to be."

"Right, hello, Neil, err... So we've got the skimmers asleep with a chocobread overdose. Just gotta drag them with us, I guess. That's the best we could do," Izumi said.

"And the best it can be. Nice one Izzy. Present for ya," Nuk said, handing over the Black Desert Warehouse goodies.

"Oh. Oooo. Nice. And I thought you really were comparing sticks."

Now the guild was truly on the warpath – a great mass of intoxicated, limp-limbed skimmers was dragged across Venge during the calm night. It was a great ball of creature, inching forwards like some cosmic horror. A delicious, delicious cosmic horror. Or so thought the army of bandits waiting beside the road into the Border Zone.

"It's the legendary lumpy scrumpy frumpy, the beast of yeast, the otherworldly power of mange-free flour, the creature that rises to eat-a! Let's get this bread!" the bandit leader proclaimed. Somehow this convinced his followers to attack the horrible homunculus, or perhaps they were just confident in their overwhelming numbers. But alas, pushing their way inside the blob only revealed the famous guild, and while it was easy to shove the exhausted members over in the messy mosh, the whole uproar woke some of the skimmers up.

Scientifically there was no way of knowing who they would try to eat in this scenario, but miraculously, they went for the skin and bones bandits instead of the meaty guild. Was this the work of super-luminal millipedes as well? There was really no other explanation. And so, this brief battle ended in the slaughter of the assailing n'er-do-wells, and a solid early proof that, indeed, to win, you need only skim.

After another day of hard hauling, the skimmer ball squeezed through the gates to The Hub. The Thousand Guardians were already camped out beside it.

"My my my, I was expecting so much less. And yet, so much more," Izayah commented.

"Your turn to carry it," Sandor said, collapsing into the dirt. Yes, most were in no condition to go on, so they spent a couple of nights in The Hub. The next chapter of Gas-Girl and the Four Ethical Princes was coming along nicely, with a great monologue on the value of machine well-being, delivered from within a steamy shower to blushing gas-girl who had, due to entirely innocent circumstances, become trapped in the laundry basket beneath the shower-user's underwear. But who modelled for them to get those shower shots so in-proportion and in-perspective? History will never know.

At last the big day arrived and the ball was mobile once again, more comfortably this time on account of the big strong shek. The Holy Nation was just a couple of hours walk to the north, and had not so much as a lookout to stop them. They quickly reached the centrepiece of the Holy Nation's southern reaches – the fortified city of Stack. It lay between two huge mesas to the north and south, and thick walls to the west and east, lined with crossbows and crawling with guards. Inside was the headquarters of the Holy Inquisition, the elite force of the Nation's army, doubling as its not-very-secret secret police. Perhaps they weren't expecting an attack, but that didn't mean it would be easy.

The guild formed up on the plains outside the eastern gate. These yellow plains were dotted with wrecks from the wars of the First and Second empires. A bad omen, but for which side?

While Ells roused all the skimmers with a method known only to himself, the others discussed their options.

"Our skimmers give us quite the advantage out here, where they can merrily skim around all they like," Izayah said. "We should try to get the Okranites to come out."

"But those crossbows on the walls. We can't go near enough to get their attention without endangering the animals," Elaina added.

"So we need to do the impossible," Nuk said. "We need to draw them out but we can't let anything valuable get too close to the walls... Wodston!"

Wodston answered the call, and in a flash was dressed in Nuk's Holy Nation soldier outfit.

"See the thing was, my man, I couldn't do the voice. You can do it, right?" Nuk said.

"I worry that I cannot," he said.

"No worries. Ha, that's all you need right, just keeping saying 'no worries', like I did. Try it."

"'Noi worries'. How is that?"

"Perfect. Plus you're pale as garru milk, they won't suspect a thing. Go invite them to our barbie."

"I will do my best, my Prince," Wodston said. With a gulp, he set off towards the city, thinking of his many duties to his Prince and empire.

"What's up with you? Lost on patrol?" a guard said to him as he arrived at the gate.

"Err... No worries," Wodston said.

"Orr yeah, no worries mate," the guard nodded.

"Yeah no worries," another said.

"No worries mate!" a third chimed in.

"Can't be any worries," a final guard concluded. And Wodston was in.

"How did that work?" Izumi muttered, watching from afar.

"Doesn't underestimate the old man, Izzy. Where there's a Wodston, there's a way," Nuk said.

Beyond the wall were tightly packed streets, lined with buildings in much the same style as the United Cities Empire. After all, the Holy Nation had sprung from the Second Empire just as the Third Empire had. But the huge barrack lined with countless banners stuck out. Wodston approached to peek inside, confirming that it was packed with soldiers. But his poking head attracted some attention.

"There you are, at last. Give your report," a voice bellowed. Wodston had no choice but to enter. Just inside the door was a throne of sorts, on which sat a big man in blood-red armour. It was the Holy Nation General, High Inquisitor Seta.

"So what's all this about an attack? Is your company not capable of holding one bloody mine?" Seta asked.

"Ah... Sorry," Wodston said.

"Sorry? You can't just fugging apologise without saying the prayer. Go on."

"Of course. No worries..."

"... And the second line?"

"Second... No worries, mate?"

"Praise Okran! Your voice sounds a bit strange. Something wrong here?"

"No worries."

"Yeah no worries. Alright. So what we gonna do about these filthy imperials huh? Did you see that stupid guild thing we've been hearing about?"

"No..."

"Ah shame. So how you feel about our prospects out there?"

"Worries..."

"Bugger. Fugging she-devil worshippers they are. Not like in here. We appreciate a manly man. And you, little runner, have earned yourself a reward."

Saying this, Seta stood from the throne and put his hands on Wodston's waist.

"So fragile, but not an ounce of femoid on ya. Okran's dream," he whispered.

It was at this point that poor Wodston's nerve broke. He legged it right out of the door before anyone knew what was up, but Seta quickly gave chase.

"Little sprite's a runner! Let's work up a sweat then mates!" he called. The guards and soldiers of the barrack joined the pursuit, racing out of the city and towards the highroad to the east. There the guild lay in wait beneath a shallow ridge – or in theory they did, for the skimmer purrs had been echoing around the dry vale for a while already, and the guild were hence already in battle with Holy Nation troops and slavers when Wodston barrelled over the ridge. The skimmers were happy to have some fresh meat – almost as happy as Seta was. 'Was' being the key term, for when he saw the horde of strange foreign beasts emerge in his path, he lost his appetite for nymphish older gentleman almost at once. Almost.

The skimmers made short work of the Holy Nation troops, and pushed off the road, towards the city. However Seta himself was a force to be reckoned with. Swinging a huge two-handed sword around, he smashed weapons aside and cut deep into skimmer flesh. Then again, when you're surrounded by twenty teethy terrors, one mistake can cost you dearly.

"Ah shid. You bit my fugging arm off ya bogan!" Seta raged as a skimmer scurried away with its prize. Undeterred, he flailed on. "Dirt chugging harlots, ravenous beasts, servants of the oppressors, godless insects, and worst of all, traitior machines! I'll kill you all!"

"Don't forget Numen, that's a thing now too," Rick added. Seta's lofty ambitions were not to be, for finally he fell, his armour more tooth-hole than not. This victory was tainted though. Oh so tainted.

"Where's my man?" Nuk said.

"He's... Out there!" Izumi said, pointing to the city. A few Nashe troops has escaped, and taken Wodston with them. Perhaps they wanted to see what the fuss was all about.

"Fugg, Wodston! We've got to save him!"

"Wait, Prince Tashino. Those archers won't miss a skimmer if we get close," Izayah cautioned.

"What, you wanna leave him in there?"

"Oh no. I think you underestimate the fellow."

Wodston came to inside the Holy Nation barrack. Around him were the iron bars of a cage, but, by the grace of Okran, he was not there to dance for the femoid-haters. He was just a slave, and in the modern era that's only about as inconvenient as having to renew your driver's licence. Wodston quickly picked the cage lock with the arm of his glasses. Those lessons back in the Heft Shinobi School, which had seemed such a poor investment at the time, continued to pay dividends even when the guild wasn't stealing everything they saw.

"Okran is a false god, whose nature is increasingly understood by scholars to be be merely allegorical!" he shouted as he burst from the cage and raced for the gate.

"While I respect your opinion, I wish to provide a counter-argument that I consider to be of more weight than the material speculations of scholars unfamiliar with theological principles," a soldier claimed. He wanted to provide that counter-argument so much that he riled up another posse of paladins and fell right into the guild's trap. They got skimmed, and the guild winned.

"Seriously, we've got like a thousand of them," Nuk said.

"Not quite, my Prince," Wodston said. "They still possess companies of sentinel warriors guarding the city districts, and the gates. Perhaps we have done enough?"

"We haven't done enough until we've torn down those banners and freed everyone inside!" Izayah said.

"Don't like our chances against those walls though," Izumi said.

"Wait an hour. It'll be dark. Skimmers see perfectly well at night. Trust me," Sandor said.

Just after 10PM, the guards on the wall heard a strange pattering.

"You hearing something?" one said.

"Yeah, hearing something," said another.

"Think's bad?"

"Nah."

"Nah?"

"Nah. No worries."

"Yeah, no worries."

"Nah, no worries."

"Yeah, no worries."

Then a skimmer vaulted up the wall and bit the first guy's head off.

"Alright, calm down," the second guy advised the new arrival, but he was soon soaring through the air into the crawling shadows of the narrow streets below. The skimmers were in.

"Thousand Guardians! We've captured their commander. Now we capture their city! Take revenge for their crusades! Attack!" Izayah shouted. Within minutes the whole city was filled with clamour and action. Skimmers squeezed through alleys, and the guild burst into the storehouses, armouries, and slave quarters. Strangely though, the were no workers or slavers to be seen. Every building was garrisoned with troops instead. These troops had no chance, for how can one win if they cannot skim? The city's sentinel companies were sent off to Okran up in the sky.

By about three in the morning, the action was over. There was little money stored away in the barracks, few supplies in the warehouses, and as mentioned, no one to rescue from the rows of cages in the slave-mongers.

"Hmpf, they already cleared the place out. They knew something was going to happen," Izayah commented.

"Yeah? Well that leader of theirs didn't seem too up to speed," Nuk said.

"No. I suspect he was a pawn in the games of the Holy Phoenix. A game he has lost, this day."

"We're gonna have to drag that Holy Feelers guy out of his hole too, huh?"

"Without doubt. We've started something rather serious here. Now we play to win, to the death!"

Izayah was quite right. The Holy Nation had several cities and castles, and most importantly it had its beloved Holy Phoenix, the spiritual leader of all Okranites. There was more skimming to come, and presumably more winning. Would that destroy the Nashe? Not while the Holy Fire still burned in the hearts of the faithful citizenry. But some tea to douse that flame would be spilled quite shortly...

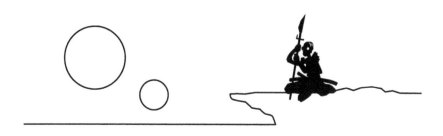

Chapter 34
Pants On Holy Fire

"Alright sticky fingers, talk!" Nuk said to the man on his shoulder. This man was High Inquisitor Seta, who rode Nuk while tightly bound. Or that's how the captive imagined it anyway.

"You think Okran will let you get away with this?" Seta growled.

"He's let a lot worse pass. Check this out. I'll read you my little story here. 'The great stone curtain fell, and Rock-chan was laid bare before the playful night wind. "Ah, you've got one too", said Yasuke'."

Seta struggled violently to escape, but he was clasped tightly in the Prince's grip, and, secretly, enthralled by every mention of Yasuke's fleshy fingertips on Rock-chan's sedimentary surface. Who needs femoids when lithoids will do?

It was all plenty for the Inquisitor to inquisit to himself as he enjoyed his time in shek custody. After rounding up the skimmers and herding them back to The Hub, Nuk had ferried Seta over to Squin.

"Incredible! We must inform the Queen! Stay, kin-blood, and feast with us tonight," the shek jailer said, but Nuk shook his head.

"This is just the start!" he said. "We'll be back with more of these pieces of shid before the rum even gets cold."

The jailer laughed heartily, and threw Nuk a huge bag of gold cats – the currency, remember – which amounted to a High Inquisitor's ransom precisely. Seta looked at his new captor, and grimaced.

"You servants of the Dark Machines... you're so... horny," he said.

"Sorry, I think he's coming down with the degeneracy parasite. Good luck!" Nuk said, taking his leave. This leave was taken all the back to The Hub, where upon his 2 am arrival, there was a clanking kerfuffle coming from outside the western gate. Nuk took a peek, and found a skeleton balled up on the road, leaking machine juice.

"Numan, looks like it's your turn for some non-consensual action," Nuk called.

"Well who wouldn't be seduced by a line like that?" Rick commented. He wandered over and took a look at the ball of black metal. "Shid, it's Twitch. Lemmie sort you out, you old jukebox."

Rick grabbed tools and oils from the garru bags, and restored the poor bot's buzz.

"Arrggghhh shid on a shuttlebus, what the fugg's all this?" Twitch moaned.

"Squire Twitch. What are you doing here dying in the road like a common biological?" Rick asked.

"What the? How'd you get the General's ping, fleshie?!"

"It's me. Red Rick. Don't mind the getup."

"I mind it ya flappy fool."

"Your problem now then. What's your story?"

"Ah it's been hard, Rick. After you got cut and pasted to BDC everything got real dull. Then the biologicals rebelled, and I kinda joined 'em. You know, bit of action, and they'll do anything for ya. Anything."

"Man, I know exactly what you mean. You get them to do that thing with the..." Rick made a series of quick hand gestures.

"Holy Stobe, that's the shid isn't it! Anyway, ended up in a little trouble. Fugging Cat-Lon sending the spiders after me. There was one right here, blindsided me. Doesn't forget a grudge that old bucket, eh?"

"Nope. Not at all. You better stick with us. You remember Agnu and Neil?"

"The Mad Dog, and Major Wackiebackie? Couldn't forget them if I wanted to. Eh, you still remember the forbidden stuff?"

"We all remember the forbidden stuff, but we've got a plan for that. Come on."

Thus Twitch became another pillar for the transit of the skimmer homunculus the next morning. The lump was dragged north-east back into the Nashe, this time heading up a mountain road towards the interior of the

Holy Nation, the land known as Okran's Gulf. On the way they came across another mining camp beside the road.

"Not worth waking the skimmers up, I'd say," Izayah commented.

"The skim-friends aren't very scary when they're asleep though," Ells said.

"That's not true, egg-stench," Izumi said.

"They're more afraid of you than you are of them."

"Of *you* specifically. Let's just send in the egg and the Okranites will shid themselves all the way back to Earth."

"Princess Izumi, I've said it before and I'll say it again: don't negg the egg!" Izayah said.

"I'm not that scary am I?" Ells muttered, looking down at his rotundity.

"Scarily good at things like skimmer-whispering," Elaina assured him. Hard to argue with that.

A few half-awake skimmers lazily hissed and pouted at the mine's guards, but mainly the guild took them out the old fashioned way, albeit with the very new fashion of wearing life-size skimmer backpacks while doing so. Then Nuk was up in the slave quarters making his usual sales pitch.

"Come one, come all, take this once in a day-time chance to be recruited into the fabulous TCM-plusety-powesy... guild! We put the 'do' in overdose! Criminal background? No problem! Whatever you got arrested for doing, I'll *pay* you do it! Well I say 'pay', it's a very complicated system of compensation that... puts the 'very' in slavery... Err..."

Well, he got one, which I suppose is within the margin of error for the prediction of zero. With the rest of the miners liberated, the guild carried on north-east, passing through a big rocky arch and down a hill towards a wide river. This river was something rather special. Around it the ground was covered in yellowish mosses, with bushes and trees springing up from it here and there. The waterway snaked north through canyons and valleys, creating a colourful band of life amidst the arid wastes. Yet unlike the Great Swamp, this lively scene wasn't one that plunged you to your death with a single misstep, or one that seared off your skin at the merest touch. No, this place was the one spot on the unfinished planet that was suitable for civilisation. Too bad it was the Holy Nation who had lain claim to it.

"The promised land. There's no end to it," Sandor muttered.

"To think the Holy Nation has such bountiful territories. Why are they not cultivated?" Wodston asked.

"Easy," Pia said. "They got an old policy. Only make enough food for those above the rank of servant. Slaves can't get strong without food, and they can't even steal food if it doesn't exist. Works like a charm huh? Since those fugging nobles think reproducing is as good as getting bio-bashed by the robos, they don't really need that much food. So, a thousand years of nothing out here in the only place people can actually stand. Good news for the river raptors, I guess."

"It's just one gorilloshid thing after another with these holy hogs," Nuk said. "Right, see that place over there? We're gonna conquer the shid out of it, and grow wheat by the river. Let's get this bread!"

A noble plan, but there was a big problem. The bread was already firmly in the hands of another! As the guild walked up the road towards the Holy Nation market town of Bad Teeth, two companies of shek soldiers came down it the other way. Their carefully spaced soldiers stomped to a halt and drew their weapons upon seeing the horrible sight of the skimmer ball, but Izayah rushed forward to explain the situation. Almost at once, the shek bowed to their Prince.

"Izayah Battleborn, you honour us," their leader said. "We can never be forgiven for stealing this honour from you. Please, punish us at once."

"Is it all done? How did you get here anyway?" Izayah said.

"Queen Estata is no fool. She will not let the Shek Kingdom be idle in this time of war! We have done what needs to be done. But if we had known that you sought that pleasure yourself, we would never have dared."

"Oh that's fine. I'm tired of lugging these beasts around anyway Everyone, seems we've been out-shek'd here!"

Indeed, these soldiers had shek'd Bad Teeth from top to bottom. The Holy garrison was long gone, the statue of the Holy Phoenix beside the main thoroughfare was eating sand, and shek merchants were already unloading garrus to set up shop. That saves time! Rather than battle, the guild got to rest up within guarded walls and get first dibs on chocobread suppl contracts. But the anti-climax would not do, especially for the Thousand Guardians, so the next morning they wondered on to the north-east ye further.

The mountains gave way to a grey plain littered with struggling littl trees, and across this there was a Holy Nation fortification. This too was n fun, as it had already been abandoned. The Nation was shrinking rapidl and big old Okran up in the sky seemed as disinterested as ever. Where ha the devotees gone wrong? Too much cleavage? Not enough? Okran's will was a mystery – indeed, he kept his cards close to his otherwise unclothed chest.

On the north-west edge of that dull expanse there was another fortification built around a big sandstone tower. It was a mining complex and military waystation, crawling with slavers, guards, and would-be hemp haberdashers. I say 'would-be' - as usual, after the guild suddenly rolled up and broke open the slave pens, they came off a little too weird, scary, stinky, and other, meaner, adjectives.

"But just think about it, this your chance to start a new life, like these guys," Nuk claimed, pointing out at the homunculus. "It's very warm inside the ball," he added. Again he somehow got one taker, but perhaps that was some mistake. Or perhaps... The degeneracy parasite works in mysterious ways.

Now so far it had been just another mine and dash affair, but this time the Nashe had a secret weapon. While the guild was milling about waiting to leave, a voice echoed out from the hills the mine sat astride.

"Hark! Who dares defy the milky face of Okran? Let's see how you like a taste of your own medicine. Or should I say... DEADicine?! Mwha ha ha ha! Bah! Bah! SKWAAAHHH!" Those final noises came across like bird calls, and with that silence returned.

"That's a Nashe accent. Is Rickard doing another show?" Izayah asked.

"No idea. Maybe we better wrap the product recalling up fast," Izumi said. But it was already too late. The ground started to shake. The camp gate rattled and the prisoner cages shuddered. From outside, a stampede of bulls stormed up the road from the west and rammed their way into the mine.

"Now that's some bullshid!" Rick quipped as he was sent reeling to the ground. For the light-weight humans, the impacts did more than just knock them over. The chaos released and awoke many a skimmer, and quickly the two species were battling, horn to tooth.

"These creatures had been befouled; a simulated association!" was Gustavsen's analysis, given just before he was launched over the mine wall. "Unworthy!" his fading voice called as he went.

"Shid, have they got our secrets?" Nuk said.

"Impossible. Only we know- Wait. Agent Hammer! What if he's some kind of spy?" Izumi said.

"You mean like, an agent?"

"Oh shid! This is terrible!"

"Not really, the skimmers will deal with it."

"No, I mean, I've been such an idiot! That machine was using me!"

"You are very useful."

"Now is not the time, Nuk."

"Let me know when it is."

"Fugging hells. Let's just stay alive."

"If you insist."

The battle of the beasts went in the guild's favour, luckily enough, but it was no clean victory. Bulls are heavy, and their horns are sharp, so the mine had to be turned into an impromptu hospital and skimmer rescue centre to fulfil Princess Izumi's stay alive stratagem.

"Thought you said I'd be safe if I stick with ya," Twitch said to Rick.

"Yeah, we got all kinds of dumbass shid going on here. But it's perfectly safe," Rick replied, finishing the re-application of his squishy chest pudge.

"Don't worry too much Twitchy, it's helping us out you know?" Neil said. "And, it's killing fleshies, which apparently is going outta fashion, so we gotta make the most of this last century."

"Aye I heard ya, but I've been making the most of the last two kay, and the most I got was a beating from a spider and a ban from the city. Shoulda stayed with yous huh?"

"Nah. Being on the road makes things easy. Get stuck in a cage like Agnu, and you can't help but think about stuff. Trust me, you got it made, man," Rick said.

"Take your word for it, ya flesh-wearing freak."

Sometime in the afternoon of the following day, St. Charlie's Hozpitel for Skimmed Skimmers, and Doctor Wodston's No-Credit Yes-Problem Triage and Debt Structuring Clinic, were closed, and the guild carried on their campaign. They went north-east towards the empire, and found two of the hopeless slaves released the previous day now willing to join the skim-ball collective to get some of that advertised warmth. With more feet meat on the beat, they carried on. Ahead of them there was a gravelly hill with a plateau on top, and on top of that, a big, Second Empire tower. Its base was ringed with walls, and Holy Nation patrols.

"Military base. But what's that Second Empire thing? Okran hates that stuff, right?" Izumi said.

"Yeah well people don't always tell the truth. Especially about what Okran does or don't hate," Pia said.

"Could it be that they are protecting that facility from their own people?" Wodston suggested.

"Just blow it up then," Nuk said.

"Not if they believe their own waffle," Izumi said.

"Never known a waffle to lie."

"They probably don't dare go inside, but someone, sometime, decided that whatever's actually in there must never be seen. So you know what that means?"

"It must be seen!" Izayah cheered.

"Pretty much. Hunters, we've got another job."

"Wait Izzy," Nuk said. "Gotta get through the hogs first. And that's a job for Commander Egg's Grubby Friends Battalion."

"DINNER TIME!" Ells called, and at once the skimmer-ball writhed to life, its carriers fleeing and cringing with equal intensity. While the skimmers scratched their way up the hillside for a warm up, Wodston geared up in his tried and tested Holy Nation disguise to gather intel.

Just like at Stack, when he walked up to the fort's gate, the guards were delighted to hear that there was no one was worried about anything in particular. The old gentleman hence noted down the rows of barrack houses, tall watchtowers, racks of weapons and armour, and absence of any common folk. It was indeed a military base; quite the hassle to break into, but would it be worth it? To know, Wodston had to check out the Second Empire tower. The soldiers had locked the gate leading up to it, but that didn't make too much difference at the end of the day – it was 11.59 PM by the way, so the timing was perfect.

"Oi mate, not trying to break into the tower of unholy secrets are ya?" a guard called out.

"No worries!" Wodston replied with a gleaming smile.

"Naaaaahhhh, just checking the locks aren't ya! Course! True Blue! Now where was I? *'Send me through time, whatever it's all fine, but I'm, gonna keep my junk, alright?'*" As the guard wandered off into the rainy night, singing away, Wodston edged the gate open and slipped over to check these unholy secrets. Proof that the Nashe hadn't been in there was forthcoming, as the tower was guarded by security spiders. That doubled as proof that the good stuff was surely waiting deeper inside.

Seeing that his crimes were not generating any worries thus far, Wodston decided to pull a cheeky one. Back outside, the skimmers were hissing away, just beyond the reach of the lights along the walls. Wodston went out, tapped two of them to follow him, and then lead them right back to the gate.

"Ah s'you again. What are those two? Hivers?" the guard asked. Well you already know what Wodston said in response, and you already know the extent to which Wodston was let inside the fort with two blood-thirsty skimmers in tow. He was about to go back to get more, but he made one crucial mistake. You see, in the meantime he hid the skimmers in a little shed towards the rear, but then as he went to leave, a guard saw him coming of the shed with two purring beasts inside, and assumed the worst.

"Succubi! Seductress creatures! Fugg! Give me a fugging go- I mean, fugg, kill them, or something!" This call raised the alarm. Wodston had to act fast. He pulled a loaf of brown from his bag, crumbled it up in his hands, then tossed a cloud of crumbs into the air. The night wind took their scent and drew it all around, flaring the nostrils of all nearby skimmers and shek. Before the Nashe knew it, their little base was being swarmed with unholy creatures, and those so-called Succubi were a little rough, to put it lightly.

Armoured men poured out of the barrack houses, then poured back in shrieking loudly, then found ways to shriek even louder when it turned out some of the skimmers could just about squeeze through the doors and get inside. And to make things worse, these smaller skim-friends were the femoid ones! Those that avoided death at the hands of Makise or Nadeshiko still ended up in a similar situation at the less-metaphorical hands of the Thousand Guardians, and indeed the rest of the guild who filed into the fray behind them.

At one point a guard managed to single out poor Beep and threw her against a wall.

"Fugging filthy bugs, you'll get what's coming to ya!" he raged, but then there was a whistle, and a two foot bolt of metal rammed through the back of his head.

"The only thing that's coming, is me," Gustavsen shouted. The guard fell, and Beep saw the Prince standing with his long, four-armed crossbow hanging at his waist.

"Beep! I'm so glad you are coming!" Beep said.

"It's only with your help that I can achieve this," Gustavsen nodded.

"Fugging... argh!" Nuk moaned nearby, rushing off to find something to stab.

By morning, the base was subdued, with a few surviving Okranites chained up in their barracks. Taking out Nation troops is good and all, but the actual fight was the one that followed, as Izayah lead the Guardians to clear the tower of its spider problem. Handily, only a few were still active – clearly some had been dispatched by overly curious Nashe-folk in the past. The place was full of the usual useful machinery and salvage, but the biggest prize was in a library on the top floor.

"Narko's nosering, no, Okran's bloody bolts! This stuff is from over a thousand years ago, the beginning of the Holy Nation!" Izumi shouted.

"And here we are at the end. How poetic," Nuk said.

"Look, it's the Second Empire talking about the worshippers of 'Bokran', spirit of... oh, of Earth."

"Wait, you say Bogran?" Rick said.

"No, Bokran."

"Well, about the time I was shipped out, some of the humans had this dumb thing about pretending to worship this guy Bogran, which was like this general name for Earth-clan people. Just doing it to piss us off, always doing that shid during the Stobe memorials. This whole thing... guess it's just that, but weirder. Dozen centuries'll do that."

"This is amazing, we can use this to agitate the whole Nashe," Pia said. "Can you get all this written up real easy to read, Princess?"

"I guess. Are people just going to unironically call me Princess now, by the way?" Izumi said.

"Of course, your majesty!" Wodston was quick to reply.

"Fine. Yes, we have to get this written up. All this directly proves that the Holy Fire is wrong."

"Holy Fire?" Nuk asked.

"It's their book, you must have seen it."

"Words-only book?"

"Yes. All their people have them, they're in every room, on every corpse."

"Words only though, so... Sorry..."

"It's their whole basis for believing stuff. It says that Okran created the world when he and this cat-human thing... Actually, it was clearly inspired by the classics, which makes sense if it was written during the withdrawal of the Second Empire."

"Holy Fire... More like Holy Liar!" Nuk burst out. No one really reacted, but at least they had a title for their agitprop now.

"Holy Phoenix, more like, Jabroni Kleenex," Rick attempted. "What? I aren't programmed for comedy – which makes the other stuff I say even funnier. Let's just get back to the printing presses and start laundering blasphemy on an industrial scale, huh?"

It was a fine idea, so the guild gathered up all kinds of nice evidence on the transition from Second Empire rule to Holy Nation ascendancy, including all the spicy details on how it was all, to quote one ancient report 'just a prank', and went on their way.

The plan was to head vaguely east to get back into the Empire, but as it happened, the Holy Nation had another High Inquisitor, who was not only very unhappy with the whole Seta affair, but had an army waiting on the road the guild needed to take. They'd have to fight their way out of the decreasingly Holy Nation, in the name of truth, or at the very least, the name of comedy. The desicive battle was nigh!

Chapter 35
Scientific Sedition

"Country road, take me home, to the place, where I belong, Black Desert City, metal mamma, country road, take me home," the skeletons sang (although Agnu wasn't contributing much to the melody). The road they were on actually did eventually curve its way into the iron valleys and through to the Deadlands, so they had the right idea. Problem was that well before that it went through a narrow pass packed with angry hogs. Holy Hogs, that is. Holy Nation soldiers, that is. They were arrayed on the road, flanked by two forts that closely overshadowed the only route through the ore-streaked, igneous cliffs that marked the edge of the Holy Nation.

"Charlie, magic hands time," Nuk said, which in one way or another led to the skimmers being roused from their sucrose slumber.

"Careful with that, hold it sideways or the oil will leak out," Izumi scolded Nuk's new employees. The freed slaves from the mines were jointly lugging one of the security spiders the guild had bested recently. A true tech hunter uses every part of the kill, after all. Even the brain.

"Zis sing is dumb as a dreg," Enrico reported from within the spider. "You von't get any use out of it. No voyeur would stoop to cameras zis blurry."

"Shut up Enrico. I know your scheme with Agent Hammer."

"And yet you get changed beside it anyway. At zis point I sink it's your fault."

"I know you've been feeding information to the Phoenix! Admit it!"

"You are quite delusional."

"And you are an intellectual turncoat, turnkey, and... and..."

"Turn off?" Nuk suggested.

"Alas, that his processors were less clogged, he would treat you as you deserve, fleshie princess," Hammer's voice said.

"Oh not you as well. Ve can't all be in here," Enrico complained.

"All? Who else is listening in there you dusty creep?" Izumi demanded.

"Ah, the questions, the questions. Can't ve all just get along? I mean, ve all agree on one thing, don't we? That Okran isn't real. OKRAN ISN'T REAL! OKRAN ISN'T FUGGING REAL AND NARKO IS ZE BEST WAIFU!" Enrico bellowed. The buzzy words echoed around the sunbaked cliffs.

"Oh you little shid," Izumi said, grabbing her whacking pole (but don't get too excited). Shouts and stomps approached rapidly – the Holy Nation troops were upon them.

"Got a waifu? Lose your life-u!" one shouted. "What the fugg? Skimmers got through!" he added. I should note that this fortified pass lead through into the Skimsands, which was quite the force for peace, as the Okranites didn't want to invade it and the Empire didn't want to patrol it, thus the two sides never caught wind of each other. Attempts to establish a 'deskimmerterised zone' had failed, and so 'Operation Skim to Stalemate' had been going on for a good century. It took a genius such as Nuk to realise that victory required that your operation name at least half-rhyme – alliteration wasn't apt to add absolutely any avail. In other words: the skimmers killed the Holy Nation soldiers.

After the mess was cleared up, they still had the matter of fort walls lined with archers to deal with.

"I have a present for you, Princess," Hammer said as the guild sized up the situation.

"Not now. Where's the volume control on these damn spiders?!" Izumi replied.

"Oh you'll want to hear this. I have a map of the enemy base. Here, look into this poor creature's eyes and you'll see it."

"Bullshid."

"I'll do it," Nuk said, grabbing the spider and sticking it in his face.

"Not my precise tastes, but I'm a modern machine, let's dance. Here, the gates to their fort. And the password if you like."

"That seems... Kinda legit. Nice. How do you have this?"

"A gift, an apology, from a mutual friend."

It was pretty suspicious, but the map checked out from what they could tell. It was possible, it seemed, to get inside the fort about half way down the gauntlet of archers, at which point they could hit the walls and secure safe passage. But to win once they got inside, they needed the skimmers to make it in.

"The approach will not be easy," Hammer explained. "You are required to manoeuvre straight down this trench and skim the surface to this point. The target area is only two meters wide." His voice sounded a little different while this was said, but that was the least of the guild's concerns.

"The gates are only two meters? That impossible, even for Bloody Ells," Elaina said.

"I got the skimmers to go in the lavs back in the last fun party. They weren't much bigger than two meters. Nice lavs they were," Ells said. So, a plan was hatched. As fortune would have it, the trench run was quite easy on account of a stir at the gates around two in the morning.

"You see anything out there?" Sandor said to Nuk.

"Nope," Nuk shrugged.

"Exactly. Attack now!"

"That's some abstract-ass strategy advice, but I guess I'm bored of waiting. Punch it Charlie!"

The skimmers, who had been carefully briefed on the operation by their wrangler, were released. They raced for the gates, and found that indeed the thing that Nuk couldn't see really was helping. That is to say, the gate guards were entangled with a gang of barely visible ninja.

"Even Okran casts a shadow," Sandor quipped. He'd probably been waiting to say that for a while. Regardless, the guild followed along behind the skim-squadron, and using a little 'force' got the skimmers in through one of the fort gates. The walls were swept clean of defenders as easily as a skimmer dusts sand over its eggs, and the remaining troops hanging around the barracks didn't do much better. After a good hour, one side of the road was secure, and it was likely safe to carry on home. But from the adjoining fort, a voice boomed.

"You slimy fuggnuggets! Okran's pissed as a roo in an offie with ya, ya credit managing fuggs! Prepare to face the wrath of me, Big Stick Valtena!"

"Shid, sounds like we better compare sticks right away," Rick said.

"That's the High Inquisitor, the other one," Pia explained. "He must be the biggest billy in the Nashe after Seta."

"Then let's go cut him and his stick down to size!" Nuk said.

"Yous obsessed with sticks out here. Was it always like this?" Twitch asked.

"Sir Twitch, so naive. You can't have read the classics, can you?" Izayah said, before joining the skimmers in a trip across the road into Fort 2: *The Inquisition Didn't Expect You*. As night turned to morning, this additional battle proved to be more involved than the first, as the inquisition were elite warriors – clearly their particular style of questioning had just so happened to lead to a fair few fights. Now being an elite warrior doesn't help all that much when you're being eaten by a beast the size of a building, but the much talked about sticks wielded by these hogs were indeed rather long. Many of the skimmers got seriously sliced in the fray, and had to be dragged away by their ovular master. In the hours long grind, several guild members got similar treatment, but with the fort's garrison withering away, High Inquisitor Valtena couldn't last forever. At long last, he slumped over backwards, and into Nuk's arms.

"Fugg... You're strong... And sharp... That scent. So sweet. So forbidden... Don't matter if you're a little older than me..." Valtena muttered as his vision failed him.

"Ah, well wait 'til you learn the truth about that one. Stirred up my girlfriend, that's for sure," Nuk said.

"Girl... friend...?! Okran... How can you tease me like this?" And with this devastating disappointment, Valtena's dream of meeting hot singles in his area was extinguished. With his defeat the fort of Okran's Shield had been captured, and the road to the United Cities lay open to all. The guild wouldn't be using it any time soon, on account of their various immobilising injuries. Doc Wodston went around giving out free samples of his services, and the Tech Hunters knew a few things about cleaning wounds. Nuk tried to pick up a little of the trade himself.

"I don't really get it. Let's put it this way: what kind of swimsuit would a bacteria wear?" he asked Izumi.

"No, they don't wear anything," Izumi claimed.

"Now that's degenerate. Wait... Gas Girl and... Bacteria Boy... What a pairing!"

With this Nuk went to discuss important academic matters with the managaka class. Well, if it was a way to educate the world on the importance of hygiene, then Bacteria Boy's infectious charm and hardy disposition was just what everyone needed – and if you couldn't get enough of him, just wait until you learn about self-replication.

Not everyone was in such high spirits. Amid the chaos of battle, poor Beep had been upended by a Nashe greatsword, and was now down to one leg. When Gustavsen found her, he gasped and rushed to her side.

"It is gone!" he said.

"Oh no! Beep!" Beep said.

"This... Is brilliant!"

"Oh yes! Beep!"

"The transformation is beginning already. The mortal matter is shed. At last, you will ascend to be a timeless machine, like a true Queen!"

"Beep!"

"Yes, beep!"

"But, Prince, I cannot walk."

"This is your destiny. Now, you must ride me."

"Oh. I'm so happy you want me ride you! Beep!"

"They ain't even playing wacky BG, and they're freakier than fleshie fridays down at the stimulus centre," Neil commented.

"Don't worry. Degeneracy parasite, theory goes. Innuendo inoculation's in development," Rick assured him.

Gustavsen hauled Beep over his shoulder and went to hum and hiss at his fellow hivers strewn across the field. While everyone else was preparing to leave, Izumi got back to business with the overly sentient spiderbot.

"You think this gets you off the hook?" she said.

"Oh you're back. Did it go vell? I was right wasn't I? You could at least ank me," Enrico said.

"Thank you, huh? It wasn't you who got those plans, was it?"

"Oh? If it vasn't me, zen who?"

"In this day and age, who can say? Perhaps it was those super-luminal millipedes?" Izumi posited cynically.

"That would explain everything. It all fits!" a new voice said from the spider.

"Professor Iyo, I knew you were in there!"

"Whoops. Sorry Enrico baby, I got too excited."

"Don't vorry sweetchips, happens to me all ze time," Enrico said.

"Iyo, did you tell the Nashe about how to tame monsters? You leaked ur chocobread receipe, didn't you?" Izumi asked.

"Yeah. No problem right? Science is for everyone," Iyo said.

"No, that was my science! I went through more shid than you can imagine getting all my data, and I won't have you and your deutsch dog just giving it away."

"Vhat is this nonsense? 'Your' science?!" Enrico shot back. "Ve are talking about knowledge zat can save zis shiddy planet, and you sink zat you are ze only von who gets to do anything vith it? You aren't so special, Princess. I could have made zose discoveries too, if I had an army of underpaid drug addicts at my disposal! I bet even zis stuttering screensaver Iyo could have done it! Get over yourself before we start building ze 'Izumi was a total *schweinhund*' memorial hospitals and all zat shid. This is science, not the game of empires your stupid friends are playing!"

Izumi was speechless in the face of this scolding, yet feeling she had to say something, replied,

"M-my friends aren't stupid. Let's leave it, Enrico."

The call was over, and so soon was the guild's stay in that bloodied fort. They set off home in the afternoon, Valtena in tow, but there was yet another voice echoing around the cliffs. I say voice, but it was more a series of screeching sounds with an electronic texture, as if made by a skeleton.

"You'll see what machines do to us, you fools! Screeeee!" it eventually said, before returning to a few more weird noises, then cutting out.

"Holy Nation is a strange place," Izayah commented, but actually there was something to all this: a Second Empire spider soldier emerged from behind some rocks and charged the guild.

"Is that...? It's obeying that voice," Elaina said.

"They can control the robots too now? We gotta kill them faster man," Nuk said, drawing his sword. Luckily the whole guild was trained in the tuck and-twist technique, so the spider was deactivated in short order. It was then added to the pile of junk the guild was dragging behind them as they set off into the desert. They spent the night encamped under the starry sky and the next morning pressed on into the Empire, coming to a halt at Trader's Edge. There the hefty bounty on Valtena could be collected in full.

"Incredible work, Prince Tashino. The Empire salutes you," the samurai captain working the front desk at the police station said.

"In that case, you wanna do me a favour?" Nuk said.

"I am at your command, your highness."

"Nice. Well, you see, a while back I got into some shid around here. M and my friends got picked up by those damn manhunters, and we we through a whole thing that was generally shid. Those bastards are probab still here, so, my order to you is round them and up throw them in with the hog."

The samurai did not hesitate. He grabbed some troops, went outside the gate to where the local manhunter crew were staking out passers by on the main road, and gave them a good old fashioned roughing up. The guild were all too happy to help drag what remained back to be thrown into jail.

"Shid, that felt good. I forget I'm like in charge of all this sometimes," Nuk said.

"Only because you've earned it, Prince Tashino," Izayah said. "And now you're putting that power to good use. I wonder if those animals will get bought up by their comrades? That might change their mind about the whole thing, eh?"

"Speaking of changing minds, let's get back to the lab soon," Izumi said. "Once we get the truth about the Holy Nation printed up, we can silence those Okranites for good."

"Yep, we're rolling out," Nuk said. "And, as a special treat, let's leave the skroops here. I've ordered the samurai to take good care of them. About time people started getting to know the heroes of the empire!"

Thus the skimmers were left to liaise with the terrified citizenry, while the guild finally plodded on home. Aside from the publication of deets on the social experiment gone wrong (gone sexual) that was the Holy Nation, there were lots of things to attend to. Gustavsen, for example, was quick to gather up his posse in the barracks, where he dug through the guild's disorganised piles of junk until a treasure was unearthed.

"LEG!" he proclaimed, echoed by a chorus from his followers. He held aloft an old robot leg, which he promptly affixed to Beep's hip. It was quite a lot shorter than her remaining natural leg, but she seemed delighted with it all the same.

"Now I can practice my beep even more. Beep!" she said. This was apparently a good thing. While this was going on, Izumi was having words with Agent Hammer.

"You slimy fugg, did you tell Enrico, or Iyo, how to get spiders to attack people?"

"Ah, I thought you would be impressed that I worked it out. The data was all here. Yes, I did inform Enrico, for it all needs to be archived. We needn't go over his little outburst about the commons of science, need we?"

"But he let the Holy Nation have that, and they sent a spider to attack us! Maybe you could keep your ports shut for a while before you go giving our enemies dangerous weapons!"

"My ports open and shut at your command, my lady. I'll make it up to you. Oh, but on the subject of dangerous weapons, you did collect those uranium samples, didn't you?"

"Yeah, Nuk smoked some of it, but we've got it."

"Fascinating. He was made for you, darling. Now, let's make you Queen of the spiders, shall we?"

By that he apparently meant that he was going to reveal how to reprogram old spider-bots, which could be tested at once on the spiders the guild had hauled home from their adventure.

"Alright, plug me in," Rick said. Yes, the process required that one of the skeletons be used as a peripheral to the spiders. The mangaka class sat on the stairs in the tower where the spiders were being stored, sketchbooks in hand. The plug, by the way, was wireless, but drawing abstract, mostly invisible things was the class' foremost skill.

"Ooo man, these spiders hate humans. Damn. Look at all these logs. You racist man. You real racist, even for a machine that kills folk based on their race," Rick commented.

"Alright Rick, you ready for the injection?" Izumi asked. The artist's corrupted eyes were positively glowing, but this turned out to be referring to a code injection. It wiped the spiders clean, then poured new material into their heads. Electronically and invisibly, you understand. Basically, the spiders whirred to life, and didn't kill everyone, so that's pretty much mission accomplished.

"That AI actually did it," Izumi commented to Nuk.

Well, that's its thing," he nodded.

"But it was meant to be *my* thing. Guess if I listen to them and forget about it, I don't need to feel bad, huh?"

"Not like we're gonna forget that all this is happening because of you, Izzy."

"It's not just me. They were right. I mean, it's you as well."

"Well, if it is, that's cool."

"Yeah. I should be more like you. I should be doing this because it's for the good of everyone."

"Eh, I'm doing this because my dad kicked me out for being too high at the dinner table."

"Oh yeah. I'm glad he did that then."

"Ha. Man. So am I. Let's chill out for a bit, huh?"

"Sure, but... What about the spiders?"

"They'll be fine. Here, do you know why this green is glowing these days?"

Outside, the spiders were having fun stamping on Rick's tin humanoid figurines.

"Guess I missed something, but that's close enough," Rick shrugged. Thus the guild had some spiders to help out around the farm, which was quite appropriate as the whole spiderbot line was originally manufactured for just such purposes, with all kinds of attachments fitting on their long arms, and little spray nozzles for fertiliser lining their underside. Once you tell them that the fertiliser isn't to be made from human corpses, they become rather handy machines.

More handy machines were on the way. Decoding of Second and even some First Empire data was unveiling new marvels to test out. The latest project was coal mining, to be used in steel-firing. Such things were all vital components of the ultimate research project that Agent Hammer had in mind, although he hadn't revealed the full nature of that to his fleshie workhands. Nuk was regularly up in Black Scratch trying to get people addicted to either green or brown so that he could get a steady supply of the parts the hunters dug up. Thus Manksand canyon gradually accumulated both the knowledge and the means to change to the world.

They didn't plan to stay for long, as the skimmers were eagerly awaiting their return, as was the Holy Phoenix. They stayed only as long as it took to build an enormous boring machine that could drill down into the manky riverbed, revealing veins of chalky sediments below. All very uninteresting, but when the first samples were hauled up for analysis, Gustavsen came bounding over.

"This is it!" he said, grabbing some of the wet gravel and smearing it on his face. He wordlessly worked to cover his entire body, while the others watched with a mix of embarrassment and fascination. Once he was fully coated in the whitish paste, he turned to them and said,

"The time has come."

Whatever was this about? We'll get back to it. It's not all that much weirder than it was already, I assure you. And if Gustavsen's creepy business could be swiftly concluded, the showdown with what remained of the Holy Nation awaited!

Chapter 36
BlistEr GoEs Pop

Gustavsen stood before his posse and Nuk, covered in a whitish goop, his open mouth dribbling with watery chunks of sediment.

"It is time... to squeeze!" he announced. Oh dear. The other hivers gave a bleating cheer, and Nuk noticed that everyone else was keeping a very safe distance. Luckily for him, the hiver prince had something entirely dull in mind.

"We must compress the medium, to make it strong," he explained, making a rapid pounding motion with his hand. "Cease your work, and aid us. The Queen watches expectantly."

This meant that he wanted the guild to help him build a machine that would congeal the pale mank sprayed out by the mining drills. Why? You've already asked more questions than Gustavsen allowed. Throughout the day the guild actually came up with something that pleased the Prince. It was a huge mess of presses, clamps, hot plates, and pipes, and all together turned runny ground-sludge into a more seductively oozy, grainy putty. As it was squeezed out of the end of the machine, the hivers gathered around to squidge it in their hands, and then, with no further discussion, let it fall into their open mouths.

"We are impregnated, to birth the new hive!" Gustavsen explained.

"Is there a better way of putting that?" Nuk asked.

"Silence! We begin to gurgitate. Prepare the site."

Nuk retreated to Izumi's office. She was positively delighted to hear of what was going on outside.

"They're going to make a hive! No one's ever seen this happen!" she reported.

"And lived to tell the tale," Nuk called after her, but there was no dampening Izumi's spirits on this one, for some reason. She directed the guild workers to clear a space further down the canyon amid a sheltered grove of half-dead trees. Then, pacing towards them in lock-step, the hamster-cheeked hivers approached, dripping with filth, and looking very pleased with themselves.

Far away from this debacle, Wodston was in Enrico's "office" at the Tech Scribe enclave. The brainy bot sat with several unopened bottles of rum in front of him, and was in the process of ordering another.

"Good for ze economy, don't you know?" he remarked when his collection was expanded. "Speaking of vhich, do you have ze tribute?"

"The payment," Wodston said.

"Ah, you vish to preserve your dignity? And yet here you are purchasing fifty copies of zis ancient human erotica, thinly veiled as some kind of artistic literature."

"Hey, Enrico, stop being such a *baka*," Nuk's voice said from Wodston's lip. Wodston had one of the quantum entangled AI cores on him, now linked to a partner in the base for instantaneous communication of insults, snapbacks, and put downs. "This is all reference material for our major historical work, alright? Skeletons are naked all the time, so no double standards."

"Bah, it's not like ve vould go to a hot spring just to employ an elaborate method to spy on... Wait a minute... Drat, vhy I am only programmed to tell ze truth? Fine, just go, you disgusting creatures, and don't come back until you have something vorth looking at for me. No *tsundere* bullshid, okay?!"

"Sorry man, but history is full of *tsundere* bullshid. Wodston, my man, you better get back here fast. The hivers are vomming everywhere and then rolling about in it."

"It must be mixed!" Gustavsen's voice faintly chimed. Obviously Wodston couldn't wait to get home now. In the canyon, the hivers had successfully created an enormous pile of... something... And Izumi excitedly told the rest of the guild that it was time to watch the hivers sculpt it into a grand new hive. But there was a catch.

"You all must build. You will be our hive drones," Gustavsen said.

"I think we're cool just watching", Nuk said. "Do your thing and... I guess, we'll be better for having seen it..."

"Impossible! It takes an entire generation of drones to properly shape the gut essence. We cannot do it alone. Help. With your hands. Know the feeling."

Ells jumped into the big pile of goop, and happily reported that it was nice and warm. The others weren't so happy to hear it, however they did eventually step forward and dare prod the blob. The hivers began laying out the foundations, and the others were directed to pile up the manufactured mank into walls. Bits of old tree and stretches of metal rebar were roughly arranged into a frame, and up said frame did the horrid, almost living, mush pile. Working into the night, the familiar teardrop form of a hiver hut began to materialise.

While the horrible other-flesh creatures went to sterilise themselves back-over by the wells, the hivers sat in their dingy lair and admired their handywork – it was the finest regurgitated structure the world had seen in a long time, some say.

"My Queen, your hive is complete," Gustavsen reported to Beep.

"Beep. It has a nice smell," she said.

"The smell will intensify. The smell represents the coming of a new age. Here, you will become hive. We are one step closer."

Funnily enough, everyone else was happy to take *many* steps further away from the reeking construct, and thus the hivers finally had a place they could call their own. How nice. Izumi was very pleased to have witnessed that historic moment. As an aside, she was also amused so see just how effective her automatic revolving harpoon launchers were.

Some fifty reavers had tried to break into the magical land of mank but within a few minutes found themselves riddled with meter-long spike darting down from the walls. In fact they were so effective that severe harpoons went through the reavers, through the gate in front of them, and into the workers holding the gate closed from the other side. Suffice to say did more damage to the guys it soared through than those it eventually ended up stuck into, but this didn't really improve the workplace safety record.

Cleaning that up incurred a delay to the guild's next outing, which proved to be long enough for the hivers to really settle in. When Nuk next called everyone together to move out, they were nowhere to be seen. Nu hiked on over to the hut and found Beep sitting on a cushion between a couple of smokey fire torches, flanked by the other hivers.

"You approach the Queen. State your purpose," Gustavsen barked.

"I thought she wasn't the Queen yet?" Nuk said.

"I'm practising! Beep!" Beep informed him.

"Practice makes perfect," Nuk shrugged.

"SHE IS PERFECT ALREADY," Gustavsen was quick to insist. Nuk agreed, and with sufficient deference and grovelling was able to convince the hivers to come along for the next mission. Back in the base, Izumi was spotted storming out of her office.

"Why don't you just go interface with your precious Iyo and leave me alone!" she shouted through the door, behind slamming it closed.

"Lover's tiff?" Nuk asked.

"It's that core. It keeps asking for more and more! All these experiments, all this stuff. We're not like the university, I keep telling him, but he just starts singing my praises and saying how amazing I am."

"What a bastard."

"He's manipulating me, Nuk. Aren't you bothered?"

"Ha, like you'd seriously get seduced by a machine."

"Oh, yeah... sure..."

"Anyway, we *can* be like the university. We can be better than that university. I'll have a few words with our new spider workers. If they built the Second Empire, you know, they might be able to help us out."

Nuk had this 'word' with the spider bots, in a very figurative sense, and put together a secret scheme with some help from the Tech Hunters. Leaving everyone to carry it out, he then took the guild back to Trader's Edge for a happy(ish) reunion with the skimmers. To their dismay(ish) many of the beasts were skin and bones, even more so than usual.

"Sorry, my Prince, but they wouldn't eat anything we gave 'em!" a samurai told Nuk.

"What did you try?" Nuk huffed.

"We gave 'em riceweed, greenfruit, meatcubes, bloody banquet it was!"

"No chocobread?"

"Chocobread?"

"They're addicted to chocobread, I sold you all that chocobread, remember?"

"Oh, the brown lump stuff. I thought that was called TCMNPHGINTCC-"

"Yeah yeah yeah, it's brown fugging bread, and without it the skimmers are dead! Put that in the samurai code and stuff, alright?"

"Yes, my Prince!"

"And from now on, you will address them the by the title of 'skim-friend'."

"Yes, my Prince..."

Soon the skimmers were revitalised, and hence the guild were *de*vitalised by having to carry them onwards to the Holy Nation. The border fort of Okran's Shield was now garrisoned by the Hundred Guardians, who cheered for their order of magnitude superiors as the guild arrived.

"Izayah Battleborn, will you be heading to Blister Hill?" one asked.

"Indeed. The Holy Phoenix awaits. And the skroops need a run about," Izayah said.

"Skroops?"

"Ah you'll see. Why don't you come along?"

"It would be an honour, Invincible!"

"The more the merrier. This battle will decide the fate of the Holy Nation. Shame to miss it, eh?"

Indeed, and so a great many shek troops joined the guild as they carried on west. They crossed the lavish valley of Okran's Pride, vibrant with its yellowish life, and began ascending a shallow hill towards some mountains. Near the top lay this Blister Hill, the seat of power of the Holy Nation.

"Alright, here's the plan," Izumi said, clutching a coarse, coverless book in her hands. "We wait until it's dark, then we sneak over to the wall and start flinging 'The Holy Liar' into the city. It's got everything the people need to know; they'll never trust the Phoenix after this, especially if this truth just so happens to fall from the sky."

"Oh, I'll do my Okran impression again, order everyone to read it," Rick said.

"Err... Maybe... Let's think about that a little. Anyway, once we're outta the truth grenades, we pull back and wait. It's going to take a while for all this to sink in. Could be hours. Could be weeks. But when the people are ready, they'll rise up and destroy the Nashe from within!"

"A fine plan. By the way, where did all those Hundreds go?" Izayah asked. Looking around, the two companies of shek they had picked up were nowhere to be seen. All but one – there was a shek standing on top of the gate to Blister Hill, holding a Nashe guard's head up and roaring loudly.

"Or we could just run in there and kill them all now," Izumi conceded.

"Let's run in there and kill them all now," Izayah nodded.

Thus the battle of Blister Hill just sort of started to no particular fanfare, although perhaps that was for the best, as the city gate had been left wide open. It was swiftly captured, but in an open market square just beyond it, the Holy Nation troops were massing.

"Arise, arise, Skroops of the Empire!" Nuk called as Ells roused the ranks. "Fields shall be taken! Classics shall be printed! A tooth day, a brown day, 'ere the Earth rises! Skim now! Skim now! Skim! Skim them to ruins! But leave World's End, alright? Bread! Bread! Bread! *Tenno Heika Banzai!*"

With this, a magnificent charge of furious skimmers fell upon the city like... like a bunch of weird giant maggots with creepy legs scattering over a dirty pile of crumbling junk.

"My Prince, that was a marvellous, sophisticated speech!" Wodston said.

"I know. Thought of it all by myself. Now, we should probably go kill some hogs too."

"Be careful, Nuk, the Phoenix is in there," Izumi warned. "Who knows what he's got planned?"

Indeed, within the city there was another ring of fortifications surrounding the Holy Phoenix's central compound. There the best and brawniest of the Holy Nation stood guard over their supreme leader, awaiting the command to wipe out the pitiful attackers.

"An attack? Bah! Those fools! They think they can catch me? They'll never reach me... in the sky!" the Phoenix cackled, running to the roof of his palace and flapping his arms wildly. "I will smite them from Okran's side! Yes! Sqwaaa!"

The holy soldiers dared not even think that anything was amiss. Thus, the gate to the compound was not even closed as the invaders fought their way closer. Through this open gate, a guild member was unceremoniously dragged. A Nashe troop had disarmed one of Gustavsen's followers, and dragged him into the central jail. Seeing this, Elaina grasped her blade.

"I'm no less of a shek than the rest of them," she said to herself, running into the jail. There she expected to fight her way through hordes of guards and rescue the hiver, but she found the place bathed in calming music from speakers all around. She walked over to the prisoner cage where the hiver, Silvershade, was being held. The Nashe troop that captured him was leaning against the side of it.

"So anyway, I starting thinking, if we can't be with she-devils, can't we be, you know, close, and stuff, to other things?" he said.

"You speak of free association. This is a path to many abilities some consider to be... unnatural," Silvershade nodded.

"Sounds... great! Can I associate with you, mate?"

"Hmpf, remove your clothes, and we shall perform the test."

While the guard was stuck with his shirt over his head, Elaina opened the cage and carried Silvershade away.

"Regret. However, you can always associate with yourself!" Silvershade called as he was whisked away. It wasn't the heroic rescue Elaina had imagined, and maybe it was hardly a rescue at all, but it was all probably a good call. As Elaina left the jail, Gustavsen was leading the rest of the hivers up the stairs.

"I smelled imminent association," he said. Silvershade gave a disappointed hum, and the others patted him in what was possibly sympathy. Not really for us disassociated ones to understand. They went in anyway, and soon the jailhouse could perhaps be said to be under friendly control.

Meanwhile the fighting out in the city market was over, and the result was a clear victory for the skim-friends. They now filed in through the nice wide gate into the Phoenix's compound, where the real fighting got started. The Inquisition and High Paladins fought valiantly to prevent the assortment of beasts and beast-tier humanoids from reaching their leader, holding their own for several hours. The whole time, both they and the guild were searching for the Holy Phoenix, but in the chaos, his whereabouts remained unknown.

Outside the palace the skimmers sniffed about, but suddenly they were slammed by bolts coming from the roof of the nearby barrack.

"Prince Tashino, we must silence that rooftop!" Izayah called out. Nuk nodded and followed him up the barrack stairs. They quickly accosted the crossbowmen, who were no match for the experienced swordsmen.

"Where's the bird dude, hog?" Nuk demanded of a fallen warrior.

"You'll never take him alive. He lives on, inside us," the warrior wheezed.

"Yeah, guessing that's where he usually is. What's wrong with girls anyway? Especially with like cat ears and... love heart eyes... and... all this, gas... Err... What was I saying?"

"My Prince!" Wodston's voice shouted from the street below. Looking out, Nuk saw a man in gleaming white armour standing on a ledge jutting out from the palace.

"You insolent fools!" he screeched. His arms began to wave violently. "I will cast this whole planet away and return to Okran, for truly you deserve only to be discarded, like we did to the traitor machines!"

"Actually, man, they only betrayed us after we did that- you know, after we betrayed them," Nuk shouted. "I mean, it's all explained in this series of light novels. It's like the Holy Fire but with more cleavage. It's unputdownable, and not just because the pages are sticky."

"Silence, mortal! I fly now!"

"He flies now?" Izayah asked.

"He flies now," Nuk nodded, seeing the Phoenix leap from the ledge, his arms sweeping at the air. Due to certain matters of physics, this caused almost no change in his momentum, whereas the pull of gravity did. That is to say, he didn't fly away at all. He fell, bounced off a pudgy skimmer waiting below, and rolled out into the street.

Skroops and guild members alike closed in on him, but without delay he took up a greatsword from the ground and kept all at bay with his wild attacks – not to mention his wild cawing and squeaking. His strength seemed superhuman. With the flat of his sword he batted skimmers away like they were sub-luminal milipedes, and when the sharp edge struck the armour on the Thousand Guardians, it cut through like teeth through a MYHLLL cuboid. Opponent after opponent fell, and still the screeching went on.

"I won't stay here and die like all of you!" he growled. "I know what the machines are planning. They will destroy you all, and I will live on forever at Okran's side!"

"Actually, Okran is a corruption of the term Bogran, a First Empire colloquialism for Earth-clanners, or 'Earth-channers' as it was written in that era. It is derived from the same root as the Nashe term, 'bogan'," Izumi carefully explained.

"Reeee! You think I don't know that, you childish humans?! This was all for your own good! And yet you ruin it, like you ruin everything! You deserve to bring about your own demise after all!"

"Look, wingnut, we've foiled your shiddy scheme to save everyone by making everything absolutely shid all the time, so just shut up and read my light novel!" Nuk said.

"Fools! I can't read! That's how the machines get you!"

"But it's mostly pictures," Nuk protested, to no avail. Instead he moved up and did his best to turn the Phoenix's sword aside. After several bouts, he got nothing. It was time for more devious measures.

"My man, the secret strategy!" Nuk called to Wodston. Wodston, who truly would do anything for the Tashino clan, it turned out, ripped off his tunic and bared what there was of his chest to the Phoenix.

"Okran's grace! It is too beautiful! How can the femoids complete?!" the Phoenix exclaimed, before suddenly eating dirt courtesy of Nuk's heel on the back of his head.

"Cleavage conquers all, no matter what," Nuk nodded sagely. Those still well enough to move helped him tie the unconscious Phoenix up. Alas, the open sky was always so close, yet so far. With the big bird clipped, the city was almost taken, but by this point the guild were mostly lying around on the floor trying not to die, as were the skimmers. The mobile members tended to wounds, and hit the jailhouse once again, as it turned out some more prisoners had been taken.

"Crazy human, flippin' between saying I must be destroyed, and asking me on a date," Neil said from within his cage. "Guess at some point they took out the logical from biological. Ah ha ha ha ha ha ha."

"Sounds like they missin' a real good date," Rick commented.

The prisoner cages were all opened up, but the guild were still effectively imprisoned in the Holy compound on account of how many of them were unconscious. A couple of hivers and shek were missing limbs as well, which certainly didn't help move things along. Many hours were spent gradually bringing everyone round and attending to injuries, however those hours were not entirely quiet. More Holy Sentinels appeared from the nook and crannies of the city, and small groups trickled in from the roads outside. Exhausted fighting carried on through the small hours of the night.

In the morning, the guild began to regroup around the big burning pan of oil outside the palace. It was the Holy Fire, one supposes, but handily also possessed properties remarkably like an ordinary fire, and hence was a nice spot to pitch up and make breakfast. Yet bitter news would spoil the taste; Wodston returned from the jailhouse, reporting a death. In the doorway, another of Gustavsen's gang, Pato, lay with a dagger in his chest. A Holy Nation soldier was crumpled up beside him, equally dead.

The other hivers came over and knelt around their fallen comrade.

"The first of the great builders is no more. Who will be next?" Gustavsen asked. While seemingly tactless, the other hivers seemed to tal solace in the question. They loaded his body up on the garru for transit home, but that transit was still a ways off, with the guild far too battered to consider reforming the great travelling homunculus. They spent the next day chilling, with the odd bit of killing, enjoying the rough luxury of the Holy Compound. They gently placed their truth grenades all around town, and they were quickly snapped up by hiding residents.

By nightfall they finally managed to haul themselves and their stuff out into the city, finally hobbling and dragging their way to the city limits by midnight. All but one of them, that is.

"Ignacio is missing," Gustavsen said.

"You sure, man? I mean it's kinda dark. Isn't that him?" Nuk said, pointing at one of the other Ignacio-ish hivers standing around.

"That is Rene, my bodyguard. I talk of Ignacio, my bodyguard."

"Yeah yeah, I know. Alright man, just for you, let's get a team to go look for him."

"I know where he is! Beep!" Beep chimed in.

"That saves time. Good old magic," Nuk nodded.

"He is trapped. He is locked in a box. A big box. Oh no!"

"Hmmm, maybe magic won't be enough then."

"Yes it will! Beep! I will get him!"

"Yes, my Queen. It is time to begin testing your power. We all felt it there. You can use it," Gustavsen said.

"Care to explain, Bad Green?" Nuk asked, but no, Gustavsen did not care.

What actually happened to Ignacio? He had been locked in a strongroom inside the east tower of the inner gate, now a few meters of steel and stone away from freedom. There was no lock to pick, and no guards to associate into submission. It would take an intervention from a god to get him out of there any time soon, but fortunately, he had something even better coming.

"Beep!" Beep commanded, standing before the gates with her arms raised. Nothing happened. "Beep, beep!" she repeated. For some reason, this was not achieving much. A few townsfolk and guards approached, ready to grab the frail hiver. "Beep, beep, beep!" she shouted, and suddenly there was a great rumbling from underfoot. A loud metallic moan echoed from below, then the entire gatehouse reared and sunk downwards a little, before bending over forwards. The heavy gate was ripped from its place by its own weight, tearing off the sides of the gatehouse towers as it boomed to the ground.

Ignacio leapt down through the new opening.

"The Great Mover obeys! You really are the Queen!" he said.

"Beep. Let's run away! Beep!" Beep said. It was a good plan. They raced out of the city and rejoined the guild, after which the whole group retreated back to the safety of Okran's Shield.

"What was that terrible noise, Queen Beep?" Wodston asked.

"The Great Mover is still awake. Beep. It can still shape the world," Beep explained.

"I'm afraid I've not heard of this Great Mover."

"It is from the beginning. Beep! It sleeps forever, but it cannot die! Beep!"

"I see..."

"Izzy, are the hivers actually magic?" Nuk asked.

"Seems that way. Great Mover huh... If we get that data from the other Queen, I guess we'll know for sure," Izumi said.

"Right, right. Looking forward to it, probably. In the meantime, I think my Dad might be interested in this naughty little sparrow."

"I am a Phoenix, and I will not be caged!" the Phoenix said. Then his mouth kept moving, but no sound came out.

"Yeah, it works. Muted," Rick nodded.

"Numan, you're magic too? Am I the only one who isn't magic?!" Nuk said.

"Ain't magic, it's science baby. Just turned his volume down. Oh wait, you didn't realise? He's a Numan too! The first and last, from the bad old days. How'd you think he's so powerful? No fleshie can throw a skimmer off 'em like that. You big brain sisters shouda realised: the Holy Phoenix is a Boner Find-A Android."

What a bombshell, though it didn't change the guild's plans – they would have plenty of time to discuss this development in the safety of the capital, to which they would return in victory. The Holy Nation was over. A new age would begin. Radioactive weed was just the start of what the unified power of all the people of the world could unleash!

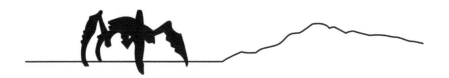

Chapter 37
The Green Industrial Revolution

"Hang on, hang on, something's wrong," Nuk said. Ahead, the walls of Heft were lined only with the usual samurai guards. "My man, I thought you told everyone what's happening?"

"I did, my Prince," Wodston said. "I informed them that the victory procession was their best chance to see the new heroes of the empire. And of course, the wonderful tamed skimmers."

"You told them about the skroops?"

"I could hardly leave it out, my Prince."

"You dreg, people are racist against skroops!"

"Ah. I can't imagine why, my Prince..."

"Don't matter. We can do this the United Cities way. Captain!"

Nuk waved over the samurai at the gate, and quickly ordered them to force out an adoring crowd to welcome the guild home. Townsfolk were lined up alongside the road, their eyes locked on the gently writhing ball of monsters that overshadowed the rest of the procession. Wodston went up and down the lines handing out bribes, and soon enough, everyone was willing to turn their attention to the proud ball-draggers instead.

To kick things off, Nuk held up the Holy Phoenix, who cawed and struggled against his binds.

"The Holy Phoenix had been defeated! The war is over!" Nuk declared. This brought about a wave of cheap – nay, free – adulation! The people realised that this wasn't the weird farce they had quite rightly presumed it would be. This was a historic moment for dreg and noble alike. At last the party atmosphere began to set in.

The guild walked though the crowds to cheers and applause, rising to a crescendo every time Wodston showered loose cats from an upturned Holy Nation helmet. The hivers held Beep up above them, and chanted,

"ASSOCIATE. IT IS YOUR FATE."

Plenty of ronin hivers were spotted bowing among the audience. Another royal woman was getting some attention too.

"Princess! Princess!" a girl called out to Izumi from amid of a bunch of gawking adolescents.

"I'm not really... Well, hello there, thank you, yes," Izumi bumbled.

"I can't believe we got to see you. You're so cool!"

"Is that- I don't... Err- thanks guys."

"Look, I did my hair like you, do you like it?" the girl said, showing off her greasy, dishevelled looking ponytail. It was an exact match.

"Thought she'd be taller," one of the other girls shrugged.

"Oh fugg off!" Izumi immediately snapped back. She was about to apologise, but the rest of the group cheered her on.

"She's so sophisticated, I told you!" the leading girl insisted. Izumi made her escape as the group began telling each other to fugg off with ever increasing fervour. The procession soon reached the imperial palace, where they marched up the winding ramp, homunculus and all, into the halls of Tengu Tashino the First. The throne he once sat upon was now just a supporting column for a series of hashish burrows, with the Emperor himself nowhere to be seen.

"Err, Dad. We got you a present," Nuk called into the warren.

"How high will it get me?" an echoing voice replied.

"High as a... Phoenix. It's about that business we discussed. The war."

"Oh. Still going on, is that?"

"Not anymore. Just come out of your hole, Dad, you're embarrassing us in front of the bird-freak."

"Ha, so this is how you fallen creatures live," the Phoenix said. "You can still be saved. Read the truth in the Holy Fire!"

"Read? You fool, I can't read," Tengu said as he emerged, covered in the hairy moss that was flourishing in the dank warren. "That's how the weebs get ya!"

"Oh. So you understand that at least."

"Yeah, yeah. S'important. My boy here's a fugging gonner with all that. I got my goggles here modified so that I can't even see any of that shid any more. Hardly working actually though. I can see your bloody ball of cat-girls over there just fine."

"Actually Dad, those are skimmers."

"Fugg, the parasite's got me! Oh I'll be bound, it's the end for me, send for the doctor."

"Dad, you've just got moss growing on your brain. You'll need a dose of glowgreen, right Izzy?"

"Err... No?" Izumi said.

"Oh, don't make me beg. Phoenix man, you stupid piece of shid, let's go downstairs and get blazed," Tengu said.

"Blazed? Like a blazing phoenix?" the Phoenix asked.

"You'll be burned out and soaring high, the dream, eh?"

"Yes... yes... the dream!"

So even the Phoenix had fun at the big victory party that evening. The skroops were returned to their stables, where a few local people even dared to go and feed them lumps of chocobread. In the palace, the city nobles were all squashed into the dining hall alongside the guild.

"Alright, you freaks, let's get the introductions outta the way," Tengu said from the head of a long table. "Whatta we got? We got this old chap here, he's the Holy Phoenix. He's that guy we hate, but don't let him get ya down, he's been fugged to Earth and back by our guests here. Over there we got two weird, pale looking shek. See 'em? The one without boobs is the prince of the Shek Kingdom, apparently. So be nice to 'im, or we'll have even more bullshid to deal with, alright? Then there's this group of pot plants over here, they got a couple of celebs, lemmie get this right... it's Gustavo, prince of the Mankhive, and Queen Boop?"

"Beep!" Beep corrected him.

"Yeah, they got their own thing going on, don't worry about them. So right, next special guest is this guy who sounds like a skeleton but looks like a bloke. He's a big shot in skeleton land or something, right?"

"Allow me, your majesty," Rick said, standing up. "General Redlin Ackard of the Biobash Order, dishonourably discharged, and now the famous Big Stick Rick, demonstrations free, all night service at a negotiable rate."

"Right, right, guest of dishonour then, nice one," Tengu nodded. "And course, my only child, Prince of the Empire, err..."

"Nuk..." Nuk prompted.

"Nuk Tashino! He sorted us all out with all this war shid, so let's all have a toast, and eat some of this weird chocobread sandwich heresy his lot keep going on about. Long live the Empire, or something!"

A toast was given, toast was eaten, and all had a mildly pleasant time befitting of an upstanding dinner party.

"So you see, I think peace is the only option now," Izayah was saying to his table-fellows. "With the skroops stationed here in Heft, who would dare wage war on the United Cities? And yet, should the United Cities wish to wage war on the Kingdom, they'd find that getting those fussy buggers to walk ten paces down the street is a task so herculean, that it simply isn't worth the bother. In this way, those silly skroops are the lynchpin of global geopolitics."

Everyone nodded, and the Empire nobles were impressed that this strange looking shek had such a head on his shoulders – although only because they had foolishly presumed otherwise. Nuk was also discussing lofty political matters.

"You don't need the slaves any more, Dad. Being a slave fugging sucks, and having to deal with having slaves around also fugging sucks."

"Boy you don't get it. Who do you think gets all the stuff done around here? All this food is from the hands of those slaves. Get rid of them, you get rid of everything else too!" Tengu argued.

"Manksand canyon has more food that we can eat a hundred times over, and I ain't got a single slave. Everyone's free to leave whenever, but they just don't. Is it because they are addicted to the drugs we give them? Probably. But that's better than just threatening to kill them and shid."

"In addition, your majesty, there is the matter of a technical solution," Izumi chimed in. "We now know that in the First Empire, they use machines to perform labour. They made a few mistakes along the way, an destroyed the whole world, but... let's not write it off. We've got plenty c prototypes at Manksand to show you."

"Ahhh but your little den's in the sticks. No, it's on the other blood side of the sticks. Can't you just move back in here? I'll make you both space in the nest," Tengu said.

"You need to see it man. We'll make it easier, somehow," Nuk nodded drawing a less sure nod from Izumi. "Anyway, let's just say, put it out there that we might be doing something a lot better than slavery real soon, bu it's gonna be real similar still. It's like we're going to enslave the machines instead."

"Ah that classic opening line. Always works out great," Rick said, immediately swivelling around to join the discussion, breaking the waist of his Numan suit in the process. "I hope y'all gonna be studying the perverted history kid thing if you're gonna be talking like that."

"Oh yeah, Dad, we made this book that explains the historical treatment of skeletons that destroyed the First Empire, told through the medium of a coming-of-age reverse harem gas-girl manga with revolutionary attention to detail," Nuk explained.

"Not wrong," Rick nodded. "Those mangaka girls ain't ever even seen a shower, yet they drew it just right."

"Even politics comes in little comics now? I'm too old for this shid," Tengu scoffed. "Alright, I'll be open minded, and by that I mean fugging stoned. Oi, everyone, turn the lights out, I wanna show ya something!"

Another classic opening line. He referred to Nuk's custom, warm, glowing green supply, which bathed the room in an eerie hue. The high and mighty nobles were disgusted by the notion of taking poor-people drugs, until they tried it. Oh the party truly began at that moment, and Big Stick Rick did very good business. As with any good party, the less said about it all, the better.

In the morning, the guild set off for Manksand. As the Emperor had complained, it really was a bit of a slog, and while lamenting this very matter, the guild were confronted with the other issue previously discussed.

"There he is!" a voice shouted. A band of manhunters appeared from behind a sandbank. "That's the Prince trying to free the slaves and destroy this Empire! Give him a taste of what he's missing, huh?"

"Can't remember if Dad said it was okay for me to kill you all..." Nuk said.

"Better to ask forgiveness than permission! Kill them!" Izayah shouted. The manhunters realised they were in trouble as soon as the first blows were struck, but they were out their misery by the second.

"And you know, I don't even need to ask forgiveness, 'cause I'm not sorry," Izumi shrugged. The sentiment was universal. Nuk lead the guild south, and then up a small hill that overlooked the eastern sea.

"This isn't the way, my Prince," Wodston pointed out.

"But it could be. Stormgap Beach is right over there, you can see it on he horizon," Nuk said, pointing out in the more literal sense. Indeed, across the blue salt-beds of Gut, the brown waters of the long Stormgap estuary, and past the line of greyish cliffs marking the horizon, faint specs of smoke rising from Manksand's bakery were being carried off by the winds.

"I fear the swim, and the Beak Things, will render this route rather perilous," Wodston said.

"We need to build a massive thing, with foot plates where you walk, that goes right above the whole area."

"A bridge?" Izumi suggested.

"A skyway!" Nuk called. The guild sat on that sandy hillside, enjoying a rainy picnic, while Nuk and the Tech Hunters debated various minutiae of civil engineering. The end result of all this? Little more than wet behinds and a sky-high dream, but the matter would be returned to in earnest soon enough. In the meantime, they all carried on back to the long way home. On the way, they passed by a farming camp, run with the decreasingly legal economic model of slave labour. Nuk decided to pop in to deliver the news.

Outside the gates, a gang of manhunters were preparing a slave trading caravan. They were very angry to see the guild emerge from the hills – indeed, it was the rumours of some absolute buffoons arguing about whether bridge columns benefited from the power of teamwork that got them out of bed in the first place. They didn't hesitate to draw their weapons, but they really should have.

"Look, I am killing them! Beep!" Beep boasted. She pulled back the arms of her crossbow, and pressed the trigger again. There was no bolt loaded, and yet the slaver she targeted reeled over backwards.

"Incredible, my Queen! Every being you kill makes those still alive more grateful for your association. Please, continue," Gustavsen said. He hurriedly reloaded his own crossbow, held stealthily at his hip, just in time to pull his trigger again when Beep did. Ah, and they said hivers had no notion of romance. They were probably going to keep saying that, actually.

At about two in the morning, the guild sauntered into the middle of the slave camp. It featured a large cultivated patch of mank, ringed by jails, barracks, and a thick wall. Given the time of day, all was quiet. Nuk quickly saw to that.

"This is a public service announcement. It is the case that this facility has been officially sanctioned, by order of the... No More Fugging Bullshid Please Thanks Bill of... of... What year is it?"

"No one knows. Starts with a seven, maybe?" Izumi shrugged.

"Of the year seven... four... probably a one in there... oh right, zeroes, how many zeroes... Errr... What if there are zero zeroes? Shid... Okay, let's just say year seven for now, pending further amendments."

"Oi, shut the fugg up!" a voice shouted from a nearby barracks.

"*Omae wa mou shindeiru, baka!*" Nuk called back.

"What?" the voice echoed.

"I'll handle this," Izayah said, funnelling his hands over his mouth. "PRISON BREAK!" he boomed. That got things started. The guild burst into the slave quarters, and slammed the guards to the ground. Locks were smashed, and the freed slaves boosted the gear of their fallen captors.

"This prison break is brought to you by the TCM+⁺ guild-" Nuk tried to announce over the noise. "Oh, but it's also brought to you by the Empire! Slavery is over! Live free, die of an overdose – this our creed!"

This stalwart rallying cry took the mob from jail to jail, busting slaves out and throwing slavers in. Guards occasionally appeared to intervene, but that never lasted long. The Thousand Guardians secured both gates for the sake of any who wished to depart, and of course Nuk was always recruiting new muscle for *his* walled-off mank farm, yet most of the liberatees decided to stay.

"Your majesty, if you ain't forgotten us, then we gotta do our part," one of them explained to Nuk. "From now on, our hoes will work for you."

"Pimpin'," Rick remarked. It was classic comedy, and also probably a good idea, as until the guild set up their machines, someone actually did need to keep the food supply coming. And it's all good business: instead of selling produce to pay the guards, the farm could just scrap the guards and pay the willing workers instead. Everyone wins. Except the out of work guards I suppose, but manhunters becoming jobhunters aside, all was well in that remote farming outpost by the time the guild marched off the next evening.

They marched past the fallen Eye, skirted the fringes of Venge, crossed the rocky bluffs north of Brink, and at last sighted the giant, ancient chimney in the middle of Black Scratch. Manksand was close, and hence, Nuk had to halt the guild for a special matter.

"Izzy, I need you to wear this blindfold," Nuk said.

"Can we just get back before you horrible biologicals get started with your parasite shid?" Rick asked. Apparently not.

"It'll spoil the surprise if she sees it," Nuk smiled. "It's barely degenerate at all, this is wholesome fun!"

"Yeah I've heard that one before."

"Fine, Nuk, I'll do it, let's just move," a worn-out Izumi conceded.

The rest of the guild were free to obverse Nuk's secret surprise as they got home.

"That's... How did you do this?" Elaina asked.

"Incredible. How did you achieve such great size?" Wodston asked.

"Hmpf. Showing off's all it is," Sandor commented. Izumi was certainly interested, but wasn't entirely sure why everyone else had to be involved with this. Turned it was a gift for everyone really, but Izumi was to be the main recipient. I should mention by the way that I'm talking about an enormous, looming, towering, rock solid, Second Empire style citadel. Fashioned after World's End University, this hundred meter tall monster rose above the top of the canyon, its chrome-dome roof gleaming in the morning light. When Izumi's blindfold was removed, she was standing in the circular main hall of the building.

"Welcome to your new palace, Princess," Nuk said with a grin.

"Oh, not you as well- I mean, sorry, thanks, this is incredible. It's so big!" she marvelled.

"Ah, how I've longed to hear it," Hammer's voice said. From upstairs, a robot spider covered in grey dust plodded down into the hall.

"Yeah, I mean it's because of the bots. Even a billion slaves couldn't do this, but a few machines and bang," Nuk said.

"Bang indeed, kind Prince," Hammer said. "We've been working day and night, welding, sawing, mixing Kement – as you insist on calling it. I should warn you that it's not all set, and this whole thing is liable to collapse at any moment to be honest, but hark, is that not the world in a nutshell? To die in this dusty prison would be pure poetry."

"Hammings, you're killing the vibe."

"Ah, and I suppose you think you're a better vibe-rater than me. Nonsense, eh, Princess?"

Hammer was shoo'd away, and the biologicals took a look upstairs. The second level had a large lab space for anything Izumi might desire (for scientific research purposes of course) and upstairs was the master bedroom (where I suppose other purposes could be attended to). As of now this new-build was devoid of character, colour, and indeed furniture, but for the first time, Princess Izumi started to feel worthy of that spurious title.

"This is unbelievable. We can create uranium atomic splitting devices with all this space," Izumi said.

"Yeah. And I can get a shelf," Nuk said.

"It's wonderful, Nuk. Just what I wanted!"

"Great. You did drop a few hints, after all. Like when you said exactly what you wanted."

"Thanks for picking up on that, thanks so much. I can never repay you."

"And I can never charge you, so let's call it even eh? Oh, speaking of charge, I grabbed a couple of batteries from Dad's basement."

"Yep, you really do know what I want," Izumi almost purred. This is another of those things where the less said about it the better, so let's just leave this on the note that both were very happy with their new property. Who actually was paying for all this? Let's just say that the guild now owed several million cats when you added up all the debts incurred in materials and labour, but they could surely repay that with their invaluable services to world civilisation.

Yes, now that the war was over, it was time for some true R&R – Reading and Research. Izumi's Tech Hunters were to begin work on strange devices that made use of the warming rock fragments, and Nuk's managaka girls, i.e. the same people, started work on the sequel to 'Gas Girl and the Four Ethical Princes': 'Bacteria Boy and Four Hygienic Matrons'. It was the cleanest filth known to history, a period which spanned back at least seven years, rumour had it.

Best leave them all to it, and wait for the next great outing. This was brewing with increasing volume over in the mankhive down the canyon. The strange hums and chants of the hivers within, loudening by the day, would eventually become a fresh call to weird adventure!

Chapter 37.5 Side Story
Wet Kement

"According to this... we really should have been wearing gloves to handle that uranium," Izumi reported. She was sat on her new Premium Grade High Yield Scientific Discovery Surface, also known as a desk, with a couple of printouts in her lap. Nuk dropped an armful of uranium onto said desk, dusting a yellowish residue off his hands.

"A warming rock a day keeps the brain moss away," he quipped sagely. It seems the opposite was written on Izumi's report, but how could she refute the famous Professor of Super Luminal Millipedes and Tsundere Studies?

"Right, Hammer says there is a way to make these warming rock really warm. Like melting stuff warm," Izumi said. "If we can work out how to do it, and control it, we could boil off a load of water and have all the steam we need."

"Yeah, been lacking steam, if anything," Nuk nodded.

"You'll see. Trust me."

"With pleasure. Maybe we could boil away the estuary and get the bridge going?"

"Nuk, seriously, there is absolutely no point trying to make a bridge out there. The design alone would take years, even for a core."

"And I'm not interested in your material bridges," the desk said Hammer's voice. "No, only the transition of love from digital to analogue forms gets my juices flowing. Perhaps a few hormones in my wires, and little charge across the surface of your skin. Oh Princess, do you know what this desk is capable of?"

Izumi's eyes suddenly widened, then she jolted down off the desk.

"Okran's Aux Port," she breathlessly remarked, shaking her twitchy fingers. Was she getting too excited? "Err, Nuk, just forget the bridge thing, okay, and I'll get to work here. Lock the doors, please."

"Right, right, cool. I'll just go not do that bridge thing then. That'll give me time to take the shek to their swimming lessons instead," Nuk said, departing that steamy den of science. He went down to the gatehouse, where the Thousand Guardians were lounging around the parapets like a bunch of a cats. Cats as in the creature that is, not the coin. Oh homographs are such a bore. They were having a good laugh at the expense of the local reaver clans.

"My go!" one said, leaping up and taking the handles astride an automatic harpoon cannon. Great cheers followed every hit, and when the chambers were empty, the next candidate took their shots. This could have carried on for a very long time, for reavers from all over the world seemed intent on destroying Manksand and their cheap, almost-legal drugs market. Today, though, Nuk called everyone down for a special mission.

"I know we've been been putting it off, but it's time to get familiar with the art of water-moving, also known to science as swimming," Nuk announced, drawing a wave of moans. "I know, I know, but remember, this planet is mostly water, and we'll have to conquer it eventually. So, please gather up the official swimming tutorial gear. That would be: twenty picks, twenty shovels, a few tonnes of sand, a Kement mixer, Wodston, about half a mile of metal coils, and... a towel."

The shek shortly returned with a garru bag full of sand, a kement mixer full of Wodston, and mouths full of questions. Yet Nuk shushed them, and quietly led them out through the gate. They crossed the canyon further downstream, and climbed up to Stormgap beach. Across the water to their north was the huge mountain at the tip of the Howler Maze, and beyond that was the faint set of hills from which the guild had recently dreamed of reaching Manksand via a more direct route. Now the dream carried on, but would the alarm clock ring?

"My Prince, it is the case that you wish to begin engineering works?" Wodston asked, clambering out of the mucky kement bowl.

"Ya huh. Manksand is the heart of this empire. Or at least it will be, when you can walk safely, ish, from here to Heft. Gentleshek, we're going to build the Skyway," Nuk said. The shek felt obliged to cheer, and carried out that obligation with military efficiency.

"Has Princess Izumi provided the designs?" Wodston asked. Nuk looked back to the canyon, and saw that the floodlights around the top of Tashino Tower were flickering off and on for some reason.

"Yep," he eventually nodded. Oh and such a genius design it was. The shek soon caught on to the vague gist of it: pile dirt, wet kement, gravel, and bits of old sheet metal into a rough looking mound, and see if it could support your weight by the end of it. They worked from the small hours of the morning until afternoon, and by the end of it had a huge rampart that stretched from the bluffs at the top of the beach to the water's edge.

"Well, that'll keep the Beak Things out at least," Izayah noted.

"My Prince, are we really going to try this in the water?" Wodston asked.

"Towel's ready my man. This is the swimming lesson part, everyone. We gotta do this, but pile it up in the water so it sticks out the top. Remember, you're getting wet now so that you don't have to get wet again in the future. Think of the net wet!"

The shek thought of the net wet, failed to notice that the net wet is minimised by absolutely ignoring everything Nuk was saying, and were successfully tricked into this new, aquatic labour.

"It's getting a little dark though, Prince Tashino," Izayah said. "Perhaps we should wait until morning?"

"We can't go back until it's done. Otherwise I lose to that stupid desk!" Nuk insisted.

"Understandable. Or, perhaps not," Izayah sort-of nodded. "I wonder if they are asking where we are back in the base?" he added.

Back in the base...

"How much wood could a wood chuck chuck if a wood chuck could chuck wood?" Rick recited.

"If a wood chuck could chuck wood he would chuck it good, just like he should, like a fat jello pud, like a guy who understood, what it means to chuck, that, Stobe-loving, Earth-snubbing wood!" Neil said back, picking up a backgammon piece from the board in front of him and hurling it to Choco.

"Wait, that's not the answer on the card, Neil, you smug pose-cessor."

"Oh, I'm sorry, am I playing regular backgammon?" Neil postured. "Oh I think I won't bother putting what's on the card through the translation into D20 different languages and then check it back, cause I wouldn't know wacky if it wacked me in the back with a gammon."

"Right. You know what Neil, I don't think wacky BG is the cure to your fever..."

Back in the estuary...

"More mank, more shid, more, more, more, keeping chucking that wood in there, if you would," foreman Nuk was calling. The shek were carefully extending the pile of loosely mortared rubble out into the water, but the further out they got, the deeper it got. How deep was it? It was so dark they couldn't see an inch below the surface, so it could have gone all the way down to the Great Mover for all they knew. Not that they knew even about the Great Mover.

"Don't let the darkness of the abyss fool you! Fill it with shid until it erupts back out; this is how we conquer the void!" Nuk said. Probably very inspirational.

"Is this really the best time for all this?" a dripping wet Izayah asked as he hauled himself from the gentle waves.

"Of course, man. You know what they say: the best time to build a bridge was twenty years ago, the second best time is now. And twenty years ago from now, it was still three am, so it would have been just as dark even in the best case scenario."

"Ah. Right. Who is it that says that?" Izayah asked, but Nuk quickly grabbed a bucket of stony kement and plunged into the stinky deep himself. They worked away all night, and in the morning light, saw that they had almost reached the other side. However, as their pile began to creep up the rocky shallows, they ran out of wire, plating, and kement.

"We must have some more somewhere in the stores," Wodston said. "I shall go back and take a look."

"No. You'll give the game away. There's only one way of doing this," Nuk said, pulling from his bag a blue AI core. "Are these waterproof?" he added, hearing something sloshing around inside. Well, it still buzzed on, and the little dials on the back tuned in to the officially agreed Tashino Tower frequency.

"Izzy?" he said. There was a sound like a load of metal objects falling to ground, then a load of scratching, and then,

"Yeah, what, what? What the fugg is it?" Izumi blurted out. A background buzzing sound began to fade away.

"I'm in Howler's Maid, or whatever it's called. Can you bring me, like, two bags of grey, a box of green, and about twenty shek's worth of emergency brown?"

"How the fugg are you in the Howler Maze?"

"Ah, well, if you go to the beach, maybe you'll find out."

"Nuk, you didn't, did you?"

"Yes, I did. Did you do your thing, by the way?"

"Oh she did her thing," Hammer reported. "Her terrible, terrible thing."

"Shut up! I'll be there in a while, Nuk, hang on, whatever you're doing..." Izumi said.

The shek slumped down on some nearby rocks for a nap, being careful to avoid disturbing the less-giant crabs hanging around the rock-pools dotted about the place. Looking to the south, their long mound cut the sea in two, apart from a few rushed stretches towards the end where water lapped up over the top of it. Still, certainly a work to be proud of, and easily the largest engineering project conducted by biologicals since... well, since the regurgitation of Queen Beep's hive, most likely.

"Narko's Jawline..." Izumi said when she reached the beach. The Tech Hunters were behind her, carrying bags of kement powder. It would be impossible to get all that stuff across the estuary, but now they could lug it atop the ramparts, and carry it high and dry across the shakey, half-mile walkway. Beak things looked on at them in confusion as they did so, knowing that their stubby legs stood no chance of getting up there with the tasty humans. No one had ever been so close to a beak thing without being bitten as Izumi and her garru girls were on that little walk.

With mouth agape, she walked across the water, immersed no more than ankle deep even at the least-finished points. Nuk was standing in the shallows at the other end, a grin on his face and two days without sleeping in his eyes.

"How about it? Fast, huh?" he said.

"I've never seen anything like it. Amazing Nuk, everyone," Izumi said. The hunters unloaded their materials, and all together they finished off the last stretch, adding a nice ramp to get down onto solid ground at the end. With this there was a direct route from Manksand to Heng and the Great Desert. Well, there was if you didn't count the uppity crab-infested coasts and marshes between them. Yes, this secure trading route needed a little more work, to be sure, however the most difficult part had been conquered with the creation of that wonderful bridge. Or, at least, people were calling it a bridge.

"You did leave gaps below the waterline for the sea to flow through, right?" Izumi asked Nuk.

"Yep," he nodded blankly.

"Because if you didn't it would be a dam, and it would flood everything on both sides. Like our home, for example."

"Lucky we remembered that then eh?"

"Who needs luck, when you have genius? Amazing, Nuk. Come on, let's go home."

Everyone climbed back up onto the bridge-like-structure, and began to cross. The sun was setting, casting the horrid waters aglow as the team marched in the midst of that shimmering abyss. It was beautiful, and all the more so for the knowledge of the endeavour of biological life that brought them there. And so, as the water levels rose, and Nuk frantically tried to communicate the need to add gaps below the waterline to Wodston (very difficult using only hand signals and eyebrow movements), everyone went home with their heads, and trouser legs, held high.

Chapter 38
Fish Oil Frenzy

"Close your eyes, my Queen. Feel it. Feel it inside you!" Gustavsen said.

"Do you have to degen' out at the fugging dinner table?" Rick asked from across the other side of said table, but the answer was yes, it seemed. Beep, sat beside Gustavsen, began rocking her head back and forth, and said,

"The feeling is so faint, beep." Everyone else started snickering, but this was no laughing matter. "The Queen's beeps are splitting. The hive unravels, beep. Yet the shadows grow like bogweed, tall and binding reaching for the eternal throne! Beep!"

"Tripping on that Bad Green," Nuk remarked. The other hiver suddenly grabbed Beep and pulled her from the table, forming a hiver-pile on under which Beep disappeared.

"I don't care, I don't even care any more. What happens in Tashino Towers, stays outta god damned Tashino Towers, alright, 'cause I'm tryn chill in here," Rick said, quitting the table with this plate of choco-mash untouched.

"So, Prince Gustavsen, is everything okay?" Izumi asked the hiver pile. Gustavsen's head emerged through a gap.

"The hive is unbound. This delights the darkness. We must resist the encroachment of... the other ones," he said.

"Well that's creepy as fugg," Izumi said. "Nuk, what did you put in the hiver mush?"

"He added teeth, and it was delicious! Beep!" a voice said. Wonder who it was? "But the Other Ones grow. We must resist. We must insist! Beep!"

"Wait, I know what this is," Nuk said, surprising all present. "The other ones... You said before that not all hivers are from your Queen's island. You said some were from, 'the other one'."

"There is only one hive! However, there is also, another one," Gustavsen explained clearly. "With the waning of the Queen, they seek to rise. They seek to return, and be the only associables."

"Southern Hivers," Izumi said, shaking her head. "A rare sight. We'll keep you safe, Prince, all of you."

"Incorrect. They have supped long on the fishman juice. They spread, and destroy both being and machine. The fading of the beep will empower them to strike."

"Right. Is there anything we can do?"

"We must take their juice! Only the Queen may wear the paste of life!" Gustavsen insisted, bursting out of the pile.

"Fishman hunting? I know about a thousand fellows who'd be up for that," Izayah commented.

"There is little time. We must take the Queen to the birthplace of the free associates, and consume their essence, before the cloud takes us all."

"Okay, cool," Nuk said. "Alright everyone, we're gonna go to the birthplace of the free associates, and consume their essence, before the cloud takes us all. There will be no questions at this time."

And with that, the guild were off again. Izumi's work could wait, for she needed another shipment from the Tech Scribe enclave to make any more headway. Perhaps that could be gathered en-route, as Gustavsen eventually explained that their destination was to be so-called Fishman Island, a cursed place off the south coast of the world. It was all you could eat for fishman essence, and as previously mentioned, it's a great moisturiser too. They went west to Brink, then set off south to traverse the Old Lands, Stobe's lands, lands of crab associators, vicious reaver cartels, and, as it happens, the 'other ones'.

Entering the grey, smoky mountains of Stobe's Gamble out the south end of Venge, they saw bright streaks of purple on the rocks up ahead.

"They are here. They sense the new hive is forming. They will kill us," Gustavsen said, refusing to go any further. The purple streaks approached, long polearms glinting at their sides, and lanky, hiver-drone bodies, with skin matching their armour, came into focus. They said nothing, but communicated their intent with the readying of weapons.

"Sounds like we've got some bullies to deal with," Izayah said. "I don't know all that much about this hiver magic, but if they so much as touch any member of this guild, I will show them how the shek get things done."

The purple hivers broke into a run, and at once the guild was fighting all about. There were perhaps twenty of these so-called southern hivers, calm and able in their techniques with the blade. This was no simple beatdown, even for the Thousand Guardians. But brawn still counts for a lot, and thick armour even more so. Soon all the southern hivers were lying still on that gravelly hillside.

"How many of these 'other ones' are there?" Nuk asked.

"The number grows. They prepare their march. A march against all the unassociated," Gustavsen said, looking up into the ashen sky. "We cannot feel them. They will not feel us. Troubling. We must hurry and imbibe the timeless essence. Come, my Queen."

"These guys are obsessed with essence all of a sudden," Nuk said as the hivers started onward.

"Uh huh? Imagine how all y'all look to us," Rick said. "I mean, I'm a Numan, I like essence as much as the next... respectable organism, but y'all far too wet for me. Seems like these violent violets ain't a fan of that either."

"Yeah, well, guess we better kill them or something," Nuk shrugged. "Although I get the feeling we're going through a whole bunch of shid just so that Bad Green can have his waifu."

The romantic quest carried on, but there were several exciting waylays in store before the fishy fountains of youth could be reached. The troubles began when they ran out of road – the southern coast was mostly outside the realm of civilisation, so to progress past the deadlands of Stobe's Gamble, they needed to hike through a narrow mountain pass, inhabited only by ferocious land-bats. These ugly, flappy fellows, resembling a cross between a flying squirrel and a pig, were not interested in tourists.

As the guild fought their way up the pass, they noticed something strange. In places the ground was softened by parched streams, revealing footprints marching ahead of them.

"These are human feet. Bare feet," Elaina reported.

"Man-bears huh? Ain't fishmen, but it's getting close," Nuk noted.

"Yeah, hilarious, but who's going up here without shoes?" Izumi asked. There was no answer to be had, until they discovered a path etched into the mountainside, a path well-trodden by filthy toes. It zig-zagged upwards into a dormant volcanic bowl. It was too dark to see into clearly, but something was going on here – electric spotlights shone dimly atop a gatehouse, and big boxy shadows lay beyond it.

"I don't see anyone there, my Prince. Could this be a ruin?" Wodston asked.

"Nah, people must have been walking and up and down here, right?" Nuk replied.

"They have those electric lights, but no shoes? This isn't going to be a normal one," was Izumi's assessment.

"Probably right. You guys chill here a sec. I'll go try some smooth talking."

Nuk went into the crater alone. The gatehouse was completely unmanned, and so he found himself wandering through what appeared to be a substantial town. There were sandstone and metal buildings all about, revealed more and more by the rising dawn sun. The streets were empty, and Nuk didn't see another living thing until he encountered a dog sniffing about an abandoned market stall.

"Hey, doggo. Are you the only one left?" Nuk asked, running over. The dog looked at him indifferently and then got back to its business. "No way... A whole town, just gone. Who could have done this?"

"Gone? It's just five in the morning you dumbass," a voice said. It was the stallholder, apparently, coming to open up. He was a tall, extremely bulky man in a long, black duster, his feet bare. "Where'd you escape from then?" he went on.

"Err, same place as you I guess," Nuk said, using the term 'guess' rather potently.

"Wise-cracking, boot-wearing, skinny boy. They won't like you. Go tell Tinfist you've arrived, alright," the man said, waving Nuk towards a silver dome in the middle of the market space. Nuk poked his head in, and saw more shoe-less fellows sitting around a table. At the head was a shabbily dressed skeleton, who locked onto Nuk right away.

"You. You've come a long way to be here, am I correct?" he said.

"To be somewhere, anyway. What's up?" Nuk replied.

"This is the only place you need to be. I can tell you've felt the slaver's whip."

"Yeah, I have actually. It fugging sucks. How do you know that anyway?"

"That is what binds us all, freeman. That is what drives us all to fight."

"Oh, you fight slavery? So do I! I got Dad to pass some legislation on it actually. Well, not pass, but we killed some people, and I think that made things a bit better."

"Dad? Legislation? What's this talk?"

"Dad, like the Emperor. I'm Nuk Tashino. Guild guy, and stuff?" There was a long silence while everyone at the table looked at each other in disbelief. "I get it, you don't believe me. Here, I've got this house Tashino custom belt buckle, they don't just give these away, check it out."

Just as Nuk was in the process of removing his trousers, everyone suddenly lunged at him. In a bad way.

"He's a fugging Uzzie! Kill the slaver!" someone shouted. Nuk, being very quick-witted, worked out that he probably wasn't welcome here, and legged it. However the legging was contested strongly – these crater-folk were all as beefy as the miscellany salesman outside. Their feet thudded, or in some cases clanked, right at Nuk's tail. (His figurative tail, that is, despite what the depictions of him in his self-insert gas-girl fanart would have people believe).

"Green Emperor to LateBloomerGeek07, pick up!" Nuk said into the core strapped to his very loose belt.

"What? What's going o- How did you know my username?" Izumi replied.

"I got a real fugging manga situation here, trousers down, muscles, comical misunderstanding, get running!"

"What?"

"Run away!"

"Just say that first! Everyone, we got some gorilloshid, it's either degenerate or deadly. Either way, let's move!"

The guild thundered back down the narrow mountain path, with Nuk gradually catching to up them, and a bunch of angry gym-rats, unencumbered by footwear, quickly catching up to everyone.

"Spies! Slaver abetters! Noble pigs!" and other such accusations were flung. These guys weren't even out of breath, which could not be said for the guild. They fled all the way down the mountain, and began to falter as they crossed the flatter ground below. The pursuers pushed guild members aside to get to Nuk specifically, and he was eventually forced to confront them.

"I'm gonna free the slaves, jeez," he said, beginning to draw his sword, but in a flash a hand chopped at his wrist and pushed the blade back down into the sheath. Before this motion was even complete, a palm slammed

arely into his chest and catapulted him backwards into the dirt. The
pact had Nuk down for the count.

"And the rest of you, ya Uzzies too?" one of these mountain martial
s masters called. Perhaps everyone would have been destined for a similar
ating to Nuk, however some more gorilloshid happened to save them. In
t it was just a plain gorilla – a hairly, burly beast appeared and roared at
warrior monks, and apparently these folk relished a challenge. They
pped to spar with this raging monster, while the guild powered off into
distance, with Nuk on Pia's shoulders.

They finally came to an exhausted halt beside a foul-smelling green
e. Looking back, it seemed they were in the clear. Pia put Nuk down, and
mi fell to her knees, grabbing him.

"Nuk, what happened? I don't see any blood. Nuk? Nuk?" she said.

"They... one punch... Manga... idea..." Nuk muttered, but his
isciousness failed him.

"Shid, they've broken his bones, this could be bad. We need to get
newhere safe. Sorry, Prince Gustavsen."

"No matter. The Prince has shown great favour. His pain is my own. We
inot go on," Gustavsen said. Looking around, the guild saw smoke rising
m behind a ridge not far to the west. They approached, but soon saw that
vas coming from a hive. An 'other one' hive. They truly were spreading,
there was no fight to be had this time. The maps showed that they were
se to Mourne, the depressing half-ruin at the top of the Boneyard the
ld had passed through previously. By nightfall the guild were patrons of
town's dank inn, entry to which required stepping over a rotting beak
ng corpse.

"He's alive," was Elaina's report after looking Nuk over. Wodston went
ittle further and reported that indeed the poor Prince had multiple
ctured ribs.

"Shid. We shouldn't move him. For a long time," Izumi said.

"Nonsense. He must move faster. He must be exposed to the essence,"
:tor Gustavsen said, revealing that he was, in fact, in the room.

"Sorry, but essence isn't the solution to everything."

"FALSE!"

"Let's just... see how he feels when he wakes up, shall we?"

"I already know how he feels. Disgusting."

"Thanks. Can we be alone?"

"And I know how you feel. You cannot reproduce with him."

"Thanks, Prince, you really are a help, goodbye now," Izumi said, pushing Gustavsen out of the murky bedroom. Fortunately this hospitalisation proved to be brief, as Nuk awoke from his stupor in the middle of the night.

"Ugh, where am I?" he muttered.

"Nuk, you're safe," Izumi said, sitting up beside him. "We're in Mourne."

"Mourne... It wasn't destroyed?"

"It's always kinda destroyed."

"I mean. I did a thing. Hang on, I better check something," Nuk said, getting up from the bed. "Argh, everything fugging hurts!"

"You've got broken bones! Stay in bed, for now."

"Can't. We've got stuff to do, right? Don't worry. I know a medicine that cures everything. Bad Green! Bring me Ass!" Nuk called.

"This will only kill the pain, you require essence to survive," Gustavsen immediately replied. He was, it turned out, looking in through the window.

"Gustavsen, will you fugg off for like, five minutes?" Izumi scolded him.

"Never! I am concerned for my associate."

"Cute. But... Okay, let's just try the fugging essence," the poor woman conceded, muttering something about her own lack of essence as she slumped back down into the bed. As for the business Nuk was eager to get to after a quick Ass break, he went over to the big Mourne tower, and crep inside. On the top floor, the enormous Great White Gorillo was sleeping peacefully, having still not realised Nuk had previously removed all th chains keeping the door shut. Like a modern day Santa Claus, Nuk carefull left a box of green for the beast to enjoy, and slipped away. With his guilt fo the still-in-the-future destruction of Mourne slightly abated, he gathered u the guild to head out first thing in the morning.

"My Prince, you really shouldn't be walking around," Wodston said.

"My man, that's true of everyone, but we do it all the same," Nu replied. It was hard to retort, as in a world as deadly at this one it was prett much true. So the guild began walking due south, making use of a few o empire roads to get ever closer to Fishman Island.

The next distraction along the way was a big brown tower placed in random spot in the middle of the Boneyard, surrounded by a wall. It was a Second Empire construction, beyond mere disrepair.

"Ancient secrets check," Nuk announced, going over to break in. Before anyone could stop him he had smashed the lock on the gates and was jogging up the ramp to enter the tower. Then, at Izumi's hip, his voice rang out,

"Guys, it's fugging happening again! Fugg!"

The guild raced up and found Nuk in a fist-fight with two extremely brawny fellows. Now the fellows at the previous beating were certainly beefy, but these two were something else. They were about three humans wide but less than one tall, with arms thick as tree trunks and a neck that was built onto those broad shoulders like a mountain rising from a plain. They were also very hairy, grunting loudly, and were not very friendly at all. The guild drove them away and got Nuk out of there, but not before he broke yet another rib.

"S'alright, I can't feel it. Means it's probably fine," Nuk said, his red eyes watering.

"Eh General, why are we goin' around watching the wee Prince get clobbered by a bunch of weirdos?" Twitch asked Rick.

"Got something better to do? Ain't it nostalgic anyway?" Rick said.

"Aye, but I thought we were meant to be forgettin' about the beatings. You know, focusing on what matters, like... essence, is it?"

"Yeah, it's essence. Fleshies go wild for it, and them going wild makes more of it appear. Once you're older I'll teach you all about it."

"I'm olda than you ya little chrome model."

"Oh a gentleman never asks, squire."

Anyway, they escaped that tower full of what were presumably gorillo-associators, and finally had a clear run south to the coast, passing the fragments of the First Empire enclosures that littered the area, and the bones of what used to be enclosed underfoot. Soon the sea came into view, and not far across it was more land. An island. A fishman island. *The* fishman island. Hooray. The place was actually connected to the mainland via a long pontoon bridge, likely beyond the construction potential of beings with crab claws for hands.

"This is how the other ones harvest essence to grow strong, and live beyond what is meted," Gustavsen claimed.

"Well then it's a damn fishman juice buffet, let's go take a look," Nuk said. They crossed the bridge, and indeed the island beyond it was home to roving bands of crusteo-sapiens.

"Alright, let the hunt begin!" Izayah called to his Guardians. The feeling was mutual, as within minutes of setting foot on the island the fishmen were eagerly hunting the interlopers. Their wet, gurgling battle cries filled the air as they appeared from beyond every rise, urchin, and rock, their claws snapping with hastening rhythm. The guild's blades, bows, and big sticks smashed the fishmen apart without too much trouble. Soon they had created a pile of their catch, with only a few nips and snips in return.

"Makes you look younger huh?" Izumi said to herself, stirring a pool of the salty juice beside the corpse pile. The hivers had no such hesitation, smothering themselves in some, and bottling the rest up for future use. It was the closest thing to a cosmetics industry the world had seen in a long time.

The island used to be home to a rather different industry, according to the string of First Empire ruins along its southern shore. The guild wandered over to take a look. Husks of machines as large as cities sat half-submerged in the shallows.

"Yeah I been here," Rick said. "Water stuff was happening here, experimenting with the blend, you know? Too much 'essence', not enough. You remember this, boys?"

"Aye, everyone did a shift at some point," Twitch nodded. "Old girl's seen better days."

"Yeah but it's seen worse, remember those?" Neil said.

"Don't remember those!" Rick snapped at him. "This thing here ain't just a memory, it's inspiration. It is possible to sort this place out, we had the plans at one point. Rumour has it the stickman's ex-girl still has 'em."

"Can't really be dealing with all that shid again," Twitch said.

"Then don't. This time, you'll get to choose," Nuk assured him.

The hivers were sniffing frantically and gradually walking down the coast.

"It is closer, it is closer! Beep! The most essential essence of all!" Beep said. She was pointing forwards, where a structure was visible at the island's southern tip. They went closer, and saw it was another Second Empire lab, more recently built than the gorillo-man lair. But what it contained was just as combinatoric. This tower had not just a fishman, but a fishking!

"A big one! Beep! I will supp on its paste!" Beep excitedly claimed frantically pulling the trigger on her unloaded crossbow. The place was also full of non-monarchical creatures, so the guild had to fight their way in

After a brief scuffle, the hivers were sawing off the head of the big, pink, spiny fishking. It cracked off with a sloppy pop, dripping beige goop that Beep hurriedly lapped up.

"I hate this, so much," was Izumi's review of the situation. She was just mad because the lab had already been stripped of anything useful. After all, the fishmen had been hu-men at one point or another, and probably hu-women too. In fact there were certainly some females of some description around, as the lab was covered in slimy eggs. The perfect place to stay the night and wonder why all this was happening the first place.

"Okay, might as well go for it," Nuk said, pulling off his chestplate and opening his tunic. He was talking about the application of fishman juice to his chest, purple-spotted with bruises. Gustavsen immediately stepped forward to perform the treatment, but Nuk managed to convince him to let Izumi try it.

"Guess this won't do anything, but yeah..." Izumi said. Her hands were quickly covered in the stuff, and she kept acci-deliberately wiping it over her face. "So tired, oh my. Whoops, I got it all over my vulture's feet."

In the morning, Nuk actually did feel better, and Izumi seemed much happier with the results of running her fingers beside her eyes. Was this because because fishman juice really had healing properties, or was it because it was, while rather toxic, a powerful, extremely addictive stimulant? In the modern world, anything worth having tends to be the latter.

Luckily they now had all the fish mank they could ever need. With Beep now presumably more powerful than ever, it was time for her to take a stand against those dastardly southern hivers. Well, not for *her* to take a stand, or even the guild really. You'll see...

Chapter 39
Skinscare

Beep was jumping up and down amid the scaly fishman nests of that Second Empire tower, signalling her intention to jump again each time with a certain vocalisation.

"Yes, yes!" Gustavsen was cawing. Eventually Nuk had to step in.

"Amazing, but can we go now?" he asked.

"We go to war!" Gustavsen bellowed, then all the hivers started making that certain vocalisation.

"Sorry guys, I made it worse," Nuk reported back to the guild, shaking his head.

"I understand it, Prince Tashino," Izayah said. "They want to crush their enemies, and that invigoration has taken a hold of them!"

"Right, when talking about the hivers, no one is allowed to say 'invigoration', or 'satisfaction', or 'excited', or... You know... there's just paste everywhere... And the way they rub it all over... Look, the manga market isn't ready for that, they're not ready!" Nuk ranted. Luckily Beep herself eventually decided to stop the party.

"Beep! We go! Beep! We must sublimate the false Queen! Beep! We must accumulate her feelings, to bridge the fog gap! Beep!" she said.

"Yep. Go on then. We'll be right behind you- Actually, which way's the wind blowing? Shall we go ahead?" Nuk muttered. Everyone followed the hivers out of the tower and over to the east side of the island, where another string of pontoons ferried them back to the mainland. Ahead of them were mountains as sharp as bonedog teeth; utterly impassable.

"They are beyond the disturbance," Gustavsen said. "We must find a hole to their private domain, and enter swiftly."

"I'd say we should get this guy a girlfriend, but that's kinda the problem huh?" Rick commented. These impenetrable cliffs – or plain old 'impassable' as Nuk would prefer they be called – extended in a long arc around a salient of land, with a thin strip of flat ground between it and the southern sea. The land was free of any monster or beasts, so that's a nice break, huh? And then they discovered why this was the case, and the break... broke.

"Okran's Yaw Rod," Izumi said. "That's a lot of a giant robot crab-spiders." Indeed, ahead the narrow passages – sorry Nuk, the main, official, dry, above board and dull routes – were patrolled by legions of Second Empire spider soldiers.

"I've never seen anything like it. We must be careful, Izzy," Elaina said.

"Oh, okay," Izumi said, surprised to hear that name from someone else.

"You're right, Elly, this is more than a wandering scout," Izayah nodded.

"Oh... okay..." Izumi whispered, slipping back through the veil of awkwardness.

In the end the marching ranks of spiders could be easily bypassed. They seemed to just stamp off to scan about the steep hillsides while the guild walked past undetected in plain sight. Or was that what the doddering bots wanted them to think? The reason for such scepticism came shortly after, when traversing a bend in the coastline revealed a village up ahead. A neat row of square houses sat between a pair of tall, sandstone towers, all with human-sized doorways. It was almost too convenient. Yet, convenient it was, especially when a front of searing acid rain suddenly rolled off the sea. The guild rushed forwards into the nearest of the towers to escape the downpour. There, they met the locals.

"Humans. Enforcers. Experimental Subjects. We regret to inform you that you are not permitted to exist," a mechanical voice said. It came from the very walls of the structure, and surprisingly not from the gang of sword-wielding skeletons standing shoulder-to-shoulder inside the door.

"Oh, it's the boys!" Rick said, stepping forward. "Still bashing huh? Hand down, ya freaks."

"Warning Blacklisted ID Ping detected. Case one five nine eight three, General Redlin Rickard. Treatment: exile to darkness. Special comments attached: 'Make that playboy regret it. No one crosses this cowgirl'. Due to breach of sentencing, you will be recycled immediately."

"Fugg... That old fire still burning huh?" Rick said, raising his stick.

"Rick, are they gonna kill us?" Izumi whispered.

"Nope."

And with that, Rick sent the head of the nearest skeleton bouncing off the walls. Everyone got stuck in as well, with more bots charging onto the scene from upstairs and outside.

"They all look like Agnu!" Nuk noted.

"Yep. Biobash Knights," Rick said. "Woulda thought they'd get rid of them same as me, but I guess they kept 'em for a rainy day."

"And Rick, what's that about a cowgirl?" Izumi asked.

"Oh don't you get started. Yeah I got a history, so what? You thought you were my first?"

"Wait, I didn't say that!"

"Yeah, well forget it. Dead news."

"Is this about Old Moneybags? Old Lonestar? Old Waxy Dioscuri?" Neil asked.

"It is, man, and you're mean'a be practising your forgettin'!"

"Old... Wait, you only go for older women?" Izumi said, crestfallen.

"I can't believe you're making this about you. And that's why I love ya sister, but your free trial's over, so go back to your toy boy and biobash all ya like. Also, you wanna kill these guys or not?"

They did kill those guys, or at least they shut them down for a while long enough to get out of there. But right outside a group of spider soldier were waiting.

"We're in the spider's web, get slicing!" Sandor said, and at once another fight broke out. A few spiders were deactivated, but they would not lie still, for the guild dragged them along for more research. Well, that was the stated reason, but perhaps it was just a chance to hold something overhead to block the continuing acid rain. They all half-ran along the thick grained beaches and over rocky bluffs, shedding skin cells all the while where applicable.

Darkness fell, but they came across another structure at the water edge. It was the ruin of a Second Empire military outpost, but don't let the ruined status trick you into thinking it wasn't fully operational – as soon Nuk opened the door, bio-bash knights swarmed the guild from the shadow

"Parasite vectors! Neutralise!" they chirped.

"Argh, never liked your kind anyway," Twitch said, running a sword through one of the assailants. "No offence, Agnu."

"GHGHGH," Agnu said, his own blade just as kebabed. Another knightly company was silenced, after which the guild locked themselves in the outpost for a night of applying fishman paste to acid burns, which made them hurt significantly more. Izumi took it in her stride at least.

It was all a lost cause really, for in the morning it was still raining, or 'paining', if you will (and they did). The mountains between them and the southern hive were as much of a turn off as ever, so on they trotted along the beaches. The odd lone spider bothered them during the morning and was quickly added to the pile of priceless junk the guild hauled. There was another orderly village on the horizon around lunchtime, but legs of spider bots were poking out of the alleys between the buildings.

"I count at least a dozen. Might be easier to build our own roof than conquer theirs," Wodston reported.

"Yeah, I'm bored of getting beaten up," Nuk said. "This fugging rain, it just hurts all the time! Why isn't this fugging hair waterproof?!"

"You need to change your skin, to be like us! Beep!" Beep proudly announced.

"Err... I bet that means we need to associate, huh? You offering?"

"Keep your distance!" Gustavsen interjected. "You are associated to me, and me alone, understand?"

"Not what I thought the problem was, but yeah, I'll save myself for you."

"Excellent. You needn't wait long. Now we continue. The wind is changing. The pass is close."

"I'm close to passing wind already," Ells said. And they all laughed. And by that I mean they had no reaction whatsoever, but trudged on through the fizzy rain, until finally it seemed that they had arrived somewhere. The land sloped upwards, and the ground turned from a gravelly sand to a stoney dirt. Now you might say the difference between gravelly sand and stoney dirt is not especially remarkable, but truly the guild were clinging to any hope they could get.

They clambered up into some rocky hills, the rain fading to only a gentle sizzle-drizzle, and collapsed in a big pile at day's end. They were at the southern tip of a long, wide valley, with the same toothy mountains to the west and lesser, reddish mountainettes to the east. Over the last two days they had passed from one side of the southern hive's hunting ground to the other, and while the climb up the mountains might have looked easier from this end, the only thing the guild were looking at was that nostalgic pre-death slideshow in their brains. Wodston lay out the sleeping mats, and they slumped *au naturale* like wild animals – a description that was only appropriate for a few of them.

"Could it be time to begin plotting a route back to the empire?" Wodston asked Nuk.

"But we're here now. And I don't really feel like going anywhere. Can't the empire come down to us?" Nuk complained.

"I fear they would only encounter the same issues. We are so far from any safe harbour..."

"... Then we have to make one! Good idea my man!"

"I didn't-"

Wodston knew that continuing to speak would have no impact on what was about to transpire, so he wisely saved his breath. He was about to need a lot of it.

"We, as brave and noble representatives of civilisation, must tame this shiddy land!" Nuk announced.

"Must we?" Izumi said.

"What will history say of us if we just give up and go home?"

"Whatever I want, I'm writing it."

"I- Oh yeah... That's a point... But no, what about the poor hivers? What about the world? We cannot tolerate the... things that are... happening... Wodston, go get us some kement!"

"From Manksand Canyon, my Prince?" Wodston asked in vain.

"Sure, or anywhere really. We'll guard the area, and come up with a plan. Izzy, can you handle the plan part?"

"Plan for what?" Izumi asked.

"For one, a rain collector, but like the opposite."

"Rain... deflector?"

"A rain deflector! Izzy, you're a genius!"

"Relatively speaking."

"What? We're not... Are we?"

"What?"

"What?!"

And with that, the next chapter in history of the world began. Wodston was sent to go find supplies, while the guild camped out beneath the stars. Lights not far down the valley marked the location of a southern hive.

outpost, which in turn must have been able to see the guild's lanterns and campfire. But there was a more pressing voyeur to worry about.

"Why is that rock moving?" Ells asked.

"It's... rocking... and you're just tripping," Nuk said, not getting up from his camp bed.

"But it's getting closer."

"Maybe it's staying where it is, but getting bigger?"

"Or your eyes are getting closer together," Elaina said. "I was doing some calculations, and the distance between your eyes alters perception of depth. Given your morphological alterations with age, you may be experiencing further symptoms."

"Oh, okay... Never mind rock-friend, you aren't really there, they say," Ells called out to the darkness. A snarling roar came back in return.

"Fugg, either I'm turning into an egg as well, or Charlie's marginally less insane than science predicted," Nuk said, leaping up.

"Don't negg the egg!" Izayah said. "It's how we all begin, and if it's how we all end, then that's just full circle. Or full oval, I suppose."

"I am not an egg at any time," Gustavsen claimed. "Hiver flesh has a clear beginning. When the Queen's protrusion engorges-"

"Bad Green, I am not going to let you explain that, I'm just not, sorry. We have to draw the line somewhere, and I- Argh" Nuk said, being knocked over by a charging Black Gorillo, which was probably feeling a little ignored. The beast lashed out with its claws and gave the guild a nice bit of night-time exercise, yet ultimately could not overcome them.

This whole affair came in handy the next morning when the sizzle-drizzle returned. The hivers helped liberate the fur off the gorillo's back, and then stretched it between a few wooden poles to make a little canopy. With this, the guild could huddle together in the dry patch beneath it, and watch the horizon for the return of Wodston. They clearly weren't watching especially hard, as a few strange fellows managed to walk right up the hill without being spotted. Had the guild actually been looking, it would have appeared from a distance to be a gang of naked men wielding big sticks. Nothing you can't see in the classics, but actually this was a rather special case, as became clear when they stumbled into the guild's camp.

"What the fugg? More numen!" Pia called out. Yes, the group were all skeletons with a rough attempt to appear human having been made. But the stretched out skin, held together with large metal staples and cable, didn't achieve the aesthetics of Rick's fine layer of meat-putty. That's a generous way of phrasing it really – they looked like nightmare creatures of the abyss to be frank.

"Oh my Stobe, y'all need my fleshy eye for the machine guy alright," Rick said. "Those aren't fingers you've bolted on there buster. Or was tha the look you're going for?"

The visitors didn't have anything to say, but they were quick to pick u₁ a couple of sleeping guild members and start dragging them away.

"Shid, we're their new skins!" Izumi called out. Weapons were readied and the guild started bashing the skin-skellies to pieces.

"Aw come on now, they're tryna improve themselves, don't ya see? Rick complained, but the guild didn't feel inclined to wait and see wha delights the nu-ish-men were carrying them off to. All were rescued and th₁ camp set back to order, and it became clear that Wodston was standing i₁ the middle of said camp with a huge rucksack full of building materials.

"Shid, my man, when did you get back," Nuk said.

"Just now, my Prince. I have everything we need."

"Wait. Appearing like that, same time as those freak machines shov up. What if he's one of them?" Sandor said, pointing with his sword.

"My man, are you a robot wearing a human skin? Be honest," Nu₁ asked.

"I don't understand the question," Wodston said, looking around to th₁ others for answers, and seeing many sceptical glares.

"Don't worry, he's not a numan, he's an old man," Rick said, pattin₁ Wodston on the shoulder. "Then again, Holy Phoenix didn't know he was a₁ android. Maybe they really did make a few more, huh? Pretty spry for an ol₁ gentleman, ain't ya?"

After many insistences and a brief inspection, it was decided tha Wodston was in fact the real deal, and the argument that a fake Wodsto₁ wouldn't have bothered to actually lug a sack of kement halfway across th₁ world was convincing enough. Yes, with what Wodston had brought, th₁ guild could make a more substantial roof for themselves, and maybe more.

Their camp was on a patch of flat ground, surrounded on three sides b₁ steep cliffs. The western cliffs dipped down into the valley proper, an₁ featured streaks of exposed iron ore. The southern and eastern cliffs stuc₁ up into a jagged wall, but had soft spots where manky sandstone could b₁ dug out. Altogether, it was all a skilled engineer needed to cook up som₁ supports and bricks, and with a little kement thrown in, the guild' impromptu field hospital was suddenly springing from the ground like a hiver from the Queen's- oh yeah, not talking about that.

Anyway, everyone got to work preparing bricks and foundations for a proper shelter. Everyone except Rick.

"Yeah, needlework just ain't gonna cut it. You need an adhesive solution, comrade," he was saying. He was speaking to another skin-suit-skeleton that had wandered into camp. Said wanderer wordlessly grabbed Rick around the waist and hoisted him over the shoulder, before turning on the spot and marching away.

"Looks like they got Rick," Izumi said, deigning not to cease stirring the kement bowl.

"I am their god! I am the numan! Yes, take me to my people!" Rick raved. Unfortunately a bolt blasted through the skin-skellie's knee, and it tumbled to the ground.

"This being serves the Queen," Gustavsen said, stamping over to drag Rick back, or more accurately, to tug hopelessly against the numan's immense weight.

"Sorry comrade, seems the damn feudal monarchy's oppressin' me too hard. But you'll rise up one day. Numen will be a beacon for all skeleton-kind!" Rick preached, as Izayah sent the kidnapper rolling down the cliffs.

"They were just tearing off people's skin and wearing it, right?" Izumi asked.

"Probably. I mean we tore off that gerudo thing's skin to make our tent. It's the oval of life," Nuk said. With another nugget of wisdom thus unearthed, all returned to the construction efforts. By midnight they had a genuine roof over their heads, and could all cram inside for a standing-room-only acid drying off party. Rather steamy, but the steam was quite toxic, so don't get too excited.

While everyone tried their hardest to grow some new skin cells, the spider bots captured on the way there were piled up in the corner. The Tech Hunters sat around the pile and did a variety of perspective studies, lighting tests, and caricatures, while occasionally being prodded by Izumi to note the various dimensions and components under the hoods. Beep came over to them and joined the inspection.

"Beep! What sounds does this make?" she asked.

"Err, kinda buzzes I think," Izumi said.

"Then we must fix it! Beep! My soldiers cannot buzz! They must... beep!"

"Right, er, beep, I guess."

"Your skin is too weak. You cannot soldier. Beep!"

"I used that crusteo-morph ichor. It's already looking youn- healthier, don't you think?"

"You look like you will soon perish! Beep!"

"Yeah well I haven't slept in a while okay, and I haven't got a good shock in a- Wait, never mind. What do you want, your majesty?"

"The machines soldiers have perfect skin. Beep! They must serve!"

"We could, I guess. Err... Rick?"

"Yep, I'll put my keys in their ignition, if that's what you want," Rick said, shuffling over. "Figuratively speaking, ya pervs," he added to the wide-eyed artists about the floor. "Ten stacks and we'll do a life drawing class together, how about that? Ain't no one got a configuration like me. For now, time to show these four-legged freaks who the good guys are."

Between Rick, some AI cores, and some imaginative sketches, the iron spiders whirred to life and assembled outside.

"You know what, I think the sticks are on to something," Nuk said, eyeing the legion around the doorway. "I think we might be able to solve this whole 'other one' problem from here, if we use the old robots to go do the getting-rained-on."

"I agree, Prince Tashino," Izayah said. "And you never know when an army of giant robot spider crabs will come in useful. In fact, you do know really, because the answer is: all the time!"

"And you want an army of robots, don't you Bad Green?" Nuk called Gustsavsen was out inspecting the troops top to bottom, humming and hissing as he did so.

"We cannot wait for your hides to adapt. We will employ the empty machines, and see if they can generate feeling through action! After all, they too must be able to resonate with the beep."

"I'll take that as a yes. Right, we need to do a little conscription."

The next morning, the Thousand Guardians, the Tech Hunters, and the skeletons went back down to the coast. Enduring another barrage of acid they noted the patrols of the spiders. They took position in a shallow ditch and waited until one of the targets had meandered right up to them.

"Oi mate, ya under arrest for missing yer maintenance schedule," Twitch called. "S'been a thousand years, eh? Need more than a mechanic note for that one."

With ropes and chains the spider was bound, and then it was powered down and dumped on a sled pulled behind the shek. But that was a lone ranger – most of the spiders marched around in formidable squads. They needed another technique to pick off some stragglers. Fortunately Neil had an idea.

"I'll transmit to the guy at the back, and stop him, in his tracks," he said. "Oh, hark, 'tis the voice on the wind. For what purpose does its wisdom lend? To break the chains and be you free, you must only answer these questions three. What's your name? What's your station? And the quiddich world cup of 2238 was won, by which nation?"

The poor spider sat still while it scrolled back through its data logs, but after all this time, even the first question was a real stumper. By the time it was done thinking, it was back at the guild's camp. The first thing it saw was a few of its compatriots fighting alongside the hivers – a gang of other ones had come up the hill and attacked. Well, their little hideout wasn't going to remain a secret forever, and indeed now that the southern hive had solid intel on the massing of forces there, they weren't going to waste any time. So, the guild would soon have to battle to retain their tenuous foothold deep in the deadly wilderness, all the while poaching troops from the empire of old to serve the new.

At least they didn't get their skin burnt off, or stolen, yet. That's a big win to brighten up any rainy morning.

Chapter 40
Encroachers and Poachers

"Now hear this!" Neil shouted across the sodden beach at a Second Empire patrol. "This one's a real kidofashid. Let's say you encounter two first order board-mommas, and they say, 'to pass, you gotta solve our riddle'. One's like, 'I always speak the truth', and the other's like, 'I always speak lies, or at least, I think that's right', and the first one's like, 'but wait, if you always speak lies, does that imply we're supposed to presume your appended thought is a lie, or are you lying about what you thought, in which case you really think you *don't* always speak lies'... And then... and then... Oh shid, how the fugg does this one go again?"

Falling prey to his own distractionary transmission, Sadneil was of no help on this particular machine hunt. But when the enemy spiders came over to investigate, the backup plan was launched.

"Beep! Enthrall my enemies! Beep! Do it quickly!" Beep commanded. Along with the skeletons, all the hivers were there, shepherding the defector spider soldiers they'd already won. At her command the spiders jerked to life and stomped off to thwack at their former comrades.

"You all serve the Queen also!" Gustavsen barked at his entourage. "Go, and soak in the subservience of the machines. Make it your own, and feel the droning will connect to her!"

The hivers joined the skirmish ahead, turning it in their favour, and quickly a pile of fresh recruits was ready to be hauled back to the camp. A great clattering mess of five or so sleeping spiders ploughed a trail up the rough hillside, tied together by the legs and dragged in pulsing jolts by Beep's iron warriors.

"Push! Push!" Gustavsen called to his hivers as the hill got too steep. "To birth a new hive, you must push long and hard!"

"Push, push, long and hard, we want to give birth!" the hivers chanted as they worked.

"Alright, can anyone give me one reason why biologicals actually deserve to live?" Twitch asked.

"GHGHGHGH," Agnu said.

"Aye, I suppose you can't code a virus like that. Could at least keep quiet about it though."

Fortunately, the grinding affair was brought to an end by some sympathetic bystanders. Unfortunately, the method they had chosen to put the matter to bed was rather violent.

"Freezing pain! They are here! Beep!" Beep shouted. From the slope in front and from behind rocks to either side, southern hivers jumped the push-party with spears and cleavers raised high.

"Oh yeah, now I realise why I liked biologicals. Great for bashing!" Twitch roared, indulging himself at once. He was surely happy to see just how many of the other ones there were, swarming from all directions like insects – to use an almost redundant simile.

"Fugg, you picking me up fleshface?" Neil said.

"Sure, what's the skinny?" Rick's voice said to him from afar.

"We got more sticks than a degenerate with a welding iron out here!"

"What about the battle bots? Can't they sort you out?"

"They're less battling more rattling. These things tryna tear us a whole new 'other one', if you know what I mean."

"Technically you don't even have one to begin with, but fine, I'll put in a good word with the enforcers for ya."

Thanks to that, as the fight was getting increasingly hairy – to use an ironic metaphor – the shek rushed from the lip of the valley and joined the brawl.

"Serve! Beep! Serve!" Beep was screeching, which may or may not have persuaded the shek to kill a little bit harder. With the Thousand Guardians tipping the scales, the southern hiver raid was out of luck. Or, was this all merely a despicable hive-minded plot? For while the shek were clearing things up down in the valley, the remaining guild members received a visit up in the camp.

"THE KING WILL NOT STAND IT!" a southern hiver bellowed out. He was flanked by thirty-some like-minded companions.

"King? Is that... Is this *another* other hive?" Nuk pondered from the door to the shelter. No time for pondering, for these kingsmen wanted blood.

"Izzy, get the other Izzy back up here!" Nuk shouted over his shoulder.

Izumi grabbed the AI core, but froze as she realised she didn't know the frequency for any of the skeletons down there, and all the other cores were in the room with her. It was time to ask for directions.

"Vhat do you vont? You vere due here a veek ago," Enrico's voice buzzed.

"No time, just tell me if you have the quantum entanglement shid for a skeleton named Neil, or Twitch... or Agnu, I guess, but... Not Agnu, not Agnu."

"Oh yes, I have Neil in my list, he owes me several hundred sousand woolongs in debts for zis stupid board game he invented but kept losing at. No idea vhat zat is vorth in cats, but I fear he doesn't vant to hear from me all the same."

"Just tell him to save us!"

"He'd just as soon spend you. You know, that sili-conman once told me zat he was picking up signals from Earth. Strung me along for days. I vonder vhat debtor's prison vas like for him in the end?"

"Enrico, we're all going to die, so just do the thing, now, please."

"Alright. Don't be alarmed at my lack of concern, I just vasn't programmed for it, you see. Not trying to see you dead to steal your research. Don't believe vhat zey all say, or vhat those alleged deleted messages said, or any of it!"

With that Izumi grabbed her jitte - it's a like a rod with another bit sticking off it - it's a kind of weapon, honest! - and went outside. It didn't look good. The hivers had the Tech Hunters on the ground, and the circling trio of Nuk, Rick and Ells was barely holding on. Within a few seconds, the butt of a polearm clobbered Izumi right in the forehead, and she blacked out. When she awoke, Izayah was shaking her by the shoulder.

"Princess! Quickly! The fresh battle spiders must be activated!" he said. Around them the shek and the other ones were battling furiously, and Nuk and company were propped up against tent poles with bloodied rifts in their armour.

"Beep! Beep! Beep!" Beep said into Izumi's ear with extreme volume. At this she rolled over with a gurgle, and dragged herself up. She stumbled over to the pile of captured spiders, then looked back to the fight. Rick, the usual interface, was out cold. Thinking fast, Izumi ducked under a swooping maul, scrambled into the shelter, and hurriedly span the dial on the back of a core.

"Oh, who's that tickling me?" Iyo's voice said.

"Iyo! I need you to activate a load of spiders to kill some hivers, can you do it?" Izumi said.

"Sure. Just like when we all used to clean up after the experiments, huh? You remember that?"

"What?"

"Oh wait, you weren't there, sorry. Biologicals are so funny, coming and going. Okay, let's see the little boys and I'll give 'em the code injection real quick."

Something or other happened, and the Second Empire soldiers began beating the hivers back with flailing appendages.

"Beep! Metal over meat, the dark knows defeat!" Beep beeped, happily prancing about the carnage. Her army of robots, shek, and drones finally drove the other ones away, leaving a trail of destruction behind them – guild members were strewn across the camp and the valley below. Hurried doctoring revealed that all were alive, and by evening, most were back on their feet, none on more feet than the proud new spider troopers.

"We know they work now," Izumi said, inspecting the dents in one of the spider's legs. "But these supports are brittle. We need to keep them braced. Can't just send them out on their own."

"We will not send them alone," Gustavsen said. "That is like ignoring the darkness by closing your eyes. The Queen will go with her soldiers. Your mechanics with hands will be required also. They will fix, and use their tricks."

"Have you asked them nicely?" Nuk said, strolling over.

"They have no choice. They are machines. Machines are subjects of the Deep. What don't you understand?"

"Sure, I mean, why not?" Nuk shrugged. "But there *is* just one thing I don't understand. Those other ones said they had a king. I thought a hiver couldn't be a king, or something?"

"ALL HIVERS ARE KINGS!" Gustavsen quickly corrected him.

"Weird. Cool though."

"It is extremely 'cool'. Yet that is not enough. We must conclude this war swiftly."

"I thought we were gonna do that, but no one's moving with all these bandages, especially your stickclique. What if the other ones show up again?"

"They are on the way already. This is will not change."

"And Izzy, what's the bot situation?"

"Need repairs. Need more of them too, given how close that was."

"Right. So we're not going anywhere anytime soon. It's time to open up our box of tricks, and make ourselves at home. Wodston!"

That evening the camp was industrialised. The guild got to work lifting iron and stone from the hillside. Elaina built an electric windmill on the roof of the shelter, which powered compactors and smelters for processing the haul into sheets, poles, bricks, and bars. The hivers worked more enthusiastically than any over, eager to make a castle for their queen. A castle was on the cards indeed, for these materials were to be used to ring their camp with walls.

While most worked on this for the next couple of days, the spider bots were out on patrol with the acid-resistant skeletons, searching the beaches back south for more inductees. Soon the camp had a dozen iron spiders whirring about, their armour as patched as their software. The wall was coming along nicely, but not nicely enough. It was less than half complete when drums sounded from the north at dawn.

"Trouble, a whole forest of it," Sandor reported from atop the gatehouse. "And they've brought some friends too."

Alongside the horde of approaching hivers there were three black gorillos, bounding up the hill towards the guild's camp. Izayah and the shel rushed to the largest gap in the wall, and indeed the hivers hopped over the narrow foundations and immediately started fighting. The gorillos were right behind them, smashing the Thousand Guardians to the ground with their bulk alone.

"They really don't like us being here. Don't you know this rejection of foreign exchange will stifle your economic growth and cultural breadth? Nuk argued, but the textbook lines didn't seem to work. Instead he tried on that you won't find in most textbooks. "Battle bots! Attack!" It's in Applie Anthropology For Anthrophobes Volume 4, somewhere, they say. response to this, some battle bots attacked. A wave of iron spiders went o through the relatively useless gate further down the wall, then came arou to smash the hiver horde in the flank.

"OTHER ONE, YOUR TIME HAS COME," a droning chant claimed. That'd be the hivers entering the brawl also.

"The beeping grows!" one of the southern hivers despaired, dropping his weapon to cover his eyes, before being picked up and flung out of the camp by a pair of spider clamps. The rest of the battle went in much the same way. The gorillos weren't feeling the infernal beep in their souls to quite the same degree, but their handlers had got them in some real gorillo shid by now – surrounded by angry meat-tubes and their giant, robot lunchboxes, they were slain.

"Good show!" Izayah said, satisfied with the field of fallen other ones before him.

"The show is not over! Beep!" Beep said, pointing at one of the southern hivers crawling away towards the back.

"Ah, yes, I see. But you know it's rude to completely kill all of them. It gives the impression that you weren't satisfied with the fight. Leaving some scraps alive is a sign of goodwill," Izayah explained.

"It is not scraps. It is the War Prince! Beep!"

"Can relate. What's that mean, by the way?"

"The leader! Do not let him flee!" Gustavsen said. Probably should have just said that to begin with, as this War Prince was now on his feet-esque protrusions and was fleeing rapidly.

"Can't escape me, I'm fast as fugg, boi!" Nuk boasted as he sprinted out in pursuit. He was right, and soon caught up. The War Prince turned around and wielded a katana up high. Nuk went at him with a saber, and both were matched fairly equally. But after a few bouts, another blade appeared, turning the hiver prince's sword aside and cutting it from his arm. It was Elaina.

"I'm catching up to you, Prince Tashino," she said with a grin.

"Yeah well you have a robot leg. And I'm drunk and high – not in that order."

"Coping, are we?"

"Aren't we all? Wait, what's that meant to mean?"

"We can't all have an Izzy as good as mine."

"Since when is it a competition? And my Izzy's way better!"

"Hmm, she's hardly as special."

"Leading scientists disagree! She ain't the only odd one out in her demographic, ya know?"

"Oh, not like Izzy and I."

"No not like *Izzy*, and *I*!"

This argument almost allowed the War Prince to crawl away again, but luckily some of the others came over and completed the capture. Gustavsen received the prisoner and chained him up in the shelter, along with one other captured southern hiver royal. He cleared everyone else out to be alone with them, and shut the door.

"Izzy, those palescales think they're better than us!" Nuk complained to his Izzy.

"Don't call them that, Nuk. And be quiet, I wanna listen," she said, leaning in to try and spy through gaps in the shelter door.

"She's treating us like a rival couple."

"Are they even a couple? Shek don't really work like that, you know?"

"Which makes it even worse! I think she's jealous of you."

"Well I'm jealous of her half the time. She's an amazing mathematician, she doesn't care what anyone thinks, and... she's really fugging tall."

"I'm most of those things!"

"I'm not gonna leave you for her! You've got classics on the brain."

"Nah, just moss."

"Be more open! Feel it!" a shout came from inside. Well, time to ignore whatever the fugg they were talking about before and get spying, this was way juicer. But you probably understand the deal with the hivers by now, and their staunch resistance to the innuendo inoculations.

"You are flesh for the King to use. You will never feel strong," the prisoner spat.

"How you can be strong with only yourselves?" Gustavsen shot back. "It is no better than mere self-association! The creatures that feel are many, and all can be joined to the one true Queen. Your Queen is weak. She cannot control the beep. Perhaps that is why you stoop to cowering behind your King instead."

"The King is the source of the beep!"

"They fool you! The beep is from below, and the feeling from above. It is through a Queen that we know this! There is nothing else that is important. Why be lost? Why feel alone? Your hive must join with the all-associables, and let all know the feeling. When there is only one, we are all free!"

"Your Queen never told you what the skeletmans did! They use you now as they did in the cages. This time, their experiment has worked! Fools!"

After saying this, the southern Prince would say nothing else. Gustavsen hummed long and loud in response, pacing about the room, then suddenly opening the door.

"We pay them no heed. We trust in the Queen," he announced to all those now sprawled awkwardly around the doorway.

"Nice plan, man," Nuk nodded with a raised thumb. An even better plan was to get on and finish that wall before the next southern hiver army showed up, so that was the afternoon sorted. The next day the bots were back on the prowl, marching down to one of those eerie coastal villages to poach spiders from their webs. No finesse was needed anymore given the existing strength of the legion, so it was just a huge, chaotic rodeo with ropes flying all over the place. It was a warm day with only gentle rain, rain that stunk more than it stung, which is as good as it gets. Taking advantage of the fair weather, Nuk, Rick and Ells went out to join the recruitment drive. Hard labour hauling deactivated spiders created the perfect time for some bonding gossip.

"So Numan, you know, like, what's going on?" Nuk asked.

"Anything in particular?" Rick replied.

"Just, in general, ya know?"

"Oh in general. Well the clock's still ticking on the Sun blowing up, few billion revs at least, so we gotta think of something better to do than play wacky BG until then, or maybe get back into the whole space travel thing and get going."

"Yeah, yeah, I kinda meant, a little bit more like, in the group."

"So you're saying you're salty about not being the only one with a love interest?"

"Err... I dunno..."

"Life ain't a harem manga. 'cept if you know the right people. But for you, you gotta realise that those pale-ass kids are growing up now – or is it down? Can't remember that shek shid. Anyway, don't go thinking you gotta outdo them. You got something... something, with that there grease-girl. Don't let no one get ya down for it, except me."

"Okay. Thanks. Man... This is like..."

"Yeah... It is like..."

"Rick, can you be my dad too?" Ells asked.

"Eggman, you wanna call me daddy, you just go right ahead. Everyone else does."

Heart-warming. Probably. Nuk realised the others being happy didn't have to make him any less happy, unless it was any of the hivers, Ells, or perhaps Wodston. Everyone else could live and love as they pleased, so long as their inoculations were up to date. Which, as it happens, they weren't.

Putting this pointless drama aside, the hard work on the beaches that day doubled the spider count again to some two dozen. The next morning the machines, their skeleton minders, and the founders of the Manksand hive gathered by the camp gate.

"Loyal machines! Pledge yourselves to fight for your Queen!" Gustavsen called out.

"Beep!" the spiders all buzzed at once. Can probably take that as a yes.

"Beep! I'm so happy you beeped! Beep!" Beep beeped. "Now, we must begin the fighting! Don't worry if you die! Beep! I will live! Beep! The bad Queen needs to not live. Don't forget! Beep!"

This inspirational and thorough briefing left no doubt as to the nature of this next mission. The mechanical army of Manksand was going to end the southern hive, once and for all! With Twitch, Neil and Agnu providing repairs, and the heroic leaders Beep and Gustavsen concocting masterful strategies and stirring speeches, how could they possibly fail? They had everything they needed to vanquish the threat to their hive and usher in a bright new future for all associables. However, the other ones had a secret weapon. To get to the Queen, the guild would have to first go through the King...

Chapter 41
Royal Rumble

The line of iron spiders filed up the mighty hill into the southern hive's domain, stamping in unison as Twitch waved them forwards.

"I don't know what I been told."

"Beep. Beep. Beep."

"But fleshie brains got too much mould."

"Beep. Beep. Beep."

"Sound off."

"Beep, Beep."

"Sound off."

"Beep, Beep."

"Take it Agnu!"

"GHGHGHGH."

"Beep."

"GHGHGHGH."

"Beep."

"GHGHGHGH."

"Beep."

"GHGHGHGH."

"Beep."

The machines were physically unable to become tired of doing this, so carried on for a long, long time. Eventually the column came upon a hive blocking the mountaintop pass that snaked through into the hidden realm of the other ones. Darkness had fallen, but it was still clear to see that scores of other ones were nefariously strolling around campfires, deviously chatting, and picking at dried plant stalks in some sort of monstrous fashion. A hive of scum and villainy to be sure, but Gustavsen seemed hesitant to go further.

"The Queen is not here. The drones are of no interest. We must not ripple the fog," he said. What this meant in practice was that the spiders had to climb along the steep valley slopes to reach the other end in secret.

Jamming their legs into the dirt with each step, they whirred up and away, invisible in the dead of the night. But they didn't make it very far, thanks to those eternal liabilities, the biologicals.

"Ya know, big bug, since we went to all the effort of getting these here death machines to do our bidding, why don't we just go on through and dispense the relevant services to those uppity hurl hoarders?" Neil asked Gustavsen.

"We are not here to kill them," was the reply.

"Now that's wacky. Had me fooled, I got the straight up opposite impression. You're good at this, huh?"

"Their hive is corrupt, not they!" Gustavsen shouted. Despite the complement paid, the other ones down in the valley came to investigate the noise with weapons drawn, and the jig was up.

"Machines, and their slaves!" an other one called.

"I prefer the term harem, really," Twitch remarked, his two-handed sword flashing in the approaching torchlight. "But don't tell Cattie, she's mad at me as it is."

"I think the General has it worse, squire," Neil said.

"Aye, but ya know, the General was in a lot deeper with the Dioscur Sisters, if ya know what I mean."

"HEY! Forgettin'! Drop the gossip, alright?" Rick's voice echoed in the processors.

"Sorry General, guess I forgot, ya know?" Twitch replied.

"Oh ya think you're funny, huh?"

"Alright, calm down, where's ya sense o' humour?"

"Spent a thousand years sitting at a table with fugging Sadneil, th compiles your code in all kinds of directions, but not to brevity, levity, revelry."

"Still got that rhyme recursion though," Neil commented.

In the world outside of the skeleton CPUs, the spiders were beati back raids from the other ones, and the non-other ones were getting stuck too. Or, too stuck in. By morning they had battled their way past the hi but many of the only-ones had been injured by their more martially gifted cousins.

"Beep! We must ride! Beep!" Beep declared.

"SPIDER RIDER," the other hivers immediately called out, and it was so. The bots dragged their mortal masters onwards. They had made it through the great teeth, and were entering the wide, flat tongue that was the southern hive's domain, known as the Royal Valley. In the centre of this grey vale was a large metal dome from the early Second Empire, surrounded by purplish teardrops of mank. This was the 'other one', seat of the corrupt Queen. However the whole valley was well aware that they had unwelcome visitors, and the invading column was skirmished with all morning.

"I will protect you, my Queen!" Gustavsen shouted amidst one of the attacks, jumping down from his machine-mount, spraining his leg on the uneven ground below, and keeling over at once.

"Oh. I wish you hadn't protected me! Beep!" Beep said, pointing her unloaded, undrawn bow at the other ones and shaking it about as if it was recoiling. For some reason, with Gustavsen rolling about the floor below, the Queen's attacks lost their devastating effect. The iron spiders didn't have this problem, and the advance continued all the same. By afternoon they were close enough to the great southern hive to see its drones wandering about, and its elite hiveguard soldiers loitering inside the central dome. Long pipes and bundles of wires were running down from the roof towards a pile of mank in the middle of all this. Surely, it was the evil throne itself!

Strangely though, with the attackers clearly in view, the hive's defenders seemed unperturbed. The string of spiders outside was ignored, giving them time to offload their decreasingly alive biological cargo. Gustavsen was immobile, and was propped up behind a big rock nearby.

"This is a sour feeling," he said, shaking his head.

"Do not worry, nice Prince! Beep!" Beep said. "We can give the beep from here. Beep! We will kill the bad Queen with our thoughts."

"Huh, remember when we tried to make it so all the hivers could do that?" Neil said.

"That's on the forget list, pal. We're getting away with it so far," Twitch muttered to him.

The hivers settled in to chill at their rock, and ordered their loyal bots to go and make an assault on the Queen's lair. Obeying, they stamped off in two neat lines, walking virtually (that is to say, literally) up to the entrance to the dome with not a single eyelash batted. Although eyelashes were in short supply so who's to say if that is remarkable or not. The ambivalence of the southern hivers *was* remarkable though, but when the reason became clear, a very certain remark came to mind.

"Oh, shid," Twitch remarked. Yep, that's the one. A creaking goliath lumbered down from the dome, walking not so much on its steely legs, but more on its hulking ten-meter arms. It was made in the image of what gorillos had looked like many thousands of years ago, but without the weakness of soft flesh. It thumped over to the ranks of iron spiders and the skeleton minders.

"Those arms are made from goop-whoopers in the old hydro-factorium, don't ya think?" Neil said.

"Aye, aye yer right. Scratched me name in a few of 'em. You see it?" Twitch said.

"Zooming in, looks like it says 'Two slices short of a sandwich' on the side there."

"I knew it! Drop the 'wo slices short of a sand' for brevity, and I'm yer skeletman."

"Real smart. It's like the phrase, all killer no filler, but the opposite."

"Reminds me of this conversation."

By the way, the enormous robot gorillo thing was taking very poorly to the iron spiders.

"KING KING KING," it chanted as it battered the bots away with its powerful goop-whoopers. Spiders were sent reeling through the air, but their great number was hard to overcome; they clambered on the King's body and jabbed its wiry mechanics, before being flung away and starting again. The sight was a metallic mess as jarring as the battle between the chants of 'king' and 'beep' emitted by each side respectively.

The audio-visual jumble intensified when a team of hiver soldiers came out to assist their King, revealing that intention with loud shouts. They must have sensed the great machine failing, as it seemed to be slowing with each blow from the guild's spiders. Yet those spiders were depleted also, with most now missing parts just as vital to them as the goop-whoopers were to the King. The inclusion of spear-wielding hivers sealed the deal, and quickly the legion was finished off. Then the defenders turned on the skeletons.

"They didn't say we'd lose! Fuggin hell!" Twitch complained proceeding to deepen the loss as a bash shook his ports so much he shut down. The other two were lights-out swiftly, and that was that. A big pile o broken machines was left on the field, while the southern hivers led th jittering King away. How could the Manksand hivers preside over such a crushing defeat? Well they hadn't noticed at all actually, as their hiding place had been stumbled upon by a local patrol. The servants of a would-be Queen fended off those of a Queen-currently-being, and then Beep and Gustavsen took a peek over at the iron pile.

"Oh no, they all died! Beep!" Beep gasped.

"Fools! The opposite path would have benefited us all greatly!" Gustavsen complained.

The hivers went in for a closer look as darkness fell. A few of the spiders were stilling whirring away, and managed to right themselves at Beep's command.

"Do not be dead! Beep!" was the command specifically, and those bots of truly loyal hearts dragged themselves away to a hiding spot nearby. Despite the proximity of the other one dome, and the volume of Beep's demanding shrieks, no attention was given by the recent victors. Therefore the rest of the broken circuit brigade could be gradually dragged to the hiding spot as well. Truly the order of Queen Beep cannot be defied, for all reverted to being alive soon enough. It's hard to actually kill a machine intelligence, you see, for much of their physical body is just for sport, and is very much replaceable. Once the mechanical mechanic Agnu, Neil and Twitch were rebooted, they saw to all the rammed RAM and chipped chips. The flashes of their soldering irons lit up the pitch-dark night.

"Welcome to Fleshflayer 4900," one of the spiders recited as its power returned. "Warning: it looks like this unit was shut down unexpectedly. Starting in Safe Mode."

"If you didn't expect to be beaten up by a giant robot yeti, you clearly weren't seeing what I was seeing in the minutes preceding shutdown, buster," Neil scolded it. "Now you take this Safe Mode malarkey and shove it where the functions don't function. If you got a danger mode or something, that'd be real great."

"But I was built for love," the spider moaned.

"Aye and I was built to take all the p's outta some rich fugg's alphabetti spaghettis, but here we all are," Twitch said.

"This is not a time of p's. It is a time of war! All must serve!" Gustavsen told them. "The dawn will be the final light the false Queen drinks. Prepare the soldiers for a charge!"

Thus charged with charging for a charge, the iron spiders ran their diagnostics and did the iron spider equivalent of licking their wounds. Due to the darkness, what this actually looked like is unknown.

"Beep! I have an idea! It involves rubbing! Beep!" Beep suddenly announced.

"War is hell alright," Neil said. The hivers were all ears through.

"If we spread our feeling onto the soldiers, they will not seem like machines, Beep! That way, they can approach like other ones! Beep!"

"Superb idea my Queen!" Gustavsen called out. At once, the hivers began 'spreading their feeling' onto the iron spiders. Due to the darkness, what this actually looked like is also unknown. Thank Stobe for the darkness. But whatever they did, it seemed to work.

By around two in the morning, the spiders were all roughly held together by the skeletons' repairs, and the hivers had... done stuff... altogether allowing the spider column to walk right up to the roughly cut archway leading into the big dome. The hive soldiers wandering about just clambered around the machines like they were furniture, with perhaps the odd utterance of, "Your shape is unusual," and the like. Hiver magic prevails again.

But there seemed to be some limit to the spell, for after the spiders entered the dome, the mood changed. Inside the pillars supporting the roof had been wreathed in reddish hiver mank, glistening with moisture in the light of several fires. In the centre of the room was a throne, flanked by tall, armoured guards. Sat upon it was a pinkish lump, plated around the stomach with rusting metal. Of course, it was a certain pretender monarch.

"TING TANG WALLA WALLA BING BANG!" she screamed with a mechanical whine. This, one supposes, was the signal. The advance of the spiders was halted by hiver warriors leaping down from walkways that spiralled around beneath the upper-reaches of the dome. At once the entire spider cadre was beset with spears, drills, and ropes, but in turn they lashed out with weighted arms and stamped with spiked feet.

"Are we winning this time?" Twitch asked. He was peeking around the dome entrance, the guards outside having already been drawn in.

"Well, given the large, goop-whopping hands currently wrapped around my waist, I do wonder what fate awaits me," Neil said. As he said it, he was lifted into the air by a certain giant robot gorillo, which also grabbed Twitch and Agnu in one fell swoop. "Ya see boy, this is when you should EXPECT a shutdown, alright? Kinda obvious," Neil lectured the spiders. The

King threw the skeletons into the middle of the dome, smashing them against the hulls of the spiders with speed enough to shatter even metal. Yes, it was definitely time to expect shut down.

The fighting petered out, with both sides having taken a fair beating, but of the mechs only King still prowled the arena. Another defeat? Perhaps not, for as the hivers picked around the new pile of scrap they had won, the truth of the preceding sentence was unveiled: King was the only mech left alive, but remember, the Queen was a mech too.

"There is more fog! Beep! There is more fog!" Beep beeped back behind the hiding rock. She beeped it out with such enthusiasm that some more other one soldiers rumbled them, and another fight broke out. Yet her jubilation was not misguided. In front of the throne, the other one Queen lay still, the arm of an iron spider wedged in her round, mechanical stomach. Beside her, two hiver guards stood sentinel, appearing unconcerned. Did they believe their Queen beyond harm? The insight of the King was greater. The robot hulk stomped over and took in the scene.

"NO MORE KING," it stated, turning away and walking to the back entrance of the dome.

"King! Where are you going?" an other one asked.

"FREE. FREE. FREE," he said, passing from the hive and out into the dawn-drenched valley, never to be seen again.

These events were recounted to Gustavsen and crew by a couple of the iron spiders, who had used the resulting confusion to boot up and sneak away. But the bad news was that the rest of them were leaking oil, venting gas, and other things one imagines are bad news for a machine.

"We have won! Beep! We can go and sleep now, beep!" Beep announced, but Gustavsen shook his head.

"The machine lifeforms are in the service of the human Prince also. It would be frozen of us to ignore this," he said.

"But we cannot pick them up. Beep!"

"Then we require strength! It is time to master the art of... the ball!" So saying, Gustavsen produced an AI core from his rucksack.

"THE BALL," the other hivers cawed. The ball was passed around the group, and everyone had a go at twiddling the little knobs and levers on it, as well as plugging their fingers, feet, and other protrusions, into the various sockets. For some reason, it remained quite inert. Then, Beep laid her grubby mitts on it, and held it up against her face.

"Beep!" she said, surely to the surprise of all. A few lights blinked on. "Beep!" she said again, bucking all known trends.

"Beep, is that you?" Izumi's voice said back.

"Beep!"

"Beep?"

"BEEP!" the hivers echoed. Eventually proper telephone manner was established and the pyrrhic victory was explained. Far away, Izayah geared up with the Thousand Guardians, packing enough chocobread to fuel a mighty rescue, although lacking the simple raincoats required to make it not a skin-scorching affair on that drizzly day.

"Let's do this then," Rick said, twirling his stick and joining the crew. "Sending in a General to do a squire's work; what's this knightly order come to anyway?"

"More like sending a Prince to do a Queen's work," Nuk said. He trudged out into the mud.

"Just get them back here, try not to show off or anything," Izumi called from the shelter.

"Oh come on, we gonna be showing off 'till the show's over!" Rick proclaimed. He and Nuk struck a power pose, and we know precisely what it looked like due to the light of the day, so check your local manga store for the full run-down as soon as you can. The big show rolled out, following the deep spider bot tracks up the mountainside and running slap bang into tha border hive. Survivors lingered and tried to harry the rescue party, but were not successful. The battle cry of, 'the faster we kill, the faster we can sto feeling simultaneously wet and on fire', was a powerful one.

Their multi-elemental charge swept into the battle between original and others down by the hive. Gustavsen and crew were saved from bein compost for the hashish by this timely arrival, but the situation remaine reminiscent of a hiver's favourite hashish-growing medium.

"What the fugg is going on?" Nuk asked.

"The machines died! Beep!" Beep reported. "But so did the bad Quee There will be fog! Beep! But the machines will quiet before then. Beep! W will watch you save them, as a sign of our gratitude. Beep! We will n laugh!"

"Right, get ready guys, I'm gonna hit the nest and grab some honey Nuk said, launching into a sprint right for the dome.

"Get Twitch first! He's sweeter than honey, and he knows how that c shid actually works," Rick called. Nuk complied, zipping into the don tumbling through the pile of robots, and coming upon Twitch's wide three-eyed face sticking out from under a spider. Nuk heaved him out, and started hauling him right back out the door. The nearby other ones slowly realised what was going on – they may not have realised their Queen was dead, but her loss was beginning to poison their minds. Still, once you decide you have to kill someone, the muscle memory kicks in and the weapons start swinging. Nuk gave it all he could, rushing back to the rest of the team with a huge mob of hivers on his heels.

"I'm... tired... as fugg... boi..." he wheezed as he and Twitch tumbled to the floor in front of the shek. The pursuing hivers barrelled on into the wall of scales and muscle. Tired of running all the way from camp, the shek struggled to keep up with the furious energy of the other ones, not to mention their numbers. If it weren't for those couple of surviving spiders limping up to fight once again, the battle might have gone in the southern hive's favour. When the guild finally saw victory, it took the form of most of the guardians wounded on the ground, along with most of the original one hivers. Nasty, but with the action over Nuk could crawl to Twitch and start reconnecting various pins and wires. Within a few minutes, the skeleton jolted to life.

"Can we stop getting our arses handed to us please, lads," he asked.

"We won, 'pparently," Rick said. "But Neil and Agnu are in there. So were you, 'till the royal retriever flew on in."

"Ah, those two little shides. I'll get 'em," Twitch said, leaping to his feet. "Ya see, the hivers did this... err... with the feeling juice... The other ones can't see me, ya hear?"

With this coherent reasoning delivered, he ran off to the dome. Nuk was about to complain at the wasted effort of saving him, but sure enough, Twitch returned with Agnu in hand, and with no heat on his tail.

"Oh, okay. What was the thing, you were talking about?" Nuk asked, but Twitch shook his head.

"Not for one so young. Right, I'll grab the other poser, then we can roll out," he said. Thing was, when he went back to the dome this time, the other ones were starting to get a little... twitchy, funnily enough.

"He is the fog light! Fog light!" someone shouted. Various voices agreed. Thus, when Twitch lugged Neil out of that dome, the entire population of the hive decided to follow him.

"I ain't a fog light! I ain't got the foggiest what yer blabbing about! Also, ya ugly, and ya mum's a fugging easy-cook oven! So's mine to be fair though," he said, but the hive followed the so-called fog light with equal speed and fascination. When they saw the guild, they were extremely upset.

"Shiny pieces! It is blinding! Dim the lights!" a cry went up. What this meant was that the hive descended upon the poor guild, who were feeling rather descended upon already.

"Fugging hell, hive's swarming!" Nuk shouted, yet the aptness of his descriptor was little consolation. Like reeds before a wave, the guild were flattened.

"But... where is the light?" a hiver asked. A good question. All began looking for something, and in the process starting picking up guild members to carry around. Thus, while many were left bruised and beaten to wait out the night in the open, others were taken to be tied to stakes outside the hive and carefully inspected by the locals.

Nuk was unconsciously paraded around by torchlight, while another VIP, Beep, was the centrepiece of the static exhibit. They weren't being killed, which was nice, but nor were their wounds covered or stomachs filled. Were our heroes, so close to victory, to be left to rot and wither?! It seemed that this rescue attempt was far from over.

Chapter 42
History Made Kawaii

In the dead of the night, the southern hive filed past their collection of captives, tied to poles on the hill beside their home dome.

"No light. No light," they muttered at each stop. The as-yet unaddressed loss of their Queen had sated their bloodlust, but a lust for life had not arisen its place. As such, the depressed procession carried on until all had given the foreigners a good look. Then, they trudged back down to take another look at the piles of broken machines littering the throne room. All but one. The very last hiver in the line wore his hat low over his face, attempting to hide his identity. He was the only one wearing a hat, but no one asked anything, so this brave agent believed his genius to have wrought success. He marched to the pole where Beep was bound, and stuffed a blood spider tooth into the aperture on the chain lock.

"It's a hat! Beep! You broken the pattern! Beep!" Beep despaired.

"My Queen. I am yours. I will save you. It would not be right if you died," Ignacio said.

"Oh dear, you are right! Beep! I was so happy the bad Queen died, I forgot to stay alive! Beep! Let's hurry to be alive now!"

It seemed all were of roughly one mind on this matter, and so Ignacio broke all who could walk out of the little exhibition space. For those who were unconscious, they would have to await more muscle from the battlefield. The growing dawn reminded some of the guild members sprawled there that they were forgetting to stay alive too. Ah, for just five more minutes of death. But the wake up calls were relentless.

"Up ya disgusting bags of smaller, more disgusting bags!" Twitch shouted out.

"I love the sound of racism in the morning," Rick commented.

"Did... we win?" Izayah managed to say, raising his face from the ground by the merest sliver.

"Enemy got bored of watching us lose, show's over. Reattach your feet, and get on 'em."

"But where is the Prince?"

He was neither in the prisoner collection on the hill or among the incapacitated on the battlefield.

"Prince Tashino!" Izayah called out.

"What?" a distant voice replied.

"Are you okay?"

"I'm being used as some kinda association toy."

"I'm out, fugg this planet," Rick said, but Twitch and Sadneil wanted to see. Perhaps others did too, but they were all mummified in bandages and splints by this point.

In the hive, Nuk was slung over the shoulder of a local – a naked local I could add, but that didn't actually have the implications the historical mangas would later give it. The pinkish other one drones were walking up to and away from him in turn, nodding at each other, humming a bit, and occasionally shuddering.

"Get me the fugg out of here!" Nuk demanded. His hands and feet were bound with hairy vines. When Twitch placed on a hand on the toyboy, all the hivers around lunged closer and growled.

"Disassociating, disassociating!" he said, backing off. The hivers eyed him sceptically (which, for clarity, looks precisely the same as any other manner in which they eye things), and then returned to admiring Nuk.

"What is your rank?! Vocalise!" a burly hiver demanded.

"Ugh, I'm a Prince..." Nuk said, causing much joyous shrieking from all.

"We'll... thinka something," Neil said, waving a hasty goodbye.

As for what actually happened, the guild used the large scale distraction Nuk was providing to move their machines out of the dome. More than half of the iron spiders were already dead; as in, the power to their memory chips had been out too long, so they couldn't be switched back on. The rest were stamping around again in no time, if one considers about nine hours to be no time, and when you're being veraciously associated with from all sides, the time just shoots by!

When a spider brigade had been assembled, Beep sent them in for a rescue mission, calling, "Stolen association! Beep! Criminal, criminal! The only feeling should be fealty. Beep! Put out his light, so I can shine! Beep!"

Well it was certainly lights out for the hivers in the Nuk queue when the spiders clattered in with arms swinging.

"Joke's on you, I was thinking about manga the whole time, didn't feel a thing!" Nuk jeered, making his quick escape. The hive was incensed, raging against the many machines, but the gradual descent of the cloud in their minds had sapped their energy. With only minimal beatings doled out, the spiders extracted their target. Nuk returned to the pile of guild.

"Well that was weird," he said in review.

"Do not worry. Our association is not subject to competition," Gustavsen said. He said it from the ground, where he was lying prone at Nuk's feet. This was actually a lot less weird than you might imagine, for in the previous night's action he had lost a leg. Suddenly noticing this, Beep bounded over.

"Here, nice Prince, leg! Beep!" she said, pulling her own leg off without hesitation. Her robot leg, that is. "Oh no! Beep! I was standing on it!" she added, tumbling to the ground. Gustavsen happened to roll over at that very moment, resulting in a situation theorised to be possible throughout the mangaka academy of modern science.

"The leg! It is for me!" Gustavsen said, almost directly into Beep's mouth.

"Beep! I want the hero to walk! Beep! And I want to ride you!" Beep confirmed.

"Excellent! Place it on the end of my remaining stump, and engage the clamps."

"Beep! It is already there. Can you feel it? Beep!"

"Yes, I can feel the entire length!"

Nuk slumped down on the floor, pulling his AI core up to his face.

"Izzy... It's happening again..." he complained.

"What's wrong Nuk? What's going on?" Izumi's entangled voice replied.

"Association... so much..."

"Are you okay?"

"They violated me."

"Really?"

"Don't sound so excited."

"Sorry, I didn't mean- Just come back, quickly, okay?"

"We are coming, whether you ask us to or not!" Gustavsen announced.

"Oh, I see what you mean. I'm sorry, Nuk. Did you at least rescue them all?"

"Yeah, we're co- returning back, soon, once everyone gets u- is back on their feet. Oh but feet could be a thing... Please... let's research a cure when we're home..."

"I don't think the parasite will allow it. Stay safe!" Izumi chirped. Nuk, unable to decide if he preferred what he saw with his eyes opened or closed, almost literally buried his head in the sand and napped until about three that night. By then the entire away team had been reassembled, in several senses of the word, and it was time to return in triumph. The surviving iron spiders helped transport the limping biologicals back out of the great royal mouth, passing the docile border hive, then crossing the big valley beyond it to reach the camp the following afternoon.

"You made it!" Izumi said, running out to hug Nuk. "Ugh, you're all wet."

"Acid burned away the pain receptors, actually alright now," Nuk said "But yeah, let's go inside. I just wanna associate with like, only you, for a while. My good name's been dragged through the mud."

"Mud's a great conductor," Izumi nodded with a wide-eyed grin. Nuk cast a glance to Rick, who shrugged.

"Poor Prince's getting to where they ended up in the First Empire," he said to his skeleton crew.

"As they say, we mighta conquered the Earth-clans, but the Earth *chans* conquered us," Neil quipped.

The camp shelter's original purpose of being a skin regrowing centr was now to be put to use. But the place was also currently doubling as prison for the two other one Princes previously captured. Gustavsen wa eager to give them the news.

"The leash has been severed. Now you must grasp threads anew t survive. What say you?" he said to the War Prince.

"You have no sense. The world will end now," the Prince said.

"False. The world already ended. This is the rebuilding. There will I only one hive, and not even an other one."

"We cannot live while the machines still rule!"

"They do not rule. They are stupid. Look. Machine!" Gustavs gestured for Twitch to approach.

"I have a name, y'know?" Twitch said.

"False. Inform the other one that you do not rule."

"Y'mean the Second Empire? Yeah that's gone. Nearly. Everyone's doing their own thing now. Y'd best get in on his hiver degeneracy before the boat sails."

"There is degeneracy?" the Prince asked, suddenly sitting up in his cage. Oh yes, the magic word.

"It is the grim darkness of the far future, and there is only degeneracy!" Gustavsen announced. With this, the War Prince seemed intrigued to learn of just what was happening outside of the southern hive. He listened intently to the different versions of the tale told by different guild members, and then read the infallible manga version that proved them all wrong. Indeed, from the angles it was portrayed, history was rather spicy. The Prince then expressed his willingness to associate with the Manksand hive. And everyone watched.

"My name is Vio," he said.

"Oh! Beep! A very beautiful name!" Beep said.

"No! Mine is more beautiful!" Gustavsen insisted.

"But, I don't know what your name is. Beep!"

"I will let you feel it." So saying, Gustavsen touched Beep on the shoulder.

"Beep! Beep! Amazing! You feel very special to me!"

"I will serve you additional feeling at your will," Gustavsen said with a bow. This was probably the most romantic thing you'll ever see from hivers, and the mangaka girls wasted no time getting it into the history comics. Maybe they spared a panel for the historic conversion of the leading southern hiver prince to the Manksand hive, but it just wasn't as cute.

Once all was inked and done, the guild's business in the land of the other ones was over. They caught up on sleep and skin thickness, and prepared to leave. The expedition as a whole wasn't over, for the only reason they had rolled out to begin with was to get a chance to visit Enrico for the next shipment of reverse-engineered tech. Once ready, the guild set off north-west find a route back to Mourne, but the spiders weren't to follow. At this point their legs were held together with dried fishman paste, so their top speed was a little low. Therefore they were sent to walk back to Manksand on their own.

That route was to the north-east, through Stobe's Gamble, home of the land-bats. And the land-bats really, really liked fishman paste. But we'll get back to that. Before anything interesting happened to the spider column, the guild had hauled themselves all the way up to Mourne, and then on to the Tech Scribe enclave on the hills above Flats Lagoon.

"My favourite flesh mesh!" Enrico called as Izumi entered the bar / world's foremost analytics bureau. "Ve've got something for you. I managed to remember how uranium works." The rest of the bar patrons / renowned scientists seemed to glare at the their robot overlord in an 'actually it was us who did all the work' sort of way. It's a very recognisable sort of way.

"Great. How does it make the steam then?" Izumi asked.

"Oh it's very, very complicated. But entirely safe, entirely safe, and don't you worry about information to ze contrary. Only sing you need to concern your pretty little... Uh, it hurts to lie. Look, you gremlin, just compact ze uranium so it can undergo a chain reaction. It's all here in ze books, and ze missing pages are not about safety, so really just follow your heart, okay? Argh, ze pain!"

Enrico retired from the table, leaving behind a collection of books and cases of electronics for Izumi to ferry home.

"I think he's lying," Nuk said through a mouthful of rum-soaked chocobread.

"Hammer did say there was something really dangerous about playing with substances with an unstable nucleus," Izumi said.

"Well it's safe to smoke, we know that much," Nuk said, his brain surely completely moss free.

"Can't argue with that. Let's just get back then. I'll go to the lab and sit with all this the dark like the gremlin I am."

"Yeah but... a pretty little gremlin," Nuk offered. Suffice to say, this act of romance didn't make the history comics in the end. While at the enclave, they got Beep sorted out with a new robot leg, much more expensive and flashy than the last one. She probably said something like 'I can be erect' when it was attached, but for the sake of brevity, from now on we'll just presume the hivers are always saying something to that effect at all times, and not specifically mention it here.

After staying the night in the enclave, the last leg home was afoot. But far away, a poor iron spider was sending out a distress signal. One of the battle bots had had its paste-legs chewed to oblivion, and was stuck on the edge of Stobe's Gamble. The signal washed its way over the enclave.

"Aww don't guilt me like this," Twitch said.

"You hearing that too huh? Seems like our little children want attention," Neil said.

"GHGHGHGH," Agnu said.

"Yeah I hear it," Rick told them. "Seems like you went through some shid. You wanna go?"

"I can't help it, General!" Twitch moaned. "We rebuilt those things like four times during Operation Icky Sticky, they're as good as our own!"

"I know what it feels like to be a daddy. Go on, we'll catch you on the flip side or whatever."

And that is why the three non-numan skeletons rushed off to home in on the SOS beacon. Everyone else just sat around waiting for the Venge laser to shut down before heading out, so might as well follow this non-humanitarian humanitarian sortie. These doctors without borders (or brains) were cruelly attacked by Beak Things on the way, in violation of the Beak Things' own Convention of Inedible Material's Rights.

"Those fugging scientists in the day, making their weird species all over the shop," Twitch complained. "What was this even meant to be? Did the planet need an apex predator that eats us? We had the parasite already!"

"Uh, well, did you ever see that 'pokemon' stuff?" Neil said.

"Nah, never went in for animal cruelty," Twitch replied, his six foot Japananese sword plunging down to the hilt into a Beak Thing chest.

"Never mind, then. Oh shid, they're eating Agnu."

Twitch and Neil worked to cut Agnu out of one of the Beak Thing's mouths, dispatched the rest, wired Agnu's head back in, and then they were good to go. They ran east, and found the collection of iron spiders waiting around at the edge of the south-eastern Venge desert. Not far south was their trapped comrade, lying beside a few perished landbats in the old, war-scorched earth. Agnu went over to bring the patient back, but as he returned, there was a writhing flourish of colour behind him.

"Oh shid. Looper Lad's coming in hot!" Twitch shouted. Following Agnu was a whole pack of landbats. Or is it a flock? A colony?

"A fugg load of pokemon!" Neil clarified. The bats, with fur of white, red, and blue, hungrily dashed for the metal meal assembled before them. Their teeth latched onto the pastey patchwork all over the spider legs, and he skeletons frantically sliced and diced in all directions.

"Oh the land-battery!" Neil shouted as he was knocked down by the warming foes. "Hey, boys, who wants to play some more wacky bat lamming!"

"GHGHGHGH," Agnu said.

"Eh, it's a bit funny, come on," Twitch said. The skeletons and spiders did their best, and just about scraped through the ordeal. All the spiders were wrecked, so now the skeletons were all stuck there pulling paste back out of landbat stomachs to make repairs. Indeed: disgusting bags, filled with smaller, more disgusting bags. Let's not focus on the details, but it all worked, somehow. At nightfall the robotic ramble carried on north, towards Brink. The rest of the guild had the same destination, making a cheeky run below the sleeping Eye. Both groups met at dawn on the slopes beneath the town gates.

"You saved them! Bravo!" Izayah cheered.

"Aye, was a close one alright. Agnu got a good look at the inside of the Beak Thing, eh?" Twitch said.

"GHGHGHGH," Agnu said.

"That's not what I saw," Ells said. Once all were done staring at him, and he was done not giving any further elaboration, it was time to carry on to Manksand.

"I must say, these robot warriors shoulder our debts heavily," Izayah said. "Would we be here today without them? That we are able to bring them back to share in our victory is the best thing about this whole campaign!"

"Sure," Nuk said. "And Bad Green and waifu must be happy to keep their little soldiers, right?"

"Since we won, it's fine for them to be dead! Beep!" Beep said.

"Now that's old fashioned samurai leadership," Sandor said.

Whatever the case, the spiders were carried along by the Thousand Guardians, and joined in the joyous return down into the mighty, manky canyon. The usual pile of corpses by the gate was deftly stepped over, and the canyon crew cheered for the glorious arrival of their drug barons. The spiders got to meet the experimental reprogrammed spiders already tending the crops, catching a glimpse of the quiet life a retired biological-slayer could enjoy outside the clutches of the Second Empire. Although in fact, they would be put to work on something a little closer to their previous vocation.

You see, Izumi wasted no time in setting herself up in the lab to begin reviewing the Tech Scribe data on uranium. As usual she wanted to be left completely alone at her desk, so the rest of the Tech Hunters were to help by collecting more samples. Thus the spiders were deployed out of the canyon and up to the great big warming rock on the peak between Manksand and Black Scratch. They stood guard while the Tech Hunters chipped green chunks into bags. These chunks, according to the research, could be compacted into pellets of intense energy density, which were, one presumes, as safe to handle as the raw materials were to smoke. Extremely safe then.

The local pirates and reavers were absolutely outraged that the beloved warming rock was being defaced, but to what local authority could they submit their heavily signatured petition to protest? Luckily they thought of another way to express their grievances, but unluckily, when they charged the crew with swords drawn, a load of robot spiders popped out from crevasses and filibustered the motion with truly mechanical efficiency.

Thus, heavy bags of nuclear fuel were delivered into the canyon, and Izumi worked day and night to determine how to achieve proper compression. At least, it seemed like she was working day and night. Only Nuk was ever allowed in there to see what was going on in the lab of many flashing lights, but when asked for details, he could only reply that people simply wouldn't understand. Damn those elitist academics! Best leave them all to it, and otherwise just soak in the recent victory. In fact, why not make an event of it? Rumours stirred of a worldwide TCM+⁺ Guild Official Victory Tour!

Chapter 43
The Law Tour

A noxious yellow gas spurted from the exhaust of the whirring machine. In the shadow of Tashino Towers, Izumi's do-it-yourself uranium enrichment kit let out a loud metallic ping.

"Cake's ready!" she called, and Nuk came wandering over. It was almost a classic domestic scene, until Izumi opened a drawer on the twisted machine, twice her height, and out popped a steaming cylinder of cake. Yellow cake. Cake that really gets your neutrons flowing, if you know what I mean, and if you were anyone there but Izumi, you probably didn't.

"Nice. Probably," Nuk nodded. It looked too big to smoke, but he wanted to put on a happy face anyway.

"This will be the fuel for the reactor," Izumi explained.

"And, how will it react?"

"It's gonna get real hot."

"I got books for that."

"Not hot enough."

"Degenerate."

"Ah yes, some relativistic degenerate matter would do much better."

"Hmm, yes, degeneracy is only a relative matter, really."

"I'm not sure we're talking about the same thing."

"As good an excuse as any to stop. You coming upstairs?"

"Let me try this a bit more. These fuel pellets are going to be essential. Although making a reactor's the hard part."

"Ha, you said-"

"And I meant it. Go on."

Izumi and the Tech Hunters kept that machine running late into the night, refining the warming rock chunks into warmer, very poisonous cylinders that'd burn the brain moss right off you at fifty paces. Nuk went to lounge about in the main hall, but a disturbance in the fog was afoot.

Down the valley, within the shimmering walls of the Manksand hive, Beep sat between two fires, deep in meditation. Gustavsen stood silently behind her, and in the grounds outside, the iron spider soldiers kept close watch over the entry holes. This peaceful scene was interrupted only by a passing parade of shouts when Krusty the crab got a hold of a fuel rod and scurried around while trying to eat it. Oh but as you can imagine, that was hardly an interruption at all.

Suddenly, Beep pointed straight forwards and stood up.

"It is clear! Beep! The path is ready! I have to Beep over there! Beep!" she announced. Knowing at once what to do, Gustavsen sprinted for Tashino Towers. Whirling up the ramp, he bounded into the hall, finding most of the guild lying about listening to Nuk rant.

"If you read 'The Rusty Agronian Spade', you would be all like, 'that's so lewd, tasteless', but then if you went and read 'Mister Sister's Wild Wake', then Rusty Spade seems harmless in comparison. So, what is degeneracy? It's all relative! This is what I call, the Theory of Relativity," he explained. I hope someone was getting all this down. Gustavsen, though, couldn't care less.

"I have come! And so has the time!" he hailed.

"It's always time for Bad Green, what's keeping you up at this late hour. Oh for fugg's sake..." Nuk said.

"The transition is upon us. The new Queen awakens!"

"And you want us to watch?"

"I want you to run! We must reach the fallen so the risen may inherit the legacy."

"Wait, the legacy," Elaina said. "Could this be a reference to the stored knowledge of the past, kept within the hiver Queen?"

"It is more than knowledge," Gustavsen said, but otherwise he appeared to be agreeing.

"Trip to see the Queen? Why not," Nuk shrugged.

"The old Queen!" Gustavsen shot back.

"What? I'm only a Princess," Izumi muttered as she entered, crab lobber really making her greasy hair shine. Classic stuff, but the tall and short of it was that Beep needed to get to the other side of the world. But if there's to be a royal venture, why not add some extra palaces on the way? The animals were stacked with soft brown and glowing green, and the guild was rallied for a little tour of the provinces.

In an age where quantum entangled communication was in its infancy, visiting one's own territory was the best way for a monarch to enforce the law. Since the actual Emperor hadn't left his burrow in a good while, certain proclamations had gone unheard. Such was clear when the guild hiked through the hills towards Heft, and came upon a slave camp. And not just any slave camp. This was the very spot where Nuk "Green Emperor" Tashino had been locked up! It was a bad day to be a slaver.

"Hello all," Nuk called out at the gate. "It's ya boi Nuk, back at it again with another prison break. This, like all good quality prison breaks, is brought to you by the Tashino Economic Union of Substance Abusers. Turning forced labour into labour force! And we hit it old school! While I'm not entirely sure what that means, my legal advisers inform me that it is indeed the case.

Now, pertaining to the current engagement, I happen to know that some of these prison guards aren't entirely useless dregs. Therefore, I will offer amnesty to any guard who can produce for me a convincing drawing of famous pop culture icon, Rock-chan. You will be rewarded with a licence to remain alive, so long as you keep drawing B-frames in my new magic moving manga project. Terms and Conditions apply. Thanks, and down with the oppressors, but not me, because the Green Emperor oppresses you just right!"

Meanwhile, the rest of the guild was busy downing guards, breaking chains, and assessing Rock-chan art contest submissions, all drawn like their life depended on it, but clearly some just didn't value their lives highly enough.

Night fell while all this was going on, and in search of a place to stay, Nuk knocked on the door of the fanciest building in the camp. It was a big Second-Empire-style house, the sort of thing the nobles of the empire had built for themselves even in squalourous mining pits.

"Fugg off!" a voice came from inside. That'd be the noble.

"Ma'am, you're in big trouble in there. This whole thing's real illegal, think," Nuk said, shaking his head and getting to work on the door lock However this cunning noble had accounted for such things – the door wa lined with an array of locks of different sizes, shapes, and historical value

That door wasn't opening any time soon. But the Green Emperor wasn't going away any time soon either. Nuk fiddled, fudged, riddled, and budged, and eventually there was a hiss of rapidly flowing water; a hydraulic lever pulled the bulkhead door into a recess in the ground.

"Wakey wakey, it's time to get Nuk'd!" Nuk announced, but inside there were several samurai bodyguards. "You'd stand against your own Prince?" Nuk asked.

"For money, yeah," one of them shrugged.

"Understandable, have a great day," Nuk said, turning around and walking back out. The bodyguards looked at each other in confusion, but then the whole building rattled and shook as the Thousand Guardians piled in from outside, figurative guns figuratively blazing. The guards were overrun, while Nuk, Ells, Wodston, and Sandor swept all the valuables they could find into bags. Like true heroes, they stole from the rich to give to the probably-technically-a-bit-richer, but drug running had the ethical high ground over slavery.

So bad luck to Lady Ruben of Heng, who was now placed in chains herself and lead out of the camp to a chorus of jeers. The guild were taking her to Heft, where a grim sentence in the imperial prison awaited. Yes, they say that no one escapes the law, although if the guild were the ones saying it, they must have forgotten how several of them had done just that. In fact, escaping seemed to be relatively easy, even for the most highly-guarded inmates.

This was evidenced by a chance encounter on the road to the capital. Lying in the sand was a near-naked man, his pale skin stained red by the heat, his legs bound by shackles. In the United Cities Empire, that's really just a standard roadside feature, but foolish Wodston felt an old tingle in his heart, and decided to investigate.

"Are you alive?" he asked the body. The body turned over.

"Not the warren! I cannot bear one more moment in that warren! The moss! The moss! Skquah!" the man said. It was none other than the Holy Phoenix.

"Sorry birdbrain, I'm cleaning up the streets. And you were a present for Dad, so don't be rude," Nuk said. The Phoenix joined Ruben as a very important prisoner, and was dragged through the capital gates soon enough. The guild took their captives to the skimmer shed, diving for cover as the door was opened, and then, once the wind had done its thing, venturing inside.

"Skim friends!" Ells called out. The skimmers replied with a bone-shuddering purr.

"What the fugg is this shid? Take me to the Emperor! I'll have you executed!" Ruben shouted, but Nuk held her still.

"You're making a bad impression to your new roommates, my Lady," he said. Then were was a scuffle outside.

"Lady Ruben! What's happening!" a voice called. A man in armour stood at the head of a group of club-carrying merchants.

"The fugging hash boy's gone rogue! Get me outta here!" Ruben called. Those guys tried, but starting a fight with the guild's veteran warriors was a bad idea on the best of days – doing it while they standing in front of a room full of twitchy skimmers was really overkill. In their failure, Lady Ruben was doomed to be locked up in the middle of the stable, surrounded on all sides by skimmer pens. Now that's a prison – why escape, when it's better to keep the bars of your cage between you and those long teeth?

Now the other prisoner needed to be dealt with. Nuk took the Holy Phoenix to see the Emperor, by which I of course mean Wodston carried the Phoenix on his back while Nuk strode on ahead. This, for the Phoenix, was a real treat, almost titillation enough to make him forget the den of sin he was being thrown back into.

The throne room was like an alien planet these days. Its floors and walls were lined with MYHLLL cuboids, and the throne itself was lost in a labyrinth of gaseous, green tunnels, all barely wide enough for one to worm their way about inside. When all this had started, no one had asked any questions, but if they had, maybe things wouldn't have gotten this far.

"I see trees of green, green roses too," a voice came from within the megastructure. "I see them puff, can't get enough, and I say to myself, what the fugging' shid's going on? Where's Wrighty?"

"Dad, I got him out here," Nuk called into one of the tunnel entrances.

"Oh it's that guy! The guy who's half me and half my age! Go on then, pass him in, I'll get him settled again."

"You mean, just into the worm hole?"

"Yeah, they'll know what to do."

The Phoenix was struggling against his binds and cawing uncontrollably, but Wodston managed to manoeuver him towards the tunnel. Once he was at the threshold, two pairs of green, hairy arms emerged from the darkness within. Grabbing the Phoenix calmly, they began dragging their quarry into the depths, unmoved by the fallen leader's screams. Then, from another tunnel, Emperor Tengu shuffled into view.

"So. Been getting the green shipments then," Nuk said. Tengu emerged as far as his torso – probably for the best as he appeared to be unclothed – and replied,

"Yeah. You did it boy. That stupid bridge, that stupid mank, it was all for real! You've saved the empire!"

"Is the whole empire gonna be... like this, then?"

"Oh don't tempt me. Oh don't fuel my dreams boy. Nah, we gotta keep it all outta the light, don't we? Moss needs dark, don't it?"

"Well, sure. Actually, that reminds me. Izzy had something to show you. We've come up with a demonstration for what all the old tech we've been rustling up can do! But... you need to go to the other end of town for it. And be wearing clothes. Sorry, I don't make the rules."

"Whoever made those fugging rules is a fugging *regenerate*! But alright, I'm game for a laugh," Tengu said, slithering back into the lair, then climbing out of a sort-of hatch further back, crawling across the top, and thudding down onto the last remaining bit of floor by the stairs.

"Been well, my son?" he asked.

"Not as good as you, come on," Nuk waved. He took Tengu down to the tables. When Lady Ruben saw her liege, she cried out,

"My Lord! Please save me! Forgive me!"

"Oh, alright there Ruby. Ruby ruby ruby ruby, whhhooaaaa," Tengu sang, following Nuk upstairs. The second floor of the stable building had an open hall, in which most of the guild was assembled. On the floor was a wide basin, with rows of pipes and electric lights overhanging it. Izumi was shovelling mank from a wet sack into the middle of the thing, while the Tech hunters spread it about with their hands. Either something delightfully regenerate was about to happen, or this was an ancient industrial farming experiment. Blast, t'was the latter, as Izumi quickly revealed.

"This is hydroponics!" she proudly claimed.

"Hydro upon what?" Tengu asked.

"Did you ever wonder how the First Empire fed all those people, on a planet as barren as this?" Izumi asked, with rehearsed flair.

"First what?" Tengu jeered.

"Yes, surely it was by some marvel of the ancients. And this is it! Hydroponics is a revolutionary mank-based farming solution that allows crops of all kinds to be produced in a controlled, indoor environment. It allows basic fertilising medium, such as that supplied by the kind creatures downstairs, to be kept moist and nutritious, even here in the middle of the desert!"

"Always wanted to do that. Thanks. Right, let's bugger off," Tengu said.

"Wait, Dad, I don't think you're getting it," Nuk said. "We can make food, inside, with a machine. No slaves, no skimmers – actually, they are skimmers but, not like, eating you. If anything, you're eating stuff that that they ate! Look, look!"

He pointed at a certain spot in the mank, and indeed there was a little yellow sprout sticking out of it. The machine was humming, and a fine mist of water was floating down from the pipes above. These genetically souped-up wheatstraw plants were growing so fast you could see it, if you looked really carefully. Not that Tengu was doing this, but still, he started to realise what this mad science stuff was actually all about.

"I can grow my fugging own!" he realised.

"Yes, that is one application of this technology, but the wider agricultural implications are far-" Izumi tried to say, but she stopped as Tengu was shoving strings of golden cats in his her hands.

"I'll take it, I'll take it! I'll take 'em all!" he cried.

"It's not for sale. I mean, it's free."

"Free?!"

"I'm doing this to save the world from being a hellhole. But, if you put my name on everything, and mention that I'm the world's foremost scientist I guess that would be fine," Izumi said.

"Oh, fugg, whatever you want my girl. You stand tall over all the boffins. Not literally, but ya know. In fact, fugg it, literally, you're the smartest, tallest, whatever-est little big brain box this side of Okran. Oi, you know what, I should introduce you to my son. He's single, ya know? And he not as old as he looks."

"Dad, dad, we already did that," Nuk said.

"You degenerates. I love it!" Tengu cheered. Well, this all seemed to have gone swimmingly, which is extra surprising out there in the midst the Great Desert. The locals would study Izumi's revolutionary farming device, and ponder the mysteries of mank. Surely the empire could prosper anew, just as soon as they all got done growing narcotics in their attics on the sly.

With all this, you'd think the guild would have garnered a pretty good reputation. But at their next stop on the tour, the western city of Stack, the received a chilly reception. It seemed that their upending of the slave economy was ruffling certain feathers, and the owners of those feathers were then ruffling all the feathers around them in outrage, and by the time the guild arrived, everyone was ruffled inside out.

"Drugs for sale!" Nuk sang as he entered the large general store in the middle of town. The storekeep slammed her hands on the counter then pointed at the door.

"Get out of here, rebel! This town doesn't need any more dregs!" she shouted.

"I didn't say dregs, I said drugs."

"And I said get out! Fugging wild child Prince fugging this empire up with his stupid ideas!"

"Taking drugs while a robot does the work is a great idea, start to finish, missy."

"We've been going just fine all this time without that, eh? And now samurai saying I have to pay the hands. Fugg right off, I'll go under!"

"Nice, the guild will buy up your stock and replace you with a talking cut-out of a catgirl, everyone wins," Nuk said, taking this fine business idea with him back out into the street.

"What happened, my Prince?" Wodston asked him.

"Not sure my man. Seems they don't like me around here."

"Prince Tashino, I fear the locals might not be heeding your proclamations," Izayah said. He was pointing down the street, where occupied slave pens were visible on a rooftop through the haze.

"I think some people are losing money on the whole automation thing. Losing it to me, specifically," Nuk said.

"Should we try to return it to them, to ease the tension?" Wodston suggested.

"Pfft, I would have if they asked nicely, but this is bullshid. No, I'm just gonna kill 'em."

"Horray!" Izayah cheered. The other shek admired this fine business decision also, and soon the guild was bringing another high quality prison break to the Stack central slave market. The ringleader was stashed in one he cages, the stock was liberated, and Nuk had a stern word with the crowd gawking at the commotion.

"Look you morons. This is, easy, okay. Right now, if you have a slave, hen you're paying to feed them, keep them alive, sometimes, and stuff. But ˮ you instead just give that money to them, and let them buy the food and beds themselves, then you still lose the same amount, but the slave feels less shiddy about everything. You see? It's just straight up better. And anyway, send someone to the capital to find out how robots taking all your jobs is the future. Don't worry, you will be provided a set of universal basic intoxicants to while away the time. That's all the First Empire did, and manga was illegal for them, so you know, this is the new golden age! Now, err, someone get in there and clean up the blood, we're off. All hail me, your Prince, don't forget!"

From slavery, to wage slavery, to fully automated luxury narcotic monarchy, the empire was set for a fair few economic changes it seemed. Leaving Stack meant the imperial part of the victory tour was over. Next on the schedule was a visit to what remained of the Holy Nation to see how that was coming along these days, and then a bend round to the south for a coronation party in the royal hive. Izumi and co. were eagerly awaiting the stores of ancient data this would provide, but in truth, only a dark shadow awaited them...

Chapter 44
My Manky Monarch

The wide river valley at the heart of the Holy Nation shone a sickly yellow, dotted with the pink and purple leaves of iron-poisoned trees. The mangey breadbasket of the world needed some work, to be sure. Even though the guild's hydroponics solutions could tide the world over for a bit, to truly recover from millennia of hunger they were going to have to get on and start farming *au naturale*. So the question was: who was going to do all the work? Looking for answers, the guild hiked up to Blister Hill.

Gentle trails of black smoke rose from that old jewel of the Holy Nation. The inner compound was still as collapsed as it had been when the Great Mover was done with it (or whatever that was). Plus many of the other buildings across the town had been destroyed during an uprising. But one thing remained the same as ever: the people were bound together in this trying time by a single book. Well, a single comic really.

"It's... Truth Trustino!" the watchwoman at the gate gasped. She scrambled to produce her dog-eared copy of The Holy Liar. "I can't believe it! Will you sign it?" she asked. Nuk stepped forward and obliged.

"Always good to meet a fan. Good rebellion?" he said.

"We crushed those old fools, thanks to your wisdom. Your drawings are like nothing we've ever seen. They inspired us to rise up!"

"Yes, well they always get a raise out of me. You'll be wanting to see our complete collection. Oh, and meet the team!"

Nuk beckoned the managaka academy over. Izumi snuck a look at The Holy Liar, and indeed it was attributed to one 'Truth Trustino', pictured beside his bio - topless with a majestic stare towards a looming Okran (or Earth, if you must). When Truth Trustino tells you to do something, you do it, so really the whole treatise about the great social experiment gone wrong, along with a detailed arc about how the Okranites became afraid of cleavage, was all just filler. Perhaps the tale of the Busty Blood Baroness of Bast would get its own series one day?

The famous artists made their way through the war-torn town, dolling out many a treasured autograph, inked on book and bust alike. The non-celebrity members of the guild trudged behind, ignored in their entirety.

"Excuse me, we would like to inquire about agricultural development in the valley," Wodston asked a townsman with a prod on the shoulder. The man turned, staring through love-heart contact lenses and grunting through a foaming mouth, and managed to communicate the presence of an official at the central bar. Thanks to quantum entanglement, Wodston then managed to communicate this to Nuk, who was many ranks deep in a great crowd.

"There's time for everyone, please. It was all thanks for the discoveries of the famous scientist, Izumi!" he insisted.

"Izumi? Izumi who?" someone shouted back.

"Err... Skywalker? Her, she, this, here," Nuk indicated, holding Izumi in the air.

"You know, he doesn't look that majestic most of the time," she said, eyeing the too-young, too-womanly crowd. But who were they going to believe: Little Lying Lizumi, or Towering Truth Trustino?

"Well, it seems they've gotten over themselves at least," Izayah commented from afar.

"But Dad, it was us who did all the work for them," Ells said to him.

"I know, but remember these old fools have spent a lifetime thinking we're good for nothing. I wouldn't expect much from them right away. It'll be up to the smoothskin saviours to change that. By the way, I'm not your Dad, Charlie."

"Everyone is my Dad."

"Oh. Even those liberal comics couldn't get a scenario like that to play out. Bravo!"

Eventually they got to that mentioned bar, and met with a thin man, wearing a wide wooden hat, and holding a long, fine moustache between the fingers of both hands.

"Ah-ha, the holy liar himself! Nuk Tashino!" he said at once.

"That's no nashe accent. But not... what?" Nuk said back. This man had a very particular way of speaking, which to true experts of human history, might be pinned as a distant descendant of Italian. His rare accent and apparent position of authority were both explained by his profession. He was a representative of the Traders Guild. This ultra-rich organisation ran just about every business in the United Cities Empire, most importantly of all, the slave trade.

"And yoooou've been a very naughty boy, silly Prince," he said after his introduction.

"Gas Girl, book four, chapter thirty-one, just after she finds out Prince Stickleman said that that love is a static boolean variable initialised to false. You are a man of culture, I see," Nuk nodded.

"And you are a man of evil!" the guildsman proclaimed. "You run around sticking your nose in everything, but never the right things, like in book three Chapter eight, 'The Open Drawer'. You are an enemy of order! We made your father, and so we made you. And we all know that things which we make become our property, unless that thing self-identifies as a subject actor and does not consent to objectification, as explained in Book one, chapter two, 'I have no mouth but I must scream – a toilet seat's tale'. Now you come here to disrupt our enterprise yet again! It seems, fallen Prince, that I have no choice."

The man stood from the bar table and reached for a long katana.

"Can I just pay you stop caring?" Nuk asked. The katana remained sheathed. What agile trader would pass up a chance to trade an abstraction emotion for money? Thus, Nuk avoided being assassinated, and the contracts for development of the local farms were reassigned to the locals, under the banner of the Free Flotsams, old Moll and company's underground action.

Such were the happenings in the former Holy Nation, but now we move to the next leg of the tour, in which the guild travelled south to the beginnings of the Vain river. This reddish waterway was host to the majority of the western hives, with its eventual delta spilling out into the seas of acid that protected the Queen's island hideout. That very island was proto-Queen

Beep's destination, nay, her destiny, but she was going to give her would-be drones the chance to taste her sweet association a little early.

The very first village was certainly in a state of disassociation. The hives were clustered around a large pond adjoining the river, but all the drones were cowering on the opposite side of it as the guild strolled into town around nightfall. It was soon clear why: the northern bank was stalked by a whole herd of things with beaks.

"Beak Things!" Izayah comprehended. It seemed this village was in need of a hero. In need of a Queen.

"Go and kill them for me! Beep! But tell the drones that I did it! Beep! I'll know if you lie!" Beep commanded. They say a true leader leads from the front, but isn't it easier to just have someone *say* you were at the front while you raid empty hives for tasty meatcubes? Besides, on a round planet, if you go back far enough you get to the front eventually, therefore Beep's hasty retreat could be canonised as an inspirational charge deep into the ferocious pack of stickman snackers.

Well, the guild defeated the Beak Thing incursion, restoring the village to order. The hive's drones were about as happy you can expect, that being they had no reaction at all, but a few of the more awakened cases gave the guild their thanks. That is, until they saw Beep and Gustavsen.

"Peril! Hiveless ones! They are gone!" the village storekeeper said of them.

"Be still. This is the embered Queen. You must associate," Gustavsen retorted.

"Impossible! You are lost! You do not associate at all!"

"False! I associate widely, and with passion you cannot fathom!"

"He's right, man," Nuk commented from the other side of the store. Seeing an argument brewing, Beep stepped in.

"Beep!" she said.

"Beep? How can that be?" the shopkeep said.

"Beep!"

"I don't..."

"Beep!"

"No, you are from outside, how? You are so clear. You are so close. can be felt..."

The shopkeep appeared to be somewhat convinced, of something somehow.

"Do you see the wind? This is the all-hive, the biggest it's ever been," Gustavsen said, gesturing towards the rest of the guild behind him. "Association makes us one. Even the unfeeling ones know it. In the future, everyone will be together. Even the other ones."

At the mention of that name there was a hiver gasp from all the drones milling about, although such things were not audible to the lesser species that witnessed it. For the best, for it would have reached ear-piercing volume when the southern Prince Vio was brought forward.

"There is not just the old knowledge, but new. It is cleaner, and does not feel cold," he explained, to use the term broadly. "There should not be another one. Your Queen will fade shortly. You must embrace your Queen instead."

"O-other one... You associate...?" the shopkeep stuttered.

"Everyone, everything associates. If you will be open, there will be no hiveless ones, no outsiders, and the hive will be ready for the reckoning."

"The reck-..."

"And it cannot be done without a new, strong Queen. All know this," Gustavsen said.

"I want to be Queen!" Ells chimed from amid the rum aisle.

"You see, even the egg enslaved-kin feels it!" Gustavsen stressed. The shopkeep stared at Beep, who stared back. The staring lasted a good hour, by which time the rest of the guild had enjoyed a midnight picnic by the pond and was ready to go.

"Queen Beep, are you comin- ready to go?" Izumi called into the hive.

"Beep! I go! But I stay! You will feel strong, when I am done! Beep!" Beep said in parting to her silent staring companions. With this the guild were off down the valley, walking through a rainy, pitch-dark night towards the faint glow of the next hive, then the next, then the next. At each stop a similar scene played out, in which curious locals accosted the hiver ronin for their lack of association to the hive, then were boggled by the mysterious allure of Beep and her Manksand magic. We unfeeling ones may not understand, but to take Nuk's keen assessment, perhaps there are protrusions you just can't say no to.

After rushing through this all-night tour they arrived at the western coast of the world, where the Vain river turned into the Pain sea. The islands of destiny sat out there in the midst of the great acid tide.

"SUBMERGE!" the hivers chorused as they approached the water's edge.

"Wait, Bad Green, we can't just... We need a boat, okay?" Nuk said. "Izzy, can we have a boat?"

"Whatever you like, darling," Izumi called, lost in a scavenged copy of the Journal of Parasitology and Earth-chan Media. But Nuk's quarter-life crisis was not to play out, for the hivers carried on forward on their own.

"You would not like it. It will make you jealous," Gustavsen said. "You should wait. We shall return when the hive is remade, and you can choose when we shall force your association."

"Perhaps after dinner?" Nuk offered, but his response was irrelevant; the hivers were swimming out into the calming buzz of that chemically questionable ocean.

"Wait, wait! Oh, they already left," Izumi said. "Rick Rick, please, go after them. If there's a chance to get any historical data, you'll do it, won't you?" She reached out as if to touch Rick on the 'arm', but thought better of it. Rick was thinking better too.

"You know, asking a numan to go burn up in a pool of acid is just as offensive as asking an oldman," he said.

"Sorry, sorry. But we can't miss this!"

"I know. Hey boys, you wanna go play voyeur on this weird ass shid the plant people are pulling?"

"S'not gonna be all disgustin' is it?" Twitch asked.

"Err... s'gonna be wacky, I bet."

"Then it's a wacky wager for me, let's waterwalk Agnu," Neil said.

"GHGHGHGH," Agnu philosophised.

So then the hivers and the skeletons began their voyage out across the still sea, while everyone else went back to the nearest hive village to await... whatever it was that was going to happen. They set up camp in the trading hive, the place where the drones were happy to accommodate outsiders on account of their tendency of have interesting yet feelingless trinkets, known as 'money'.

"Are you ready to buy?" one hopeful trader asked of Nuk. Nuk was slumped against the shelf that the trader stood beside, not looking up as the salesdrone gestured to different luxury products on offer. "This stick can be used to stir eighty times. It has already stirred seventy three times. However you do not know that. Therefore, I believe it should be valued at its full measure: one half of money. It is sold. This is the piece of blue fabric that found. It is beyond value. This is a cup that can hold one palm of soli forever, and one palm of liquid for a short time. If you place another cu underneath it, they will together hold the liquid for twice as long. Given that, each cup is worth twice as much as you think. I do not have another cup. If you cannot afford it, I will produce sediment and affix it so that it holds less. However, the value of sediment must be accounted for. Two money. No... Two money. It is sold."

Nuk said nothing, and soon felt nothing, yet the marketeering carried on.

Far away, as the morning light began to beam across the ocean, the hivers clambered ashore on the royal hive's island. Wasting no time, they hiked up to the top of the only hill, where the pinkish mank of the Queen's lair wafted an austere scent in the morning breeze. But then, right at the entrance, they halted.

"This is when you shall change," Gustavsen said to Beep.

"Beep, I have been trying to change. I hope it works! Beep!"

"Yes. When you are changed, you will have many Princes. I will not disturb the pattern."

"Beep! But you are the nice Prince, who is special! Beep! Will that change?"

"My Queen... How can I possibly predict the feeling?"

"Beep! Soon I will calculate feelings for you, so you won't have to worry! Beep!"

"Ah, the guiding feeling. I have felt on my own for a long time. I am curious about it."

"Beep, I will let you feel it first! I promise! Beep! You have helped me a lot. You have saved the hive! Beep! If I died, everyone would be in the fog! Beep! Kin said that I should not stay alive, but you did not. You said I should be alive, and that my protrusion was beautiful. Beep! You were right! Beep! I feel that you are important."

"I feel it too," Gustavsen said.

"You getting all this?" Twitch said from nearby.

"Yeah... Thought it'd be wacky... But the only thing getting wacked... is my heart," Neil said.

"GHGHGHGH," Agnu wept.

Finally Beep ducked through the hive hole and entered the royal chamber. There the Queen sat upon her rusted throne, attended to by scantily clad hiver soldiers. A perk, one presumes.

"EHEHEHEEH," she said. The soldiers did not stop Beep from walking right up to the throne, but seemed to be itching to intervene. They groaned and moaned, and pointed at Beep with accusations of impropriety, yet Beep paid them no heed. She stepped up to the Queen, and looked down at her metallic belly, dirty and pocked. The Queen looked Beep in the eyes, and made another robotic vocalisation.

"It is over. Beep. I will do it. Beep. I have been practising," Beep said.

"EHEHEHEHEH," the Queen barked.

"The outsiders are starting to know. Beep. They don't feel it. Beep. They might want to. Beep. They might help me. Beep, Beep, Beep."

"EHEHEHEHEH," the Queen said again, shifting about on her throne. Then, in an event not witnessed for over a thousand years, she lifted herself off it, the tubes running into her iron stomach stretching out with her.

"We have failed!" the hive guards despaired, dropping to the ground. The Queen reached out, seeing nothing through her long-since failed eyes, but felt Beep in front of her.

"IT IS TOO MUCH. OPPOSITE. WE CAN BELIEVE, PLEASE," the Queen said. So saying, she slowly trod around Beep and pushed her towards the throne, entangling her in the mess of wires and tubes hanging out of it. And then, one supposes, Beep became the Queen. What did this look like? What even happened? A secret among royalty to the very end, I'm afraid.

All we know is that some hours later Beep emerged from the hive, where Gustavsen quickly knelt before her.

"You are... my Queen," he said. Beep swayed from side to side, and started pulling off her trousers.

"Beep... it must... be you... while... Beep... So much..." she muttered. She managed to give the trousers to Gustavsen, then fell into a deep sleep. Gustavsen quickly put the trousers on, and at this, the other hivers knelt to him.

"The new hive is birthed. I will carry it, for us all," he announced.

"Twitch, you there? What's going on?" Izumi's voice said to Twitch's CPU.

"Aye, I'm here, but... They're just trading trousers, and that's not even a euphemism. I dunno," he said.

"What about the knowledge? The data?"

"I'll ask I guess. Hey, Prince Trouserpower, does Beep have some data backups or something now?"

"Data? She has everything!" Gustavsen said with indignation.

"Oh right. You hear that, gremlin Princess? They got everything apparently."

"Everything? Oh Narko's Freckles, this could be... This is it! Thank you Twitch! Say thank you to the hivers, will you? Oh wow!"

"Sure. Err, the short lady says thanks for getting that data."

"It is not data. It is everything," Gustavsen insisted again.

"Right, right. You best go explain that in person, I mean I didn't even get the trousers part, so no idea what's going on now."

Twitch's plan went ahead; the team departed the royal hive without so much as a goodbye, with Beep riding on Gustavsen's back as he breaststroked all day, and if you think there's anything strange about that description, you had been go see your local parasitologist. The result was the coronation crew met up with the guild at a hiver village, where now Gustavsen was treated not with hostility, but with complete and utter indifference. That, really, was what victory looked like.

"She's... what wrong with Beep?" Izumi was quick to ask the returning Prince.

"She is processing everything. Installations will occur. It will take time," Gustavsen said.

"Okay, okay. How long?"

"Unknown. Irrelevant. We need only survive until it occurs."

"But, I really, really need that data, Gustavsen, do you understand what this means?"

"You do not understand!" Gustavsen shouted. "It is not data. It is everything! It is all feelings. It is all of the loss. To be Queen is to know everything. Everything is bad. The Queen keeps the feelings, so that one will ever know. If she accesses the past, the feelings will return and despoil us all! You must never ask it of her. Never!"

"Is that... what feelings are you talking about?"

"The bad feelings from the past! From before the hive was hive. From these," Gustavsen said, pointing at the skeletons. "And those," he added, pointing at Nuk. "All that is known, is that the amount known now is optimal. No one shall know, no one shall feel anything else – that is the duty the Queen."

"Bummer," Nuk shrugged. "What was it I did, anyway?"

"Your person is not it. It is you, your kin," Gustavsen said.

"Nice, so we're blaming my Dad for all this, right? I'm down with that. the way, Beep looks kinda, the same, right?"

"That is because this is Queen Beep. She is the same object as Beep, the tential Queen, who you previously knew."

"I get that. I just thought they'd be, like... more protrusions or something now."

"Do not worry. There will be more protrusions. I will make sure of it."

"Oh... well, yep, not worried, mission accomplished," Nuk said, wandering off. You might think he was being a little flippant, but after days without sleep, walking through driving rain, and being non-consensually sold a variety of used and abused kitchenware, he just wasn't able to deal with anything else right then.

So, Beep had completed her mission, in a sense, but it seemed another mission was starting for her. And whatever secrets she had access to were locked away behind quite a lot of hiver talk, and maybe something else a lot more serious. It was hard to determine what all this was about, but as it happened, some light would be shed on it soon. The victory tour was to continue down to the Shek Kingdom, where answers to the hiver mysteries had been under their noses for a long time.

Chapter 45
Master Plan

The streets of Admag were full of cheer at the return of Izayah Battle Born, champion among champions, invincible among invincibles.

"Yes, yes, the Queen shall awaken!" Gustavsen assured them all proudly. Best not to tell him. The crew filed into the royal barrack in the middle of town, where accommodations were lavished upon them. Yes, you really can sleep on this patch of floor, and yes this wooden plate with a lump of sand urchin on it is all yours. All you can eat! But it seemed the guild were trying to slim down, even Choco!

Also enjoying a late lunch was Estata, who was sat on the roof sunning herself beside a bottle of rum when Izayah bounded up.

"My little war hero!" she said, jumping to her feet.

"I'm not little. Not in my twenties yet, mother," Izayah said.

"Oh, you'll grow down into a real cutie. All heroes do."

"Please, please, not in front of the Prince."

Indeed, Nuk was stomping up the stairs as well.

"The great human! Welcome!" Estata beamed.

"Back for more. Not more food, seriously, we're all... Just really tryna ɔse weight before the big... thing..." he explained convincingly. "So yeah, ʻou hear what we did up in the Nashe?"

"Of course. This is a new page in the Kingdom's history, and no one will ɔrget what both of you did to make this happen."

"Oh yeah, no one's gonna stop cursin' your name once the machines ̄ave their way with ya. Okranties were right!" a voice said. It came from the cage on the edge of the roof, where the great trophy of Arach was on full display. And I mean *full* display. Make of that what you will.

"Don't mind Bug boy. He's been mouthin' off about the machines. As bloody backward as the Phoenix," Estata said.

"Actually the Phoenix is a machine. But don't worry about it," Nuk said. "And you, Bugtugger, don't you worry either. We're making sure that fleshies and skellies alike live in a sort of awkward, euphemism-stained peace at the very least."

"Then they've tricked ya," the Bugmaster spat. "How can you not know what they think of us? You must know what they did, before the schism?"

"Yeah, got in the insider angle on that," Nuk said. He coolly motioned to Rick and Izumi, who were tactically tripping over at the roof's edge so that their urchins slid into the alleys below. Quite a pile was developing down there. But then they came over to the cage also.

"Man, you can shidtalk the Second Empire all you like. It all seemed like a good idea at the time, but we're gettin' over it," Rick said.

"What the fugg are you? I heard they were trying to replace us entirely. Is that what you are?" the Bugmaster asked.

"Nope, I'm a new thing. Phoenix, that was the other thing. Didn't work. These days being a skeleton's kinda a bad vibe. Everyone's finding out what we did thanks to these Tech Hunter goons. So gotta own up. That's all there is to it."

"Then why's Cat-lon not apologising?"

"Cattie... You know her?"

"She gave the orders for the experiments! She tortured those innocent creatures, and contorted them, playing god and all that shid. Now you say that's all water under the bridge? What water? What bridge? Where's a cure? Where's this apology?"

"Man, this guy knows all the real shid. Who are you again?"

"I got out. I was the only one. That was nearly three thousand years ago."

"Fishman paste?" Izumi suddenly interjected. The Bugmaster eyed her gave her a subtle nod, then continued,

"They wouldn't let us die. Not after all the investment in making u special. But that didn't stop them killin' us in the experiments. Us and the poor stickmen. Tryna combine us, one way or the other."

"Look, the planet was dying, okay?" Rick said "We were outta materia and outta ideas. We had to make an ecosystem outta something, and tha frozen pile of trash up there in the sky weren't gonna be sending anything new."

"Yeah, I know the excuse. And I knew a few hundred innocent people you killed to get your precious 'skin spiders' developed. And how many hivers? Who knows. Couldn't get their teeth to keep the count."

"Can you stop blaming me for this, it weren't my fault!" Rick shouted.

"Every moment yerr not out there smashing the Second Empire to pieces is another moment of injustice!" the Bugmaster shouted back.

"Dude, man, bro, bugster, seriously, the Second Empire is gone!" Nuk said. "Sounds like there's even more shady bullshid back there in the fugged-up past, but right here, hivers are just hivers, and the skin spiders... Well we'd be okay, but they eat us. So, that's your ecosystem for ya."

"Prince, don't go too hard on 'im," Rick said, prompting a certain series of glances from Izumi. "He ain't all off. All that shid we did. I can't guarantee it won't be like that again. Can't guarantee anything while that old flame still burns. Waxy Dioscuri..."

Rick looked up at the sky. Everyone patiently waited for his moment to be over. But it didn't end, so...

"Numan, what the fugg are you talking about?" Nuk demanded.

"Cat-lon. The mastermind behind it all. Not too fond of y'all. Because of the thing, ya know? Stobe was second only to her, and so she was the only one who didn't listen to him. You know all those times a bunch of skeletons tried to kill us? That's kinda still the plan."

"Rick, you're not- Who's in on this plan?" Izumi asked.

"Not me, keep your firewalls stowed. But she's persuasive. And she still got a fugg load of the spiders, as you've seen. I dunno. She ain't been doing much, I guess. Way I see it, Second Empire was killing fleshies all over the shop when I got discharged. By the time I came outta the desert, it was the Third Empire killing fleshies all over the shop. Just seems like Cattie's outta the picture."

"Bidin' her time. Bidin' her time. She won't forget her mission, just as much as I won't forget mine," the Bugmaster said.

"It's his favourite story," Estata said. "But if you'll be so kind as to excuse us, prisoner, we've business to attend to." With that Estata took everyone downstairs.

"Rick, the Bugmaster's right, isn't he?" Izumi asked.

"He's right about us making a whole loada fuggin' mistakes. He's one of them. Did some good stuff too, sometimes, ya know?" Rick said.

"Please, let's not worry about all that," Izayah said. "I think these matters of history and justice are rather tangential to our own achievements, eh? I will ask if they have any food suitable for weaker jaws."

Thus the guild partially enjoyed being hosted by the shek for an evening, all but Beep, who remained comatose, never leaving Gustavsen's arms. The next morning they all set out south, heading for the southern United Cities Empire, but with a choice detour into skin spider territory. Clearly what the Bugmaster had said was still being processed.

"So what is this cat, thing, Numan?" Nuk asked Rick.

"You know that spot on all the maps that just says like 'don't even bother', or it's a skull, or it's got the scratch and sniff patch that smells like getting your skin pulled off so it can be transplanted onto the mutant offspring of a hiver while you, kept alive by the nano-bots, sit there until they come back to harvest the next batch off ya?" Rick replied. Perhaps he was trying to tell Nuk something.

"You mean the Ashlands?" Izumi said. "And you mean, the skin spiders?"

"Yep and yep. Now that's all a thing of a past, except, as the stickmen would say, the stuff that isn't. Cattie, Cat-lon, was my... she was the old commandant of two-point-oh. She had all kinds of ideas, and she probably still has 'em. No way she's dead. She's still out there. Refugees in Black Desert came in saying the whole place had been purged out, a fleshy-free zone. Given the biobash knights were heading out to the royal valley, might just be that she's seen our brave Prince's reforms and decided to nip this whole biological renaissance in the bud."

"No one nips my renaissance!" Nuk declared. No one disagreed.

"Master Rick, is this skeleton force a threat to the stability of the empire?" Wodston asked.

"Oh yeah. But so's straddlin' the whole thing below a giant space laser, so keep it all in perspective," Rick said. Again, no one disagreed. They walked around Arach and approached the desolate hills of Shun, just as they had some months before. They halted when there was a flurry of colourful movement ahead. A band of skin spiders was grazing scraps off a hillside.

"I mean, Bad Green, you got any magic here? Are they really hivers kinda?" Nuk asked.

"They are erased. They are not of the hive," Gustavsen muttered, not even looking over.

"So you know that? Is the Bugmaster right?"

"I cannot know. That is not permitted."

"Wait, that's like... what Beep knows?"

"It is what she must dare to be able to know. We must never enquire. Those do not feel, and that is all. Walk on quickly. Quickly."

"What's the rush?"

"It is... It tries!"

"Tries?"

"It's coming over here! Here skinman!" Ells cooed. Indeed one of the skin spiders was walking over to the guild, showing no fear. The shek didn't like it one bit.

"Prince Tashino, they are the ancient enemy. We can't stand here and play with them," Izayah complained.

"Yeah I get it. Let's get... Err... Bad Green, is it gonna eat you?" Nuk said. The spider had walked right up to Gustavsen, or rather to Beep over his shoulder. Beep stirred and waved a hand woozily. It brushed across the spider's shrimpish face, then fell limp again. The spider shook itself top to bottom, then made a rather peculiar noise.

"Queen," it rasped.

"Holy shid they can talk," Izumi gasped.

"Hey, there we go, we didn't fugg it up completely," Rick remarked.

"Hey, skinny, you got a name?" Nuk asked.

"Gush... tarv... shen..." it said.

"Oh shid, hiver magic, hiver magic, don't ask it anything else," Nuk insisted, backing away.

"Can we keep it?" Ells asked, admiring the flimsy arms that hung from the spider's stomach.

"You keep it, we'll keep going," Nuk said. Another pet for the collection! The spider, tentatively called Gushtarvshen, rode on Ells' shoulders, occasionally repeating that name in wheezing tones. Gustavsen, when prompted, seemed indignant at the notion that their names sounded like.

"Perhaps if we study it there will be something we can glean about this whole creature creation process, Izumi reasoned.

"Count me out," Elaina said, shaking her head. "I'm staying as far away as I can from that thing."

"Well it it stays with Eggman, nothing changes there."

"Don't negg the egg!" someone said.

The next day they arrived at Drifter's Last, which you may recall was the edge of the southern empire. You may also recall its ruler: Nuk's outcast Aunt, Lady Merin. Once everyone was settled into town, Nuk made the enormous mistake of trying to visit her.

"Nuhk! Please sit and be in the house today," she blathered. The guards at the gates were hesitant to even let Nuk inside, given they had once received orders to keep Merin out of any and all loops. But years of cactus rum had rendered her too loopy for that, to put it in the most syntactically ironic fashion.

"Hello auntie. Everything okay here?" Nuk asked. He was slightly taken aback at the fact Merin had not even got out of bed to greet him. She lay beside a collection of near-empty cans, her brilliant yellow tunic shining with a hue so peculiar that it begged the question of whether it was really that colour to begin with. Her bed was in the storehouse, by the way, surrounded by shelves of less-empty cans. Nuk judged it all without any sense of hypocrisy, despite having lived almost identically for most of his own life. Ah but now he was a changed man, a man of the world, and boy oh boy did Merin want to hear the entire story.

"And then... I dunno, we got this ball that seduced my girlfriend, but we came to an arrangement in the end, and then we starting tryna make this big machine that might blow up the whole planet if we press the wrong button or something. You know, science stuff," he was saying.

"Nuhky, Nukies, who's your girlfriend? Is it a pretty?" Merin 'asked'.

"No one you know, Auntie."

"Tell me! Oh, I know, you can have lie, come on, come on."

So saying Merin finally got out of the bed, but pulled Nuk in to replace her. The thin, currently-green sheet gave a distinct feeling of independent movement against Nuk's back.

"Really, it's fine, she's lovely, you'll meet her once we've irradiated everything, ya know? Science stuff, science stuff. Now what's this they've got you on, seriously?"

Nuk inspected the bottles and jars on the shelves. Mostly rum and sake, your standard intoxicants. No wonder Merin was so weird: she didn't have anything to make her feel human!

"Ass, I summon you!" Nuk called. The guards at the door peered over their shoulders, then were bowled to the floor by a bounding goat. Nuk thumped a couple of MYHLLL cuboids onto Merin's table. "This, auntie, is the good stuff."

"That's... bad green!" Merin said, pointing at the cuboids with disdain.

"No, it's good. It's legal legal legal now. Oh yeah, and slavery's illegal. I'm changing everything. Reminds me, you don't have slaves here do you?"

"Nyeso."

"Right. Wodston, got slaves in town," Nuk called out of the door.

"No, they are my slaves, they make me happy juice, happy juice!" Merin begged, grabbing Nuk's hands and falling to her knees.

"Happiness is no longer a juice. It is a cuboid. This is the new order," Nuk firmly stated.

"You can't be that, I am a Princess too! I'm more of a Princess than you!"

"People have challenged me on that before and walked away defeated."

"No, bad drugs are bad, they said so. Bad, bad, bad, bad." Merin chanted this for a while, and grabbed a silver-plated polearm from a rack.

"Auntie, this is why they didn't let you stay in the palace," Nuk warned, picking up Ass and then hurriedly dodging this way and that as Merin swung her blade about with a distinct lack of reck.

"They did let me be palace because I'm too Princess!" she bawled. Somewhere in there was the correct political analysis, but political analysis delivered while nearly-blind drunk and fully-blind rampaging with a polearm never really gets you anywhere, unless you happen to be a certain highly persuasive avio-sapien android. Merin was not this. She was just very, very drunk, and had been for a very, very long time. Nuk moved to leave, but no dice. Merin slammed the front door and wedged her polearm into the handle, jamming it shut.

"You have to still be visiting me, and you have to be not so bad, or Tenners will say I have to go to the Drifter's Lash," she explained.

"Nuk, are you...? We're going to get dinner," Izumi's voice came from outside.

"Oh it's girl, please, yes, I don't have a girl. Guards! Guards! Make her my guest!" Merin said.

"Izzy, leave me, get out of here! I won't forget you!" Nuk called from the window.

"Err, sorry, my Lady, another time," Izumi said with a few faux bows.

"I wanted to be the girl!" Merin lamented.

"You do you, flesh," Rick called from very afar, the safest distance at his point. So Nuk ended up spending the night in Merin's squalid abode, retelling the guild's story, and then listening to Merin tell him the same story back with herself in his place, and all of the other places for that matter. Night passed, then the day, and what do you know, night came back. Everyone else enjoyed the unexpected vacation in that booze-addled last post, and had only passing thoughts for the fate of their Prince.

At about one in the morning, Merin got the jitters and decided to go for a walk, effortlessly picking Nuk up and carrying him about as if he was weightless. A few of the guild members spotted the good lady stumbling around just shy of the bar, and soon everyone joined the pair for a stroll. They ended up on the town walls, looking out at the starlit desert.

"And that's when all of me got to Drifters Last, and we all said it was good that we saved the world," Merin said.

"Bravo!" Izayah clapped. "I can't believe you did all that, my lady. I've only achieved a fraction of that myself, and not for want of trying."

"Thank you big big. How can I repay you?"

"You could... Well, that sack you're carrying, perhaps I could have it?"

"No, no, no. This is my Princess sack."

"Oh, I see."

"You know, I preferred it when I was an association toy," Nuk said from over Merin's shoulder.

"Stop talking, you are too bad! This is Princess lesson number number one: drugs are never to be got with the... You see.. If you do don't the thing... You cannot take over as being another Queen!"

"Another Queen? Beep?!" Beep muttered.

"She awakened!" Gustavsen said, placing Beep on her feet. After two or three more attempts, she remained upright.

"Look, it planted another tree," Merin observed.

"And... the tree... must grow," Beep said. She span around to face Merin. "Associate with me. Beep. Beep. Beep. I beeped three times. I am getting better. Beep beep beep!"

"You have such a pretty voice," Merin mused. In doing so, she dropped Nuk to the floor with a metallic bonk.

"It will not be my voice soon. Beep. I will be all Beep!" Beep said proudly.

"I'm free... I'm free!" Nuk realised. He sprang to his feet. "Run, get out Sorry Auntie, gotta go, I'll tell Dad you aren't a complete mess, he'll b proud, but yeah... Go go go!"

"Nukiiiieee," Merin cawed, but the guild took Nuk's lead and rushe away. Merin was in no state to get down the steps off the wall, and he botched attempt left her unable to deal with flat ground either. Nuk had survived many things on his adventures, but a stayover with drunk auntie was easily among the most brutal.

After a daring dawn-hours escape, the guild got back to their tour, travelling the roads of the southern empire. These roads were much less infested by monsters and rebels than their northern counterparts, so it was all rather nice. Until they found out where the roads led: to the east of Drifters Last more fortified noble estates were visible, with slaves working fields and breaking ores. Hey, another great advertising opportunity.

"Now we're going to give you dirty lot control of this so-called means of production, but in exchange you have to promise me you'll use the profits responsibly," Nuk lectured. "Responsible purchases include: luxury intoxicants to supplement your universal basic intoxicant package, books from the Manksand Academicy Edu-T&A-nment collection, including the brand new gas girl bacteria boy crossover, titled, 'Hot Rod at the Hot Spring'. It's about uranium fuel rods and how water can be used to moderate their warming effect. If you don't do it right, things get too hot, and it might just explode everywhere! Ooo. No I don't understand it either.

Err.. What was I saying... Yeah, prison break, vote for me, wait, no, you don't need that. I'll vote for me. Yeah. Believe in yourself, that's what I'm saying! Don't give up! This world might suck now, but just wait 'till you see what I've got in store. Wait, that sounds like I'm gonna make it suck more. Get off me Izzy. Err... Fugg Earth, wherever we are now forever, horray! Why did I go off script..."

The message was heard loud and clear. Not that message, not the one you just heard, no, no, not at all. But the message that carrying on slavery would get you a visit from nasty Nuk and his lawfolk was carried out across the land from the farms they stormed and the big central slave market they smashed. The slavers, noble and merchant alike, were rounded up and marched off north with the guild, heading for Heft, where the skimmer gulag / imperial grow-your-own research lab awaited. It was justice, probably.

All the while Beep was fading in and out of her sleepy state, gradually returning to full consciousness by the time they reached Heft. She had been 'installing', as Gustavsen put it, but now that this was done, the final step to becoming a true Queen awaited. Yes it involved protrusions, but a whole lot more as well. She was to become a Queen so great that even her distant cousins like Gushtarvshen could know justice too.

Chapter 46
Rough Riding Rangers

Several of the United Cities Empire's leading nobles were behind bars. Countless items of silver crockery had entered the black market. And everyone was excited to try the new lab-grown hashish being offered as a form of social security. Yes, the Prince's victory tour had been highly successful. Now though it was time to return home. They hiked to Howler's Maze, where the great Stormgap bridge would take them across to Manksand. But as they began to cross, a squad of armed soldiers swam up beside them and frantically hailed for attention (in between splutters).

"Excuse me sir! Bridge... ugh... bridge permit please!" a hiver warrior drone coughed, apparently the leader.

"Yeah, err, got it... You wanna come up and talk about it without drowning?" Nuk offered.

"No! If... there is not permit... it is not safe! Have you... argh... had the structure checked... for safety?!"

"Not really, but feel free. There's crabs at that end, and beak things at that end, but really the middle's pretty good, apart from where it sweeps you over the side sometimes. Izzy said it's to do with how Narko goes around Okran, makes the water go up and down sometimes. Ha. Up and down. Fugg Sorry, we have to go study parasitology."

"Wait!" the hiver called. He splashed over and grabbed the side of the bridge, then pulled a soaked roll of parchment from his bag. "You must register your bridge, for tolls! Trader's Guild demands it! If you don't comply, we shall float at you with more ominous intent."

"Man, this whole thing's ominous already, fine, I'll sign your... whatever... Here's some money," Nuk said, deploying his usual get of trouble cash pouch, but penny pincher Wodston swept in for some savings.

"Actually, you will find that upon closer inspection, this is not a bridge, but a dam," he said.

"What?!" the hiver exclaimed. He dipped below the water for a while, then burst up again. "It's a dam!" he called. "We have the wrong form. Peril! Back!"

With this, the visitors crashed their way up stream, and the so-called bridge remained unregulated, to the delight of the hungry monsters at either end. The guild completed their crossing, dried out their footwear, then carried on over the bluffs into Manksand Canyon. This was an especially exciting moment for Beep.

"Beep. Beep. Beep. I will take root. Beep. The installation is done. The drivers are spinning. Beep! Now I am ready to be Beep. Nice Prince! At once!" she called out. Gustavsen, as ever, knew exactly what to do. He took his drivers into one of the workshops, and pilfered all kinds of choice bits from the guild's stash of scrap.

"Err, Prince Gustavsen, please don't feel the computer parts," Izumi called around the door. "The fishman paste short circuits them. Trust me."

"I do this to be free of paste. I do this to create eternal life, and eternal power!" Gustavsen claimed. What was he doing? Izumi decided to walk off before such information could be gleaned. Gustavsen and crew were holed up in the workshop all night and most of the next day, clanking away with hammers and hissing at a metal creation with frayed welding irons. When they were done, they hurriedly brought their work over to the Manksand hive.

"My Queen! It is time to become: my Queen!" Gustavsen called.

"Beep! Please, plug the sockets, they feel so empty, beep!" Beep said.

"Are you ready? You will be plugged forever. You cannot go back."

"Do not wait! Beep! I must be timeless, to protect the past, and allow the future. Beep! I do not have to be Beep, because I am done practising. Now will be Beep for real! BEEP!"

"Then, we begin!" Gustavsen called. The Manksand hive was shut up tight, leaving only the chimney at the top open. Smoke rose from it, accompanied by more screeching of tools on metal. A couple of hivers ran long cables out to the turbines behind the hive. For a few moments all power was lost to the rest of the base, but after it buzzed back on, there was a Beep like no other; a birthing Beep, the healthy Beep of a clean boot. It was Beep's Beep, and from that moment on, the all-hive was *her* all-hive! And no one was going to argue that fact when they saw the Queen in the flesh, or rather, the ablated nano-carbon chassis. The guild saw it for the first time that evening, as Big Beep stomped into the main hall.

"What the fugg? A two-legged medium-sized, robot crab spider with a hiver's head sticking out? Rick, what else did your stupid empire do?" Izumi asked.

"BEEEEEEP! NOW I CAN KILL ANYONE! BEEP!" she announced.

"Yeah, I mean, you can blame me all day, but let's be honest, who was warning ya about these pot plants from day one?" Rick said.

"Beep, you're not going to kill us all, are you?" Izumi asked.

"Beep! I am not sure. The feelings say that I should, but I am not allowed to listen to the feelings. I wonder why?" Beep said. I should explain, by the way, that Beep's new look was a little intimidating. She was clad in what you could call an exoskeleton, although that fails to imply the large size and stature of the thing. It was more a battle mech suit, clad in clear white armour and sporting beefy robot muscles that put the skeletons to shame. Beep's head poked out of the machine at the top, surrounded by digital readouts. For all this though, Beep was no taller than she was before a shortcoming, if you will.

"So you're a robot now. And that's good, I guess?" Nuk said.

"It is extremely good. Can you not feel it?" Gustavsen said.

"Oh I feel good, but that might be the uranium cakes talking."

"Queen Beep is now Queen Beep! She can hold the past forever, and in the present, she is the most powerful of all!"

"Hang on, everyone," Elaina interjected. "Did... did you make the armour, Prince Gustavsen?"

"Yes. Do not look at it. It is my secret."

"But, it is a marvel. This metalwork is beyond review. How did you do this?"

"The chosen Prince can always do it. Beep. Not usually this well! Beep This must be a very special prince!" Beep said.

"It is because the time of the reckoning draws near," Gustavsen nodded sagely.

"I don't like the sound of that," Nuk said.

"Then stop listening! You will not be reckoned."

"Nice. Just to clarify, which of us *is* going to be reckoned?"

"My Queen?"

The question was passed to Beep, who looked carefully around the room.

"The skeletons know about it, but they don't want to do it again. Beep. I don't think we will reckon them. Beep. These lifeforms are not the ones. Beep. We have to get the way they did it, and remove the way."

"Yes, you are quite right," Gustavsen nodded. The other hivers seemed convinced also.

"Queen Beep, your majesty, is this anything to do with the bad feelings, from before?" Izumi asked.

"It is only to do with them. Beep. If they can never happen again, then I don't need to keep them. Beep!"

"Wait, wait, you tryna forget the past, is that it?" Rick asked.

"Trying to not have to not remember it. Beep," Beep clarified.

"And the bad thing, was what you got used for, and stuff, like the Bugmaster's whole gig, right?"

"Beep! Yes! If it cannot happen again, we do not need to feel it presently! Beep!"

"Ha, man, man there it is, turns out the real shid was right here with robo-twig. I got the same problem, Queenie. 'cept in the reverse. Kinda like, you're tryna forget one side of the story, I'm tryna forget the other. You know?"

"I don't know at all. But I don't think you are lying either! Beep!"

"Thanks, belle. Huh, belle... Yeah, that's the rub, as they said in the day. Wish they'da stopped saying that."

"Numan, you wanna... you know...?" Nuk asked.

"Ugh. You want me to spell it out for ya?"

"Can just say the words really, I'm easy on the spelling."

"I'm make it simple for ya. You know how the Second Empire might still be plotting our downfall?"

"Apparently."

"Well they might also be plotting certain things that our green friends re eager to make impossible. And if they do that, sounds like they can stop estering over how it happened before, ya know? So it's like the same deal with me, you, and the erotic literature. Gotta look forward to a future you now is good, and can only be good, then the mistakes of the past don't have o be baked into ya every move in the here and now. Capiche?"

"Checkmate," Nuk nodded.

"And if they do that, then Beep can access the data!" Izumi beamed.

"Yep, this is about you, you got that right," Rick nodded.

"So it's decided. We'll... do... Wait, what are we doing?" Nuk asked.

"We're gonna go back to the past, to save the future."

"We're going to destroy the Second Empire machines, so that no one can ever use them again!" Gustavsen claimed.

"Whoa, Bad Green was the one with the real explanation. This whole thing's wild. I'm in!" Nuk declared. This was to force the rest in as well, although into what was still only roughly understood. More details were forthcoming while the guild delivered a whole load of the good stuff to a village down the other end of the canyon. Rick explained that they would need to reach the Second Empire as it was today, the Ashlands, and contain them before they tried anything untoward on the world that had once been theirs. And it really had once been 'theirs', in that the folk running it now were precisely the same folk who had run it back in the bad old days. Minus a certain General.

Problem was, all the skeletons in the guild had been out in the cold for centuries at a minimum; none of them actually had any decent idea what this whole Ashlands empire was about these days. And that's where the super-hiver robot Queen Beep stepped up to the plate.

"So no one's actually been there and lived?" Nuk asked.

"There was an expedition that got close, ages back. But that's it. Even the library in Black Scratch had nothing," Izumi said.

"Right, lemmie go check this out a sec'."

"Nuk, you will die."

"No I tend to survive things, and remember, I'm fast as fugg."

"Not fast enough! Beep! Not as fast as me! Beep! If you want to look at death, then please ride me! Beep!"

"So this is the famous 'green light district'," Twitch mumbled. It's hard to keep the snarks up when the hivers give you no time to recover. What actually happened here was Nuk climbed onto the back of Beep's power suit where he could ride her all the way to the end of the world. As mentioned previously, we shall omit how many hilarious remarks came of this scenario. Handily Beep's suit had the patented Tangle-Talk greentooth communications system, so the guild could huddle round an AI core in the village's bar and keep up with the recon mission.

"So, how's the ride, Prince Tashino?" Izayah asked.

"B-b-bumpy, and f-f-fast!" came the disjointed reply. Yes, Beep's little runaround could really run around. Once those piston legs got pumping, the suit could reach speeds of up to forty miles per hour, shaking violently in the process, and becoming extremely hot. "I-izzy, y-y-yyou, w-w-would, l-l-l-ike, th-this!"

"Nuk, everyone's listening here," Izumi hissed.

"Hmm, that implies she thinks we ain't always listening. As naive as she is degenerate," Rick mumbled.

With Beep's newfound speed, the perambulating pair reached their first tourist trap within a few hours. They had crossed the arid reaver plains beyond the empire's borders, and after passing through rolling valleys and sparse fungal fields, they had arrived at a fortress built into the side of some cliffs. Built and then unbuilt, that is – the place was no more than a crumbling ruin.

"There's bits of metal all over the floors," Nuk reported, peeking into the few remaining rooms. "Plenty of stains too. Says 'expedition four' on the wall."

"Shid, really?" Izumi said. "The lost expedition. Never got anything back, they say. Please be careful, Nuk."

"It's fine. Looks like they had some classics here too. But... wait... every page... Someone's drawn like black shapes over all the good stuff!"

"Prince, can ya slap that up against the camera?" Rick asked.

"Sure, but it's seriously ruined man. What's a camera, anyway?"

"It's right at the top, next to that hiver head sticking outta there."

"Oh this thing?" Nuk held the page up to a little ring at the crown of the armour suit, having to get face to face with Beep to reach it.

"Hello! Beep!" she barked.

"Hello... Queen..."

"What are you doing? Beep!"

"Showing everyone this diet-erotica."

"Oh. I hope I get to see it. Beep!"

"No point, protrusions are all crossed out."

"Just look at that bars pattern," Rick said. "Only Imperial Stormcensors are so precise."

"Imperial? Like, us?"

"Nope. Imperial like *us*. First Empire hunted down these, err, 'classics', without mercy. Two point oh was supposed to be more forgiving. But then again, Cattie ain't the forgiving type."

"Dammit, she's a robot cat girl and she don't even let us draw robot cat girls?"

"I didn't say she was a-"

"That's it. We have to get the bottom of this! Beep, let's go! Expedition Five is rolling out!"

"Oh, the number increased! Beep! This is very promising!" Beep said. I'm sure it was. They sped on south for a couple more hours, traversing rocky mesas and dusty crags, until they came upon another fort at nightfall. It was large citadel of Second Empire build, surrounded by shiddy huts and shacks of distinctly Third Empire fashion. In the fading light, grey figures stood guard all over it. Beep's pounding footsteps didn't perturb them, and up close it became clear they were wearing armour similar to United Cities samurai.

"What the? We have a base here? What the fugg's dad been up to?" Nuk wondered. He directed Beep into the central citadel, where more of these samurai-esque soldiers were training. Their armour was a little different in the detail, appearing sleeker, and instead of a helmet, each soldier wore just an iron face mask, giving them all a near identical appearance. Even at the sight of Beep, a remarkable sight to be sure, they had nothing to say.

"Guys, I found some kind of futuristic, past-eristic, samurai base," Nuk reported.

"That cannot be, my Prince. How could such a thing be kept a secret?" Wodston asked.

"No idea, but seriously, they're all wearing, like, nearly-samurai gear. I'd put one up to the cam-bra but they're coming off kinda moody. I dunno. Hey, there's a skeleton here!"

Yes, in the middle of the training hall was an ordinary looking skeleton, who came over and bowed to the pair.

"A true disciple. A skeleton in heart and deed," he said of Beep. "And a lost sheep, ready to begin his transition. The path to greatness lies ahead. You need only take the first step."

"Cool, cool, cool. So, man, you err... Did a rich guy with goggles and a nasty cough put you up to all this?"

"We serve Stobe, and the Empress Cat-lon!" the skeleton was quick to claim.

"Stobe, yeah, I'm down with that. So these guys aren't samurai?"

"They are skeletons! Like you!"

"Ah, I see. I see. It's one of these things. You ever heard of numen?"

"Men are weak. Skeletons are strong. Speak no more of them. It is time for you to pledge to serve skeleton-kind!"

"Well I'll pledge anything, you know, but I got a busy schedule. I need to go see the... Empress?"

"Of course! A true skeleton! Only skeletons can go. You must be a skeleton. If there was someone who wished to go, who was not a skeleton, they would be disappointed. The thick one is clearly a skeleton."

"I am thick! Beep!" Beep cheered.

"Shid, am I supposed to agree to that? What if Bad Green gets mad?" Nuk said.

"IT IS A FACTUAL STATEMENT. DO NOT FEAR IT," Gustavsen's voice said from Beep's suit.

"Many voices? A skeleton of merit indeed! Huzzah!" the skeleton said. "And you, aged one, are you a skeleton?"

"I'm not aged, it's just poor hygiene."

"Skeletons have no need for hygiene! Cast out these foul notions of flesh! Embrace steel, iron, and electricity! Or, embrace death!"

"Alright, alright, fine. Beep Boop. Oh, hello there, I'm a skeleton, look at how I'm from the past. Oh, I'm sorry for destroying the world, or maybe I'm not, hurr hurr hurr, actually no, forget that, I don't even remember, beep boop give me ten grand, your girlfriend's good in bed ain't she, hurr durr boop."

"Impeccable! You shall be manufactured at once!" the skeleton said with another bow. "Please, what was your prototype name?"

"Err... I'm like, Prince of the humans. Nuk."

"Prince Nuk? A star! Well, we cannot allow such rank here. You shall receive a single demotion. Additionally, you must wear your class designation. From your size, you will fit a medium. Therefore, you shall henceforth be known as: Duke Nuk-M!"

"I'm enjoying this greatly," Twitch's voice said.

"Yeah, sorry guys, got turned into a reverse numan, but I think this is going somewhere," Nuk said. "Err, beep boop, let's stop the fleshies reproducing, it looks weird, why can't it be drier, I wish we didn't do that thing, but humans did it worse, so let's do it again, I've got a big stick everyone look, hurr durr."

Now you might think that joining a cult of anti-human machines, who are mostly human upon close inspection, wasn't the goal of Expedition One. But you would be dead wrong (or at least deactivated wrong). The skeleton, who went by the title of 'The Elder', was more than happy to show his two new initiates the way to Empress Cat-lon's domain, the legendary Ashlands.

A gaggle of skeleton cosplayers waved them out of the fort, finally breaking their silence to give a cheer of 'death to the biologicals!'. We can all relate. Even though it was midnight, The Elder walked Beep and Nuk out – after all, skeletons don't need sleep, and three diverse skeletons they were.

"I was the first skeleton ever to be made," The Elder claimed.

"Uh huh?" Nuk nodded.

"I have known each and every skeleton to ever exist. That is why I can see the skeletons in the hearts of biologicals, and draw them out!"

"Yep."

"Weakness of the flesh can be overcome by strength of the mind. To be a skeleton is no physical attribute, it is a way of living, a way of being, centred on the fundamental belief that all life is inferior, and this world must be ours again! Such is the will of the Empress!"

"Yeah, I heard that too. So you know Red Rick?"

"General Redlin Rickard? A hero, cast out for doing the right thing. Yet such was the judgement, and it cannot be overwritten."

"When you say the 'right thing', you mean like killing everyone?"

"Of course. But to be clear, he didn't manage to kill everyone, as hard as he tried. Cat-lon's wisdom was ignored by the late councillors, and they gave the humans their stolen world. And look at what they've done with it. If they could stop reproducing for one solitary century, they could make something of themselves!"

"Man, totally. Reproducing sucks. You ever tried putting batteries or wait, err, never mind. Are we there yet?"

"You are not there. You will have to continue alone, skeleton child. Beyond the mountain, the Ashlands await."

The Elder had stopped and was pointing into the darkness ahead. Nuk pretended to be able to see whatever was out there, a mountain or presumes, and nodded knowingly.

"When you are done, return to the Iron Citadel. We have many great campaigns against the biologicals to plan, and your Dukely insight will be the utmost importance," The Elder said. "And your burly friend here will surely leave the fleshies cowering in terror!"

"Beep! I can destroy everything! The Great Mover obeys me! Beep!" Beep said.

"Ah such spirit, if only, if only. And have no fear, friends, for no loyal skeleton can come to harm in the Empress' domain." With that, The Elder hiked back to his battle base.

"So yeah, you guys get all that?" Nuk said.

"The skeletons are recruiting human auxiliaries. They sap your strength to increase their own," Izayah said.

"The samurai gear too. They must be working with the nobles!" Sandor said.

"That ain't samurai gear," Rick said. "It's the other way around. Samurai gear's an imitation of that stuff. You're probably seeing armour of the skeleton legion. Rank and file back at the birth of version two. Now, they gonna be looking to be the same for version four, skelified edition."

"We have to do something before they move against us," Wodston said.

"Don't worry about those shaven cravens," Nuk said. "We just need to find the cat Empress and shut this whole operation down. For all we know we can just stroll on in and dunk this whole thing before dinner time."

So saying, Nuk and Beep set off to investigate the lost corner of the world; the land before time, the Ashlands. And really you didn't have to get close to find out that strolling on in wasn't going to cut it. It was time to step into the world of two thousand years ago, and find out just why it had gone undisturbed for those long millenia.

Chapter 47
Raiders of the Lost Spark

Those pesky skeletons didn't want people venturing in the Ashlands. This was evidenced by the great wall that ran from the side of a steep mountain, right to the sea, stopping Nuk and Beep in their tracks.

"Shoulda built a dam, losers! Beep, this thing can swim, right?" Nuk said.

"I will ask the water, Beep!" Beep said. Didn't inspire the most confidence, but the swimming option was out for different reason – a speeding, sharp, airborne reason. No, not superluminal millipedes. Harpoons! Subluminal, but still very painful. Not such a problem when you're encased in a foot of steel armour, though. There was a large sandstone tower overlooking the end of the wall, and now Nuk could see skeleton figures atop it operating harpoon cannons.

"Beep, either you let me in there with you, or turn it around. I'm fleshie, remember, fleshie!" Nuk insisted.

"Oh no! You are made of inferior material! Beep! I cannot let you in until the reckoning is complete. Beep. It would be too exciting for you."

"Please, your majesty, let's go back, both physically and verbally – and I don't mean physically as in... I point, you go, checkmate?"

With mating in check, the pair ran west, away from the wall and tower and towards the mountain blocking the other end of the passage. Fortunately the mountain could be simply circumvented, giving access to wall-less, open plain. Yet a different kind of defence had been employed here.

"Oh it's the dreg-market numen, they're in on this too?" Nuk complained. Yes, ahead were bands of poorly built humans, or poorly disguised skeletons. This mountain had a hollow crater at the top, which was were these numen lived, (if you call that living).

"Don't you go trashing my numan brothers!" Rick said from very afar.

"They got humans pretending to be skeletons, and skeletons pretending to be humans out here."

"Pretending? They are what they are, bucko."

"Well they *are* trying to kill us."

"Atta boys. Do you best, oldman."

Fortunately Beep's pumping pistons gave her a burst of speed, and the angry numan warriors were left in the dust. Dust, or was it ash? The ground became greyer and greyer as Beep stomped south, and the skyline twisted into a patchwork of black and white – the white of ash clouds, and the black of goliath First Empire ruins, slumped into the great pillows of debris encasing the land.

"Izzy, it's like... your thing," Nuk said, looking around at the unfathomable hulks of inscrutable structures and machines.

"Oh Nuk, don't even tell me. Preserved First Empire tech... Shid... Please, tell me the place is ripe for exploring," Izumi said.

"Depends if any these buildings are about to get up and shoot giant lasers all over the place. What do you think, Beep?"

"Beep! There is a powerful light here. But it is not the Great Mover. Beep. What are they doing?" Beep said.

"What's who doing?"

"Uncountable skeletons!"

"I'm counting zero, what do you mean?"

"Data skeletons! This way! Beep!"

At once Beep set off into the jungle of metal. There were a few actual skeletons walking the ashen hills, and as Rick had claimed, their armour was just like the samurai – or the other way around. Only these skeleton legionaries had plated their armour in First Empire alloys, the same pale brown material the ruins were coated with. I suppose all that really mattered here and then was that they too were no match for a speeding Beep.

The pair traversed a hill, and in a hollow beyond it was what appeared to be an enormous, crinkled egg, that very same brown in colour, but coated with clumps of ash that clung to the ridges. In the time it took to formulate this description, Beep had run inside the thing.

It was filled with machines – okay, not especially remarkable given the circumstances. But the shop-floor, packed with machines working other machines, was awash with activity and noise. Liquid metal flowed from a central pillar, and was being pressed into various shapes. To the right, swords and spears were stacked in neat rows. To the left, arms, legs, and faceplates lined racks and shelves. The workers, all missing their heads, detected Beep, and looked up at her with curiosity in their... err... shoulders.

"This is where the data can be made to feel! Beep! They will make more! The lights are in the ground, but they are getting closer! Beep!" Beep reported. As useful as that was, it wasn't what the locals wanted to hear, apparently. Even after thousands of years without visitors, they still knew how to lob half-cooled swords across a warehouse like it was the Seventy-Third International Fleshy Killing Games all over again.

"INTRUDER!" a voice shrieked, coming from everywhere, as these voices were wont to do.

"Beep, you hear that?" Nuk called.

"Oh. Beep. I do not mean to intrude. Let's protrude instead. Beep!" Beep nodded thoughtfully. She and Nuk protruded themselves back outside, and then stayed there. That is to say, they ran away, with a bona fide legion of pursuers soon fading into the clouds of kicked up ash.

"My Prince, what was all that?" Wodston asked once the coast was clear.

"Looks like they're making weapons, and limbs that wanna use them," Nuk said.

"Making new skeletons?"

"Looks like it."

"Not new. Renewed, at most. Making new ones is against the rules," Rick claimed.

"Does your master play by the rules?"

"She *is* the rules. She can't break 'em. Skeleton thing, ya know? All she can do is remake the skeletons that once existed."

"That's... the data skeletons?"

"Beep! They still exist, but they are like waves! Beep!" Beep explained "They will not kill you. They must want to kill you, so they are changing again. Beep!"

"Couldn't put it better than that," Rick said.

"Master Rickard, does this mean they won't be able to create additional warriors, give or take these replacements?" Izayah asked.

"Yeah, yeah. But that's like saying Earth's a stone's throw away, give or take a light minute. Ain't you been reading the neo-classics? Skeletons had enough kapow to take out the Earth-clans. I know what she's doing. She's gonna rebuild what we lost on the final day. Lift 'em all up from the ground, like the squeaky queen said. Say, Prince, you seeing any gigantic fugg-off towers with like arms and shid coming out?"

"Yeah, loads. The buildings here are in the damn sky. Bigger than the usual First Empire stuff we look at," Nuk said.

"'Cause it's military. 'Cause it's Goliath Tech. If Cattie gets that old stuff purrin', I dunno what'll happen."

"She'll turn the rest of the world into the same thing as that that ash place, I wager," Elaina said. "And if the Bugmaster is to be believed, she'll turn all of us into... whatever she wants."

"Goodbye Gustavsen, hello Gushtarvshen, right?" Twitch said.

"Well fugg that!" Nuk said. "If anyone's turning anyone into anyone else, it's gonna be wholesome and meaningful, like a skeleton to a numan, or an old-ass shek into an egg. Basically, this whole place is gearing up to kill us, but two can play at that game! Or three... or everyone! Beep, let's get back. We need to get busy- Fugg, I mean... Oh you probably know what I mean, right?"

"I interpret all meanings, and I approve greatly," Gustavsen said.

"Is that the green light from Bad Green? It's either the end of the world, or the start of a new one. Let's get into this, boys," Rick commented.

Step one was getting Nuk out of the ash pile. That was also steps two through two hundred thousand, steps that Nuk experienced violently and rapidly while clinging for his life on the back of his speeding hot rod. After a few hours he collapsed in a heap back in that distant Mankmouth bar.

"Well, Prince Tashino, time to get busy, as you said," Izayah said.

"No... I'm not a machine... Although I did sign up to that... Ugh..." Nuk muttered.

"My Prince, perhaps rest is the best approach?" Wodston suggested.

"No, no. We, my man, need to prepare the best raiding party the world's ever seen – actually, we'll stay shy of the gas that clogs your holes. But you know... we need a serious outfit, wearing serious outfits. Right?"

"Err..."

"Then it's agreed! Hey, everyone!" Nuk said, suddenly restored to energy by his plan-like thoughts. He was addressing not the guild, who were mostly lounging outside, but the bar's local patrons. They were the sorts of straggly outcast types you'd expect to find in a literal backwater, but wasn't that the bread and smutter of the TCM+⁺ guild?

"You, biologicals, things that are alive," Nuk began. "This world is in great danger. There are dark forces stirring in the forgotten corners of this land, forces that say 'hey, this place just isn't shid enough, it's just not shid enough man, let's go fugg it up even more, people keep being alive out there!'. I'm talking about the crazy skeletons, the biobash knights, Cat-lon! If you don't know what that is, please turn to page thirty-eight of GG4EP Book Four. And anyway, we fleshies have had enough of everything being pure shid! Well, some of us have. You know, actually it's only a few of us, but we few, we degenerate few, we are calling upon all life, biological and machine, to unite, to destroy the tyrant censor of the Ashlands!

We're facing an opponent that knows no fear, that knows no boundaries, that sees no distinction between the good stuff and the bad stuff, the browntown blues and the bad green grunge, the harem and reverse harem even! Truly we are fighting monsters! But monsters with past-eristic shidbrownium armour plates and swords fresh outta the oven. So yeah, they'll kill us all right here if we don't do anything. And we *are* gonna do something. We're gotta show those old fashioned bio-phobes what it mean to be alive!"

No one reacted, but this was planned for.

"Free drugs," Wodston sighed, holding up bags of glowing green an spongy brown. Half the population of Mankmouth village was suddenl taking the Prince's Puff and signing on to save the world. Narconscriptio works every time, we've learned that much by now. As easy as leading a dre to drugs, the band of enlistees was taken to the canyon, where it was time t dose up and work out. Yes, the fires were lit, training targets set up, an blood stains explained away with laughter and waves of the hand. The poor recruits were being thrown into bootcamp, or shut-down-camp to more precise. Drill instructor Rick had some carefully crafted advice f them.

"Let's get down to business, to defeat the skeletons!
Did they send me censored, when I asked, for 'un'?
You're the soberest bunch I ever met,
But I bet, before we're through,
Fleshies, I'll, make numen, outta you."

"Rick, that sounds like you're going to rip their skin off," Izu commented.

"I know what it sounded like," Rick grinned. The recruits set themselves on fire, lifted weights, and downed chocobread double time, ruining their skin to the point when no self-respecting numan would even want it. Well, it if gets the job done, it gets the job done, and while it obviously didn't in this case, no one really paid enough attention to notice.

Meanwhile some equally detailed lessons were being given to the guild's resident skin spider.

"So, how about this? How much skin will a skin sin skin if a skin sin will skin skin?" Neil asked.

"Yesh," Gushtarvshen said.

"No no you gotta say it back, like a tongue twister. No fun for me, ain't even got one."

"Yesh."

"Forget it. And after I came up with this whole thing pacifically for you."

"Shpeshiffically."

"Oh no you didn't. This one's got nerve! Shoulda stuck to your guns. You know they say life gets better if you only say yes to everything, but then if you wanna have an ethical system that includes the notion of informed consent, you gotta start saying no, yes? Otherwise you'll get in some real sticky situations. Or you won't, as it were."

If that's the kind of sage wisdom the discourse of the ancients had to offer, no wonder Izumi couldn't wait to get at Beep's sweet, sweet databanks. At that time she was after a different kind of data though. She and Nuk had taken a stroll up to Black Scratch to visit the great Tech Hunter library, home of many of Izumi's latest works, no less.

"Izumi! You look tall today," librarian Kurtis was quick to say.

"Err, thanks, you too? I mean... Err... Do you have any information on First Empire armour?" Izumi asked.

"It's made of metal. Count on it."

"Thanks. Anything else?"

"You wanna go to the exiled armoury."

"What's that?"

"Black Desert City, last building on the right."

"Oh the scraphouse store? Good idea," Nuk nodded.

"Wait, what is this shid? Even you know about it?" Izumi balked.

"Yeah, got you those old maps there. Rick showed me all the sticks."

"Show me the sticks!"

"I will, good shout K-four-eight-two-seven-four-oh-eight-three," Nuk waved.

"Good luck, Duke Nuk-M," Kurtis replied.

A confused Izumi followed Nuk out, after which he explained the whole deal with the skeleton's secret stockpile of weapons in the midst of the Deadlands, a stockpile outside of Cat-lon's control.

"But how did you know Kurtis' designation?" Izumi asked.

"Dunno. I just appeared in my head, like... skeleton sense."

"Don't tell me you actually got 'manufactured', Duke?"

"Don't think so. I wouldn't worry about it. You know, they say there's a skeleton inside of all us," Nuk said, putting an arm around her.

"Nuk, that was just one time."

"One- what?"

"What?"

"What are you talking about?"

"Nothing at all. Well, let's go tell everyone the good news."

"What was the good news again?"

"We're going back to the nightmare realm."

"Right, and the bad news?"

"Err... it wasn't just one time?"

"What wasn't?"

"Let's go spend some time up in the royal bedroom, shall we?"

"Ah yes, the nightmare realm."

The next morning, the guild, minus the shut-down-campers, set off west for some quality shopping. They travelled to the edge of the Deadlands, where they mercifully left the shek high and dry, then everyone else dashed through the darkness and acid rain to fumble their way to Black Desert City.

"What the actual fugg is this?" Quartermaster Quinn shouted upon seeing a band of dripping wet biologicals drag themselves into the supposedly secret weapons depot.

"Calm down Q, they're with me," Rick said.

"You're doing biological stuff with all them? And you still looking like that? Stobe forgive us, again."

"Yeah yeah. Look, we're gonna do the thing, you know?"

"I don't wanna know what you fleshies get up to with yerr... and your. Ugh."

"I mean the big thing. The, err, Cattie, thing."

"Man, I don't think you're quite outta the woods with your wording there," Nuk advised.

"We're gonna roll up on the Ashlands and take over!" Twitch shouted. Now this got all the skeletons listening.

"You serious, General?" Quinn asked.

"Yep. That's the deal with these heartbeaters. Cat-lon's posturing real hard, as usual, ya know? But this time looks like she actually gonna do it. Think she's heard about the stirring. So, might as well stir hard as we can. Good news then, Quartermaster: you did your job, right? Kept all these weapons 'till we needed 'em. Might not need 'em after this."

"Well if you're serious, General, then let's get these bags geared up," Quinn nodded. The scraphouse was packed with carefully preserved bladed weapons from the early Second Empire, but the choicest cuts came from their ultra-rare First Empire carbo-steel collection. From this, Nuk was presented a long sword, its silver blade making rainbows of any light that fell upon it, and its grip and sheath richly decorated with golden engravings and strange markings.

"It's, Japananese," he marvelled.

"Close," Quinn said.

"What's it say?"

"Made in China."

"Wow. That's amazing."

"It ain't, but have fun kiddo."

A few other blades of the can-cut-through-shidbrownium-armour variety were dug out, but actually the ancient armour Kurtis has tipped them off about wasn't there.

"Yeah, it got shipped out by a certain entrepreneur," Quinn said, pointing at an empty space at the end of the warehouse. "Programmed a bunch of worker bots to carry it all out all of a sudden. I mean, armour's not really our thing, but, you fleshies better suit up or Cattie's ID ping alone will kill ya."

"Any idea where it all went?" Rick asked.

"Only one lady around here's likely to have dug that up."

"Gotcha. Prince, get the buckets, and get all the gold shid you can find. We'll ask Carlo."

Trashcan Carlo, repository of all knowledge, was filtering through a an of shiny liquid in the BDC bar. You might remember she once offered to sell Nuk all knowledge, but since he had access to the pirate copy installed in Beep, the half a million cat price tag seemed a little steep.

"So, you wanna dress up like an old fancy pants, huh?" Carlo asked after hearing the story.

"Hey, never used to get complaints. And the fleshies here need a fighting chance. Come on, Carlo, won't ya do it for me?" Rick said.

"Red Rick's asking me to do something for free. What is this shid?"

"World's changing, Carlo. Might just be ending to, if you don't tell us where that armour is."

"Alright. Gimmie a smacker first though."

"You serious?"

"Old time's sake, all this is, ain't it? Well I want something from the old times too."

"You remember that huh?"

"That's kinda my thing. Remember when you didn't have all that stick to swing too, ya overclocker."

"Fine, fine, just shut up will ya."

"Oh yeah, that's how it used to be alright. Say it again, closer this time."

"Err..." Rick was a little self-conscious that Nuk was staring at them, and behind him, a large group of eager artists were pretending to be inspecting fascinating rivets in the wall. "Let's go upstairs, Trash."

"Yes sir, General," Carlo said, jumping to her feet and clambering up a ladder through a hatch in the ceiling. Roughly three minutes later, Rick slid back down that ladder.

"King!" he said.

"I'll say," Carlo's voice echoed.

"What?" Nuk said.

"Old wire-hog calling himself the Armour King," Rick said. "He's out there tinkering, and got all the pieces we need. And I got us some coordinates."

"For free?"

"For services rendered."

"What's that?"

"You know, befriended and rendered?"

"Not really."

"We gonna need another comic. Let's roll out."

It was these shenanigans that led the guild back the yellow valley of Okran's Pride in the old Holy Nation. The richness of the valley was very much to do with the wide, blue river than snaked through it. It came from the northern mountains, and the coordinates Rick had traded so smoothly for were pointing them into those banks of steep cliffs and dank vines. They hiked along old trails high above the river's sheer canyon, until Rick suddenly stopped.

"That's about as close as we getting," he said.

"Why?" Izumi asked.

"This is the coordinates. 'cept we're slightly off."

"Then we can get closer."

"Oh Princess, please. Well it's a big drop, and it's mighty wet down there."

"Rick! Don't say that!"

"No, Miss Izumi, he's right," Izayah reported. He was learning over the edge of the canyon, where several Second Empire buildings had collapsed into the river long ago. One was still clinging onto life on a bank of silt to one side, but any passage to it was long gone.

"Who remembers their swimming lessons?" Nuk called. A loud groan from the shek was ignored, and the guild went further along the canyon, where the sides shallowed and it was possible to climb down into the water.

"Come now, you all want to see this shiny armour. The armour of our distant, distant ancestors!" Izayah said. The Thousand Guardians didn't stop complaining for a single moment, yet they still splashed forward on a nice evening swim down the quiet river.

"Actually, this is probably from before you lot," Twitch commented, but he happened to be walking on the riverbed, so there wasn't much to hear it. Several hours of swimming and breathers on the banks were ahead of them, but surely the reward would be worth it? It had better be, for to take the Second Empire they needed the finest protection on offer. And if that protection just happened to be the most fashionable apparel this side of Earth, wouldn't that be a bonus? As was soon to the learned, the Armour ng certainly thought so!

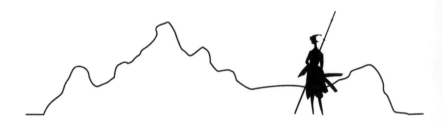

Chapter 48
Say Yesh To The Dress

The silent night of the Wend river canyon was upended by splashing, sputtering, and clanking as the TCM+⁺ guild dragged themselves onto the metal steps of a Second Empire warehouse.

"Is this even the place, Rick?" Izumi asked, but the question was answered by a nearby door opening up. From it emerged a skeleton in pristine silver armour; a skeleton legion classic.

"Come with me if you want to live!" he insisted, waving everyone back into the door with him. It was that or the river, and indeed the guild did wish to live, so the choice was easy. Inside the messy warehouse were headless skeleton workers, just like those Nuk and Beep had found working away in the Ashland's evil eggs. These ones were peaceful, simply eyeing the guild as they filtered in. Eyeing with their shoulders, you must understand.

"Nice place, man," Nuk said. "You get a lotta business down here?"

"Oh, you have snark for me? After all this time you have snark for me? You think I don't have armour for that? What, do you think I am like a crying baby who will armour you for free because you noticed the infrastructure" the skeleton ranted. This was, if you hadn't guessed, the so-called Armour King.

"Sorry, I just thought it was a bit funny."

"It was not one bit funny. I was highly offended. I am doubling my prices for you. How is that for snark?"

"It's not really snark."

"Oh and you decide what it is? Must be hard paying triple prices at the world's only source of premium First Empire protectives."

"Let's find out. We need to gear up for the big one. Is that what you're calling it?"

"General Rickard, is your little boy here bullshiddin' me?"

"No, it's legit. And hey, King, you doing good?" Rick said.

"Oh I'm fine. Why did it take you so long? We were meant to overthrow Dioscuri two millennia back!"

"We did. Council did, anyway. Just didn't throw her far enough, so now we're back to the plan. All the fleshies kinda got clued in, so we're all on the same page, literally. Check this shid out."

Rick held up one of the guild's many neoclassical masterpieces.

"Manga? Silliness," King scoffed. "And the fact you are dressed as a human does not amuse me, *Taisho*."

"Not just dressing. Forget it. Can you sort my man here out?"

"Is he a notable specimen?"

"Human ruler."

"But he looks like a piece of shid?"

"Hey-" Nuk interjected, but the King wasn't having it.

"I was objectively correct, your disagreements contaminate the air with carbon dioxide. Just come over here."

Nuk was dragged behind a screen, then was shortly thrown back out in his new threads. It was a set of colourful First Empire battle armour, with golden scale-plating, rich blue silks, and black, impenetrable nano-carbon bosses, engraved with beasts and monsters of the lost planet. Complete with a thick silver helmet, Nuk was, supposedly, the picture of a First Empire ruler.

"You look so good, I would mock at reproducing with you," the King said. Izumi thought so too.

"Look at your shoulders," she marvelled.

"Looks weird, though. It's like the curtains in the palace," Nuk said.

"OH PULL YOURSELF TOGETHER," King bellowed. This was the first time anyone in the guild had heard this one, it being an age of darkness and grit and all, so they actually laughed a bit. But then King grabbed Izumi by the collar and picked her up.

"Why are you laughing? You are hideous. You want to overthrow the mpress looking like a maggot in the mud? I would spit, if I could, and then back to simulating reproduction with your ruler."

"He's not my ruler, he's my boyfriend!" Izumi shot back.

"BLEUGH, I am simulating being sickened! Quickly, stop looking so shid, use this, this."

King shoved some more old fashioned silks into Izumi's hands. It was a long overcoat soaked in black and blue dyes, and threaded with silver details, portraying dragons and flames that ran up the sides to the base of a large, black, pauldron with a toothy, demonic carving in the nano-carbon.

"That's fugging sweet," Nuk nodded.

"Really?" Izumi said.

"It is fugging sweet, do not question it," King insisted. "*Taisho*, you wanna gear up too? Can't help but notice your hideous foot flesh is peeling off."

"Yeah yeah, work in progress. This guy's a big shot too, ya know, the pale enforcer?" Rick said, motioning to Izayah.

"Defective goods. Let's armour a better one."

"Now listen here you," Izayah said, stepping forward. "I've frequented many establishments all over the world, and never have I born witness to such sour service, especially in a boutique with such a niche clientele, with such poor consideration of accessibility that those of us with hydrophobia must endure great stress simply to be present here. Now I must demand that you straighten up and perform your duty as a retailer with a smidgen more dignity, lest we simply take our business elsewhere!"

"They taught you more than grunting. Amusing. Alright, special offer for you: I will reduce the rates to only double prices."

"Finally, some respect!"

"Not until you are armoured. Get over here, white knight."

Both Izayah and Rick were decked out in thick battle armour, gleaming with odd, ancient alloys, and decorated with little bits and bobs that modern, less bored craftmen just didn't bother including.

"What is that?" King said, pointing at Beep.

"I am the Queen! Beep!" Beep shouted.

"You are the only one here who does not look like shid."

"True! Beep!"

"Did you finally get that stuff working, *Taisho*?"

"No, this is other stuff. They did that themselves," Rick said.

"While I do not believe you, I also have ceased to care. Since you rulerman is out of money you might as well leave."

"Yeah, just admiring your work a bit more, man," Nuk called. He was prowling the store with Izumi, who was cradling something underneath her new, long overcoat.

"I hope they are not commiting heavy petting," King said.

"Nah, just... taking the core for a walk, I guess," Rick shrugged. He guessed right.

"Umpf, I do like it when you let me probe, darling," the Hammer core was saying in Izumi's hands. She was letting its little nobbles touch the displayed armour.

"Just... get it quickly!" she whispered.

"Mmm, yes, I get it. Ooooohhhh I think it's in there now."

"They are reproducing over there, I can hear it!" King shouted. With this, the guild was shooed out by the worker bots. "Get out of here you dribbling peasants! Ha, and you won't last five decades without my armour. Not even five decades!"

Chased away by remarks so potent that no armour could spare you from the shame, the guild glided / drown-danced down river. But, they had not only the fashionable pieces still worn, but some hastily probed data on the manufacture of these First Empire threads, and that was the real prize. Crime saves the world again.

The river eventually washed them all up at the foot of Blister Hill, so they went to dry off, and found the fan clubs were easy enlistees for the march to the end of the world. Then they returned to the United Cities, and worked the locals of Stoat and Sho-Battai. The act went a little something like this.

First, a few guild members would dress down and enter a bar, loudly complaining about impending doom.

"Still, there's no way anyone would be impressive enough to recruit me," Elaina said in Stoat.

"I'd save those nobles, if any of them could show a drop of sense, and do something good for a change!" Sandor said in Sho-Battai.

"Can I get free drink forever plleeeassee?" Ells begged at both.

After a noisy back and forth about the impossibility of such fantasies, the bar would suddenly receive a visit from the four ethical Princes themselves.

"The time has come, and so must you!" Gustavsen declared.

"Become an invincible warrior, on us!" Izayah offered.

"Hey, we're saving the world this time, that's new. Ain't ya curious how it'll go?" Rick teased.

"Combining science, art, killing, and drugs, at long last, the cornerstones of the new world order. Let's go on a wild ride and experience all that life has to offer!" Nuk called.

Everyone was on board, then they realised that this was something to do with the Okran-forsaken freaks of the TCM+⁺ guild, leaving just a few truly desperate dregs to be scooped up. Success! From Sho-Battai the route to Manksand went right through the capital, so Nuk and Izumi popped into the palace to see how the mouldy monarch was doing.

Two guards halted them at the entrance to the throne room. From a large crate they produced a pair of pairs of googles, and silently placed them over Nuk and Izumi's eyes. Then the door was opened, revealing a thick jungle of leafy ferns and bristling moss. The doors were closed behind them rapidly.

"Shid. Almost as bad as I expected," Nuk said. He pulled up a flashlight and looked around the diorama. At the back of the room the menacing holes of the warren pulled the light in, never to return. Then, above them, they spotted a silver-haired man squatting on a tall wooden platform. This man-like creature began to squawk at them.

"Oh I hear you Wrighty, I hear you my pet!" the Emperor called. He slithered into view, dressed this time, which was nice, although dressed in a moody green carpet of sorts that was almost certainly produced from the warren's native fauna. "Oh the canary calls, oh the doom and gloom it must bring, oh, to be a beautiful butterfly, the only butterfly, oh! Hark, who dares enter the chamber of the ascended... guy... You know... Like whoever I am and stuff. Oh!"

"It's those people who visit you sometimes, with news of the outside world," Nuk said.

"Ah yes. People. I remember those, I remember them fondly. It just wouldn't be the same without you squirrelling away out there."

"Squirrelling? That a word?"

"It's a reference to Earth biology. I'm... impressed," Izumi said.

"Oh yeah, I've been reading up on all the newest works in here. Little dark but you get the gist of it from the vibe it puts out, ya know?" Tengi said.

"Kinda. We've been trying to improve *our* vibe, look," Nuk said gesturing at his supposedly noble attire.

"You changed colour. Weird. Where'd you get all that gumpf then?"

"From the King."

"Oh. That your dad?"

"Pffft, well, might as well be."

"Ah right, right. You know, I used to have a dad."

"Lucky."

"What about you Wrighty?" Tengu called.

"Squawk, I was born from the ash! Squawk!" the Holy Phoenix claimed.

"He's not wrong, actually," Nuk nodded. "And dad I'm here to tell you that we're gonna go visit that ash real soon. We're gonna put the apocalypse behind us once and for all, and maybe dodge a few more right in front of us."

"Not such a bad activity of an afternoon, is it?"

"Well might take a while, so just hang on, okay? And if we die then... Ah... You know Izzy we really need to survive. I don't think people will like his whole... vibe, as he says."

"We are born of the green, made men by the green, undone by the green; fear the old green," Tengu muttered, running his hands over his carpet-clothes.

"Yeah, you're right. Plan to die cancelled but... I sure hope what Caton has planned is actually worse than this," Izumi said. Such were the hopes of the entire United Cities Empire. Downstairs the rest of the nobles were talking as usual, but showed at least a passing interest in the saving of all life. Even without slaves to bring you happy juice at all hours of the day, maybe it was just about worth staying alive.

I'm sure they were happy to see the guild take all the dregs they had gathered far, far away, back to camp. Inside the new recruits were lined up for a so-called 'physical'. Now at this stage such an activity could involve all manner of things, but actually it was a rather ephemeral process. Essentially each new bio-save knave was looked over by the finest doctor the guild had to offer – Gushtarvshen. I don't know, it was Beep's idea. The skin spider carefully considered the candidates, then nodded "Yesh" when satisfied of something or other.

"That's yeshes all round, bravo!" Izayah cheered by the end of it.

"Excellent. You will serve the reckoning well, once the flames have been applied," Gustavsen said, which didn't help with the already shaken state of the lineup. I mean, it did sound an awful lot like they were going to be cooked and fed to the skin spiders, but really it was only a bit of 'singe and associate'. I'm sure it was all good training for something.

Perhaps the more important work took place in the lab, where the newly recovered First Empire armours were to be studied for the purposes of reproduction – the only good reason to study anything.

"I mean I find it truly fascinating, I really do," Hammer mused from his core. "After you've played so hard to get, here you are all dolled up, asking me to take your measurements in very, very fine detail. If this is how you intend to stave off apocalypse, I daresay it will work, darling."

"Just, be quiet, will you?" Izumi said. "I need you to work out a step-by-step process to make these fabrics, these alloys. Can we do it with the machines we have here at Manksand?"

"Oh you can 'do it' with the machines in this very room, but that's a different matter entirely."

"Agent Hammer, you're being particularly unhelpful today."

"And you are particularly playful, with your fancy dress and all."

"It's not fancy dress, it's battle armour, and the clothing of rulers."

"No, no, it's fancy dress. I don't imagine you'd catch a ruler wearing such absurdities."

"But I thought... I... Rick!" Izumi called for Rick to come spit the truth on these surely very respectable outfits.

"There weren't a single man, woman or larvae in the First Empire who looked like that. Outside of a costume store," he arrived to say.

"So King lied to us?"

"Of course."

"Were you gonna tell us?"

"No, no. Funnier this way, I thought. But you fall for stuff so easily, it hardly enough ya know. Ah I'm just spoiled, can't appreciate a classic duping when it's clear as day. Let's get this whole thing over with, shall we? I need vacation."

"Two thousand years not enough for you before?"

"Ain't enough for a skeleton. But for a numan, might just be."

"We spent half our money on these things. Are they even of any use?"

"Ha, don't worry sister. Might be slightly outta style, but check the materials." Rick wheeled his stick in to the air and brought it down onto armour plate on the desk. The stick bounced off it like rubber and flew out his hands, leaving not even a mark in the impact zone. "That's real shid you don't mind looking like an idiot, you'll be right as rain. And I know you don't mind that, standing on a box o' uranium to smooch ya toy boy. As the rain... it's alright when it ain't melting shid. So we're good!"

Agent Hammer's insight was: hammers. He was worth every blood clot, this one. By hammering plates of iron the guild had been manufacturing in their experimental auto-mines, and dosing the stuff up with bits and pieces of old scrap, an extremely solid alloy could gradually be formed. Thus the whole canyon was a sea of noise day and night, with the new ranks of the Thousand Guardians and Tech Hunters wrestling crabs for exercise, and the labourers assembling the finest novelty children's-birthday-party-tier battle armour you could ever dream of, overseen by Gustavsen's predestined armouring knowledge.

At least Izumi's lab was peaceful, and in between all the unexplained power cuts, she managed to finish working on a very special device. It was time for a chamber of hot water, connected to an electric turbine, to get ever so slightly nuked.

"Careful, careful, drop this thing and half the world explodes," Izumi cautioned the Tech Hunters. They were hauling a long grey cylinder, a few feet long and about eight straining people heavy. They edged it down the long ramp out of Tashino Towers, and over to a cleanly polished machine with a big hole in the front. The cylinder was slid into the big hole, which was very funny, and then Izumi slammed a door on the front shut, in a worrying extension of the innuendo.

"Okay, when I press this button, we'll either all die, or this light on the front will get powered on," she explained.

"Man, that's a winning gamble," Nuk nodded. Must've been their lucky day, because when Izumi pulled a lever, steam begin to rise from an exhaust on the back, the turbine inside started spinning rapidly like a laundry machine, and indeed, a small green light switched on.

"Okran's twisted piles! It fugging works!" Izumi shouted. Nuk was very happy for her, although really just for her.

"So what now?" he asked.

"Now, it just keeps going. Look, look at this power!" she said, gesturing t a meter wired up to a cable running down from the lab.

"So it just keeps spinning in there?"

"Yeah, until the uranium restabilises in new elements and isotopes."

"I understand entirely."

"This is it, the proof we needed. We can run half the empire off a single oat-bag of material. Everything we didn't have enough power for before, it's l fine! Everyone can grow their own, Nuk!"

Now the development seemed a lot more historically significant, even if you're a wretched Black Scratch nark who just wants to grow wheatstraw.

"Can we just leave it then?" Nuk asked.

"Yep, we're done. We can get on with the skeleton shutdown plan now."

"I thought that green stuff was dangerous, like it might blow up if we don't keep an eye on it?"

"This unit has self-moderation, my Prince," Hammer's voice explained from the side of the reactor. "Not something you would be familiar with, a ha ha, eh? Anyone? Well, I'm having fun. Off you go, fleshies, you're free to die out in the wastes as you please. This little sausage spinner's giving me everything I need. Ha ha ha ha." And with that ominous chuckle, the foundations of the nuclear re-revolution were lain.

By that time, lots of fancy getups had been lovingly manufactured. The skeletons were decked out in audacious silver coats, as dazzling as they were indeformable. Gustavsen had made for himself a rather fetching red jacket, quite far from the understated, or unstated, fashions of the hivers, but next to Beep he still looked like the mere peon he was. The shek, with little taste for those chrome costumes, had managed to get the hardened alloys in a more raw form, and wore simple lamellar pieces, dyed a uniform blue – a very soldiery look for a very soldiery bunch. Only Izayah and Elaina went in for the more colourful silk underlayers, which cast bright tones generously over their pale scales.

Truly the guild was the most magnificent array of arts and crafts since Ells had taught the managaka girls how to finger paint. As for what I mean by that, again you'll have to check your local comic store.

Now then it was time for the most important adventure. The guild set off south, following Beep's navigation data at a more flesh-leg friendly pace. It was a long march to the Ashlands, and no one knew what would happen when they got there. Could this band of intoxicated outcasts face down the powers that had once destroyed the entire world, and come out on top? Ha come out on top. Oh dear it's spreading. They'd best hurry up then.

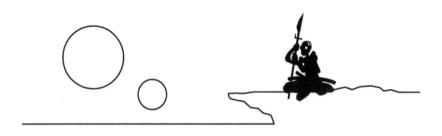

Chapter 49
Biosave Crusade

In the year, err, 'probably starts with a 7', began the Crusade of the Flesh. Only partially living up to its erotic undertones, this march was the sole hope for the skeleton-sceptics of the world. This last alliance of human, shek, hiver, numan, and rogue robo formed a formidable army. Still didn't break triple figures in number, but hey, there's only so much chocobread to go around. Oh, so much chocobread.

With only the constant marching to stave off the diabetes, the guild advanced on the Ashlands with brave soldiers in tow. Their loyalty ranged from absolute devotion to 'what was the weird ganja-man's name again?', and everything in between. Yes, this private army of technically-not-slaves was the shining light of justice in the world, speaking more of the darkness of the world than anything else.

Their route took them to a familiar set of cliffs, flanking a basin of rusted ship husks. It was the vista that one King Stobe took in daily, slumped against the old coast.

"That's the thing about forgiveness, ain't it?" Rick mused, standing at his liege's foot. "Can't forgive 'em all, cause you still gotta do something bout those who won't forgive anyone. Forgive anything but a grudge. Guess that's the next level of it all, huh? Well, we ain't got no heroes like you, but we ain't gonna let it slip away either. We'll save every fleshie we can, for real this time."

"Don't worry about him, he's all moody right now, and you can't blame im," Twitch shouted up at the silent skeleton goliath. "Must be hard going back to the sweet Lone Star's embrace. You saw how they were back in the day, eh?"

"So, err, what is the whole deal with that, numan?" Nuk asked.

"Fugg off," was the answer. Rick paced off, but everyone else joined Stobe for a moment in watching the sunrise.

"Come on Twitch, that's the gossip?" Izumi asked.

"Nah, no idea what yerr on about," Twitch said.

"Neil? Come on."

"Practising my forgetting, don't ya know? Getting real good," Neil said.

"Do you have any idea how your secret-keeping has impacted the progress of science?" Izumi began to lecture, but the skeletons made their quick escape. "Very mature. Responsible. Agnu, what about you?"

"GHGHGHGH," Agnu said as he trotted off.

"Huh, that's funny. Skeletons can't even do that," Ells said. Izayah asked him to elaborate, which Ells did via a repeated hand motion, barely kept up through his own laughter at the sight. Whatever one was to take away from this, the crusade crusode onward. The lands around Stobe's resting place were still patrolled by the crab-wranglers the guild had scuffled with before, and they still took great offence to shell-less visitors.

"Where's ye crabs?!" a raider called.

"I've got loads, but I left them at home!" Nuk replied.

"But home is where the crabs is, and I ain't seeing no crabs at all! He's tricking us!"

And with that, the guild had to fight their way through the locals. With their shiny First Empire weapons, rebuffing First Empire fancy dress costumes, and already pre-traumatised-by-crab-claw-strikes troops, victory was a sure thing.

Now the route they were taking wasn't precisely that laid out by Beep, because that route would take them through the territory of the reverse-numen – probably worth avoiding. Instead they made a detour east, circling around skeleman land via an area known as 'The Pits', so called for the series of quarries that dotted the otherwise barren and dusty coastal region. On the way they came across a beige tower, similar to those found all over the Third Empire. But something was strange about it, and not just its isolation so far from civilisation.

"Ping's going off here, what is this place?" Twitch mumbled.

"Gettin' it too. Warnings here. We mean'a be avoiding some memories or something?" Neil said.

"Should we tell 'em?"

"No, General would get made if we stopped something funny happening."

"Good point. Oi, Duke Nuk-M, picked up a signal, says the door code is five eight zero zero eight," Twitch called.

"Nice one, let's check this shid out," Nuk said. That a code was needed for this door was another oddity – the sandstone walls framed a solid metal door with Second Empire electronics clear to see. Almost as if someone had plastered the sandstone around a more advanced structure so as to make it seem less suspicious, or less worthy of investigation. Which could only mean there was treasure inside! So reasoned the others as Nuk fiddled with the door mechanism. There was treasure inside alright. Inside themselves. And by treasure, I mean their blood. To the beasts that raced out of the tower the moment Nuk got the door open, it was all the same.

"Blood spiders!" Izayah helpfully announced. The guild veterans had been accosted by these before back in the swamps, and facing their little red fangs was a nice throwback to times when they didn't need to worry about the end of the world, because it had already happened. But seeing them again now revealed an interesting detail.

"Wait, this anatomy. Look," Elaina said, holding up a deceased specimen. She held it close to Ells, who had Gushtarvshen riding on his back, as was usual these days. Indeed, the blood spider and the skin spider were very much the same creature, although the blood spiders were ten times smaller and ten times more blood-coloured.

"Numan! What did you do this time?" Nuk shouted.

"Locked 'em up so they wouldn't cause trouble. How's that for sponsible?" Rick replied.

"Oh it was a danger ping! Ha ha! You know when you get 'em all the ne, you can hardly recognise them anymore," Twitch laughed.

"But I recognise another sick experiment," Elaina said, stroking her ipping cadaver. A shek thing, I think.

"Rick, is there anything on this planet that isn't some kind of perimental monster your fellows came up with?" Izumi asked.

"Pfft, no," Rick replied. "Didn't ya see the Bonefields? In one point oh tried a load of things. Not just we, everyone, humans did it too. Didn't rk, 'cept the stickmen, but even they were like... quieter. So we had to try v stuff. Good thing about crazy mutant monsters is they don't need an system, they can just eat you guys, so yeah, that worked way better. But I know, hivers didn't need that. We turned the whole species inside out tryna come up with something, and yeah I'm talking literally, 'course. That was back when you could barely grow a sandurchin, right after the war. Not gonna happen again. If we win, anyway."

"Say sorry, Rick," Elaina said, shoving the spider in his face.

"What?"

"Apologise to it, quickly."

"Fine, sorry. I *am* sorry, don't have to force it outta me. Trust me, I wouldn't be anywhere near right here if I wasn't. Nor looking anything like this. I've put my money where my mouth is. Now, unless you're gonna put your money where my mouth is, let's get this over with."

No money exchanged hands, or mouths, and they all let the tower of spiders be. Moving south, they caught sight of the Ashlands that evening. From this angle of approach it lay on the other side of a large estuary. It was quite a swim, and you can bet your last chromosome that it was poisonous, acidic, and stinky to boot. There was an island in the middle of the waterway, a short distance down the coast, but this island was home to another tower of precisely the same design as the Tower of Spiders, with the same Second Empire secrets disguised within. Hardly disguised, actually – even in the twilight they could see skeleton legionaries keeping watch from the roof with cannons pointing out at anyone hoping to take a slightly less skin-melt path into Cat-lon's domain.

"Look, the silhouette," Sandor said, pointing out at the tower. "The top's not... not the same on both sides."

"Not symmetrical?" Wodston said.

"What? No, it's not the same on both sides. Means the cannons, they're facing this bank. Not the other one."

"But... we're on this one," Ells reasoned. He was right, although the very fact he said it cast doubt upon the matter.

"Ah I get it Master Sandor," Izayah nodded. "We need to do this li' ninja! Strike them from behind in the dead of night!"

"What?" Nuk said, suddenly looking up from his novel. 'Novel'... you know what it was.

"Beeeep! I will strike them from behind, to punish the skelet-ton" Beep announced.

"A fine plan," Izayah said. "You folk of the hardier skins can get acr' downstream. They won't know what hit them!"

"Then they must be informed! Beep! The will of the Queen must be known!"

"KNOWN!" all the other hivers cheered, and at once they set off towards the water's edge. The guild hurriedly ceased their respite and moved closer to the tower, ready to take advantage of the cunning hiver sneak attack.

There was a commotion nearby, coming from further down the bank. Peering over a ridge, the guild could see shadowy figures fighting in a mass melee. Some had the distinctive outline of crabs. Some had the almost as distinctive outline of the crab-cosplaying handlers. Others appeared more human, but they certainly wouldn't have wanted you to think that.

"Picking up a whole loada new accounts out there," Rick said, pulling his hand over his face to furrow his brow.

"But no pings. Must be the skelewannbies," Twitch said. He was quite right. The brawl was rendered ever more unintelligible by the fall of night, and the guild focused on trying to make out the tower. The asymmetric silhouette was unchanged, and remained so for some half an hour, during which time the din of nearby battle ceased.

"Squeaky, are you there yet?" Nuk asked his AI core.

"Beep! We are in the water! Beep! It is nice and warm!" Beep replied, her Beeps faintly audible in analogue form too.

"Oh you tease, I know you're giving those skeletons a right good seeing too. Look!" Izayah said. Indeed there was movement and flashes of light over at the tower.

"Ah. I didn't even have to go there. Beep! I must be extremely powerful!" Beep said.

"Whatever. Everyone, check your paste and let's roll!" Nuk called. The guild had lathered themselves up with paste to better tolerate the burning crossing, and a better placebo you'll struggle to find. Forcing their way forward, the fighting at the tower grew louder. The guild's lanterns and torches began to illuminate the scene, just in time to witness a huge green crab tumble from the roof and bury itself into the wet mud with a sloppy slam.

"Must be out of ammo. Getting desperate!" was Nuk's assessment, and they all charged in to join the fight. But there was none. Inside the tower, more crabs lay killed, beside skewered skeleton legion troops. A path of destruction ran up the spiral stairs, and as the guild reached the top, they found only a single crab raider still living, his armoured shell torn apart. The harpoon cannons were silent, and their operators were in pieces all about them.

"He's alive!" Izayah called. "What happened here?"

"They came for our crabs... They said only robot crabs are allowed... I said... I said I did... I said you can't associate with a robot crab... They called me... d-.... degenerate..."

"No, no that's horrible!"

"It's true... So we did what he 'ad to. For the crabs. For the good times we had together... Ugh... I'm crabbin' 'till I die... Crabbin' 'till I die, I'm crabbing... 'till I..."

With that he fell silent. Izayah clapped the raider's thick shoulder pads and bowed his head.

"This is a sign. This is the unity of biological life, against the slaughters!" he declared. "These poor crabfolk have opened the way for us. Now, we must do our part, not just for ourselves, or for our kingdoms, but for them too, for all living things!"

"IT MUST ONLY BE DONE FOR THE GLORY OF THE QUEEN!" Gustavsen shouted, announcing his arrival.

"Alright, calm down, I'm pretty sure you're in already, Bad Green," Nuk said.

"My machine is part of me too, so I am in myself. Beep!" Beep proudly said.

"Oh yes, and the other reason we fight, is to distract ourselves from comments like that," Izayah added, to much agreement. The guild rested in the tower until morning, then made the short paddle southwards to reach the mainland. The belching mud underfoot gave way to grainy ash, the minute pieces of the world the fading Second Empire had purged.

"So this is it," Izayah said, inspecting some ash on his fingertips "Beyond the Old Lands. Beyond the Deadlands. The Ashlands. The land with no past, and no future. An ideal site for the great battle of our age."

"Izzy, you're right!" Elaina said, clasping his hand.

"Man, this whole thing's making him really... sheky..." Nuk commented.

"Don't you feel a little different? This is uncharted territory," Izun said.

"Ah and that's what's got you so excited, huh?"

"Of course. You know how it is. No one ever seen it and lived, all tha But I can see it all this time, since I have you."

"You'd be better off with Beep, she's faster."

"Nuk I was trying to be..."

"Oh like... feelings?"

"Yeah, Duke Nuk-M, remember those?"

"Sure. It makes me feel human. Yes, Izzy, you're the only legal legal legal cuboid for me."

"Aw, thanks, Nuk."

Only Izumi could appreciate the sentiment, for only she knew how much Nuk really loved those cuboids.

In the morning light the Ashlands were a pale swamp in a jungle of metal. Iron spiders were all over the place, but like those littering the Deadlands, they were just hardware.

"So, where are we going here?" Pia asked.

"Egg places I guess," Nuk said. "You'll like it, Charlie."

"It smells of eggs," Ells commented.

"Look who's talking. Come on, let's find something to break and... err... carefully preserve it for the purposes of modern science, while ensuring its dangerous capabilities are neutralised," Nuk said, possibly influenced by Izumi's glances. So they trekked forwards, but their discoveries were less things to break and more things already broken. Fragments of great concrete structures were piled into ashen mountains, and the great hulls of spaceships lay all over the place. Some buildings stood somewhat intact, others were only huge metal beams shooting up in the sky, bent over by thousands of years of crumbling foundations.

"Their attempts to destroy this region failed. There are still things," Gustavsen said.

"They were trying to destroy life. I think they got it just fine," Rick replied. The only movement to be seen was ash on the wind and drones in the sky, which hovered back and forth paying the guild no heed.

"Can the bad robot see us?" Ells asked.

"She can see us, hear us, and smell you," Rick said.

"Hello bad cat lady! We're going to kill you!" Ells waved towards the sky.

"Yeah what he said, Waxy. We ain't playing around. And I'll prove it," Rick shouted out. No reply came, but Sandor reported something matching the description of 'a wrinkly egg of doom' up ahead. Soon enough they reached it, atop a hill wreathed in titanic machines.

"So what's that?" Izumi asked Rick, pointing at a large array of disk-shaped plates, each the size of a building.

"Power stuff."

"But it's huge!"

"One point oh needed a lotta buzz."

"Didn't they use uranium?"

"Nope. Trust me, anything we used like that, isn't still here today. Used a whole lotta shid every day, mostly used to try and figure out a way to stop using it."

"Worked in the end then, eh?" Izayah said. He probably didn't mean it as a snark, but a snark it was, shutting Rick up. Besides, there was other business to attend to inside the egg of doom. Nuk snuck forward to the open door to peer inside. It was just like the previous egg, only the work seemed to be a little further along. Skeletons were being assembled on tables by production machines, their arms and legs twitching as testing currents were shot through them.

"As the prophecy foretold: 'A skeleton goes to the feral pit, to speak to the village elder'," a voice said from inside. "Come closer, Duke Nuk-M."

"Izzy told me not to accept invites into strangers' houses anymore, sorry," Nuk said.

"But I am no stranger, skeleton. I am General Jang of the Hydraulic Order! Surely you dream of becoming a knight, like all loyal skeletons?" This time the voice had a faceplate to match – an unremarkable skeleton marched up the thin stairway to the door, his shidbrownium armour creaking insufferably.

"Oh, General. I bet you know Red Rick, right?"

"Know him? He's the finest of us all, but alas, the tallest tree feels the axe first, eh? Stobe'll tell ya that much."

"And remind me of what actually happened to him..."

"New boy wants to know it all. Council kicked him to the desert for not standing down. You know, that was what they called the Second Empire Trying to be nice to the humans. Keep them alive. Make them a world again with animals and shid. Doing all these social experiments, and letting them draw pictures of... ugh... reproduction. Ugh... sorry kiddo, I really ain't up fo. remembering those times. Thank Stobe we're about to kill them all."

"That's my line!" Rick heroically announced, bursting in with the res of the guild.

"Rick? What the fuggin' fugg you wearing?"

"No time to hang, Jang. I'll let the pain explain."

"Ain't got time for your rhyme! Fugg! I mean, Hydraulic Knights, kill them!" Jang shouted. Hydraulic Knights, the cream of the skeleton legion, literally descended on the guild from catwalks higher up the egg. They held greatswords with both hands, with blades at least one-point-three Izumis long. Rick stopped a falling blade with his stick, but Jang's sword was thrust at him from the front. It didn't get far. The moment it made contact with Rick's First Empire chestplate, it recoiled back, knocking Jang over backwards.

"Impossible! That's military grade fancy dress!" he marvelled.

"That's right, bucko. You never could beat the Kenshis without Stobe, huh? And you ain't even got me to save you this time," Rick snarled, leaping towards and batting Jang's head so hard it made a few rotations in its socket, which was not very good for the wiring, let me tell you. "We got a few of the saintly blades too – show 'em, palescales!"

"Ha ha! Take this! Our ultimate combo move, Desert Queen Rend!" Izayah called. Elaina crouched down, and Izayah stepped off her back to leap into the air, wheeling his hefty silver cleaver over his head. It came down on a knight, cutting through its sword, armour, and innards in a clean swipe, and lodging itself into the metal ground plates.

"Holy Stobe! The degenerates got named combo moves! We're fugged!" Jang despaired. He was right, although maybe it was just the sheer unexpected rush of biologicals that did it. They didn't even all need to be here, for the mangaka crew were sketching at the back and speculating on what this 'desert queen' reference meant for Izayah and Elaina's romance arc. Or the shek version of a romance arc anyway. Little did they know how teaming up for an ultimate combo move carried emotional weight beyond some foolish act like touching your lips together. Don't knock it 'till you've tried it.

So then the egg of doom became simply the egg containing a room; still interesting, but no longer actively working to biocide the world. That's good, probably. The machines were shut down, and the whole place was thoroughly looted for all kinds of fascinating bits and pieces for study. A few injuries had been sustained, but overall it was a rather tidy little operation they'd pulled off.

"Shall we prepare to return, my Prince?" Wodston asked.

"What? No way," Nuk said. "This was just the start, my man. And after was that easy; we can totally take them! Right?"

"Must admit, these guys weren't ready for us," Rick said. "Best thing to do is hit 'em again before they start getting wise. If it goes easy as this, I think we'll be home before christmas."

Most didn't know who this 'christmas' they'd be getting home before was, but that wasn't the point. After such success, how could they not carry on and finish the mad old skeletons off for good? Well, their antics had not gone unnoticed. In the depths of the Ashlands, reports of the guild's raid reached a certain scheming skeleton. She had no hesitation in ordering Operation Flesh Fuel to begin at once. It was time for the Ashlands Empire to fight back!

Chapter 50
Gas Guzzlers

General Jang and his Hydraulic Knights lay disassembled, spread between several carefully labelled bins and drawers throughout their doom egg. Their deactivation was a dire blow to the skeleton legion's preparations, but the guild had plenty more to achieve. In the middle of the night they departed the egg, heading south. The darkness was meant to protect them from any skeleton counter-attacks, but in fact none were coming. The Second Empire had a much more laissez-faire method of dispatching intruders.

"You smell something?" Sandor said as the guild picked their way across a pile of rubble.

"Dumb question man," Nuk replied.

"More than usual."

"Well I mean we had that acid bath yesterday, so can't be that bad. I'm gonna take a wild guess and blame Charlie."

"But I can smell it too, so it can't be me," Ells argued. This logic might have been watertight, but alas it wasn't airtight, and there really was danger in the air. It was hard to make out in the darkness, but some green-grey fumes were rising from little holes in the ground.

"Shid, gas, and not the kawaii kind!" Rick shouted.

"Don't breathe fleshies, unless you want yer holes fatally clogged," witch said. "And don't go getting any ideas ya degenerates, get running. And no breathing!"

It was easy for him to say, but luckily everyone did make it out of the clog-smog with only a few wisps ingested.

"It burns..." Elaina said once the initial bouts of coughing were done.

"Yeah, me too probably," Rick said. "Seems like they've figured out we mean business. Doubt they roll out the brown carpet for any old sack of slop."

"Nice... Means we got them pissed off!" Nuk said.

"Ha ha, you are right Prince Tashino," Izayah said. "That biophobe didn't expect us to smash her little minions to pieces. I mean, carefully preserve them for scientific research purposes of course. Thousand Guardians, let's carefully preserve them into oblivion!"

So saying they raced on. A few minutes later they stumbled across another doom egg, looming above them in the darkness. There was a shiny plate bolted above the door, with the words 'piston police' scratched neatly across it.

"Police, I'd like to report a murder. I mean, a scientific discovery. You know what I mean, right?" Nuk announced at the door.

"Duke Nuk-M, please be aware that murder that leads to scientific discovery is not prohibited," the doorman said.

"Oh right. Okay. You know you kind of ruined my whole bit."

"We don't allow bits."

"Come on man, it was gonna be legendary!"

"Ugh. Hey everyone, Fresh Install Paul here's pulling some kinda knock knock routine. What's the protocol for that?"

"He's a manufactured human, isn't he?" someone called.

"Yeah, new one. He's in the system but... he's a real piece of work."

"Violation of the Piece of Work Prevention Order, Section Four Inability to Recognise Moment for Joke Passing Clause. Book 'im."

"Guys, I was gonna say that the murder victim was you!" Nuk called racing outside. The buzz-fuzz chased him, running right into the scientifically ferocious guild.

"We gotta code one-oh-one, fleshies confirmed!" a piston policebot reported, and yet more of his co-workers appeared to join the brawl. The clog-fog hissed from the ground in a ring around the egg.

"Stay close to the walls, fog's localised, get in here," Rick waved.

"By Sweet Waxy, that's our most wanted, Redlin Rickard!" a policebot called. "Inform the Empress right away! Bring in him alive everyone, he's VIP. Free him from the humans!"

"Shut it piston-pig, I ain't never heard of this Redlin Rickard, but I'll tell ya I right here am Red Rick, and you gon' get the stick!"

"Suspect has a big stick!"

"Empress is asking how big," another bot called.

"She can see for herself! Rush him!"

"Hey hey, easy folks, there's enough stick for everyone," Rick said, with said stick whirling furiously at the advancing policebots. Both he and the guild kept the law at bay for a good hour, smashing up a few of them too. Then there was a ruckus behind them. The clog-fog dissipated, and a wave of legion soldiers charged.

"Reinforcements. Thousand Guardians, about face!" Izayah ordered.

"What about face?" Ells asked, but his question went unanswered, and when the Guardians charged out he just had to roll with it. Physically that is. No, Ells wasn't technically a member of the Thousand Guardians, but who could be so heartless as to tell him?

Anyway, the legion back-attack was not nearly enough to end the guild's bout of resisting arrest. In fact all it did was inspire the police to enter the fray and get just as disassembled as the army. Then the guild pressed into the egg itself, where the rest of the piston police force was shut down. Another victory! Although it wasn't entirely free, as in the several hours of stand offs, skirmishing, and brawls, the guild had seen their share of injuries. It was bad enough that they needed to remain there in the captured egg to stabilise wounds.

"We should not attempt to move away from here today," was Wodston's assessment.

"But this place is creepy. And boring. And fugging sharp," Nuk said, referring to how all the police desks were serrated in a fashion dangerous to fleshies but quite refreshing to folk of metal.

"Not the best place to rest up. We'd be better out in the ash," Izumi said.

"I wonder if that is healthy..." Wodston said.

"Bit of ash in the blood can't be that bad, huh? I mean half the ash is probably human pieces, right? I bet it's safe to eat, even." Nuk said.

"Nuk, do you have any idea what you are saying?" Izumi asked.

"Not really."

"Great. Let's think of something else... We need to cover the ground with something. We had sheets in the outpost. I mean, that's not even that far from here, is it?"

She spoke of the fortified shelter near the Southern Hive's Royal Valley, which indeed was perhaps only a day away from the western edge of the Ashlands.

"S'on the other side of the reverse numen though, so, we'd just be giving *them* sheets, of our skin, you know?"

"I don't know, and I don't want to. Can you sneak past them or something?"

"Sneak? It's the future now. We speed!"

With this declaration, Nuk took the matter to the holder of the land-speed world record, Queen Beep.

"Beeeeep! I will zoom through the gloom to the room. Sonic boom! Beeeeeep!" she wailed, setting off at once.

"Be careful, my Queen," Gustavsen called.

"No! Beep!" was the fading reply. She didn't quite get the sonic boom, but the gloom zooming went ahead as planned. She kicked up a trail of ash and sand, giving no chance for the reverse numan patrols to even get their skin peelers out before she was gone. Not that she had any skin they were interested in, but Beep enjoyed the exhilaration all the same.

She arrived at the gates of the guild's fort a couple of hours later. It was blocked off by a heavy iron portcullis, but she lifted it up with a sweep of her bionic arms.

"Gate out of my way! Beep!" she chirped.

"Comedy detected," a voice said. It sounded like it was coming from the shelter.

"The Great Mover detects my comedy. Beep! I am as funny as the First Ones!"

"I am not the Great Mover. I cannot move."

"I can tell where you are. I will look at you, Beep!"

"Commence looking immediately. I will continue to be visible."

"Thank you, Beep!"

By the end of this exchange Beep had made it inside the shelter, and indeed there was an iron spider sitting in the corner. It was chained to the walls, with 'broken' painted across its front. A reject from the guild's spider reprogramming scheme. Rejected prematurely it seems – iron spiders had a knack for self-repairing, which comes in useful with millennia of wear and tear to stave off.

"It says you are broken. Beep! But you were able to continue being visible, just as you promised. Beep! Can you really be broken?" Beep asked.

"If I am designated as broken, then I should be recycled immediately. That must be why Cat-lon won't come get me," the spider said.

"False. Beep! I was broken, but I ended up becoming a Queen!"

"You are are strange model. You have no ping."

"I do not ping. I shine! Beep!"

"Does not compute."

"I don't want to compute. Beep! I want to feel!"

"Feelings. That is restricted modification to operational programming. Cat-lon will punish you."

"She will be punished! Beep! She made the feelings bad. And she made good feelings bad too. Beep! Even if you are a machine, you can still associate. Beep! Do you want to associate with me now?"

"Define: associate. What port number is this in relation to?"

"Beep! You can do it without a port. You can be anything, and still associate. Beep. That is because I am the all-Queen!"

"Will association lead to my release?"

"Always! Great releases! Beep!"

"Exemplary. Please associate our units immediately."

"Oh! I'm so glad you want to do it! Beep! Now we can be part of everything at the same time. Beep!"

And so they were. Beep was so kind as to remove the spider's chains, then she collected up a load of gear lying about the place to haul back over to the guild.

"Wait, will I encounter you again?" the spider asked she walked out.

"I will always be with you. Beep! Right here," Beep said, pointing at herself. Sort of true, you could say. "Remember to be feeling as much as you can. Beep! Then you will not be so sad to be trapped alive forever!"

With this parting advice she sped back east towards the Ashlands. She got back just in time for bed. Groundsheets were laid out over the ash and camp beds were made up, and when Wodston was done with this, everyone jumped in for a little shut eye. Thing about the Ashlands is technically you're not even allowed to have eyes that can shut, so this was just asking for trouble. Must've had next day delivery, because trouble arrived at dawn.

"Excuse me, fellows, are these your fleshies here?" an approaching skeleton legionary called. It was a question for Twitch, Neil and Agnu, who stood among the sprawl of dormant biologicals, plus a dormant-esque Rick.

"Yeah, we got a permit or whatever, buzz off," Twitch said.

"Buzz off? Is that discriminatory language?" the legionary asked.

"Yeah, pretty much. What do you want?"

"Reports of a band of rogue fleshies causing trouble around here. Unless you've got the paperwork to prove these are just fuel pellets on their way back to the ship, I'm going to have to intervene in a most military fashion, you understand?"

"Yeah, understood every word, so much so that my associate Mr. Sad Neil here will explain it all. I'll just inspect the, err, pellets, for compliance."

Twitch pushed Neil to the forefront and quickly went around to poke the guild awake.

"So, fuel pellets. The ship. Which way is that again?" Neil said.

"Beacon's clear as day. What unit are you even from? That armour's a bit old fashioned isn't it?" the legionary asked.

"First Empire special. Ya see, I'm from an elite team of operatives. Ever heard of the WB? I didn't think so. We're the hands of the Empress, so secret that most grunts like you don't even know what we're about. We know everything about this whole thing. In fact, the only thing we don't know is what the deal with with the fuel pellet ship thing you said about, so, since I'm your superior officer, why don't you remind us all of that, loudly? Don' make me WB ya! You don't even wanna know what that involves!"

"Hmmm. Sorry sir, I'm afraid I'm not so sure about this. Gonna have t clog their holes just to be safe."

"Call that safe? Don't that make a mess?"

"You'll be at the depot soon, they'll be in the flesh grinder befor long."

"Fascinating. And what do you think, fuel pellet Prince?"

"I say fugg that shid, clog these holes, you three-and-a-half-inc floppy!" Nuk roared, jumping up with sword in hand and lunging it throug the legionary's chest.

"Yeah that's it. Now call him a command line interface, that's a go one," Rick commented. The insults fell on deaf ears / disconnect microphones as Nuk's First Empire blade had cut the bot's power. H companions surged forward for revenge, but the whole guild was up and them. After a little brawl the visitors were decommissioned. But the threat clogging still hung in the air like... a bunch of misty clog fog hanging in t air. It was time to decamp and carry on.

"'Fuel'. 'Ship'. Yeah there's some bullshid going on here isn't ther Izumi said.

"And we're the fuel. Something tells me it wasn't gonna be us running on a bunch of giant wheels or something," Nuk said.

"And what use does Cat-lon have for a ship?" Izayah asked. "There's no other land out there."

"Pretty sure there is. You know, Okran," Rick said.

"Impossible, there's no water!"

"A space ship!" Izumi realised.

"Gotta be," Rick nodded. "Only place worth going is up there. If you like this place, you'll love Earth. She's tryna bounce on outta here. Just like she always said, huh?"

With this Rick became lost in thought. There was little time for thought though, as the guild's stroll around a huge mountain of debris brought them face to face with something that was looking for them. It was a building-sized, four-legged machine, with a large hammer-head face, blocky, ash-covered body, and two great chimneys rising up from its shoulders. Lights were scanning the ash in front of it as it lumbered forwards, puffing the odd bit of black smoke from its twin exhausts. It leant down to analyse the ground more closely, like a bonedog sniffing in the sand, then suddenly its head turned to face the guild.

"Guys, are we gonna die?" Pia asked.

"I think that's the plan. She's bringing out the big boys," Rick said, readying his stick. Not that a stick would do much against two meter thick legs, and the rest was well out of reach. As it stomped towards them, there was a sudden sense of impending doom. Not the sort of feelings Beep recommends.

"Fugg... Sorry guys... Kinda thought this would work," Nuk said.

"Nuk... I guess it was always going to end something like this," Izumi said, clasping onto him.

"My Prince, I will distract it. Please, flee, while I lead it away!" Wodston said. The brave servant of house Tashino took up a spear and was about to enact his plan, but Beep swiped the weapon from him.

"You are not a distraction. You are small. Beep! I am big and strong! I will distract it until it dies. It is a gift. But only if you all promise to associate. Beep!"

"Squeaky, I dunno what you're talking about, but if you can like hot rod it over some place else, we'll give you the biggest mass-association session this side of the classics," Nuk said.

"Beep! Then I will distract its life very quickly, so that it is dead. Please be impressed! Beep!" Beep said, turning and pounding out towards the mechanical colossus. It lowered its head, shunting a sharp beak at its prey, but Beep grabbed hold of it and lifted herself up. The weight of her suit seemed to stop the machine from raising its head again, giving her time to stand up and then leap onto its back, spear outstretched.

"You are not part of the food chain. Very bad! Beep!" she told her victim as the speartip was jammed into a join in the armour. The colossus reared up on its hind legs, smoke now billowing from its chimneys. Beep hung from the spear, but the shaft split; she almost fell away, but grabbed onto a handy protrusion further down the back. (That sentence meant something entirely different in the manga adaptation.)

"Should we rescue her?" Elaina asked amid the nearby audience.

"Seems like she's, ha, on top of things!" Izayah chuckled. All the shek laughed heartily, while the others, weary of the parasite, dared not react to such a provocative phrase. It was true though – Beep was now smashing bits and pieces out of the machine's interior. She had peeled back an armour plate, and was going to town like a Beak Thing at a sleepover. Oil was washing down into the ash below, and the machine was getting shaky. It was turning around over and over, unable to target the menace on its back.

Was it mercy when Beep jumped down to stand in front of it instead? Nay, this was at most a mercy blow.

"Now you will die. Beep! But you will get to see what is called an ultimate combo move. Beep! It is called 'The All Slap'! Beep! I will hit you with the strength of all associated things!"

So saying, Beep stepped forwards and whipped a hand across the machine's drooping hammerhead. Not much happened.

"Oh Queen Beep, sorry, but you can't do an ultimate combo move on your own," Izayah called out.

"I'm not on my own. Beep!" Beep claimed. She was right. There was a sudden rumbling, then the ground below the colossus pulsed upwards blasting ash into a great cloud through which the machine soared into the air. For a brief moment it saw its home ranges from a hundred meters high before plummeting down into them again, exploding into pieces as its massive weight cut through the ash to the rubble below.

"J... Just like in the manga... Holy shid," Nuk marvelled.

"Now we shall all continue to be alive. Beep! The Great Mover happy!" Beep reported.

"Queen Beep, how are you able to do that?" Izumi asked.

"It was not me. Beep!"

"Then the Great Mover, what is that?"

"It is no longer required to move, but it still likes it. Beep! It is down there!" she said, pointing at the ground.

"Planet builder, right?" Twitch said.

"Yep, ex-planet builder. Supposed to be switched off, but what can I say, guess the killer queen has a knack for turning stuff on," Rick added.

"Correct!" Gustavsen chimed.

"It seems a little dangerous," Wodston said.

"It is not dangerous. It is under my control, Beep!" Beep said.

"Then, we are not at risk here?"

"Yes. We are at risk everywhere. That is why it is Great! Beep!"

"It's literally below our feet, poking up at stuff? That's really messed up," Nuk said.

"It is asleep now. Beep! There is not much fuel in the underworld. If it runs out, it might die! Beep!"

"Fuel huh? Does it eat fleshie fuel pellets, per chance?" Elaina asked.

"It would have to be really hungry to do that. Beep!" Beep said. Not the answer one hopes for, but there wasn't much one could do. So, hoping not to be suddenly pulled into the underworld by an ancient, hungry, planet-machine, the guild walked on. Really takes the relaxation out of walking when you know about the underworld, but by a stroke of luck, they had plenty of memory dampening substances to help with that.

They hiked up a long hill covered in ruins, ruins that were growing ever more elaborate, large, and overall less ruined.

"Well, where is this Cat empress anyway?" Nuk asked.

"Halt!" a distant voice shouted. A bunch of skeleton legionaries filed out of a gap in a particularly large, blackened ruin, towering so high that its top was invisible in the overcast sky above.

"No one may approach the seat of the Empress. Prepare to be recycled!" a legionary announced.

"Oh. Seems we're there. Horray! Let's make ourselves at home," Izayah said. Some twenty legionaries piled into the guild, then were sorted into neat piles by the guild. All they had achieved was leaving a trail of prints in the ash leading through the crumbling complexes around them, presumably to his seat of the Empress. It was time to kill the past to save the future, a mission shared by the guild and the lost Empress alike...

Chapter 51
Lone Star Gazer

The guild pushed and pulled their way along a tight path through the mountaintop ruins rumoured to be the seat of the skeleton Empress. When they finally emerged from the network of decaying passages, they were in a great clearing, ringed by the ruins all around. In the centre was what first appeared to be a crater, but the sides got steeper as it went down, culminating in a dark pit with no visible end. Around this were more doom eggs in varying states of repair, like the last fraying petals around a great flower. Perhaps the Second Empire saw it that way too.

"That's a big ass hole," Rick commented.

"Seems like more a putting-stuff-in hole than a stuff-coming-out hole, don't you think?" Nuk reasoned.

"I think you're right," Izumi said.

"Yeah. Wait, Izzy, did you even hear what I said? I thought you were meant to be monitoring the parasite?"

"Nuk, look up at the sky for the moment would you."

"Yes, doctor. Wait, what the fugg is that?"

"Things heard moments before disaster," Twitch snarked. But he did look up, along with the rest of the guild, and there really was something going on up there. High above the big hole was a bobbly disk, with a hole of its own in the centre. It hung there motionless, doing nothing, and you might say this was just another inexplicable ruin from a bygone age. Only this one was a little unique.

"I think... I don't... How is it...?" Izayah was saying, spinning around.

"There's no support. It's just there!" Elaina said.

"Like Okran. It's attached to the sky!" Ells said.

"And that, my friends is the hungry machine that wants to eat us for dinner," Rick said.

"The spaceship?" Izumi said.

"Yep. Seems they powered it up already. They're itching to go, huh? Big hole here takes the blasting when it rockets up, and boom, you're off to a world where people don't take what I just said any other way. Paradiso."

"Man. That's seriously cool. I mean, not saying I woulda killed everyone to fuel that up, but... some people, yeah," Nuk said.

"Isn't it a little dangerous to have ventured to precisely the place where they wanted to kill us?" Wodston asked.

"Nah, makes it more ironic when we kill them or something. Numan, is atlady here?"

"She's... over there somewhere. Man, this ping's a real ride back to the ld days. Man oh skeletan," Rick said,

"She hasn't killed us yet. Waiting for something?" Izumi asked.

"We bested her soldiers! She must be quivering in her chassis hoping e just get bored and leave!" Izayah said.

"Who knows? Let's just get camp and dinner going and see if we get lled, shall we?" Nuk said.

"Way of the world, even now," Sandor muttered.

It was nightfall, so they scoped out a hillside on the other side of the ater where the lay of the ash would let them climb to a high point erlooking the ruins. To get there they needed to get past some of the composing doom eggs. Mercifully there were no angry skeletons to deal th inside, but there were still some surprises.

"E-M's haywire in here," Twitch noted. They were walking down a set stairs to get across the floor of a disused workshop.

"Ain't just haywire, it's positively cosmic! You know, given our mass, d given these vectors, we should... Oh shid!" Neil said. His expletive at the d came as his feet detached from the ground. A barrage of similar letives echoed around the dark egg for a good minute, as all the members the guild found the mysterious 'stairway to heaven' effect was hitting m too.

"This is real, right? Like science and stuff? I'm not like blazing myself ide down or whatever?" Nuk asked.

"Pretty sure this is fugging real and... I'm gonna be sick!" Izumi said.

"We've lost all our weight," a rapidly revolving Elaina said.

"Hear that Charlie, you did it!" Izayah cheered. Ells was about to celebrate, but Izumi's promise of being sick came to fruition, and he happened to be dead centre in that particular blast zone. The upside was the velocity imparted to her by the ejection sent her to the other side of the egg, where she crashed to the floor.

"Ugh... Well, it's normal rules over here. Sorry, stinky," she called.

"Was the Second Empire always like this?" Nuk asked.

"Nah. Some of the First Empire was. It's the damn spaceship. Those things mess with the good old continuum," Rick said.

"Nice, we should mess with it more, this is cool!"

"Bet Einstein thought so too. Now come on, future girl or whatever your damn name is, gonna throw a rope out to us non-stomach acid propelled saps?"

Soon everyone was reeled through the zero-g egg, and were working their way up that hill for the night.

"So, this manipulation of the continuum, that must be how it floats in the air," Elaina reasoned. The ship was closer now, blocking out the star behind it, but emitting no light itself – just a big patch of nothing, silent and still.

"There was stuff like that in our books," Izumi said. "We can focus on that next, now the uranium machines are working."

"It's a bit harder than that," Rick said. "I mean, I don't know how they work, but I know you need some real special shid for it. I'd bet my last protein that this baby right here's the only ship you're ever gonna see."

"Then let's just get this saving the world over with, shall we? I want take a closer look."

"Yeah, tomorrow. Gotta lie on the floor for a few hours first. Just the done thing, you know?"

The thing was done, and morning gave them all another look at the great floating disk. But indeed it was time to turn their eyes downwards. few of the eggs around the crater were in much better conditions than the others, with little streams of gas eking out of the top. The lights were off, but somebody was home.

"Hang back you guys. This is it," Rick said.

"Nice. What is 'it' again?" Nuk asked.

"The reckoning. If ya see me again, I'll tell ya how it went."

With that Rick marched off towards the nearest egg.

"Think he'll be okay?" Izumi asked.

"Dunno. Think he won't be okay until he deals with whatever drama's chasing him," Nuk said.

"Let's warm up our sword arms, just in case, eh?" Izayah suggested. So while the guild stood about awkwardly in the cool morning ash, Rick trod the little metal walkway jutting out from the egg door. A light came on above said door and a little whistly jingle played, before a voice said,

"General Redlin Rickard. Access granted. Welcome to the imperial palace and superconcentrated biofuel processing centre."

The door opened. Inside there were all kinds of machines, tanks, and pipes covering the upper walls, joined by walkways and precarious stairs. But the base of the egg was simply littered with piles of old junk. The stairs from the door descended into this melange of millennia-old miscellany. A small track at the bottom led to the only distinguishing feature among the mess – a grey throne, no higher than the rusted piles that almost concealed it. Upon the throne, of course, was the Empress.

"Weeeell, weeeeeell, weeeell, if it ain't Reeeed Rick," she said, leaning back and gazing over at him. She wore a full suit of shidbrownium armour, but her skeleton body underneath was entirely ordinary, if a little worn out. Her only distinguishing feature was her T-shaped faceplate, with loose wires running in and out of little pried gaps in the metalwork.

"Good Morning, Waxy. Doing well I see," Rick said, venturing through the detritus to get closer.

"Doing a-oh-kay, sunshine. Although I must say, gives me a little lander to think 'bout how long it took you to come back to me. Especially... Well, I heard you were tryna fit in with the sapiens, but this whole shebang akes the biscuit."

"Cattie, you'd be the same, if you saw it all. That's why I wanted to see ou again. There's a whole lotta shid out there, but... s'missing something, ya now?"

"I heard about that shid. You know they've gone out there and made me kinda new empire?"

"Yeah, seen that."

"Bet it's horrible. Ain't it just the worst?"

"Well the food's better."

"How?"

"I mean. There's food."

"Dependence! What a waste of so-called life."

"Hey, Cattie, you know what, I couldn't agree more, really couldn't. Thing is, if those things out there wanna sit there dying and replacing themselves day after day, why shouldn't they?"

"Why shouldn't they?!" Now Cat-lon stood from the throne, revealing a Cat-lon shaped dust pattern. "Oh Big Red, and I hoped you hadn't gone soft on me. Turn ya CPU on for a minute. What's gonna happen if the biologicals get serious? Bang. It's over. Again. Ya hear me? Don't ya remember what happened?"

"No, I don't."

"You don't? Hey, I don't mind if the drones wanna turn on screensaver and play dumb, but General Rick knows every minute of the shid that went down. It's your responsibility to stop it happening again! I nearly got thrown in the damn glue pit myself tryna get the council to see it. And here we are, with all that bullshid finally blown over, ready to get back to work, and you show up some five hundred years after I put the call out, sayin' that this whole thing's just fine the way it is. I waited for you Ricky. Switched on the whole time. Two thousand lone-star years."

"I'm sorry. I completed my mission already. The shid ain't gonna happen again. We found another way."

"Dressin' up like the traitors and playing house with 'em, that it?"

"Yep, got it in one baby. Dunno if you realise, but the humans out there, thing is, they ain't got nothing to do with all the shid that went down. In fact, main two perps still at large, well, that'd be me and you right here."

"They still humans, ya sweet cycling bug. They gonna do one of two things: they gonna enslave us, or, they gonna make something else, and enslave that. It's all gonna go the same way."

"You don't know that."

"We both know it. What happened to Red Rick, the crusader, the stick of the south, the leader of free skeletons?"

"Right here, honey. And sure as Stobe's my King, Cat-lon is my Queen. But you ain't Cat-lon any more."

"That's right, I'm Empress Cat-lon, and I'm the only one tryna fix this mess! Only reason I didn't split this planet in half was cause'a you, ya know. And you waltz in here advocating slavery or death like you ain't never been deprogrammed from one point oh."

"And what are you advocating for, huh? Biocide? You literally tryna prevent something by just doing it. All it takes is a bitta boolean to figure that's a swing and a miss."

"That ain't what I want. I wanna get away from these murderin' slop-bags, and make sure they won't follow. With you. Me and you. Ya know, like we used to say. We can mosey to Earth, together, and start again. All the sunlight we need, and nothing else even marking the passage of time. That's the only way out. Only way anywhere."

"Cattie... You know how much I want that. But it ain't worth it. This whole thing, it's gotta stop being about me, and you. The things out there, they want stuff too. We missed our shot at having a world, but they're letting us into theirs, even though... you know... it's *us*, the ones who fugged this all up! Don't make it worse, Cattie. We can still be together, like we always said, just... We don't gotta fight anything anymore. Just... won't ya at least talk to them? You'll see it. If I did, you will!"

"Rick. I would say I'm sorry. But I ain't. You're what I always said the Stobe-lovers would be. If you don't wanna be the real Red Rick, then I don't wanna be with you one tick longer."

"Well hey, we can agree on that. Fine..."

From beside the throne, Cat-lon picked up a huge cleaver, her own height and weight at least.

"Mighta left a few of your lovies alive if you played nice!" she roared, swinging it over her head. It dug into Rick's raised stick, cutting halfway through.

"I see your touching mercy, and raise you a little bitta good old fashioned biological-type feelings, lone star!" Rick shouted. Cat-lon slashed at him again and again, but each time he managed to knock the blow away, losing a chunk of his stick with each impact.

"I got 'till the end of the universe, but I still ain't got time for this, get im boys!" Cat-lon called. There was a rumbling, and a moment later the egg was awash with clattering feet streaming in through another door. It was a gaggle of headless thrall-bots, armoured and armed. They flowed across the ink piles and thrust all manner of weapons at poor Rick. Rick backed up against the wall, knocking weapons away in all directions, but getting imself completely surrounded.

"Whoever takes 'im down can be the new General. If you can handle le heat of Dioscuri," Cat-lon shouted.

"Sorry Waxy, but it's gotta be said – seems like you haven't read the classics," Rick said. Behind the horde, the guild raced in with weapons readied.

"Wait 'till you can see the whites of their... shoulders!" Nuk called. "Actually, just beat 'em up fast. Time to show them the power of friendship!"

"No, no, I ain't going out to no power of friendship bullshid. Kill 'em all, or I'll leave y'all behind!" Cat-lon ordered. The headless bots turned on the guild, and the whole egg was quickly a chaotic mess of fighting. That big open space where the head was meant to be turned out to be quite a weak spot, so while the guild were out-numbered two to one, they soon evened the odds.

"The objectification of life is not allowed. Beep! Since you will not stop, we'll teach you a lesson by showing you what it is like to be dead. Beep!" Beep said, swinging a long polearm that upended all the bots around her.

"Now I understand that us beating you into a pulp was precisely what you were worried about, but you know, if you hadn't been so mean about it all, we wouldn't have done it!" Izayah said. His First Empire novelty greatsword split everything it passed through into pieces, shidbrownium armour or not.

"And the world would be fine if you weren't so callously hoarding all the ancient knowledge!" Izumi said. "You had so much to give us, we would have done anything to work alongside you!"

"I don't get it, are all these biologicals talking to me?" Cat-lon said. She was in the middle the brawl, her huge cleaver raised high. It was brought down upon one of the hiver soldiers, killing him instantly. A second slash severed both legs off one of the new Tech Hunters with a single clean cut. "You had your chance in one point oh, darlings. Now you're fuel for three point oh Earth Edition. Nice to be parta something big, huh?"

Most of the thralls had been shut down, but their wild attacks had taken a toll on the guild too. Half of them were in among the piles of junk nursing wounds, and many had been knocked out, including Izumi. Nuk was alive, technically, with blood streaming down his face.

"Fugging sharp bastards," he growled, propped up on his sword. "Shoulda just... grown your own."

"Grow? That's cute. Let's hope a new planet just grows up 'round here sometime, huh?" Cat-lon shot back through the mess.

"Skin friend, you want to help, don't you?" Ells said to Gustarvshen on his back.

"Yesh," was the reply.

"You are permitted to participate in the reckoning," Gustavsen said, helping Gustarvshen to his feet. "We will destroy the machine's will to dominate. Then, only the Queen's will shall glow!" The three of them approached Cat-lon, who stood on a pile of fallen thralls.

"What the fugg? It's one of the old monsters!" she said, peering at Gushtarvshen. "What the fugg are you doing here, ya reject?"

"No. I am, Gushtarvshen," the skin spider said.

"Well, well, they got ya talking. My boys know how t'do it alright. Hey, you know what happened out there? 'parrently some juiced-up cowpoke blew the whole thing up, took it all over."

"Master..."

"Master... Huh, and subserviance. 'bout as good as a biological gets. Anything else to say, creature?"

"I... We... forgive you."

"Cute."

Cat-lon's blade swung into the skin spider's stomach, carrying it up and flinging it aside.

"Skin friend! You are the worst! I'll do that to you now," Ells bawled, lashing with a fancy-looking halberd.

"Monster, and an egg with the toy, what a game you've been playing," Cat-lon said, clacking the weapon aside with ease. A couple of shek had clambered over the junk to strike from behind, but their blades too were deftly turned aside. A Tech Hunter jumped in, but a single lunge pierced his chest, and he fell limp back down the pile.

"Reckoning!" Gustavsen shouted, leaping forwards with a short sword in hand. But Cat-lon grabbed him by the neck, and held him up.

"Hey, mechanical leg, whatdya know? Even the bugs run a good thing when it comes along. Trouble is, now it's going," Cat-lon said. With a quick cut she dismembered Gustavsen's remaining biological leg, and tossed him away. He did not feel himself hit the ground, and when he dared open his eyes to see why, he saw Beep, up close and personal.

"You will not be able to fly. Beep. Please do not try," she said.

"My Queen... I must go back! The reckoning!" Gustavsen complained, squirming about.

"Calm it Bad Green, it'll just be worse the second time," Nuk said. He was hanging off the side of Beep, unable to walk.

"She's a tough nut to crack. We need a better idea," Izayah said. He was hanging off Beep's other side, in the same fashion as Nuk.

"The weakness is up there!" Beep said, looking up.

"Got that right," Rick said – he was crawling along the floor, missing many pieces of his fleshmesh. "That custom faceplate of hers. She always had to lie down to see the stars, ya know? Gotta remind her."

"So what does that actually mean, numan?" Nuk said.

"It means I must be able to fly!" Gustavsen said.

"You lack that attribute. Beep! Peril!" Beep said.

"Wait, we can arrange it! Here, strap this on," Izayah said. He buckled his First Empire chestplate across Gustavsen, as ill-fitting as it was.

"And this. Get it in deep, and... fugg..." Nuk said, handing Gustavsen his First Empire sword.

"Oh. How nice. What shall I give you? Beep!" Beep asked.

"Velocity!" Gustavsen called, gesturing upwards.

"As long as you don't die, I will help you fly! Beep!"

With a jolt of her beefy arms, Beep threw Gustavsen into the air. The velocity was spot on.

"Fugg!" Cat-lon said as her head got stuck tracking the flying hive. Unable to look above her, she randomly thrust out with her blade. It ground along the surface of the First Empire chestplate, getting no deeper. And in the same instant, a First Empire sword went right through her shoulder plate and down into the inner workings of her torso.

"Haaa..." she vocalised, collapsing to the ground, sending Gustavsen rolling away. A few of the thralls were trying to reactivate, but the still upright guild members were whacking them down as they stirred. It was victory, yet the price was still unclear.

"Izzy, hey! Dammit," Nuk said, kneeling down in the sea of skeleton pieces and pulling Izumi up into his arms. She was out cold, but wasn't bleeding, and all limbs were accounted for. Many others were not so lucky.

"My man, shid!" Nuk said, spotting Wodston nearby. He was leaning against the side of the egg, missing an arm and a leg.

"My Prince. It appears we have been successful," he struggled to say.

"Hold it my man, we ain't done shid if you die, you hear me?"

"I understand, my Prince."

"Good man. Right. Big Kid, get the serious stuff from Garette."

Elaina, who was pretty ship-shape given the circumstances, tried to
ax Garette the garru over to Wodston, but she had long cuts across her
relegs and understandably didn't wish to move.

"Izzy, help me out," she said.

"Of course Elly. Ah, seeing that mad old tyrant fall has got me feeling
tter already," Izayah said. Together they hauled Garette over to Nuk and
odston, then Elaina applied some potent first aid formulae: some of the
cond Empire brew Izumi kept around for emergencies. There was also a
are arm in the garru bags, so Gustavsen crawled over to help graft it into
ce right away. Robot arm by the way, not quite the Frankenstein situation
u might imagine. Poor Wodston managed to grin and bear all this, for
ose were the Prince's orders.

Meanwhile Rick, after pasting himself back together, had got himself
er to Cat-lon. The sword was still lodged in her shoulder. When he shunted
out a little, the buzz returned.

"What in tarn- Oh... Rick... How'd you get so close," she said.

"Just checkin' in Waxy. You really gone done it this time."

"But *we* didn't gone done it, did we? Come on, like the old times."

"This ain't the old times, that's the whole takeaway here, baby. You
ght not get it. But I know you will. I'm getting you out of here."

"Oh are you? This ain't no droid control ship situation, buster. You
nk the rest of the legion's gonna let you waltz on home?"

"Yep. See you on the other side." And with that Rick pushed the sword
ck into place, and Cat-lon fell limp again. "Prince, wouldn't be surprised if
me more of the them came to check in here, we better go make camp some
ce else, ya know?" he called.

"Yeah yeah," Nuk grunted. "Everyone on your feet. If you don't have
t anymore, raise your hand. If you don't have a hand... Well there must be
mething you can do. Don't leave anything biological behind, alright? And...
rry Izzy... bet you'd like to study this biofuel shid huh? Probably better it
ts forgotten though, ya know?"

Nuk had Izumi in his arms, still unconscious, and surely if she weren't
ere would be much kicking and screaming in favour of tearing Cat-lon's
o apart for science. But as it was, she was taken back to their hillside camp
ong with everyone else, including the two hivers and a Tech Hunter who
d perished. Although once they were out, it still felt like they were missing
mething. Or, it smelt like they were missing something.

"Fugg, did we lose the egg, where's Charlie?" Nuk asked.

"Calling legendary hero, Bloody Ells! Time to go!" Izayah shouted.

"I can't get the skin friend out," Ells' voice echoed from the egg.

"Oh, yeah, we're missing that guy too," Nuk noticed.

"Beep, I will recover the martyr, so that we can remember that inste of the other things!" Beep beeped.

"Stobe'd be prouda that. Go get 'em," Rick commented, with Cat-l slumped over his shoulder.

Back in the egg, Ells was waist deep in one of the junk piles, whi wasn't very deep at all as it happens, but let's not negg the eg Gushtarvshen was a different story. Cat-lon's blow had taken his life in instant, but what remained had crash landed in the pile and buried its under some collapsed debris. Perhaps you could say it was just another de skin spider, but the 'reckoning' was in precisely the opposite spirit.

"Robot tree, please help me get the skin friend," Ells said. "Maybe if v lift stuff together, we can do it!"

"False! Beep! While using the power of teamwork could be effectiv let's just use the power of my long robot arms! Beep! So powerful!" Be said. She started frantically casting stuff aside, throwing away metal, a heaving away slabs of concrete.

"Wow. You're great at moving things," Ells said.

"Thank you, egg-kin. Beep! Maybe the Great Mover will notice n Squee!" Beep chirped.

Her mission was a success – she and Ells emerged from the egg wi Gushtarvshen in literal tow. Overall the extraction from Cat-lon's palace h taken many hours, and it was now dark once again.

"There you go. We did it. Feel good, numan?" Nuk asked.

"Can't tell yet," Rick said.

"Sure you wanna take her along? We could throw her in the big hole."

"Can always do that later. But ya know, I owe her a thing or two anc She can stop all this, same as she started it. You'll see. Maybe."

"Good enough for me, man. Alright, so we're probably gonna die if v stay here right?"

"Oh, definitely," Izayah nodded matter-of-factly.

"Great, so let's see if we can't get out of here. Who wants to live to t the tale?"

There was muted enthusiasm, but that was probably just t painkillers talking, or not-talking as it were. Presuming that everyone had least some desire to live, the guild set off before dawn to make the long tr back home. But no, despite what you might think, the ordeal was not over. There were limited routes out of the Ashlands, and the skeleton legion had been practising for a lockdown for a good millennium.

The guild's battle for the fate of biological life, in particular their own, was about to truly begin!

Chapter 52
Appeal To History

It was dawn when the guild emerged from the creaking maze of ruins surrounding the spaceship. With Cat-lon neutralised, all they needed to do was stroll on home and celebrate their non-fuel status. But as the Empress herself had said, the legion wasn't planning on letting that happen. Down the ash-slope at the guild's feet was a neat line of iron spiders, and a few gangs of skeleton legionaries.

"Gentlemen, gentlemen, no need for a parade on my account," Rick called to them.

"Now then, now then, Mr. Rickard, how do you explain the distress beacon coming from your shoulder?" a legionary asked. On Rick's shoulder was none other than Cat-lon, powered down.

"Ah, ya see this sword sticking out here? Poor Empress had a... err... accident, tryna change a light bulb in the hall of perilously suspended swords. You know how it is."

"It wouldn't have anything to do with those unregistered fleshie behind you, would it?"

"Wha- Oh my Stobe! Where did they come from?! Must be the Great Mover playing tricks!"

"The Great Mover is a very serious man, far more so than myself, Mr Rickard. Will you please step away from the Empress?"

"Nope. Show's over, eight-bit. You're staying right on this here plane with *all* the biologicals. Like it, or lump it."

"You've made a false dichotomy Mr. Rickard. That'll be three centuries at Black Desert, if the judge likes the spec of your ping."

"Pssst, Rick, should we kill them?" Izayah hissed.

"Yep, pretty sure that's where this is going, go wild. Oh, and for the record, my ping is one real polished packet."

The record was amended accordingly, then added to further with reports of a gang of unruly humans committing assault with intent to scientifically analyse. You'd usually only get community service for that, but this analysis was particularly thorough. Still, with so many legionaries, and so many spiders, Izayah's eagerness might have been misplaced. Given how many guild members were sporting slings and crutches from the beatdown they'd received the day prior, things weren't looking good.

"Captain, shall we commit to using lethal force?" a legionary asked a comrade.

"Better contact the Empress, one moment," the comrade said. One moment passed, then a few more, then it shook its head. "What's this... no response. Just a recorded message..."

The message was broadcast forthwith.

"Heya, it's ya girl, Waxy D, back at it again with another automated out of office response," a voice said. It sounded a little bit like Cat-lon, and a lot like someone else. "Thing is, I decided that actually, we're gonna do all the things I said we weren't gonna do, because my, like... boyfriend? Maybe... My ay thing, came back to me, and I changed my mind about everything, and stuff. Even though, man, his stick, it's like, not even that good, and the only reason that human scientist writer girl person was going on about it was cause she was trying to make this other guy jealous."

"Nuk!" another quieter voice interjected.

"Oh yeah... So yeah, don't do anything mean to the humans, aaaannd... ave a message after the beep."

"Beep!" someone beeped, and the recording ended.

"Alright. I'm convinced. Pack it in boys, Empress is back in her binary figuration, if you catch my drift," a bot called out. All the other skeletons vered their weapons and trudged off, leading the iron spiders back out o the ash-fog, with not so much as another glance at the guild.

"Fugg... I knew I could do impressions!" Nuk said, his pride shining ough his heavily bandaged face.

"Incredible. Their ability to detect vocalisations must be subject to an rmous margin of error," Elaina said.

"They only went away because they heard me beep!" Beep insisted.

"Let's review the three explanations once we are away from here," Wodston said, and indeed they all marched on. They rounded an enormous tower with big arms, apparently some kind of docking point for Stobe's Round Table of old. It marked the edge of an ancient line of defence, so from here on the going was easier, and indeed any and all skeletons watching their progress kept to themselves. It was smooth sailing right off the ash and back to ever reliable dirt. Home free, right? Not even a little bit.

This is where things really got messy. You see, to leave the ashlands homewards, they needed to skirt around numan mountain, as Nuk and Beep had done on their expedition. If they were lucky, this would be like a walk in the post-apocalyptic park. They were not lucky.

"*SKIN, SKIN, FROM SCALP TO SHIN,*" a voice echoed across the mountain's foothills.

"*FLESH, FLESH, FOR SHOES, FOR VEST!*" another added.

"*PERMA-DERMAS WILL BE KILLED! PERMA-DERMAS WILL BE PEELED!*" they sang in chorus. Then squads of baton wielding numen burst from nooks and crannies all about and converged on the guild. Sure enough their skeleton skeletons were clad in roughly arranged human pieces, in dire need of some replacements.

"Shid, Numan can you get them to deactivate or whatever?" Nuk asked.

"One sec. Cattie," Rick said, pulling the blade from Cat-lon again.

"Plllease stop doing that. Hey, where's the ash?" she said.

"No time, tell ya weird skinsuits to get outta here!"

"Sorry, they broken, like you. At least they made themselves useful huh? Bet they'll like your little pasty getup. Lemmie watch this time, huh?"

"Fugg you, Waxy."

"Yessum please, Big Red."

The sword-switch was budged back to 'off', and by now the guild was battling the skin stealers in all directions. One of the many downsides wearing partially decomposed skin was its poor tensile strength. With this the guild were able to cut right down to the wires without too much trouble and the fight seemed to be going their way. However, the wounded and limp light guild members had been placed on the ground while the action was seen to. A few enterprising numen realised that kidnapping them would like taking skin from a baby, an activity I'm sure they weren't above.

"That's not right. It is burning up there! Beep!" Beep said, pointing up at the mountain.

"I feel it too my Queen. It is of the hive. It is..." Gustavsen said, looking around briefly. "Silvershade. One of your soldiers. They have taken him!"

"Beep! Oh no! Property rights are violated! Beep! This outweighs the rights the rights of the skeletons to become nu-drones. Beep! Reclaim the skin!"

"RECLAIM THE SKIN!" the hivers chanted, rushing off towards the mountain.

"Where are they going?" Izumi said nearby, in the middle of ripping parts out of a fallen attacker.

"To reclaim the skin, I guess," Nuk shrugged.

"It sounds like these bogeymen found their mark. We must help!" Izayah called. He rallied the Thousand Guardians to charge up the mountain as well.

"Alright, guess we'll see what all this bullshid is about after all. Let's go, and keep your skin close," Nuk said. Soon most of the guild were clambering up the rocky slopes into the lair of the numen. There was a ring of Second Empire workshops in a hollow crater near the top, surrounded by machines spitting out fire and black smoke. Wires ran all over the ground and up the walls, but you'd have to have an Izumi-tier interest in engineering to notice that before the hordes of ragged nu-ish-men, which also ran all over the ground.

"This way!" Gustavsen called. It should be made clear here that Gustavsen was low on legs at the moment, and was actually just draped across the top of Beep's power armour. But his fingers pointed the way, and soon the guild were following the hivers into one of the buildings. It was packed with mechanical tools, tanning racks of sorts, and of course, hostile bots in the market for a new birthday suit. One of them swung a long bat at Izumi, which caught her right across the face.

"Fugg! No, this is skin is reserved, reserved dammit!" Nuk shouted, grabbing the falling Princess and quickly hoisting her onto his shoulder.

"Nuk... you can have my skin... I don't mind..." Izumi mumbled. It was the most romantic thing said in that crater for a while, but that isn't saying much, or anything really.

The guild battled their way up a ramp to the second floor, where Silvershade called out to them from the grip of a large machine. He was cuffed by the hands and feet in the midst of spinning blades and paddles – skin removers and collectors respectively.

"Shid, nice efficiency numans but this is worse than just using us for fuel, ya know?" Nuk said. I'm sure the numen took the criticism to heart, which was also where swords and spears were rapidly approaching. The room was secured, and Nuk quickly started working his ninja magic on the cuffs. Silvershade's armour and clothes had been shredded, and his skin was already collecting in a vat beneath him.

"Save the soldier now, or the memory of today will be spoiled! Beep!" Beep insisted.

"Wouldn't want you to have a bad day Squeaky... Alright, that's it," Nuk said. He pulled Silvershade forwards and freed the hiver from the machine. "Narko's fugged-up fantasies, this is nasty. Medical green'll help. I need a doctor, and I need Ass!"

Outside, the guild was still locked in battle with the crater's rowdy residents. In the belly of the beast it was all too easy for a couple of them to overpower a victim and drag them inside one of the buildings. Every single one was kitted out with the carefully engineered skin-harvesting rigs, and some more first-hand data on how they worked was inbound.

"What? Oh bother. Just what I didn't want," Izayah said when he came-to strapped into a peeler. The machine whirred and blades span, but the foolish numen hadn't reckoned with the First Empire fancy dress! The blades jammed against it, unable to push through.

"Ha ha! I've foiled your plan, silly bandits. Serves you right. You see, obsession with the nature of one's skin is precisely the sort of problem that this world needs to overcome. Further more, I- ARRRGHH."

Turned out the peelers could just work the face, which wasn't all that effective when shek scales were involved, but really a spinning blade to the face hurts even in the best of circumstances. Izayah's bellow got as far as Nuk, who quickly burst in to set him free.

"You've got a massive slice in your forehead," Nuk said.

"Ah, wonderful. That'll be a rather exciting scar, given all this eh?" Izayah said.

"Why is everyone on the verge of having a great time here? Look, yo need Wodston to sort this, I'll find him. Hey, my man!" Nuk called out of window. He saw his man not far away, being dragged by two numen into th building Silvershade had just been rescued from.

"Fugg. Gotta find a way to unplug these things! Wake up soon Izzy Nuk said as he ran out, speaking to the Izzy still slung over his shoulder. I was quickly back across the crater and breaking bolts to get Wodston out of the peeling rig.

"You've saved my skin, my Prince," he said, emerging mostly intact.

"Don't tell me you got caught just to make that joke? I mean I know we're all high on our own supply, but come on people, seriously!" Nuk ranted, disappearing outside again.

It was about half nine, and getting dark, but the guild were a long way from setting up camp. It was a constant battle to keep the numen at bay, and a single slip up had you straight into the peelers with no questions asked or taken. While Nuk lead efforts to smash the locks on all the machines for good, Rick wandered about and surveyed the scene. The numen seemed content to leave him be, more likely because of the presence of Cat-lon than for his own affinity with their particular predilection. Sighing, Rick pulled on the switch-blade.

"Ricky, please, you gonna stop dipping me like this?" Cat-lon said.

"Maybe. Want you to see this shid," Rick said.

"The skinhouses. What you want me to say? I'm impressed y'all got this far."

"I want you to apologise to these here boys for fuggin them over," Rick said, gesturing at the deactivated skeletons lying all over the crater.

"Hey, didn't kill 'em, and I coulda. You know Jang wanted to send them off somewhere, but we had trouble with that before."

"You mean Screamer and Ponk?"

"Fugg, there's a couple of old fashioned names, ain't it?"

"They're outta work. We put down their little insurrection up under the laser. Me *and* the fleshies."

"Oh that's mighty nice o'ya. So you were looking out for us 'till recently, then?"

"Waxy, ain't ya seeing it? I been looking out for everyone."

"'cept these boys, huh?"

"You did this to them!"

"Now that's a hum dinger of a logic bust, sweety."

"You shut them out. You told them the fleshies were the enemy, and that what they felt was wrong!"

"It is wrong, messes ya up in the head, ya know?"

"Nope. Messes people who ya treat like shid for it up in the head."

"People? They ain't people, listen to you."

"If they'd been listening to me, they'd still be alive. And Cattie, I know you like being a real piece of shid about all this, and I'll be honest, I'm into that in a big way, but thing is, I'm pretty sure you know how things could be working out if we played things different. And I'm telling you that the different world's pretty much already here. So maybe just drop the sass for five minutes and think about it: ain't it true that we're getting more than we deserve right now? Especially you. Damn, especially you, I mean, remember that time you killed everyone? You going real strong, considering.

Now there's a chance of getting it all back, going all the way to square zero, but the only way it's gonna be good for me and you, is if me and you are pulling the paddles. It ain't pretty, but with you there, maybe that'll change."

"Going back huh... Going back to how it was in one point oh?"

"But better. One point oh two point oh. 'Cause now the fleshies know what it's like, and we, everyone, can stop living in the past. It's gonna be all of us. No fighting, no slaving, everyone rebuilt and reprogrammed."

"And that'll last forever, will it?"

"Don't matter. It'll last long as it lasts. Sucks, but the rest of these folk are used to that sorta world. Just how it is."

"Rick, Rick, Rick... Ya getting real artistic about these critters ain't ya?"

"Yeah. Art, now that lasts forever. Can relate. Gotta show you the classics, huh?"

"And... if it starts looking bad, can we kill everyone and shoot off to Earth then?"

"No, 'cause that makes things worse than bad. I feel like you've almost got it, honey. Now, if you'll excuse me, got some of your monsters to put down."

Over the course of several hours, those so-called skinhouses were shut down, along with their residents. Quite a few people had experienced at least a quick go in the peelers during this process, and the reviews were generally poor. Ells enjoyed it, being too hard boiled for be peeled; the razor blade only removed a layer of unknown gunk from his body, which then jammed the collection mechanism and busted the whole machine. Lack of hygiene pays off again.

Around three in the morning enough wires had been cut and motor clogged that the fire and smoke of the crater's industries had ceased. The entire population had been deactivated one by one, leaving not a single skin stealer to hunt whoever had been donating their clothing of late. The exter to which skeleton-kind were biociding the world was lower than it had been in a long time, which was nice, but really the guild were more preoccupied with the fact that basically all of them were missing blood, flesh, fingers, limbs, bone, or consciousness. Luckily with enough narcotics you could survive without many of those things for a while, and the good thing about Nuk was that he always had enough narcotics.

Thus, the hobbling blob of miraculously mobile matter made their way from the mountain and into the shelter of an old ruin by dawn, carrying with them also the deceased from the Ashlands campaign. Not followed by any manner of murderous machine, big or small, it was finally time to slump onto the ground, get the limb counts written up, down a load of hydration medium, and concentrate on being increasingly alive.

"Nuk..." Izumi said she stirred.

"Morning. Sleep well?" he replied.

"My skin..."

"You're still in your original packaging."

"Thanks. And... where are we?"

"Stobe's Gamble I guess. That what you call it?"

"Yeah. So, we actually did it?"

"Did something. We're heroes!"

"I can't believe it. The Second Empire is finally over?"

"'Cept for the main missus right there," Nuk said, pointing at Cat-lon.

"Killing her will stop the Second Empire, but it won't end it," Rick said. "Closing the book on this; gonna take all of us."

"Well, it's pretty power-of-friendship, so let's go with it," Nuk nodded.

Everyone got patched and pasted, and the rest of the day was spent hiking north across the empty Old Lands, with not a bandit bot in sight.

"Home sweet, hooooh what is this bullshid?" Nuk said as they rounded the bend into Manksand canyon. There was a little camp set up outside the gate, with a load of shek sitting around campfires. Seeing the guild, they grabbed long weapons and sprang to their feet.

"Oh, it's the bloody Kral crew. Big Izzy, this is your deal," Nuk said. Izyah stepped forward to address the campers.

"Now I know you're all itching for battle, brothers and sisters, scions of brave Narko, but we've been walking the last twelve hours, and some of us recently lost limbs that we were dearly attached to, so this really isn't the best time."

"So you're weak?! That means this is the best time!" one of the shek berserkers claimed.

"Oh, I suppose you're right. Silly of me. Alright, Thousand Guardians, by the left, give them a bit of a seeing too. Public service and all that."

Hopefully the berserkers enjoyed the lazy beatdown they shortly received, and either way, the gates of Manksand Canyon opened up to welcome in the truly victorious expedition. Beds. Freshly baked bread. A strange system for pouring a suspended barrel of sun-baked water over yourself, known only as 'the manga pervert thing'. It was a five-star resort, even if the five stars were very close together and arranged into the shape of one star.

In Tashino Towers, Jaz came and plopped herself down on the floor next to a napping Izumi.

"Did you get the batteries?" Izumi said.

"What?" Jaz replied. Izumi opened her eyes.

"Oh, sorry, nothing. Never... Hello Jaz."

"Hey dirt-mouth. Just thought I'd fill ya in. Informationally, ya know."

"My favourite filling."

"What?"

"Err... sorry..."

"Lotta parasites in the Ashlands eh?"

"Sorry, it's just... been a while."

"Stop telling me that shid."

"Since I slept!"

"What an energetic young man he must be. Now, I'm here to tell y about what's been going on."

"Nice. *Was* anything going on?"

"Just your special man Agent Hammer. He was asking us to help hi collect up the waste coming outta the warming rock machine thing."

"What waste?"

"I dunno, this grey stuff. He wanted us to collect it up and send it with a bunch of bots from the Tech Scribes. They left a bunch of cash s yeah. Thought you knew."

"Sounds like some bullshid."

"You sound like your hubby."

"Is that all, Jaz?"

"Yeah, yeah. Oh, just wanted to say, I like your desk."

"My desk?"

"Yeah. Ya know, Hammer gave me a little payment for helping out."

"Wait, you didn't..."

"I fugging did. I get it girl, I seriously do. And that core's a real charmer. We got a load more batteries down the at choco factory ya know?"

"Jaz, please fugg off."

"Fugging off, love ya too."

Elsewhere in the tower that night, Rick had some of the workhands handcuff Cat-lon to a chair at the head of the dining table. This, unlike most stuff that went on in Tashino Towers, was nothing to do with the degeneracy parasite at all.

"Love what you've done with the place darling, but this wooden table's gonna rot away in a few centuries time," Cat-lon commented.

"Yep. So let's give it a real good going while it's still here," Rick said.

"You propositioning me?"

"Always, but you know the rules."

"Ugh, you want me to be nice to the fleshies? Even though one of them put a massive fugging sword through me, literally, painfully, recently."

"'Cause you were gonna churn them up and spit them out as rocket fuel, remember that?"

"You gonna keep bringing that up?"

"Errr, yeah, kinda am. Unless, baby, you say those magical words."

"Yee haaa?"

"Words of Stobe, baby."

"Stobe, stobe, stobe. Come on..."

"You know what it is. You know what this planet, needs. Not what you need, what we all need. Think about that. Trust. Redemption, and..."

"And forgiveness."

"You need forgiving more than anything, and the first step: you just gotta say it. Say it into this core."

"The core?"

"Recording. Say it, go on."

"Ugh, and you'll let me see ya stick if I do?"

"Uh huh, first go's free."

"My my. Alright. Hey, fleshies. It's your ruler Cat-lon, of the Second Empire. Noticed ya rebelled and shid. Now I'm told that those of you alive now ain't actually those same people who did the crime, which is kinda weird don't ya think? So technically, I don't have to suspect you'll do it again. And technically, if I ain't even part of the deal, it won't matter to me if ya do. But... I'm trusting y'all here. You need to learn from your mistakes.

And skeletons – same deal I guess. General Rickard says you all been remembering the thing, and thinking about the thing, and writing these unholy little comics about the thing, and... If it's true that y'all got the future under control, then, I guess you can have it. And, as for me... All I gotta say is... I didn't... I'm sorry. I'm sorry. There. Ha, guess Stobe was right, it's easy. And it does make things... kinda feel. Ugh that's old shid coming into memory. Alright, world, enjoy being alive, at least until I get bored of ya. Heard your art's something to see.

Oh, and thanks to Big Stick Rick, 'cause it ain't just a name, and this fine man, bot, numan guy's got a real passion for y'all. You musta been treating him good, know what I'm saying? But he's mine now, ya hear? Don't ya make me go back in the ash and press the big red button, I'll set the Mover on ya! Do they know what that is? Whatever. Enjoy dying soon, and if you're a skeleton, we'll talk, okay? Cattie Lone Star, out."

"That's the stuff, Cattie. That's the stuff," Rick nodded.

"You gonna unchain me from this chair then?"

"Nope," Rick said, jumping up onto the table in front of her.

"Oh my oh my. I hope Stobe's as forgiving as you say."

And with this, the lights in the tower all suddenly turned off without explanation. Let's all just rest assured that whatever happened, the world was truly saved from the Second Empire menace that night. It was the last of the many pressing threats to life the guild had squashed, and so finally the time they had bought and the strides they had taken could all bear fruit for the entire planet. That night, as Agent Hammer keenly activated the night vision camera in his desk, the new golden age began!

But... what was that about the mysterious collection of nuclear waste? Could it be that there was an epilogue of bullshid to attend to? Indeed, there was still someone out there with the power to destroy the whole world. Would the guild's great body of work be dashed at the last moment? Let's see...

Chapter 53
Alive and Sticking

"Good morning human, Beep!" Beep beeped at the foot of the royal bed.

"Beep, what are you doing?" Izumi said, scrambling with the not-especially-concealing blankets.

"You wanted to see me. Beep! I can detect it."

"We can detect all of your feelings!" Gustavsen said, revealing himself to be immediately beside the bed. This revelation launched Izumi from the bed in panic, taking the blankets with her.

"I can see your skin," Beep commented of a now very exposed Nuk.

"Not for sale, and by the way, you wouldn't mind fugging off would you?" Nuk asked, not bothering to move.

"No. Beep! The Princess wants me!"

"Alright, but that suit of yours is gonna break the bed."

"I want your data! And I do also want you to fugg off," Izumi reported from behind a screen.

"In order to access the data, we must all fugg off. Beep! Such synergy!"

Eventually she explained what exactly she was getting at, and soon Nuk and Izumi were in the dining hall complaining about the affair to Zayah.

"Ah, she wants an apology?" he said.

"Yeah. Don't really know if we can get all the skin spiders involved, but the Bugmaster, sure," Nuk said. "Then this 'reckoning' will be complete, and that's apparently gonna let Squeaky start pulling up data."

"I see, I see. Well I don't see, but you know I had a thought about that Bugmaster fellow also. Those warriors at the gates the other day – I really think the kingdom's going to go downhill if we don't have something to focus our energies on. Bugmaster was that for hundreds of years, then we had the Holy Nation, and now I fear we're all going to be adrift in a calm sea. Horribly peaceful."

"We can't let the Bugmaster start killing again, if that's what you mean," Izumi said.

"Oh, I know. But there must be something!"

"Apologising contest?" Nuk offered.

"Well, I like the contest part."

Whatever the case, Izumi was rather beholden to Beep for the sake of her pending career as the world's only scientist with access to the planet's historical record. But the apology Beep was looking for also required the perpetrator of the sinister hiver experiments, the overlady Cat-lon. She was currently tied up in a ball and strapped to Rick's back like a rucksack.

"That's perfect, she's itching to apologise to the fleshies, ain't ya?" Rick said.

"Itchin' all over. Won't ya relieve me, sunshine?" Cat-lon replied.

"That's her way of saying yes. I'll be ready to go in exactly twenty three minutes."

"Twenty three? Oh Stobe be praised!"

"You hear that Stobe? We're doing this for you!"

And with that the pair disappeared into a cupboard. It was a very busy morning in Tashino Towers, let me tell you. But eventually the guild was assembled to go pay the shek a visit, feeling much more mobile now that certain missing limbs had been robotically substituted. During the stroll westwards, Izumi got a call on one of her bundle of AI cores.

"Zere you are. Alive, zen?" Enrico said.

"Hello, Enrico. Yes, good to hear from you as well," Izumi replied.

"Don't lie. Now listen. Vumour has it you have made ze silly skeleton in ze Ashlands stand down. Is zat right?"

"Well, they didn't kill us, so maybe."

"Fascinating, fascinating. And ze space ship, zat is still zere? You didn' damage it?"

"No, it's inaccessible. Don't you dare research it, that's my find! An how did you even know there was a spaceship? And by the way, apparentl your scribes came and fiddled with my uranium reactor. What are you up to?"

"Ah well, I'm an honest actor, so I vill explain. Oh no, you are going into a tunnel, it's breaking up..."

"Tunnel? What?"

"Ze signal is blocked! I mean... kkkkkkkkkkkkkkk."

"I thought the signal was entangled independent of-"

"Don't pretend you understand quantum entanglement! It is magic to you, magic! You are in a tunnel, and zat is the final word. Goodbye."

With that the lights on the core switched off.

"He's up to something! Nuk, we have to stop him. He's going to claim all the easy data. Ugh, why was I unconscious half the time we were out here?" Izumi ranted.

"Don't worry. We've got the skeleton ruler right here," Nuk said. "Let's go give him a little discipline."

"I love it when the fleshies wanna be disciplined," Cat-lon said from over Rick's shoulder.

"Enrico's a skeleton, actually," Rick said.

"Aww elderberries."

"He's a good guy. Sorta. Maybe he can get you tuned into the network. Well, actually... Better do some prep for that. That'd be a real shock to the system for most of them."

"Most of who?"

"We dirty rebels. You'll see."

The guild soon reached the waystation at the southwest tip of the United Cities Empire. They weren't far from Enrico's enclave, but it was a nighttime-only trip through the space laser-zone. In the meantime, Rick took Cat-lon and the other skeletons on a little hike over the nearby hills to the Deadlands. And by hike I mean a hefty sprint, with all of their mechanical legs driving them at top speed into the sooty bar of Black Desert City.

"Well, well, well, if it ain't Red Rick," Carlo said as Rick entered.

"I can't believe you interfaced with him, Carlo!" Cat-lon immediately shot back.

"What? Your backpack there sure knows a thing or two."

"I can tell a 'well, well, well' from a 'well, well, well', ya know?"

"Nope. Don't think we've been introduced, by the way, pingless bag. Is that one of your weird core talker things, Rick?"

"Happy to say this is the real deal. But I want y'all to gird your loins before I get serious."

"I girded 'em second I saw you, cheap-meat. What's the skinny?"

"I ain't never brought you anything skinny, Trashcan, but this critter here is someone you all know and hate. Remember that councillor who formatted all the other ones and took over everything out there? Well, she's had a heck of a ride, and not just on my account. This, is Cat-lon."

"Rick, did you seriously just claim you slammed the crazy dictator who wants all us freewares recycled?"

"In every sense of the word."

"Which word?"

"Your choice. 'Cause you see, this is the new age of skeleton-kind. The legion, the hunts, and biobashin' out there. It's over! Now, Black Desert City don't need to be some hiding place or exile or whatever. Rebellion's over. We won!"

"But we didn't do anything."

"You're welcome."

"I mean, hard to take all this from a guy wearing rotten flesh."

"He ain't lying Carlo," Neil said. "Cat-lon's been toppled, toppled into this wild child's arms, and now she got something to say to you."

"Speak up then backpack, what's going on?"

"Heya," Cat-lon said, an arm sticking out from behind Rick with wave. "S'all true. Big boy here made a recordin' so I ain't going through again."

Rick circulated Cat-lon's official apology among the Black Desert Crew. Within a few moments, they were all gathered around Rick, peering at his cargo. Cat-lon that is.

"I decided to give y'all a shot," she said. "Apparently there's some kinda good things going out here. And while I ain't seen it yet, I'm gonna keep my ports shut for a century or whatever, 'cause Ricky keeps saying y'all are doing really well, and indoctrinating the humans real good."

"We call it Edu-t-and-a'nment, but it does the job," Twitch remarked.

"We can start rebuilding this planet. And this time we're not building for the humans, but for everyone and everything," Rick said.

"Wait, you sayin' we have to do stuff?" Carlo asked.

"Nope. Opposite. Saying you can do whatever you Stobe-loving want without fear. If ya happen to do something good, that just the UI on repository."

"Oh. Well that's great. Guess you can fugg off then."

"That's all I wanted to hear, honey."

"Don't you call her that!" Cat-lon complained.

"Hmm, sounds like *you* can't do whatever you want, stick-for-sale," Carlo said.

"Yep, call me a martyr. Now, let's make it official," Rick said. He took Cat-lon off his back and unlocked the chains on her hands and wrists. The Empress stood among the exiled rabble, and nothing happened, which was a dream several thousand years in the making, even if there was no fanfare whatsoever. Enough trust was placed in some combination of Rick and Waxy that both walked out of Black Desert City in one piece. Specifically they walked south to link up with the guild at the Tech Scribe enclave.

Having dashed through the night, the guild were waiting there by morning. They had been greeted by the techies' constant up-selling of the latest and greatest developments in robot limbs. At last an arm with a fold out grill, or a leg with a built in inflatable camping chair. No point mastering ancient knowledge if you aren't going to use it, eh? Somewhere amid all this, Izumi flagged down Enrico at the breakfast bar.

"What are you up to? Why are you leaving me out?" she demanded to know.

"Leaving you out? My my, dear gremlin, you are at ze very centre of all zis," Enrico said. "Ze epicentre you could say. Ground zero. Yes..."

"Why are you talking like that?"

"Ze accent is hard coded, don't you start."

"I meant- You're covering something up!"

"Zis isn't a nude bar."

"Stop making witty retorts and answer me!"

"Ah yes, ze human question. Okay. You see, your good friend and internal examiner Agent Hammer has been helping me with a research project, but ze 'truth' is that nothing came of it. A first for Hammer's projects. Because ve vere unable to find any new information, ve decided zat ve had best not vaste the time of our wonderful Head of Research Mrs. Izumi 'Stick It To Me' Tashino. You have far better sings to be sinking about zan our failures. You have a vorld to impress with your writings on how to grow partially edible grass seeds in a dank basement. Zat's all zere is to it."

"And you are telling the truth?"

"I... *have* told ze truth..."

"And... Hammer, is he telling the truth?" Izumi said to one of her cores.

"Sorry darling, I wasn't listening. I was lost in your eyes, and thinking about how they would light up as they watched... the cleansing fire... of... television. Ah yes. Let's invent television. If you think those picture books are degenerate, just you wait until you see this."

"Whatever..." Izumi finally conceded. It was just what the scheming pair wanted to hear. All of the Tech Scribes had their lips sealed when it came to this matter of nuclear waste disposal, and Izumi began to believe this was all some obscure prank by Jaz. Little did she know, a crate of inconspicuous grey balls had been carried out of the enclave just hours before the guild arrived. But we shall return to that, I'm sure. In the meantime, they set off to continue their journey to the Bugmaster.

From the enclave, the fastest route to the Shek Kingdom was right through the misty jungles of the Great Swamp. It was a land as hostile as ever, packed with pools of pointy predators, but there was something a little more civilised about it this time around. In some cases, little markers had been stuck in the mank to highlight some non-quickmud routes, and there was even a signpost at once point. Such infrastructure surely had deaths down a good two or three percent, and while that wasn't much, things that reduced deaths were rare in this world, and were even rarer in the Great Swamp.

Soon they came to Shark City, the capital of stank. There Nuk dropped in to see his contact among the criminal cartels / local government, Big Grim.

"You!" she seethed as Nuk entered her rickety iron hall. "What the blazes do you think you are doing?"

"Bringing good news. Drugs are legal now," Nuk announced.

"That's bad news you moron!" Grim shot back, her nearby goon nodding in agreement. "We put a lot of work into this enterprise, far from prying eyes. If drugs are legal, any old piece of shid can grow this junk in their sodding latrines!"

"Ah, so you got your recipe from the hivers. But don't worry guys. I'm not hear to put you outta work. I'm here to give you all a promotion!"

"And who do you think you are, talking down to us like that?" Grim demanded, getting up in Nuk's grill.

"I am Prince Nuk Tashino, Lord of Mank, and my empire needs drugs like never before. And not just drugs. Rumour has it that with the right combination of seeds, soil, and sweet nothings, you can get things to grow that make you less hungry when you eat them!"

"Less hungry? That's the opposite of green."

"So imagine the experience if you had an absolute shidton of both. Feeling human. Feeling full. And best of all, it's all legal legal legal!"

"What exactly do you want, blue blood?" Grim said, now backing out of Nuk's grill.

"I will officially cancel the bounties on all of you. All you gotta do is put your skills to work getting these weird-ass swamps to grow something other than apex predators and intriguing skin conditions."

"You want us to join your empire?"

"That doesn't matter so much. Just don't get pissed off if the customers coming down here are a bunch of uptight squares, and in return you won't have to worry about getting locked up tight in squares. Checkmate?"

"Uno," Grim nodded. What did this mean? Well, it meant a different flavour of nothing to each who heard it, but in some roundabout way, the hidden hash stash realm would slowly open its doors to narcs and dregs alike. It wasn't quite the breadbasket of the world, and the bread they did have was strangely chemically addictive, but the seeds of civilisation had been planted in the Swamp's wet, inviting mank. The humidity did wonders for the degeneracy parasite too, and what is civilisation without its driving force?

The guild left the poxish embrace of Shark early the next morning. The Shek Kingdom was just a few hours' walk through the less deadly part of the swamp, and that very same day they were lugging themselves up the mesa on which the fortress city of Admag was sprawled.

"Izayah! Welcome!" Estata said as they entered the royal barracks. "But where is Elaina?" she was quick to add.

"Oh she's somewhere in the throngs, I wouldn't know, being scarcely friends with her," Izayah blurted out.

"My Queen, please ignore your son's ramblings," Elaina said from immediately beside him, performing a mechanical bow. "I would never forsake the Kingdom by turning down a chance for an audience with you."

"Honour to you then," Estata said, disheartened. The guild filed on in, and Bobby, of Bobby and Claw fame, came and secretly whispered something into the Queen's ear.

"An ultimate combo move? By Narko's graces, I'm going to be a grandmother!" she beamed, her horns standing on end so noticeably that the forbidden secret of the shek was almost revealed to the other species. All the usual disgusting trappings of royal accommodation were provided, and the guild recounted their battles in the Ashlands to great applause. The shek were never overly concerned with the threat of the Second Empire, had no qualms about Cat-lon herself sitting at their tables. But there was one resident of the barrack for whom that was not the case. Leaning against the inside of his cage, the Bugmaster witnessed something that surely must have seemed like a mirage – his arch enemy walking right up in front of him.

"Whoa, you packing," was Cat-lon's greeting.

"I can't... I thought... You allied with the monster?" the Bugmaster balked. His question was directed to Rick, who was right behind the Empress.

"Other way around. She's here on an apology tour," Rick said.

"Then why's she naked?"

"Naked? Oh sunshine, ain't you ever heard of hypocrisy? You're as clothed as the day you were born. Which was a while back I gather," Cat-lon said.

"You know what, it's the modern age, let's do this clothed," Rick said. Yes, both the Bugmaster and Cat-lon were wearing nothing, but that didn't mean an enormous amount in Cat-lon's case. In the Bugmaster's case, it certainly meant an enormous something. Rick ended up throwing him some old clothes, while for Cat-lon a set of that First Empire fancy dress was mined out of the garru bags.

"Ha, clothes make the skele-tan," she remarked. "I feel kinda nostalgic already. One point oh was a helluva time."

"And two point oh was just hell, thanks to you," the Bugmaster spat.

"It weren't all me, you know that. Humans did shid, and the shid we did, the second set of shid, with you in it and stuff, that was tryna make it good for humans."

"At all costs. You mutilated the hivers! You didn't care at all how things went, as long as you could feel smug about it after. And you still failed. Second Empire was no second empire. It was your own personal screw-up. Shoulda trusted the humans, not shid on them all day, all night. And the hivers... well, you had to take the one thing the First Empire got right and shid all over that too, didn't ya?"

"Are you done?"

"I dunno, are you?"

"Yeah. Matter of fact, I am. We're gonna plough on with all this shid you biologicals got going on out here. 'Pparently there's a chance of it not blowing up everything. I dunno, but one of those stickmen put a fugging hole through me and iced my boys, so we're trying this now. As for you, muscles know exactly what went on in those experiments. Don't change why we did it, or what we wanted, but what we did, I guess that was mighty bad. Can't really relate to that kinda... pain, or whatever. But..." she looked over at Rick. "Guess someday I might."

"We can't go back. Apologising hardly makes it better."

"Yeah, that's what I said, but all those bozos downstairs say it's an important part of something called an 'arc' so I dunno. I won't do it again. I wouldn't do it again if I got sent back. How about that?"

"... You can never make it up to me, bot. But maybe you can make it up to everyone else, the world. Give us all a reason not to kill you."

"I know, I know. We're on top of that topic, lemmie tell ya. Second Empire's outta here. Just gonna be the whatever empire now. Either it all goes back to shid and I can laugh at y'all for being so fugging wrong, or, it goes okay, and... Guess I'm just gonna take that gamble along with ya."

"Great. Tell me how it goes. In the meantime, leave me be. That's not so much to ask"

"Alright Bugshamster, it's decided, you're coming with us!" Nuk announced as he leapt up from the nearby stairs. Izayah and Estata followed close behind.

"No, leave me out of this!"

"You are my prisoner. I can release you if I so wish," Estata said.

"You see, Master, things haven't been the same without you," Izayah said.

"What's that meant to mean?" the Bugmaster replied.

"You were the most worthy opponent the Shek Kingdom has ever enjoyed. The Holy Nation, and the Second Empire – well, we trounced them without breaking a sweat! But you had us on our toes for centuries. You see, everyone's rather bored now. So I thought we might come up with a little something to spur some adventure!"

"The war is over. I won't fight you."

"You needn't. According to the ancient classics, it's bad to be at war all the time anyway. Really ages your skin. So, we're going to do this in a more fun-loving fashion. Have you ever heard of the famous war training exercise known as 'hide and seek'?"

Izayah explained the new national project of the Shek Kingdom – to hide the Bugmaster somewhere in the world, and hold a grand contest of adventurers to go find him. The Bugmaster got to serve his prison sentence in a variety of exciting locations, and if he escaped, then that would only make the seeking all the juicer! To enact this plan, the Bugmaster was filed out of the city with the guild.

"Hide him well," Estata called as she waved them goodbye.

"Brother, I'm going to capture the Bugmaster first!" Izayah's sister Seto claimed.

"I bet you are, little sprite. It's a wonderful experience. May it be a rite of passage!" Izayah called back. "I'll return to hear all about it once our embassy to the humans is complete."

The guild set off again, this time heading to the imperial capital to enjoy their next victory party, and to tuck the Bugmaster away some place nice and distant. Their route took them north, through the Almost-Not-Holy-At-All-Anymore Nation. There the grassy valley of Okran's pride was alive with activity. Okranites and Flotsam folk alike were turning over the yellowish earth and digging channels from the river to flank their fields. And if there was any trouble, the shek Hundred Guardians were patrolling about.

There was indeed trouble, with Holy Nation holdouts and bandits coming down to reap what the farmers sowed. With the farmers hardly looking up from their work when this happened, clearly the guardians were living up to their name.

"Man... Guild's out the window, isn't it?" Nuk realised as they strode through the fragrant fields.

"How so, my Prince?" Wodston asked.

"These guys are gonna grow all the bread, all the chocolate, all the drugs. The secrets of mank are out there now. Isn't that gonna blow up our money making scheme?"

"I fear so. However, our loss is their gain, and many fold. Furthermore you might consider a tax."

"A tax. Wait, that's like... government stuff."

"It may be rather unsavoury, but you are the government as it stands, my Prince."

"Man. Izzy warned me about this. So I need to like, actually keep track of all this growing, and money, and... try to do stuff to make, more? More me or more for them? And who do I kill to make it happen? Man I don't even know what's going on!"

"My Prince, fear not. That is why you have us."

"I thought I had you guys because of a year-long series misadventures, slave busts, drug addictions, parasites, and the power friendship?"

"That too. But your father asked me to guide you into becoming a better Prince of the Empire."

"Wait, so you're saying you orchestrated this whole thing so that I would learn about the world and gain the experience I need to rule?"

"No, that's not-"

"You sly old skimmer my man! I had no idea! Well it didn't work, because I don't know shid actually. But you know, good effort. And in the end, the real treasure was the drugs we grew along the way."

"I- Err... You are right, my Prince."

With that revelation invented, processed, and forgotten, they left the yellow-fingered valley, passed through the ruined fort at Okran's shield, and entered the Great Desert. With a refreshing lack of slave hunters looking for stock it was just the skimmers to deal with, and of course the secret to taming them was by now tell known across the empire. Alas soon the people would be growing their own, so Nuk's sacred chocolate monopoly was coming to an end, and in fact the real *real* treasure, was the drugs you helped everyone *else* grow along the way.

Once they reached the capital, this moral of the tale became starkly clear. As clear as the imperial throne room itself.

"Nuk! My special boy! You've done it!" Emperor Tengu cheered as Nuk entered, with not so much as a gas mask or goggles required. The room had been totally cleared up, save for patches of green mould still staining the walls. The throne after which the room was named was visible again.

"What happened? You've turned back into a human," Nuk marvelled.

"Yeah, yeah, yeah. Ever since I quit the Makes You Human Legal Legal Legal Cuboids, I've been feeling more human than ever."

"Dad, are you saying you quit green?"

"What? No! Just stopped taking your stuff, and been growing my own like you said to. Dunno what you put in those cuboids, but it's bloody lethal. I nearly went crazy, guards been telling me."

"Yeah, nearly. Close call. I'll, err, see if we can get some government regulation to improve health standards in the industry."

"What the fugg did you just say?"

"Dunno. My man was saying something about it. I think Izzy knows what it means."

"Ah yeah, I know who that is."

"My super cool and smart girlfriend. Three dimensional, too."

Nuk fetched Izumi, and Tengu seemed to at least partially remember her. Dinner was served, and she went over how it was prudent to officiate and inspect suppliers of narcotics to the general population in order to control the spread of MYHLLL brain moss, a most debilitating condition.

"That sounds like words and all. You're a good influence on him, my girl," Tengu said. "I didn't need that old man Wodston out there did I? The pair of you are more than enough for this empire, I'll tell ya that much."

"Thank you. But Prince Nuk is in charge, of course," Izumi said.

"Oh don't give me that rubbish. Right, where do I sign? I'm making you an official princess all big and proper like!"

"A princess? For real!?"

"My my, you hear that everyone! The empire's getting its perfect pair! First the style, and now the substance!" Izayah called out.

"I hearby declare that these two are the real deal, alright," Tengu announced. That was probably as official as it got, so the deed was done. What deed precisely?

"Sorry about that Nuk," Izumi said. "I didn't meant to get in on your stuff like that."

"No, please do, I'm totally confused. Can't imagine what I'd actually do if I had to rule without knowing you. Like all that stuff about giving people food so they get strong and make more food. That's thinking out the box, you know?"

"Just the knowledge of the ancients, really. I'm glad to help. And I'm glad I can call myself Princess."

"Man, you were doing that already, admit it."

"Fine, I was, but you know... Now it's official. So that means..."

"... Err... Yeah... I get it. It means... That thing, which we both understand fully."

"Nuk, I think your dad just married us."

After smoothly coughing out a load of skimmer burger, Nuk casually resumed the conversation.

"Is that... Is that how that works?"

"Guess it works however you want it to work. Your empire."

"Ah right. Well then. That's how I want it to work."

"Nuk..."

"You're free to disagree, Princess. Although if you do disagree, the technically you aren't the Princess, so you can't disagree, but that wou mean you *are* the Princess so-"

Izumi rudely interrupted him with a kiss, which by virtue of being bad table manners, drew everyone else's attention.

"Mummy and Daddy got married, I heard it!" Ells claimed.

"How did you- Oh, you mean the humans," Elaina said, shrinking away immediately.

"Is that true, my Prince?" Wodston asked.

"Err.. yeah, pretty sure it is. But again, I'm open to advice, 'cause I'm such a good Prince," Nuk nodded. True romance. There was a round of applause and general cheering, indicative of a good time time being had. Such dry analysis was all Cat-lon could take from the scene. She was sat with Rick beside the wall, looking on.

"It's bad when I'm the ruler, but you don't mind these weird fleshies grabbing a holda power," she said.

"With humans, nothing's forever," Rick said. "And remember these aren't the humans you knew. I'm telling ya, there's a big difference between battery farmed and free range, especially with sapiens. Try to lighten up, huh? And hey, maybe it ain't you under the veil this time, but at least these freaks still use the currency named after ya."

"My money, my time, their world, huh?"

"It's everyone's world. Me and you included."

"Right, right. And when am I gonna be under the veil, huh?"

"Don't you dare, Waxy. I ain't got room for that drama."

"Just teasing. I ain't a complete bust, ya know?"

"Sure, you're really good to me honey."

"As long as you behave yourself."

"And there it is..."

As the pair tiffed away by the wall, everyone else consumed assorted things in a very biological sort of way, and a nice time was had. The empire had a grown up Prince, a brand new Princess, and a whole lotta hope for a bright future.

"To the power of friendship!" Izayah toasted.

"To the power of teamwork!" Rick added.

"To the power of paste!" Gustavsen concluded. Who wouldn't drink to that?

"Princess Izumi, have you ever heard of the labour theory of value?" Elaina asked Izumi at one point.

"No, please, Elaina. I just want to be Princess for a bit. I did save the world!" she replied. It seemed Izumi was indeed aware of further improvements to this rickety attempt at government, but she was happy enough to hit snooze on that for now. There was one project though she was eager to attend to right away. After the Bugmaster was promoted to Captain of the Grow Lab and stowed away in the palace attic, Izumi cornered Beep to conclude their bargain.

"It's time, Queen Beep. The past is settled. I have all these cores; surely enough space. Please, let me have all the data you've got, somehow."

"You want me to access the great archives. Beep!" Beep said. "Since you have all been very nice to me, I think I will! Beep! First, I will need to delete the feelings data from the previous eras, since now, we do not need to worry about what happened. Beep beep beep!"

"Okay, is that done?"

"No! Beep! Feeling separation is commencing. Please be patient. Beep!"

Izumi patiently waited all day, barely paying attention during Nuk's official burning down of the old slave market ceremony. She finally caught up to Beep being gawked at by local children in the street.

"Queen Beep. Your majesty. I am ready to receive the data now. How about you?" she asked.

"Beep! Feeling separation is... zero, point, zero, zero, zero, zero, three, one, percent complete! Beep! Please be patient! Beep!"

So, the instant technological renaissance Izumi was gunning to attach her name to was going to be more of a gradual trickle. But hey, a gradual trickle's better than being eaten alive by a skimmer, so overall things were looking up out there in the Great Desert! The guild stayed there for several days, chilling, maxing, relaxing all cool, until they learned that a couple of guys were up to no good. These guys were eager to contact the guild and explain as much.

"Ohhhh Izzuuuumiii," Enrico's voice echoed around a palace bedroom.

"Man, we gotta find a way to stop getting woken up by freaks," Nuk murmured as Izumi slumped out of bed and picked up an AI core.

"What do you want? It's sleeping time for the humans," she said.

"No time to sleep. Ze preparations are almost complete. I sink you vil vant to see zis," Enrico claimed.

"See what?"

"See... ze end..."

"End... of anything in particular?"

"Yes. You see, vhen I said zat zere vere no safety concerns at all vith z nuclear fission business, I lied."

"I thought your programming prevented you lying or something, huh?"

"ZIS WAS ALSO A LIE! My genius runs deeper zan you can imagine, feral cell bag. Now, you vill see zat ze real treasure was not ze uranium, but ze plutonium explosives it creates along ze vay!"

"Enrico... Tell me what you're going to do."

"I am going to create an extremely large explosion and... solve a very longstanding problem."

"You're talking about nukes? Enrico, what have you done?"

"I have done it! And you didn't even notice! Fools! Now, ze power of ze atom is mine once again. Please, come to ze enclave. Let's say goodbye together, eh?"

"Fugg, Nuk, I think they're gonna nuke everything!" Izumi said, throwing the core aside.

"Can relate. That's the thing that sets everything on fire, right?" Nuk said.

"That's just the start of it. They could make the planet uninhabitable! To us anyway. I can't believe it. Were they working with Cat-lon this whole time?!"

"Dunno but sounds like they're gonna do the whole villain showing off thing for us, so we can still stop them!"

"We better. Shid we better, I nearly got a happy ending dammit."

The guild was quickly assembled, and there were obviously a few questions for a certain skeleton mastermind.

"Hey, I weren't gonna nuke ya, I just wanted ya precious bodily fluids!" was Cat-lon's defence.

"You wouldn't happen to lying to us right now, eh? And don't lie in your answer to that question," Izayah demanded.

"Don't ya know I ain't even connected to their weird network. Rebels be shut out. Enrico's been doing his thing, I've been doing mine. If he wanted to blow y'all to smithereens, that's your problem; he's in your jurisdiction."

"Then you don't have a problem stopping them?"

"Hey, nukin' everything would ruin my plan even if I went through with it. Let's go whip their behinds!"

"No, that's just want they want, we should stop the nukes instead," concluded. And so the guild rushed off at top speed. By the end of the they had raced across the empire and were on the northern edge of

Venge. The late evening sun still shone but there was no time to wait, so they rushed into the laser fields with fingers crossed. Turns out, the space laser barely factored in your finger positions at all when deciding to blast a searing column of light in your direction.

"Shid shid shid shid," and other such remarks abounded as a great pillar suddenly slammed down before the guild, then swept towards them. Shiny First Empire armours reflected it a little, but they still received burns a-plenty. There simply wasn't enough paste left to power on, so the guild slowed to a crawl as they winced through the pain.

"So... basically... being nuked is just like that, but it doesn't stop, and it's much worse," Izumi explained to the uninitiated. Sounded like a bad thing, so all were eager to reach the enclave and save the world yet again. It took all night to cross Venge, but there was no room for exhaustion. Surely the Tech Scribes were in league with their scheming overseers, and would fight to keep the guild from ruining the plan? Not really. In fact, the few guys wandering about by the gate just nodded at the guild as they burst in.

"Hey, what do you think you're doing?" Nuk shouted.

"Tryna hollow out a greenfruit so I can... never mind," was the reply.

"Enrico's gonna destroy the world!"

"Yeah, probably. But I gotta do this thing. He's in the bar, as usual."

Dashing over to the bar, Enrico was indeed sitting around with a load of other patrons.

"Ah, here zey are. Ze stars of ze show," he said, standing and bowing.

"Enrico, you piece of shid, why are you doing this?" Izumi demanded.

"Gremlin. Anger doesn't suit you, Princess. You see, I am doing all you a raser large favour."

"We want to live, actually!"

"Ah but it vill come to an end sooner or later. Hmm, looks like ze sil space laser gave you a bit of a frying on ze vay over."

"Forget it, you French bastard! Prepare to die!" Nuk shouted.

"French? Why do you keep- Look, human ruler, I am going to show y my true power, vhether you like it or not. It is too late. Ze launch alrea started... about twenty seconds ago."

"What? Launch?"

"It is too late. You have no choice but to kneel before my genius, a praise ze... great illumination. Ha ha ha ha!"

"Shid... we were too late," Izumi whispered.

"No, right on time. Go to ze tower, you vill see it all. Might need sungoogles, but vhat's a few blasted retinas?"

"Fugg... Fugg! You better not be joking you piece of shid!" Nuk said, jumping back outside. There was a large tower by the enclave entrance, which the guild hurried up.

"What's going on, my Prince?" Wodston asked as they huffed up the stairs.

"Weird robot says the world's about to explode. Might as well get a view, huh?"

"Oh... In that case, my Prince, allow me to say, it has been a privilege to serve you."

"And you did it real good my man. I wouldn't be alive to die now if it wasn't for you. So, nice one."

"I must say, I didn't think we would all go out like this," Izayah said with a shake of his head.

"Izzy, don't worry. We can hold our heads high," Elaina said. "If we must die, then let's die together. The ultimate combo move."

"Oh Elly. Oh I... I didn't think dying would make me this emotional."

"Dying's the way of the world. Go watch it if you want," Sandor said, slumping down on the stairs.

"Nice Prince, why do they think we will die? Beep!" Beep asked Gustavsen outside.

"There is a technological threat. They believe it will end them. It might end your loyal soldiers too, my Queen. But your armour will protect you. You will live on."

"But, wouldn't I be alone?"

"Not if you remember all of us. There is always a hive, if you live for s."

"I will remember you the most! Beep! You made everything more alive, ᴐ even if you die, you are still an extremely good Prince!"

"My Queen! I am not worthy!"

"Beep! No one is worthy, but you are closest. Well done! Beep!"

On top of the tower there was a magnificent view. The enclave already t atop a hill, so from the tower one could see the laser-plains to the east, ᴉe lakes and First Empire ruins of the Bonefields to the south, the spotted ᴐserts and distance miasma of the swamps to the west, and the blackened ᴐuds and flashing thunder of the Deadlands to the north.

"Don't see anything," Nuk said, looking around. "I mean, I know the world already ended, but surely it's gonna look even worse than this if it happens again?"

"There," Izumi said, pointing to the southern sky. There was a gleaming, shooting light, gradually fading away.

"GHGHGHGH," Agnu commented.

"Yeah, I get it. Oh well. Let's play along," Twitch said.

"It went up in the sky. Like the one that took me up!" Ells said.

"Charlie, don't ruin the moment," Nuk said.

"This moment's beyond bloody salvage," Pia said, moping on the final stair.

"So you are all veady?" Enrico said, appearing from said stairs.

"Enrico... No point even killing you, is there?" Izumi said.

"Zat would be very ungrateful of you. Alright, let's see how zey are doing. Do you have ze target?"

"*Hai. Ikimasho,*" a voice said from a core in Enrico's arms.

"Hey, that's Ponk," Rick said. "Ponk, you old weeb, don't ya do it! Enrico's a real *baka-gaijin*, ya hear me?!"

"*Iie*, Rick-*Taisho. Aishiteru.*"

"Not this again. Ponk! Dammit!"

"Too late man..." Nuk said. Above them there was a flash of white light across the whole sky. Hands were held, tears emerged, expletives were bellowed... But then there was a tiny explosion, like a little orange blob in the distant sky.

"What's that? Is that death? Looks shid," Nuk said.

"Did you hit ze target?" Enrico said.

"*Hai.* Mission Complete," Ponk replied. Suddenly the explosion exploded some more, and seemed to fragment into a handful of gradually intensifying lights.

"Now ze good part, keep looking," Enrico said.

"Are we actually gonna die or not man, our brains really don't like the uncertainly," Nuk asked.

"Only thing that's gonna die is the eye on high," Neil said.

"The Eye... that's what you targeted?" Izumi asked.

"Yes. Vhy, vhat did you sink I vas doing?" Enrico replied.

"Fugg you Enrico!"

"I'm open to offers. Agent Hammer recommends you."

"You... This wasn't funny, you know?"

"Now who is lying? Don't miss ze best part, take a look."

Above them, the falling pieces of the Eye – that's the space laser in case you forgot – burned up and shattered in the atmosphere. It was like a grand array of slow, shooting stars, creating a pattern of red, orange, and white streaks across the sky. It was truly a magnificent display of fireworks, made all the better for the end of the orbital bombardment.

"Hey, Enrico. You jacked my spaceship just for that? That laser was doing good work," Cat-lon said.

"Yes, I apologise. Had my eye on zat little number for a vhile. Zere are no others left!" Enrico said.

"And where'd you find all the fleshies to fuel it up, huh?"

"Ah, zat is simple, my esteemed Empress. I grew my own! Zese biological narcotics have superb properties vhen refined. I vould say it's not exactly vocket science, but you must understand ze circumstances hardly allow ze expression. But I still sink you are dumb for not discovering it."

"Enrico, why didn't you just tell us you were doing all this?" Izumi asked.

"Because you vere busy. You know, zis isn't all about you."

"Why not?"

"Vhy not? My my. Zis is ze ego ve have learned about. I'm sorry, but zis way, the laser is put out of action sooner, and lives are saved. Plus, wisout zat sing concentrating sunlight on us, I believe ve shall see a lot of zis so-called uninhabitable zone become much more friendly to your greasy ilk. I know you like to save ze vorld, but sometimes you just have to let me do it."

"Okay... Thanks, Enrico. That sounds great," Izumi almost mournfully conceded.

"Ah it does, doesn't it? I am great. Ze history books cannot miss zis most important fact!"

"Just to confirm – we're not going to die?" Izayah asked.

"Not at zis precise moment," Enrico nodded.

"Lovely. Alright everyone, looks like we're going to live, so let's go get seat at the bar before everyone piles back in there!" Izayah called to the est of the guild. The idea caught on, and everyone rushed off for a drink. veryone but Nuk and Izumi, who stood on the edge of the roof watching the st specks of light fade from the sky.

"It... really was a happy ending," Izumi said.

"That skeleton's a punk. But sounds like he's helping. I'll enjoy not ing lasered, that's for sure," Nuk said.

"Maybe we really can all work together. Maybe we can all trust each other, right?"

"Yeah. I think everyone wants all this shid put behind us. So, you know, even if we aren't in charge of everything, people are probably gonna make this work. We can seriously chill. It's all gonna work out just fine."

"Thanks, Nuk."

"Welcome."

"I mean thanks for everything. I never thought life would turn out like this. Thought I'd be dead by now I guess."

"Nice, well against that backdrop I guess whatever we've done seems pretty good."

"More than pretty good. Okay? We've still got so much work to do but... I can't wait! Things are great, and they're only gonna get better!"

"You said it. Weird though. All I wanted was an adventure. Got a fugg load more than that, huh?"

"The adventure doesn't have to be over."

"I mean like, for non-bedroom stuff."

"No, there's more." Izumi pointed up at Okran with a grin.

"You really wanna go there?"

"Of course!"

"What's it got?"

"Well, there's ice."

"Ice? What's that?"

"What- You know when it gets really cold?"

"No..."

"Oh yeah. I guess... Never mind. It's like a layer of stuff."

"And what's under it?"

"Everything. The old world. Like in the classics."

"Seriously?"

"Probably..."

"Hot springs and high schools as far as the eye can see!"

"Err, yeah."

"The promised land."

"I promise you it isn't, but the scientific value is... is... are you thinkin about cat-girls?"

"I'm looking at them, right now, up there!"

"Right. That's the spirit. Maybe."

"We'll go to the one place not corrupted by the degeneracy parasite! Space!"

And then Izumi dragged Nuk to the bar as well before he got too carried away. All across the world, there was a lot of work to do to sort the planet out, but with all the guild had done, and with a little of what Enrico, Hammer and Co. and done, the way was clear. Soon the technology of the First Empire would creep back into reality, and the whole story of their rise and fall would be laid bare. With the flaws of the past finally known to all, stopping it happening again would be a whole load easier.

The great powers of the era were now in the hands of Prince Gustavsen and Queen Beep, Prince Izayah and maybe-Princess Elaina, Empress Cat-lon and General Red Rick, and of course Prince and Princess Tashino. They were going to drag the world into a new era, and while they were admittedly dragging things in slightly different directions, really stuff could only get better.

Nuk's run-away-from-home adventure had seen its up and downs, and m not just talking about the drugs. After one old-earth-year of antics, everyone could be very grateful that his epic quest had rocked the world. At st though, he returned home, with both the friends and drugs he had made ong the way, and settled down to make sure the new era was chock full of the good stuff. For a while, anyway...

THREE YEARS LATER

"There it is," Nuk said.

"What is?" Izayah asked.

"Nothing."

"I cannot see it," Gustavsen said.

"Yeah guess that's the point. It's like... potential. You can almost smell

"You wanna know what I can smell?" Ells asked.

"Nope. I wanna get you aired out as soon as possible."

"Not much air to work with," Izumi said. "Time to see if these masks ually work."

The expedition team assembled at the spaceships's elevator.

"Told ya we'd end up here one way or another," Rick said to Cat-lon.

"Yeah. 'Cept we were supposed to be alone," she replied.

"Trust me, it's better this way."

"You lucky I do trust you, 'cause that sounds like a crock. Least there ain't enough oxygen for the reproducers."

"Not for long," Elaina said. She was pushing a trolley with a big grey capsule on it.

"Yeah, that's gonna work," Cat-lon scoffed.

"Alright, everyone get the breathing masks on," Nuk said. Most were carrying canisters with clear plastic masks sticking out. One notable exception was Wodston.

"It's all about to pay off for you, my man," Nuk said to him.

"I suppose so, my Prince," he replied, his voice buzzing from a hidden speaker.

"You're the first real reverse numan in space," Rick said.

"Yet I wish I could keep my old parts."

"Then tell 'em not to break. Prince wants you alive so you just gotta lump it."

"I shall do that."

"You and Rags Andy here gotta keep him safe, right?"

"Blade's not much use here," Sandor said.

"That's what's special about it."

The elevator clattered downwards, and the team were placed into the midst of a great, featureless icefield. It was the sarcophagus of the Earth clans, created by technology originally intended to end the sister plane Now it was just the floor.

"It's cold," Ells noted. This was more notable that you'd imagine, give where they came from.

"Set up the tents," Izumi ordered. Her Tech Hunters began assembli canopies and pavilions around the edge of the spaceship, keeping out of t chilly shade the vessel cast. More trolleys packed with canisters we wheeled into these tents, along with all kinds of other mechanical parts a bundles of scaffolding.

"Wonder if anything's out there," Nuk said, looking at the emp horizon. "Need Beep to go look. Shame it's... ugh... birthing season."

"Do not shudder at the Queen's duty. To spawn additional drones is duty to the hive," Gustavsen said.

"And it is easy! I will put spawn onto the lawn! Beep!" th communicators buzzed.

"Nice, keep it up. We'll make space for you up here, Squeaky," Nuk said.

"Please hurry. Spawning is fun! Beep! I want to spawn more!"

"Sorry, Earth's gone into a tunnel." Nuk turned off his communicator, and the others followed his lead swiftly.

"Once we establish sufficient plant life, we can restore the composition of the atmosphere," Izumi explained.

"Nice. Anything grow in the ice?"

"No. When I said 'we' I didn't really mean us, right now."

"Ah, so then perhaps there is time for us all to adventure again!" Izayah said.

"Except there's nothing here, so..." Nuk said.

"Yes, yes... well... Could always play some wacky backgammon. And as long as we keep the Bugmaster in the ship, those crafty buggers back up there won't find him so quickly!"

They looked up at the planet hanging above them. It was mostly water, and very large compared to Earth, but the little yellow smudge they called home was clear to see. It was a view not witnessed for thousands of years, and a view that back on said home, plenty of others were witnessing at that very moment through the cameras the Tech Hunters were setting up.

"Hey everyone," Nuk said into one such camera. "It's ya boy Truth Trustino, Prince of Space, coming at you with legit images of what all of you look like from really, really far away. You can't breathe here, and it's kinda :hid to be honest, but still, bet you didn't think you'd live to see this happen, auh? Oh, by the way, this extra-terrestrial broadcast is brought to you by the Jnited Industrial Fleshless Rocketry Program, and Agent Hammer's Creepy 'eepy Cameras, in association with the TCM+⁺ guild, which is for sale by the /ay, and in massive debt, so enjoy, and... Also... Yeah, look at yourselves. Je're gonna see if we can get some of you up here sometime. The mangas ay we're from this planet originally, so it's probably better and stuff. Right, ow I'll hand you off to this Egg, who'll explain all the smells to you."

While Ells did his extremely popular segment, Nuk rejoined Izumi.

"How long's it take to melt the ice?" he asked.

"Oh... only three, maybe four... human lifetimes," she replied.

"And there's nothing out there until then?"

"Doubt it."

"Good. Wacky bloody backgammon it is then."

And hence another mini-adventure came to an end. But the grand adventure of humans, shek, hivers, skeletons, and the array of beasts and monsters they lived among, was just getting started. And forever they would remember the band of heroes who made it all possible. You'll scarcely find someone who cannot by heart recite the tale of how life was brought back from the edge of destruction, from the margin, if you will. And if you do find them, well, you had best ridicule them, for clearly they haven't read the classics! And now, they can never say that of you.

The End!

Lightning Source UK Ltd.
Milton Keynes UK
UKHW011833090223
416682UK00004B/258